A Luciferian conspiracy

NIMROD
TWICE BORN
LYN J PICKERING

ISBN 978-0-620-50057-9

Forest of Lebanon Publications

Cover design by Jordan Pickering

Website: nimrodtwiceborn.com
GMail: lyn@nimrodtwiceborn.com

To my father – a soldier.

Web page: http://nimrodtwiceborn.com
Gmail: lyn@nimrodtwiceborn.com
Kindle: http://www.amazon.com/dp/B009BCB17O
Smashwords: https://www.smashwords.com/books/view/443131

"I shall give a propagandist reason for starting the war – never mind whether it is plausible or not. The victor will not be asked afterward whether he told the truth or not. In starting and waging a war it is not right that matters, but victory.
Close your hearts to pity! Act brutally! Eighty million people must obtain what is their right…The stronger man is right…Be harsh and remorseless! Be steeled against all signs of compassion…Whoever has pondered over this world order knows that its meaning lies in the success of the best by means of force…"
Adolf Hitler

"From the days of Sparticus-Weishaupt (who founded the secret order of the Illuminati on May 1, 1776) to those of Karl Marx, to those of Trotsky (Russia), Rosa Luxembourg (Germany), Bela Kun (Hungary) and Emma Goldman (United States), this worldwide conspiracy for the overthrow of civilisation and for the reconstitution of society on the basis of arrested development, of envious malevolence, and impossible equality, has been steadily growing. It played a definitely recognisable role in the tragedy of the French Revolution. It has been the mainspring of every subversive movement during the nineteenth century: and now at last, this band of extraordinary personalities from the underworld of the great cities of Europe and America have gripped the Russian people by the hair of their heads, and have become practically the undisputed masters of that enormous empire."
Winston Churchill (1920)

Although they may pierce you
Fight, resist, stand by.
You yourself may perish
But keep the banner high.
Others may win the victory
When you're laid to rest
And shall gain the glory
To which you aspired.

Heinrich Himmler

Character list – in order of appearance.

Chaim Freiberg	League of Nations
Michael Segal	Writer & lecturer
Gabriele Hoch	Music lecturer; friend of Michael
Herod Antipas	Tetrarch of Galilee and Perea
Herodias	Wife of Herod
John the Baptist	Forerunner of Jesus
Philip the Tetrarch	Half-brother to Herod
Salome	Daughter of Herodias
Walther Krauss	Friend of Michael and Chaim
Matthias von Ingolstadt	Soldier WW1
Dieter von Lossow	Matthias' friend in Poland
Herr von Lossow	Dieter's father
Anna Lejkin	Friend of Dieter
Herr and Frau Segal	Michael's parents
Tetrarch Philip	Herod's brother
Pontius Pilot	Roman governor of Judaea
Chuza	Herod's chief steward
Joanna	Wife of Chuza
Mikolai Slowacki	Clerk
Simon the Magus	Samarian magician
Frau von Ingolstadt	Mother of Matthias
Hermann von Ingolstadt	Father of Matthias
Greta von Ingolstadt	Anna's assumed name
Marianne von Ingolstadt	Matthias and Greta's daughter
Hester	Walther's fiancée
Heinrich Himmler	Future Head of SS
Ernst Röhm	Captain of SA
Yeshua bar Joseph	Jewish designation of Jesus
Mary Magdalene	Follower of Jesus

Judas Iscariot	Betrayer of Jesus
Simon the leper	Father of Judas
Helen of Tyre	Consort of Simon Magus
Margaret Boden	Himmler's wife
King Abgar V	King of Edessa
Shaphan	Temple priest
Hiram of Tyre	Builder of Solomon's Temple
Lazarus	Raised from the dead by Jesus
Mary and Martha	Sisters of Lazarus
Peter	Disciples of Jesus
Matthew	
John	
Nathanael	
Philip	
Andrew	
Horst von Ingolstadt	Son of Matthias and Greta
Reinhard Heydrich	SS intelligence head
Thaddeus	Disciples of Simon Magus
Marcus	
Nicodemus	
Joseph of Arimathea	Members of the Jewish council
Caiaphas	Jewish High Priest
Karl Wolff	Obergruppenführer, member of Himmler's inner circle
Lina Heydrich	Wife of Reinhard Heydrich
Oswald Pohl	Members of Himmler's inner circle
Gottlob Berger	
Malchus	Servant of the High Priest
Annas	Father-in-law of High Priest
Bar Abbas	Barabbas of the Gospels
Otto Rahn	Explorer and writer
Bérenger Saunière	Village priest in Rennes-le-Chateau
Wolfram von Seivers	Head of Ahnenerbe
Walter Buch	Nazi legal expert

Walter Schellenberg	SS Obergruppenführer
Cleopas	Follower of Jesus
Ruth Lieman	Prostitute
Hans	Forger of documents
Lucius	Disciple of Simon Magus
Joseph	Uncle of Simon Magus
Marie Denarnaud	Housekeeper to Bérenger Saunière, village priest
Klaus Barbie	Gestapo "Butcher of Lyons"
Tobias	Jew in Edessa
Aggai	In the service of King Abgar V
Demetrius	Disciple of Simon Magus
'Mary of Magdala'	Consort of Simon Magus
Jacques	Follower of the Magdalene
Sarah the Egyptian	Also Helen, Priestess of Astarte
Caligula	Roman Emperor
Herod Agrippa	Herodias' brother
Salomon	Disciple of Simon Magus
Caesar Claudius	Emperor of Rome following Caligula
Messalina	Claudius' wife
Joseph	Disciple of Simon Magus – 'Joseph of Arimathea'
Salomon	Consort of Herodias
Sarah	Daughter of Simon Magus and Helen
Rene de Bar	Also Alain, leader in Paris underground
Simone	Underground agent
Dr. Felix Kersten	Himmler's masseuse
Nero	Emperor of Rome

Dr. Kraus	Plastic surgeon
Paul of Tarsus	Apostle
Alexander the Coppersmith	Follower of Paul
Menander	Leader after Simon Magus' death
Muhammed	The Prophet
Abu Talib	Uncle to the Prophet Muhammed
Father Michael	Catholic priest
Khadija	Wife of the Prophet
Waraqa	Cousin of Khadija
Ernst Karltenbrunner	Successor to Heydrich
Godfroi de Bouillon	Claimant to Jerusalem's throne
Peter the Hermit	Monk from Calabria
Jean Cocteau	Parisian playwright
Jean Marais	Cocteau's lover
Bernard	Cistercian Abbot
Pope Urban II	Odo Abbot of Cluny
Alexius Comnenus	Byzantium Emperor
Peter Bartholomew	Monk - discoverer of the lance
Hugues de Payens	Grand Master, Order of Sion
Baudouin de Bouillon	Brother of Godfroi, King of Jerusalem
Dr. Graf	Obstetrician
Frau Zeigner	Midwife
Michel Hervet	Successor to de Bar in Paris underground
Everard de Barres	Templar Grand Master - France
Charles de Bar	Father of Rene de Bar
Martine de Bar	Wife of Charles
Frau Giesler	Farmer's wife

Robert de Bourgogne	Grand Master of Templars – Outremer
Malik Abu Hanifa	Ismaili
Ali ibn Wafa	Ismaili leader
Fulk d'Aguilers	Templar
Udo von Woyrsch	Obergruppenführer
Karl Gebhardt	
Ohlendorff	
Von Herff	
Hedwig	Himmler's mistress
Sibylla	Queen of Jerusalem
Guy de Lusignan	King
Gerard de Ridefort	Templar Grand Master
Raymond of Tripoli	Regent to Sibylla's son
Saladin	Kurdish General and Sultan of Egypt
Captain Thomas Williams	Commandant who arrested Himmler
Colonel Michael Stokes	British Intelligence
Alexius IV	Byzantium Emperor
Jean de Bar	Son of Rene de Bar
Heinz Halder	Informal tutor to Jean
	Assumed name of Himmler
Henry II	King of England
Philippe II	King of France
Richard the Lionheart	Son of Henry II
Herr Groener	Lawyer

Introduction

In the year 1199, the Teutonic Knights wearing the black cross superimposed on their white surcoats thundered across the pages of history. Jerusalem had fallen and the need for such an order seemed to have lost its relevance yet this new order of knights was formed with the blessing of the pope. It was a military Christian order combining the rules of the Templars with the Hospitallers, the Order of St. John, and their role was to colonise and to Christianise the German east. The Teutonic Knights worked in close association with the German burghers and both protected and participated in trade. Because the Order was free from feudal ties and the influence of lords it became an elite body, unconditionally loyal to the Emperor. Entire territories were entrusted to the administration of its knights and the Teutonic Grand Master belonged to the inner circle of the Emperor's advisors.

The Nazi Order of the SS intentionally bore a striking resemblance to the Teutonic Knights.

In 1937, Otto Rahn, who died two years later in unusual circumstances, sent a special consignment to Heinrich Himmler. Rahn had studied the sacred geography in the Montségur area and believed that his most important find was the Holy Grail. Yet Adolf Hitler, in a last ditch attempt to save the Third Reich, later sent men into the Montségur region of France in his own desperate search for the Grail. The year was 1944; a year that Hitler believed marked a significant turn in historical events, a change that took place every seven hundred years. He also asserted that, according to German legend, a hidden treasure would rise to the earth's surface, and he connected this treasure with the Grail.

The fulfilment of the promise of the Grail was brought to pass in 1944, but not in the manner that Adolf Hitler had anticipated.

The last Reich is unfolding even now, right before our eyes, but this time we are dealing with a Reich not conceived openly in ritual and power, but one that eats into our midst, with stealth.

Prologue
Twice-Born

1988

It was not the first time since Chaim Freiberg's death some thirty years ago, that Michael Segal wished he were still around. Except for a handful of souls who chose to use it as a reference in their study of the Turin shroud, his own book was long since published and forgotten but Michael had never lost his fascination for the subject. Freiberg would have brought his level-headed approach to the present report and between them they might have reached a conclusion.

The issues defied any logical answer. Why had the Roman Catholic Church twice chosen to release findings pertinent to the Turin shroud on the anniversary of the suppression of Order of the Templars? First the STURP findings on 13th October 1978 and now, exactly ten years later, this present report on the carbon 14 dating. Obviously the Mother Church was speaking but exactly what was being said was more difficult to discern.

Segal's book, written during the Second World War, had been one of the earliest investigations undertaken but since then there had been a number of significant advancements in the study of the shroud, not the least Dr. Max Frei's report on the pollen samples. Frei, a Swiss criminologist of international repute noted for his work on the analysis of microscopic substances, was granted permission in 1973 to collect dust samples from the linen cloth. The result was an extensive list of pollens, among them plants typical to the area around the Dead Sea, specifically adapted to the high salt content of the soil, and species indigenous to the area around Edessa, modern day Urfa, as well as to Constantinople, or Istanbul. His results had gone a long way towards strengthening Michael's theory that Edessa's Mandylion concealed the full length shroud under its tapestry backing.

Gabriele looked into the room. "I know you need time alone," she said, "so I've arranged to meet the girls in town for lunch. There's a cold meal for you in the fridge."

"Ever the diplomat," he laughed. "Come and give me kiss before you go."

He put his arms around his wife and looked down at her with affection. Her blonde hair was now grey but the curls were as irrepressible as ever and, to Michael, she was as lovely as when they first met.

"Enjoy your day, and give our grand-daughters my love."

"I will."

He heard the door close behind her and settled back to his desk littered with dozens of clippings and copious notes.

The carbon dating report, which set the time of the cutting of the flax for the shroud between the years 1260 – 1390, made nonsense of Frei's findings - and of his own less scientific study. Interestingly, only three of the initial seven laboratories chosen to perform the tests were ultimately given the go-ahead; England's Oxford University, a lab in Zurich and one in the United States. Typically, Michael thought, the Catholic hierarchy had proffered no reason for the exclusion of the others. This report placed a firm lid on the subject. The single conclusion that could be drawn from the carbon 14 dating was that the shroud was a clever fake.

Michael Segal returned to his own body of more circumstantial evidence and to Max Frei's data, which clearly, if not conclusively, demonstrated that the linen cloth had followed the route from Israel via Edessa and Constantinople to France and Italy. What Renaissance forger could have foreseen the need to source fabric in Israel for the manufacture of his fake? And what of the documented presence of the shroud in Constantinople in 1201, well before the cloth was said to have been made? The keeper of the relic collection in the Pharos Chapel had declared its presence, claiming that it 'wrapped the mysterious naked dead body after the Passion'. Could he have stated that the body of Christ was naked except for the evidence of the image on the shroud?

Two years later, a Frenchman, Robert de Clari who, as part of the Fourth Crusade, had been brought to Constantinople on a Venetian ship prior to the attack on the city wrote:

"There was another of the churches which they called, My Lady St. Mary of Blachernae, where was kept the sydoine in which Our Lord had been wrapped, which stood up straight every Friday so that the figure of Our Lord could be plainly seen there…"

These and other testimonies clearly suggested the existence of a shroud, which bore the image of Christ, before the carbon 14 dating evidence said it could have existed.

Was it then possible that someone had tampered with the shroud samples or the dating results?

The Vatican's go-ahead for the shroud's testing had been given in October 1987 and specified that the tests were to be carried out by technicians who knew nothing about the identity of the cloth until after the experiment was complete. A centimetre wide strip, eight centimetres in length had been cut from the linen cloth and three strips of 1.3 centimetres were submitted for testing on April 21st 1988. But although the findings under the accelerator mass spectrometer would have been received almost immediately, they were withheld for several months.

There were two possible ways that any 'fixing' might have taken place, Michael surmised. Either the samples were switched and replaced by a cloth known to be of a far later dating, or the lab technicians were persuaded to provide a different date. The former, presumably, would have been simpler to arrange than the latter. The question remained, why? What would the Roman Catholic Church possibly have to gain by deliberately manipulating the dates of arguably its most sacred relic?

And there, for a long time, Michael Segal was stuck. He ambled into the kitchen made himself a cup of strong coffee and fetched his lunch from the refrigerator although it was still only 11.00 o'clock and ate the cold chicken and salad absentmindedly.

If the Catholic Church believed that the shroud of Turin was genuinely the burial cloth of Christ, it would surely not be in their interests to do anything to undermine that belief. Yet the deliberate nature of the release of two sets of reports, ten years apart, on the date of the attack on the Templars, had the immediate effect of disassociating the shroud from the time of Christ, setting it in a different time frame. The first even before the carbon 14 dating had taken place, as though, years before, they anticipated the test and its result.

Why, what was their game? Was the research of those outside the Church moving too close to the truth of the real nature of the shroud? Had they stumbled unwittingly to the edge of a new discovery? Or was the intention of Catholic hierarchy to draw adherents to a new faith, one no longer founded on the old tenets of belief in the death and resurrection of Christ but on the mysteries surrounding the Templars and the continuance of the Order beyond the time of their demise? Relic worship had, apparently, been designed to drawn devotees of Catholicism into a belief in Christ; had the focus subtly shifted?

Perhaps, Michael Segal thought, as he drained the last of his coffee, the true face of Catholicism is about to be revealed. The Catholic faith, like the shroud of Turin, rested upon an iconic reflection of Christ Jesus. If the Turin shroud, the Catholic representation of his death and resurrection, was discovered to be based on a false premise, the emphasis could always be shifted to suit the new face. Those faithful souls which had followed the teachings of Rome could find that their foundation, built on an indistinct image of Christ Jesus, had shifted like sand. They would be worshipping the one Twice-Born.

PART I

Chapter 1
Twice-Born

It pleased Herod Antipas to have the Baptist in his cells. It was like holding a wild bird captive in a wicker cage; he could at any time create a pretext and go down to see the man. Lacking the freedom of the common people, Herod had had to content himself with hearing about the prophet while being prevented from observing him at first hand. He was younger than Herod had expected, perhaps only in his early thirties; heavily bearded, and his hair was long and unkempt. And if the Tetrarch had anticipated that the Baptist's eyes would be those of a mystic or a mad-man, he was disappointed. No outward welcome of his captor was extended in his expression but neither was there any rejection; he seemed to accept Herod's presence in the dungeons of Machaerus without question. Why would the Tetrarch not seek him out? He, the Baptizer, had the words of the Living God.

Indeed, something about John bar Zachariah continually drew Antipas back. Learned Jews, and Pharisees in particular, had always looked upon Herod the Tetrarch with undisguised contempt yet, surprisingly, the Baptist's gaze held understanding. He was completely unaffected by Herod's status and spoke to him with an artless honesty as he had never been spoken to by any other man. He read him as though he were an open letter. Herod would sometimes slip down to the cells and converse with him, less as gaoler to prisoner than as proselyte to teacher. It was cool in the cells below Machaerus and the nights were often intensely cold. One of John's followers had brought him a cloak and Herod himself often brought food, which the Baptist accepted from his hand with no show of humility. Antipas suspected his prisoner knew his charity to be the act of a man with a bad conscience.

From the first appearance of John the Baptizer in his territory Herod Antipas had been fascinated. Here was a prophet and, by many accounts, a genuine prophet – the first since Malachi four hundred years before. Some said that Malachi's final words had come to pass in the person of John bar Zachariah.

Behold I will send you Elijah the prophet before the coming of the great and dreadful day of the Lord: and he shall turn the heart of the fathers to the children, and the heart of the children to their fathers, lest I come and smite the earth with a curse.[1]

"Do you believe this could be the return of Elijah?" When John first wended his way down the banks of the Jordan River challenging all who cared to listen with his preaching, Antipas had asked Herodias that question.

"Superstitious nonsense! The man is our enemy! Do you wilfully choose to ignore what he's saying about us?" Herodias tossed her head. "It's evident that you admire him! Does it not concern you that he condemns our marriage as incestuous?"

"In Jewish eyes it is. You were my brother's wife."

She shrugged contemptuously. "Half-brother! And I was Herod Philip's niece when I married him, but I never allowed that to bother me. What has it to do with some ill-clad peasant, anyway?"

He took her by the shoulders and kissed her. "Don't allow him to disturb you," he said, "he can't damage us with words."

"Words have the power to destroy kingdoms," she warned him. "Agrippa my brother is in Rome awaiting the right moment to seize your territory and that of Philip the Tetrarch. If this Baptist arouses the people against us, Pontius Pilot may well report the matter to Caesar and you, my dear husband would be ousted in an instant."

Herod Antipas' smile failed to disguise the unease her words aroused in him. At the time of Herod's marriage to Herodias, only Roman-ruled Judaea stood between Antipas and the remainder of his father's realm. The government of Judaea had changed five times during Herod Antipas' thirty-one year rule of Galilee and Transjordan, and it was not unlikely that Rome would extend the Tetrarch's rule in order to bring stability to the region. One false move, however, could turn everything in the favour of Herod Agrippa. It was this fear that was encouraged and fanned into flame by Herodias.

---

[1]Malachi 4:5,6

"I don't believe John is a rabble-rouser," he protested. "He seems sincere to me. By his words, he intends to return the Jews to their keeping of the law. I don't see him as a danger."

Herodias drew away from him making no attempt to disguise her irritation.

"You are more of a fool than I realised!" she spat.

He raised his hands and dropped them helplessly, "What do you expect me to do about the man, imprison him for preaching?"

"If you want to protect your position. Yes!"

"I can't do that, Herodias. I know he has upset you, but I can't throw him in prison because you don't like what he says."

Her eyes met his and locked them in her glance. "You are afraid to do it," she said with scorn. "There's still too much of that Jewish upbringing in you. What do you imagine will happen if you get rid of the man? That your God will strike you down?"

He turned away from her, humiliated by the sting in her words. There was truth in what she said. His father had insisted that he and his brothers be schooled in the Torah more, he knew, as an expedient and training to rule as king over Israel than as a code of conduct. Something, some superstition perhaps, had remained. If there was a god who governed this universe it was unlikely to be one of his wife's gods of stone and precious metals, but far be it from him to suggest that Herodias herself might be involved in superstitious practises. She was iron-willed and prevailed against him in every argument. He sighed as she left the terrace.

From the first moment of Herodias' marriage to his brother, Herod-Philip, a businessman from Caesarea, Herod Antipas had lusted after her. A witty and vital woman with intelligence that far outweighed that of her husband, Herodias was, of her choosing, the hub and focus of every gathering. She was intensely beautiful, with lips perfectly shaped, and dark, smouldering eyes. She wore her black hair loosely braided and in those moments when her eyes had sought his, flirting with Herod over the unwary head of her husband, she would finger the plait and allow the hair to escape from its bands only to gather it up and restrain it again. It would command all of Herod's will-power to keep his mind on his brother's conversation. It was obvious to him now that Herodias had used Philip as a necessary stepping-stone in her ambition for power. Herod Antipas' position suited her purposes better than Philip's and, when she judged the time to be right, she had seduced her husband's brother and left him thirsty for more.

Within weeks Antipas had divorced his Arabian wife, the daughter of Aretas, and taken for himself the wife of Herod-Philip his younger half-brother. Herodias brought a sixteen year old daughter, Salome, into this new union.

Herod's hope that John the Baptizer would leave Galilee and never return did not materialise and it was more than his life was worth to threaten the tenuous security of his marriage. At Herodias' insistence, Herod Antipas had sent some of his men to warn the Baptist to cease speaking about his marriage on pain of imprisonment.

Chapter 2
Twice-Born

1918

Matthias von Ingolstadt was twenty-two years old when the Great War ended. He crawled from his trench like a rat from its hole and attempted to see the devastation in terms of his new found liberation. It would take nature a long time to heal the scars that their weapons had inflicted on the countryside. It was divested of almost all colour or life. Trees had been stripped to grey leafless stumps; the raw earth blemished and pitted. Around him, the men were simply a reflection, he supposed, of the way he looked. Their eyes, set into the muddied masks of their faces, were flat and lifeless. Had there been a victory to celebrate, perhaps there would have been some jauntiness; some of those battered frames might have been able to hold themselves with pride. As it was, nothing could be salvaged from those wasted years and wasted lives.

Von Ingolstadt was tall; half a head taller than most of his friends, and the muscle and sinew across his shoulders and upper arms granted a suggestion of power to a body that was too lean. Blonde hair, closely cropped against lice, dusted his skull, emphasising the smudges of shadow hollowing his eyes and cheekbones. His hands were of the sort never intended to handle a weapon. They were gentle, with long fingers made to coax the best from a violin, or create ecstasy in the face of a woman. They were the hands of a poet and a dreamer, but now, mud-encrusted, they appeared little different from the gnarled and broken stumps of the trees. The war had generated men that were machines of slaughter and trained them to kill. Von Ingolstadt lifted his hands to his face for a moment, almost without recognition, only to drop them loosely to his sides. Would they ever respond again in human terms without the touch of death overshadowing every action?

From the front, the men began to go back home to their families. After a four-year trench-war, their self-esteem was shattered, their spirit broken, and little remained of their national pride.

Demobilisation was sporadic and, when at last Matthias von Ingolstadt arrived in Berlin, it seemed that life had normalised for most people, rendering the remnant of the returning army an embarrassment. Nobody needed to be reminded of what amounted to Germany's defeat.

The butler met Matthias at the station and loaded his baggage into the waiting taxi. Lack of income meant that most of the servants had been dismissed and home had become a shabby parody of its pre-war grandeur. Even his parents unaccountably seemed like a familiar, faded image on an old photograph. His mother dressed in brown silk and white lace, stood tall, slender and brittle as always, beside her husband in the lobby. His father's moustaches were sharply waxed and his white collar freshly starched but his eyes had become weak and rheumy beneath grizzled eyebrows; his skin was pale as parchment and deeply furrowed.

The welcome lacked warmth; gestures of affection and genuine words of endearment had never come naturally to his parents and von Ingolstadt had not expected anything to have changed. His mother returned to her weekly routine of tea parties with chosen friends over the silver tea service in the drawing room and Matthias made plans to leave. Any sign of weakness was frowned upon and he was locked in on himself, seeking to cope with memories that exhausted and threatened to engulf him. He wanted to sleep until the feelings were gone, yet sleep was no longer restorative but haunted by night visions, sometimes elusive, often vivid with horror. That which affected him most was the one that should have left him untouched. In a village on the Meuse, he had stumbled across a cat, probably used by the last troops for target practice. It was wandering aimlessly through the street with its face half-blown away, its remaining eye pleading with him to end its misery. He had killed it with a single shot to the heart but the cat lived on in his dreams. All the terrors of war had become bound up in that one image, which would not be erased.

The German High Command had sought the Armistice, not because their armies were being overpowered, nor even because of the stalemate in the ongoing trench war, but because of an imminent Communist uprising in Germany. Just one year after the Bolshevik Revolution, Rosa Luxemburg and her predominantly Jewish Spartacus

Bund planned to repeat Lenin's Russian success on German soil. By 1918, Spartacus agents infiltrated the German fleet. Rumours were spread of an impending battle against the full might of the Allied forces. The purpose of the battle was to cripple the allied fleets so that they would no longer be able to defend Britain's coastline against a German military invasion.

"The British have developed a secret weapon," the crews were told. "They've got a chemical that can be fired from shore or dropped from a plane that will create a sea of flames. If we don't die from the flames and the heat, we'll die from lack of oxygen."

The cells introduced their poisoning of the crews drop by drop until it became obvious to them that the only way to prevent certain death was revolution. On 3rd November 1918, the German seamen mutinied, and a few days later, on their way to the Western Front many more deserted ship, believing they were to spearhead the final sea battle against Britain.

In Germany itself, uprisings had caused industrial shut-downs and in the ensuing conditions of defeatism, the Kaiser abdicated and the Social Democrats formed a Republican Government. The Armistice signed on November 11th 1918 was a prelude to a negotiated peace. Germany never intended it to be unconditional surrender.

Rosa Luxemburg's agents created chaos throughout the armed forces. Forcing the government to order the immediate demobilisation was her trump card, which ensured that the revolution could take place without military intervention. Everything was in place for the final assault planned for January 1919. Luxemburg's failure came as they prepared to launch their onslaught. Only then did she realise that she had been double-crossed by those who had financed Lenin's revolution in Russia. Spartacus had been betrayed. The failure of Rosa Luxemburg, Karl Liebknecht and their Jewish-dominated revolution resulted in immediate reprisals against German Jews. Thousands of men, women and children were rounded up during the night and executed. The attempted revolution was confirmation of a Jewish-led revolutionary movement and Hitler would use these events to consolidate German hatred for Jews and Communists in the years that lay ahead.

Exacerbating Germany's sense of isolation and hatred were the demands from the Allies for restitution; Germany must be made to pay - to be squeezed dry for what she had done. The armistice, which President Woodrow Wilson said should make the world safe for democracy was destined to create the discontent which would spawn Europe's dictators, and pave the way for the more horrifying war to come.

Matthias von Ingolstadt joined the Freicorps within the first two months of his demobilisation. There were few jobs to be had, and the ranks of the Freicorps swelled with such misplaced officers and soldiers. For some men, after the war, the return to normal society was plagued with difficulties, others never managed to make the adjustment. They missed the comradeship of the army that had become their home or, like Matthias von Ingolstadt, they needed the imposed discipline of the army as a bastion against an inner emptiness, until such time as they were able to move back into society on their own terms.

As a further backlash against the German defeat, the ranks of the Freicorps followed whatever flag happened to be flying, content to be soldiers of fortune, and their regiments obeyed or disobeyed government orders at will.

Von Ingolstadt had little desire to make the army his future. The Freicorps however, welcomed him in and, on the strength of his past record, made him a senior officer. Matthias von Ingolstadt had taken a step destined to be his first towards a long army career, which, ultimately, would result in a move into the German SS.

Berliners had chosen denial as a means of assuming change and a superficial, hedonistic society began to emerge from the confusion and pathos of the war. A revival of the arts focussed on the flippant and the fantastic. Billboards and posters depicted lean, sensual women and men who were suave and well-groomed. Multitudes had perished, Germany had been humiliated in the sight of the world, but those who survived shook off the memories and rose up with a grim determination to wring everything from the present.

Chapter 3
Twice-Born

John the Baptist struck a strange figure. He was strong, fit and suntanned, and his hair surrounded his face like the feathers of an eagle, almost indistinguishable from his untrimmed beard. He dressed in camel skins belted at the waist, and lived on what the desert area offered – wild honey and locusts. An inquisitive crowd had followed him to the banks of the Jordan River close to the northern end of the Dead Sea where he was baptising all who would respond to his message. His voice bellowed across the water as he waded out from the bank and the sun caught the ripples creating a kaleidoscope of fragmented light.

At Herodias' insistence, a group of several soldiers, clad in the distinctive blue tunic of the palace guard, had been assigned to watch the Baptist and report back to Herod anything that was spoken against him. Their presence was designed to pose a threat to every meeting, but John would not be intimidated into softening his message or leaving the area. From his position on the banks of the river Jordan he would deliberately project his voice to include the silent line of men spread out across the ridge. Within days there were those soldiers who were personally touched by John's call to repentance and they approached the Baptist afterwards.

"As soldiers sworn to obey a commander, what do we do?"

"Do violence to no man," John counselled them. "And don't accuse anyone falsely. Be content with your wages."

The little gathering that had listened in fascination throughout the morning, turned curiously to watch the approach of a group of Pharisees who had come to judge for themselves this man whom the people were proclaiming a prophet. John looked up, shading his eyes against the sun, the better to see the black-clad delegation that stared coldly down at him.

"You brood of vipers!" he yelled, "Who warned you to flee from the wrath that is to come?" The eyes of the Pharisees hardened and they glanced at one another silently. They were accustomed to man's acclaim; never to open scorn. It was certain that this could not be a man of God if he poured contempt on the chosen religious leaders of Israel.

"Produce fruit in keeping with repentance!" the Baptist cried, but this time his appeal was to the whole crowd as though they were more worthy of his attention than the Pharisees. "Religion is not outward show; it's a circumcision of the heart. What good is your giving of alms, what good are your tithes if it's done to impress people with your good works? If you do things to impress men, your reward will be from men only."

The Pharisees bristled, recognising that he was using them as a public example but, faced with an exposure of their behaviour, they were powerless to protest.

"Don't imagine that being a child of Abraham is enough to save you from God's wrath! The axe is already laid to the root. Every tree that does not bear good fruit will be cut down and tossed into the fire."

John had a way of taking the Torah and the writings of the prophets, absorbed from an early age at the feet of his father, and presenting it to the common people in a manner that touched their conscience.

"What can we do?" a young man asked. It was the cry of many who recognised that their lives simply did not measure up to the high demands of the Law.

John smiled. Fleetingly, the gesture revealed a gentler side to one known for his isolation.

"If you have two cloaks give one to a person who has none. If you have food, do likewise. And," he raised his voice to include a group of despised tax-collectors who, as acknowledged pariahs, stood a little way apart from the rest of the crowd, "exact no more than that which is appointed to you!"

One by one those convicted of their sin waded down into the water to be baptised while the Pharisees, watching from a safe distance higher up the river bank, discussed among themselves whether the rite that John was introducing was pagan. Baptisms of the mystery religions were carried out in secrecy but John was openly calling Jews to recognise their need of repentance and to return to the purity of their faith. Although the Jews used water for ceremonial cleansing, baptism was practiced only when a new proselyte was absorbed into the faith. Was the Baptist seriously intimating that there was a need to bring Jews into a new relationship with YHWH? There was only one other possibility. They all knew the scriptures associating Messiah with repentance and spiritual cleansing.

"Who are you?" one shouted giving voice to the unthinkable. "Do you claim to be the Christ?"

"I am not!"

"A prophet then? Tell us who you are so that we can give an answer to those who sent us."

"I am the voice of one crying in the wilderness; make straight the way of the Lord."

The familiar words of the prophet Isaiah called for a way to be established through the desert for God to bring back the people of Israel from their Babylonian exile, but there was a Messianic implication that could not be ignored.

"Why then do you baptise if you are not Messiah, Elijah nor the Prophet? Do you claim to prepare the way for him?"

"You say so," John replied. "There is one coming whose sandals I am not worthy to unloose."

Those Pharisees who had not known John's father, Zachariah, had heard of him. The angelic visitation, foretelling the birth of his son, had struck the elderly priest dumb as he performed his duties in the temple. His wife, Elizabeth, was barren and past child-bearing age when this took place, but within the year she gave birth and Zachariah regained the power of speech when he called for a slate and named his child.

The story had evoked much speculation and, inevitably, the young man had been watched to see whether a new prophet was set to rise in Israel after the long dry period of silence since the prophet Malachi four hundred years before.

Once more Israel was under the oppressive yoke of a foreign state. This time the oppressor was Rome; a harsh and unyielding nation. Had John become a Pharisee or a priest like his father, the religious leadership may have heeded his call; instead he was subjected to cool scrutiny and even animosity as he developed his own unique direction, and it was the common rabble that was drawn to his teachings. He was, as he said, just a voice, crying out in the spiritual wilderness that Israel had become.

None of John's words could be faulted; there was no obvious deviation from the writings of the Law and the Prophets, but his contempt for those in authority had been noted.

From their vantage-point above the water, the Pharisees gathered their robes around them and departed with dignity to report back to the Sanhedrin.

John's attack against the marriage of Herod Antipas continued unabated and he demanded that Herod, as tetrarch of the region of Galilee and Perea, repent and put away his brother's wife. Much against his better judgement, Herod again sent out the guard. Those who had gathered to hear the Baptist watched the soldiers' approach in silence; a co-ordinated band on horseback, their clothing and banners a brilliant blue against the rust and gold of the sand. Something in the determination of their approach forewarned the knot of John's disciples that this time meant trouble. They screwed up their eyes against the sun to follow the progress of the dust cloud kicked up by the horsemen as they approached across the desert. Dismounting, the soldiers left their horses on the ridge and made their way on foot to where John stood. It was green around the river: a cool, solid green against the unbroken red and yellow of the hills. Men and women stood in silent clusters in the shade of the trees and watched uneasily.

"John bar Zachariah. You are under arrest."

Some of John's disciples resisted at first, protesting volubly and shaking their fists at the soldiers but the Baptist stopped them with a word.

"Have I not told you to do violence to no man?" he asked them calmly. "If Herod's conscience is troubling him, what is that to me? I will grant the Fox the pleasure of my company at his palace."

His followers watched in stricken silence as John was led away. Gradually the group of onlookers, some of whom had gathered to hear him preach and others who had come simply as spectators, began to disperse. It was, for the most part, a long way back to their villages, and they bore tidings that would cause great consternation and excitement.

Chapter 4
Twice-Born

"Shabbat Shalom."
"Shabbat Shalom," Chaim Freiberg's voice echoed down the empty corridor of the Yeshiva. Michael stood looking back into the classroom that had been his second home for the past three years. The usual neat rows of desks and chairs had been left in disarray after the earlier celebration. It was over. He cast his eyes over the dingy green walls and the scuffed brown linoleum; the overflowing ashtray on Rabbi Cohen's desk with its familiar line of burn marks on the edge closest to his seat, before turning to leave.

Michael followed Chaim out into the sunlight and the doors swung shut behind him.

He stood overlooking the field where the practice game was drawing to a close. The sun glinted through the leaves of the oak trees and cast long shadows across the grass. Young men walked in small groups, a hand thrown companionably over another's shoulder, laughing as they rehashed some salient point of the match. One youth took leave of the others and ran up the bank, tugging his jersey over his head as he did so. His torso, caught in the late afternoon light, glistened with sweat. He was broad shouldered, muscular, a perfect specimen of early manhood. Michael noted all this in the instant before the footballer collided with him, almost knocking him off his feet.

"Watch where you're going, will you!"

His assailant back-pedalled for a couple of steps, flashing an unabashed grin in Michael's direction.

"And you – watch where you're standing!" he countered, before disappearing in the direction of the change rooms.

After the cloistered atmosphere of the Yeshiva, Frankfurt University had proved to be exhilarating and overwhelming, thrusting Michael into a world of alien and often hostile attitudes. Academics proved no problem. Years of in-depth reading on the subjects of history and philosophy had prepared Michael well beyond the level of most of his peers, while his Talmudic studies had grounded him in critical analysis, and study of the Torah, a strong moral base.

His father had tried to warn him about the social and ethical issues that would inevitably arise from the unfamiliar environment.

"Everything you have learned to hold dear will come under siege, Michael. They will test every belief and attempt to undermine even the foundation that has been laid from your youth. Ignorance leads men to destroy what they don't understand."

"It will be fine, papa."

"It will be the test of your foundation, believe me! Don't imagine that you won't be shaken. You will be. But you have made this choice, Michael, and I trust you will cope with it."

The choice had included shaving off his long side locks, and the conscious setting aside of his Judaic manner of dress. Rabbi Cohen had not understood, but Michael Segal had his father's support. Yes, he would refrain from the drinking, womanising, and sports, inherent in the university life. He had only one pursuit in mind, a degree that would launch him on his chosen career.

"So, the football player is also a philosopher?"

The young man glanced at Michael and then his face broke into a grin of recognition.

"Perhaps, but I may be better with the ball." He stuck out a hand, "Allow me to introduce myself, I am Walther Krauss."

"Michael Segal."

"And I gather, Michael Segal, that you do not play football."

"I think I may be better at philosophy."

"Then it is possible that a mutually beneficial friendship could develop," Krauss laughed.

Michael responded instantly to the keen humour conveyed in those hazel eyes. Walther Krauss was more than a head taller than Michael, who had never considered himself short, and he had managed to tame the light brown hair, which was now slicked back from his broad forehead and temples.

"How are you finding the course?" Michael asked.

"Somewhat challenging so far. Look, I am going to get a cup of coffee. Would you like to join me?"

"Sure."

It was the beginning of an unusual association for Michael. Walther was the first German he had considered a friend since his pre-school days when race had still played no part in relationships.

Despite his protestations, Walther had a fine mind for philosophy, what he lacked was the desire to study, preferring to kick a ball around the football field. He gave up trying to persuade Michael to join the team, and swore it was their head to head discussions that got him through classes rather than anything else. Michael enjoyed his company. Krauss' outgoing nature attracted people wherever he went and knowing him made Segal's path easier through his first year. It was not the basis of the friendship, but a valuable spin off.

Chaim Freiberg had also gone on to university but his courses differed from Michael's and their paths crossed less frequently. Chaim was intent on carving out a political career for himself, which, after the war to end all wars, was still a slim possibility for a Jew.

They saw one another during Saturday prayers and occasionally Michael invited him home for lunch after synagogue. In the afternoon the two of them would gather with Michael's father for a lively discussion over a passage from the Torah.

In 1922, there were few rumblings of what was to come. The war was over, the economy was in tatters, and most Germans were attempting to put the pieces of their lives together once more.

Like most Germans, Michael knew the constraints and heartaches that war had imposed upon his family. His father had fought until he was badly wounded at Cambrai in November, 1917. After his discharge, he was sent home to convalesce. He was back at his accounting job but still limped heavily and Michael and his mother could see, written in his face, the pain he suffered both from the leg and the injury to his intestines.

"Have you decided what you want to do when you leave university?"

"Yes sir," Chaim replied without hesitation. "I want to join the League."

"The League of Nations?" Herr Segal looked faintly amused.

"Why?"

"Well, sir, I agree with all their principles. It's the sort of body needed to prevent another war."

"Can war be prevented?"

"Yes sir. President Wilson has captured the public imagination with this. If we can indeed bring freedom to the seas, freedom of commerce, disarmament, an end to secret diplomacy and so on, we will have a fair chance at a peaceful future."

Abraham Segal smiled and shook his head. "Idealism!" he pronounced. "I don't believe it can happen. I'm not even sure that the men who are putting this forward want it to happen."

Chaim appeared offended. "I beg to differ, Herr Segal. It was this agreement that brought Germany out of a war that benefited no one."

"The Entente hasn't benefited any of us either."

"That's because the Treaty of Versailles was imposed on us in the end," Michael cut in. "Germany was promised a negotiated peace based on Wilson's fourteen points. It never happened."

"We were squarely beaten," Abe Segal said wearily. "Our High Command knew it and insisted on the negotiations for an armistice. Ultimately, they accepted the settlement to avoid military occupation of Germany."

"Treaty of Versailles aside, if all nations could accept the League's ideologies," Chaim insisted, "it would be a major step toward world peace."

"And you see yourself as part of that?"

"Yes, sir."

Segal smiled and nodded. "Then I wish you luck. I hope you make it."

Chapter 5
Twice-Born

In June of 1919, Matthias von Ingolstadt took leave to stay with a friend in Poland. The train that took him from Berlin to Warsaw wended its way ponderously from village to village, cutting a swathe through thick natural forests; then on into patch-worked fields of potatoes, rye and wheat.

The city of Warsaw first appeared on the horizon like a mirage, fluid under the haze of steam from the engine. Gradually the forms grew and solidified and then, abruptly, the view of the city was swallowed by the once pompous station buildings, blackened and besmirched by the smoke of many engines. Warsaw had grown up around the banks of the Vistula River; a random agglomeration of buildings, many of them painted in ochres and pastels softening the more austere domes and spires of the inner city.

Herr von Lossow was a German banker who had established his interests in Warsaw before the war and, despite the Second Republic, seemed set to maintain and strengthen his position in the country's capital.

Matthias' friend, Dieter, had inherited his father's looks and his mother's light-hearted approach to life. Both men were tall; their faces lean with a high forehead and well-defined nose. Deep grooves extended from cheek to jaw that were accentuated when they smiled. Dieter's eyes were an unremarkable shade of green and his hair, which was swept back off his face, a soft brown, while Herr von Lossow's eyes receded behind steel-rimmed spectacles and his hair had turned a steely grey. His expression as he examined his son over the rims of his glasses was resigned.

"He tells me that your coming warrants a party," he observed dryly to Matthias von Ingolstadt. "And when I commented that according to my observations, you have never cared much for parties, he insisted that we should have one anyway."

"How else can he get to meet everyone he should meet in such a short space of time?" Dieter asked.

Matthias laughed. "You told me that I was to come to Warsaw for a rest," he said accusingly.

"And so it will be a rest," Dieter parried lightly, "afterwards! But first you need to play a little."

His father shook his head disapprovingly, set his newspaper down on the table and stood to his feet. "If it was rest you wanted young man, Dieter is the wrong company for you. I trust you will join me for a drink later?"

Even in his immaculately cut dark suit and bow tie, Dieter's insouciance, so much a part of his character, was infectious. He took Matthias by the arm.

"Come on," he urged. "I've invited all the best people and you've got to meet the lot!"

Matthias smiled patiently and allowed himself to be propelled across the room. The quartet Dieter had hired for the occasion was playing one of the new waltzes.

"Dieter, won't you dance with me?" The blonde was dressed in black, with a red rose pinned to one shoulder. Dieter glanced apologetically at Matthias as he slipped an arm around her waist.

"Get yourself a drink and introduce yourself!" he ordered. "I'll be back in a moment."

Matthias helped himself to a glass of champagne from a waiter's tray and perched on the back of a sofa to survey the company.

He singled her out of a group of willowy young women who were engaged in conversation in one corner of the room. With Paris fashion making its influence felt on the rest of Europe's major cities, many of them had already cut their hair short and wore it curled around their ears. They were dressed in ankle length silk sheaths that clung provocatively to their breasts and hips and they twittered and fluttered like a group of highly coloured birds. Against them she almost appeared plain. Her thick, dark hair was caught up in a chignon, framing a small earnest face which lacked the sophistication of the women he had become accustomed to meeting at any of Dieter's parties. Even her dress was simple and thoughtful rather than flirtatious, as though the consideration of her sexuality was not of any great importance. Matthias von Ingolstadt was instantly attracted to her and when at last she moved away from the other women, he approached her.

"Can I refill your drink?" He spoke awkwardly, aware that his Polish was clumsy.

She glanced up at him, surprised.

"Thank you."

Her eyes were large and grave, dark-brown, fringed with dark lashes. When he returned from the bar she was standing at the door to the terrace,

looking out into the night. She accepted the glass from him and smiled her thanks.

"I haven't seen you here before," she said.

"I'm a friend of Dieter's," he said by way of explanation. "May I present myself, Matthias von Ingolstadt.

She laughed lightly and replied in fluent German. "But of course, the party's in your honour isn't it? What part of Germany are you from?"

"I'm a Berliner," he replied, "But you haven't told me your name."

"Anna. Anna Lejkin."

The band was playing a waltz and many young couples were taking to the floor.

"Shall we go out onto the terrace?" he asked.

She threw him a grateful glance. "Thank heavens!" she said, and her mouth pursed with a touch of humour he had not noticed before. "For a moment I thought you were going to ask me to dance!"

He laughed. "Don't you like dancing?"

"I don't dislike it," she replied, "but I don't dance well enough to make a grand impression."

The sound of voices and laughter spilled out with the light onto the terrace, but at the rail became more muted. The night was warm, the heat of the day tempered by the rain that had fallen earlier. The pungent smell of damp earth scented the air and now that they were beyond the noise, persistent insect sounds began to impinge on their senses. A haze had formed around the outside lights. Drops of water glistened on each leaf, rolling with infinite patience towards the tip where they hung poised and waiting for the inevitable moment of release.

As he leaned with his hands on the balcony rail, Matthias became aware of his companion's slight build; her head scarcely reached his shoulder.

"Where did you learn to speak German?" he asked.

I was brought up in the West of Poland," she said. "Close to the German border. Most of us learned to speak both languages. Have you been to Poland before?"

"Twice," he replied, "But I haven't seen much of the country beyond Warsaw."

"Do you like it?"

"It's a very unusual city."

She laughed. "It sounds as though you haven't taken to it much."

"I'm sorry, that wasn't what I meant. Warsaw has a great deal of charm, but I find it very complex."

"We have a complex history that has helped to create an unusual people."

He nodded, looking out into the night, knowing that her words implied an unspoken accusation against him as a German.

"It will take time for the country to get back on her feet and re-establish her identity," he said at length.

"Perhaps not so long!" she retorted. "The Polish people have never forgotten who they are, despite having lived for so long under the thumb of others."

"I feel that I should be apologising," he said ruefully.

She laughed and he warmed to the sound.

"No, I should be the one to apologise," she replied, turning to face him, "for attempting to shift the responsibility of your nation onto your shoulders." She changed the subject abruptly. "Are you enjoying the party?"

He smiled. "I am now!"

She shot him an amused glance. "Am I right in thinking Dieter used you as an excuse?"

He laughed. "I doubt whether he ever needs an excuse for a party. But you haven't told me anything about yourself. Do you live in Warsaw now?"

Her expression closed and at first he thought she was not going to answer.

At length she said: "I moved here after the war. My parents were killed."

"I'm sorry."

He sensed that although she appeared vulnerable, she was far from weak. There was pride in the set of her expression that rejected any suggestion of pity.

"If you would like to take me onto the dance floor and bear the consequences, I would be happy to dance now," she said.

"It would be my pleasure."

Despite her protestations, Anna danced gracefully, although without the polished performance of many who were already on the floor. Dieter approached them with a different young woman on his arm.

"There you are!" he said. "I wondered where you had got to. Are you enjoying yourselves?"

His partner reached up and whispered something in his ear and Dieter laughed. They danced on by without waiting for an answer to his question. Anna looked up at Matthias and smiled. She was warm and exciting in his arms. He could smell the soft perfume of her hair and feel the light touch of her body against his own. The music created a gentle backdrop of sound and for the first time since the war, Matthias von Ingolstadt experienced the joy and challenge of life flow through his veins. Their eyes met and suddenly it was as though everything else receded and they were alone in the room.

"I'd like to see you again," he said hesitantly.

Chapter 6
Twice-Born

Machaerus, the palace fortress of Herod Antipas, Tetrarch of Galilee and Perea, emerged triumphantly from a striated mound, isolated from the surrounding hills, several thousand feet above the Dead Sea. Its strategic position was designed to afford a clear vantage point and an invincible military stronghold against raiding bands of Arabs or Moabites. The precipitous ascent to the citadel so exhausted the horses that parties en route to Machaerus were usually forced to leave their carriages and walk the final stretch. Any discomfort was soon forgotten though, as Herod was renowned for his lavish hospitality and an invitation to Machaerus was not lightly refused. Herod Antipas may have been brought up in the ways of Judaism, but as a Roman citizen, he entertained in the style of Rome.

Far below the fortress, the sea that by day lay like a brilliant azure jewel in the arid palm of the desert, would darken and fuse with the landscape. The raw sterility of the surrounding hills softened to cinnamon and rose pink in the evening sun, diffusing the day's unrelenting heat into long shadows and, as small breezes began to toy with the blue, purple and silver drapes and banners within the palace walls, the evening's festivities would begin.

It was Herod's birthday and many important guests, including some of Galilee's tribal leaders, had gathered at Machaerus. In the early part of the evening the women banqueted with the men and only withdrew to the women's quarters when the customary social drinking began, accompanied by a time of entertainment.

Salome, the daughter of Herodias by Herod's brother Herod Philip, the businessman from Caesarea, had filled out into a voluptuous young woman since Herodias' marriage to Antipas. Herodias had watched her husband's growing attraction towards her daughter without comment, aware that Salome openly encouraged him while silently challenging her mother to intervene.

Her opportunity to use this relationship to her own advantage came on this night of celebration at the time when the men were becoming bawdy with too much wine. Those less inclined towards such entertainment had retired with quiet apologies hours ago. Herod Antipas, sprawled out on his couch, replete and red-eyed from an excess of food and drink was in good spirits but the evening's entertainments were drawing to a close and the remainder of his guests, although not yet showing an inclination to leave, were becoming noticeably bored. Antipas turned to Philip[2], his brother, Tetrarch of Northern Galilee.

"Salome is a fine dancer. Better than the girls we have seen here tonight. I wager she will dance for us if I summon her."

Philip's eyes lit up. He had been watching Salome with considerable interest since his arrival at Machaerus.

"Will Herodias permit it?"

There was a momentary hesitation on Herod's part but he answered with a confidence brought on by the wine.

"Certainly she will permit it!"

He summoned a servant and spoke a few words into his ear over the noise of the banqueting hall. The man nodded and left the room. Voices were raised in loud conversation and laughter almost drowning the lively sound of the instruments of the musicians. Torches flickered and smoked, casting an array of mobile shadows on the stone walls. The servant returned and spoke to Herod who smiled and clapped his hands.

"Gentlemen, I have reserved the best for last. My daughter, Salome!"

The lust in his eyes as she entered the room was anything but fatherly. Salome was clad in trousers of the sheerest fabric and low-cut halter, which exposed the seductive curve of her breasts and the soft flesh of her belly. Fine metal chains adorned her hips and her dark hair hung loose. At once the room fell silent; there was a breath of expectation as the tempo of the music changed at a word from the girl and she swirled across the room, tossing her long hair off her face.

Salome's first dance was one of passion: the fire-dance of a peasant girl, which set the blood of every man in the room pulsing

---

[2] Philip the Tetrarch, brother of Herod, not to be confused with Herod-Philip, uncle and first husband of Herodias and father of Salome.

through his loins. The second dance was pure seduction; her hands and lissom arms drawing her audience; her belly rising and falling to the rhythm of the music. Salome's eyes were locked upon Herod Antipas, and he was held captive under her spell.

The room exploded into applause as she fell at Herod's feet at the climatic ending of the song. Herod reached down and took her by the hands, drawing her to her feet.

"Salome!" His voice was husky. "That was wonderful! Let me make you a gift." He looked round the room for support and the audience cheered appreciatively. Herod's words slurred drunkenly; his eyes were on the bosom of his step-daughter, which still rose and fell with the every breath after the exertion of the dance. "Let me give you a gift little one," he said. He still had her by the hand although she was half-turned away from him as though to leave. "A gift, by heaven – even to half my kingdom!"

Salome smiled, "My father, you are kind. There is no need for any recompense. I danced for you."

"A gift!" Herod insisted, swaying a little on his feet. "Certainly, my child! Let me give you your heart's desire."

She kissed her fingertips and touched his mouth, "Thank you father," she said, lowering her eyes. "But let me first ask mother."

Herod smiled but a sobering chill of premonition touched him. He had declared his intention by an oath before all these men that he would give up to half of his kingdom and there could be no backing down. Herodias was a woman of subtlety who would be unafraid to ask for whatever she wanted.

Salome returned to the room within minutes, walking lightly on her sandaled-feet. She bowed before Herod and her mouth puckered into a mischievous smile.

"Mother says that we desire the head of John the Baptist to be sent up to this feast on a platter."

There was silence and all eyes were fixed upon Herod Antipas. He gripped the edge of his couch and his face became bloodless.

"My dear child, your mother of course is not serious. There must be something else I could offer you…" His voice tailed off, knowing already that there was nothing that Herodias wanted more.

She was punishing his interest in the prophet, his refusal to bow to her continual insistence on his death, and finally she was humiliating him publicly for lusting after her daughter.

Herod compressed his lips and looked at the ground; finally he clicked his fingers summoning an officer of the palace guard and gave the order. The banquet fell silent and, at a sign, the musicians began packing away their instruments. The Tetrarch was at once clear-headed and completely sober. Fifteen long minutes dragged past: conversation was muted but no man stood up to leave.

Herodias gathered her robes around her and hurried down the stairs to the dungeons behind the officer. She waited while the Baptist was awakened roughly from his sleep and watched with grim satisfaction as he stumbled clumsily to his feet. As he caught sight of her in the flickering light from the torch, held high in the hand of a servant, his mouth tightened.

"My God," he said quietly, "I commend myself into your hands. Let it be done in accordance with your will."

A youth, who had earlier waited at tables, came down the stairs behind Herodias bearing in his hands a silver platter. He looked uneasy as though his presence was an intrusion on a scene which he had no desire to witness.

Iron doors clanged violently as they were opened and shut. Prisoners clung to the bars of their cells staring in silence as the wooden block was carried into the Baptist's cell. John's eyes rested on the woman and his expression mocked her.

"My head will bring you all your desire, my mistress. And it will, of a certainty take you to the depths of hell."

"Hold your tongue!" the officer shouted.

"There is none who can silence me but the God of Israel, Isaac and Jacob," John retorted. "You may take my head if that is your purpose here, but He will take my soul. My blood is on you and the evil hands of your mistress and it will not leave you guiltless."

Two swift blows from the soldier's fists doubled the Baptist over clutching his broken nose. Blood streamed from between his fingers.

"Enough!" The command came from Herodias. "Kill him!"

The officer unsheathed his sword and another forced the Baptist to his knees. The weapon was raised high and the blade whistled through the air. There was a resounding clang of metal at the same instant as the swift blow severed the head and the officer of the guard regarded his shattered sword in amazement. The second soldier laughed shortly and picked up the other half of the blade.

"Give it to me," Herodias said. "I will make sure you receive another. Let the head be taken to the banqueting hall. She pushed the frozen youth forward impatiently and he held out the platter to the soldiers. Herodias carefully wrapped the sword with its broken blade in her veil and took the stairs from the dungeons without a backward glance.

Footsteps clattered on the stone floor as two members of the guard entered the room. The unkempt head of the prophet was borne on a meat platter and set down on the table before Herod Antipas. The eyes of the Baptist were still open and the dish swam with his blood. Herod, pallid and sick to the stomach, nodded briefly to dismiss them and summoned Salome. The daughter of Herodias made obeisance before her step-father and, as she arose, the torchlight reflected the ice in her eyes. She was, Antipas realised for the first time, entirely her mother's daughter. He bowed his head towards his guests and announced an end to the evening's festivities then, drawing his robes around him, Herod Antipas left the room.

Several days later, Herodias announced Salome's betrothal to Herod's brother, the Tetrarch Philip.

Chapter 7
Twice-Born

"Have you read it?" Michael asked Chaim Freiberg thrusting the book under his nose.

"Philip Dru: The Administrator?" Chaim nodded. "Of course!"

"Then you know that Woodrow Wilson reorganised America's financial and legislative structures in accordance with it?"

"And founded the League of Nations along Philip Dru's lines?"

"Exactly! Doesn't that bother you?"

Chaim sat down under one of the trees and unwrapped his sandwiches.

"Not really. Like everyone else, I was fascinated to see that Mandel House had written it."

Michael viewed his friend in amazement. "President Wilson's closest advisor writes an anonymous book outlining legislative and fiscal policy and you are unfazed when it's adopted as a directive for the United States? It's a novel, for heaven's sake!"

"And Mandel House is Wilson's advisor. I'm sure they cooked it up between them. House probably had pretensions as a writer and they saw it as a way to project their intentions and to influence the nation towards the changes they proposed to make. Is there anything particularly sinister in that?"

"When Wilson signed the charter of the League three years ago, its aim was to bring about world government. Wilson saw himself becoming President of the World. Who knows where we would be today if the senate had ratified it."

Chaim was munching his way resolutely through his large pile of sandwiches but his jaws stopped moving for a moment as he considered his answer.

"In the end, if we are to prevent a war like the last one from recurring, we need to end all forms of constitutional government. The only way forward is to replace them with a world dictatorship. America has chosen to stay out of the League anyway. I personally don't think

Wilson was the man for the job, but world government must come. It's inevitable."

Michael Segal's shoulders sagged in disbelief.

"I don't understand what's got into you, Chaim. Don't you see that you're being an idiot? You set up a one-world government and sooner, rather than later, you will have a megalomaniac at the helm. It's a recipe for human enslavement!"

Chaim had returned to an almost morbid mastication of his lunch and he shrugged off the interruption.

"I think that's a somewhat narrow and hysterical viewpoint," he said. "Not really worthy of you at all, Michael. As I see it, the League has a vital role to play and world government is the inevitable result of the formation of such a body."

"And as I see it," Michael retorted, "it is downright dangerous!"

The last of the summer days had passed. Almost without warning, the air became crisper with just a hint of winter to come. On the campus grounds, oak leaves turned gold and russet, and fell from the trees.

Carpets of dried leaves crunched and rustled underfoot as they walked down the road towards Michael Segal's house. Walther, who had suffered the death of his father during the last semester, had become noticeably quieter. He had sisters at home who were taking care of his mother, he said. He was glad the football season was over as money was short and it freed him to take on a part-time job

On an impulse Michael had invited him home to share the Sabbath meal. His father met them at the door and shook hands a little stiffly as the introductions were made.

"It's kind of you to have me, Herr Segal."

Inside, the curtains were drawn and the table was set with the best white linen.

"Mutti?"

Michael's mother was bustling round the kitchen but she wiped her hands on her apron and took Walther's hand.

"Welcome," she said. "Michael's told us so much about you. Dinner will be ready in just a minute."

They sat in the parlour savouring the aroma wafting through the house as the finishing touches were put to the meal. Conversation with Abraham Segal was stilted. His father was defensive; his underlying antipathy towards the Germans, Michael realised, still ran deep.

Frau Segal lit the candles and the Shabbat prayers were intoned. Once or twice, Michael glanced at his friend but he need not have worried. Once the formalities were over, Walther slipped back into character; his quick sense of humour soon won Michael's mother over and even Herr Segal allowed himself the occasional smile.

Afterwards, while Frau Segal busied herself with the dishes the men returned to the parlour. Herr Segal lit a cigarette, inhaled deeply and blew the smoke towards the ceiling.

"Michael tells me you play football."

"That's right, sir."

"What position do you play?"

In moments the two men were embroiled in a discussion on the finer points of the game and Michael left them to it.

He took a cloth off the rail and began drying the dishes.

"I didn't know papa knew so much about sport!" he confided with a laugh. "It seems he and Walther have found something in common."

"He seems a nice young man," Frau Segal said. "You must invite him back. Such a shame about his father!"

They packed away the last of the dishes and rejoined the men just as Walther was preparing to leave. Michael walked him to the gate. The gas lights were on, forming broad circles of yellow light down the length of the street. Walther put his hat on and buttoned up his coat against the chill.

Herr Segal nodded in approval as Michael returned to the house and shut the door behind him.

"A good German," he commented. And his tone suggested that it was an unusual phenomenon.

Chapter 8
Twice-Born

The haunted look had gone from Matthias von Ingolstadt's face in the
months that had passed since the Armistice although, trapped behind his
eyes were unsolicited memories, which came and went like shadows.
The Freicorps had been good for him. Knowing that he was not bound
to stay, the echo of pounding explosion, the sick shock of broken flesh
and the stench of death had begun to recede. His thin frame toughened
by years of hardship, had become hard and sleek with muscle, but there
was still something in his bearing and his expression too gentle to be
exposed to the practice of war.

From the relationship with Anna Lejkin, there came the touch of
healing. In the weeks since the party they met almost daily and spent
hours in one another's company. Matthias was in love as he had never
been before and certain in the knowledge that this was the woman he
would marry. He cursed the swift passing of time that would soon take
him away from her.

Anna lay on the grass beside him with her head in his lap. He
traced the outline of her face, and caught up her hair in his hands
allowing it to sift through his fingers.

"Anna."

She smiled up at him. Matthias' face was strong, though not
handsome, with a clean-shaven well-defined jaw line. His hair, which
was shaved close to his head above the ears, thickened out and fell in a
wave over his forehead. The grey eyes that looked down at her were
serious.

"I want to leave the Freicorps when I get back," he said, "and
find myself a civilian job."

"I'm glad. They have a bad reputation here in Poland."

"I know. Part of the Freicorps has begun to take the law into
their own hands. They've become a bit like the old Vehmgericht."

"The what?"

"The Vehm, a secret society from Charlemagne's time. Men who used to carry out their own trials and executions. A dagger under the tree where their victim was hung acted as a warning to others that there was to be no investigation of the murder."

"Who were their victims?" she asked.

He shrugged. "Heretics, rapists and Jews."

Anna sat up and wrapped her arms around her knees. "There was so much support for Germany during this war," she said unexpectedly. "Jewish intellectuals in Britain almost without exception supported the German fight against Russia. Did you know that many Jews were reluctant to fight against Germany because of that?"

He shook his head, puzzled by the turn in conversation.

"When the Germans arrived in Russia, Jewish villages had been razed by the Russians and thousands of Jews were rounded up and sent to Siberia. The Germans were said to have been wonderful to the people. They gave the children sweets and biscuits. The Jews saw them as conquering heroes. Yet as a Polish outsider I've seen so much anti-Semitism in the Germans."

He shrugged. "I haven't thought much about it, but I suppose you're right."

"You know that in this war, the Jews in Germany fought as the Germans fought. They died side by side on the battlefield. Did you know, Matthias that something like twelve thousand Jews gave their lives as Germans in the war against Britain?"

He looked at her, puzzled by her obvious anger. "I know there were Jews in the army with us. I have no idea of the numbers."

"Then you are probably also unaware that after 1918, when we Poles suddenly found ourselves in a new country and serving under a new flag, of the attacks made by the Poles against the Jewish community?"

"I read the papers," his tone had become defensive.

"So you know that more than fifty Jews were killed in Lvov, and that seventeen hundred were slaughtered in Proskurov and that by the end of the year Simon Petlura's gangsters had murdered possibly sixty thousand Jews in this country? Their only crime, Matthias, was that they were Jews." She fell silent and turned her head away. A chill had fallen on the afternoon. He had no idea what Anna was driving at, but he knew that the conversation had not gone at all as he had intended. A strand of her hair had fallen across her forehead and she twisted it between her fingers and pinned it back into place.

"Matthias, do you know that I am Jewish?" she asked suddenly.

The blood drained from his face and he was unable to respond. He felt as though he had been dealt a blow to the solar plexus.

"You didn't," she said and her voice was flat. "How stupid of me, I assumed you knew."

She stood up and smoothed her dress, stooped to retrieve her scarf and began the long walk up to the house. The mauve silk caught the wind and trailed from her clenched hand, fluttering softly behind her.

Matthias made no move to stop her. Years of deeply entrenched prejudice had been in one instant thrown into question. The Jewish race had never been more to him than a bad joke, a people he had consciously avoided. They were a stain on his nation and every nation with which they came in contact. A grasping avaricious race of money-lenders that had arisen by some freak accident, in the same way as weeds grew and choked wheat, or fleas fed off dogs. But not Anna. Anna who seemed to him to be everything that was innocence and purity. How did she fit into the picture he had painted for himself? For the first time Matthias von Ingolstadt wondered whether there was some intrinsic delusion at the very foundation of his beliefs.

"Why didn't you tell me that Anna was Jewish?" The question was accusing.

Dieter set his glass down on the table and turned to face him.

"Would it have made a difference?"

"Of course it would have made a difference!" Matthias replied irritably.

Dieter shrugged. "Look, I've always known your feelings," he replied, "I don't much like Jews myself but in my father's business we have to socialise with them. It really didn't occur to me to mention it when you were having such a good time. Anna came to the party with Jewish associates of my father's. "I've met her on a couple of prior occasions."

"Damn you!" Matthias said. He stopped pacing and slumped into a chair, his mood changing abruptly from anger to despair. "It would have been alright if it had simply been 'a good time', but it's already gone much further than that."

"You mean you've slept with her?"

"I don't mean that I've slept with her!" Matthias retorted with exasperation. "I'm talking about how I feel about Anna. It's different for me this time, Dieter."

His friend laughed. "You're always much too serious, Matthias," he said. "If you like her, forget that she's a Jew and get on with it. You're leaving in a couple of weeks anyway."

Not for the first time Matthias wondered how two such different characters as Dieter and himself ever came to be friends in the first place.

He shook his head. "It's not that simple," he said quietly. "I want to marry Anna."

"You'd consider marrying her even though she's a Jew? You have got it bad!" He sat down opposite Matthias and appraised him speculatively. "So, have you asked her?"

Matthias shook his head. "I've made such a mess of things that I doubt whether she'd have me," he replied. "I've thought about it all afternoon Dieter and I don't know how it would be possible anyway. Can you imagine my parents' reaction, or what living in Germany in a mixed marriage would be like?"

Dieter grimaced. "There are mixed marriages and I presume they work."

Matthias von Ingolstadt ran his fingers through his hair. "I don't think I could do it to her," he said. "I don't want her to bear the brunt of the sort of prejudice that I've been guilty of."

Dieter raised his eyebrows perceptibly and his narrow face creased into a smile. "It sounds as though you've undergone one of those religious conversions," he commented cynically. "And here you are, a transformed man!"

Von Ingolstadt refused to rise to the bait. "It occurred to me today that I've never actually known a Jew before. I've simply spewed out the stuff I've been fed!" He sat quietly for a moment, thinking back on the conversation with Anna. "Her parents were killed," he said. "Have you any idea how they died?"

"In one of Petlura's uprisings, I believe. Anna was away from home at the time. Look, Matthias, there's no need to rush this thing. Passions have a way of fizzling out after a time. Give it a few months and see how you feel."

Matthias stood up. His limbs suddenly felt very tired. He had no idea what the solution would be, but he knew he wanted Anna and he would accept her now on any terms.

Anna Lejkin had known what it was to be despised, degraded and set apart and she bore that knowledge in her eyes: the touch of sorrow that is often the mark of the Jew. It had been a simple to thing to pretend that Matthias von Ingolstadt had known her racial background. What, in the first flush of their attraction to one another had hardly seemed to matter, had become a stumbling block that she had actively sought to ignore as her feelings for him had deepened. Now that it was in the open and she had witnessed the shock that the news had afforded him, she simply retreated. She was hurt, but resigned to the inevitable.

Anna was not a practising Jew, her family had carried out some of the ritual of the feast days but without conviction and, as an adult, Anna had allowed even that to fall away. She was Jewish simply by an accident of birth or by a cruel design of fate, but she considered herself emancipated beyond the need for the encumbrance of a God, and especially one who, by choosing a nation had destined it for such persecution and hardship.

The next evening, Matthias was waiting for her outside the bank where she worked, as though nothing had happened. Her heart lurched when she saw him.

"Anna," his voice was uncertain. "May I walk you home?"

She looked up at him and the tilt of her chin was defiant. "Are you sure you want to?"

He took her arm, leading her back into the doorway, away from the flow of pedestrians on the pavement.

"I have to talk to you."

She nodded and averted her eyes, wishing suddenly that he had not come. It seemed pointless to attempt to breach the divide between them; it would only reinforce the pain she was already experiencing. A clean break would be far simpler.

"Anna," he was pleading with her. "I'm sorry about what happened yesterday. Will you forgive my stupidity?" He took her face in his hands forcing her to look at him. "Can you ever forgive me?"

"Perhaps I should be the one to ask forgiveness," she said hesitantly, "for not having told you."

He shook his head and drew her to him, holding her close, oblivious of the curious glances of the passers-by.

"Come," he said at last. "Let me take you home."

She held onto his arm as they crossed the road, securing her hat with the other hand.

Although Anna felt proud to be seen in his company, it was not his good looks that had first attracted her to Matthias von Ingolstadt, but his vulnerability.   Most Germans she had met appeared insensitive and controlling.   Their primary loyalty seemed to be in nationhood as if they were threatened by interpersonal relationships and chose to take refuge in a higher ideal.   As a people, they seemed to Anna a little like a child without a father, finding a front in bravado rather than tears.

There were steps from the street up to the front door of the house where Anna roomed.   Here it was quiet and gnarled trees grew at intervals along the edge of the street, carpeting the pavement with white blossoms that grew opaque as they were bruised underfoot.

"In less than two weeks I go back," Matthias said.   "I want to come back for you, Anna."

She looked up at him, startled.

"I know," he said.   "It's too soon.   But I love you and I want to marry you."

She laughed softly.   "Matthias, I don't believe you've thought about this at all.   You don't have a job apart from the Freicorps and little chance of getting one with the economy in such a shambles.   But apart from that, have you any idea what it would be like being married to a Jewess?"

He shook his head.   "I don't," he confessed.   "But I'm willing to find out and I promise that somehow I'll find work."   He took her by the shoulders.   "Anna, before you say anything else, there's one thing you haven't told me.   Do you love me?"

It was a moment before she spoke, but he could read the answer in her eyes.

"More than my life," she said simply.

It was she who made the suggestion, so lightly that at first he was convinced she was joking.

"Is it important that I marry you as Anna Lejkin, a Jew?" she asked.   "I could always change my identity, you know, and become an Aryan."

He smiled at her.   "It sounds as though you've got cold feet," he commented.

"Icy!" she retorted.   "The thought of facing your parents and a long line of relatives and friends scares me half to death."

He looked at her curiously. "Even if it were possible, wouldn't it be painful to renounce your background?"

She shrugged. "What would I be renouncing; Judaism? I'm not a believer. My race? I've never been allowed to care for it." She linked her hands and looked down at her upturned palms. "I wouldn't be renouncing a nation because without a country our identity really only lies in our religion. What remains then is my family."

"And you no longer have a family," he said softly.

She nodded and when she turned to face him there was a touch of the defiance in her expression that he had only seen once before.

"So, if I marry you and return with you as a Jew to Germany, I will be setting you at odds with life as you have always known it. Since the collapse of the Spartacus Bund, Germany is blaming the Jews for the Versailles Treaty and Lenin is saying that Rosa Luxemburg was responsible for the new wave of anti-Semitism that is sweeping across Germany. As a Jew, I would only make your life unbearable. What would be the point?"

He sat down next to her on the sofa. "I believe you're serious!" he said incredulously.

"Of course I'm serious!" she answered, pushing her hair back off her forehead. "I know exactly what we'll be facing in Germany. You can't possibly know!" She turned to face him. "Could it be done?"

He stood up restlessly. "I've no idea. I know there are ways of assuming new identities, but where one would begin…" His voice tailed off and he looked thoughtful, then he sat down and took her hands in his. "There may be a way, but are you certain you want me to try? What if you regret it later?"

Anna shook her head. "It would be a ticket to freedom," she replied.

Chapter 9
Twice-Born

Herod's wife was fascinated by the head and took satisfaction from the level of revulsion the story had aroused in Judaea. Inevitably the news had spread swiftly across the country. Herod was both embarrassed and angry and for many days after his birthday party refused to speak to Herodias. She remained unconcerned. It was he who was guilty of allowing his daughter to dance, something normally reserved for peasants and prostitutes. He had lusted after Salome therefore he had received his just desserts. His humiliation was limited to the elimination of a Jew; he had rightly chosen to protect the honour of his word over a worthless life. Herodias vowed to keep her talisman and when John's disciples came to Machaerus to claim the Baptist's body for burial she refused Herod's request to surrender the head.

Herod's relationship with Herodias changed after his unfortunate birthday celebration. Salome had been married to his brother with almost indecent haste and Herod was left in no doubt that Salome's match to Philip was part of his own punishment. He had publicly displayed undue affection towards his step-daughter and Herodias intended to make him suffer for it.

Although not everyone had been attracted by John's teachings, few sympathised with Herod's slaying of the Jewish prophet. Pontius Pilot had heard of the outcome of Herod's birthday celebrations and had sworn that he would have nothing more to do with the man on a personal level. Politically, situations would arise requiring some interaction, but Pilot's sense of decency was outraged by the callous act that had taken place in the name of entertainment.

The rift between the two men was deepened and Pilot's antagonism further incensed in another incident. In order to honour Tiberius Caesar, Pontius Pilot had had golden shields made and hung in the Herodian Palace in Jerusalem. There was no image on the shields, simply a dedication to Caesar. Nevertheless, a delegation composed of members of the Sanhedrin as well as Herod Antipas and his three brothers had arrived one day at the Herodian Palace to meet with Pilot. Their complaint was that the shields offended Jewish religious sensibilities and violated their law. When Pilot refused to remove them, Herod Antipas and the chief priests had taken it upon themselves to write their complaint to Tiberius. The incident had almost resulted in Pilot's recall to Rome.

Chuza, chief steward to Herod Antipas, had a wife named Joanna, who served Herodias. It was Joanna who had told Herodias on the day following the banquet, of a man who was an adept in the ancient Egyptian art of embalming and Herodias instructed her to summon him to the palace immediately.

Joanna was a woman in her early thirties, with a thin face, prominent cheekbones and a long nose. She would not have been unattractive were it not for stringy shoulder-length hair, devoid of any real style or colour, and a sly attitude that found expression in her eyes. It had delighted Joanna as much as it had her mistress when John bar Zachariah was arrested and thrown into the cells beneath Machaerus, especially as she knew the act would cause her husband pain. And, although even she was secretly shocked by the murder of the prophet; she would never have given expression to an attitude that might have caused her to lose favour with her mistress.

For Chuza, Joanna had proved an unfortunate match. He was an upright man, well suited by his integrity to his high position in Herod's service. His marriage to Joanna had been arranged for him by their respective families and it had led to years of torment. Many times he had considered putting her away quietly, especially when the marriage had proved childless, but divorce was not encouraged within Judaism and he was reluctant to take such an extreme step.

Chuza had gone several times to hear the Baptist preach, at first out of curiosity but on the second occasion he had waded out into the tepid waters of the Jordan River to receive baptism as he repented of his sins. Joanna laughed when she heard what he had done and mocked him as a fool. He expected no less of her and had never mentioned it again in her hearing.

The embalmer was an intense man with black fanatical eyes that seemed to see past the ordinary and penetrate the dimension of spirits beyond. Herodias was struck as he worked, by his dexterity and the unusual length of his fingers.

"How can I be certain that the work you are doing will last?" she questioned at length. Her tone was imperious, she was anxious not to suggest familiarity by her absorption with the intricacies of his task.

He did not look up. "This head will outlive you by many generations when I have finished with it!" he assured her. "I learned my art at the feet of the priests and magicians of Egypt and my work is of the finest quality. In that country, the process is one of keeping the body whole until their journey through the realm of the dead is complete. This man, of course, was not an Egyptian but a Hebrew prophet." He shot Herodias a glance out of the corner of his eye as he bent over the dismembered head.

She shrugged.

The embalmer was removing the brain piece by minute piece from the cranium through the nostrils with a long metal instrument; a slow, tedious process, which required skill as well as patience. He had set amulets about the head and incanted spells as he worked to protect himself against spirits from the realm of the dead. At length he was satisfied, and by the insertion of a second implement, proceeded to scrape the cavity clean. Still working painstakingly through the nose, he coated the inner skull with a dark resinous fluid, plugged the nostrils with two strips of cloth and coated the skin in camomile oil.

Once he was certain that the work was complete, the head of John the Baptist was presented to Herodias wrapped in a white linen cloth to be stored in a camphor chest complete with amulets prescribed by the embalmer. More than a week had passed since his arrival. As he prepared to take his leave he bowed and his thin lips drew back off his teeth in a smile that was both ingratiating and devoid of humour.

"I know a man, one Simon the Magus, a magician of Samaria who is able through his power to make this head a god."

Herodias had no hesitation. "Tell him to come to me," she ordered.

Chapter 10
Twice-Born

July 1919

Herr von Lossouw sucked on his pipe and eyed the younger man speculatively.

"What makes you think I would have any part in such a scheme?" he asked. "If you ask me, the idea is hare-brained enough to have come from my own son. I must say, I expected better from you, von Ingolstadt."

Matthias bit his lip and when he spoke again he chose his words with even more care. "I realise, sir that I have asked far more of you than I should have done and I apologise. But you were the only person I could think of who might have had the means to help."

Herr von Lossouw knocked the loose tobacco from his pipe into an ashtray.

"Is it because of your parents' reaction to the girl that you want to do this?" He removed a pipe cleaner from the small wooden smoking cabinet at his elbow and began the task of cleaning the stem of his pipe.

Matthias von Ingolstadt shook his head. "Not entirely sir. I realise they will be upset, but I'm prepared to face that if necessary. It's really for Anna."

Von Lossouw shot him a glance. "For Miss Lejkin? In what positive way would this deception possibly benefit her?"

Matthias von Ingolstadt looked uncomfortable. "In fact sir," he said, "she feels that it would be easier for me to be married to an Aryan, rather than a Jew. I'm sorry, this was a mistake. I should never have presumed on you in this way." He stood up and clicked his heels. "With your permission sir, I'll leave if I may."

Von Lossouw ignored his outstretched hand. "Sit down, von Ingolstadt," he said gruffly. "I hope this is not something I will live to regret, but I have to admit, this Jewish thing is carried to extremes at times, and Miss Lejkin seems a nice enough young girl."

Matthias sat down obediently and waited while von Lossouw refilled his pipe.

"I can't promise anything," he said at last, "but I'll make some enquiries for you. Obviously, it goes without saying that I will require absolute silence from both you and Miss Lejkin. Anything said at this stage could compromise the investigation and land several people in a great deal of trouble. That, of course would include myself and my family."

He stood up and placed his pipe on the rack in his tobacco cabinet. "I will speak to Dieter myself and I would ask you not to discuss the matter with him any further. "I'm certain that despite any shortcomings my son may have, he can be trusted to be discreet when the occasion requires it."

He waved away von Ingolstadt's thanks.

"I'll see you at dinner." He turned away ostensibly to examine the titles on his bookshelf. The subject, for the present, was closed.

Matthias von Ingolstadt had approached Herr von Lossouw naively, believing that somehow, from his position of power as a banker, he would have access to people and positions that he, von Ingolstadt, would not. But it was not as a banker that Herr von Lossow chose to work. He was indeed a man of influence, wielding far greater power than Matthias von Ingolstadt imagined. Herr von Lossow was a 'Knight of the Pelican and Eagle, and Sovereign Prince Rose Cross of Heredom', which grandiose title attained in the service of the Great Architect of the Universe, made him a Freemason of the Eighteenth Degree.

It was a comparatively simple thing to obtain lists of Freemasons from the Grand Masters of the various lodges, and to check who was 'on the square' in the Warsaw Civil Service.

Mikolai Slowacki was a Third Degree Master Mason and a clerk in the Registry of Births and Deaths. At the end of July 1919, at Herr von Lossow's request, he met with him in Lazienki Park.

Warsaw wore the pristine face of a city resplendent in sunlight after several days of rain. The old buildings along the Royal Axis that ran parallel to the Vistula seemed freshly restored and the river carried their images deep within itself, except where water birds and insects disturbed the surface, breaking it into facets of reflected light.

Slowacki was a slightly corpulent figure in his late forties. He was dressed in a dark grey suit and grey felt hat, with a fob watch chain hung from his breast pocket. Apart from the slight bagging of the material at the knees and elbows, he might have passed as a businessman rather than a white-collar worker.

Herr von Lossow returned his handshake, acknowledging the slight pressure of the third finger, a sign of his Masonic affiliation.

"Thank you for agreeing to this meeting, Herr Slowacki."

"I assure you, the pleasure is mine. How can I be of assistance to you, Herr von Lossow?"

"I have a somewhat unusual request to make of you."

"Shall we walk?"

They took the path along the water's edge in the direction of the Summer Palace, the warmth of the sunlight on their backs.

"I have a friend who needs a favour and I believe you may be in a position to help."

Mikolai Slowacki glanced at his companion curiously. "Obviously, as a brother, I will do my utmost to assist," he assured him.

"I think you may find our association to be mutually beneficial. I believe you have been seeking promotion within your department for some time?"

Slowacki's expression brightened perceptibly. "This friend of yours, Herr von Lossow, what can I do for him?"

"How difficult would it be to effect a change in identity?"

Slowacki fingered the waxed end of his moustache thoughtfully. "In fact it would be remarkably simple," he replied at length, "but it would depend on the manner in which such a change is handled afterwards as to whether it's uncovered or not."

"Perhaps, before I continue, I must give you my personal assurance that this is not an attempt to evade the law. This person is not a criminal. It is simply, in fact, a young woman who wishes to make a fresh start in a new country."

A knowing look crossed Mikolai Slowacki's heavy features arousing a surge of irritation in von Lossow.

"What one could do," Slowacki suggested, "is to draw up a

death certificate for the young lady and then find someone recently deceased, who is of similar age and background."

They sat down on a bench and Slowacki stretched out his legs. Herr von Lossow leaned on the head of his cane and looked out across the water. Ducks paddled swiftly towards them and watched them from the shallows, in the hope of food.

"You say she would be leaving the country?" Slowacki asked.

"She's intending to get married in Germany." Von Lossow replied frigidly.

"I see." Slowacki was aware that he had lost favour and when he spoke again his tone was ingratiating. "I will require certain information on the young woman. Birth certificate and that sort of thing."

Herr von Lossow nodded. "I have it with me."

He produced a manila envelope from the inside pocket of his jacket. "If you need anything further, you can contact me here. He scribbled an address on the back of the envelope and handed it to Slowacki. "How soon can I expect to hear from you?"

"It depends entirely on how easily I will be able to match her with a deceased person. May I assure you though, sir, I am delighted to have made your acquaintance in this way and I trust I shall be of service to you."

Herr von Lossow nodded, and then as if it were an afterthought, added: "Oh yes, the girl is Jewish, and I would like the person whose identity she assumes, to be Aryan."

Mikolai Slowacki gave a slight bow and doffed his hat as von Lossow took his leave. He watched him walk away across the park, shoulders held stiffly erect and his step a little uneven as though the act of walking was painful to him.

He examined the birth certificate and shook his head incredulously. Obviously the attraction must be money, how else would a man of his age appeal to a young thing like this? Smiling, he walked back towards the road, his mind filled with the prospect of promotion.

Chapter 11
Twice-Born

The almost legendary power of Simon Magus had spread beyond the boundaries of Samaria into Galilee at a time when Judaism in its purity teetered on the brink of extinction. The Herods' had been responsible for building cities such as Caesarea Philippi and Tiberius, in which religious Jews refused to dwell, and under the Roman occupation in combination with the enormous Greek influence, ancient forms of worship had sprung up afresh and new cults abounded.

Herodias received Simon Magus eagerly. It had been two weeks since the embalmer had completed his work and she had awaited his promise to send the Magus with ill-disguised impatience. When he at last arrived, the outer courts of Machaerus were already heated by sunshine that lay white-hot over the desert and leeched the colour from the Dead Sea many miles below them. Simon Magus was granted time to change his robes, stained from the long journey, before being ushered into the women's quarters of Machaerus where he was received by Herodias alone.

He was a man in his thirties with an expressive, sensual mouth and eyes that were a light sea-green. His beard and hair were washed and perfumed with some expensive unguent; a smell that was both pervasive and seductive. Magus took Herodias by the hands and bowed his head in deferential greeting but as he raised his eyes they locked onto her own and tugged at her soul. She deliberately turned away from him, gesturing that he should be seated. Refreshments were brought, and sweetmeats arrayed on the low table.

Dressed in a white gown draped from the shoulders to display her smooth olive skin and the curve of her breasts, Herodias reclined on her silken cushions and watched him through lowered eye-lids. She had expected a peasant, but Simon Magus was a man of learning and cultivated charm; despite the outward display of subservience, he was obviously not in the least intimidated by her position as wife of the Tetrarch.

Simon Magus had studied at the feet of many masters and the gods had given him great mastery among the Samaritans. His words broke the last threads of discernment between good and evil, captured victims and held them in his web. Some allowed themselves to be bound in his thread of control knowing what he was; others remained without a fight believing him to be what he proclaimed himself to be. Few fought to free themselves once Simon Magus assumed control of their lives.

It was the magician's voice that captivated her. His tones were the call of a flute; of water over the rocks in a brook. Herodias was transported as he spoke; his eyes ensnared her and his perfume aroused her senses like the heady smell of loam off a forest floor.

"How can I know that you are to be trusted?" she asked.

He smiled at her, displaying perfect white teeth. "I have travelled to the great cities of the world; to Damascus, Alexandria, Rome and many others, my Lady," he said. "I have seen many wonders and learned the arts of illustrious men. Many bear witness to my powers and they speak truly."

"I need a demonstration," she said. "I would first prove you to see if you are indeed a magician of stature."

Simon Magus bared his perfect teeth in a smile.

"What is your desire, my Lady?"

Herodias nodded towards an object wrapped in red cloth, which lay on the table.

"I have a sword that has shattered," she said. "Do you have the power to make it whole?"

Without a word, the Magus unwrapped the cloth. The sword with its severed blade glinted in the sunlight and, as the magician picked it up, reflected light played across the ceiling.

For several moments Simon Magus was silent. He sat with his eyes shut with the two parts of the sword resting on his hands. Then he began to mutter words in a foreign tongue and Herodias felt her flesh creep as an unearthly chill gripped her chest. At once the body of the Magus stiffened and his words became more strident, he lifted the sword above his head as if in supplication to an unseen deity. Laying it back on the cloth, he matched the two parts together, holding them there for several seconds while his hands trembled and the sweat poured off his brow as though the process afforded him great physical effort.

"My Lady!" He lifted the sword by its hilt and handed it to her. His eyes mocked her. "This sword, which has shed a prophet's blood will become the sword on which all else hinges," he said. "It will be the desired possession of kings. Twice it will shatter before the pieces are brought to the spring and healing comes once more to the nations."

The warmth of the sun again poured into the room and the abject fear Herodias had experienced only moments before slipped away. She raised the sword to the light and gazed at it in awe. There remained no suggestion of a break and no visible sign of the join.

"How did you do it?" she asked.

Simon Magus grinned at her. "Madam, nine virgins heated the metal with their breath and brought about the fusion."

Herodias laughed and laid the heavy weapon down gingerly.

"I will have it engraved," she said. "You must design the pattern for this 'desire of kings' and I will ensure that the workmanship is of the highest quality."

She toyed with the braided hair that snaked over her shoulder knowing that by the end of this encounter she would give her body to him and aware that he knew it. Simon Magus exercised a sexual mastery that was to control Herodias from that point forward.

"And if you can do what I ask of you, what reward do you seek?"

His eyes were bold; the Magus had deliberated this matter very carefully. The patronage of the Tetrarch would be of great value to him.

"My Lady," he bowed his head. "I would require a dwelling beside the sea of salt. A place from which I could continue my work."

"What manner of work?"

"The practise, my Lady, of certain sciences."

Herodias nodded vaguely but did not pursue the conversation further. Her mind was set on things of infinitely greater consequence.

At a word, Joanna brought the chest and set it before Simon Magus leaving the room on slippered feet, as silently as she had come. Herodias knelt down and removed the linen wrappings and the Magus lifted the head from the box and held it up to the light burying his hands in the tangled hair and beard of the Baptist. The head exuded a pungent smell from the spices and oils used in the embalming.

"The head of a Jewish prophet! What a trophy!"

"He died a man and a prophet. I want you to make me a god."

"It is likely to take some time."

"But it can be done?" Herodias spoke with thinly disguised eagerness.

"I can do it."

Simon Magus sensed for the first time the vital importance of this mission, and he listened within himself until the whisper of the gods became a clarion call.

'You were born for this moment,' the voices told him.

Simon Magus set the head onto its linen cloth in the box and turned to Herodias. His eyes strayed over her body.

"You will need to be involved in this magic," he told her. "We will use love to invoke the power of the gods."

Chapter 12
Twice-Born

A condition that Herr von Lossow had placed on obtaining a new identity for Anna Lejkin was that all ties with him and his family were immediately broken. Anna and Matthias had accepted this with an unexpected sense of relief. Anna stepped out of her past and discarded it like a sloughed skin, experiencing at the same time an exhilarating sense of freedom. Her new identity papers stated that she was Greta Plessen, born into a Roman Catholic home and baptised as an infant. Matthias tentatively suggested that she should receive a genuine baptism, but she had dismissed that notion immediately.

"Because I have left my faith does not mean that I can in any conscience adopt yours!" she told him. "I don't want shackles, Matthias. I don't want anything, beside you, that will exercise a hold over me."

He backed away from the suggestion reluctantly, hoping that at some time in the future she would change her mind. His love for Anna was so deep that he was afraid that her death might mean more than physical separation.

Frau von Ingolstadt, Matthias' mother adamantly refused to accept her son's choice of wife.

"The girl has no social standing. What on earth was Matthias thinking when he decided to marry a Pole?" she asked.

"Her background is German," her husband answered somewhat wearily and not for the first time. "Greta may have been born across the border, but she is not Polish."

"It wouldn't surprise me if there wasn't mixed blood there somewhere." Frau von Ingolstadt sniffed. "I disapprove of this match and I will make sure Matthias knows it!"

"If you reject this girl you will lose your son," Herr von Ingolstadt warned. "You will need to decide whether that is what you want."

"Matthias says she is not even a practising Catholic, Hermann.

Do you really want him to marry someone who had no interest in attending Mass?"

"Surely, my dear, for Matthias sake we can put our considerations aside and accept the choice he has made? He is not a child any longer and neither you nor I can make this kind of decision for him."

Frau von Ingolstadt rose to her feet with dignity. "You have absolutely no idea what you are talking about. I will not accept this young woman, and that is final!" And she swept from the room like a ship under full sail.

Once he and Greta were married, Matthias maintained the divide between his parents and himself with little regret. At first there was the occasional uncomfortable visit but in time it became simpler to stay away. There was an irony to the situation that did not escape the young couple. If Matthias had presented Anna the Jewess as his wife, acrimonious division would have been a certainty, yet it appeared on the surface that nothing had been gained by the change in identity. Anna though, was content to become Greta von Ingolstadt and what was at first the self-conscious enactment of a part eventually became second nature. To Matthias, Anna remained Anna.

"If people ask, we will say it is my pet name for you. I'm not calling you Greta!"

"It will be the one reminder of our secret," she said.

The only job available to Matthias upon leaving the Freicorps had been that of a shoe salesman. His enlistment had prevented him from pursuing a career and opportunities for advancement were extremely limited in post-war Germany. For a man of Matthias' intelligence the work was mind-numbing.

In 1920, Matthias' father died of a heart-attack and shortly afterwards his mother's ill-health necessitated a move into a nursing home.

"It's been a great shock, Matthias." Frau von Ingolstadt dabbed at her nose with a lace handkerchief. She was seated in a bath chair and her son pushed her dutifully down the narrow pathways through manicured lawns and immaculate flower beds. "His death was so sudden; there was absolutely no warning of what was to come. It has upset me more than I can say. You have no idea how I have suffered!"

"I know it must have been very sad for you, Mutti."

"It has left me weak," she said plaintively. "My nerves have been damaged."

Matthias was silent, recognising, not for the first time, that it was all about his mother. She had reduced his father's death to an inconsiderate and somewhat spiteful way of inconveniencing her and now he was beyond her reach for eternity. No wonder her nerves were bad!

"You must leave that job immediately, Matthias! I can't abide the thought of you working as a shoe salesman. You will have to study or go back to the army. At least there you were an officer!"

"I have a family to support," he reminded her.

"Well, I want you to take over the running of the house and you can't do that while you are still in that ridiculous job!" she said. "You must ensure it will be properly looked after until I am able to come back home. I suppose," she added reluctantly, "that your wife will have to go as well."

"Unless Anna goes with me, I won't be going anywhere at all," Matthias said grimly.

His mother waved her lace edged handkerchief disdainfully. "In that case you'd better take her."

Anna was four months pregnant with their first child when she and Matthias moved their few possessions into three rooms of his parents' home. Neither of them had much liking for the house in Heiligerstrasse. It was big and old-fashioned, heavily damasked and furnished with uncomfortable period pieces. It was only after von Ingolstadt's will was read that Matthias realised that there was still money in the estate, some of which had been left in his hands. He obeyed his mother's order thankfully and quit his job.

Most of the work in the house was undertaken by a competent housekeeper, but Anna insisted on cooking.

"I have to do something, Matthias," she protested when he argued.

"What about tea parties?" he asked mischievously.

"Definitely not!"

What she failed to admit was the sense of isolation she felt. German society was rigidly divided; separated by unwritten codes in which any intermingling of classes was an invitation to disorder. Although Greta Plessen was a von Ingolstadt by marriage, she was also Polish and therefore an outsider. It would take years before she felt accepted at any level.

Their first child, a girl, was born in 1920, a year after their marriage and they named her Marianne. Shortly afterwards, Frau von Ingolstadt suffered a massive stroke from which she never recovered and Matthias inherited the house in Heiligerstrasse and with it the sizable sum of money left to his mother in his father's estate. Although he would still need to consider his future, he and Anna were now comparatively well off.

Chapter 13
Twice-Born

Heavy rain was falling, beating against the grimy panes of glass on the windows of the studio and partially drowning the intonations of the lecturer. Outside, Michael could see how the steady drip of water from the trees snaked between the raked piles of dead leaves forming muddy puddles along the pathway.

Several students had arrived late showering the floor near the doorway with water from their mackintoshes and umbrellas. Now the radiators overpowered the autumn chill creating a muggy atmosphere within the confines of the room. Eventually, even the professor seemed to realise there was little to be gained from fighting the elements and lapsed into anecdotes for the remainder of the lecture.

Walther Krauss grimaced as he and Michael left the studio together.

"Nasty weather."

Michael shrugged into his coat.

"I have to go down town. Some errands to run."

"So, I'm to have a companion on my walk home?"

Michael flashed him a grin. "If you'll have me."

The streets were steel grey, slick with water and reflecting the shop lights. Michael hunched into his coat, head down, hands thrust deep into his pockets against the sting of the rain. Water rolled off the rim of his hat and blew back into his eyes.

Once in the main street they took shelter under the overhang of a shop frontage. Michael took off his hat and shook it.

"I'll buy you a cup of coffee," he offered. "Anything to get out of this rain."

"Why not. I'm not in a hurry."

It was warm in the little corner café and steam fogged the thick, uneven panes of glass in the front windows. They hung their dripping rain coats on the pegs beside the door and sat down. Michael ordered coffee and looked up as the door bell tinkled again. The young woman waved a greeting and both men stood up as she came across to their table.

"Walther, I thought it was you! I was over the road."

"Michael, this is Hester."

He looked into eyes that were a cool shade of blue.

"May I join you?"

"Of course."

She ordered tea and carried on a light-hearted conversation with Walther until it arrived. It was obvious that they knew one another well.

Michael stirred his coffee and glanced at the girl. Sleek blonde hair was done up in a loose bun in the nape of her neck. She was the modern German mädchen, healthy rather than pretty, with a clear skin and well-drawn features. She would tend towards fat later in life, Michael decided critically; there was an indication of it already in the broad sweep of her back, which seemed intentionally directed at him; in the somewhat heavy upper arm and the hint of a double chin. But Walther's eyes were only on Hester and he seemed oblivious to any shortcomings. Michael drank his coffee moodily and tried to decide how to leave without making his irritation too obvious.

He set his empty cup down on the saucer.

"Walther, I must go, I have things to do while there's a lull in the weather."

He stood up and shook Michael's hand but Hester did not even glance in his direction. Michael felt for the coins in his pocket, paid the bill and left.

Outside the rain was still falling heavily, the lull, if it had not been just his wishful thinking, had past.

On Monday morning he bumped into Walther in the corridor outside the studio.

"Hester asked me to thank you for paying for her tea on Friday."

"You've never mentioned her to me," Michael said, trying to keep the note of accusation out of his voice.

"We haven't known one another for long."

"It seems serious?"

Walther shrugged but his colour heightened. "I don't know.

It's all happened very quickly."

"So, where did you meet?"

"Through a friend of mine. A friend of the family." He seemed anxious to drop the subject. "Look, Michael, if you have time before Thursday's exam, could we run over Spinoza together?"

"I'm free tomorrow afternoon."

Michael took off his reading glasses and rubbed his eyes slowly with his fingertips.

They had discussed Benedict de Spinoza's Pantheistic doctrines in *Ethics* at length and he could see that Walther had had enough of philosophy and was anxious to turn the conversation in a different direction.

"If I told you my relationship with Hester *was* serious, what would you think?" he asked abruptly.

"I would say it's your life."

"No, seriously, Michael."

"I am being perfectly serious. But I might add a warning note."

Walther raised his eyebrows.

"To take things slowly. You have time. Male/female relationships tend to lead to life commitments."

"Hester doesn't approve of you," Walther said suddenly.

"She doesn't know me."

Walther shook his head. "I mean, she doesn't approve of my association with you and Chaim."

"As Jews?" It was suddenly so obvious that Michael wondered why it had not occurred to him before.

Walther looked at him wryly. "Sorry. It's not that she is unreasonable, but not many Germans have Jewish friends."

Michael laughed. "It hardly warrants an explanation."

Walther looked embarrassed. "To me, these things mean nothing, Michael. You know that. I had hoped that she might try to get to know you as people – to forget about racial issues but I don't think she would be easily persuaded."

Michael remembered the coldness of her eyes and felt certain Walther was right.

As he looked in the mirror that night, Michael assessed himself critically. Now that his sidelocks were shaven, he did not even look particularly Jewish. His hair was light brown, tending towards blonde and there was even a dusting of freckles over his nose, which was more Roman in shape than Semitic. Dark brown eyes peered back at his reflection behind tortoise-shell spectacles. He pushed his glasses onto his head and surveyed his slightly blurred image. Good well-shaped brows, a firm chin and neat ears: he was not the caricature Jew, neither was he dashingly handsome; but presentable, attractive even.

Logically, he knew anti-Semitism was not about appearance, it was primarily about race. Yet he knew that even if he denounced Judaism and attempted to assimilate into the German culture, it would make no difference to people's perception of him. He sat on the edge of his bed and thought philosophically about the conversation he had had with Walther. If his relationship with Hester endured, it would certainly mean the end of their friendship. Perhaps it was inevitable, a Jew and a German, oil and water, surely there could be no mix.

Chapter 14
Twice-Born

In August 1922, Heinrich Himmler passed his final examinations, qualifying at the Munich University as an agriculturalist. At twenty-two years of age, his ties with home had begun to weaken and life became a little more enjoyable. He joined a fraternity during his first month at university and worked hard at being accepted by his fellow students, but the association dropped him from their membership at their next election. They were not interested in socialising with a youth that would not drink with them and had ethical problems with duelling and womanising.

One Saturday evening at the Lowenbrau Keller, still in uniform and sweating after his drill, he was sitting with some of his young comrades when Captain Ernst Röhm came over and joined them. Himmler stood quickly to his feet and clicked his heels. Captain Röhm was all a man should be. Outgoing, resourceful and, above all, he exerted the sort of brute strength that earned him respect from his men. Röhm was the first person in years that had taken Himmler seriously and did not publicly humiliate him. He listened to his conversation as though his opinion was of some importance, and Himmler idolised him.

"Are you enjoying the Reichsflagge?" Röhm asked him this evening, clapping a hand on the young man's shoulder.

"Very much, Herr Captain," Himmler assured him.

"And you're ready to face some action?"

Himmler's eyes brightened. "You're anticipating action, Herr Captain?"

Röhm shrugged. "There are things in the wind," he replied. "Hitler's ready to move at any time and we must be prepared to back him."

Himmler's shoulders straightened perceptibly. "I look forward to the opportunity, Herr Captain."

Röhm stretched out on the seat next to him and put his feet up on the table. Taking a slim silver case from the top pocket of his uniform, he lit a cigarette.

"So Himmler," he asked conversationally. "Are you going out with any young woman?"

Himmler coloured slightly. "Not really, Herr Captain. I had a girl, but it broke up a while ago."

Röhm laughed. "But a man must have a sex life," he said. "You must see someone!"

Himmler attempted to meet the older man's eyes, but in his discomfort he was forced to look away. He glanced quickly around to see whether anyone was listening in to their conversation, but the others had withdrawn in a group to the bar, leaving them alone.

"Of course," he said, attempting to convey the maturity that he felt was expected of him. "I do find it difficult being without a woman, but for the moment, I would rather wait. It's too early to settle down."

Röhm laughed again, loudly and heartily. He took a swig of his beer and set the stein down on the table.

"Who's talking about settling down?" he asked. "I'm talking sex!"

Himmler placed his hands carefully on the table in front of him as he sought the right words. It was important for him not to jeopardise his relationship with the captain, but he had no wish to compromise his own moral standpoint.

"You don't think that it's better to keep sex for marriage?" he asked, taking refuge in a question.

Röhm's expression was incredulous. "You're a damned virgin!"

Himmler raised his chin defensively. "Well, Herr Captain, I have attempted to maintain certain standards."

Röhm snorted. "Standards!" he said, "Don't you realise boy, that's what is wrong with your life. You have roped yourself in with your church beliefs and your phoney standards. What you need is a bit of real living!" He regarded Himmler thoughtfully for a moment. "What is the one thing you really want in your life, more than anything else?"

Himmler answered without hesitation. "Power, Herr Captain. The sort of power I see in your life, that makes men sit up and listen."

"You don't get power by sitting on your backside moralising," Röhm said. "But if you're serious, I can give you what you want."

They were an oddly assorted couple, this intense young man and the battle-scarred war veteran. Himmler looked up at him cautiously.

"What do you mean, Herr Captain?"

Ernst Röhm said nothing for a moment. The cellar had begun to empty, the hour was late and soon it would be time to close. He knew he could use this moment to advantage. When at last he looked at Himmler, there was something in his eyes that the younger man was at first unable to interpret, but he found himself strangely disturbed under the captain's intense gaze. Excitement coursed unexpectedly through his loins as Röhm began to speak.

"I can show you how to get that power more quickly than you think," he said softly and he placed a hand on Himmler's shoulder for a second time that evening. Now, the gesture was intimate.

Heinrich Himmler realised for the first time, as he read the expression in Röhm's pale eyes, on what the captain's relationship with him was based, and he experienced a mixture of unexpected pleasure and unbelievable revulsion.

Chapter 15
Twice-Born

"Chuza told me about a woman who is a disciple of the Jew, Yeshua of Nazareth." Joanna was tending the feet of her mistress, Herodias. She massaged the toes of one foot slowly, whilst the other soaked in the bowl of warm water and herbs. Joanna was a gossip and Herodias seldom discouraged her. It was through Joanna that she gained useful insight and knowledge into the community, which she often passed on to Herod, or used to her own advantage.

Much had been learned about Yeshua through Chuza, who had turned, after John the Baptist's death, to following this itinerant preacher at every opportunity. The Nazarene's disciples were also baptising proselytes in the Jordan River and Jesus, as the Greeks called him, was preaching a similar message of repentance. Herodias was both intrigued and repulsed by what she heard and took every opportunity to report anything to Herod that may bring about his downfall.

"He's a dangerous man;" she had warned her husband a few days earlier, "the sort that will cause another insurrection if you don't act swiftly to stop him." Herod as usual had shrugged off her approach in such a way as to annoy her and muttered some superstitious nonsense about the Baptist returning from the dead.

"The Nazarene is a magician," he had told her uneasily, "who performs miracles and heals the sick."

"Fool!" Herodias replied scornfully, "You are ruler of Galilee and yet you live in fear of the people. You are afraid to act – even when there is a threat. I have heard it said that Yeshua of Nazareth was born to reign over Israel. Get rid of him unless you want him to be your downfall!" She had turned and left the room.

Herod had summoned Chuza and asked him the question that was troubling his thoughts.

"During the reign of my father, Herod Agrippa," he said, "there was an incident that you may remember. Astrologers from the east came to the palace and spoke of the birth of a child whom they said was born to be king of Israel."

Chuza nodded. He was a short, stocky man with a receding hairline and a stomach that had begun to protrude. His face was unremarkable in its features but his quiet temperament suited Herod and, although he would never have admitted it even to himself, his steward was his closest confident and friend.

"That's right, sire. They claimed to have seen a new star in the heavens and they followed its path from Babylon to Judaea. These were men of high birth who had learned something of the prophecies from the Jewish community in Babylon and they believed Messiah had been born."

"Why did they approach my father?"

Chuza smiled gently. "I suppose, sire, they assumed firstly that the birth would have taken place at the palace. But when they realised that was not the case, they asked where Messiah should be born in accordance with the prophecies."

"Beit Lehem!"

"Precisely, sire. Bethlehem, the House of Bread. Your father immediately called in the priests to search the scriptures diligently and that was the answer they gave the wise men."

Herod turned away to hide his expression. "Leave me, Chuza!" he ordered. He remembered the story now. Somehow the astrologers had known there was murder in his father's heart and when they failed to return, Herod had sent a contingent of the palace guard to Bethlehem. Their instructions were to kill all the male children under the age of two. Not long afterwards Herod had died a terrible death, his body ravaged by maggots; it was whispered among the Jews, that this death was an act of righteous vengeance of the God of Abraham, Isaac and Jacob. Not for the killing of the innocents only, but for the deliberate attempt to eliminate God's Messiah.

Had the temple priests ever enquired in Bethlehem to see if such a birth had taken place, he wondered, or were they so shocked by the slaughter, which had resulted from their revelation of the prophecy, that they were ashamed to seek the truth. Could such a child have survived? It was said that Yeshua the prophet, was about thirty years of age, which would accord with the time of the event. But his followers claimed he was a Nazarene. Was it possible his parents escaped from Bethlehem with the child and settled in Nazareth?

Herod looked down at his own hands which, in his mind were still stained with the blood of the Baptiser. If his father had tried to kill Messiah then he, Herod Antipas, on the whim of a woman, had killed one of God's prophets. And he knew Herodias. The further he stayed away from the Jewish teacher the better if he was not to bear responsibility for the death of another righteous man.

In the women's quarters bright sunlight pierced the window forming geometric patterns on the flagged floor and drapes of silver and blue stirred momentarily in the hint of a breeze. Joanna turned her attention now to the massage of Herodias' left foot after carefully towelling dry the right.

"Mary was born in Magdala. It's a fishing village on the northern coast of Lake Kinneret[3]."

Herodias shrugged impatiently. "I know the village. Tell me about the woman!"

Joanna nodded unperturbed. "It is said that she was possessed by seven devils!"

Herodias glanced at her with renewed interest. "I thought you said that Jesus of Nazareth gathered upright followers around him. Do-gooders like your spouse, Chuza."

Joanna laughed. "Chuza told me that Jesus cast the demons out of her. She was rolling on the floor, foaming at the mouth as they fought for possession of her body and soul. Some of the devils cried out in terrible voices as they left her and for many moments Mary Magdalene lay there on the ground as one who is dead."

"And she's become a follower?"

"Oh yes, a close follower." Joanna patted the right foot dry and slipped Herodias' sandals onto her feet.

Herodias made a mental note to repeat the story to Simon Magus. It was obvious that this Nazarene exercised unusual powers. "So, this Mary, is she young?"

"I am told that she is both young and beautiful."

---

[3] Lake Harp, or Sea of Galilee.

"And, as Jesus has, for some reason, chosen to remain unmarried, she has no doubt demonstrated her gratitude by becoming his lover."

Joanna's expression was quizzical. "Chuza expressly says that there is nothing of the sort between them. He says the teacher treats her with great courtesy and compassion but offers himself in that way to no man or woman."

"Impossible!" Herodias retorted. "I don't care what Chuza thinks. If the man is involved in magical practises he is sexually involved."

"That's what I said, but Chuza is adamant. He says Jesus of Nazareth, like the Baptist, has been a follower of the Jewish law from childhood."

Herodias was thoughtful. "I've heard it said that he refused at first to baptise this Yeshua bar Joseph, because he considered himself unworthy?"

"The Nazarene persuaded him though." Joanna said importantly, parroting words she had heard her husband speak. "He said that it must be done to perform all righteousness. Chuza said there was a thunderous voice when Jesus rose up out of the water, and the Baptist saw the Spirit of God rest upon him in the form of a dove."

Herodias exhaled her contempt from pursed lips. "I will hear no more of this superstitious nonsense! Joanna, I need a spy within the Nazarene's followers and I think you would be well suited to the task. The Baptist made it clear that he anticipated Messiah. If this is the man, he is a danger to my husband and he must be stopped before he inflames the people to rise up against the Romans. I'm giving you a very important task, Joanna."

"My mistress! A spy! That would mean leaving your service." Joanna was crestfallen. "Please don't send me. There must be many others who could join with the Nazarene and report his actions to you!"

Herodias ignored her. "I will tell Herod that I have dismissed you. We will say that it is for theft. Chuza will be only too glad to see you leave Machaerus I think. He is always so concerned about your indiscretions."

Joanna grasped Herodias' feet. "Please!" she appealed. "I want to stay with you, my mistress. How will I survive without my quarters here; without my husband and without an income?"

"I will see to it that you have a very handsome income, Joanna and in due time, when this man has been conclusively dealt with, I will advise Herod that you have been forgiven and returned to my service. Now, we must plan this carefully. Bring me the Baptist, Joanna. We must beg his counsel."

Joanna fetched the camphor box and set the head on the low table before Herodias. Her misery was temporarily forgotten as she knelt entranced, then both women prostrated themselves in supplication before the gruesome relic. Simon Magus had done his work well. Now, whenever the idol was brought out, the women sensed that a dark presence entered the room with it. The head had become a god of force excelling any of the gods of stone or metal which were in Machaerus. Manifestations occurred when it was worshiped; objects in the room inexplicably moved; often an eerie glow appeared around the cranium and facial features appeared to change as though amorphous masks were shifting over the inanimate visage. Both Herodias and Joanna now feared the deity that had been created but were bewitched by it as one might be hypnotised and captivated by the gentle movements of a venomous cobra reared to strike.

They waited, eyes at first downcast, until something prompted them to gaze up at the face. A grotesque leer seemed to shift across the countenance and for the first time, a voice emanated from the image causing both women to cast their faces to the floor again in terror.

"I know Mary of Magdalene intimately. Watch her but do not reveal yourself to her! Through the Magdalene, the man Jesus will ultimately meet his destruction."

Chapter 16
Twice-Born

The wind, edged with sleet, swept in with the newcomers who entered the Arzberger Keller and they stamped their feet against the cold, knocking the snow from their boots. Captain Ernst Röhm shrugged out of his greatcoat and hung it on one of the pegs by the door. The entrance smelt of damp, and films of water lay in the ruts of the unevenly flagged floor. But as they opened the door and descended the stairs to the cellar, noise and laughter rose invitingly up to meet them. Smoke clung to the underside of the arched ceiling and formed soft haloes around the lights, the pungent smell of it combining with the reek of old beer.

Someone shouted and waved a stein in greeting. Ernst Röhm lifted his hand in recognition and nodded to the others.

"They're over there."

He strode across the room and voices were raised in welcome.

"Röhm! Wie getz?"

Ernst Röhm struck an imposing figure. He was a familiar sight to many Bavarians and was hardly a character to be ignored. When he entered a room, heads invariably turned to follow him. The captain was short, square-set and solidly built, abounding in energy. His skull bristled with a thin covering of hair, which tended towards red. An old bullet wound had cut away half his nose and burnt a livid scar into features that were thick and fleshy, a disfigurement which he wore proudly, like a badge of honour. Most of his comrades looked up to him as a true soldier, a heroic figure, but there was an earthiness about Röhm, a coarseness of speech, which repulsed some and fascinated others.

Young Heinrich Himmler followed Röhm somewhat self-consciously. He was not accustomed to attracting any attention. In comparison to the captain he appeared slight and almost effeminate with the sort of face that youthfulness rested upon awkwardly. His skin and eyes were too pale and despite many attempts before the mirror to prime his mouth with definition and maturity, he had achieved little success. A pince-nez gave him a short-sighted, owlish appearance and he was still apt to blush awkwardly in difficult or embarrassing situations. In all, Heinrich Himmler still fell far short of the exacting standard he had set for himself.

A waitress no more than a girl, leaned over the table in front of Röhm, setting the foaming steins of beer down on the long table, her bosom provocatively exposed above the bodice of her dirndl. Two blonde plaits had been caught up to form a coil around a face that was white and delicate.

"Hello sweetheart!"

Röhm cupped a hand under her breast. She coloured and drew back in confusion as the men at the table shouted with laughter. The captain picked up the beer she had placed in front of Himmler.

"Here, you can take this one away liebling, this man can't take it. It's his stomach!" He rubbed his own stomach expansively to bring the point home and his voice was sardonic. "Bring him a glass of water will you?"

"Doctor's orders," Himmler explained apologetically to anyone who would listen.

"So, what did you think of the parade, Major?" Röhm asked, the girl's discomfort already forgotten.

"Excellent! There was a good turnout. I sense the people are ready for a change." Major Angerer wiped the corners of his mouth between finger and thumb.

"My feeling entirely. We must exploit the mood."

"The response to Hitler was good," Angerer said, "He has a way with words."

"I'd say we have our man!" Röhm lit a cigarette and lifted his beer stein in a good-natured salute to the Major. He turned his attention to Himmler.

"This is where we first met, isn't it?" The words were quieter, intended for the youth's ears alone.

Heinrich Himmler squirmed uncomfortably on his seat and attempted a smile. He had always recognised and admired the captain's control and domination of every situation but his hero-worship of Röhm as the epitome of the military man had been thrown into confusion.

"I remember it well, Herr Captain."

Röhm shifted to a higher tone in mimicry of the younger man's voice. "I've seen you here often, Herr Captain. I'm a great admirer of yours." He had developed a way of insulting Himmler, mocking him, yet at once maintaining a seductive intimacy from which the youth found it impossible to extricate himself. Initially, Himmler had interpreted Röhm's gentle attitude towards him as paternal affection but he now recognised it as the seductive charm a man would display toward his woman.

A grin split Röhm's scarred face. "What was it you told me? Something about my shrewdness?"

Himmler twisted his hands together. "I believe I said I had followed your career closely," he replied uncomfortably.

"And when I questioned your conclusions?"

Himmler looked him briefly in the eye and turned away, reddening under the explicit gaze of the older man.

"I said you were a shrewd man and a born soldier, Herr Captain."

Ernst Röhm threw back his burly head and laughed. "And have I given you any reason to doubt that since you've got to know me better?" His voice was raised now, demanding an answer that everyone around them could hear.

Himmler tried to smile. "I've had no reason to doubt it, Herr Captain."

"Have you met Major Angerer?"

Himmler shook his head.

Röhm leaned across the table and clapped the Major on his shoulder. "Major, meet a new friend of mine, Heinrich Himmler. Himmler has just joined the Reichsflagge. The bastards in the SA wouldn't have him!"

The major glanced at the earnest features of the boy on the bench beside Röhm without any pretence at interest. It was obvious to him that the hardened war veterans who did the recruiting for the SA would not have considered this desirable material for their ranks. He addressed a few polite words to Röhm and returned to his conversation with the man next to him. Himmler averted his gaze. He had come to anticipate rebuffs without yet having come to terms with the inner response they elicited. People had always expected more from him than he was able to give. His father had conveyed on him, the name of a former student, Prince Heinrich of Wittelsbach and the prince had graciously consented to act as Himmler's godfather. But every effort he made to live into the image his father had created for him had failed. He was a victim of his poor eyesight and weak body, and while he had developed into a young man who was always dependable, carefully moral and meticulous, he was also the sort of bore that people consciously avoided.

Himmler positioned his hands neatly on the table in front of him. They were too small for a man; soft-skinned and very pale, and by their very immobility, they conveyed his uneasiness. Röhm was drinking heavily and with every stein he consumed, the danger of his indiscretion increased. His jokes had become coarse and his laughter too loud. Himmler felt his own personality fade as though utterly consumed by Röhm's flamboyance. Once or twice he shot a glance at the captain's flushed face and vacuous expression. He was afraid of him; sick to the gut of the things he did when they were alone, and yet unwilling to break free. He was certain what Röhm was offering in exchange for his favours was real - access to unlimited power.

It would have been a simple thing to leave early, but as the men slowly dispersed later, Himmler was still at the table. Röhm turned to face him.

"Shall we go?"

Despising himself for his weakness, Heinrich Himmler stood up.

Chapter 17
Twice-Born

Simon contracted leprosy shortly after Judas' thirteenth birthday. At first he had refused to acknowledge the evidence of his eyes and successfully hid the disease even from his wife, gazing in morbid fascination when he was alone, at the growing white spot in the skin of his inner thigh. He recoiled in shock when she had entered his room one morning before he was fully robed.

"Get out, woman! Get out of here!"

Judas, who was returning with a bundle of firewood, had heard his father's voice raised in fury and, as always when there was a quarrel, found himself irresistibly drawn to the scene. He slipped closer to the house pressing himself against the outer wall of his parent's bedroom so that her quiet protest came to him quite clearly.

"Why Simon, what is wrong?"

His father was clearly visible in the shaft of early sunlight that fell through the opening. He was holding his black robe in front of him as a shield and his features were twisted with rage.

"You have no right to walk in on me like that!"

"Tell me what's wrong? Why are you acting so strangely?"

"Get out! I'm telling you to get out!"

There was a moment's pause and when she spoke again his mother's voice was flat and toneless.

"What are you hiding, Simon?"

For a moment it seemed as though his father would continue to remonstrate but unexpectedly he dropped the robe; his hands clawed at his beard and his face crumpled.

"Look at me!" he sobbed. "I'm a leper!"

For Judas, the moment brought his childhood to an end. He had studied with his father the teachings in Leviticus on leprosy and knew the implications. The disease was unclean and because of the nature of its contraction he would have to declare himself to the priests and be driven from the village to live away from society. It was unthinkable to imagine him becoming one of those pitiful men and women who wandered like ghosts in the wilderness. Simon had spoken so often in open condemnation of these lost souls who were forced to forage, beg or steal to stay alive.

"They've brought it on themselves, Judas," he said. "Sinners, all of them. Leprosy is an outward symptom of a sinful lifestyle. They don't deserve our pity!"

By his words, Simon had condemned himself and in Judas' eyes his relationship with his father was fractured and would never be fully restored.

* * *

It was after Joanna was sent out in apparent disgrace from the palace of Machaerus that Herodias asked Simon Magus to provide her with a priestess for the head. The request seemed to please him.

"I will give you Helen of Tyre," he told her. She will be your companion in the place of Joanna. She is a priestess of Astarte and she will do well with you."

The Magus had found Helen in a whorehouse in the city of Tyre and he at once recognised in her a spiritual kinship; an attraction that even surpassed his physical desire. He called her Ennoia, from the Greek, which meant First Thought, Mother of All.

"God's first thought was woman," Simon Magus said as he lay watching her on the love mat in her room. "The angels and the demigods were brought into being through woman."

Her dark body was sleek and supple, and glistened in the soft light of the moon that spilled in through the window. It was a body made for dance.

"The gods created the earth under the instruction of Ennoia, but they rebelled and trapped her in matter so that she became part of the material world." He reached out and caressed her. "Ennoia was held captive in a series of female forms and, like you, Helen, she was subjected to devastating humiliations. She was forced to continue bound through the ages. Your namesake, Helen of Troy was one of the incarnations of First Thought."

She smiled and, against the dusky hue of her face, her teeth were as small and white as the shells washed up on the beaches of Tyre. In this gentle light her almond-shaped eyes held the mystery of ages past and her face, the hardened beauty of an African mask, smooth and high-browed.

"The gods drove you to prostitution, and through the gods I have found you," he told her. "I will take you away from here, Helen of Tyre, back to the land of Samaria. You will see how the power of Simon the Magician will possess you to dance as you have never danced before!"

The full divine power of Simon Magus, priest-king could only be achieved under the sexual anointing of a queen-priestess and the compulsion at the core of his being had driven him to find his partner.

"Prostitutes are the sacred servants of the gods in temple worship," he told her. "The men who visit the temples can only experience the divine through a process known as gnosis. The body of the temple whore is the gateway to the gods."

When she came to Machaerus as priestess, Helen of Tyre entered in the persona of Ennoia, or Sophia, Wisdom. She came, not into Herodias' service but to be served and at first Herodias did not realise the full implication of Helen's arrival. She was a difficult and sometimes terrifying woman, given to all-consuming passion, intense self-centredness and sudden rage. When she arrived, her dancing was already legendary in Samaria. Salome could ignite men's passions by her dance but Helen danced with all the fire of the gods themselves. There were times that she danced before the head of the Baptist wearing chains around her semi-nude body. When Simon the Magician was present, such dancing led to orgiastic and Bacchanalian practises within the women's quarters, designed to bring spiritual enlightenment through Helen, the initiatrix; to increase the stature of the Magus, and to add to the growing spiritual powers of the head of John the Baptist.

Chapter 18
Twice-Born

"So," he said to Himmler, "Have they improved your office yet, or are you still stuck in that little hole with all the files?"

"I'm still there, Herr Captain."

Ernst Röhm glanced at him in amusement. Himmler was demonstrably unable to break away from the indoctrination of his youth. He shared Röhm's bed, yet he still referred to him as Herr Captain and clicked his heels in the proper manner when they met in public. The fact that their liaison had cost him the youth's wholehearted respect hardly concerned Röhm; he was not a man motivated by sentiment.

Gregor Strasser had been responsible for employing Heinrich Himmler as secretary to the National Socialist Party somewhat impulsively when he discovered that Himmler through his association with Röhm, had carried the Old Reich war-flag during the Beerhall Putsch, and was also a fellow chemist. They had spent a large part of that first afternoon discussing common interests but, characteristically, Himmler's brief spell of self-confidence melted away once he entered the organisation. His pedantic awareness of rank and his servility irritated Strasser.

After two years, Himmler's meetings with Ernst Röhm had become more sporadic, yet he still found that he looked forward to them with a paradoxical mixture of longing and loathing. The depths of his turmoil after those early encounters went beyond anything he had ever experienced. He felt humiliated, degraded and filled with such an immense self-loathing that death would have been a welcome release. If he could have remained aloof from the experience it would have seemed bearable, but he despised his puny body the more for being aroused. No doubt, at any point, he could have called a halt and Röhm would have let him go, but there was a goal to be attained and he had discovered his stepping-stone.

Röhm's promise had not been empty. He knew the methods of

developing power and it amused him to adopt a loser as a disciple. The change would not be instantaneous. For Himmler it would involve time and commitment: for Röhm, pleasure.

"Perhaps I should put in a word for you to the Strassers. Or to Hitler! What about Hitler?" Röhm stood up, clothed only in a pair of under-shorts, and paraded the room before Himmler. "How about it, Reichsheini?" He delivered the name they had bestowed on Himmler at the office with considerable relish. "I will say, 'Herr Hitler, your secretary is my lover, and I'm opening him to the powers of the will. Kindly furnish him with a larger office.' It would give you a better place to hang your portrait of the Führer."

Himmler winced inwardly, but his expression remained inscrutable.

"I've always looked up to you, mein Führer, but now I'll be able to look up to you literally," Röhm mimicked Himmler's voice in the high pitched tone he used to bait him. Himmler was stirred by a familiar wave of anxiety as he remembered Gregor Strasser's hilarity when he had caught him addressing his small joke to the Führer's picture.

"That's right, Heine," he had shouted for all to hear. "Let Hitler keep an eye on you while you're working, that way you won't be able to get up to any mischief!"

As always when they goaded him, Heinrich Himmler had smiled politely, deliberately masking his expression to cover his embarrassment. Heine-baiting was the main sport of the Nazi offices in those early days, but secretly everyone was impressed enough with his administrative abilities to realise they needed his input.

"He's like a damned walking index-card system!" they would say. "You can't fault him on a thing."

"I was joking!" Himmler told Röhm defensively. "But Adolf Hitler is a fine leader and I'm proud to be associated with him."

"He hasn't even noticed you've moved into the offices!"

Himmler replaced his pince-nez carefully on the bridge of his nose. The jibe had found its mark as Röhm knew it would.

It had long ago become a simple matter for Himmler to believe the image of himself that others projected. He was a pathetic nonentity, destined for nothing more in life than to be a background figure and something of a joke in poor taste. Even the authorities had overlooked his participation in the abortive Beerhouse Putsch in which sixteen National Socialists had died. They had not considered it necessary to disarm the pale youth with the puffy features, who had clung to the flag with such grim determination throughout the disturbance. Arrest would have been a noble end to the day but Heinrich Himmler had been left to walk home.

At the office, when it seemed the time for introduction was inevitable, Adolf Hitler's pale blue eyes had bored right through him and he had left the office without even bothering to ask who Himmler was. Heinrich Himmler still idolised him. The speech Hitler made in his own defence after the Beerhall Putsch had stirred Himmler providing the final impetus for his move into the political arena. Here was a man he could serve and emulate. One who exuded strength and conviction, and simply by the power of his personality could gather supporters, imbue them with vision and enflame them with passion for a new and mighty future for their Volk. He had known without a doubt that Hitler was destined to be Führer of a united Germany. Equally certain was the conviction that one day his own name would be irreversibly linked with that of Adolf Hitler.

A small flame of passion burned momentarily in Himmler's eyes as he looked up at Röhm.

"Herr Hitler will come to know me," he prophesied. "In the future I will serve at his right hand."

"No doubt," Röhm answered matter-of-factly. "I was the one who discovered Hitler at the outset and although he's hardly the spotless being you imagine, he's the man for the job ahead. As for you, everything you are, everything you will become, is my creation. When I've finished with you, you and Hitler will probably do well together."

Röhm glanced contemptuously at the small figure so neatly arranged in the armchair, but he was unable to read Himmler's expression behind the light that reflected off his spectacles.

Ernst Röhm was a master of the art of employing sex to raise the level of human consciousness. Little by little he was perverting Himmler's feelings of rejection and repugnance to hatred using it as a motivating force in the development of his will. It was of no interest to him that the emotions he was nurturing in Himmler might be turned back on himself. He was a man accustomed to facing an enemy. By creating something that might at any time attempt to destroy him, added lustre to the game: like the mating dance of scorpions.

His mood changed abruptly and he smiled at the young man in the armchair.

"I've made you angry." Momentarily his tone was cajoling but it was short-lived and he switched from lover to mentor. "Already I'm seeing strength in your emotional control. Soon it will rise up in you like a beast, cold as steel and twice as strong. Then, when the anger becomes a part of your will, there will be nothing to stop you. Your body may never be your strength, but you will display power that will make men tremble."

Himmler said nothing. Once he became what the seething undercurrent of his thoughts was telling him he could be, when he had achieved the power he desired, he would use it to undercut and destroy everyone who had scorned, belittled and ignored him. He stood up to face Röhm, knowing that the captain still exerted a terrible influence over him. Röhm used his body and his tongue as a cutting edge to humiliate and break him, yet in the next breath would work to sculpt a god from the ruins of the man. It was in these rare moments that Heinrich Himmler came to Röhm on equal terms.

Chapter 19
Twice-Born

Tiny delicate leaves caught in the morning sunlight formed an iridescent tracery along the boughs of the oaks. Crocuses and primroses bloomed in well-composted beds and fruit trees exhibited a mass of pink and white blossom.

Michael had not been surprised by the announcement of Walther's and Hester's engagement during the first week of spring. Congratulations seemed cynical but he and Chaim offered them anyway.

"We intend to marry at the end of the year when the course is over," Walther told them shifting the pile of books under his arm awkwardly.

"Hester's father would like to see me in a job before I take his daughter away."

"Do you know what you will be doing?"

"Only that it doesn't include football," he said ruefully.

"There is a price to pay for love," Michael laughed. "By the way, did you know that Chaim's found a place in the League of Nations? If he continues to pass with distinction, he's in!"

Walther glanced at Chaim sharply. "By their own admission, the League is a hive of Freemasons."

"What do you mean?"

"If you read the report by Brother Barcia when he returned from Geneva last year, you will be left in no doubt."

"I've never heard of him," Chaim said defensively.

"He's past Grand Master of the Spanish Grand Orient and he made it known that all the French and Americans delegates were Masons. Even the secretary-general of the League, Joseph Avenal is one of the Brotherhood!"

Michael glanced at Chaim but his expression was closed. He obviously knew Walther was speaking the truth.

"Co-incidence, Freiberg or a common goal?" Walther was

goading him.

Chaim spoke quietly and very deliberately. "Why don't you spell it out yourself, Walther? What do you think the League is about?"

"Revolution! Freemasonry and Communism are obvious bedfellows to anyone who cares to make a study of the subject."

"Come on, Walther, leave him alone," Michael said. "The League's whole emphasis is peace among nations after the last war. That's all Chaim is interested in achieving, you know that."

Walther swung round and Michael saw that his eyes were blazing.

"Their aim is world government. A Freemasonic world government. They care nothing for peace! You Jews should check your history," he said. "You're the student among us, Michael. Take a look at the Rothschilds, the Morgans, the Loebs, and the rest."

"Men that have made good here and abroad."

"*Jewish* men, Michael. Most of them from the ghetto in Frankfurt."

"What have they got to do with the League?"

"If you want to know where the League of Nations originated, it was from the Frankfurt ghetto. The plot for world domination began there."

"You're talking like an idiot, Walther."

"I've never been more serious in my life. I challenge you to research the history of these men, Michael. They have attained great heights; above royalty in some cases. They've seized banks and they control governments."

"This is pure propaganda, and you know it!"

"You're the historian. Check it for yourself!"

Michael glanced at Chaim's set expression and back at Walther.

"I will," he said quietly.

Glancing at the clock over the steeple of the university building, he collected his books together and headed for the lecture room.

Chapter 20
Twice-Born

It was the illness of his father, Simon, that brought about the meeting between Judas and the carpenter's son from Nazareth, Yeshua bar Joseph.

Judas had known of the reputation of Jesus as a healer for months before he plucked up the courage to seek him out in the region of Galilee. Certainly the man would reject him; the stigma attached to his relationship with a leper would see to that. He had hung about on the edge of the crowd for days before realising that there was no other way but that he declare himself. The preacher had looked at him searchingly when Peter introduced him.

"Where are you from?" he asked.

"Kerioth, a village south of Hebron, Rabbi,"

"Ish Kerioth," Jesus said and smiled. "The man from Kerioth."

And Judas was surnamed Iscariot from that moment. Still, he had waited and watched Jesus closely before petitioning him. This was a man markedly different from any Judas had ever known; there was an indefinable quality about him, something that set him apart from, and yet not above, all others. On the contrary, he was approachable and demonstrated no pride or arrogance. An enigmatic character, Judas decided – a man with great qualities of leadership. If Jesus would have him, he would endeavour to join his followers.

Judas Iscariot slipped away early one morning to find his father, only returning much later the following day.

Simon, devastated by the shame of his disease had moved away from Kerioth to a leper colony in the wilderness close to the Sea of Galilee. The move was strategic. He knew of Jesus, the itinerant preacher who was performing miracles among the sick, everyone was speaking about him. If Judas would intercede on his behalf, perhaps there was a possibility that he too might receive his cleansing. He had looked on himself with increasing loathing as the leprosy spread through his flesh to encompass almost every part of his body. Simon was a Pharisee, a man of great learning, and one who had known what it was to be elevated among the people. Why had this happened to him of all people?

In one day, after the priest had examined the depressed white blotch in his skin with undisguised distaste, Simon had lost everything. He had left behind his family, his possessions and his wealth. But even more damaging, he had been deeply humiliated; he had lost his dignity and his status in the community and had, in an instant, been reduced to nothing: the off-scouring of Jewish society.

Judas alone had not entirely forsaken him, and now his son became the link to his one remaining hope, Yeshua the Nazarene.

Thousands had massed on a hill near the northern shore of the lake to hear Jesus.

"Where have you been, Judas?" John called. "The Master was asking for you."

"Every one of us was challenged by his words today," Peter said. "We have all reconsidered our understanding of the Law."

For a moment, Judas allowed himself to hear what they were saying. There could after all, be no misunderstanding of the Mosaic Law.

"What do you mean?"

"If anything, Jesus deepened its meaning," John said. "He said that if a man looks with lust on a woman, he has already committed adultery."

"He also said that anger against a brother is the same as murder." Peter added. "The Master said it is not in outward actions alone that the law is kept, but also in the attitudes of the heart."

"That's right!" John agreed. "What he was saying exposed man's deepest motivations. No one could possibly believe, after hearing this morning's sermon that they were right before God. Yet his words did not condemn but encourage."

Judas nodded briefly, but without much interest. There were other things on his mind besides the teaching that had taken place on the mount. Jesus was sitting a little way off, in conversation with Matthew and Andrew. Judas waited until they had moved away.

"Rabbi," he could not bring himself to meet Jesus' eyes. "I

have a request to make. One of great importance to me."

"Your father?"

"You know?"

Jesus' look was steady and Judas sensed that he knew all that there was to be known about his father and still looked upon him without judgment. He was emboldened to continue.

"He has been a leper for seven years. I don't know if it's possible to heal him now."

"What do you think, Judas?"

"I would like to believe, Master."

Jesus stood up. "Let's go and see him."

As the handful of men picked their way down the hillside, groups of people called out, picked up their belongings and followed. Judas glanced back at the crowd and groaned inwardly. What he had desperately hoped would be a private affair between his father and the Rabbi looked increasingly as though it would become a public humiliation.

Simon was waiting beneath a tree some way from the main path. Judas was relieved to see that he had trimmed his hair and beard and put on clean robes but he still viewed his father with a deep sense of shame that no amount of outward grooming could dispel. Simon hobbled towards them; his feet were swathed in bloodied bandages, a sight that could not be disguised by his robe. Still at a distance, he fell to his knees and beseeched Jesus. Judas cringed.

"Master! If you will, you can make me clean!"

To everyone's amazement, Jesus walked over to him, reached down and touched the leper, something which no other person had wittingly done since the priest had positively diagnosed the sore in his body seven years before.

"I will, Simon," he said simply. "Be clean."

To Judas, in that frozen moment, it seemed that all creation held its breath. Simon looked up wonderingly.

"Master!"

Jesus lent down and helped the man to his feet.

Behind them, the crowd gasped in shock, seeing only that the preacher was unafraid to touch an outcast, a man unclean in accordance with Hebraic Law. Jesus laughed.

"Take off the bandages, Simon," he said. "You will have no further need of them. And go show yourself to a priest. He will declare you clean."

The mother of Judas had returned to her father's home in Kerioth with Judas' younger sister shortly after her husband left the village. Her own reputation had been irrevocably tainted by her husband's disease and when Simon's healing took place she had no desire to return to him. He had always been a difficult man, given to sudden bursts of self-righteous anger if he was crossed in any way. In the years of their separation she had become accustomed to the pitying glances of their neighbours and the coolness with which the women treated her whenever she went to draw water at the well. It had become simpler to deal with the familiar than with a man who had been a stranger even during the years of their marriage. So Simon found lodging in Bethany, a village not far from Jerusalem, and because of his deep knowledge of the Torah, was soon received back into the fold of the Pharisees. It was with some pleasure that Judas Iscariot viewed his father's reacceptance among his peers. Jesus often appeared to misjudge and disparage this Jewish sect. There had been times of open confrontation with men, who were, after all, part of a holiness movement within the religious leadership. He put it down to the Master's misunderstanding of some of the tenets of the Hebraic Law. Jesus was self-taught and some error was understandable. Judas was sure that, in time, Simon himself would set Jesus back on the right path.

The disciples Jesus chose were a disparate group of men, including fishermen, a tax collector, a zealot, and Judas Iscariot, son of a Pharisee. In his heart of hearts, Judas believed he had been chosen because the Master did not really know him. In fact, Jesus chose him because he did.

* * *

For the first few weeks, Joanna, wife of Chuza, followed the disciples of Jesus at a discreet distance. She attracted little attention among the crowds, which gathered daily to hear the Nazarene speak or to see some miracle performed by him. She kept a close watch on the one known as

Mary of Magdalene to discern whether there was any special relationship between her and Jesus, and once every few weeks she returned to Machaerus, ostensibly to visit Chuza who rejoiced, believing that his wife had become a true follower of the Nazarene, while in actuality her visits were to report back to her mistress. Herodias greeted her eagerly, hungry for news that would cause Jesus to stumble.

Joanna found her difficult to satisfy. Even his enemies found it impossible to accuse this enigmatic Jew, although learned men with minds far craftier than Joanna's, sought every occasion to trip him up with his own words.

"So, what of the Magdalene woman?"

"There is no trace of impropriety. He treats her with gentleness but otherwise much as would treat any of his disciples."

Herodias was exasperated. "Come Joanna! There must be more to it than that."

The woman pushed at the lock of hair that had strayed onto her face then twisted her hands nervously together. "I tell you mistress there is nothing that I can see."

"Tell me then of his words. Does he incite the crowds to action?"

Joanna shook her head. "Of course I don't manage to keep up with him at all times, so there may be things I miss. Much of what he speaks is in parables; they say he explains things to his disciples more clearly when he's alone."

"Earn your wages, Joanna!" Herodias said sharply. "I am paying you well to follow this preacher and this is all that you can tell me?"

Joanna shuffled uneasily. "He's a strange man," she said. "Not like anyone I've ever seen before. I don't know what sets him apart from others except that he seems so contented! John the Baptist was often angry but Jesus seems to like the people that crowd around him."

"He likes the attention!"

Joanna looked bemused. "No mistress, I'm sure he just likes the people."

Herodias dismissed the statement with an impatient wave of her hand. "What does he speak about, Joanna. I need solid evidence against him if we are to protect Herod's position."

"He speaks a lot about a kingdom that is to come."

Herodias grasped her by the arm. "And he is to be king of this kingdom?" she demanded.

"I can't be sure. He doesn't seem to refer to an earthly kingdom in the sense that we understand it to be. He says it is like leaven in dough; it spreads and grows of itself. Or like a mustard seed that starts off very small and becomes a big plant. He tells his followers that they must seek this Kingdom of God and his righteousness first, and all other needs will be met."

Herodias laughed. "Kingdom of God!" she said, "So, he says he's a god! Well, Augustus Caesar claimed to be a god and I don't know that it did much for Rome. But this is good news, Joanna. It's just the sort of information that I am looking for. Sit down and tell me more."

Joanna told Herodias of the gathering of the crowds on the hillsides; of the disciples who sat at their master's feet and drank in his words.

"Most people that I speak to come to see a miracle. Jesus once fed more than five thousand who had gathered in a distant place. It was after the Baptist was beheaded, but I was not there at that time. Jesus had heard the news and sought to find a quiet place to mourn his cousin. They followed after him in their masses and as it became dark it was too late to tell them to return to their homes."

Herodias, fascinated by anything that pertained to the Baptist listened intently.

"Jesus asked his disciples to bring what food was available, but only a young boy had brought food with him. Some loaves and a couple of fish."

"So?"

"They said he raised his hands heavenwards, broke the bread, prayed and the disciples fed the crowd. Afterwards they collected twelve baskets of bread and fish that remained."

"It's obvious that like Simon the Magus he's a magician of some stature. Who is woman that imbues him with his power? Is there any other beside the Magdalene?"

"There are women of course, who follow him. But I see nothing of an intimate nature between them and the followers of Jesus."

"Then you're a fool! I order you to get closer to the group, Joanna. I want the evidence of the one who is Jesus' partner. If he is practising magic, there has to be such a woman working with him."

Chapter 21
Twice-Born

Himmler arrived in Garmisch during a Bavarian holiday and parked his motor cycle outside the Gasthof. The seventeenth century buildings of the town had roofs with deep overhangs, which were supported on carved poles. They cast shadows onto walls elaborately decorated with pictures of German knights and ladies.

Men in lederhosen with short jackets over their embroidered shirts gathered to chat in the high street. Children scampered towards the town square where a brass band was playing, followed by the women wearing white bodices with pinafores over their full skirts and lace caps over their plaits. Himmler, who had adopted the vestige of a swagger, drew admiring glances from some of the younger women and a knot of children followed him begging to be allowed to hand out his pamphlets. In the square, he waited until the dancing was over and the band members had set their instruments aside in favour of elaborately decorated steins of beer.

Himmler stood up, aware of the rushing of blood in his ears as he prepared to address the crowd; a feeling of panic that he would never entirely conquer, even in those years ahead when public speaking became a major part of his existence.

"Ladies and Gentlemen," he began. "Let me introduce you to National Socialism…"

The new level of power in Himmler's life had become more evident prior to the May 1924 elections. His physical energy increased as did his unexpected oratory skills as he campaigned around the Bavarian countryside, delivering harangues against the Jews and the stock-exchange capitalists who were enslaving the workers. For many at this time, Himmler was the only outwards sign of the Nationalist Socialist Party as he rode from town to town on his motor cycle, on some occasions delivering several speeches a day.

The youth in particular were drawn to this new political creed. Germans had experienced economic ruin and the humiliation of the censure of nations following the last war and National Socialism vowed to advance Germany to its God-ordained destiny; a Germany in which all classes were bound together in loyalty and unity; strong and feared again by the nations. There was a swelling resurgence of pride in their country and as a result the movement of the Brown Shirts was growing.

Heinrich Himmler revelled in these times of working alone. It was his word that drew the people. By his speeches and his uniform, he commanded respect and represented a growing German dream.

Although Adolf Hitler was obviously aware of Himmler's value to the Party as a campaigner and administrator, he continued to regard Himmler as just the local manager of his speaking tours and treated him with every outward sign of contempt. It was Goebbels, who in 1926 was the rising star.

Moments before, the clouds overhead had been piled dramatically against a brilliant blue sky so that the shower, when it came, caught him by surprise and he was drenched in an instant. Turning the collar of his coat up and pulling the rim of his hat well down, he took the steps to the hotel two at a time and, pushing through the double doors, he nodded briefly at the bellboy.

A woman was approaching across the foyer, her blonde hair neatly dressed under a small grey hat. The suggestion of a veil dealt mystery to eyes that were unmistakably blue. Heinrich Himmler felt the breath catch in his throat, feeling, as he said later, that he was in the presence of one of the Valkyries. This, he was certain, was perfect woman, strong and purposeful and yet imbued with grace. Sweeping off his hat, he clicked his heels and bowed, then realised to his horror that he had showered her with droplets. She reacted with surprise, then merriment.

"Forgive me." Himmler reached into the inner pocket of his coat and offered her a handkerchief.

"Don't apologise. I'm fine, really! I was about to venture out anyway. I hadn't realised how hard it was raining!"

"If you're not in a hurry, perhaps you would join me for a cup of coffee?"

"I'd love one."

The waiter sat them at a corner table and brought coffee in a silver pot, setting delicate china cups on the starched white cloth.

The warmth of the room was causing Himmler's face to flush and he felt desperately uneasy after the initial moment of boldness. He wished fervently that he had been in uniform.

She reached out across the table and lightly touched his hand. "Do you realise, here we are having coffee together and we haven't even introduced ourselves. I'm Margaret Boden. Everyone calls me Marga."

"I'm sorry," Himmler said, "What could I have been thinking! I'm Heinrich Himmler."

"You're apologising again," she laughed.

Himmler was aware that his smile was stiff, but she did not appear to notice. He watched her hands as she poured their coffee; they were strong and practical, hands that had seen hard work. She interpreted his glance.

"I'm a nurse," she explained as though a question had been asked.

"Where do you work?"

"I have my own private clinic here in Berlin. I try to work as far as possible with natural remedies, herbs and that sort of thing."

He was instantly captivated. "That's amazing! I'm an agriculturist and herbal remedies are a passion of mine!"

Marga smiled in delight. "What do you do? Are you farming?"

Himmler straightened perceptibly. "I've recently moved into politics," he replied, "I'm with the NSDAP. Actually," he added self-effacingly, "I'm deputy Gauleiter of Upper Bavaria and Swabia, so my work carries me round the country a bit."

"So you're with Adolf Hitler? Have you met him personally?"

Himmler raised his eyebrows. "Hitler and I work very closely together," he assured her, making no attempt to conceal the note of pride that had crept into his tone. Marga leaned across the table towards him. Her eyes were alight but he was aware that her excitement was for Hitler.

"What is he like?"

"He's an amazing man, perhaps the greatest brain of all time!" he replied enthusiastically. "He fully understands the needs of the Volk and I'm convinced he will lead Germany back to greatness."

Their eyes met and for a moment there was a flash of communication between them. Marga's face was strong-boned and her features were uneven but the overall effect was nonetheless attractive. Fine lines had begun to develop in the skin around her eyes and there was a greater maturity to her expression than he was accustomed to in the young women he knew. Himmler placed his cup on the saucer with exaggerated care. He was annoyed to discover his hands were shaking.

"Are you staying here in the hotel?" he asked as she refilled his cup.

"I came in to see a friend."

"And I came to take shelter from the rain. I'm staying at a hotel a few blocks from here."

"An opportune meeting!" she replied smiling. "Perhaps we'll see one another again before you leave Berlin?"

He wondered later if he would have had asked her out if she had not offered that word of encouragement. The fact that an older woman had shown an interest in him was flattering. They took dinner together at the same hotel on the next evening and wrote to one another during the following weeks of separation. Later they met in Munich and slowly a relationship began to develop. Marga had a gentle teasing manner of speaking to him that was at once maternal and erotic, but even her flighty, inconsequential patter failed to annoy him.

Himmler waited resignedly for the change in attitude he had come to expect from everyone who came close enough to him. He was still convinced that she was in love with the image he sought so desperately to convey; an image that could not possibly survive for long at close quarters. Ultimately he was certain he would lose her. He nevertheless proposed hesitantly one evening in the living room of her lodgings.

She laughed aloud. "Liebschen, can you imagine what your parents would say if I accepted you?" "Not only that I'm considerably older than their precious son, but I'm also a divorced Protestant!"

He recognised the truth in her words and experienced the old, familiar pang of anxiety. Only a few years before, he had been instrumental in breaking up an unsuitable relationship between his older brother Gebhard, and the daughter of a Weilheim banker. Himmler had ordered a Munich detective agency to investigate Paula's past, and armed with the damning information he received from this and other sources, he had confronted Gebhard. His brother capitulated and the engagement was broken off.

There was a difference of course. He had proven that Paula was a girl of loose moral character and he would expect his family to recognise that the circumstances bore no real resemblance to his own. Nevertheless, Himmler was later to confess to his brother that he would rather clear a hall of a thousand Communists single-handed, than face the introduction of Marga to his parents.

"It may take a little time," he conceded at length, with a confidence he did not feel. "They're good Catholics with firmly set ideas and it may not be easy for them to adjust."

"It's alright, liebling, I'm willing to wait, if you think the obstacles can be overcome. But not too long! I want to be with you. We could buy ourselves a small plot of land somewhere and grow our own herbs and vegetables. And we could raise chickens!"

"And what about children?" he asked. "We must have several. Living like that, in the country, close to the soil! It's the ideal way for children to grow up."

She smiled up at him and he took her in his arms. He had been able to resist other women in the past, but not Marga. It had been the awe in which he held her maturity and experience that had driven him over the edge.

He lay in the dark listening to her even breathing. She slept with one arm thrown across his chest, so that he dared not move in case he woke her. His feelings towards her were always ambivalent once they had made love. He became unaccountably angry, disgusted by her womanliness and her dependence on him. But the emotion would soon fade and he would desire her again.

When at last Heinrich Himmler found the courage to confront his parents with the news of his relationship, they were appalled. It was not until July 1928, two years later that they finally stood back and allowed the couple to marry. Marga sold her clinic and with the proceeds she and Himmler bought a piece of land at Waltrudering near

Munich. They built a small wooden house and Himmler erected a chicken coop. Eventually, it was decided, they would run a chicken farm.

Chapter 22
Twice-Born

It was during the time of Joanna's absence that, at Herod's insistence, they went to Jerusalem to participate in the feast of Booths. Herodias cared nothing for the feasts and despised the comings and goings of the chief priests at the palace but it was always a pleasure to escape the intolerable boredom of Machaerus for the streets and the shops of Jerusalem. Herod clung to the outward show for the sake of the priesthood and even fasted in accordance with the law on the holy day of Yom Kippur. When his wife protested this foolishness, he would silence her by pointing out the importance of living like a Jew if he was to rule over them. Once the week was ended, he returned to Machaerus, but Herodias stayed on in the city. Salome joined her at the palace and Simon Magus sent word that he would also soon be in Jerusalem.

When the letter bearing the royal seal of King Abgar V was delivered to the Hasmonean Palace therefore, Herodias received it on behalf of her husband from Ananias, a trusted servant of Abgar.

"King Abgar suffers with an incurable disease," the messenger told Herodias. "He walks now with difficulty. I, myself, told my King of the Galilean who performs great miracles of healing."

"Has his fame spread so far abroad?" Herodias was genuinely amazed.

"I was in your country, my Lady, travelling to Egypt. I saw the man at a distance and when I asked why he was accompanied by so great a crowd, I was told of his miraculous powers."

"Herod Antipas will locate the man you are seeking and deliver the letter by his own servants," she told him. "I will write a reply to King Abgar in my own hand to assure him of our service."

King Abgar V of Edessa, an independent principality, which owed allegiance to the Parthian empire, was unknown to Herodias but she felt certain that Simon Magus would see possibilities in this communication with Jesus the Nazarene and she could hardly wait for his arrival at the palace. The Magus laughed aloud when Herodias told him the news.

"Let me see the letter! Have you opened it?"

"I waited for you. Herod would be furious if I opened it."

Simon Magus shrugged and broke the seal with a table knife.

"He won't know, my Lady, because you are not going to tell him."

The letter was written in Aramaic, a tongue in common use, and the Magus had little trouble in reading it.

"'Abgar the Toparch of Edessa,'" he read aloud, "'sends his greetings to Yeshua the Saviour who had come to light as a good physician in the city of Jerusalem. Your deeds have come to my notice and your healings performed without either medicine or herbs...' This is pure gold," the Magus declared. "Pure gold!

'Having heard of all these deeds, I have thought that you are God, come down from heaven or that you do these things because you are the Son of God. For this reason I have written to ask you to take the trouble to come to me to cure me of my disease.[4]'"

The Magus completed his reading of the letter and set it down.

"Tonight we will consult with the head of the Baptist and see how the letter must be answered."

"Will you require an answer from Yeshua the Nazarene?" she asked. "I could ask Joanna to deliver it into his hands."

He laughed again. "My Lady, you amaze me with your innocence! The Nazarene will never be apprised of this letter or its contents, but I will reply in his stead. I have a sense that this is a god-given opportunity and from it will flow such things that we can only begin to imagine."

It was a full month before Joanna returned to Machaerus and immediately Herodias set eyes on her she knew that she was not the same woman she had sent out. Physically, not much had changed, although she had caught her hair up into a knot in the nape of her neck, a simple act that greatly altered her appearance. It was something less overtly discernable, which made Herodias uneasy when Joanna entered the room.

"Where have you been, Joanna!" she demanded testily. "Why

[4] Porphryogenitus "Story of the Image of Edessa" A.D 945

have you stayed away so long?"

"I have been with the Master."

The words jolted Herodias and she glanced sharply at Joanna. Her handmaid laid a soft leather pouch down on the table.

"I have restored your money in full, my mistress. I can no longer continue in your service."

"What do you mean?"

"I have become a follower of Jesus of Nazareth."

"Joanna!" An angry flush suffused Herodias' face. "Where is your loyalty to me and to Herod, your lord?"

Joanna momentarily looked down at her sandaled feet. Then her eyes met those of Herodias.

"I have only one loyalty now," she said. "And that is to the Father that Jesus has revealed to me."

Herodias was stunned into silence, but only for a moment. When she was able to speak once more her voice was raised to a scream, which could be heard beyond the walls of the women's quarters.

"You belong to me! How dare you commit yourself to another?"

"I am a freed-woman," Joanna reminded her quietly. "I was never in your service as a slave. Yet, Jesus showed me clearly that I *was* a slave."

"You said yourself that you were a freed-woman!"

"But a slave to sin. I have never known until now what it was to be free. Do you know that I too was possessed by demons, Herodias? The Rabbi looked at me, into my soul and he saw immediately that I was in their bondage. He asked me if I wanted him to make me free." The steadiness of Joanna's eyes unnerved Herodias and she was forced to look away. "At that moment I knew I wanted the sort of freedom that the Master offered, more than anything else on earth. I saw myself, Herodias, like a serpent writhing in the dust. I had to be clean! I wanted it with my whole being.

"Jesus commanded the devils that were in me, and they left. For the first time in my life I knew what it was to be without whispering in my head. Without a desire to do ill, or to think disgusting, evil thoughts. It's not that I never sin now, Herodias, but I have been forgiven and I want to walk righteously. I don't ever want to go back to what I was."

"What do you imagine you will live on if you follow this man?" Herodias asked contemptuously

"Jesus tells us to take no thought for what we will eat or drink. I think I told you before, he teaches that all needs are met when you seek the Kingdom of God and his righteousness."

"In a very short time, this man will be dead!" Herodias spat. "If Pontius Pilot doesn't make sure of it I, Herodias, will ensure that Herod acts against him! You are a cretin, Joanna. You are giving up everything! This preacher can never offer you the power that I have here!"

Joanna shook her head. "The power that you offer me is devilish and evil," she retorted. "I want nothing of it! Repent of your sin, my mistress, before you are lost forever." She turned and left the room. Chuza was waiting for her outside and he took her protectively by the arm. Behind her they heard Herodias' wild laughter degenerate into cursing.

"Come, Joanna," Chuza said. "I have Herod's permission to walk with you." He turned her to face him. "Promise me that you will never return to Machaerus."

She smiled up at him. "I have nothing here except you. Promise me that you will seek the Master often. I will be there with him."

Chapter 23
Twice-Born

Michael Segal sat at his desk staring blindly at the open book in front of him. A chest-of drawers and a bed with a patchwork quilt took up one end of the attic, which was divided into sections by the great rough-hewn beams sloping from apex to wooden floor on either side of the room. A dormer window let in enough daylight to study by if he tied the chintz curtains back during the day, but now the lamp burned and outside its circle of light, the beams cast giant shadows.

He had spent the months since Walther's challenge investigating his Ashkenazi Jewish heritage. The first question he had been forced to ask himself was whether the Ashkenazi were true Jews. Historically, they were associated with the Scythians who originated on the steppes of Russia and were known, among other things, to have co-operated with Cyrus in the capture of Babylon. Some descendents settled in Israel at Beth Shean, also called Sycthopolis and, presumably, had adopted Judaism. If this was the history of his antecedents, he could hardly class himself a true child of Abraham.

The second question was how deeply Ashkenazi were involved in the conspiracy to world government, if indeed such a conspiracy existed.

Here the evidence was well-documented and overwhelming. The five sons of Mayer Amschel Rothschild were sent out to Europe's banking centres with the express purpose of commandeering them for their own purposes. Nathan, Mayer's third son, achieved the greatest triumphs in his adopted city of London, where he discretely took on Napoleon through the purchase of consolidated annuities for Prince William of England. He went on to buy gold worth eight-hundred-thousand pounds from the Dutch East Indian Company and, in conjunction with James, the youngest of the brothers, based in Paris, moved it through France to Spain under the nose of Napoleon. At this point brother Kalmann took over, transmuting the metal into bills in support of Wellington and the British allies. The Rothschilds had created between them the first great international clearing house.

But it was Waterloo that scooped Nathan his supreme victory. Their private intelligence service carried the information of Wellington's victory to Rothschild's ears several hours before the British envoy. He stood at his favourite pillar in the Stock Exchange and dumped his Consols. Other investors took note and sold theirs. Moments before the official reports of England's victory was made public, Rothschild began to buy. It was a brilliantly orchestrated panic and one the brothers were to become masters at performing.

Nathan Rothschild loaned England eighteen million pounds, and another five million to Prussia from his stock market gains, to repair the damages of war. And by the time of his death in 1836, he had secured control of the Bank of England.

But the Rothschilds presented only one facet, albeit a scintillating one, of the whole establishment.

Germany's Jews had left for greener pastures in great numbers, each of them, in time, achieving great heights. Joseph Seligman rose from being an immigrant foot peddler to financial advisor to the American President. August Belmont who channelled Rothschild funds into the United States Treasury in return for government securities was, in 1844, appointed United States Consul General to Austria, bringing him in close touch with the Rothschild's Vienna branch at a time when the Rothschilds indisputably ruled the economies of Europe.

Then there were the Loebs, the Kuhns and the Warburgs, the Goldmans and the Sachs, and many others, who intermarried, formed partnerships, and moved into such strong financial positions that their influence over the United States policy formations and fiscal decisions was unchallengeable.

Whether they were Freemasons or not, Michael could not discover, but their calculated imprint upon modern history had left him with the uncomfortable certainty that it could not simply be put down to co-incidence.

He recalled a scripture in the book of Obadiah, which spoke of a confederacy or conspiracy. The hidden things of Esau, it said, would be searched out. He took his Bible out of the desk drawer and looked it up.

All the men of your confederacy have brought you to the border:

the men that were at peace with you have deceived you and prevailed against you. They that eat your bread have laid a wound under you...

Men that the Jews trusted, men that appeared to be one with them had, the scripture said, conspired against them. And they were not Jews, but Edomites, sons of Esau.

Nehemiah, cupbearer to Cyrus the king, had been incensed to discover the intermarriage of Jews with those of the surrounding nations when he returned from Babylon to rebuild the walls of Jerusalem and he insisted that they put away their foreign wives and children.

The question that disturbed Michael as he considered this poignant application of the Mosaic Law was his own position. Would he be accepted by the God of Abraham, Isaac and Jacob, if he were not a true Jew?

His friendship with Walther Krauss had withered and all but perished in the course of the year, unable to survive Hester's influence. Michael and Chaim recognised the change and kept their own company. They were, in any case, working towards final exams and neither needed any unnecessary distractions; nevertheless Michael was hurt by the slight. Jewish by an accident of birth, he was rejected by the average German and could not be allowed to assimilate. Yet, he no longer could claim to have the assurance of his faith. If he was neither Jew nor German, what was he? He had become a stranger, even to himself.

Early in the following year, Michael Segal left to take up a teaching post in a Berlin college. Chaim Freiberg had already left Frankfurt shortly after Christmas. He was pleased to be stepping out and getting on with life, he said, and was certain that Geneva would offer great new opportunities. Particularly, he was glad to be leaving Germany behind. He was tired of the growing anti-Semitism and Switzerland, he was sure, would be more enlightened.

Michael immersed himself in his teaching and studied further in his spare time but made little move to establish relationships beyond the college.

In 1929, he heard of an opening in the history department of the University of Berlin and applied for the post.

"I will be moving at the start of the new semester," he wrote to his parents later. "I feel that I have reached the pinnacle of my career. It's more than I could have hoped for in a country where so much hostility still exists towards us. Perhaps, after all, there is hope for Jews in the new Germany!"

Chapter 24
Twice-Born

1929

Röhm had not only initiated Heinrich Himmler into the secrets of power, but also into the essence of Nazi politics and beliefs. But it remained necessary to carry the process a little further. The bonds holding his young protégé to the Catholic Church were not difficult to shatter once Himmler had compromised his deeply-held moral beliefs. Guilt and the horror of the confessional kept him divorced from the Catholicism. The gnawing sense of shame could not be revealed to any priest and Himmler lived in constant terror of exposure. So, while Röhm had succeeding in removing him from the Church, it was not as easy to remove the Church from him: the fear of an eternity in hell was at first all-consuming. Death lurked in Himmler's dreams and taunted him with its imminence. Each day he persisted in sin; each failure to attend Mass, condemned him to an ever-increasing sentence in Purgatory.

Röhm worked skilfully to replace the old beliefs with something demonstrably older, esoteric and infinitely more satisfying. It was guaranteed to sear Himmler's conscience and release him from guilt. Paganism was not a belief system adopted by all Nazis, but its seeds were built into the German nation and Himmler, when once he was initiated into it, stepped out to the brink of godhood.

While Adolf Hitler was in Landsberg prison, Ernst Röhm had continued to build up the Storm Troopers known as the Stormabteilung, or SA and, by the time Hitler's sentence was up, the force numbered thirty-thousand strong, in comparison with its previous peak of two thousand. Röhm wanted to unite all military groups under a single Ministry of Defence, over which he should preside. His refusal to let the SA become involved in party politics, or to allow his commanders to accept instructions from a political leader, caused Hitler to recognise that he had on his hands a dangerous power that could at any time have ousted him from position. On his release from Landsberg, he worked indefatigably to gather the leadership of the Party back into his own hands and to create a state within a state, an organisation such as Germany had never seen before.

Out of Hitler's determination to build up a dependable fighting force of his own, the Schutzstaffel, or the SS, was born, comprised at first of only eight men, a personal bodyguard. The position of the SS was discouraging. It was not permitted to form units in places where the SA was not up to strength and no SS unit was allowed to exceed ten percent of the strength of the SA.

The SS was as good as dead when Hitler, perhaps recognising Himmler's pre-occupation with titles, made him Deputy Reichsführer SS. It is possible that Adolf Hitler, aware of Heinrich Himmler's unmistakable organisational abilities, had actually hoped he might restore the languishing Schutzstaffel. However, even the dour Rudolf Hess is said to have slapped his thighs with laughter at what Himmler's colleagues considered the biggest joke in the history of the Nazi Party. The office boy had received his ultimate promotion.

Himmler never saw the joke. He had within his grasp his first real opportunity for power. 'Reichsheini' knew that his potential was underestimated and his training under Röhm had schooled him in a most precious commodity - patience. He was able to outwait them and to outwit them and he knew it. Let them think him a fool and he would oblige them by being one until his time was right.

Himmler's historians have suggested that he became 'a depersonalised abstraction, an inanimate embodiment of the National-Socialist police state.' Heinrich Himmler was holding his own masked ball.

Himmler arrived at Waltrudering unexpectedly one morning. It had been snowing and the sound of the car's engine was muffled. Small pockets of snow that had gathered in the needles of the pine trees broke away leaving liberated branches shuddering in newfound release.

Their small wooden homestead came into view as he rounded the last bend and beyond the house Himmler could see Marga's figure wrapped against the cold. She was bending to feed the chickens and she straightened slowly as she heard the vehicle, placing one hand in support of her lower back. The bulge of her pregnancy seemed to

Himmler huge and disproportionate even against the weight she had gained over the remainder of her body. The physical attraction he had once felt for her was irretrievably lost. He felt nothing but repulsion.

Her face broke into a smile of welcome and for a moment the strain disappeared from her features and he saw a flash of the old Marga. She came to meet him.

"Heini! This is a surprise! What brings you home?"

His smile was cool and he returned her kiss briefly. "I have some news I thought you might like to hear. Shall we go inside, it's cold out here?"

She stoked up the stove and set a pot of coffee on to percolate.

"So liebling, what is this news?" she asked as she sat down heavily in the chair beside him.

"I have been made Reichsführer-SS."

Her hands fluttered to her face. "But that's wonderful! It's time they gave you some recognition after all you've done for the Party! Can you imagine what the villagers will say? I will be Frau Reichsführer." She pushed a loose strand of hair off her face and patted it into place. "Will this mean more money for us Heini? The chickens are simply not paying and there are so many expenses."

Himmler experienced a swift surge of anger. "The coffee is ready," he commented tersely.

She stood up obediently and began setting out cups on a small wooden tray. Dough was rising under damp cloths close to the heat of the stove and he noticed with irritation that there was a smudge of flour across her cheek.

"Heini, liebschen, I'm so excited!" she said again. Setting the tray down on the table between them, she poured the steaming coffee into the cups. Her expression darkened suddenly.

"Will this mean you'll have more duties to keep you away?" she asked in a tone that had become plaintive. She reached for his hand. "Please Heini, with the baby here I'll need you here more often. It's so difficult to cope on my own."

He pulled away from her. "When you married me," he replied coldly, "you knew I would be a politician first and a husband second. What do you expect me to do? Turn the Führer down so that I can spend more time with my wife? You complain that you need more money and when I finally reach the point of being able to provide it, you want me to stay at home!" He stood up abruptly leaving his coffee untouched on the table, walked over to the window and looked out across a landscape devoid of colour.

She was silent for a long moment and when she spoke, her voice was miserable.

"My life is lonely here, Heini, and it's hard. I spend days at a time hardly seeing a soul and with little more to lighten my time than a kick from the baby."

The guilt she made him feel whenever he was with her aroused him to cold fury. His response was to become increasingly aloof.

He turned to face his wife. The kitchen was warm and pleasant. Copper pots gleamed over the wood stove and everything under Marga's capable hands had the appearance of cleanliness and order.

"It's only a couple of months until the baby is born," he told her flatly. "Then you will have plenty to occupy you."

"Is that really what you imagine my problem to be?" she asked tearfully. "There's more than enough to keep me busy, even without the baby. What I want is to share my life with you, but you're never here!" She stood up and put her arms around him. "Heini," she pleaded. "Let's sell Waltrudering! Let me come back to Munich with you."

He shook her off angrily and turned away, his shoulders taut. "We've put everything into this place. We're not going to sell now!"

"I've given everything up for you!" she shouted. "I gave up my clinic and put the money into a smallholding that can't pay because there's no man to help me run it. I gave up my life in Berlin so that I could be abandoned to this." She put her face in her hands and shook her head wearily. "Liebschen, please let me come with you."

Himmler looked at her and the light from the window glinted off the lenses of his spectacles. Her face was blotched and ugly with weeping. The lines, which he had first seen as a flattering sign of her maturity, had etched permanently into her features. Marga was a middle-aged woman. He had met her in the last triumphant flush of her beauty, but what now remained was a weak and foolish female, trying desperately to grasp something that had already passed her by. He had been afraid at first that she had loved an image of him and that as the image faded, she would come to despise him. Now he realised it was he who had loved an image and with its passing, nothing remained.

He took his hat and coat from the hook by the door. "There will be a ceremony," he said. "An inauguration. I will let you know how it goes."

He left the house and closed the door behind him.

Chapter 25
Twice-Born

I give you the end of a golden string
Only wind it into a ball:
It will lead you in at Heaven's Gate,
Built in Jerusalem's wall.
William Blake, Jerusalem

And he brought me to the door of the court; and when I looked, behold a
hole in the wall. Then he said to me, Son of man dig now in the wall: and
when I had digged in the wall, behold a door.
Ezekiel 8:7,8

"What do you know of the Temple?" Simon Magus asked Herodias.
She shrugged. "It was built initially by King Solomon, son of David,
for the Jews to make sacrifice to their God."

"I heard it said that Solomon brought a craftsman from Tyre to
oversee the work?"

Herodias glanced at him sharply and then laughed.

"For a moment I wondered what had inspired your interest," she
said. "But now I see. A man was brought in and I believe he was of
Tyre."

"Why would Solomon, a Jew, have brought in an outsider,
surely there were men of equal ability to be found in Israel?"

"If you want to know these things, Chuza, manservant to my
husband, is versed in the scriptures. I am unable to enlighten you
further in such matters."

"Then, if you will, let him speak to me," the magician said. "I
have a great desire to know more."

It was obvious that Herod's manservant spoke to the magician
under some duress. He had no love for Herodias and even less for the
man of unsavoury reputation who was consuming the passions of
Herod's acerbic wife. The Magus chose to ignore Chuza's coolness.

"Tell me what the Jewish scriptures say concerning the man from Tyre who helped to build the temple of Solomon," he said.

"There are two accounts," Chuza answered reluctantly. "They differ slightly in detail."

"How so?"

"In each, Solomon communicated with King Hiram of Tyre his intention to build a temple for the name of the Lord God. Hiram had been a friend of King David, the father of Solomon, and Solomon desired that wood for the building should be sent from Lebanon. He also asked the King of Tyre for a craftsman. And the king sent his namesake Hiram, son of a widow, of the tribe of Naphtali."

"Then he was not of Tyre?"

"According to this first account, his mother was indeed from Israel, but his father was from Tyre. There is a strange inconsistency in the second account which says he was a son of a woman of the daughters of Dan." He shook his head. "It is not often that these things arise, but I am unable to explain this difference."

A smile played around the mouth of the Magus but he held his peace. "I am told that the King of Tyre referred to Hiram, a humble workman, as Hiramabi, Hiram my father," he said. "What can you tell me of this?"

Chuza shook his head. "Only that he was held in great esteem by the king," he said. "Solomon too later referred to him in the same manner."

The Magus drew back his lips in an incredulous smile. "The great Solomon, said to be wiser than any man on earth, referred to a craftsman of Tyre as Hiram, my father!"

Chuza, who had begun to relax as he expounded the scriptures prickled under the sarcasm.

"The God of Abraham, Isaac and Jacob had indeed given the king great wisdom," he said defensively, "but perhaps, in this, Solomon sought a source of wisdom, forbidden of God. David, his father, would have looked for a man among the Jews with the skills necessary for building a holy place."

"And if no such man existed?"

"For the preparation of the Tabernacle in the wilderness God himself equipped men for every task. Solomon had only to ask."

Simon Magus raised his eyebrows but made no comment with regard to the manservant's simplistic faith in his God. He could see that Chuza desired more than anything to leave his presence but the Magus still had one more question to ask of him.

"Solomon married many wives," he said. "Among them was the daughter of Egypt's Pharaoh yet, according to Jewish Law this is forbidden. If King Solomon was given a gift of wisdom from God, why did he not conform to the Law? Is a king above the Law?"

Chuza looked down his nose at a man who wore a very thin cloak of righteousness as a cover to his nefarious activities.

"No one is outside the Law. All men are judged by it, whether they know it or not. Solomon made fewer obvious mistakes than David his father but David was the man after God's own heart. For all his sins, he loved God and knew what it was to repent. King Solomon allowed his foreign wives to turn his heart away from God. And perhaps Hiram the man of Tyre, whom Solomon called his father, also turned the king's desire from heavenly things to earthly wisdom. If this was so, Solomon's sin was like the sin of Adam!"

"The daughters of Dan!" the Magus exclaimed triumphantly after Herodias had dismissed Chuza from their presence. "The widow woman may have been of the tribe of Naphtali, but she was an adherent of the daughters of Dan."

Herodias laughed. "What are you saying?"

"King Danaus, the son of Belus. He and his daughters went from Israel to Arcadia where they established the cult of the Arcadians. If Hiram of Tyre was indeed known by two kings as their 'father', he was far more to them than a craftsman."

"What then, a priest?"

"More than a priest, one who had opened their eyes to the Mysteries. He would have left certain signs. I must examine his works within the temple for myself."

"Impossible," Herodias proclaimed at once, "You are a Samaritan. You would never be admitted beyond the outer courts."

"Nothing is impossible," the Magus replied with equal certainty. "Did not Herod the Great, rebuild much of the temple? He was no Jew yet, doubtless, there was no part of the temple that escaped his scrutiny. What of Herod, your husband, does he not offer sacrifice?"

"Even Herod is not exempt from the Jewish Law."

"Then you must bribe someone. I will see this building!"

"Herod speaks of tunnels and secret rooms beneath the mount," Herodias said. "Perhaps what you seek is not in the buildings above."

Simon Magus ceased his pacing and turned to face her. His eyes gleamed with excitement. "If the gods will it, we will uncover the hidden things in the secret places," he said. "I am certain that this great adept, Hiram, who had the ear of kings, would have known that to undermine the Temple of the Jews is to undermine the Jewish God. If, under the foundations of this building mysteries are concealed, they are mine to discover."

Herodias set herself to the task of finding a man who would take Simon Magus into the passages and chambers beneath Jerusalem's Temple. The situation was delicate, requiring that servants of her own, whom she could entrust with the assignment, work within the community. It was months before she could confidently declare that she had a man in her pay who had undertaken to disclose the secret places to the Magus.

"I have discovered that there is a cabal of priests that worship beneath the mount," she told him. "They are followers of Hiram. You must go this night and meet with one of these priests on the steps of the Court of the Gentiles. He will make himself known to you."

"You are a woman of wonders!" Simon Magus said. "Does this man have a name?"

"He is called Shaphan," Herodias said. "I know nothing more."

Simon drew the hood of his cloak over his head so that his face receded into deep shadow. The night was cold and clear. A myriad stars shone overhead sharply defined against the blackness of the sky. The Magus knew the patterns of the stars and the meanings of the constellations but tonight his mind was occupied with more earthly things. He was filled with heightened expectation that bordered the edge of fear. His mouth was dry and his heart pounded. Flaming torches burned in holders at the temple's outer court creating shapes which metamorphosed uneasily in the wind.

"Simon?" He had been watching but still the arrival of the priest startled him. He nodded.

"Follow me."

Leaving the city through the Fish Gate, they took the narrow path that led down into the Kidron Valley. One moment Shaphan was walking ahead of him, the next he had disappeared into the darkness. Simon Magus faltered and glanced around him. There was no sign of the priest. He took a few uncertain steps forward gasping with shock when a hand reached out from the rock of the cliff face and gripped him roughly by the arm.

"Come in here."

Beyond the concealed doorway were steps that opened into a passage. The way before them was black as pitch. Keeping one hand on the rough wall of the tunnel for support, Simon Magus groped his way forward, feeling with his feet for the treads, which were followed by lengths of tunnel and more steps; always aware of the cat-like footsteps of the man ahead of him. The passage terminated in a blank wall.

"Turn around."

The Magus obeyed listening to the slight scrape that indicated the opening of a door.

"Come!"

The dead-end had given way to another corridor and then, before long, a second door. The priest opened it without comment and lit a torch. Simon Magus gazed in amazement at the sight before him. It was as though he had been transported back to Egypt and found himself in some rich Pharaonic tomb. The walls were richly inlaid with a mosaic of images, predominantly in shades of blue and gold. All the gods and idols of the Egyptians were inscribed there: hooded serpents and figures of men with the heads of beasts. A domed ceiling supported by intricately carved pillars was encrusted with sapphire to convey the vault of heaven, while carbuncle marked the position of the stars of the zodiac. As he walked around the sanctuary the quick eye of the Magus took in other details. Magical symbols were woven into the cloth that draped the high altar and, predominant upon it was a goat's head and the star of the god Shalem[5]. Ciphers were inscribed on the lids of several deep stone boxes, which had the appearance of the caskets of the dead. As he paced the room under the watchful eye of Shaphan, the Magus saw that a mosaic pattern was inset within the great circle of the floor. Again, he realised it was triangle interlinked with triangle – the star of Shalem.

"Yeru Shalem," he said. "Yeru meaning foundation, of the Canaanite god, Shalem. Is this then the underlying foundation of the Jewish holy city?" His voice held a note of mockery to cover the deep impression made on him by the temple.

The priest refused to answer.

"It is enough that you have been brought here," he said. "I can do no more than that."

"Tell me one thing and I will ask nothing else. Is this the work of Hiram of Tyre?"

The priest looked at him sharply. "This is the true spiritual temple established by the Master," he said. "He was cruelly murdered and the women still lament for him as they did for Tammuz. His priests turn their back on the temple and worship facing the east as it was from the beginning of time."

He wore the full beard, untrimmed locks, the robes and the headdress of a Jewish priest but he was an adept even as Simon Magus himself. The Magus determined that he would come to know the man better in order that, in time, the secrets of this place should be revealed.

Many hundreds of years had passed since the building of Solomon's temple and that first edifice was destroyed by the Babylonians and rebuilt later under Nehemiah. Herod the Great repaired and extended the Second Temple yet, beneath the foundations, this secret place had endured undetected and preserved by a committed priesthood.

The memory of Hiram, the father of kings was kept alive; the women still wept for the Master as they did for Tammuz. Simon the Magus desired that same legacy, and one yet greater than that of Hiram. Future generations would remember him and weep; they would remember him and worship. He would ensure that it was so.

---

[5] See postscript.

Chapter 26
Twice-Born

1930

Matthias von Ingolstadt slipped his arms around Greta's waist and held her close.

"It's a new unit," he assured her. "Very small at the moment and nothing like the SA or the Freicorps."

Her body was rigid against him. "You said you wouldn't go back into the army."

"Try to understand, Anna. I have nothing else. The war stole the years that I should have been preparing for a career."

"There's your father's business. You just need to hold on a little bit longer."

"It's dead, Anna. Face it. It's another war victim that will never revive."

Abruptly, she pushed him away. Angry tears were streaming down her face. "It will lead to trouble!" she said. "The German war machine has always spelled trouble."

"This is different. The SS has been formed to restore the imbalances of the SA and the Wehrmacht."

She shook her head bitterly. "Why are you so blind, Matthias? Can't you see what Hitler is doing to this country? The SA Brownshirts are thugs, why do you suppose the SS will be any different?"

He shook his head in frustration at her intransigence. "Heinrich Himmler has set out to create something quite different. The Schutzstaffel is an elite command."

"An elite based on Walther Darré's image of the glorious German male," she returned sarcastically, "for men of pure blood. Wake up, Matthias! Think about this clearly for a moment. You might be just the sort of man the SS would welcome in. An officer of the German aristocracy. I'm sure they made you feel right at home! But you have a Jewish wife – tell me what they would say about that!"

For a moment Matthias looked abashed. "They will never know Anna, unless you choose to tell them," he said.

Greta von Ingolstadt gazed at her husband with contempt, and then swung round and left the room. Matthias made no move to follow her. He was reminded of when she had walked away from him in Poland. At that time he had not known she was Jewish; in joining the SS, he had chosen not to remember.

Almost all who had served in the World War were initially welcomed into the Schutzstaffel but gradually Himmler tightened his process of selection, although the introduction of a minimum height requirement of five foot eight inches did not pertain to the old soldiers.

"I am applying the basic principles of the nursery gardener," he said to his officers in the mess sometime later, "to reproduce a good old strain which has been adulterated and debased. Obviously the principle of plant selection is the place to start. I am not ashamed to admit that I have begun a process of weeding out those men who will not help to build up the SS. Of course, height is a good place to begin," he laughed shortly. Laughter was never natural coming from Heinrich Himmler; it held an element of embarrassment and discomfort. "I am aware that height is a good indication of the sort of blood I desire in my men."

Generally, Matthias was unperturbed by Himmler's anomalous world view.

"He's what the English would call an 'odd fish'," he told Greta some months later when she had grown a little more accepting of Matthias' position in the SS. "Every new applicant now has to submit a photograph which he scrutinizes personally with a magnifying glass. I'm told he spends his time looking for indications of foreign blood, like cheekbones for example, which might denote a Mongolian or Slav background." He spoke lightly, expecting her to be amused.

Greta raised her eyebrows cynically, "Perhaps you should draw his attention to his own features," she snapped. "And his height and colouring for that matter! Heinrich Himmler seems to have a personal blind-spot."

Matthias smiled. "The Reichsführer couldn't pass the physical on any level to make it into his own Order," he confessed. "He insisted on undergoing the examination but those who tested him had to tamper with the results to prevent any further humiliation."

"So, why humour him?" she persisted. "If the Reichsführer

can't lead by example it must demoralise the men."

"It doesn't," Matthias said shortly. But, not for the first time, he wondered how it was that no one else seemed to notice the paradoxes, which Greta would not allow him to ignore. "But the thing is, without the Reichsführer, the SS would not be what it is today."

Greta gave a bitter laugh. "The German male is easily seduced by elitism," she said. "In the past, it was purely social. Good breeding; the right name, possessions and education, that sort of thing. Himmler's changed all that. Now we're asked to accept a German racial elite. All that skull measuring has apparently proved that Aryan superiority is a cut above the rest of humanity. Germany's nobility has become purely based on idealism, a racial aristocracy!"

"Race is just one minor aspect of the SS," Matthias said, "It's really a protective organisation, one that will apply checks and balances to the other movements. The Führer knows the value of our organisation. We have never let him down."

Greta von Ingolstadt who recognised Matthias' parroting of the Reichsführer; gave her husband a withering look and began to vigorously chop the onions for the evening meal.

Chapter 27
Twice-Born

Edessa and the surrounding region of Osrhoene prospered under King Abgar V. Caravans travelling from the east, passed through the city bringing abundant trade in silks and spices. However, the king's illness inevitably cast doubt on the future stability of the region.

The reply to his letter from Jesus of Nazareth arrived some weeks after his own messenger had returned from Judaea. The annoyance the king experienced at first, in having heard from Herod's wife instead of the Tetrarch himself was ameliorated somewhat by receipt of the reply from the Judaean prophet. However, the king was disappointed. Yeshua the Nazarene would not, he said, come to see Abgar himself, but would send one of his disciples.

There were thirty men and women in the innermost circle of Simon Magus' followers and included among those was the priestess, Helen of Tyre. Helen alone was not of Samaritan or Idumean birth.

Herodias, wife of the Tetrarch of Galilee and Perea, had been initiated into the second tier of this coven and later Salome, the daughter of Herodias would join her. These circles alone saw the head and worshipped it, but there was also an outer circle of adherents who, although they were not privy to the deepest secrets, witnessed the unmistakeable power of Simon the sorcerer and were prepared to follow him to the death.

After sending the reply to the king of Edessa, Simon Magus stalled.

"The timing is wrong," he told Herodias and Helen. "Something else is to take place before we send anyone to see him."

"I don't understand why you don't go yourself," Herodias said petulantly. "Who can you entrust this mission to if you are not even certain of the purpose."

"I will know when the time is right, my Lady. We are to wait and to listen. The head of the Baptist will speak a word in due season."

"Waiting will be of little use if Abgar is dead!" she retorted tartly but she had learned to respect his leading and she held her peace.

Herodias had granted Simon Magus his building on the shores of the Dead Sea but she remained ignorant of the nature of his experimentation. The black art of alchemy was something the Magus had studied for many years and it suited him to work under Herodias' patronage and protection. Under Mosaic Law, wizardry was punishable by death and although he had practised his art safely in Samaria, the present aspirations of the Magus required the sort of money that could only come from Herodias.

He worked assiduously with metals using the skills taught him by the Persians and the Arabs and the knowledge obtained from the great library of Alexandria. The Greeks had gained access to many formulas, including those of ancient Egypt, some of which were written and some were passed down through high initiates. For the alchemist, the quest to create gold, symbolic of the sun, from base metals, such as tin, which took the symbol of Hermes, was paramount. This represented, always, an allegory of the alchemist's own pursuit of godhood.

Simon the Magician was already an adept initiated into the Mysteries of Osiris in Alexandria. Like Plato, the Magus had spent three days and nights entombed in the Great Pyramid at Giza, a time of symbolic death and rebirth before emerging a god in his own right.

The Great Pyramids were temples of enlightenment, khuti, meaning 'glorious light' and it was believed that the all-seeing eye of Horus overshadowed the apex of the pyramid. These Egyptian temples of initiation were built to commemorate an occurrence around 4000 BC, in which Osiris, who was one with Lucifer, fell as a blazing star from the heavens. After the fall, both Osiris and Lucifer were represented by the sun and certain stars. It was prophesied that the intense light of such a star would be seen again in the heavens six thousand years after this portentous event.

After his days of entombment, Simon had been brought out into the soft pre-dawn light by an adept of the Great White Brotherhood whose head and features were covered. The Magus had stood for a moment, breathing deeply and feeling the touch of the warm desert air on his face. He still held his cloak protectively around him as he had while in the chamber in the depths of the pyramid, a ward against three days of spiritual onslaught that had left him weak and trembling in its wake. Only the strongest adepts underwent this supreme test and not many men came out unscathed. Panic and madness stalked a very close path to those already weakened by the lack of food and water. Terrifying visions and powerful feelings of dread haunted every moment: sleep was more dangerous than waking, any lack of vigilance meant that the mind could be seized and destroyed by the powers of darkness. Only the application of the most highly-trained will could withstand the pressures of the King's Pyramid. Simon had come forth in victory and, standing between the massive paws of the sphinx, an ancient rite was performed by faceless men, themselves adepts of Khufu.

Lucifer was the light-bringer, star of the dawn, announcer of the rising sun. Arms outstretched towards the early rays, they proclaimed the second birth of Simon the Magus.

"This is given to you as a sign of new life," one of the priests said. With care he withdrew something from a black pouch and handed it to the Magus."

Removing the object from its wrapping of soft cloth, the Magus took it between finger and thumb and held it to the light.

"Glass!" He felt a momentary nudge of disappointment. Glass was well-known among the Syrians and the Egyptians, and was used both to make vessels and to beautify objects. But this circle of thin glass, which was about six millimetres in diameter, had been finely honed and skilfully shaped; concave on the one face and convex on the other; a strange token such as he had never seen before. He looked round uncomprehendingly at the members of the Brotherhood.

"Quartz glass," the priest replied. "It is a cunning invention of the ancients, an art that was well understood many ages ago, but in the mists of time, except to the very few, its purpose was lost. These glasses were placed before the eyes of the mummies of kings to allow them to see all things in this world and to give them sight in the underworld. If you are chosen by the gods you will discover its properties."

In the years that had passed since that day, the Magus had

discovered many applications for the little piece of glass, not least its ability to gather together the fire-making rays of the sun. Placed just before an eye that was weak, if the other eye was covered, it could in many cases bring improved sight. Simon had experimented with the making of similar glasses himself but had been unable to invent a method of honing it to such fineness. The ancients had taken their secrets to the grave with them.

Because of its enigmatic quality, the delicate quartz lens was Simon Magus' most treasured possession. It was a message from the gods but one which he was yet unable to interpret.

Chapter 28
Twice-Born

Gabriele Hoch was Michael Segal's only close friend at the University of Berlin in the years between 1930 and 1933. There had been a gradual freeze towards the sprinkling of Jewish professors by their German colleagues. Nazism was taking hold of Germany like a vine, which would ultimately overwhelm and strangle the tree. Despite Segal's hope that at university level the intellectual giants of the nation might remain untouched, he knew that the first heartbeat of Nazism had been triggered in Berlin University's hallowed halls. Throughout the nineteenth century, philosophers and historians had fed their doctrines into the lives of Prussia's intelligentsia each contributing towards a subtle shift in ideology. Hitler was pouring out a distilled potion of these same philosophies on the working-classes and they had become intoxicated.

The talk in the university was not on the crass level of Julius Streicher's newspaper, Der Stürmer; no one called Jewish professors lascivious Jewish goats – at least not to their faces. Talk focussed more on the manipulative role of the Jewish bankers and the shared goal of international Jewry and Communism. There was no doubt, so it was said, that there was a Jewish conspiracy towards world domination. One had only to look at the role of Karl Marx, a German Jew, in the formulation of Communism or at the Rothschilds' in European banking to know that there was a conspiracy. Colleagues frequently pointed out, as Walther had, that an examination of history showed Jews had consistently influenced European affairs. They had been expelled from almost every country in Europe because of their unscrupulous moneylenders.

Many evil geniuses, both financial and political, had already arisen from the Jewish community in Germany alone, how many more lay latent? From the Universities, there was no call to barbarism but, it was reasoned, Jews must be barred from higher education: an educated Jew was a dangerous Jew.

"Hitler's gleaned ideas from a variety of sources," Michael told Gabriele on one of their midday walks. "Most of which first found expression here."

"Fichte and Hegel?"

"That's right. Fichte was in Philosophy. His success after Napoleon's defeat was making the German people think that they were a superior race with a superior and unique language. The only race possessing the possibility of regeneration. Hegel followed Fichte. His thinking revolved around the glorification of the State, and of course Hegel believed war to be the great purifier." Michael Segal sat down on their favourite bench under an oak tree and motioned to Gabriele to join him.

"There's no real indication that Hitler would lead Germany into war."

He shrugged. "I think, in line with Fichte and Hegel's philosophies, Hitler believes he's the one chosen to lead Germany to greatness. War is the next logical step." He took Gabriele's hand tracing her long fingers with his own. They were artist's hands that flowed across the piano keys like the waters of a stream. He delighted in her music and was increasingly drawn to Gabriele the woman. A group of students approached and Gabriele drew away from him, smiling an apology.

"And it was Hegel who believed the end justified the means."

Michael nodded. "He taught that the State must crush any object in its path without being hindered by moral issues and that Germany should be led by a small elite, free of any moral constraints."

Gabriele raised her eyebrows. Her shoulder-length hair tended towards copper and sprang into natural curl, reflecting the irrepressibility of her character. Today, as she often did, she had chosen to wear it caught up in a soft bun, creating a bouffant frame for her face from which curls escaped like tendrils of a plant.

"Hitler's Brownshirts are certainly not known for restraint," she commented. "Moral or otherwise." She picked up a dead leaf from the grass and twirled it between her finger and thumb. "Every good German longs to be a hero. It comes from listening to tales of Nordic mythology."

"Or Wagner."

She smiled.

"What about Heinrich von Treitschke?" she asked.

"He was professor of history and very popular. There were always enthusiastic gatherings at his lectures, staff officers and Junker officials included. Treitschke was tougher than his predecessors and more Prussian than the Prussians. He claimed that war was the highest expression of man and the common people were to be little more than slaves. It didn't matter what you thought, as long as you obeyed. As far as Treitschke was concerned the idea of peace was not only absurd, it was immoral. Peace would lead to decay."

"These things are deeply entrenched," she said. "Germans learn total obedience at their mother's knee, and I'm not sure that we're ever taught to discern who we should obey. Adolf Hitler is stirring up terrible hatred, especially against the Jews, and his followers are multiplying."

"The National Socialists are still a small party."

When her passions were aroused, as they were now, Gabriele's entire body was engaged. She spoke with broad, sweeping gestures to make her point.

"These men are louts, Michael! They're provincial boors with no breeding. They've simply created an enemy as a means to an end. Hatred attracts the sort of adherents that they're looking for."

"They're also wooing the industrialists, Gabriele, and increasingly more of the intelligentsia is drawn into their ranks. The danger is their fanaticism. Hitler is a man of frightening charisma."

She nodded soberly. "But Michael, if you read their propaganda, they're appealing to the basest human emotions..."

"Of which we all have a portion!"

"I haven't seen you attracted to National Socialism yet."

He grinned. "I don't think they'd have me!"

She laughed obediently but spoke more soberly.

"You've made it clear that you know where it's going. I heard only yesterday that Nazi Party officials have been ordered to whip the peasant's natural aversion to Jews and Freemasons to a frenzy. From what you've told me, the German soil has been carefully prepared for this moment, and for this man. I'm afraid for you, Michael. If Hitler manages to overthrow the Republic, German Jews will be in grave danger. Please think about leaving."

Chapter 29
Twice-Born

An icy wind whipped through the porticos of Solomon's Porch and the disciples hunched into their woollen cloaks, bowing their heads, their eyes narrowed against its sting. The Master's presence in the temple courts attracted immediate attention. This time, it was a group of scribes who saw Jesus arrive with his disciples. They walked purposefully towards them and it was obvious they intended trouble. There was no preamble.

"If you are Messiah tell us!" they demanded.

"I have told you already and you didn't believe me," Jesus replied. "My works that I do in the name of my Father bear witness to who I am."

Immediately there was jeering from the growing crowd.

"You don't believe because you are not of my sheep," Jesus said, raising his voice over the howl of the wind. "My sheep hear my voice. I know them, they follow me and I give them eternal life. No man shall pluck them out of my hand or out of my Father's hand. I and my Father are one."

There was a roar of anger from the scribes.

"Law breaker! Stone him!"

Peter glanced at Matthew. The mood was volatile. There was pushing and jostling, while the smell of sweat in the air mingled with the taste of dust. At the back of the crowd some of the men had stepped off the walkway into the gardens looking for rocks among the trees. Matthew nodded, his face was pale; it was time to leave if they were to escape with their lives. The disciples stood stunned by the swift turn of events. Andrew plucked at Jesus' sleeve urging him to leave. The Master, however, remained calm and unruffled.

"I've shown you many good works from my Father, for which of these do you intend to stone me?"

Several voices were raised in a clamour. "For blasphemy," they shouted. "For declaring yourself one with God!"

If I don't do the work of my Father then don't believe in me. If I do, even though you refuse to believe in me, believe by my works that the Father is in me and I am in Him."

If the mob could have safely dragged him from the temple precincts they would have killed him and claimed that his death was justified under Hebraic Law, but they feared arousing the ire of his many followers. Matthew took his master by the arm, urging him to leave and the other disciples both angered and humiliated by the actions of the priesthood, formed a barrier between Jesus and his antagonists. He turned and walked away from them without a backward glance.

It had become obvious that unless Jesus retired from Judaea, his ministry would be prematurely shortened. The following morning he and the twelve disciples bade a brief farewell to the family at Bethany and began the long walk into Herod Antipas' territory, stopping at the River Jordan, just north of the Dead Sea at the place where John had baptised before his arrest. Many went out to see Jesus there and many believed in him as Messiah.

"John did no miracles," they said. "But everything he said about this man is true."

"Lazarus is ill."

Three months had passed and the disciples had begun to speculate among themselves as to whether Jesus would go up to Jerusalem to celebrate the Passover when the messenger arrived with the news.

"He is close to death," the youth told him. "His sisters have asked whether you could return to Bethany."

Jesus listened to the details of his report and, while the young man was given food and drink, retired to his favourite rock overlooking the quiet waters of the Jordan fingering his beard contemplatively. His disciples waited for the word. Knowing of their master's deep friendship for Lazarus, they were certain he would leave immediately.

A few minutes later Jesus rejoined his men. "This sickness will not lead to death," he said, "it is for God's glory and to glorify the Son of God."

"So, are we not going?" Thomas asked Matthew when the

Master had left them.

"Not yet, it seems."

Jesus had taught the crowd all morning and the disciples baptised those who had heeded the call for repentance of their sin. Now most had gathered in small groups to share a midday meal and some curled up in the shade of the bushes and slept.

"Do you remember how the Master healed the servant of the centurion?" Peter asked. "He didn't even go to his home."

John nodded. "He healed him by his word. Perhaps he will do the same for Lazarus."

"The centurion's expectation was that the Master could heal by his word," Matthew reminded them. "Mary and Martha are expecting him to go to Lazarus. The Master seems to work in accordance with the expectations of those who approach him."

"Jesus did say that Lazarus would not die," Thomas reminded them.

"Nevertheless, the sisters will be worried." John looked across to where Jesus was sitting alone on the river bank. He appeared calm and untroubled. John knew by experience that he would not be pressured by what his disciples wanted of him; he would simply do what he knew to be right. The Master's quiet assurance in every situation was one of the many things that set him apart from any other human being.

Jesus the Nazarene and his disciples had often lodged in Bethany in the home of Lazarus and his two sisters, Martha and Mary, who lived on the edge of the village. From the age of seventeen, Martha had kept house and taken on the role of mother to her younger sister who was only three when their own mother died suddenly. Lazarus dealt in spices from the East, a trade established by his father who had left him the lucrative business on his death five years before.

For Martha, the death of her father dealt another deep blow and seemed to spell the end to any hope of marriage. Mary had become increasingly difficult to control as she entered puberty and Lazarus was oblivious to anything beyond camel trains and the spice trade in Jerusalem. Those five years had been more turbulent than Martha cared to remember. In her sixteenth year, Mary had brought dishonour on their family name by an illicit association with one of her brother's business associates. The affair was discovered by Lazarus; the man who had seduced their sister was thrown out and Mary was fortunate not to have been stoned to death as she would certainly have been had the Roman occupation not weakened the Mosaic Law.

Jesus' introduction to the home of Lazarus and the women brought new life and a new focus. Lazarus was deeply honoured to have a man such as Jesus under his roof, who had thrust Galilee and Judaea into such a state of turmoil and excitement. He began to spend more time in the home and for the first time in years turned back to a careful study of the Torah. Martha waited for the visits of the Master and his disciples with unspoken longing and Mary, in the full bloom of her youth, fell deeply in love with him.

Two days after receiving the news of Lazarus' illness, Jesus woke his men early. The time had come to depart.

"Is it safe for us to return to Judaea?" Nathanael asked, giving voice to all their fears. "When we were last there the Jews sought to kill you. Is it safe to go back?"

Jesus smiled. "Aren't there twelve hours in the day?" he asked. "So if any one walks in the day he does not stumble because he sees the light of this world."

They nodded in agreement.

"But if he walks at night he stumbles because there is no light in him. Our friend Lazarus sleeps now, but I will go and awaken him."

Thomas seized on the little he had understood. If Lazarus was asleep, it probably meant he was improving. This time Jesus answered plainly.

"Lazarus is dead," he said.

The journey took them two days and although Jesus seemed fired with a sense of purpose, he did not make undue haste. When the men were tired he encouraged them to stop and rest, using the time to teach them. Increasingly now he spoke about his coming death. And from this point onward his ministry was directed less at the masses and more at the twelve. Little by little he was preparing them for his departure, but they seemed unable or unwilling to fully comprehend what he was saying. As they approached Bethany, Jesus instructed

Philip to go ahead of him into the village.

"Speak to Martha," he said. "Tell her we are on our way."

So it was that the older sister of Lazarus slipped away and went out to meet Jesus on the outskirts of the village. She embraced him and when she looked up her eyes were filled with tears and her words held a hint of reproach.

"Lord, my brother has been in the grave four days. If only you had been here, I know he would not have died! Even now, I know that God will give you whatever you ask."

He took her hand. "Martha, your brother will rise again."

She nodded slowly. "I know he will rise at the resurrection on the last day."

"I am the resurrection and the life," he said. "He that believes in me, even though he dies, yet he shall live. And whoever lives and believes in me will never die. Do you believe this?"

"Yes, Lord, I believe that you are the Son of God, the promised Messiah."

Jesus smiled down at her. "Martha, go and call your sister."

Many people had gathered in the house of Lazarus' sisters. The spice merchant was well-known, and Bethany was situated only a short distance from the city. Among the mourners were members of the priesthood who had walked from Jerusalem, as well as Simon, the father of Judas. Seeing Mary leave the house, they followed her believing that she was hurrying to her brother's tomb.

"Master!"

As Mary saw the familiar figure on the pathway to the grave, tears ran down her face. Behind her, the scribes and Pharisees, some of whom had accosted Jesus in Solomon's Porch months before, stopped in their tracks, murmuring among themselves.

"Look who has arrived!"

"It's surely possible that a man who opened the eyes of the blind could have prevented this."

"See how he loved Lazarus," one said. "He weeps."

And indeed, as Jesus stood at the grave he bowed his head and shared in the grief of the women.

The family burial place where the body of Lazarus had been laid beside those of his parents was a cave set in a rocky outcrop on the hillside. For many years, Lazarus had been both brother and father to Mary and his loss seemed more than she could bear. Martha slipped a comforting arm around her younger sister and Mary buried her head against Martha's shoulder. Her only consolation was the presence of the Master. He had come and that was enough.

"Roll away the stone!"

The command was unexpected and Mary looked up in amazement. Martha reached out to prevent him.

"Lord, by this time the body will stink, he has already been in the grave four days!"

"Did I not tell you that if you believed you would see the glory of God? Roll away the stone!"

The disciples searched the face of the Master uncertainly then Peter took the initiative, ignoring the supercilious gaze of the religious leaders who had gathered in knots willing Jesus to fail.

"Philip, Andrew!" He beckoned with his head. "Come!"

Planting his feet firmly on the ground, he set his back to the rock and Philip and Andrew joined him, straining with the effort and feeling the sweat begin roll down their faces. It shifted suddenly and began to move ponderously away from the entrance of the cave. Martha's hand flew to her mouth and Mary watched, unable to stir or to speak.

Jesus looked up, his face was very calm.

"Father, I thank you that you have heard me. This prayer is for those who do not believe that you have sent me." He looked down at the black opening of the grave and cried out: "Lazarus! Come forth!"

For a long moment there was silence and then a faint scuffling came from within the tomb. The crowd fell back gasping in superstitious dread as Lazarus stumbled blindly into the light still bound in strips of cloth in accordance with the burial custom of the Jews. Mary and Martha clutched at one another, mute and trembling.

"Loose him and let him go!" This order was spoken gently to the disciples who had rolled back the stone. "Loose him."

They moved towards Lazarus hesitantly, steeling themselves to touch him. Then Philip, sensing the confusion of the man, took him by the hand and spoke his name.

"Lazarus, I'm going to take the cloth off your face. Don't be afraid."

Chapter 30
Twice-Born

Marianne von Ingolstadt was thirteen when the German National Revolution took place and a son, Horst, had been born to Greta and Matthias two years after her birth.

For a time, it seemed that the SS would wither and die. Greta von Ingolstadt held her breath. Heinrich Himmler had been virtually ignored while his rival Gruppenführer Kurt Daluege, under the Minister of the Interior, Hermann Göring, had risen to one of the highest offices of state. Daluege was State Commissar without Portfolio and Göring promoted him to Lieutenant-General of Prussian police. Daluege would no longer take orders from Heinrich Himmler and refused to meet with Reinhard Heydrich when he was dispatched to Berlin. However, Heinrich Himmler had achieved one minor advantage. He had been made Acting Police President of Munich.

In March the Reichsführer arrested Count Arco-Valley.

"On his own admission," he stated, "the Count had planned a coup against the Reich Chancellor, Adolf Hitler."

Two weeks later he informed the press that three hand-grenades planted by Soviet agents had been discovered near the Richard Wagner memorial.

"This is a route the Reich Chancellor uses regularly. There are terrible dangers ahead," he warned. "Through information we have received from Switzerland, I can tell you that the Communists have planned attacks on the Reich Chancellor and on leading personalities in our new State!"

Adolf Hitler became noticeably more fearful. Himmler had formed protection units on two previous occasions and the Reich Chancellor called him in again. The situation had become urgent.

"One day some perfectly ordinary citizen with horn-rimmed glasses and a little beard will install himself in a shabby little attic in the Wilhelmstrasse," he told Himmler. "He will train the telescopic sight of a weapon on the balcony of the Reich Chancellery hour after hour, and day after day, until one day he pulls the trigger." Hitler's Adam's apple bobbed and he eased the collar of his uniform awkwardly with one finger. "A successful attack would have a fearful effect on the public," Hitler said. "We cannot allow the State to be thrown into anarchy if some fool chooses to assassinate me."

"We will increase your guard, Herr Reich Chancellor," Himmler offered. "Allow me to use the SS for this purpose."

At the mighty Nuremberg Party Rally in September of that year, Adolf Hitler spoke warmly of the Leibstandarte-SS. Although at first the Führer had seen Heinrich Himmler as a person of no consequence, he was, despite himself, becoming increasingly impressed by Himmler's abilities. He was a willing and efficient member of the Party; sympathetic to Hitler's needs and interests and, surprisingly, as his responsibilities grew, so did his authority. He would probably never amount to much, the Führer decided, but he was a useful man to have around and the SS was flourishing under the Reichsführer's command. The Leibstandarte-SS, Hitler's bodyguard had been officially christened and its direction was set. Partly for his own protection, Himmler would at all times conceal his personal dominance behind the SS and they would provide a convenient camouflage for the Reichsführer's nefarious activities.

Matthias became part of one of the Sonderkommandos or Special Detachments inspired by Hitler's Leibstandarte, pseudo-police units designed for the protection of Third Reich officials, a move which afforded Himmler a foothold in the police mechanism beyond Bavaria. In many areas of Germany the highly disciplined force of the SS began to win the respect of the chiefs of police and Heinrich Himmler was called on to give them advice and support.

"Papa!" Horst flung himself into his father's arms as Matthias opened the door. "You're back!"

Greta came through from the kitchen wiping her hands on her apron and kissed him lightly on the lips.

"It smells wonderful in here," he said.

"We're having a roast for lunch!"

Matthias smiled down at his son and tousled his hair.

"A roast! Is this a special occasion? Have I missed

something?"

"Only that you're back again," Horst said. "I've got something to show you, Papa." And he ran off in search of a model aeroplane he was building.

Matthias slipped an arm around Greta and kissed her.

"You've been away too long."

He nodded. "But it's good to be back, Anna," he said. Matthias' service in the SS kept him away from home for long periods of time and he missed his family. He was not a controlling father, but neither was he indulgent and the children were his greatest pleasure.

"Hello, Papa. Horst said you were home."

Matthias hugged his daughter warmly. Marianne was already tall, athletic in build and, in his eyes, beautiful. She stepped back and appraised her father critically. He was wearing the immaculate uniform of the Schutzstaffel, which had never failed to instil awe in the children; black tunic over a brown shirt, black tie, black breeches and highly polished jackboots. His black cap with the chinstrap and the silver deaths-head insignia hung on the hat-stand by the door.

"You're not the only one with a uniform now," she told him. "I've joined the Hitler Youth."

Greta grimaced over her daughter's head and Matthias laughed.

"Your mother doesn't approve," he said.

"Oh, she's fine! Aren't you, Muti?"

Greta gave a little snort of irritation and bustled off to the kitchen to attend to the lunch.

Conversation over the dinner table revolved around the children's latest achievements at school and Marianne insisted on describing the Bund Deutscher Maedel in great detail.

"The BDM do marches every weekend with heavy back-packs, just like the boys and when I turn eighteen, I will be expected to do a year's work on a farm," she told them.

"And Muti says I must ask you if I can join the Hitler Youth too," Horst said.

"I said I did not want you to join," Greta retorted sharply.

"It's not fair if Marianne is part of it and I'm not."

"Will you children be quiet now and allow us to eat in peace.

We will talk about this tomorrow."

It was only later that they were able to discuss the upheavals that were taking place in Prussia where Göring's terror campaign against the last bastions of democratic resistance had spiralled out of control.

"Göring thoroughly inflamed the SA," he told her. "Then claimed to be shocked by the violence he unleashed."

Matthias and Greta had moved from Berlin shortly after Horst's birth and settled near Munich. It had been a relief to Greta to leave Prussia. Frau von Ingolstadt had died four years after their move into the house in Heiligerstrasse without ever returning home. Shortly afterwards, they made the decision to sell up and move. As far as Greta was concerned, apart from Matthias' salary, the relocation to Bavaria was the only benefit that had arisen from his joining of the SS.

"Göring's a fool!" she replied angrily. "I've heard horror stories about the happenings in Berlin. What did he think he was doing?"

"I don't know if he realised how frustrated the SA had become but he let loose a terrorist mob. They set up fifty impromptu concentration camps in Berlin alone."

"And the so-called 'enemies of the state' were hauled off into cellars and beaten up and tortured!" Greta said in disgust.

"There are four million men in the SA with nothing to do and they're thirsting for action. It's a recipe for trouble. Göring's hatched a nest of vipers, which he'll be caught in himself, if he's not careful. Diels has formed a new unit on Göring's behalf known as the Secret State Police. It's basically a political intelligence unit that could spell further trouble in Prussia. You may have heard of it? It's been dubbed the Gestapo."

Greta shook her head. "Matthias, I'm worried about what's happening," she said. "I feel that Germany is being caught up in a spiral of violence that will sooner or later spill over into war."

He put an arm around his wife's shoulders, suddenly aware of how vulnerable she appeared. "I don't think it will come to that," he said. "The last war is still too fresh in most people's memory."

"Tell that to the SA or the Wehrmacht!" Greta retorted. "For that matter, tell it to the Hitler Youth. All this militancy can only lead to war. Please, Matthias, get Marianne out of that organisation before her head is turned as well."

He promised, knowing full well that he was not able to intervene. Heavy prison sentences had already been meted out to parents who had attempted to keep their children out of the Hitler Youth, although many simply wanted to protect their daughters from pregnancy, which had reached scandalously high proportions. If he interfered with Marianne's decision to join the Jungmaedel or tried to prevent Horst from entering the Jungvolk he would be risking his future in the SS and possibly even his freedom.

Chapter 31
Twice-Born

"When a man enters the inner chamber of the pyramid of Khufu, illumination from the sacred Eye of Horus penetrates the darkness and creates a god," Simon the Magician told his inner circle. "We know that the initiate becomes simply a reflection of the great Sun and the wisdom he receives is through the Eye."

They were gathered around a log fire at the edge of the Dead Sea. Flames leaped high against the blackness of the night, now and then casting showers of sparks like stars. Behind Simon, the sea captured the fire's glow rolling it gently over a surface as slippery as mercury.

"Incarceration in darkness is necessary to the process. If the initiate cannot withstand the forces of evil; if his mind relaxes its vigilance even for a moment, the mystery of transmutation cannot take place."

"And just so is the process of alchemy," Thaddeus commented. "The elements of earth, air, water and fire must first be removed from the base metals before sulphur and arsenic can create silver or gold."

He spoke a truth that the inner circle fully comprehended. Sulphur reeked of a journey through the Underworld, while the only road to godhood was through the bite of the serpent; the bitterest of poisons.

Simon Magus, discerning their thoughts, offered them an illustration. "Around the time of Pharaoh Djoser a festival was instituted known as heb sed, a ritual harking back to the slaying of Osiris by Set. At the thirtieth jubilee of the king's reign, and every three years thereafter, a ceremony took place in which they worshipped the head of the dead god and re-enacted his slaying. The Pharaoh, who was the presence of Osiris among his people, was wrapped in grave clothes and entombed. If he survived his night of spiritual battle with the malevolent forces, he was once again awarded the white crown of Upper Egypt and the red crown of Lower Egypt."

There was silence from the men, the lesson appeared to need no explanation but the Master remained pensive as though his story was incomplete.

"The heb sed magic is at work in the world still," he said. "Djoser's burial place ensured that the spirit world continued the work of heb sed until the end is reached."

All of Simon's men knew of the significance of Pharaoh Djoser's tomb built in ancient Memphis[6]. It was known as the Horizon of Eternity and the six steps of the step pyramid, reaching sixty meters above the desert floor enabled the spirit of the departed king to ascend to the gods and for the gods to come down among men.

Djoser's tomb was not built for the living, but for the dead, who would, for eternity, continue the rituals binding Egypt to their realm.

"What *is* the end?"

"Most understood the heb sed ritual at face value, but there was far more involved." The magician regarded them pensively. "You recall what I told you of the Giza pyramids?"

"That they hearken to the belt in the constellation of Orion?" Thaddeus offered. He was rewarded with a smile from the Master.

"That is so. The three pyramids are the three stars, Al Nitak, Al Nilam and Mintaka. The names of the pyramids tell us that the belt in the sky forms a divine horizon."

"A viewing place, similar in name to the Djoser's tomb?"

He nodded. "From which to look back towards the head of the hunter and forward to his feet. Remember, Betelgeuse is at the left shoulder. It is an ancient red star which is coming to the end of its life. Betelgeuse represents Nimrod."

"What then of Bellatrix?" asked Joseph, who knew something about the stars.

"The warrior queen. Semiramis, his consort. These were the gods of the First Time. "Osiris, and Isis his queen, were of course the Egyptian names of the same Sumerian gods."

"And Osiris is said to be immortalised in the stars in the area of Mintaka."

"At the belt," Simon Magus acknowledged. "While Isis is

---

[6] Sakkara

represented by Sirius, the Dog star." He glanced at Joseph. "What of the stars on the lower side of the belt?" he asked.

"Rigel, with Saiph on the left."

"Do you know their meanings?"

They thought for a moment and discussed among themselves. "In the Arab tongue Rigel would appear to be the foot," Thaddeus said at length, "although the star is actually at the knee of the Hunter."

"And Saiph?"

"Saif al jabbar. The sword of the giant."

"Rigel is also called Sah, by the Arabs," the Magus said. "The Approaching One."

The men leaned forward, suddenly aware of the Master's leading.

"The future king?"

"A brighter star than Nimrod, who is now almost forgotten. This Coming One will complete what Pharaoh Djoser began so many centuries past."

They glanced from one to another, bemused.

"He will unite the world of the spirit with the world of the flesh," Simon explained. "Men will become gods, as the gods come down to men."

There was an exhalation of breath. Godhood on earth was man's greatest desire. Man could live without conscience if he could once cast off the soiled robe of the flesh and fully embrace the power of the spirit world.

"Who is his consort?"

"Rigel's partner is no woman," the Magus said with a thin smile. Saiph is his partner. Rigel also is a hunter, but he will hunt men!"

"There is one more thing," Simon Magus said. "The brilliant star, Meissa, at the head of the Hunter, who does it represent?"

"Lucifer," Joseph said immediately. "He is the head of the body that gives power to the two Kings."

"Satan himself," the Magus agreed. "Power and wisdom is granted by the constellation of Dracus, the Dragon."

There was silence for a long moment. Someone absentmindedly tossed a couple of logs onto the waning fire.

"In the joining of Egypt's kingdom, the Dark Land, with the desert Red Land, there is a principle," Simon Magus said at last. "It follows that there must be an embrace of light and darkness in the completion of all things. Yet there is something that continues to evade me."

Thaddeus smiled quietly into the darkness. "If we were to celebrate heb sed in the manner of the Egyptians we are already in possession of the head."

"That is it!" the Magus said suddenly. "As the wisdom of the father is beamed through the eye of the son, the Head is to us the Eye of Horus. He will lead us into the darkness of the tomb and there he will enlighten us. No element can be without the other but we yet lack the death of the king."

For a moment he was chilled into silence. Were the gods speaking of his own death, Simon wondered, or was there another that would die in his place?

"When you look at the constellation of Orion, what do you see?"

Thaddeus looked up towards the starry sky where the outline of Orion could clearly be seen. "We know Orion is the Hunter. Nimrod too was known as a great hunter."

"In the book of Genesis, he is called a mighty hunter before the Lord," Joseph agreed.

"In the skies, he carries both bow and dagger."

There was silence from his disciples. Simon the Magus answered his own question. "It's obvious," he said. "Orion is Nimrod Twice-Born."

The Magus pursued his relationship with Shaphan with quiet determination. The priest was an inhibited man, withdrawn and distant in his dealings; cautious in his associations. He allowed no one to be drawn lightly into his orbit, but that the man was open to bribery, in itself, established a crack into which a wedge could be driven.

It had been a simple matter for Simon Magus to find the priest again and to learn the times of his service in the temple. He was armed with a harmless request. He wished to learn more about the Hebrew religion.

"Jews have no dealings with Samaritans." The rebuff was dealt with cold contempt and Shaphan turned to leave.

The Magus had seated himself on a low wall near the entrance to the Beautiful gate of the temple where the beggars gathered to beg for alms. He stood up barring the way of the priest.

"Even the Jewish priesthood has been known to deal with the despised Samaritans and Herodians if the arrangement can be seen to be mutually beneficial," he replied pointedly but without rancour.

Shaphan made no reply but stepped out to pass him by. The Magus reached out a hand and placed a firm grasp on Shaphan's shoulder. He swung round in fury.

"You fool! I have temple duties to perform!"

"Which you are now unable to fulfil," Simon said pleasantly, "as you have just been made ritually unclean by contact with a Gentile."

Shaphan glanced swiftly around to see if they were observed.

"Leave me alone," he said beneath his breath. "I want nothing more to do with you."

"I think you do," the Magus said, willing him with the power of his gaze to look him in the eye. "You and I have a lot in common."

The priest swung away and disappeared into the temple.

There were two more such embarrassing contacts before Shaphan agreed to meet with him: a measure born of fear of disclosure. The Samaritan had made no threat but a threat was nonetheless implied by his persistence.

The priest specified their place of meeting; a house in a narrow side street not far from the temple mount and when the Magus arrived, Shaphan was already there.

"What do you want of me?" he demanded, waiving all niceties. "I insist that this harassment stops, immediately!"

"I am simply seeking to know more of the Hebrew religion. I have need of a priest who will enlighten me."

"I am not that man!"

"If you were not, you would not have taken me into the heart of your temple."

Shaphan sank onto a cushion against the wall.

"Sit down," he said wearily. "I should have known better than to have trusted the wife of Herod."

The Magus smiled. "You are right. She is a woman of cunning and subtlety, but her beauty is legendry."

Shaphan ignored the comment.

"Tell me what you really want."

"Exactly what I have said. You will teach me what it means to be a Jew."

"Why?"

"When my people of Samaria called for a priest to teach them the ways of God, they were trained in the ways of Israel. I want to know the ways of Judaea. Treat me as a proselyte. When you have finished with me, there must be no discernable difference between myself and the most learned of the Pharisees."

"I do not have the time."

"Make the time. Your fellow priests might not like to hear of the disclosure you made to a humble Samaritan. In fact, most of your priesthood would be appalled if they were informed of the abomination, which lies beneath the temple mount."

It was undoubtedly coercion and Shaphan entered into his part of the agreement filled with resentment. But as the months went by his anger was tempered under a grudging admiration for the Magus' undoubted intellect and his thirst for knowledge. Paradoxically, the priest had almost begun to look forward to his sessions with the Samaritan.

Simon, the scholar, left these meetings and went on to teach his disciples what he had learned. As his Samaritans poured over the Tanakh night after night, they could have been mistaken for Jews. A step still remained.

"Circumcision."

They looked at him aghast and there was a flurry of protest.

The Magus shook his head. "It must be done! No Jew is uncircumcised."

They recognised his logic and knew that argument would be pointless against his implacability.

"When?"

"We will go to Machaerus. We will need ample time to heal."

"Who will do it?"

"Marcus is skilled with the knife," the Magus replied. "It will be given to him to perform."

The circumcisions were done and a week and a half later they returned to the city. By their dialect, they would never pass as Jews within Judaea; nevertheless a foundation had been laid. From now on, no man joining their band could do so if he remained uncircumcised.

Days earlier, following Lazarus' resurrection, a council had been called by the chief priests in Jerusalem.

"The Nazarene is performing many miracles," one said. "We hear testimony of these things all the time from people coming in from Galilee. His following is already very great and unless we call a halt, it will increase."

"We have the making of a popular uprising on our hands," another agreed. "It's obvious that Rome will act against us if we allow this to continue. Bar Joseph is endangering our religious leadership and our nation!"

"We could find ourselves acting against YWHW himself," a lone voice protested. "This man could be the promised Messiah!"

There was derisive laughter as this suggestion. "Nicodemus, you know that Jesus bar Joseph is a Nazarene," a scribe replied irritably, "Messiah will arise from Bethlehem."

"He could have escaped Herod's purge of the boy children in Bethlehem," Nicodemus persisted. "He's of the right age."

Again, the suggestion was met with angry shouting and some laughter. "Messiah will not be of Israel. We all know he must arise from Judaea!"

Nicodemus was a well-respected Pharisee and a member of the Sanhedrin. Three years before, he had met with Jesus by night, unwilling to jeopardise his position on the council by openly declaring allegiance to the man whom he deemed a prophet. Jesus had made it clear that for all his learning, Nicodemus understood nothing of the things of God.

"You must be born again," he had told him. "Except a man be born of water and of the Spirit he cannot enter into the kingdom of God." You need to thirst for the things of God, the Master was telling him, to have an unquenchable thirst for righteousness. Then, and only then, will the Spirit of God bring you the life you desire.

Still unconvinced and somewhat offended, Nicodemus had continued to follow Jesus from a distance. Now, he stood to his feet and faced the council.

"Some of you are too young to remember the prophetess, Anna, daughter of Phanuel, and also Simeon, who spoke by the power of the Holy Spirit when a boy child was brought into the temple for circumcision on the eighth day, but there is not a man among you who has not heard their words repeated many times. 'My eyes have seen the Lord's salvation, which has been prepared before the face of all people. It is a light to lighten the Gentiles, and the glory of your people Israel.'"

His speech was met by an uneasy silence. Simeon, they knew, had blessed the parents of the child and directed a further prophecy towards the mother:

"This child is set for the rising and falling again of many in Israel, and for a sign which shall be spoken against. Yea, a sword will pierce your own soul also."

The old prophet had tempered his words with a gesture, a kindly hand on the mother's shoulder but, as the young couple left the temple precinct, her expression was troubled and she held the child protectively against her breast. The incident had taken place some thirty years before, in the sight of many witnesses. Both Simeon and Anna had been respected adherents of the temple; their words formed part of the temple lore and had been greatly reinforced by Herod's slaughter of the infants.

"Our brother, Nicodemus, speaks truly! It behoves us to listen."

The Sanhedrin was hushed and all faces turned towards Joseph, the man from Arimathea.

"There were many signs at that time," he continued. "Most chose to ignore the testimony of the shepherds but even Herod believed the men from the East."

"The infant spoken of was Judaean," someone countered, but he spoke without real conviction.

"As was the child blessed by Simeon," another added. "Nothing good ever came from Nazareth in Israel!"

Joseph's words broke across the laughter that followed this statement:

"Yet, if Simeon and Anna spoke truly, is it not likely that the Living God protected the child against Herod's infamous works? Where is that child today, if he is not Jesus bar Joseph?"

"He incites the masses and will enflame the Romans!"

Caiaphas, the High priest, raised a hand for silence.

His tone was cutting. "You know nothing at all!" he said. "Don't you understand that it's better that one man dies for the people than that the whole nation perishes?"

A hush fell on the gathering as the members of the Sanhedrin digested his statement. The face of Nicodemus, however, was white with anger.

"Jesus the Nazarene has done nothing deserving of either condemnation or death," he declared. "I will have no part of this." Gathering his robes around him he turned and left the chamber.

Chapter 32
Twice-Born

Frick's attempt to centralise all Germany's police forces was at first thwarted by Göring who was always one step ahead of his enemies. Wilhelm Frick turned to the man who controlled the internal Party police, Heinrich Himmler. Within months Himmler seized command of the political police in one area after another. Prussia though, refused to submit and Göring countered by making himself head of the Prussian police. By this time, the SA was on the march throughout Germany and the threat of a military revolution was a reality. Göring, realising that he was becoming increasingly vulnerable, opened negotiations and Prussian internal affairs were placed in the hands of the Reich Ministry of the Interior. He was forced to accept a humiliating compromise; Himmler was granted the post of Inspector of the Gestapo; Reinhard Heydrich became Gestapo head and Arthur Nebe took control of the Prussian Criminal Police Office.

Himmler had prevailed. The SS was now under the command of the German police. The battle may have been won but the ground had to be held against strong opposition: primarily that of Röhm and the SA.

From the moment Adolf Hitler mended his differences with Ernst Röhm and restored him to the position of Chief of Staff of the SA, Himmler knew he would have to kill him. Röhm was now in effective command of well over four million men and every attempt of the Reichswehr to control him was cleverly parried. He was treated with disdain by their generals and President von Hindenburg had even publicly refused to shake his hand. Röhm and the SA were regarded with suspicion by almost everyone except Adolf Hitler.

Heinrich Himmler had realised the extent of the danger that Röhm represented as early as 1925, when the captain sued a gigolo who stole a suitcase from him containing a bundle of compromising letters. The gigolo claimed he had left the hotel room to which Röhm had taken him after refusing to participate in a form of intercourse that was abhorrent to him. Although Himmler was not implicated in any way, he realised with horror how casually Röhm treated the disclosure of his affairs. He had since become increasingly indiscreet, even using contact men in the SA to procure partners for him that included youths from a local high school in Munich. These were first tried out by certain of his subordinates before being passed on to Röhm.

Himmler's position was further endangered by Reinhard Heydrich, Heinrich Himmler's right hand man, who had joined the Reichsführer after being tried by a Naval Court of Honour for jilting a young girl. Heydrich's arrogance condemned him and he was dismissed for impropriety. It was the end of a promising career for the young naval officer, and set the scene for the rise of one of Nazism's most dangerous progenitors.

Heydrich was the epitome of the Nazi Aryan ideal; tall blonde and blue-eyed, and it was his appearance as much as his obvious zeal that immediately impressed the Reichsführer. Armed with only a few of Himmler's files, Reinhard Heydrich set to work to create an SS intelligence service. Within a few months he had placed men of his own choosing in all SS units to deal with intelligence activities and presented Himmler with a picture of the Nazi Party riddled with spies. A purge, he told him, was becoming not only necessary, but vital. By March 1933, Himmler had promoted his ex-naval officer. But Oberführer Reinhard Heydrich was by this time beginning to build up an excellent file on Röhm's homosexual activities.

Heinrich Himmler paced the room, pausing for a moment to place a hand abstractedly on the statue of the drummer boy that stood in the corner behind his desk. He saw the carving as a symbol of his position within the Reich. In a certain sense it was a John the Baptist role; abstract, behind-the-scenes, yet a vital position of encouragement and heroism. He was the unsung hero, ill-fitted for his role and yet positive that someday his part in the making of history would be revealed.

As leader of the SS, Himmler inevitably lived with the fear of exposure. It was imperative that he come out from under the shadow of the SA, but was afraid that if he moved against him, Röhm would use the past to destroy him. The captain had nothing to lose; he held

Himmler in perfect check. At stake was Himmler's position within the Nazi Party, his reputation, his marriage and his future. Röhm was the only man who knew for certain that the rise to power of the Reichsführer SS had been dependent on his total degradation and physical humiliation. The memory of the relationship disgusted Himmler and he wanted more than anything to expunge Röhm and his perversions from his life completely. Killing him was the cleanest and most obvious solution.

He picked up the telephone and summoned Heydrich. It was imperative that he appear to be the reluctant follower and Heydrich the instigator.

"You must understand, Herr Reichsführer, that this gives us a unique opportunity of increasing the influence of the SS and purging the Party of some of its most dangerous enemies."

Heinrich Himmler nodded impatiently. "Yes, yes," he agreed. "But we must proceed cautiously. If we carry things too far, we may make enemies beyond those we are contending with at present. The Führer is squeamish when it comes to radical solutions and particularly since becoming Chancellor, he's aware of his public image."

Heydrich's narrow face appeared gaunt in the artificial light of the office.

"Herr Reichsführer, Field Marshall von Reichenau spoke to me this morning." Himmler waited his expression distant and polite. "It seems that the Chief of Staff has been a little too open in his damning of the Führer this time!"

"Röhm's temper has caused him to say things that are downright treasonable at times, but the Führer has a forgiving nature where the captain is concerned."

Heydrich's laugh was sardonic. "Perhaps if we could persuade the Führer that there is evidence of a rebellion planned by Röhm to overturn the Nazi Party, he might be prepared to take action?"

"Is there?"

"I can document the proof, Herr Reichsführer."

There was hesitation in the expression of the Reichsführer SS that might have been interpreted as doubt.

"As long as the SS continues to be an arm of the SA, it will be controlled by Captain Röhm," Heydrich said pointedly. "And inevitably, its role as an elite organisation will be tarnished."

Himmler looked directly at him for the first time.

"What did von Reichenau have to say?" he asked.

It was part of Himmler's strategy that he continued to protect Röhm in Adolf Hitler's presence and it was imperative that until the end, he would be seen by him as a loyal friend. On Röhm's birthday in November 1933, Himmler sent him a card. "It was and is, still our greatest pride," he wrote; "to be one of your most faithful followers."

Adolf Hitler had vacillated continually between the desire to disband the SA, which would inevitably mean a head-on clash with Captain Röhm, or to increase its power as a counter-balance to the Reichswehr. Röhm still had a hold over the Führer dating back to his introduction of Hitler into the German Worker's Party, and even he feared Röhm's power.

But Hitler also had plans of his own that depended on the death of Hindenburg. He wished to combine the offices of Führer and Reich Chancellor to become dictator of Germany. The Reichswehr Generals were sworn to von Hindenburg by an oath that could only be broken on the old man's death. Hitler's position would then depend entirely upon the Reichswehr. He made his decision and the machinery for the action against the SA was set in motion.

Heydrich released an avalanche of rumours and doctored documents to support the claim that Röhm was planning a coup. At the same time hit-lists were being drawn up that would effectively remove many of the prime enemies of the SS. On 29th June, Hitler received a message from Heinrich Himmler.

"The Berlin SA has completed its preparations and is preparing for action tomorrow," it read. "At 5pm sharp they plan to begin the surprise occupation of Government buildings."

In a cold fury, Hitler immediately took a 'plane to Munich and from there to the pension in Bad Weisee where he knew Röhm was staying. He arrived before the SA leaders were awake and it was some moments before Röhm answered the urgent hammering on his door. His hair was dishevelled and his face bore the confusion of one who had been aroused from a deep sleep. He stood staring uncomprehendingly at the gun in Hitler's hand.

Hitler flew at him. "You dirty traitor!" he screamed. "You dirty traitor!" His hands were at Röhm's throat. Röhm took several uncertain steps backward and fell onto the bed, his expression stunned.

"Mein Führer," he gasped, "what are you saying?"

Hitler stood over him, menacing him with his pistol. "Get dressed!" he ground out. "You are under arrest."

Himmler and Goering were conducting a purge of their own in Berlin. Among their victims was Gregor Strasser, Heinrich Himmler's employer from the early days, one of many who was to pay with his life both for working against Hitler and for failing to take Himmler seriously. Strasser was shot in his cell and his death was officially announced as suicide.

Goering was inclined to halt the bloodshed until he heard that Hitler had decided to grant Röhm a pardon. Both he and Himmler were appalled. The whole point of the purge would be defeated if Röhm were to live. They worked on Hitler until at last at midday on July 1st he capitulated and SS-Brigadeführer, Theodor Eicke, was dispatched immediately. Röhm died at Papa Eicke's hand that evening, after he had refused to commit suicide. His death renewed the orgy of violence, which was only halted on Hitler's orders after an agreement had been reached with von Hindenburg.

Eighty-three men were expunged without trial or the opportunity to defend themselves, effectively breaking the power of the SA. The Reichswehr quickly discovered the balance of power had shifted, not in their favour, but in favour of the SS.

Chapter 33
Twice-Born

Michael Segal walked through the city of Berlin with a heavy heart. Germany had changed radically and he knew it was only the beginning. The streets were decorated with the dominant red, white and black of the Nazi banners bearing the insignia of the Hakenkreuz or swastika. This was Adolf Hitler's one artistic masterpiece. By amalgamating an occult symbol with the strong colours of the old Imperial flag, the Austrian had given the German people a new national identity. Germans states were being forged into a single unit under the Nazi hammer. Predominantly, it was the youth that rallied behind the banners of National Socialism, responding to the deep-seated need in the German psyche for powerful leadership. Michael Segal's response was different. He was a Jew.

Throughout the country, police precincts had been instructed to draw up lists of all Jews under their jurisdiction, including those who were 'half' or 'quarter' Jews. Adolf Hitler's belief in violence and terror as a political tool was calculated. He knew that the average German was drawn to the strong and despised weakness. If the 'Jewish threat' had not existed, it would have been necessary to create it: the development of a super-race required the existence of a sub-race. Hand in hand with National Socialism's intention to foil the Jewish/Communist conspiracy towards world domination went the desire to create a state that glorified the might of the strong and one which would expunge the weak and the racially inferior from German soil.

In the inner pocket of Michael Segal's jacket was the letter from his faculty, calling for his immediate resignation. He had seen it coming, but it was still a shock. Somehow he had wanted to believe that the universities, traditionally the repositories of reason and racial tolerance, would resist the new order.

His initial response to being fired by the University of Berlin was anger – and a level of trepidation. Gangs of Storm Troopers roamed the city streets randomly attacking, beating and arresting Jews. Thousands of Jews and political enemies of the Nazi party had already been sent to Dachau, the newly formed concentration-camp run by the local Dachau SS who were said to be among the most savage and brutal platoons in Bavaria.

The convenient Reichstag fire, which occurred soon after Hitler became chancellor, had enabled him to set in place rules regarding 'protective custody' and he had already installed emergency measures enabling the National Socialists to expropriate Communist Party buildings and close down their printing presses. The new decrees moved Adolf Hitler towards dictatorship as he settled the score with his political opponents. It was in the wake of the Reichstag fire that Jewish professors and teachers across Germany were told that they could no longer teach Aryans.

Gabriele was waiting for him at the door when he arrived back at his apartment. He had sought her out at the university once he had cleared his desk, to tell her he had been fired.

Gabriele flopped into the single arm-chair in Michael Segal's room and leaned back surveying him gloomily.

"They're burning books," she said.

"What books?"

"Degenerate books, in Nazi parlance. In other words, mainly Jewish. There are huge bonfires outside the university and near the opera house. Some of the people gathered there were weeping."

Despite the danger to herself, she still insisted on coming to see him.

"Don't be a fool, Gabby," he implored again, "Coming here could cost you your life."

She shrugged. "So, leave the country and I won't be able to visit, it's your choice."

"That's blackmail!"

"Yes, but you know I'm right. Gather your family together and leave."

"Come with me, Gabby."

"Perhaps I'll follow later."

He knew his request was unfair on her. Gabriele's place was in

Germany whereas his, as a Jew, no longer existed. But of course she was right. Whatever had held him back from leaving had become illusionary. He had no rights remaining; no assets and, as of now, no job. As a Jew he would be forced to leave Germany with nothing, but there was nothing left to stay for; his very existence was held in the balance. Even his relationship with Gabriele could not be relied upon to stand against the building pressures of Nazism.

He walked over to her and kissed the top of her head.

"I'll get out as soon as possible but I'll need to speak to my parents."

Gabriele stood up smiling with relief. She wound her arms round his neck and kissed him. "Where will you go? To France?"

"Switzerland if I can get in."

"With your qualifications they should take you. Please do it as quickly as possible Michael. There have been so many murders and I believe there will be many more."

"We won't leave," Michael Segal's father said adamantly. "Where would we go? Germany is our home."

His mother nodded her agreement, but her eyes were troubled. Michael pressed his advantage.

"Does Mutti have a say in this Papa? Have you considered her fate if you stay here?"

Something in his resolve wavered at his son's words but the weakening was momentary.

"We will stand together in this," he said with finality. "You can go, Michael. You have your whole life ahead of you but I'm not going to let these brown-shirted brutes have the last word!"

"They won't bring *my* kingdom down!" Michael muttered to himself in an irritable parody of his father as he finally took his leave and walked down the road. He shook his head wearily. It was not as though his parents had much to abandon. A small house with its belongings, but it seemed that the fear of leaving was greater than that of facing the enemy on known territory.

"How can I go and simply leave them here?" he asked Gabriele, not for the first time.

"They've made their choice. Your father's right, it doesn't mean you have to throw your life away as well."

"You are always so logical, Gabby," he mourned.

"And so convinced that things will get worse."

He had procrastinated long enough. Every day he remained in Germany endangered not only himself but Gabriele as well. Already questions were being asked and it was simply a matter time before someone reported the relationship to a higher authority. He took her hands in his.

"You're right. You've always been right. I'll make arrangements to go."

"Now?"

"Soon," he said.

Chapter 34
Twice-Born

Mary sat in her room, her fingers resting lightly on her most treasured possession. The alabaster jar had been given to her by her father on her thirteenth birthday, the day which, in accordance with Jewish tradition she had attained womanhood. He had bought the intricately carved vessel on one of his journeys to the East and filled it with spikenard, a fragrant perfume. Her father was already ill when the gift was given and possibly sensed the closeness of death. Practically, it was intended to increase her dowry but Mary knew it was a deep expression of his love for her.

"You are like this vessel," he had said, "very beautiful on the outside but, my daughter; I want you to remember that inward beauty is of infinitely greater worth."

One finger unconsciously traced the elaborate pattern on the slender stem of the jar as Mary recalled his words and sought to control the conflict that raged within her. The man who had lain with her was much older than she was. He had seduced her with small compliments and carefully selected gifts. His eyes had drawn her, becoming bolder in their invitation whenever Lazarus or Martha left the room, until at last she had succumbed willingly to his experienced and passionate embrace. When Lazarus caught him one night leaving her chamber, she had wept bitterly for what had been taken from her. There was shame that her affair had been discovered, but it was mixed with defiance as though it was Lazarus' prying that had been at fault and not her own intransigence, and Martha's bitter weeping had only fuelled her anger. The man was not even of the Jewish faith so that her brother had not been able, in good conscience, to insist on their marriage.

The words of her father haunted her. As the value of the perfume was so much greater than the alabaster jar, she should have ascribed far greater worth to her soul. Would her father still have loved her if he had known what she had become? Would he have been able to forgive her?

Only the night before, Mary had sat at the feet of Jesus, drinking in his words while Martha viewed her younger sister with irritation.

"Lord," she said, "don't you care that my sister has left me to do all the serving on my own. Will you not tell her to come and help me?"

Mary had looked up guiltily, anticipating a rebuke from the Master. Instead, unexpectedly, he laughed.

"Martha, Martha," he said. "You are always worrying and concerning yourself with many things. Only one thing is important and Mary has chosen that good part. That will not be taken away from her."

Mary had looked up at Jesus in awe, and the Master met her glance. There was nothing in his look to compare with what she had read in the eyes of the other man. Something in that moment changed Mary. It was not her body that she wanted to offer Jesus – it was her life. But her life was tainted, defiled.

She picked up the container. She knew where her Lord was. This day, he was dining with Judas Iscariot's father, Simon the Pharisee; he who had been healed of leprosy by a touch from Yeshua of Nazareth.

The whole of Galilee and Judaea stirred in readiness for the annual Passover feast. It was a busy time of the year for the little village of Bethany, which was situated on the main route to the Holy City. Many bought provisions or lodged there in preference to the city itself. This year there was an added excitement among the pilgrims; the Teacher had been seen on the road to Jerusalem. Stories of miracles were passed from mouth to mouth. Only days earlier, on the road from Jericho, Bartimaeus, a blind man, had received his sight. But there could be no greater miracle than the raising of Lazarus from the grave and, as they arrived in Bethany, many of the Jews came to simply see Lazarus, to touch him and to hear for themselves how this great event had taken place.

Simon received Jesus into his home beaming with self-importance. He had included some of the temple priests and Pharisees in his invitation and the day promised to go well for him. Martha, a good woman and one whose cooking he had come to appreciate, had agreed to help with the preparations. She had extended his table with one of her own and added a small bowl of bright flowers for decoration.

Simon looked on with approval realising with surprise that he missed the touches that a woman brought to a home.

Jesus and his disciples were seated and chatting easily among themselves as they waited for the other guests. Simon bustled in and greeted them briefly. With him was a boy from the village who carried a basin of warm water and a towel over his arm.

"When the priests arrive, I want you to remove their sandals as I have shown you and wash their feet," Simon instructed. "Do the job properly, remember, these are very important men!"

The Pharisee met his guests from the city at the door, embracing them warmly.

"Come in! Come in! Welcome."

He made the introductions and when everyone was seated, Martha, with the help of two of her maid-servants, carried in the first of the dishes from the kitchen. There was an appreciative murmur as the savoury smell wafted through the room.

The last course was eaten and Martha's girls had begun to clear away the dishes when Mary crossed the courtyard clutching the alabaster jar in both hands. She entered Simon's house without fully knowing what she intended to do. The room was crowded with men, perhaps twenty in all and the young woman halted at the door, framed by sunlight and confused by the darkness of the interior. Then she saw Jesus and without further hesitation, crossed the room and fell at his feet.

"My Lord!"

"Mary." Jesus leaned forward and rested a hand on her shoulder. "You are crying."

"I have a gift for you, my Lord." She lifted the jar towards him in supplication then in a quick movement smashed its long stem on the flagstones. The alabaster shattered and at once the fragrance filled the room. There was a deathly hush from the men: a silence broken by the ragged sound of her weeping.

"I'm so sorry," she said. I'm so sorry!"

Everything focussed on the unseemly actions of the woman who took Jesus' feet tenderly in her hands and poured out upon them the precious perfume from the broken neck of the flask. To the increasing embarrassment of most of those present, she took the restraining pins from her hair and used it to wipe the tears and the fragrant oil from the feet of the Master.

Martha, drawn from the kitchen by the heady fragrance stood in the doorway shocked at the scene that met her eyes. A quick glance at the men in the room told her all that she needed to know of their opinions. Simon's lip was curled in contempt as he looked meaningfully at the religious leaders in the room. If this Jesus was anything of a prophet, he would have known that this woman was a sinner.

Jesus raised his head. "Simon," he said, "I have something to say to you."

"Yes, Master?"

"There was a creditor who had two debtors, the one owed him five hundred denarii, and the other owed him fifty. When they were unable to discharge their debt, he forgave them. Tell me, which man would have loved him the most?"

"I suppose the one he forgave most," Simon admitted reluctantly.

"You have judged rightly. You see this woman? When I entered your house you did not give me water to wash my feet as the custom is, but she has washed my feet with her tears and dried them with her hair. You did not kiss me in greeting, but she has not ceased to kiss my feet. You did not anoint my head with oil, but this woman anointed my feet. Wherefore I say that her sins, which are many, are forgiven because she loved much. But those to whom little is forgiven, they love little."

He lifted his hand from her shoulder. "Mary, your faith has saved you. Go in peace."

Mary's sister, Martha, covered her eyes with her hands, turned back into the kitchen and wept for joy.

"What a waste!" Judas burst out. He was bitterly angry at the slight on his father before some of Jerusalem's best known leaders. "That perfume could have been sold for three hundred denarii and given to the poor."

"Leave her alone," Jesus said. "The poor will always be with you, but I will not always be here. Mary has done this against the day of my burial and wherever the gospel is preached what she has done will be spoken of in memory of her."

"Damn him," Simon said. "How dare he humiliate me like that in my own home?"

Judas was silent but he seethed with anger. The day had been a disaster. The look that Jesus had given Judas when he had condemned Mary for her waste of the spikenard told him that the Master knew he had been taking money from the bag, which was in his keeping. How long had he known, he wondered? It seemed that not much could be hidden from the Nazarene.

"I know you have followed the man for a long time now, Judas but I want you to consider this," his father cut across his thoughts; he was bristling with indignation. "What gives Jesus of Nazareth the right to forgive a man or a woman when we know that only God can forgive sin? The man is a heretic! A blasphemer, Judas. Surely you can see that now?"

"He has done many great works, father, you know that. Yourself…Lazarus…"

"Yes, yes, that is true of course. But the man makes himself equal with God! That is a dangerous presumption and no amount of good works can compensate for the sin of blasphemy. A council met a week ago in Jerusalem and they feel that he must be stopped before it is too late."

"Too late?"

"He's gained a huge following among the ignorant. They might be persuaded to make him king."

Judas stared at his father. "There's no likelihood of that. Jesus would never accept such a role."

"Wouldn't he, Judas? You, yourself told me that he is of the royal line of David. And does he not preach that he is come to establish a kingdom?"

"A heavenly kingdom, not of this world."

"The leadership in Jerusalem do not perceive it that way. They are certain that at the right moment, when he has the people fully behind him, he will proclaim himself king. If you are not cautious, my son, you could find yourself in trouble both with our religious leadership and with Rome."

"You are mistaken, father."

"Am I? Today the man demonstrated his true nature before you in my own home! You cannot deny his disregard for the Law of Moses and for our religious leadership. I believe he intends to make his move during Passover and you cannot afford to be part of his company if he arouses the people to insurrection."

Simon read the shade of doubt in the eyes of Judas and pressed his case.

"The chief priests are willing to pay anyone who hands him over for arrest at the feast," Simon said. "It must be done, Judas. Unless he's brought under control Pontius Pilate will be forced to take action against the Jewish leadership and you and I will be among the first to suffer!"

Judas Iscariot was still in two minds when Jesus and the disciples made ready for the final leg of their journey into Jerusalem. Two of the disciples had gone into the village with instructions to untie an ass and her colt and, if they were challenged, to tell the owners that the Lord had need of them. The disciples spread their cloaks over the colt, which had never before carried a man and, with Jesus on its back and John at its head, it stepped out onto the road.

A river flowed towards the city: peasants and priests, women and children; goats and sheep: a river of colour and noise. Just before the bend in the road, several youths whistled urgently as they sought to recapture a ram, which had broken loose, amidst much bleating and shouting. As Jesus set off from the village of Bethany on the back of the grey colt, he was instantly recognised and the word went out:

"The Rabbi is among us. He is going into Jerusalem."

Could this be, some wondered, the fulfilment of Zechariah's prophecy?

Rejoice greatly, O daughter of Zion: shout O daughter of Jerusalem: behold thy king cometh to thee; he is just and having salvation; lowly, and riding upon an ass, and upon a colt the foal of an ass.

The question was flung out among the multitude as a farmer casts his seed to the wind.

"Messiah?"

And in moments the question had born fruit and become a certainty.

"Messiah, Son of David! Thy King cometh to thee, lowly and riding upon a colt, the foal of an ass."

"Our King is coming. He comes in peace bringing salvation to Jerusalem!"

"Blessed is he that comes in the name of the Lord.

"Hosanna! Hosanna in the highest!"

Judas stared in disbelief at the milling crowd. They were gathering the lulav, the branches of palm and myrtle, as was customary during the Feast of Tabernacles as a sign of the coming Messiah, and waving them above their heads. Some cast the branches on the road or laid their garments in the dust before the colt. Excited children darted out of the throng to touch the donkey shouting words of praise to the Son of David, King of Jerusalem.

"Teacher, rebuke your disciples!" a Pharisee shouted sharply.

Impotent rage welled up in Judas at these words. Did Jesus not see what the consequences would be? His father, Simon, was right. This swell of passion among ignorant and stupid men would become the excuse for Rome to crush them if it was not stemmed immediately.

"Master," he said tersely, "listen to that man! Rebuke the people. Stop them!"

"If I stopped them now, the very stones would cry out!" Jesus replied. The colt was picking its way daintily over the carpet of branches, following the ass that John was leading. The road was in an uproar and Judas became separated and was left standing by the roadside, sullen and bitter of spirit.

As the party made its way over the brow of the Mount of Olives, Jerusalem appeared before them, the temple in all its pristine beauty like a bride arrayed for the bridegroom. John glanced cheerfully back at Jesus but was dismayed as he saw his Master's stricken expression.

"Lord, what is it?"

Tears ran down Jesus' cheeks as he gazed at the gleaming temple above Jerusalem's walls.

"O Jerusalem, Jerusalem," he said quietly. "If you had known, especially this day, the things that would make for your peace!"

"Rabboni?" John let go of the rope and for a moment walked alongside the colt.

Jesus read his concern and shook his head wearily. "These things are hidden from their eyes," he said and then raised his voice and prophesied so that those who clamoured about him could catch his words.

"O Jerusalem, the days shall come upon you that your enemies will close in on every side. They will level you to the ground and your children with you. Not one stone will be left upon another because you did not recognise the time of your visitation."

John walked back troubled by the depths of the pain that he had seen in the Master's face. The ass still plodded purposefully on, dragging her rope behind her, and John retrieved it and wrapped it around his hand. The noise of the crowd seemed to have retreated, although the celebration had not ceased, and the closer they came to the gates of the city, the more they were jostled by those pouring out to meet Jesus.

"Messiah! Son of David."

Their joyful acclamation of the Master had swelled John's heart with pride that he should have been chosen to be part of this! Yet, the Master was seeing something that he, John, was not.

The smell of sweat and dung mingled with the dust and already the heat of the day was intense. The expression of many of those who craned their necks for a closer view was vacuous.

"An evil and perverse generation seeks a sign," Jesus had said once.

Some may celebrate him today but are capable of discarding him without compunction tomorrow, John thought. Is that what the Master meant when he said that Jerusalem had missed the day of his visitation? Most were drawn not to the person of Messiah, but to what they might gain from him.

It was only as they made their way into the outer courts of the temple that John truly understood. He saw the resentful faces of the scribes and Pharisees as they stood in hostile groups regarding the joyful crowd that surged around the person of Jesus and he knew what the Master had meant. Those who by their scriptures should have been most prepared for the coming of Messiah, were undoubtedly the most antagonistic. Messiah was a threat to their position; and to the perception of their own importance.

Chapter 35
Twice-Born

"I was standing outside the Hofburg making sketches of the building, when it started to rain, so I took refuge in the Treasure House. I hated that place. The whole Hapsburg dynasty makes me ill!"

Hitler's posture changed and he hunched forward, his expression becoming intense and brooding. For a moment he was cut off from the men around the table.

"And that was when you saw the spear, mein Führer?"

Hitler looked up abruptly at Goebbel's prompting, as though he had forgotten where he was. He nodded.

"There was a guide conducting a group of foreign businessmen. Something he said riveted my attention. He was telling them of the legend surrounding the spear. Whoever claims it and solves its secrets, holds the destiny of the world in his hands for good or for evil." He looked at Goebbels. "The words had been spoken for me! I couldn't believe at first that a Christian symbol of that sort, a lance that was reputed to have pierced the side of Christ, could have any bearing on my existence. And yet, this was a spear that the great leaders of the world had owned, or had coveted. Did you know it was smuggled out of Nuremburg into Vienna to keep it out of Napoleon's hands?" Hitler's eyes again took on the look of dark introspection. "When the party moved on," he said at last, "I went to look at the lance myself. I knew somehow that this was a most important moment of my life, but I was still unable to divine the reason it should have made such a deep impression on me. It suggested some inner message that evaded my consciousness. It was as though the spear was speaking to me."

"My father always had a deep interest in the Spear of Longinus," said Heinrich Himmler who had been following the story with fascination. "I've studied its history in some depth myself."

Adolf Hitler glanced at him in surprise and for the first time, Himmler saw in his expression a sign of interest or recognition.

"So did I, while I was still in Vienna. Have you been to see the spear, Reichsführer?"

"I have not been so fortunate, mein Führer, but I hope that in due time it will be restored to its rightful place in Germany, in which case I will have the opportunity."

Hitler nodded and Himmler felt the warm glow of his approval.

"When the time is right," the Führer said, "we will reclaim the Reichskleinodin from Austria. There is little else that interests me apart from the lance, but I believe that it should all be restored to Germany."

Himmler nodded enthusiastically. "Exactly, mein Führer. I have always considered this a point of vital importance to Germany."

Adolf Hitler surveyed the small group of men who had been chosen to dine with him that evening.

"I often returned to look at it after that," he said reminiscently. "There seemed to be a presence surrounding it, similar to that which I had felt with me at moments of great destiny in my life. I began to realise that it somehow bridged the world of the senses and the world of the spirit." He swilled the liquid round in his glass and held it to the light to watch it. "On the second visit, it was as though a window opened up on an event in the future. I could see a time when I would stand as leader before the people of Austria and I knew without doubt that the blood in my veins would become the vessel of the Volk-spirit of my people." His glance was now steady and confident, and he spoke with complete certainty. "At some time in the near future, I will take the Spear of Destiny as my personal possession and with it I will fulfil my role in world history."

Heinrich Himmler looked down at his plate. Adolf Hitler's statement had stirred a curious mixture of excitement and anxiety in his breast, as though the gods were whispering their own refrain just beneath the words of the Führer's. It would be a little while before he learned its interpretation.

* * *

SS architect Herman Bartels was assigned the building of Wewelsburg Castle, a Schutzstaffel training school, which was carried out under a staff of experts. The project, costing thirteen million marks, was completed in less than a year. Himmler added his own touch to the luxurious decoration of the individual rooms, each of which was dedicated to an historical figure that had at some time been in possession of the Lance of Longinus. Period garments, jewels, paintings, shields, armour and weapons were obtained to authenticate the history of each suite.

There was an unusual element to the design. The ground plan was to have incorporated the village of Wewelsburg, but only the castle itself was ultimately built. Wewelsburg, triangular in shape, constituted the apex of what was unmistakably a spear. The north tower formed the tip of the spearhead. Windows, set deep into the five-foot thick walls of what was known as the Realm of the Dead, spilled a little light into the gloomy interior. Its brick-domed ceiling climaxed in a swastika design beneath which, a sacred flame was kept burning day and night. Three steps led down to this flame, marking the castle's power point and the centre of the complex.

It was from the Realm of the Dead that Himmler envisaged the psychic force of his men emanating forth to control first Germany, then the world. It was to be the power centre of a new World Order.

Other structures, larger than Wewelsburg Castle itself were to have formed the remainder of the shaft, while the approach road became the haft of the spear. A smaller interlinking building, which was to have joined the two sections of the spear's head, unmistakably set the position of the nail in the spear of Longinus.

In 1935, three years before the genuine article was removed from Austria during the Anschluss, Himmler had an exact replica of the spear of Longinus made for himself. Even the worn leather case that the spear was in was made to look exactly like that of the spear, which lay in the Weltlike Schatzkammer, the Treasure House of the Hofburg Museum. The replica was kept in Himmler's room at Wewelsburg and as he handled it each time he was alone, he was almost able to believe that it too, was developing some strange individualistic power.

Chapter 36
Twice-Born

At eighteen, Marianne von Ingolstadt began her Land Jahr in a Labour camp near Augsburg, a city of quaint medieval buildings with stepped roofs and gilded frontages more Flemish in character than German.
Augsburg bore every outward appearance of prosperity although locals complained that the cotton textile and metal industries were suffering for lack of outside markets. The Jewish boycott was beginning to bite into the German economy. As the persecution of German Jews increased, international Jewry ensured that Germany's exports dwindled to a minor trickle.

The hierarchy of the Reich had read both the Protocols of Zion and the teachings of Karl Ritter, and discerned that the world's three most powerful institutions: the Catholic Church, International Jewry and Freemasonry, were working together towards world domination under a world leader. Single-handedly, Germany had taken them on, putting Ritter's antidote into practise and, in the process, creating enemies abroad that would cut to the heart and quietly allow the mother-land to bleed itself dry. At this point, Marianne von Ingolstadt and indeed most of German society remained blissfully unaware of the cold war that they were waging and of that that was being waged against them.

On the approach to the camp they passed small clusters of green-shuttered houses with colour-washed walls nestling among fields of wheat and brooding forests. Peasants herded cows along the narrow roads and stopped to watch curiously as the truck passed. In the back, the girls linked arms and sang the rousing choruses they had learned at Hitler Youth. This was an adventure common to them all and they revelled in what amounted to the first step towards adulthood.

In the young men's labour camps alone in the early thirties, there were more than two hundred-thousand youths in the twelve thousand camps, all of them volunteers. Even university students had made it an unwritten law that they could not take a degree without first serving six months on the labour front. Later, youth would be conscripted into the year of service by law, destroying the free spirit that reigned in the early days but, at the same time, raising the numbers of young people in the camps to eight million.

The men felled timber, built roads and helped on farms. They were lectured on subjects pertinent to the Reich, which focussed on breaking down the class barriers and building comradeship. Germans were led to believe that they were preparing defences and training soldiers in case of attack. Adolf Hitler and Heinrich Himmler were, in fact, preparing a single-minded, disciplined unit for one purpose – to wage war.

Marianne was relieved that she was given work picking vegetables on a farm rather than a year in domestic service in a city household such as was assigned to many young women. Everyone in the camp participated in cooking and household chores, and was required to attend numerous lectures.

"Mostly," Marianne wrote in one of her letters home, "they emphasise that it's our duty to bear healthy children for the Reich. However, some of the girls don't seem to be too concerned about waiting for marriage!"

There were other aspects to the lectures, which bored most of the young women and fascinated Marianne. These were the racial sciences and other esoteric philosophies espoused by Reichsführer-SS Himmler but she mentioned nothing about this in her letters to her mother who would have dismissed such things with contempt.

The ancestral cult and the focus on Germanic tribes were ideologies that were intended to replace formalised religion, Christianity in particular, but in Marianne they filled a vacuum she had not realised existed. Greta had discouraged any talk of religion in the home; having made a conscious decision to turn her back on Judaism, she was not going to allow her children to be tainted by Catholicism. Whether Matthias agreed with her or not was immaterial, the subject was closed.

The young women were lectured on religion during a visit to the Labour Camp by one of Himmler's prime men, SS-Standartenführer Reinhard Heydrich.

"When we talk about Judaism we are also talking about Christianity," he told them. "Both are effete religions glorifying the weak and the morbid; attitudes which must be entirely eliminated. Our Führer, Adolf Hitler is Germany's only redeemer and we need to remember that. He will restore men to a self-confident understanding and acceptance of their own deity." Heydrich looked around at the fresh young faces of his audience. "If Christianity is to remain in any form, it must submit to Nazi doctrine. The Church can no longer be permitted to meddle with questions of conscience or morality. We have stopped all printing and dissemination of the Bible. I want you to understand that in Germany, the swastika has supplanted the cross."

What he failed to tell the impressionable young women was the ultimate fate of the Church. Hitler had ensured that enough Zyklon B was produced to destroy twenty million people. Christians were intended to be next on the list once the Jews were dealt with.

A middle-aged Oberfeldmeister, inspector of the camps, had taken a personal interest in Marianne von Ingolstadt and he introduced Marianne to Reinhard Heydrich.

"She is the brightest of our young women," he said. "Soaks up all she's taught with enthusiasm and passes all examinations with flying colours. I believe Marianne would do well in the Ahnenerbe."

Heydrich smiled. "So," he said, his eyes locking on to hers. "That's high praise coming from Oberfeldmeister Gessler. Do you have plans for a career once you complete your Land Jahr?"

"No, Standartenführer."

"Well, perhaps you should contact me when you are ready. I will see to it that you are placed in the right job."

His glance strayed pointedly from Marianne's face to her feet and back to her face. "We would not want to waste a woman who shows potential."

He turned away and engaged Oberfeldmeister Gessler on an unrelated subject leaving Marianne blushing and unaccountably annoyed.

On Gessler's insistence, after her year was up, Marianne wrote to Reinhard Heydrich but she received no response. Somewhat disillusioned with the National Socialist hierarchy, she instead secured a secretarial post in a lawyer's office in Munich. It was almost a year later that a call came through from the office of Karl Wolff asking her to come in for an interview.

It seemed that Reinhard Heydrich had not forgotten her after all.

Chapter 37
Twice-Born

"I believe you have grasped an excellent understanding of the scriptures," Shaphan said. "I think it would be a good time to end these meetings." The pronouncement was made several months before the Passover, and the priest surveyed his proselyte with the confidence of a man who had accomplished a task and had done it well.

Simon Magus's mouth slid open to display his even white teeth in a humourless smile.

"Then we have reached a new beginning," he said.

"What do you mean?"

"It is time for you to introduce the next level. I wish to be instructed in the Cabala."

"It is enough," Shaphan protested. "I cannot be expected to go on with this indefinitely."

"We have only just begun," the Magus said. "There are mysteries in that underground temple that we have not begun to explore. You will teach me all you know, Shaphan. You will find me very receptive."

The priest sat down, confidence ebbing from his face. "I cannot initiate you into those things," he said. "You must understand that they cannot be spoken of outside the circle of confidence, on pain of death." His eyes pleaded with the Magus for understanding.

Simon Magus looked up at his teacher. He was a little older than the magician himself, possibly a man in his early forties; heavily bearded and with dark mystical eyes under heavy brows.

"What is that to me?" Simon asked without compassion. "I need to be taught and you are my teacher. If you fail to teach me, I will ensure that your fellow initiates kill you anyway. One word from me about a sum of money paid by Herodias to you to take a Samaritan into the hidden bowels of the temple would be enough."

Shaphan looked at him with raw hatred.

"I do not understand why you are doing this!" he ground out.

"It is simple," the Magus replied. "I intend to destroy the God of Israel, Isaac and Jacob. You have proven to me that you despise him yourself."

"What do you mean?" His voice was strangled.

"You have not chosen to worship him in the manner laid down in the scriptures but in an obvious perversion of his word. We are engaged in the same war."

"I have sworn allegiance to a circle of men."

"As have I. And now you will break some part of that oath, even as you have broken your oath of allegiance to Israel's God. I repeat, what is that to me?"

Shaphan the priest buried his head in his hands for a long moment and then he looked up.

"We will begin with Cabala at our next meeting," he said. "You will find it fascinating."

The methods of creating silver nitrate by adding silver to eau prime was well understood by the Magus. He had experimented with creating various metallic dyes and lustres using methods already well-known among Arab alchemists.

Simon was intrigued when he found that a cloth impregnated with silver nitrate and left in the sun to dry, retained the imprint of a fallen leaf. They hung the small square of linen on the wall of their dwelling and examined it. The leaf, although not clearly defined, was quite visible. In the following days, the two men worked with various plants and stones creating images on a variety of cloths. All the while, Simon Magus was aware that they had reached the brink of discovery.

"I am going out," he declared late one afternoon. "I need time alone."

He walked slowly along the shore, scarcely aware of the majesty of the scenery around him. Somewhere above him, shrouded in late afternoon shadow, Machaerus clung to one of the uttermost reaches of the hills, a brooding man-made edifice diminutive against the natural sculpture of the rocks.

Simon picked up a stick that had washed up onto the shore. It was bleached white by the sun like the slender bone of some long-dead animal. Absently, he drilled it into the beach sand until it stood upright. At heb-sed they planted a stick in the ground, wound about with Madonna lilies and papyrus, symbolic of the uniting of Upper and Lower Egypt. His thoughts shifted to the Great Pyramid. Khufu had become a pre-occupation, an alchemist's riddle. The Eye of Horus introduced spiritual light into man-made darkness offering a ray of illumination to the man couched within the darkened womb of the pyramid. Through the Eye, the sun captured an image within the darkness. The divine image was superimposed upon the life of the man. Could it be that the gods were saying it was possible to capture such an image?

He turned for home and as they saw him approach, his disciples came oto meet him. In his hand Simon Magus brandished the white stick aloft as if it was a sword that had just slain an enemy. His hair was swept back from his face and his cloak whipped behind him in the wind. He was shouting triumphantly.

"I believe I have the answer," he shouted. "We must prepare a room!"

On instruction from the Magus, the underground chamber was dug swiftly and secretly. A skin of stone formed the inside walls, which were painted with Judaean bitumen, while the roof rose to a single vault with a square opening at the pinnacle large enough to take a man's fist. This hole was filled with clay, into which the Magus triumphantly set the stick he had brought with him from the beach. The whole area was dressed with a layer of sand to cover any sign of disturbance. Entrance to the room was an underground passageway from a nearby rocky outcrop, its entrance cunningly disguised and covered with a stone slab.

On the day of its completion he requested of Herodias that Helen of Tyre should bring the head of the Baptist to his dwelling. She permitted it reluctantly.

That night, rituals and ceremonies of dedication were performed in the underground room and spells were daubed on its walls. The Magus dubbed it the King's Chamber.

"Tonight, a joining has been made between Upper and Lower Egypt," he said. "Now we will begin to see through the Eye of Horus."

It was to become the focus of all his new experiments.

Chapter 38
Twice-Born

Judas waited until the crowd had dispersed before making his way to Jerusalem where he knew he would find Jesus and the other disciples in the temple precincts. Years of experience had taught him how to internalise his anger and to shift the focus from himself. Small puffs of dust were raised by his sandals on the road and the heat of the sun bit into the back of his neck as he picked his way almost unconsciously between the rocks on the road, the droppings of sheep and goats, and the scattered branches.

He thought bitterly of how condemned he had felt under Jesus' quiet gaze. The master saw him as a thief! What Jesus did not know was that he, Judas, had taken money that was sorely needed. He had given up everything in order to follow the Rabbi. His home, his livelihood, was left behind – abandoned – how could he be expected to support himself and his father on the pittance that was given the disciples from the money-bag? Seven years of leprosy had devoured Simon's wealth and left him destitute at the time of his healing and Jesus, for all his supposed insight, did not appear to have noticed that! Simon could hardly be expected to live as a peasant. The degradation his father had suffered as a leper and then, just as he was finding his place in society again, his public humiliation by the Master before his guests, rankled almost as much as Judas' own guilt and fear of exposure.

Jesus had never shown due respect for the Pharisees and had openly vilified them to their faces. "Whitewashed sepulchres," he called them once, "full of dead men's bones." And yesterday he had done nothing to prevent Mary from grovelling at his feet, knowing full well what manner of woman she was, and had flung Simon's hospitality in his teeth. That was unforgivable!

The Master had compounded his folly by permitting peasants to publicly worship him and acclaim him Messiah just as Simon had predicted. There was nothing for it but to put a halt to his madness. It was an act of God, Judas felt, which had led his father to warn him at just the right moment.

In the background of his thoughts lay the motive which he could not afford to examine. 'If I don't stop him, he will denounce me as a thief before the disciples; the word will get out. I must preserve my reputation at all costs.'

Judas turned into the temple courts and stood riveted in shock at the sight of the chaotic scene that met his eyes. In a fury, Jesus was overturning the tables of the money-lenders, scattering coins across the marble floor and breaking open the wicker cages of the birds.

"My Father's house is a place of worship," he was shouting, "and you have made it a den of thieves."

In the midst of the ensuing bedlam; the beating of the wings of escaping doves, the bleating of animals and the angry cries of the money lenders, Jesus took up a whip and began driving men and animals from the temple while his disciples stood aghast, consumed with the enormity of the position in which they found themselves.

Judas positioned himself behind a pillar where he could not be seen by the disciples, and watched with malicious fascination. The Master was writing his own arrest warrant; the chief priests would never allow him to continue to preach after this. But he, Judas, must exonerate himself immediately! He could not be seen to be part of what was taking place. If he was clever it might be possible, as his father had intimated, to make some money from the whole sordid affair.

As things quietened down, Judas Iscariot slipped away to the priest's quarters where knots of gesticulating men discussed the events in heated tones. The son of Simon the Pharisee was known to many in the priesthood and he was received gladly once they realised he was as shocked as they were by the events of the day. There was no doubt that Jesus of Nazareth had done some wonderful things, but that could not be offered in mitigation of his present unruly behaviour. He must be arrested and the chief priests were willing to pay Judas, if only he would help.

"How much?" Judas asked.

"We can offer thirty pieces of silver. It's not much," they conceded, perceiving the shadow that crossed his countenance. "We would pay more if we could. But, Judas, consider this a service to the nation."

Caiaphas, the high priest, had chuckled when he had named his price to the priesthood.

"Why should we offer more from the coffers," he said. "According to the Law, thirty pieces of silver is the designated price of a slave."[7]

Herod and Herodias had come to Jerusalem to be seen by the Jews to be celebrating the Feast of Passover. For once, Herodias had insisted they go. She had heard the facts and the rumours.

Herod first received word of the Nazarene's raising of Lazarus from the dead, through Chuza his steward. The miracle had been performed right under the noses of the religious leaders who were seeking to discredit the man. Herod had, as always, listened with fascination to his steward's account.

"Many of the Jews followed the women to the grave where they had gone to meet with the Master," Chuza said. "They were greatly shocked when he called for the stone to be rolled away from the entrance. The Master called Lazarus forth with a loud voice and he came from the grave, still bound in the grave cloths."

"An apparition?" Herod shuddered in horror.

"No, no, my lord! He was alive. There was great amazement and excitement. Everyone bore witness to the event. They unbound him and took him back to the house."

Although Herod relayed none of these events to Herodias, a servant girl reported Jesus' ride into Jerusalem and the pandemonium he had caused in the temple. Herodias received the news with a thrill of premonition. Jesus' kingship had been openly declared. They would kill him now. If the Jews did not find a way, Herod would be forced to.

---

[7] Exodus 21:32

Chapter 39
Twice-Born

1935

Reinhard Heydrich was brilliant and ambitious; a man who would stop at nothing to achieve his goals. So far, he had done little more than comment lightly in passing that Himmler had spent a lot of time with Röhm during the early days of the Party. Himmler had at once recognised the insinuation and had from then on regarded Heydrich with extreme caution. Both men were to use their wits and zeal to build their own positions, knowing that ultimately one of them must make a move for power that would eliminate his rival. Neither knew for certain which was the fisherman, and which the fish, but Reinhard Heydrich believed he had been given an unimpeded view of his way to the top, on the shoulders of the Reichsführer SS.

"I want them out, every last one!" Himmler's usually unemotional features were blotched and distorted and a vein that snaked down his forehead throbbed angrily. "There are to be no homosexuals in the ranks of the SS and until we've made sure they're all out, we're recruiting no new men!" He paced the room restlessly. "I don't care how good they are as soldiers, they're finished!"

Obergruppenführer Wolff clicked his heels. "Reichsführer, there will need to be some statement to the press."

"Yes, yes. I'll leave that side of it to you."

"Certainly Reichsführer, will that be all?"

Himmler nodded distractedly and failed to acknowledge Wolff's salute as he left the room. He would clean the whole damned SS out himself, if necessary. Already in the two years since Röhm's death, nearly sixty thousand men had been dropped. He wanted no drunks, no opportunists, no men of uncertain background, but above all, no damned homosexuals. He wanted them expelled and handed over to the courts. Once their sentence was up, his men would be waiting to slap them straight into concentration camps. If possible, Himmler decided, they should be shot. Word could be put out that they had attempted to escape. Anything, as long as they were out of the SS and out of his sight.

Killing Röhm had not been enough, but perhaps by purging the SS, he could purge himself. He was washing and washing the blood from his hands, but the spot remained.

"He's a dirty Jew!" Heydrich shouted. "Look at his face, his nose! You can see it a mile away. He's a real Jewish lout!"

On the other side of the room, Lina set the last of the dishes on the table and turned to face her husband. He was pacing the room with a glass in his hand and although he had only been home two hours, he had been drinking steadily.

"He's a pedantic little schoolmaster," she said. "But you need him. He's your ticket to the top."

She walked across the room and slid her arms around his neck, but he was still distracted. She released him. He fascinated and excited her in this mood. Others might have been afraid, but she could handle him and she knew it would not be long before he wanted her.

"You haven't seen him at work," he said. "He's weak. He imagines his stupid ideas pass for intellect. If he wants to purify the Aryan race and kill Jews, let him kill Jews. Why does he have to cloak it in all this mystic shit?"

"It makes him feel important," Lina offered with an unusual flash of insight. "He knows he's a nothing, but he has to have something to hide behind."

Lina Heydrich's face was sensual but hard and her eyes held a bright hardness as though they were lit from within. They were eyes that held and dominated if they caught a glance, so that people often avoided looking at her directly. Lina was a capable actress who could pout disarmingly if it was called for, to manipulate a moment. She had used her feminine charms against Himmler at one of Goering's garden parties. Himmler had been pressing Heydrich to divorce her.

"She's impossible and ungovernable!" he had told Heydrich. "A woman of her type is a danger to a man in your position. You need someone who will accompany you to functions and remain discreetly in the background. And naturally you need a woman who will support you in your work, not become a source of upheaval!"

Lina had waited for her opportunity to retaliate and when she did, it was by using charm. She sat quietly, eyes downcast, throughout the afternoon, until at last when Heydrich left the table, Himmler leaned over to her.

"Why are you so quiet?"

"Do you really find that surprising?" she returned softly, in a voice that was just a little broken.

Himmler eased his constricting collar and stretched his chin to cover his discomfort. "Would you like to dance?"

He danced stiffly, recalling step by step those early lessons of his youth that had cost him so much in time and effort.

Lina maintained her tragic pose until Himmler had whispered to her reassuringly: "Don't worry, it will be alright."

He never mentioned the question of divorce to Heydrich again, but for Lina Heydrich it had been a moment of personal triumph.

"Come and eat," she said to Heydrich. "Dinner's on the table."

Despite the amount of schnapps he had consumed, he still walked steadily. It was difficult to tell when he was drunk. It was as if one personality became dormant and another moved to the fore and assumed the driver's seat. Far from becoming vague, his small close-set eyes glinted with malice above the long aristocratic nose. There was always a touch of cruelty to his mouth, but when he was intoxicated the twist of his full lips became more obvious, and it was said that even the Berlin whores preferred to give him a wide berth at times like this.

Lina passed him his food and watched him while he ate. He consumed it swiftly and automatically, without appearing to notice what he was eating and then pushed his plate aside. As he lit a cigarette and refilled his glass, she noticed the tremor in his hands.

"He agrees with everything I say and then he goes behind my back! I get messages from my staff saying, 'the Reichsführer says that Hitler wouldn't like it'."

Lina laughed. "He's scared of you," she said.

Heydrich observed her with interest. "Scared," he repeated slowly as though the thought was new to him. "I think you're damned right. He's too scared to turn me down, so he hides behind the Führer.

Look at our so-called leaders!" he said loudly, slopping the liquid in his glass. "Hitler's so full of fear that he can't be left alone at night. He's afraid of werewolves and moonlight and he worries about the most humane way to kill a lobster. He's so damned terrified of impurity that he gets his doctor to draw blood from him." His laughter was unpleasant. "He spends hours contemplating the vial. From what I understand, there's more Jew in that blood that he would ever want to admit. Why else would he have killed Dollfus?"

"In that attempted Anschluss with Austria?"

He nodded. "Dollfus had been conducting an investigation into his background and Hitler got wind of it. If he had nothing to hide, why was he killed?" He pushed his chair away from the table and put his feet up on the tablecloth. "Didn't even manage to capture the file Dollfus had on him, so presumably there's still incriminating papers floating around in Austria somewhere. Could be the reason the Führer doesn't sleep well at night."

It was her turn to laugh. "I've heard he wakes screaming and babbling; demanding his aides."

Heydrich shrugged. "The man's a mental case," he said. "The one minute he's claiming to be the German Messiah, the next he's calling himself a shit-head."

"Is it true he's impotent?"

"How the hell should I know?" he grinned.

"You know what I mean. You must have heard rumours."

"My dear wife, I have a personal and carefully guarded file. Nothing gets by me, not a fact, not a rumour."

"Then what?" she asked eagerly.

"Sure he's impotent. The man's sex is simply in his power of oratory. When he speaks to a crowd, he woos them and whips them and himself up into a frenzy. The man's a pervert but by all accounts he doesn't get anything together in the bedroom." He stood up and saluted sardonically. "Drink a toast with me Lina to our dear Führer and Reichsführer-SS. Seig heil!"

Lina picked up her glass, attempting to emulate his solemnity. "How can I drink a toast with an empty glass," she complained.

"An empty glass for an empty toast," he replied and tipped the contents of his own glass into the remainder of the stew. "To the Führer and his idiot henchmen, seig heil!"

"None of them are a patch on you!" Lina declared. "You've taken every opportunity that's come your way, and you've created opportunities when there were none."

Heydrich looked at his wife. He enjoyed it when she fed his ego.

"Just the beginning, liebschen. Just the beginning." He was laughing now with Lina.

"Come here woman, let's play a little," and he grasped her round the waist and pulled her roughly against him.

Heydrich's insatiable sexual appetite did not end with his wife or his liaison with the prostitutes on his nightclubbing jaunts. In 1940, he set up his own high-class brothel, the Salon Kitty in a mansion he rented on behalf of the Sicherheitsdienst in Giesebrechtstrasse just off Kurfurstendamm. It was a crib of the idea of Britain's Glass Club, which had created the scandal instrumental in bringing down Asquith's government in 1916. Microphones were installed in each of the nine bedrooms and connected to a monitoring room in the basement. In this way, Heydrich was able to combine business with pleasure, spying on diplomatic visitors to Germany, and other visitors of importance. Initially subsidised by the SD, it soon became self-supporting, and even Nazis such as von Ribbentrop visited Salon Kitty before realising it was under Heydrich's management

Even when they lay together later, Heydrich would not let the subject of Himmler drop.

"The SS are soldiers," he told Lina, "yet Himmler spends hours lecturing them on rune magic. Why the hell doesn't he let them get on with the job of soldiering?"

Lina left his side and walked across the bedroom to the dressing table. She leaned down and examined her face closely in the mirror.

"You play your part so well," she flattered him. "With your 'Herr Reichsführer this' and 'Herr Reichsführer that'. Give it another couple of years and you'll have him just where you want him. Then the pretence will stop and you will be able to walk in and take over."

She straightened up and turned to face him. "You have everything it takes to get right to the top," she said. "Play your cards right and neither Heinrich Himmler nor Adolf Hitler will know what has hit them. You'll be the next Führer of Germany!"

He lay back on the pillows watching her. It was Lina who had pushed him into the job with Himmler in the first place. She arranged the meeting with the Reichsführer-SS and insisted Heydrich take the train to Munich as though he had never received the telegram postponing the interview when Himmler needed time to consider a second man for the post. A misunderstanding on Heinrich Himmler's part secured the job for Heydrich. Reinhard Heydrich was a Nachrichtenoffizier, a wireless officer, and not a Nachrichtendienst-Offizier, an Intelligence Officer, as Himmler had supposed him to be, and Heydrich had not bothered to enlighten him. Himmler had given him twenty minutes to establish an overall plan for an SS Intelligence Service and, drawing on his limited knowledge of Naval Intelligence and the adventure stories of the British Secret Service he had read in his youth, Heydrich compiled an organisational structure that to Himmler seemed impressive. Heydrich who had until then, scorned the political world, made the shift into National Socialism.

Shortly thereafter, Reinhard Heydrich married Lina von Osten at a ceremony in which swastikas replaced Christian symbols and the Horst Wessel song was played as they left the church. His genius thrived in combination with Lina's insatiable desire for power. She centred his bitterness into a single-minded drive to achieve.

Lina swung round to face him on her dressing table stool, her long blonde hair falling like a cloud over her shoulder. In the lamplight her body was golden like an impressionist painting with deepening shadows between the thighs. Heydrich reached out his arms to her.

"Come here," he said.

Chapter 40
Twice-Born

On the second of July 1936, Himmler and a handpicked group of representatives of the State and Nazi Party made their way slowly down the main street of Quedlinburg. The grey stone buildings were hung with the red, white and black of the Nazi banners and, in the sharp breeze whipping off the Harz Mountains, they snapped and fluttered importantly, like the sails of a multitude of small yachts. The road narrowed as the group began to follow it up towards the church of St. Servatius, flanked on either side by the ranks of the SS-Standarte 'Germania'.

"I want the building stripped of all statues and any other impotent Christian icons!" Himmler had ordered. "The ceremony that is to take place at Quedlinburg must bear no resemblance to anything Christian." And even Himmler as he watched the day smoothly unfold had to admit that the arrangements could hardly have been bettered.

This was the thousandth anniversary of the death of Heinrich der Vogler, the Saxon Duke who, as founder of the first German Reich, became Heinrich I. No expense was spared in what was to be the most bizarre ceremony openly performed by the Third Reich. D'Alquen editor of Die Schwartze Korps, the official SS magazine, wrote concerning the young troops that lined the streets, their serious faces staring straight ahead:

"They were like true knights of old in the service of their lord. They may call us pagan uncomprehendingly," he continued, "but if they had seen us then, they would have experienced what real German piety is – fitting our faith and kind."

This reborn order of Teutonic knights in their black uniforms, highly polished black boots and black steel helmets, lined the cobbled streets standing rigidly to attention, rifles at their feet and hands clasped uniformly over the barrels; every soldier's eyes staring straight ahead. Even Himmler, immaculately turned out in his SS attire, diminutive against his men and pale beneath his black helmet, looked the part.

Although the focus was on the Quedlinburg Cathedral, Heinrich der Vogler's remains were not interred there. Under the vaulted arches of the crypt after the impassioned speeches, Himmler and his men stood looking down into the open tomb in silence. Gottlob Berger shifted his bulky frame uncomfortably, never quite at ease in these more public roles. Lieutenant-General Karl Wolff proudly stood to attention at Himmler's right hand. Himmler addressed him softly:

"This is more than just a ceremony, Obergruppenführer Wolff!"

"Herr Reichsführer," he said fervently, "I believe what has taken place here today, is a resurrection!"

Heinrich Himmler smiled. "We'll bring him back! This must be his final resting-place. On the anniversary of this day, we will bring his remains from the Wigpurti crypt and re-inter them here at Quedlinburg.

"Can you feel his presence, even up here?"

Gunter D'Alquen nodded and it was not simply that he felt it his duty to agree with Himmler. Below them was the Wigpurti Crypt where the bones of Heinrich der Vogler lay, but up in the castle of Dankwarode, he too sensed the presence of the first Führer.

The night sky was clear and brilliant with stars. A light breeze flowed through the trees, moving limbs and leaves and shifting their depth of shadow. The darkness was poignant as if the wind carried with it a sweet sadness; something pitched low, like an undercurrent of music. They both felt it; a presence impelled by their breathing and pulsing with their blood, a moment so delicately poised that any false movement would shatter it.

It was some time before Himmler spoke again and then his voice was hushed. "If you will excuse me Herr D'Alquen, I feel the need to visit the tomb alone."

"I quite understand, Herr Reichsführer. I will wait for you in the front lounge."

Shunning any light, Himmler made his way slowly down the garden. He waited for his eyes to adjust to the pitch-blackness that engulfed him as he entered the crypt. What he sought was not to be found using the accepted human senses. He stood beside the stone, beneath which lay the ancient remains of Heinrich der Vogler, and waited. The presence had not left him and now, at the grave, there was a discernible intensification of its power. Himmler was oppressed by an energetic force that was both frightening and stimulating. It was only by a supreme effort of will that he stayed on his feet. Gradually, using the disciplines he had acquired over the years, he prepared himself to communicate with the spirit of der Vogler.

His emotions were swept from initial pleasure to a deep, rending sorrow. Images were flashed onto a screen of darkness before his eyes that brought him close to weeping; scenes of horror and death as man tangled with man in bloody warfare. Then just as swiftly he saw Aryan children with sweet, soft mouths and blue eyes filled with laughter - the faces of angels while above them, as though a threat to their very existence, hung a sword like the sword of Damocles. Abruptly, the vision faded. Himmler was left empty and devoid of emotion and consumed by the intensity of the silence. The stillness expanded, gaining a life force of its own and out of it, words formed clearly in Himmler's mind.

"The sword must shatter!" He was aware that the words found no source in his own consciousness. "That which you have begun must be completed. Nation must be parted from nation: race from race. Cut away all that detracts from the purity of the Spring." Although you will not live to see the fulfilment of all that I have spoken, you will be called 'the Initiator'. It will be through you that the sword will be fitted together and become whole again."

Heinrich Himmler left the crypt hours later, elated in a way that he had never known and yet at the same time, burdened by the weight of the visions. But it was not until much later in a sleepless night that he recalled the source of the words that had carried with them such a nudge of familiarity.

'The sword will withstand the first blow: at the second it will shatter. If you take it back to the Spring, it will become whole again from the flow of water. If the pieces are not lost and you fit them together properly, as soon as the water wets them, the sword will become whole again, the joinings and edges stronger than ever before.' The words, he remembered, were from Wolfram's Parsival.

When Gunter D'Alquen looked up to see Heinrich Himmler

enter the lounge of the Castle Dankwarode, he was deeply impressed by a marked difference in the man. In the more sane light of the following morning, he shook off the thought as fanciful. The aura he had seen around Himmler the night before could only have been his imagination, but the increase in the Reichsführer's authority from the moment of that encounter, was not.

Chapter 41
Twice-Born

Joseph of Arimathea stumbled across Nicodemus unexpectedly as the older man sat gazing out from the temple mount across the Hinnom Valley.

"Nicodemus, you seem troubled."

"I was looking at the Roman aqueduct," he confessed.

"A remarkable feat of construction!"

Nicodemus glanced at him quickly. "I believe I can speak to you?"

"Of course." Joseph sat down on the bench next to his friend. "What is it?"

"You know that the water supply in the great cisterns beneath the temple dwindled. There was never enough, especially during the feasts, to provide for the multitudes in the city."

"The Roman consul, Pontius Pilot perceived the need and brought water to the city."

Nicodemus nodded. "Yet the people rioted when they realised that the Corban[8] had been used to increase the capacity of the cisterns and to help with the building of the aqueduct."

"It was sacred money intended for the upkeep of the temple. They believed the use was not lawful," Joseph acknowledged. He was still unable to understand why this event had caused Nicodemus to be so disturbed but he waited patiently.

"The temple treasurer, Rabbi Helcias, told our people that the money was taken forcefully by Pontius Pilot," Nicodemus said and his voice was tired. "Of course, that was not the truth. Pilot convinced the Sanhedrin that the Halakoth[9] allowed for such a purpose and the money was given into Roman hands."

"No such admission was made to the Zealots who stirred up the

---

[8] Temple tax
[9] Jewish traditional laws

masses."

Nicodemus shook his head. "The uprising brought death and injury to many but, thanks to Rome, the city now has water in abundance. Do you know where it comes from, Joseph?"

"From the springs above Bethlehem."

"Exactly. Living water from Beit Lehem, the House of Bread. One of the claims Jesus has made is that he is the manna come from heaven: the Bread of Life."

Joseph was beginning to see where this conversation was leading.

"On the last day of the great feast, when the water was poured out at the pool of Siloam, he called out to the people to come and drink of him."

"'He that believes in me,'" Nicodemus quoted, "'out of his belly shall flow rivers of living water.' A strange statement."

"There was division among the people over Jesus the Nazarene on that day of the feast," Joseph said slowly. "The crowd knew he was proclaiming himself Messiah, yet he is a Galilean. Messiah must be born in Bethlehem."

"He never gave them an answer," Nicodemus replied. "But I have spoken to his family and he was indeed born in Bethlehem. His father, Joseph, was of the house of David and he returned with his wife, Mary, at the time of Caesar Augustus' taxation. Yeshua was born there."

Joseph looked at Nicodemus in amazement.

"Born in Bethlehem, of the house of David. How then could he not be Messiah? All his words and his deeds bear him testimony."

"The Living Water has come to his Father's temple," Nicodemus pursed his lips and nodded slowly. "He has come to his own and we have not received him."

"What of the aqueduct?"

"Is it not significant that the temple cisterns, which once brought life-giving water to the people of Jerusalem, were almost empty when Messiah came?" Nicodemus said brokenly. "No wonder the leadership rejects him, Joseph; the life of God no longer abides here. Did you know that they took this new water system underground through the village of Bethlehem using part of the aqueduct made by Herod the Great? They have refused the true Living Water while willingly accepting the polluted waters of the Herodians and Rome."

"Our leadership has cut him off and would kill him."

"Exactly! Truly, Joseph, I believe this is the Messiah sent by God. We were prepared for this moment by Moses and Aaron, in fact by all the prophets. It is the culmination of all things, yet he is hated and refused."

Joseph was silent, helpless against the old man's despair.

"They will kill him and there is nothing I can do to prevent it! I have spoken and my voice has been lost like a murmur in a thunderstorm. There is nothing I can do."

"Perhaps the answer lies in the prophet Isaiah," Joseph mused. Did he not say, 'For the transgression of my people was he stricken'?"

Nicodemus glanced at him sharply. "'He had done no violence, neither was any deceit in his mouth. Yet, it pleased the Lord to bruise him,'" he quoted. "You are saying that if it pleases the Lord to make his Son an offering for sin, there is nothing that can be done to prevent this death?" For several minutes he was silent but when he turned once more to face Joseph his eyes were filled with tears. "You are right. I believe it is the will of God to prepare a final sacrifice."

Both men were silent as they gazed out over the black smoke of the Valley of Hinnom, Jerusalem's rubbish dump.

"I wish I could see a good aspect to this," Nicodemus said sadly, "but I cannot. I see a prophecy that chills my soul. The true Messiah will indeed be cut off for the sins of our nation; rejected by his own people," He rubbed his eyes wearily and covered them with his hand. Joseph of Arimathea had to lean forward to catch his next words. "But another will arise like the man-made watercourse and bypass the town of Bethlehem. I believe he will constitute a convergence of two streams, the minor stream of the Herodians and the mightier one of Rome. This is the one the Jews will gladly receive, Joseph. He may be able to bring life to the temple and claim, as signified by the aqueduct over Hinnom, to bridge hell for us, but one blast by the breath of God will be sufficient to bring him down to the pit and he will take a multitude of souls with him."

Chapter 42
Twice-Born

November 9th 1938

It was early evening, and Michael Segal was less than a block away from the truck that screeched to a halt in Ludeckestrasse. Pedestrians stopped and watched silently as SA Storm troopers leapt out into the street. There was the smell of fear in the air, or was it his own fear that he could smell? Segal knew without any need for explanation that they were after Jews and he experienced a numbing terror that, for a moment, bound him to the spot. Turning, he began to walk swiftly away only to be faced with two more lorry-loads of troops approaching from the opposite direction. Tail-gates swung open and Nazi Brown Shirts poured onto the street.

It was obvious that Jewish businesses had been pinpointed. Fifty yards away, two troopers armed with metal poles began to systematically smash the shop-front of an elderly Jewish baker. Four more in the uniform of the SS yelled obscenities as they forced their way into the shop. The baker, still in his white apron and hat, was shoved forcibly out onto the pavement and a Brown Shirt dragged his wife by the arm, flinging her onto the street behind him. There was laughter at their cries for mercy. Retrieving the pole used to shatter the shop window, one of the men lashed out with a vicious blow knocking the woman to the ground.

The baker stumbled forward shouting at them to let her alone. He grappled ineffectually with the Brown Shirt and there were hoots of derisive laughter as the soldier side-stepped, holding him at bay with outstretched arms; the metal bar gripped firmly in both hands.

"Dance, Jüden! Dance!"

He lashed out without warning, hitting the baker across the side of the head and felling him instantly with the blow. The old man lay semi-conscious in the gutter unable to defend himself against the jack-boots of the youths. His wife covered her face and sobbed.

Michael Segal drew back into a doorway. He could hear the smashing of glass as they systematically demolished the interior of the shop. There was no escape. If he attempted to go in either direction they would demand identification. He was hardly typically German in appearance. He swung around nervously as the glass door opened behind him.

"Come in here."

The young woman gripped him urgently by the arm. He found himself in the run-down lobby of an apartment building and she closed the door behind him.

"Quickly!"

Beckoning him to follow, she went up the stairs before him. A threadbare floral carpet in oranges and browns hugged the profile of the centre strip of the staircase. She opened a door off the landing two flights up and Michael followed her into a small bed-sitting room. Locking the door behind him, she kicked off her high-heeled shoes and went to the window.

"My God, they're brutes! Are you Jewish?"

He nodded. He was seeing her for the first time and something in his expression caused her to laugh. It was a jarring, bitter sound.

"Yes, I'm a whore," she acknowledged as though he had asked the question aloud.

The 'Aryan' blonde hair had been done with peroxide and a much darker root was beginning to grow through. Her make-up was too heavy on a face that, although not unattractive, was spoiled by eyes that had seen too much. She was fashionably and even tastefully dressed but the neckline was too low and the slit in the skirt too high.

"As a good Jewish boy you have probably not visited a whore before?"

He laughed. "My good Jewish mamma told me not to. But thanks. How did you know I needed a safe-haven?"

She sobered. "I'm still not sure it is safe," she admitted. "But we'll need to take a chance on that. I was watching you from the foyer. You didn't look too comfortable with what was going on out there."

"I wasn't."

"Well, you're welcome to stay until this is over, if you're not squeamish about disobeying your mamma."

"She'll never know if I don't tell her."

"My name is Ruth. And I'll tell you what I tell none of my clients. I'm Jewish too."

"The streets are not going to be safe for Jews in any profession from now on."

"I know. Tea or coffee?" She had put a kettle on the two-plate stove and busied herself with cups. "You don't need to worry," she said. "I don't work from my own premises. Far too risky." She glanced up at him. "For heavens sake, sit down!"

He grinned and perched on the edge of the bed. Ruth handed him a cup of coffee, plumped up the pillows and sat with her back against the wall, her long legs stretched out in front of her. She took a sip of coffee cradling the cup in both hands.

"So, who are you and where do you come from?"

"Michael Segal. I was a lecturer at the Berlin University until they decided that Jews were no longer needed."

"Oh!" she sounded impressed. "A lecturer! Aren't you rather young? Are you married?"

The questions were delivered without guile and Michael laughed again. "No on both counts."

He went to the window, standing off to one side so that he might not be seen to be observing the scene down on the street below. People were being herded together under SS guard. It was too dark to see their expressions but he could hear many of the shouted comments of their assailants and of a group of Germans who had gathered to watch.

"Jewish filth! Jewish vermin! Get out of Germany while you still have breath or we will get you out without it!"

"You've heard the marching songs of the SS?" Ruth asked.

"I generally try to give the SS a wide berth."

"It helps to know the mood of the Nazis. In particular their mood towards the Jews. They have a song which goes like this: Sharpen your long knives on the curb-stone. Bury them deep in Jewish flesh. Blood has got to flow."

He looked at her in disbelief.

"There are others, equally ugly."

"Spare me," Michael said wearily. "I don't want to know."

"It's time for those Jews who can get out of Germany to get out," she said.

"I have a friend who is telling me the same thing."

Down on the street the Jews were being forced at gunpoint onto one of the lorries. Segal felt an irrational stab of conscience mixed with impotent anger. Was it right that he was here in comparative safety when his brethren were under the Nazi guns? He moved abruptly away from the window and sat down on the bed again.

Ruth was rummaging in a cupboard underneath the kitchen sink.

"We will need to eat," she said. Setting a red and white checked cloth on the small table, she brought out tomatoes, bread and cheese and waved Michael to help himself.

"I don't think I have had a man to dinner here before," she said with a repeat of that small bitter laugh. "On the other hand the women who care to associate themselves with me are generally on the streets at this time of the evening."

Segal realised how vulnerable she was under the brittle veneer.

"I'm honoured! Next time I'll bring a bottle of wine." He said lightly and was gratified that her laughter took on a sweeter tone.

By the time they had finished their meal the street below them had cleared and the trucks had driven away.

Michael Segal took Ruth by the hand. "Thank you," he said simply. "What you did for me was very special. I would like to reciprocate by taking you out to dinner one evening."

Her expression was incredulous. "Professor! You would take dinner with a whore!" Her laughter followed him down the stairs. Both knew that Michael's invitation was ridiculous, as under the Nuremberg Laws no Jew could enter a German restaurant.

The street was unnaturally quiet. Michael Segal walked past the shattered front of the bakery, his shoes breaking glass shards into tiny fragments. There was a pool of blood on the pavement where the baker had fallen and his hat lay discarded and bloodied close by. The shop was in semi-darkness but he could see, in the light from the street lamp that there was glass everywhere and bread, rolls and cakes were trampled into the mess on the floor. Any undamaged goods had been looted; nothing remained on the shelves.

As he made his way back towards his room, Michael Segal was appalled by the increasing evidence that the bakery in Ludeckestrasse had not been an isolated occurrence. Street after street was littered with glass and debris. Gangs of youths were gathered on pavements abuzz with aggressive excitement. Smoke drifted over sections of the city.

Gabriele was right. Any further procrastination could spell death or imprisonment.

It was decided that Michael should obtain a vacation pass, which tended to attract less scrutiny than a work pass. Gabriele insisted on arranging it herself. Obviously Michael could not travel under his own identity as his documents were clearly marked 'Jüden' and travel was limited to his area of domicile. A friend would do it, she said, someone with connections. She knew a man with certain sympathies to the Jewish plight and it would not be difficult for him to draw the papers up without questions being asked.

"At a price?" Michael asked.

Gabriele laughed. "Always at a price!"

When she returned four days later, it was with two sets of documents.

"I hope you don't mind," she said with a twinkle of amusement in her eye. "But for this journey, you and I are married."

"Gabby, what on earth have you done? You know I can't allow you to travel with me, it's far too dangerous!"

"It's done," she said evenly. "I gave it a lot of thought, Michael, and it works out best this way. No petty official will think twice about checking on a couple on their honeymoon."

Michael smiled, but it was with a deep sense of misgiving. "Gabriele, let me go on my own," he said again. "I am prepared to take my chances, but I have no desire to endanger you."

Gabriele looked up at him. "I love you, Michael," she said. "It breaks my heart to send you away. But I know what's already happening in the camps and this is just the beginning. You must go, and this is the simplest way to do it. I have booked a room in a hotel at Singen on the Swiss border. I have the name of a guide. Beyond that, you are on your own."

He tilted her face so that she was forced to look at him and saw that there were tears in her eyes. Neither of them had ever dared confess their love for one another before. The words were too binding. But Michael kissed her now in a way that left Gabriele in no doubt of his feelings.

"Once I am across," he began. "Is there any possibility…?"

She put a finger to his lips and stopped him with a tiny shake of her head.

"We'll talk about it again," she said. "One day."

Chapter 43
Twice-Born

1936

Rupprecht, the castle warden, met each one of the officers as they arrived and arranged for them to be seen to their rooms.

Himmler had not left them in any doubt that the meeting he had called was one of absolute importance. A terse memo had summoned them to Wewelsburg Castle on the 4th of August and the Reichsführer had followed it up with a personal telephone call to each of his men.

SS-Obergruppenführer Oswald Pohl arrived at the same moment as Gottlob Berger and they exchanged nods as they left their vehicles.

"Any idea what it's about?"

Berger shrugged and shook his head. "Only that it's a matter of urgency."

"Have you noticed how damned cold this place always seems to be? I come in from Berlin and the cold hits me like a wall, yet I never seem to come prepared for it."

"Let's get inside. I'm sure our quarters will have been warmed. The Reichsführer arrived yesterday and he's not unaware of our creature comforts. Personally, I'm ready for a schnapps, care to join me?"

"The task ahead of us is distasteful and will cost us dearly in terms of our country. I think you will agree though, that anything worth achieving bears with it a price." Heinrich Himmler glanced round at the grave faces of the twelve knights of the Inner Circle who were seated at the table. "There's a lot at stake," he went on. "Few are even aware of the extent of the web that's been established. They've had a start on us that is centuries old and have established roots at every level of society. We're looking at a secret organisation that has possibly been in existence for nearly two thousand years and all we can determine with any certainty is that the heart of this conspiracy is Jewish! War is the only way to deal with this problem."

"Why would we want to steer Germany into another war while we're still trying to recover from the last one?"

There were murmurs of assent from around the table. Himmler continued, speaking in quietly measured tones.

"The only way to be sure that we break the power of this conspiracy is to rid Europe, and ultimately the world, of Jews. And there is no other way to sweep the earth clean of this vermin than under cover of war."

There was a deathly silence from the men. The last war, and its horrible consequences, was still too immediate.

"There's another aspect to this that I want to put to you," Himmler went on. "We've made Karl Ritter's teachings on the subject an integral part of our studies. His ideologies were formed to counteract to the Jewish Masonic plot towards world domination. I've known from the beginning that a time must come when we would build on his foundation."

Reinhard Heydrich shrugged. "Ritter was right up to a point," he drawled, "I totally support his reasoning that the Jewish race must be exterminated in order for Aryanism to gain control of international affairs. But his idea that winning military adventures was less important than weakening the enemy was plain foolishness! If we go to war, we go to win!'"

There were shouts of agreement interspersed with laughter from the men around the table. Himmler held up a hand for silence. "Of course we will win!" he said. "Germany does not fight to lose. But unless we follow Ritter's plan we are destined to lose the war without a battle being fought. Ritter was writing in response to Karl Marx's Communist Manifesto. He recognised that at the core of Communism lay a nucleus of wealthy Jewish internationalists who dominate banking, trade and commerce. He was also aware that Grand Orient Freemasonry was formed to further their devices."

The men were listening intently now, aware that they were on the brink of making a decision, which would affect not only Germany but ultimately Europe and perhaps even the destiny and direction of the world.

"The SS was formed for this purpose," Himmler said. "None of you are unaware of that. This Order is the new expression of the Teutonic Knights, designed to increase Germany's territory to the east and for the domination of Europe. Ritter established the ground plan. It's up to us to implement it before the Jews and Communists seize control. They have taken Russia, and they nearly succeeded in overthrowing Germany. Do we sit back and wait for them to beat us?"

They absorbed all that Himmler was saying and shook their heads.

"This is the thousandth anniversary of Heinrich der Vogler, a man chosen by the Franks and the Saxons as their king. He was a king after our own heart! A king in his own right; one who spurned the pathetic Christian anointing of the Pope. He was a man who not only understood the need to build a strong German nation but also the imperative of a pure Aryan race."

There were murmurs of agreement from the men, although they had all heard this speech before.

"Then gentlemen, it is up to us to grasp der Vogler's vision and remove the taint from Germany. You know I have communicated with the spirit of Heinrich der Vogler; without doubt he is calling us to implement a war as soon as possible to prove to the Chosen People who the Master Race really is!"

There was some laughter but the mood was sober. Oswald Pohl glanced wryly across the table at Gottlob Berger.

"There is another incentive to war that I think you will enjoy," Himmler added. "It will enable us to seize the Hapsburg Regalia and bring the Spear of Longinus to Wewelsburg."

The atmosphere around the table visibly brightened and even Reinhard Heydrich lost his distant expression. This sort of planning, with its manipulative possibilities, appealed to him.

"Hitler is vacillating," Heydrich pointed out. "At the moment he's talking peace. What makes you think you can move him into war?"

"Adolf Hitler has backed away from this route temporarily, but I know he is persuaded that Ritter's methods are right. Our role will simply be to reawaken the Führer to this truth." As if gripped by sudden agitation, Himmler left his seat and began pacing the room. Abruptly he swung back to face his men.

"For the first time, I believe we have the means at our disposal to move Hitler in whichever way we want. Using our methods of visualisation we have the ability to imprint our will on the consciousness of the Führer." He sat down again and waited for their response. His hands had begun to shake and he looked down at them as though they did not belong to him and then folded them carefully in his lap. There was a stunned silence as his men grappled with the enormity of his words. "Dietrich Eckart said that Adolf Hitler would dance to his tune, but I suggest that in future, gentlemen, the Führer will dance exclusively to a tune piped by us at Wewelsburg."

"The Führer is a powerful man in his own right," Werner Lorenz said thoughtfully. "Eckart also said that he had initiated him into the Secret Doctrine, opened his centres and given him the ability to communicate with the Powers. The Führer's fully conversant with ritual magic. He's not an ideal candidate for manipulation."

"Which is a challenge but not an impossibility," Himmler declared positively. "There are thirteen of us, whereas Hitler works alone."

"And what the Reichsführer says is right," Karl Wolff cut in with a sharp nod of his head. "The Führer must be persuaded to move towards war. The findings of the Ahnenerbe have clearly shown that there's no other way to break the power of the World Revolutionary Movement."

"Almost every Jew that holds sway over world finances today came from Germany." Reinhard Heydrich said bitterly. "Not only that, but they can almost all be traced back to Nuremburg. Our ancient laws deliberately turned them away from trades, which would have been less harmful than banking in the long run. When they were forced out of Nuremburg they moved into Frankfurt's ghetto but even that couldn't contain them. The descendents of these same families, almost without exception, comprise the international bankers and policy-makers of the world today."

"And it's obvious even to a casual observer of history that they use fiscal manipulation to dominate. It is up to us to break them,"

Berger agreed. "Most have jumped ship but their involvement in American and British affairs does not mean they're beyond the reach of Germany if she gains control of Europe."

"There is one thing we lack," Himmler said. "The spear of destiny, talisman of world power. If we seize that, it will be impossible for us to fail."

Chapter 44
Twice-Born

1936

The officer who entered Heydrich's office of the Sicherheitsdienst was in his late forties. His hair, a shade darker than it had been in his youth, was now more brown than blonde, and had begun to recede over the forehead. A greying moustache was neatly trimmed to follow the line of his upper lip in a mouth that was still full and attractive. There were lines around the eyes though, that reflected weariness. Matthias von Ingolstadt was once more caught up in a system he was learning to abhor.

Von Ingolstadt was uneasy about the summons he had received from Heydrich. This was the first time he had met the man personally but the Lieutenant-General's reputation went before him. He clicked his heels and gave the Nazi salute.

Heydrich's expression was bland, almost pleasant, but there was something in his eyes that von Ingolstadt failed to interpret. He was like a man about to attack a meal after a long fast.

"Untersturmführer Matthias von Ingolstadt," Heydrich said, making a show of checking a file on the desk in front of him. "I must commend you on your unblemished record in the SS."

Von Ingolstadt inclined his head. "Thank you Obergruppenführer." The surge of relief that coursed through him was short-lived.

Heydrich looked up and smiled but the gesture was hardly reassuring; his eyes remained pale and cold. He stood up and from a cabinet in the corner of the room picked up a riding switch, which he tapped against the palm of his hand as he spoke.

"Your son, Horst von Ingolstadt, has just applied to enter the SS," he said dryly, "which has necessitated the usual genealogical tests. You have a daughter as well, I believe, who is presently employed in the Ahnenerbe?"

"Marianne."

"Marianne von Ingolstadt, yes." Heydrich walked back to his desk and again consulted his file.

"The lineage of the von Ingolstadt line is unblemished and can be traced back to Charlemagne."

"That is correct Obergruppenführer."

"I would have been led to suppose from your records that you were a man of some integrity, but I have uncovered some glaring inconsistencies in your background that would suggest a major deception."

Von Ingolstadt licked his lips, an unconscious gesture that was not missed by Heydrich.

"I don't know what you mean, Obergruppenführer."

"Any recruit into the ranks of the SS must have a clean racial record going back over two and a half centuries and you, as an officer, are obliged to produce evidence of a racially clean background extending over three."

Matthias von Ingolstadt's skin had begun to develop a pale unhealthy appearance and he was perspiring freely.

"I think you will find I have complied with the regulations in every respect, Obergruppenführer."

Heydrich sat on the arm of his chair and looked at von Ingolstadt directly; the riding switch tapped rhythmically against one highly-polished boot.

"An SS officer takes a wife who can produce documented proof of her own racial purity." Heydrich's tone was conversational.

Matthias von Ingolstadt shifted uncomfortably. "I believe my wife's background is also correct, Obergruppenführer."

Heydrich leapt to his feet, his face contorted with fury.

"Liar!" The lash from the switch was so unexpected that von Ingolstadt had no time to defend himself. He put a hand to his cheek and felt the warm blood against his fingers.

"Liar! You know damned well what I'm talking about!"

Von Ingolstadt looked Heydrich in the face and for a moment raw hatred blazed in his eyes. Above the Obergruppenführer's desk a portrait of Hitler, possibly chosen for its intimidatory effect, glared stonily across the room.

"You must understand, Obergruppenführer that I was married many years before the race laws were promulgated..."

"Yet you married a woman you knew to be a Jewess and to ensure your position in the SS, you altered her documentation to conceal her race." Heydrich's voice still had a dangerous edge to it.

"That's not the way it happened!" von Ingolstadt protested. "I met Greta in Poland just after the war and it was then that I had her documents altered." His mouth had become very dry. "There was not the emphasis on race then that there is now."

"And yet you still chose to conceal her true racial identity?"

Von Ingolstadt lifted his chin in a small gesture of defiance. The wound on his cheek was smarting but the blood had already begun to congeal.

"Greta's identity was changed, not because I was ashamed of her or what she stood for," he said, "but because we realised what it would be like for her to live in Germany, even then, as a Jew. I will submit my resignation from the SS with immediate effect, Obergruppenführer."

Heydrich walked round the desk once again and faced him. His heavy mouth was twisted and mocking, and his small close-set eyes were filled with malice.

"Do you really think the solution is that simple, Untersturmführer von Ingolstadt? You and your tainted family belong in concentration camps. Do you imagine for a moment that your daughter will retain her position? Or that your son will somehow find his way into the SS despite the information I have in my hands?"

The cold finality of Heydrich's words caused pressure like a vice grip to form across Matthias' chest. For the first time, he realised the full implication of what this disclosure would mean to them as a family. He had been into the camps and had seen the way in which Germany's Jews and criminal elements had been reduced to human offal. He had been left with a vivid memory of a stinking valley of human bones, devoid of dignity, vision or hope. Now he faced the possibility that he might move from the anguished position of perpetrator, to the place of recipient. He knew that for his family's sake, he must fight.

"What do you want from me?" he asked.

"Who did the documentation for you?"

"A government official in Poland. He worked for the Department of Births and Deaths; it was not difficult to have the changes made for a fee."

"It seems as you say, that it was a simple job. Your petty official simply altered a death certificate made out in another woman's name and placed it in your wife's file, giving her the identity of the dead Aryan."

"My wife's family were dead. We were leaving Poland for Germany; it seemed a harmless thing at the time, Obergruppenführer."

"A harmless thing!" Heydrich exploded. He stood in front of von Ingolstadt, his face so close that Matthias could feel the heat of his breath on his face. "You fool! You enter the ranks of the SS on falsified information and you say it's a harmless thing! What about your children? Were they ever part of this scheme of yours? You've contaminated their blood, injected them with filth and yet you say that what you've done is harmless!"

Heydrich's words were spewed out with such venom that von Ingolstadt flinched. In the back of his mind he remembered the things he had heard about Heydrich's own background. There had been court-cases in which Heydrich had countered allegations that he was of mixed blood. A man in his position as head of the German secret service had had little difficulty in fighting and winning such cases, but it was not quite so simple to quash the rumours that still persisted. Under the circumstances von Ingolstadt's thoughts afforded him little comfort.

"What I did was wrong, Obergruppenführer. There is nothing I can do to change the situation of my family now, but if there is anything that can be done to spare them the consequences..."

Heydrich's expression was scornful. He sat down and perused the file, speaking as though he had not even heard the plea.

"There was just one small discrepancy that came to light when we were investigating your son," he said, and his voice had reverted to its conversational tone. "Most people would have overlooked it, but I have built my career on such inconsistencies. Do you want to know what it was that tripped you up?" He looked up to receive von

Ingolstadt's answer, his sensual mouth parted in a smile. "We checked the bank records and an old account in your wife's name was marked 'deceased'. Naturally your friend would not have been able to cover all eventualities and I'm certain neither of you ever expected such a complete check on her past. My men are trained to be very thorough, Untersturmführer, but it may interest you to know that I had no idea at all that your wife was Jewish. That was simply a calculated guess."

"What are you going to do, Obergruppenführer?"

"That depends..." Heydrich toyed with the riding switch, his presence intentionally dominant. "There may be a way that would be beneficial to both of us."

Matthias von Ingolstadt waited. He was certain that whatever Lieutenant General Heydrich had in mind would be far more to his own advantage than it would be to von Ingolstadt's. The man had him over a barrel and he knew it.

"I believe you could become very useful to me if you are prepared to co-operate completely."

"You may depend on my loyalty of course, Obergruppenführer."

"I will require more than loyalty," Heydrich snapped. "What I want from you Untersturmführer is kadaver gehorsam, the compliance of a corpse, because that is what you are from this moment von Ingolstadt, a dead man! Should you dare to cross me or fail me in any way, not only will your children discover they are half-caste filth, but I will ensure that you and your family are discredited, ruined and ultimately destroyed. Do you understand?"

It was difficult to keep the bitterness from his voice, but von Ingolstadt answered quietly.

"Completely, Obergruppenführer."

Heydrich pushed an official form across the desk towards him. "I want the details of your wife's real background. Anything you are not sure of, I will expect you to find out by some means or another. These details will be handed to me personally, at the latest by this time next week. I will be in touch with you shortly, Untersturmführer; you may be assured of that!"

As Matthias von Ingolstadt left Heydrich's offices he began to shake uncontrollably. He had sold his soul and he wondered if the one who now possessed him was not the devil incarnate.

Chapter 45
Twice-Born

"The sages say that the Khufu Pyramid at Giza opens a pinprick of divine light within those on earth who seek it," Simon Magus said. "The gods are speaking. There is a piece missing and I must be patient. In time it will drop into place."

The men had gathered in the crypt by the Dead Sea in an effort to resolve the conundrum. They crouched on their haunches around a single light that burned in the stone stoup at the central point of the 'King's Chamber'. Uneasy shadows of heads and limbs loomed and shrank on the blackened walls.

"Similarly, the room beneath the temple of the Jews is a place of enlightenment," Marcus offered.

Simon nodded. "Because it is positioned directly beneath the Holy of Holies, it focuses the light of Lucifer into the Realm of the Dead through the nexus of the temple of YWHW, so undermining its power. Those priests, who have married their scriptures to the wisdom of the Egyptian and Babylonian sages, have infiltrated light through the Eye into the hidden place. Just as we know that the King's chamber of the pyramid of Khufu is empty, signifying Osiris' birth into the stars, we are also certain that, in the fullness of days, he will re-enter the world as the Sun King, bearing the full enlightenment of Horus. His life will mean the death forever of the Jewish God!"

What occurred to Simon Magus at that moment riveted him and came to assume a vital part of his hidden doctrine. But the thought did not stem from his own consciousness. He saw the pinprick of light from the Will of the Universe penetrate the circle of the subterranean edifice in Jerusalem and strike the very centre of the star of Shalem.

He looked around him at his disciples. "The hexagram tells us more than I have realised." He was silent for a moment, listening to the inner voice that directed his spirit. When he looked up it was with an expression of triumph. "When enlightenment comes to the human heart through the spiritual pyramid, there is an integration of the pyramid of darkness and that of light." He drew a diagram in the dust at his feet.

Marcus drew a sharp breath.

"The star of Shalem from the floor of the inner temple!"

"Exactly! This star designates the work of Lucifer, the light-bearer, in the life of the initiated. It draws his power into the heart of the disciple. The qualities of that god, his wisdom, his understanding of the secrets of this age, become an integral part of him who receives the light."

"In essence, he receives godhood."

"It is so. The Greeks speak of the Dioscuri, the Heavenly Twins known as Castor and Pollux. These gods were also known in Persian sun worship as the two torch-bearers. In Canaan, Shaher was the Light-Bearer represented by the morning star and his twin was Shalem, star of the evening."

"Born, were they not," said Demetrius in a moment of inspiration, "of the Great Mother, Asherah, in her world womb?"

"Helel, the Pit!" the Magus exclaimed. "The inner temple is that womb from which Shaher and Shalem are birthed. Shaher coveted the superior glory of the sun god and tried to wrest his throne from him. He was cast down to earth like a lightning bolt. I believe these two gods also find unity in the two triangles of the star. Their power lies in conjoining the heavens with Helel, the pit. The earth is held here," he pointed at the centre point of the twinned triangles. "Captured in limbo between heaven and hell!"

Simon gazed, in silent contemplation, at the flickering lamp then he spoke once more.

"The morning and evening star are, in fact, one," he said. "They are Venus seen in her two aspects. Shaher and Shalem are at once both Mother Goddess and Lucifer." He stood up in their midst and his face receded into darkness.

"The Khufu pyramid sends us a prophecy. There is a Coming One, of whom I am the forerunner, who will complete our mission and destroy the work of YHWH. When he is revealed, there will be an annunciation. A great star will be observed in the sky and the man, the final incarnation of Nimrod, will step into the Holy of Holies in the Jewish temple to declare his deity!"

There was a hiss of recognition from the assembly.

"The temple in Judaea is the key to history," the Magus said slowly. "I have never seen it so clearly before. Imminently, it will be destroyed, and at the end of the age, before the Coming One, it will be rebuilt once more. It is our task, I believe, to ensure that through many centuries the temple remains at the forefront of human consciousness."

"There are the Jews and the Jewish scriptures..." one of the men offered.

The Magus snorted. "In a short time, most of those who have knowledge of Shalem's temple will die. We are the new Jews! We have learned the rituals and rites of the inner temple. It is now incumbent upon us to harness this knowledge in memory of Solomon's Temple and create an overarching Order that will retain these secrets and convey them to the generations to come." His shadow menaced the hunched figures of his disciples. "This will be a Samaritan and Idumean Order, although outwardly rooted in Judaism. The Jewish priests of the inner temple use the story of Hiram, Father of Secrets and builder of the first temple, to perpetuate the memory of the death of Osiris and Nimrod. We will take their rites and rituals, born of the Jewish scriptures and project them into all the earth."

"How will this be done when we are so few?"

"Did the small band of Israelites who entered Egypt not grow in four hundred years to become a mighty army?" Simon Magus thundered.

The men fell silent. The Master had a way of looking across the centuries as though he considered himself immortal.

"Temples will be built throughout the world," he continued. "Places in which men will be initiated and nurtured to full maturity in a brotherhood such as our own. Ordinary mortals, such as those humble masons who built the mighty temple of Solomon, will band together across the ages."

Marcus looked at the Magus in awe.

"And their goal?" he asked.

"The temple. Always the temple. Lucifer, the light-giver has spoken, if he is to seize control of the world from the God of the Jews, the temple is the key."

On the following day the Magus opened the square hole in the apex of the vault so that sunlight cast a greater square onto the floor and sun rays formed an elongated pyramid. He realised at once that the ratio was wrong and he called for a screen to be placed in the subterranean room and trestles on which it could rest.

"It must be set at the same level as the King's Chamber within the Khufu pyramid," he said. "The proportions can be worked out."

That night, Simon calculated the geometry, which he had learned in Egypt to set an accurate position. From this time on, experiments were conducted daily. A second screen, covered in white cloth, was set at the same distance above the hole so that the objects pinned to the underside projected an inverted, life-sized image onto the screen below.

"Now we will attempt to capture that which the light has revealed," the Magus said. But their efforts proved hopeless and, after several days of experimenting, a general sense of frustration brought the proceedings to a halt. None of the objects would project onto the silver saturated linen in the dark room.

That night sleep evaded the Magus and he rose before dawn and walked down to the water's edge. The quiet lapping of the sea soothed him and he focussed his thoughts on the rising sun. At once he was back between the paws of the sphinx surrounded by the shrouded priests of the Great White Brotherhood. In his mind he heard the words of the one who had given him the glass.

"If you are chosen, the gods will reveal its properties." He took the pouch from the leather thong around his neck and cupped the lens in his hand. Light glanced off the delicate glass. He knew that within every eye there was a natural lens, which received and focussed the light.

The Magus crouched on the beach and allowed the light of the sun to centre through the glass onto a single spot. Although the lens-makers of the ancients had taken their secrets with them to the grave, their spirits lingered, speaking wisdom into the hearts of men.

He observed how the pinpoint of light sharpened on the white pebble. So would the return of Osiris be, he thought. His presence would burn into the heart of the Holy Place in Jerusalem's temple, uniting forever the hidden with the revealed, and the God of Abraham, Isaac and Jacob would be eternally crushed.

This was the word of the ancients. How much had the lost priesthood discovered, he wondered? Wisdom existed unchanged; the gods did not forget and it was they who projected knowledge into the mind of the illuminated. If he set the lens of the Eye of Horus in its place at the apex of the pyramid, it would draw light into the heart of darkness and create a god. It was the whisper of the spirits.

Simon Magus stood quietly to his feet but with none of the jubilation of the preceding moment of enlightenment. This time he was possessed with a quiet determination. He had no doubt that he was destined to make an image. The stage was set, the ingredients were gathered. But, as yet, he had little idea of the purpose to which he was called.

Chapter 46
Twice-Born

Hans said we must travel on the slow trains," Gabriele said. "Passes aren't required at the ticket office and they're checked far less frequently than on the express trains or the specials. Often they just ask for identity cards."

On the train out of Berlin, it seemed that Michael and Gabriele Hoch had eyes only for one another. Their papers indicated that their marriage had taken place only a week before and Michael had been issued with a leave pass from the university under his new surname.

"So, Gabriele Hoch, it's not often the husband assumes his wife's name," he smiled as he took her hand. "Thank you for doing this for me."

"I could not have allowed you to go alone."

The train steamed its way out of Berlin past the last factory buildings blackened by smoke, through the remnant of shabby suburban dwellings, and into the country. Winter was approaching and the broad sweep of ground in the early morning sun was pearly with frost. Dairy cows grazed in lush grass, unperturbed by the noise of the passing locomotive and fields lay fallow after the harvest. Even nature was regimented in Germany, Michael thought, glancing out at the precise geometric patterns of field and forest. Yet, for all the precision and discipline of the land, there lay a savagery just below the surface that would not submit. Perhaps it was precisely the recognition of that wild element, which supported the Prussian desire for order.

Michael held Gabriele close. He was desperately aware that he was about to lose her. For all his hatred of Nazism, it could not extend to Germany. The land and its people had given him life and, however briefly, it had given him Gabriele.

The first check of their passes was just before Leipzig. A German sergeant rapped on the door and slid it open without more than a moment's pause.

"Identity cards, bitte."

Gabriele rummaged in her handbag and produced them with her sweetest smile. He perused them without comment, passed them back and left the compartment, sliding the door shut behind him.

Michael felt himself sweating. Each encounter was a test of the skills of Gabriele's forger, and although the documents looked authentic enough, there was no knowing whether there was anything which might give the game away. Again he was reminded of how dangerous this illicit relationship was to Gabriele and marvelled at her courage. She smiled at him.

"First hurdle successfully overcome," she remarked. "Let's see how we go on the next one."

In Leipzig they left the train, bought some bread and sausage from a grocer and ate it in a park near the station. The train for Stuttgart left at 2.00pm and Gabriele purchased their tickets while Michael carried the suitcases down to the platform. The train was already preparing to leave when she came running towards him, clutching her hat with one gloved hand.

"Is everything alright?"

"I have the tickets," she said. "There were men in SS uniform making random checks on passes at the ticket office. Someone said they were Gestapo because they had the SD sleeve-patch in place of the normal SS insignia. I waited as long as I could in the hope they would leave."

"Did they see our documents?"

She shook her head. "In the end they passed me by. But there are two booked on the train with us. They bought their tickets just after I did."

"We could take the next train," he suggested.

"No, it's fine. We're on honeymoon, remember? There's no reason for them to imagine that we're anything other than we appear to be."

Michael nodded and picked up the two ersatz leather suitcases, hoisting them up into the train ahead of him. He turned and took Gabriele's hand pulling her up after him. The sound of pounding feet caused him to look back. The two Gestapo officials were running down the platform and for a moment Michael froze. The final whistle blew and the first shudder of movement rattled life through the coaches as the two men leapt onto the train a coach away and their laughter could be heard down the corridor as they joked about their near miss.

"Come on," Michael said, gripping Gabriele by the elbow, "this is our compartment."

The train was beginning to move, the wheels squealing as they gained traction on the lines. Michael went back for their luggage, lifting it into the rack over their heads, and slid the door shut behind them. They looked at one another wordlessly; it would be a long journey across Germany with the Gestapo for neighbours.

Chapter 47
Twice-Born

It was the night of the watch before the onset of Passover, a night when men were expected to remain awake and see in the dawn of the feast, but the events of the evening had wearied the disciples leaving them troubled. Andrew's finely pitched voice led them in the *hillel*, as they toiled up the path from the Kidron Valley to the grove of gnarled and twisted olive trees, known as the Garden of Gethsemane, garden of the oil press.

"The Lord is on my side; I will not fear; what can man do unto me?
The stone which the builders refused is become the head stone of the corner.
This is the Lord's doing and it is marvellous in our eyes.
This is the day that the Lord hath made let us rejoice and be glad in it.
Blessed is he that cometh in the name of the Lord... [10]

But even the singing of the psalm failed to dispel their heaviness of spirit.

The night was clear and pierced by a myriad stars; a gentle breeze fanned their faces but the mood was sombre and, as Peter walked ahead of Jesus on the path, he was consumed by the turbulence of his thoughts. Judas was the betrayer. Jesus had spoken to John and himself over supper. As always, John had said very little and it was Peter who swore he would follow Jesus to the death. The Master's words still rang in his ears.

"Satan will attempt to sift you like wheat, Peter, but I have prayed for you. You will deny me three times before the cock crows."

Jesus was wrong. There was no doubt in Peter's mind that he was fully prepared for what was to come. He would stand and defend his Master even if all the other disciples were to flee in terror. The short sword worn by most men was a practical tool rather than a weapon but Peter had girded himself for a fight.

---

[10] Psalm 118

In reaching the garden the disciples were uneasy. They gathered together in the grove, their feet shuffling in the dust, unsure what was expected of them. The silence was complete; not even the leaves stirred now that the wind had dropped. In all the years of following the Master they had experienced security but now all were gripped by the same premonition of disaster. The shepherd was soon to be struck and the sheep would scatter.

"You men stay here," Jesus said. "Peter, will you and the sons of Zebedee come and pray with me over on the other side?"

The others spread their garments out on the thin grass beneath the trees and were soon asleep.

There is no place of greater loneliness than sorrow. Peter, James and John sensed the torture of Jesus' soul but were helpless to share in it. How could they pray for something so completely beyond their ability to comprehend?

"You watch with me," Jesus said. "I will pray alone."

He walked away into the darkness grappling with what was to come. There was humiliation before men that must be faced, but the Lord was unafraid of humiliation. Neither, though he knew what lay ahead, was he afraid of the whip and the cross, which would tear his body with physical agony. Multitudes before him had suffered agonising death and countless numbers that followed, many even in his name, would die in unbearable agony over centuries to come.

There was a greater darkness than the cross that lay ahead, and it was for this suffering that Jesus, Messiah to the Jews, bowed his face to the dust in torment in Gethsemane and sweated blood as he was broken in spirit and soul; like the olives, crushed almost to the point of death.

Twice he returned to the three disciples and found them sleeping.

"The spirit is willing," Jesus said, "but the flesh is weak." He spoke for himself as well as for them. To win this battle, the Son of Man had to be willing to drink the cup that was being offered to him. Again, he returned to wrestle in prayer alone.

Was it possible in human form to carry the burden ahead? Could he alone, in the weakness of his flesh, bear that agony?

"If it is possible, Father, let this cup pass from me! If is it possible..."

No other way. Everything in him fought against what lay ahead. Humanity's filth to be laid on one who had never known sin. Could he bear it? Would he endure without the power of God's Spirit to sustain him?

"Not my will, Father, but yours!"

There was the breakthrough; the glimmer of willingness. The force of his human will broke as he subjected it to the one who proffered the cup. "Nevertheless, not my will Father, but yours be done."

The battle was over and victory was at hand. Victory in death and victory over death was begun at Gethsemane. Calvary lay ahead.

Jesus walked shakily back to the three and shook James by the shoulder, smiling down at him in the darkness.

"Are you still sleeping and taking your rest?" he asked. "The hour is at hand."

From Kidron Valley came a sound that set a chill into the heart of the waking disciples: the tramp of marching feet, a rattle of stones, and the sound of voices. They sat up, hearing the muted calls of alarm from the other group of disciples.

"Rise, let us be going," Jesus said. "My betrayer is at hand." And he strode out to meet them with his disciples at his heels.

Judas was at the head of the heavily armed Temple Guard that had come out to make the arrest.

"It's a dark night. How will the soldiers know whom to apprehend?" the high priest had asked before they set off.

"I will kiss in greeting the one you want," Judas had told them. "When I do that, your men can seize and take him."

The glow of many flaming torches illuminated the faces of the guard and cast eerie shadows beyond the circle of light. Judas stepped out from the crowd and walked over to his Master.

"Rabbi, rabbi!" he said, grasping him by the shoulders - the touch of a comrade.

"Do you betray me with a kiss, Judas?" Jesus asked quietly and then turned to the soldiers. "Whom do you seek?"

"Jesus of Nazareth."

"I am he."

As they moved in to take the Master, Peter felt the old blinding rage rise within him. He could not allow this to happen! If the others showed themselves cowards he, at least, was prepared to die fighting. He struck a blow at Malchus, Caiaphas' servant, taking off his ear.

"Peter! Put your sword away!" Jesus commanded. "Shall I not drink the cup that my Father has given me?"

Malchus had fallen to his knees wailing and clutching at his head with both hands feeling the warm blood gush between his fingers. Jesus reached forward, touching him so that instantly the flow of blood was staunched and the gaping wound closed. Peter drew back into the darkness, stung by the rebuke of his Master. Did he not care that he had sought to protect him? Malchus, the enemy, had received healing he had not asked for, while Peter felt that he had received the sword blow. Still, although the others scattered in the darkness, he followed at a distance as the men made their way down the valley, holding their torches and lanterns high to light the pathway. John too, accompanied Jesus. He was well-known to the high priest and was unlikely to be ill-received. Malchus though, would be after Peter's blood and a word from him to Caiaphas could constitute his death warrant. He would have to be cautious.

It was the dead of night when they entered Jerusalem and the temple guard took the prisoner straight to the house of Annas, father-in-law of Caiaphas, the high priest. John entered the courtyard at Jesus' side but Peter remained outside the gate until, at a quiet word from John, a servant girl let him in. There was a chill in the air and someone had kindled a fire on the flagstones. Peter was among those drawn to the warmth. The young woman left the gate and rubbed her hands together over the flames.

"It's a cold night," she commented and, nodding her head in the direction of the prisoner: "You're one of his disciples, are you not?"

"I am not!" Peter said. He gazed at the fire, hoping that no one would detect the strong beating of his heart against his rib cage. The place was teeming with soldiers, if anyone should positively identify him as the one who had attacked Malchus there would be no escape.

Attention was drawn away from Peter as Annas arrived for the interrogation. Although Valerius Gratus, Pontius Pilate's predecessor had removed him from office, Annas was still a powerful influence in Jerusalem and many regarded him as the true high priest. Standing before Jesus, he looked him up and down posing questions in a tone that was imperious.

"Tell me about this doctrine of yours," he demanded. "And your disciples. Who are they?"

"Why?" Jesus asked. "I have taught openly in the synagogues and the temple, and I have said nothing in secret. Ask the Jews who have heard me. They know what I have said."

An officer who was standing by turned and slapped him sharply across the face.

"Is that how you answer the high priest?"

A thin trickle of blood flowed from the corner of Jesus' mouth but with his hands bound he was powerless to wipe it away.

"If I have spoken evil, tell me. But if I have spoken correctly, why do you strike me?"

Annas shrugged irritably and turned to the guard. "Let Caiaphas examine him!"

The two residences shared a common courtyard and Jesus was taken into the house to be interrogated by Annas' son-in-law. Those gathered around the fire spoke among themselves about the events of the night and their glances fell repeatedly on Peter.

"The people were behind him. You heard the cries of Messiah when he rode into the city. Insurrection was in the air."

"He was asking for trouble. It was only a matter of time before he attempted to seize power."

"They should have arrested his followers. Trouble-makers, all of them!"

"I am certain you are one of them." The man who offered the observation was one who shifted incessantly as though his robes caused him discomfort. He gave a brief shrug of one shoulder and jutted his chin spasmodically as he glanced around at the group, pleased with his own boldness.

Peter's voice was petulant. "I've told you, I don't know the man."

Two soldiers pushed Jesus roughly back into the courtyard, again diverting the attention of Peter's companions.

John, who had waited at the door, spoke a few words to Jesus and he answered quietly.

A servant of Caiaphas, a relative of Malchus whom Peter had attacked with the sword, joined the men around the fire.

"He's going to the Sanhedrin," he said importantly. "They'll have him killed for sure."

Peter's tone was sharp. "Why?" he asked. "What has he done to deserve death?"

The man looked across at Peter with interest. "By your accent, you're a Galilean. You must be one of them!" He nodded in the direction of John and the prisoner. "In fact, I saw you in the garden with him," he said, looking at him more closely across the flames. "I'm certain I did."

Simon Peter felt fear engulf him and he cursed volubly.

"I tell you, I don't know him."

At that instant, from somewhere nearby, a cock crowed. Peter looked up. The prisoner was standing on the other side of the courtyard, facing the little group that was huddled about the fire. Although Jesus' face was in partial shadow, Peter knew his Master's gaze rested upon him. Instantly, Peter recalled an occurrence on the road to Bethany several days before.

"I will be rejected by the chief priests and elders," Jesus had told the disciples. "I will suffer many things and be killed."

Peter had taken the Master aside and rebuked him.

"Then, Lord, we must not go into Jerusalem," he said. "There is no need for you to endanger yourself."

"Get behind me, Satan!" Jesus said sharply. "You have no stomach for the things of God; you are seeking the way of men."

Peter had retreated stung, crestfallen and confused.

Now there was a glimmer of understanding. Jesus had chosen this death knowing it to be the will of the Father. Peter had tried to prevent him then, and now, this night, a second time. He had compounded his sin by denying his Lord, just as Jesus had said he would. There could be no turning back to undo what he had done. Tears stung his eyes as he left the warmth of the fire. He walked out of the gate into the night and wept bitterly.

Back in the courtyard of the high priest's house, John watched in mute shock as his Master was systematically beaten by the soldiers. One of them put a blindfold over his eyes and the taunts and raucous laughter rang out as blow upon blow struck his face.

"Prophecy!" they shouted, "tell us who it is that hits you?"

In all this, as a sheep before his shearers is dumb, Jesus remained silent.

Through her retinue of informers, Herodias was kept fully informed of the events as they unfolded. She and Herod were already in Jerusalem on the night of the arrest of Jesus the Nazarene. One of his own men, they were told, had betrayed him to the leaders but the prisoner refused to speak and remained unbowed in the face of the witnesses brought against him.

"Were they credible?" Herodias demanded.

"They brought lies and distortions," the informer said. "They contradicted one another on almost every point. When at last the Nazarene did speak, he convicted himself."

Herodias smiled her satisfaction. "Tell me!"

"Caiaphas the high priest asked whether he was Messiah, the Son of the Blessed. He replied, 'I am. And ye shall see the Son of man sitting on the right hand of power and coming in the clouds of heaven.'"

Herodias' features contorted with anger. "So, what was the response of Caiaphas?"

"He tore his robe, my Lady, and convicted the Nazarene of blasphemy. Day was beginning to break when the prisoner spoke so the High Priest was able to pass the sentence immediately in accordance with the Law."

"Will they kill him?" she asked eagerly.

"He is condemned to die."

Herodias gleefully relayed what she had heard to Herod.

"The Sanhedrin has lost its power to apply the death sentence in Judaea," Herod said. "In the past he would have been stoned, but

Roman law won't allow it. Having found him guilty, they will have to take him before Pontius Pilot. But it's generally a formality. If Caiaphas has found him guilty under Jewish law, Pilot will ratify their decision." He sighed and looked away. "Personally, it doesn't sound to me as though he is deserving of death."

Herodias hissed her contempt and left the room.

Chapter 48
Twice-Born

Based on his study of the Templars, Teutonic Knights and Jesuits, it had been Heinrich Himmler's early goal to make the SS a similar Order. From men of pure Aryan blood, bound by an oath of absolute loyalty to their leader, a new order would arise, and ultimately Homo Noeticus, new man. His men rose through the ranks of the SS by a series of initiations and, at the apex of the organisation, were his twelve top Lieutenants-General strong in the esoteric powers of the pagan religion Himmler sought to revive.

Himmler had learned the art of controlled speech and he used it to confirm other people's outward impression of himself. Although he had undoubtedly grown in strength and power in the years since he had taken control of the SS, nervous energy still took its unrelenting toll on his stomach and the pain often brought him close to fainting. He was a man of masks, a porcelain face with empty eyes, yet behind the security of the image, he remained plagued by the interminable self-doubts he would never learn to conquer.

"Before 1188 the Prieuré de Sion and the Templars shared a Grand Master." Heinrich Himmler smiled thinly. "The inquisition of the Templars produced some interesting revelations. We're all familiar with what was said regarding their initiation rites. It's certain that they renounced their belief in Christ in a conventional sense and many confessed to rituals that involved the trampling and desecrating of the cross." He held up a hand for silence. "I know you all know a lot about the Templars," he said, acknowledging the good-natured banter that followed his remarks, "but how many of you know about a head that was central to Templar worship?"

"A skull or an effigy of some sort?" Gottlob Berger asked.

Himmler shook his head. "A bearded head, which was said to impart power to those who came into contact with it: a head that spoke to them."

Wolff nodded. "I've heard of it," he said. "It had a name…"

"Baphomet," Himmler confirmed. "It could have come from a corruption of the Arabic, 'abufihamet', which means the father of all wisdom. The same name is often given to the goat's head used in Masonic rites and Satanism."

"It may not have been an actual head," Berger suggested.

"We considered that, but the evidence had substance to it."

There was a murmur of interest from the men. There were seated at the great Arthurian table in the Obergruppenführersaal, the Hall of Supreme Generals in the newly constructed north tower of Wewelsburg Castle. Set into the floor beneath the table was the mosaic of the Black Sun, symbolic of Odin.

"All the Grand Masters of the Prieuré de Sion take the name of Jean, or Jeanne in the case of a woman, but the first Grand Master, Jean de Gisors, was known as Jean II. Assuming there was a connection between the two, how many Johns do we know who have lost their head?"

Reinhard Heydrich grinned facetiously. "What offers on John the Baptist?"

"That's not so unlikely," Gottlob Berger cut in. "Didn't some sort of cult develop after his death, claiming him to be the real Messiah?"

"What happened to the Baptist's head?"

"I checked it out," Himmler replied. "We know that Herodias was given the head on a platter by her daughter and John's disciples buried the body." Himmler looked around with an expression of pleasure as he prepared to make his climactic exposure. "What history tells us is that Herod Antipas was banished and his wife went with him. They went to the Languedoc region of France, a region which was to become Cathar and Templar territory!"

"With a head under their arm?" Reinhard Heydrich suggested politely.

There was a guffaw from the men. "And I suppose you're going to tell us that it was kept in a perfect state of preservation, if a little cut off." Heydrich was leaning back in his seat and he responded to the laughter with a boyish grin.

"You say that the head the Templars worshipped was able to

communicate in some way," Werner Lorenz cut in. "Surely that couldn't have been the Baptist's head?"

Himmler reacted defensively. Heydrich was the joker of the twelve but his attitude always subtly undermined the Reichsführer's authority and standing with his men in a way difficult to pinpoint or to counter.

"I am certain there were adepts attached to Herod's court with the arcane power to effect something of that sort."

Heydrich threw back his head and hooted. "You're telling me the Herods went across Europe with some sort of damned flesh and blood talking head? And I suppose they wrapped it in a blanket and passed it off as a baby!"

His remarks were treated to a roar of approval from the men and Himmler fought to retain his dignity.

"I'm saying," he said stiffly, "that the Templars worshipped a head that could have been that of John the Baptist. There was definitely some sort of convergence of cults in the South of France. The Magdalene was said to have gone there, as well as Joseph of Arimathea and many sites are dedicated to the worship of the Baptist."

"Who's the present Grand Master of the Prieuré?" Gottlob Berger asked, his fascination with the subject overcoming amusement.

"We're not sure. There are men working on it," Karl Wolff said briefly.

"The Languedoc was not part of present day France," Himmler continued. "Their education was at a higher level than the rest of Europe. Poetry and philosophy flourished. Many studied Hebrew and Arabic and there were schools devoted to the study of Cabala."

Again there was a buzz of interest from the Obergruppenführer. From the research of the Ahnenerbe, Cabala was perceived as the primary source of power of such orders as the Prieuré de Sion and the Knights Templar but also, and far more significant, of the World Revolutionary Movement spearheaded by the Jews. As such, Himmler had conducted his own investigation and personal study of Cabala and introduced it to his inner circle.

"What was the form of government in the region?" someone asked.

"It was an independent principality," Himmler said, "ruled mainly by the nobility.

"And the Church?"

"It was not a Roman Catholic stronghold."

"The crusade was launched against the region because of their Cathar beliefs?"

Himmler nodded his agreement. "The Languedoc had become a threat to the authority of Rome. The Cathar heresy was beginning to have an effect on other parts of Europe, in particular Flanders, the Champagne region of France and in certain areas here in Germany."

"But they were Christianised Gnostics?"

"The Cathars were never a cohesive body with a unified belief system," Himmler explained. He was in his element in this form of lecture in which the frustrated schoolmaster, so much part of his nature, was able to come to the fore. "It was nothing like Catholicism with a codified theology and doctrine. In fact this heresy consisted of a vast number of diverse sects loosely held together by some common principles. But there does seem to have been a common Judaic Christian basis to their beliefs."

"And the Cathars were keepers of the Grail," Heydrich offered. Despite himself, he had become fascinated by the discussion. "I remember reading about the siege of Montségur. They smuggled something out of the stronghold before it fell to the crusaders."

Himmler nodded. "It was either an object of veneration or it had something to do with the source of their power," he confirmed. "Rome launched a crusade against the Languedoc that ultimately reduced the country to rubble. Montségur was the last Cathar stronghold and it had been besieged for ten months when a deal was struck with their besiegers. Those who remained in the castle were granted lenient terms. The fighting men were to be pardoned and permitted to leave with their arms and baggage, and the parfaits, provided they renounced their heresies and confessed their sins to the inquisition would have received only light penances. They were granted two weeks to consider the terms." Himmler looked meaningfully at his men. "A festival was held in the castle on March 14th which coincided with Easter and also, more significantly, the spring equinox. On the 16th four parfaits descended the western cliff face of the mountain and escaped carrying with them the Cathar treasure. It was a precipitous and dangerous descent, especially at night."

"They couldn't have been carrying much in that case," Lorenz commented.

"That's right." Light glanced off the circular lenses of Heinrich Himmler's spectacles. "It's my contention that they were carrying a head," he said. "The head of John the Baptist."

Chapter 49
Twice-Born

Without doubt the lens made a difference, but once again the results were disappointing. After several days of exposure an image was achieved that stabilized when immersed in urine and could be brought out into the sunlight without further deterioration. But the result was so obscure as to be worthless.

"It is like a stain on the surface of the fabric," Marcus observed, "but there is no definition."

"There is not enough light," Simon said. "That which is projected off the image has to be strong enough to scorch the cloth. The dark room needs to be placed above the ground."

The men looked at the Master in dismay.

"It will require the building of a second room," he said, "but now that we have greater understanding of the task, it can be made smaller than the King's Chamber. The screen will be set in such a manner as to gain most advantage from the sun."

"An upright screen?" Lucius asked. "In which case we will be able to capture the image of heavier objects, perhaps even the image of our own faces?"

"If you are prepared to stand immobile for three or four days in the heat of the day," Marcus observed, amid general laughter.

"Never mind, Lucius, in death we will immortalise you!" Thaddeus said. His words resonated in the mind of Simon Magus and the seed of an idea was planted in fertile soil.

A smaller room was built above ground, its height and width only a cubit more than the height of an average man. Again they painted it out with bitumen, which was endemic to the region. This time, Simon Magus included pin holes on three sides of the building, which could be blocked off or opened at will in order to make full use of both summer and winter sunlight.

Immediately, the new structure made an impact on the experiments and within days far clearer images were being recorded on the linen cloths. It was noted with interest that dark was recorded as light and light as dark, while lettering was not only inverted but also mirrored by the action of sunlight through the lens.

"It is the action of the pyramid," Simon Magus explained. The lens in the Eye of Horus takes light in a straight line from the top point of the object projecting it the bottom point of the image…"

"And from the lowest point of the object to the highest point of the image," Marcus said, grasping the concept immediately. "So it creates a dual pyramid, one of light, one of darkness!"

The Magus smiled. "When we view Khufu, Khafre and Menkaure[11] we see only pyramids of darkness," he said. "We fail to see the infinite pyramid of light, which focuses upon that Eye. Seen together through the eye of understanding, the two pyramids represent the duality of God; his nature of good and evil."

Thaddeus' words to Lucius developed the germ of an idea in the mind of Simon the Magus: a desire to create an image of the head of the Baptist on cloth. There was only one reservation. Three days or more of exposure to the full desert sun on the embalmed head might well bring about massive deterioration. Was it worth the risk? Herodias would certainly not think so, yet if it was ordained by the gods it could be done. It would create an icon second only to the head itself. The idea haunted him and he could not let it go.

Now that the wraps were off, Simon Magus did not hesitate to openly use blackmail to milk Shaphan the priest of all that he knew.

There were regular trips into the subterranean temple to study the symbols inscribed on every surface and to learn the religious rites and rituals practiced there. The essence of Cabala was in the handing down by tradition and although he could not be brought into the Brotherhood, Shaphan guided the Magus through the purification rites and the three levels of initiation. He disclosed the names contained in the Tetragrammaton, the four consonants of the ancient Hebrew word for God, too sacred to be spoken. By arranging the four letters of the name, the priest taught him the manifestation of the seventy-two powers of the Great Name and its use as a talisman against evil spirits. There

---

[11] Giza Pyramids

was a disc, he claimed, inscribed with certain symbols which, hung around the neck before sunrise on the first day of the week, the day when the light of God was shed forth over the earth, would render the wearer invisible.

He showed him the ten Sephirot of the Tree of Life, connected by paths, which formed triangles, each having particular significance. At the zenith lay the crown, while in the lowest Sephirah at the foot of the tree, was the kingdom represented by David.

"In this tree, the whole essence of Judaism is captured. The created order is entrusted to our stewardship so that we may raise it to the Divine. In this way, we may place the crown upon him to whom it belongs and make the earth his kingdom."

"Messiah."

Shaphan nodded. "In ancient times, there were those in Aryama[12] who taught that all wisdom emanated from a Supreme Being – a Being of light who desired that a group of perfected men and women carry out the organisation and direction of the world under his control," Shaphan said. "These adepts of the fourth degree of initiation, who are able to communicate with the White Brotherhood, are known as the Roshaniya, the illuminated ones or Illuminati."

Simon Magus nodded and waited for the priest to continue.

"When the first temple was built, Hiram of Tyre initiated certain members of the priesthood into the tenets of the Roshaniya and, under guidance of the White Brotherhood, these men developed the Zohar[13]."

"A perversion of the scriptures given by the God of Abraham, Isaac and Jacob to the Jewish people," the Magus commented sardonically.

"Not a perversion," Shaphan protested. "They were granted illumination into the mystical depths of the scriptures."

"But not the way they were intended to be read!"

"The Tanakh was given to the uninitiated, men who followed

---

[12] Afghanistan/Iran
[13] Zohar - the principal source of Cabala, a mystical commentary on the Pentateuch, the first five books of the Old Testament, put into writing between 2nd and 13th century but possibly conceived long before.

the letter of the Law blindly. There are few mature minds in the world, which can read and interpret the things of God."

"And doubtless, you are one of those enlightened minds!"

His sarcasm was not lost on Shaphan and his face coloured. "I am, like you, Simon Magus, not one of those to whom the things of the senses appeals. Unlike the Gentiles that make sacrifice on the altar facing a stone deity, which can neither see nor speak, I believe I am able to discern spiritual truth."

"So, you are one of the Illuminated who communicates directly with the gods! What then is your goal?"

The priest was enthusiastic. "By a selective initiation into the hidden doctrine, it is possible to bring about conformity in the member. Judaea is destined to become the greatest and most powerful nation on earth through the Zohar, not by conquest with the sword but by conquest of the mind and the spirit."

"Will the power of the Jewish spirit lift the bondage of the Romans?"

"The Romans are a decaying nation. The star of the Jews is in the ascendancy. Rome will not be allowed to prevail over us forever. Messiah will come and his will be the eternal crown."

"Man's desire to be part of an elect is intoxicating," the Magus said thoughtfully. "It is true that in any study of the Mysteries those who do not reach the higher levels become part of the enslaved. The Mysteries therefore become a dominant tool by which to control the masses."

"Symbolically, of course, Lucifer is the snake or dragon, both of which symbolise wisdom," Shaphan said. "The power of thought is Lucifer's gift to mankind."

"While the veneration of wisdom is Satan worship in its purest form."

Where he differed from Shaphan was in the priest's inability to see the application of Cabala beyond the land of Judaea. Simon was not a Jew, except in name only when it pleased him, but he saw the power of Cabala and perceived with burgeoning excitement, its greater potential beyond the narrow confines of the Holy Land.

The Magus was well aware that when a tribal group embraced

the Mysteries, all adults became involved, separated by gender but generally male dominated. Its most potent device was initiation, or the rite of passage and its secrets formed a lasting bond of kinship.

While the initiate, or neophyte, was planted anew or reborn into the Mysteries, higher initiation was a promotion inspiring loyalty. It was the reward of the inner circles for ambitious men who could be entrusted with secrets. The possibilities of ensnarement and control were dizzying; properly handled, men could be enslaved, individual countries captured and their societies remoulded.

Little by little, Simon Magus was shaping the Order on which the new brotherhood of man would be based.

"You must see yourselves as stonemasons under a Grand Master," he told his disciples. "The building you are creating is a mighty edifice made of men. One stone must be built on another in a series of initiations that will cause a man to strive for perfect enlightenment. The true knowledge of god. Only when they attain the highest level are they to discover whom it is they serve."

"Satan, the god of this earth!"

"By which time they will be fully enslaved and the truth will no longer be of any importance."

Simon Magus determined to squeeze everything from Shaphan the priest and when he was no longer useful, he would spit him out.

It was therefore just before the Passover that the Magus met with a Zealot by the name of Bar Abbas and paid him a sum of money.

"Kill the priest in the market place," he told him. "In a crowd. A knife between the ribs."

Chapter 50
Twice-Born

It was the third day of meetings with his Obergruppenführer at Wewelsburg and Himmler was set to conclude with the climax of his revelations. Above them in Wewelsburg's great hall, the eight-sided chandelier formed a sympathetic echo to the black sun mosaic at their feet. He glanced down at some hand-written notes.

"What I have here was taken down during interrogation of several top-ranking Freemasonry members," he said. "Apparently there is some sort of connection between the Jewish tribe of Benjamin and the line of Mérovée, the first king of the Merovingian line."

Himmler's face was pale and his skin appeared clammy under the artificial light. Only he was fully aware of the enormity of the revelation that he was to make to his Lieutenants-General. But there was still some groundwork to be covered.

He looked up briefly. "Firstly, it's important to note that Jerusalem was part of the inheritance of the tribe of Benjamin," he said.

"So, if there was a union, the Merovingian Kings would have believed in some sort of divine right to the city of Jerusalem!"

"And in some way to its throne," Himmler concurred. "But although the first king of Israel was Saul of the tribe of Benjamin, the Benjamites had no direct right to the throne – the Davidic line arose from the tribe of Judah." It was obvious by his expression that even the subject of Jewish history was distasteful to the Reichsführer. "I have a theory as to how the alliance of David's line to the tribe of Benjamin and the Merovingian kings came about."

This time, even Heydrich remained silent and all looked to Himmler to provide the answer.

"The Magdalene cult." Himmler said. "Dagobert's first marriage to Mathilde, a Celtic princess, ended when she died giving birth to a third daughter. A second dynastic marriage was arranged for him by Wilfrid, bishop of York. Giselle was daughter to the Count of Razès and niece of the king of the Visigoths.

"There's no doubt that Dagobert's English bishop had more in mind than a convenient match for the young man. At the very least, the Catholic Church intended to make gains through his extended empire once he regained his throne." He looked at his men with a vestige of a smile. "You will be interested to know that this royal marriage was celebrated at Rhédae, modern day Rennes-le-Château."

There was a murmur from the men around the table.

"It has been suggested that the Magdalene brought with her the progeny of Jesus when she landed in the Languedoc region of France. If the Visigoth princess, Giselle of Razès, who married Dagobert II was a direct descendent of Jesus through the Magdalene we have the link that gives the Merovingian line their right of inheritance and their right of rule."

"Which would explain why Godfroi de Bouillon was painted by Claude Vignon with a crown of thorns around his head!" Karl Wolff said.

There was an immediate buzz of excitement from the Lieutenants-General.

Under Otto Rahn, the Ahnenerbe had conducted extensive research into the history and the sacred geography of the Languedoc. The Templar treasures were said to have been buried there, and the finds of Bérenger Saunière, a village priest in the area in the 1880's had aroused endless speculation.

"I have given you a long history lesson," Heinrich Himmler said and added with an uncustomary touch of humour, "but even Reinhard Heydrich has behaved himself quite well."

There was a burst of laughter from the men somewhat louder than the little joke deserved and the Reichsführer looked gratified.

"Just permit me to complete the lecture if you will, before I come to the main purpose of this meeting.

"In 674, with the support of his mother and Amatus, bishop of Sion in Switzerland, Dagobert was restored to the throne of Austrasie. Two years later a son, Sigisbert IV, was born to the king.

"Dagobert II failed to fulfil the expectations of bishop Wilfrid of York and the Roman Catholic Church was given no room for expansion under his reign. Dagobert, whose territory now included large parts of the Languedoc, seems to have absorbed the Gnostic beliefs of the Visigoths. In the process he made some powerful enemies and on 23rd December, 679 he was assassinated during a hunt and his murderers attempted to exterminate the rest of the family. Sigisbert survived and was taken into hiding, possibly to his mother's seat, Rennes-le-Chateau. The day of his murder coincided with the feast day of the tribe of Benjamin. Nothing, as you will see, is without its Jewish connection!"

Himmler stood up restlessly and walked to one of the tall arched windows that regularly punctuated the walls. He turned to face them.

"You will appreciate, gentlemen that the Order we are fighting is ancient, well-established, and has roots in every area of society. Coming into the fray in the twentieth century sets us at an immediate disadvantage. No one has yet succeeded in untangling the web that has been woven over hundreds of years. But, although we cannot fight this battle by conventional means, I believe there is a way."

Heinrich Himmler walked back to the table, removed his glasses and massaged his face with both hands. Without his spectacles, his eyes appeared vague and incomplete.

"We are already engaged in a war with the Jews, and in particular with Jewish Freemasonry and its satellite, Communism. As I see it, it will be necessary to engage them on two fronts if we are to win. Firstly, we will have to try our utmost to wipe every Jew from off the face of the earth to prevent the ultimate annihilation of the German race. Secondly, we have to recognise that it may be impossible to succeed in total extermination; therefore we have to outwit them at their own game. We will engage them on both fronts simultaneously. I have spent hours during the night in meditation and an idea has occurred to me that is so audacious…" His voice trailed off and he shook his head.

There was something in his attitude that fully gripped the attention of the twelve men and they waited expectantly.

"We know from the Protocols that they intend to introduce a world leader and I have no doubt they will attempt to legitimise him through the Merovingian claim to the throne of France first, and then Jerusalem. We can expect that this leader will claim to be, as the Protocols suggest, of the 'Seed of David'; a man who will fulfil the

Jewish expectation of Messiah while satisfying the Christian church that he is the second incarnation of the Christ."

"Would the Jews be likely to accept the legitimacy of such a claim if it comes through the line of Jesus Christ?"

"If they have genealogies to prove he is of the Davidic line, could they counter it? On the other hand, the Christian church would have few qualms in receiving a Jewish Messiah who can also lay claim to be a descendent of Jesus through Mary Magdalene."

There was silence from Himmler's Obergruppenführer and they waited for him to continue.

"For those of you who are familiar with horticulture, you will be aware of the process of grafting. A cutting containing the genes to be replicated is taken from a plant. In English, this is called a scion. Usually it would be clipped from a superior fruit producer. An incision is made in the host tree; the cutting is bound into place causing the raw tissues of both scion and stock to remain in contact. This process is necessary for the graft to take." Himmler twisted his hands together nervously as light began to dawn in the faces of some of his men. They sat forward in their seats as though to hear him better.

"I think it may just be possible to infiltrate an Aryan into the Prieuré de Sion," he said.

"Scion," Karl Wolff interjected. "It has another meaning in English, no?"

Himmler nodded. "An heir," he affirmed, "or a descendent."

"You think it is possible to graft someone in?" Wolff looked dubious. "These men are not amateurs."

"It will require a great deal of shrewdness to outsmart them. There is still a lot to be learnt about their organisation. War will be the best cover for our activities and it will be imperative that we capture France. We must attempt to trace the genealogies that were uncovered in the Rennes-le-Château region before we can set this plan in motion. Ultimately, it will hinge on one thing." He looked round at his men and smiled. "The depth of one man's greed for power."

Back in his suite, Reinhard Heydrich reclined in the armchair, stretched his legs and crossed his ankles. Linking his hands together in front of his face he sat contemplating his fingers as though they were capable of providing clarity to his racing thoughts.

"If Hitler knew what his little 'Reichsheini' was scheming behind his back, he would be a dead man!" he said aloud.

The prospect of disclosure was tempting and for a while Heydrich permitted himself the pleasure of thinking along those lines. If he confronted the Führer with Heinrich Himmler's treachery would it guarantee him the position of Reichsführer SS? The prospect was fraught with danger and besides, it was too simple – too blatant!

Himmler was so certain of his own genius. Heydrich could plainly see the workings of the Reichsführer's mind. A future glorious Germany would worship the memory of a great man. Heinrich Himmler, they would say in hushed tones, the unsung hero, single-handedly overcame Jewish Imperialism!

Did the Reichsführer imagine that he, Reinhard Heydrich, was unaware of what he was attempting to achieve with all this Quedlinburg mumbo-jumbo for example? By focussing the nation on King Heinrich I, Himmler was simply preparing Germany to receive his own empire.

Even if it were only in death, and his bones were interred alongside those of his namesake, when he received the worship he imagined was his due, it would be enough. Then Heinrich II, maligned and misunderstood in his lifetime, would be the acknowledged saviour of the German people!

Reinhard Heydrich shook his head. Undermining him would require a far more devious approach than disclosure and a mind far superior to that of Reichsführer SS, Heinrich Himmler. But undermine him he would, even if he were to die in the attempt!

Chapter 51
Twice-Born

The Herodian Palace, where Pontius Pilot and his retinue stayed, and where Pilot held court while he was in Jerusalem, lay west of the Hasmonean Palace, which was Herod's city residence.

Unexpectedly, to the annoyance of the Jewish leaders, the Roman procurator chose to reopen the case against Jesus the Nazarene. The Sanhedrin had tried him during the night in order to ensure a swift execution of the prisoner while Jerusalem was preoccupied with the Passover. To the Jewish priests, this delay constituted a serious turn of events; his followers might enflame the people and cause an uprising. It was also entirely possible that Pilot would secure his release if he found that Jesus had done nothing to warrant death under Roman law. They waited impatiently for the examination of the prisoner to get underway. Finally, Pilot took his seat and listened to the testimony of the witnesses but as he turned to cross-examine the accused there was a brief interruption and someone handed a note to the procurator.

Pilot glanced down at the message written in his wife's familiar hand.

"Have nothing to do with that righteous man, for I have suffered much this day in a dream because of him."

He glanced back at the prisoner standing before him with renewed interest. Jesus had allowed the stream of accusations to be made against him in silence, showing no desire to offer a defence. Having begun the trial, Pilot was committed. There was nothing he could do to comply with his wife's wishes, unless of course the man was not under his jurisdiction.

"Where do you come from?" he demanded of the prisoner.

"I am from Galilee."

"A Galilean! That is the Tetrarch's territory. I should imagine he is in Jerusalem for the feast?" He waited for the affirmative answer and, with some relief, ordered that Yeshua bar Joseph be taken to Herod's residence.

Herod was delighted. He had desired to see this preacher who was causing such a stir in his region and, more out of fear of Herodias than anything, had refrained from creating an opportunity. Now the man was being offered to him by the Roman governor for examination. No doubt the Galilean would be only too relieved to perform some miracle in exchange for his life.

Although it was still early morning, Herodias, and Salome her daughter had arisen from their beds in haste to view the proceedings. They watched Herod's attempted interrogation of Jesus from an adjoining room and both women were infuriated by his handling of the prisoner.

"He's so consumed with the possibility of seeing him perform some magical act," Herodias whispered scornfully, "that he forgets who he is! This man is proclaiming himself King of Israel, and my dear husband wants to see signs!"

Salome giggled. "Then let my father see Simon Magus at work. There is a man who knows how to perform the miraculous!"

The Nazarene stood silently but without servility before Herod, showing no sign of fear or even of arrogance.

"He is," Herodias remarked, "a fool. Doesn't he realise that Herod holds the power of life or death in his hands? Salome, order a servant to bring one of Herod's richest robes. A purple robe! Let it be put on the shoulders of this self-proclaimed king!"

Now that she had seen this gentle Jewish worker of miracles and preacher of truth, she hated him. The hatred was unmerited but all-consuming, and it would pursue Jesus way beyond the cross and the grave.

Herod quickly lost all patience with his captive. Yeshua made no attempt to offer any sort of defence against the charges; made no effort to perform a miracle; and remained silent under interrogation. Eventually, in frustration, Herod Antipas handed the prisoner over to his guard.

"Take him back to Pontius Pilot and tell him I find the man, Jesus, innocent of all charges and recommend he should be afforded his freedom."

Herodias stood in the arched doorway and beckoned towards

her husband. Over her arm she bore the robe.

"Have them robe the man!"

At first Herod glanced at his wife in puzzlement. Then he smiled. The act was typical of Herodias' subtlety but it served to save his face. Walking over to the silent captive he drew the purple garment over his shoulders. Turning to the assembled group of soldiers and Jewish priests he shouted:

"Behold your king!"

Herod's concurrence with Pilot's verdict and his little joke in returning Jesus dressed in his own robe was the first communication that had occurred between the two men since the episode of the shields and the beheading of the Baptist and it served to restore their relationship. The priests had gathered once more outside the court of the Herodian Palace so as to remain ritually clean for the second night of the feast. Pontius Pilot left Jesus with the guard and went out to speak to them.

"You have accused this man of subverting the people," he cried. "I find no fault in him. I will therefore chastise him and let him go!" He looked out over the crowd of several hundred people which had been gathering steadily before the place of judgment: the mood was becoming ugly. Pontius Pilot could sense their stirring anger and he experienced a nudge of unease.

He returned to the prisoner in the judgment hall.

"Do you not know that I have the power to crucify you or to free you?"

Jesus met his eyes steadily and unexpectedly he chose to reply.

"You have no power over me except that it is given to you from above," he said. "Therefore he that delivered me to you has the greater sin."

Pilot strode back and remonstrated again with the priests. "He has done nothing deserving of death. He must be released!"

"If you release him, you are no friend of Caesar's. Whoever makes himself king speaks against Caesar."

Their logic could not be faulted. Any such report from the priesthood to Tiberius could cost him his position and, after the warning he had previously received, in all probability, his life. There remained one further route open to Pontius Pilot, who was still convinced that he was dealing with an innocent man. When the power to impose the death sentence was removed from the Jewish Sanhedrin, Pilot had promised to carry out, wherever possible, the recommendations of the high priests. If they considered the death penalty was called for in the case of a prisoner delivered to him for judgment, he had sworn that he would try to uphold their decision. In return for the reduction of the Sanhedrin's powers, Pilot had also promised the release of a prisoner to coincide with the Feast of Unleavened Bread, and he still had that card to play.

There was a man, Bar Abbas, imprisoned in the Antonia, who had already been found guilty of sedition and murder. Surely sanity would prevail and they would not choose him over Jesus! He put the option to the priests and then to the gathered throng.

"It has become the custom of Rome to release a prisoner at Passover," Pilot said. "Shall I release the King of the Jews?" He listened with dismay to the screams of the crowd.

"Crucify him!" they shouted. "And give us Bar Abbas!"

"Bar Abbas is a murderer and a thief!" Pilot cried. "I will release the Nazarene."

"Crucify him!" The cry grew to a chant.

Pilot called his guard to bring the prisoner to face the crowd, hoping perhaps to arouse some sympathy for his plight. He was still wearing Herod's purple robe, and Pilot's soldiers had placed a reed in his hand in place of a royal sceptre. One of them had plaited a crown of thorns and set it on his head. The blood ran down his face in thin trickles and matted his beard.

The multitude, incensed at the sight of him, cried with a single voice.

"CRUCIFY HIM! CRUCIFY HIM!"

Caiaphas, the high priest stepped forward and reminded Pilot quietly: "We have a law, and by that law the Nazarene is deserving of death because he has made himself the Son of God."

Pilot's thoughts returned to his wife's dream arousing a stab of superstitious fear. He spoke urgently to Jesus.

"Are you the King of the Jews?"

"My kingdom is not of this world, if it was, my servants would have fought rather than give me up to the Jews." Jesus replied. "I was born for this, and for this cause I came into the world, that I should bear witness to the truth. Everyone that is of the truth hears my voice."

Pilot fought for control, knowing that it was slipping away from him. He tried to establish a note of authority but his voice quavered.

"What is truth?" he asked and he turned away before Jesus could answer.

Then he sat down on the judgment seat in the place known in Hebrew as Gabbatha, the Pavement. It was early morning on the day of the preparation of the Passover. Calling for a basin of water and a towel, Pilot took his seat and before the shrieking multitude he symbolically washed his hands of the guilt of a death that was now inevitable.

The situation was beyond him. Bar Abbas, son of the fathers' was to be released, while Bar Abba, Son of the Father was condemned to die in his place.

Immediately upon receiving news of the capture of Jesus of Nazareth by the chief priests, Herodias had sent a horseman to summon Simon Magus. She knew that the magician would recognise the vital importance of what was taking place.

He arrived shortly after the eighth hour in the morning, sweat-stained and weary from the night's journey. Herodias gripped his arm urgently.

"There is no time to bathe or change your garments," she said. "Herod has sent Jesus of Nazareth back to Pilot and I have heard news that he is to be crucified at this very hour. I cannot go to the cross, but you can." She handed him the goblet made of red jasper that had contained the blood of John the Baptist, and a bag of silver coins. "Bribe the Roman guard and bring me a cup of his blood."

Simon looked her in the eye and bowed ironically, "My Lady, are you sure I should not ask the head?"

Herodias smiled. "His blood is enough," she replied.

Chapter 52
Twice-Born

The presence of the Gestapo on the train was sobering. An early darkness fell over the countryside and Gabriele and Michael's world shrank to the illuminated compartment with its bottle green seats and grey walls. The rhythmic sound of the wheels might have been restful had it not been for the menace of the two men just a few compartments away.

"They don't give the impression that they're on official business," Gabriele reported with a confidence she did not really feel. "They are standing in the corridor smoking and chatting."

"If they were going to check passes I think they would have done by now," Michael agreed. "They're probably on their way to Stuttgart. Look Gabby, the dining car is in the opposite direction, why don't we go and have a meal? Worrying isn't going to make them go away."

When they returned to their compartment two hours later, everything was just as they had left it. As he closed the door behind them, Michael took her in his arms and held her against him; the sway of the train adding to the sense of unreality they both felt.

"Are you sure you won't come with me, Gabby?"

She shook her head. "One day soon there will be a Germany to come back to," she replied. "I'll be waiting for you." She reached up and kissed him.

They were woken by the rattle of their door and Michael sat up with a start. Gabriele stirred in his arms.

"What is it?"

"Probably a routine check. Don't worry."

He unlocked the door.

"Papers!"

"Liebschen," Michael said, "Do you have our documents?"

"In my handbag. Could you put the light on?" Her voice was sleepy and a little irritable. She passed the identity cards to Michael and he gave them to the Sergeant.

"Where are your passes?"

Gabrielle handed them over and he scrutinised them by the light from his torch.

"We'll be arriving in Stuttgart in ten minutes," he said briefly. "Newly married, huh? Enjoy your leave, sir." And he winked at Michael and moved on to the next compartment.

Michael Segal sat down and found that he was trembling both from fear and the sudden blast of cold air into the compartment from outside. He and Gabriele clung to one another in silence for several minutes before the shriek of the train's whistle warned them that they were nearing the city.

"Come on, Gabby," he said. "Let's get our things together. We're one step closer to our destination."

Singen was a short train ride from Stuttgart. They arrived mid-morning and the bus took them in the direction of the hills beyond the town. The hotel was no more than a chalet with a steep grey roof and red geraniums in the window boxes. Michael and Gabriele were shown to an upstairs bedroom with a view of the extinct volcano and the castle ruins. They could see the outskirts of the town but the border post with its wires and guards was not visible.

"From the map, I would say it's close," Michael said. "Probably only five or six kilometres from here."

Looking at her, Michael knew that Gabriele's confident façade was beginning to crumble. Faced with the imminence of their parting, and the fear of the border crossing that still lay ahead for Michael, she wavered.

"I should come with you," she said at last.

He shook his head. "You've made the right decision, Gabby. You know you have. There's your family to consider, and your job."

"And there's you, Michael," she said. "How will I make it without you?"

"You will. You're the strongest person I know. You've taught me how to be strong. I don't want you to make any promises you won't be able to keep, Gabby. Give it time. Germany in a few years may be a different country. If I asked you to marry me now, it would mean taking you away from everything that is important. I can't ask you to make such a decision yet."

She nodded, unable to verbalise or understand the nameless dread that assailed her but she wondered whether she would ever see Michael again.

There was only one other couple staying in the hotel and they were already in the dining room when Michael and Gabriele came down to supper. The woman wore her long grey hair in a single plait drawn up like a coronet over her brow and her husband's magnificently waxed moustache would have done the Kaiser proud. They glanced politely at the new-comers but, mercifully, made no attempt at conversation. Neither Gabriele nor Michael was able to do justice to the hearty country meal served by the hotel owner and cooked by his ample wife.

"Michael, I want you to leave tonight." Gabriele said later.

He looked at her in surprise. "Why?"

She shook her head in confusion. "I have no idea, I know we planned that you should go tomorrow night, but I have a sense of urgency that I can't explain."

They had returned to their room and Michael was stretched out on the bed. He sat up slowly and looked at Gabriele. Her face was tense and pale and he realised that the strain was stretching her to breaking point.

"I don't know how prepared I am," he said doubtfully. "Hans gave us the name of that guide to contact tomorrow. I'm not sure I could make it across without him."

"I have a bad feeling about it," she said. "Please, Michael, do this for me!"

He lay back again with his hands laced behind his head. His mind was racing. Gabriele sat down beside him and he pulled her down so that her head rested in the hollow of his shoulder.

"Are you sure, Gabby?"

"I've never felt so sure about anything!"

She felt his body relax as he reached his decision. "I'll leave at midnight," he said. "I'm as prepared as I'll ever be. With the map of the area I'm sure I'll find the crossing point without much trouble."

Michael caressed her gently. On the one hand, he was filled

with an exhilarating sense of purpose, but he was all too aware that he was leaving behind the woman he loved.

In the last hour, he studied the map, committing every detail to memory. Midnight came all too soon. The hotel was in almost total darkness as they crept silently down the stairs. Michael had noticed earlier that the key was left on the inside of the entrance door and the night light, which burned in the lobby, revealed that it was still there. He turned the key in the lock and kissed Gabriele goodbye.

"Leave early in the morning," he said. "Get the first train out, if you can. I love you!"

"Go carefully," she urged. "You will make it, Michael. I know you will!"

He disappeared like a shadow into the night and, locking the door behind him, she returned to their room. There was no possibility of sleep now, every nerve in her body jangled; she lay rigid, listening to the silence and waiting for morning.

A light snow had begun to fall as Michael left the hotel. There was no moon but he was aware that the terrain fell away reasonably smoothly towards the stream in the valley, which was roughly two kilometres away. As his eyes adjusted, he began to pick up the landmarks he had memorised. There was a torch in the pocket of his jacket, but it would be folly to use it, except in a real emergency. Pulling the woollen ski cap over his ears, he walked as swiftly as the conditions and visibility allowed. A night bird startled him as it rose from the snowy ground a few metres away, its wings beating in panicked flight. Stumbling clumsily over a rock, Michael paused to listen, his ears straining for any unusual sound that would suggest his presence had been detected.

He came upon the stream quite suddenly although the thickened undergrowth had warned him that it was near. The snow had almost deadened the sound of the water. He risked using the torch briefly to assess the best place to make a crossing. Just downstream, rocks broke through the flow of water creating a natural weir and, keeping the beam low, he crossed swiftly to the other side. Michael dowsed the torch and waited, feeling his heart pound with anxiety. Nothing moved. Above the natural undergrowth on the bank of the stream was a narrow belt of pine forest and beyond that, he knew, was the stretch of open ground before the wires.

He felt his way through the trees. There was no snow on the ground in the forest and he placed one foot in front of the other testing the surface like a blind man before allowing it to take the full weight of his body. Gradually there was a lightening of the sky-line, and then the trees stopped and he was out into the open once more. The snow had created a thick layer over the grass and, unless the fall increased considerably, his direction would be instantly trackable in daylight. He had checked his watch in the forest and knew that it was already 3.30am, but dawn was still a long way off and, assuming nothing went wrong, he would be in Switzerland before anyone realised he had left the hotel.

Telegraph poles, just visible in the gloom were the first indication that he was close to the road. A thicket provided cover and he lay down full length in the snow and waited. Somewhere beyond the road was the border fence and, according to the information provided by Gabriele's forger, patrols were made at regular fifteen minute intervals. About ten minutes passed before he heard the approaching motor cycle. It was travelling very slowly and the patrol guard in the sidecar shone his flashlight clearly illuminating the barricade. Michael waited until they were out of sight, before sprinting the last few hundred meters. He took the wire-cutters from the inside pocket of his jacket and cut the bottom two strands of the high barbed-wire fence. He could just make out a similar barrier parallel to the first and estimated that there must be about four meters separating the two. Rolling underneath the fence, he crawled the distance to the second; aware that he was sweating despite the cold as he fumbled with the cutters in his gloved hands. Then the strands parted and he was through into the no-man's land between the two countries. There was not a light to be seen. Michael ran, keeping within the cover of brush whenever he could, the patrol would soon be back and the breach in the fence would be discovered. Doubtless there was a second patrol on this side of the divide, but he had no way of knowing where it was.

His lungs were burning with exertion when he was caught in the powerful beam of a flashlight.

"Halt or I'll shoot!" the command was in German.

Michael stood rooted to the spot and slowly raised his hands realising it was all over.

The guard approached him warily, hidden behind the beam of his light.

"You are in Switzerland. Are you armed?"

Michael shook his head and the breath that caught in his throat was a sob of relief. The Swiss border police received him courteously and took down his details.

Germany was behind him. They had no power to hurt him any more.

Chapter 53
Twice-Born

He had not slept or changed his garments; his feet were filthy and the hem of his robe was grimy with the dirt. With his matted hair and eyes red-rimmed from weeping, Judas Iscariot presented a pathetic figure. He clutched to his breast the leather pouch with the thirty pieces of silver that he had traded for the life of Messiah. Was that all he had been worth to Judas - the price of a slave?

In the months leading up to the final Passover, when Jesus' ministry became less public, Judas had become increasingly embittered. It was apparent that other disciples were preferred above himself. When the Master went up into a mountain to pray, it was Peter, James and John who were called to go with him. They returned more secretive and self-important than ever, refusing even to speak of the things that had taken place. Something had happened up there, Judas was sure of it.

"Why were we left down here to handle the people?" he asked later. "What is so special about Peter and the sons of Zebedee?" They were walking the road to Capernaum and again the three disciples walked ahead, deep in conversation with Jesus, while the others trailed further behind. Some of them murmured in agreement. Judas voiced the resentment that had formed an undercurrent of discontent among them for many days.

"When the Master sets up his kingdom," Judas said, "*they* will no doubt want the highest place."

"One on the left hand and one on the right," one of them commented dryly and there was laughter as they remembered the petition that the mother of the sons of Zebedee had brought before Jesus, the cause of much embarrassment to James and John.

"They're no different to any of us," Judas reminded them. "In fact, Peter is a fool. He falls over his own feet to make Jesus notice him. He's always first with an answer – usually the wrong one!"

The discussion had continued most of the way back to the town.

"What were you arguing about on the road?" Jesus asked after they had eaten the lunch prepared by Peter's wife and mother-in-law.

They looked down at the table but no one ventured an answer. Jesus shook his head and smiled.

"Talitha, come here!"

Peter's two-year old daughter came to him readily. He lifted her onto his lap and she snuggled into the crook of his arm.

"If any of you desire to be first, let him be last and the servant of all," he said. "Unless you are converted and become like this little one, you will not enter into the kingdom. And anyone who humbles himself like a little child is the greatest in the kingdom of heaven."

The child slipped her thumb into her mouth and closed her eyes. The disciples glanced at one another and smiled, children were always comfortable in the Master's presence. Nevertheless the rebuke, however gently delivered had sobered the mood.

"Whoever offends one of these little ones that believe in me, it would be better for him if a millstone was hung around his neck and he was cast into the sea." As he said this, Jesus had looked directly at Judas Iscariot. Judas was incensed; the remark was unnecessary, he had no intention of hurting any child.

"If your hand offends you, cut it off," the Rabbi continued. "It is better to live life maimed than having two hands to go to hell, into fire that shall never be quenched."

"Where their worm dieth not, and the fire is not quenched," graphic words from the prophecy of Isaiah! Better, Jesus had said, to cut off a hand or a foot: better to remove your eye if it should cause you to stumble and fall away from the only one who is able to save. Everlasting torment in unquenchable fire. Judas remembered his words and shuddered. Three times, the Master had repeated his warning chilling the hearts of every disciple, while the child contentedly sucked her thumb and drifted into sleep, completely secure in his arms.

Was there any way to pay penance for what he had done; to turn back and be saved from such punishment?

"I have betrayed him!" the words were rent from him.

He ran blindly down the road to Jerusalem. Perhaps it was not too late. Perhaps the crucifixion could be stopped.

It was almost the third hour, nine in the morning, when, wild-eyed and dishevelled, he reached the residence of the priests within the precinct of the temple. Judas gripped the arm of a Sadducee who was well-known to his father.

"He cannot die!" he shouted. "He is not deserving of death. It is I that have sinned by betraying innocent blood!"

The priest shook off his hand. "What is that to us?" he asked. "It is laid to your account. The man is even now being crucified."

Judas dashed the tears from his eyes with the back of his hand. "Take this!" he shouted, "It is the price of blood. I want nothing further to do with it!" He flung down the money bag and coins scattered across the flagstones. Turning, he ran from the temple.

"And whoever offends one of these little ones that believe in me, it would be better for him if a millstone was hung around his neck and he was cast into the sea."

The saying of Jesus rang in his ears. He, Judas Iscariot had caused offence to all who believed in the Master, an offence that may even reverberate on through the ages and touch the portals of heaven.

He had no millstone, but he knew where to find a rope.

They found the bloated body of Judas three days later, hanging from a tree in a place called the potter's field. When they cut down the corpse, the stomach split and the intestines spilled forth so that the field became known throughout Jerusalem as Aceldama, the field of blood. The chief priests took counsel and bought it with the thirty pieces of silver. It was blood money they conceded and could not go back into the temple treasury. So, they fulfilled the prophecy written in Zechariah:

Then I said to them, "If it is agreeable to you, give me my wages; and if not, refrain." So they weighed out for my wages thirty pieces of silver. And the Lord said to me, "Throw it to the potter," that princely price they set on me. So I took the thirty pieces of silver and threw them into the house of the Lord for the potter.[14]

---

[14] Zechariah 11:12,13 NKJ

Chapter 54
Twice-Born

Thirty-nine stripes with the vicious Roman cat 'o nine tails could take a man to within an inch of his life, but flogging before crucifixion had the advantage of shortening the time on the cross. Jesus was scourged, then, as he was dragged staggering to his feet, they dressed him again in Herod's royal robe. The soldiers roared with pleasure at the diversion. There was riotous laughter and ribald joking. But, as their captive remained unbowed, mockery and fun turned into deepening aggression, Jesus was spat upon and beaten; hair was plucked from his beard. When at last he was led back to Pilot, he was scarcely recognisable.

"Behold," Pilot said to the jeering crowd, "the man."

"CRUCIFY HIM! CRUCIFY HIM!" thundered the mob at his feet.

They dressed him in his own garments and roped the heavy horizontal beam of his cross to the broken skin of his back. A Roman guard led the procession to Golgotha, the Place of the Skull, outside the city walls. When Pontius Pilot instructed the centurion, he gave him a sign to be affixed to the cross. On it he had written in Hebrew, Greek and Latin, "Jesus of Nazareth, the King of the Jews."

Caiaphas and the chief priests protested.

"Do not say, 'King of the Jews,'" they said testily. "Rather, he said I am the King of the Jews!"

Pilot's eyes narrowed in anger. "What I have written, I have written," he said shortly, and he turned and walked away.

Jesus was not the only one to be crucified that day; two thieves had also been condemned to die. Many of Jesus' supporters trailed behind the guard, and many more of his antagonists. Repeatedly he stumbled over the uneven ground and it soon became clear that he was no longer able to bear the weight of the heavy wooden beam. A soldier grasped the wrist of a passer-by, a well-built man called Simon who had come into Jerusalem for the Passover feast. He was a black man from the city of Cyrene.

"Hey, you! Take this man's cross!" the soldier ordered.

Simon did not attempt to argue with either the soldier or his lance. He shouldered the cross-beam and carried it for the man, Jesus.

The Magus arrived at Golgotha shortly before the third hour, which in Hebrew time was nine o'clock in the morning. He watched dispassionately as the hands of the three prisoners were nailed to their cross-beams by the Roman guard, and a spike was driven through their feet. Their agony meant little to him, crucifixion was a common form of death for criminals under Roman rule and he had witnessed it many times before. Pushing his way through the crowd that had gathered, he bought himself victuals and drink from a peddler. There was no rush to do the job he was sent to do; death could take many hours, or even days, and the Magus was tired after his long night.

In a huddled, silent group not far from where he stood, he recognised Joanna, the servant of Herodias who had become a follower of the one now nailed impotently to the cross. Simon Magus pulled his cloak up over his head and allowed it to fall forward over his face so that she would not recognise him. He watched them as he ate his bread, but they had eyes for nothing but the central cross and their dying Master. The women wept quietly, while John, one of his disciples, stood white-faced, supporting Mary, the mother of Jesus, who appeared close to collapse. An hour passed. Simon Magus listened to the loose talk around him and heard how the other disciples fled at the time of the arrest. Some said Judas, the one who had betrayed Jesus, had thrown his blood-money back at the priests and run from the temple. The Magus smiled softly to himself. An ignoble end to the Galilean, but one destined to conclusively quell his following.

There were mockers at the foot of the cross who had gathered simply to taunt the man who, only days before, had been hailed as King of Judaea.

"He saved others, let him save himself!" they shouted. "If you are Messiah, the chosen of God, come down from the cross!"

Their amusement was heightened from an unexpected quarter. The thief, crucified on the left of Jesus, forgot his own torment for a moment and joined in the mockery.

"If you are the Christ," he said, "save yourself and us."

His words were greeted with wagging of heads and hoots of raucous laughter. The second thief lifted his head.

"Don't you fear God?" he cried out. "Our condemnation is just. We have received the due reward for our deeds but this man has done nothing wrong." An uneasy hush fell over the gathering at these words and the thief strained his head to look towards the man who hung at his side.

"Lord," he said, "remember me when you come into your kingdom."

"Truly," Jesus replied, "today you will be with me in paradise."

At the sixth hour there was sudden consternation. Darkness descended without warning. It was a sign that struck superstitious dread into the hearts of the onlookers. Many turned to leave. The Magus pushed his way to the front of the crowd. Looking up to the crosses in the half light, he could see agony etched deeply into the faces of the three men. The soldiers, who had entertained themselves by drawing lots for the garment of Jesus, now shifted nervously, gazing up at the sky. Simon sidled up to one of them.

"This man was a magician as I am," he said. "It's a sad thing to witness his death."

The soldier shrugged. It was unusual for a Jew to address a Roman and he said so.

"I am of Samaria," the Magus said by way of explanation. He briefly showed the bag of money hidden in the folds of his cloak. The eyes of the guard widened but he made no comment. There was a question in his eyes.

"I need something from you," Simon Magus said. "The blood of a man who has performed many miracles would be of enormous value to me. I have a cup. If you place it at the foot of the cross of the Nazarene to receive the drops from his feet the money is yours."

By the greed in the soldier's eyes, the Magus could see he was tempted and pressed his advantage.

"There is a natural dip in the ground," he pointed out, "it could be concealed there and no one would be any the wiser."

There was a cry from the central cross and both men swung around. Jesus was breathing heavily and his body was bathed in sweat and blood. Even in his torment he was interceding for men who had betrayed him and nailed him to the cross.

"Father, forgive them for they know not what they do!"

The Magus had lost his advantage; the guard's expression hardened.

"Get out of here! You know the penalty for trying to bribe a Roman soldier? Move, I say!"

Simon melted back into the crowd. He was still there at the ninth hour when Yeshua cried out again.

"My God, my God, why hast thou forsaken me?" It was plain that he was fighting for every breath. Someone dipped a sponge in a mixture of vinegar and water and raised it up to his lips. He tasted it but did not drink.

"It is finished! Father, into thy hands I commend my spirit!"

His head rolled forward onto his chest and his body shuddered and stilled.

The centurion looked up at the cross. He had overseen many crucifixions, but this was like none he had ever witnessed before. First there was the darkness, which had not yet lifted. Then, at the very end of his life, when he was at his weakest, this man had shouted with a voice filled with power.

"Truly," the centurion mused aloud, "this man was the Son of God."

At the moment when Jesus of Nazareth breathed his last, the curtain of the temple, separating the Holy of Holies from the Holy Place, was rent in two, from top to bottom. Through the veil of Messiah's flesh, a new way had been made to the Father. The Passover Lamb had been offered; the sacrificial system of the Jews was finished. There could be no further need of a sacrifice for sin.

The disquiet of the soldiers was obvious and when the centurion gave the command to break the legs of the men to hasten their death, they moved quickly to comply. Everyone had been unnerved by the cries of the Nazarene. The soldier who had spoken to the Magus shook his head.

"Leave this one alone, it's obvious he's already dead."

A fellow soldier swung a heavy beam of wood with sickening accuracy across the shin bones of the first of the thieves. The man groaned and his body slumped. Death would come quickly by suffocation without the support of his legs. He laid the beam to the legs of the second thief and both soldiers stood looking up at the inert body of the Nazarene.

"He's dead," the one agreed, "but we'd better be sure." He took his lance and thrust it under the rib cage into the side of the limp body, and backed away watching dispassionately as water and blood flowed from the tear in the flesh. He nodded.

"He's dead. You can take him down."

Magus waited until the two guards were fully occupied with lowering the cross and removing the body. Thick darkness still shrouded the scene and no one noticed when he picked up the nails that had secured Jesus' hands to the beam, and spirited away the discarded crown of thorns and the lance used to pierce his side. He was well aware of the magical value of relics. Concealing the spear under his cloak, Simon the Sorcerer melted swiftly into the crowd.

On the night of the death of Jesus the Nazarene, a deliberate distortion of the Jewish Passover was enacted, presided over by Helen, hierodule and priestess of Simon the magician. The cup, the lance, the crown and the nails from the cross were consecrated in the same dark ritual. Herodias was at first furious with Simon Magus' failure to bring back the blood of Jesus. It was common knowledge in the Babylonian and Assyrian religious tradition that by partaking of the blood of a god, one assumed his power on earth.

"The cup has held the blood of his prophet," Magus said, "And we ourselves, have made the Baptist a god. The cup will become a mighty relic, but the lance is stained by the blood of a true god. This lance," he prophesied, "will direct the cause of men and of nations, for good or evil. We have our relics, Herodias; the head of the Baptist, the sword that dealt his death blow, the cup of his blood, and the lance. They will be used to undermine and destroy the Jewish God!"

That same night, Simon Magus knew beyond doubt that the Prince of Darkness had chosen him as his vessel. Kings and emperors held sway over kingdoms but no one would have the influence that he, Simon the Magician, would exert over the centuries to come. He would change the course of history and the final outcome of the age would be tainted by this blackest of hours.

260

PART II

Chapter 1
Twice-Born

Gabriele Hoch heard the labouring of the engine as the vehicle approached the hotel and went quickly to the window. The snow had stopped and the first light of dawn was just beginning to filter through the curtains. The landscape was devoid of colour; trees were dark smudges on a blanket of white. She could see the headlights of the car as it negotiated the long driveway to the hotel. Two men in plain clothes took the steps to the front door and she heard the urgent rapping of the door knocker. Two others lit cigarettes and stood with their backs to the vehicle watching the building.

Gabriele sat down on the bed, her heart pounding unnaturally in her chest. Their look was unmistakable – Gestapo! It was about Michael, it must be. Had they caught him? Was he alive or dead? She tried to pull herself together; to prepare herself for what lay ahead, but panic rendered her helpless. When the two officers hammered on her door moments later and burst into the room, she gazed at them mutely, feeling that her inner being had floated away leaving her body unattended.

"Where is he?"

The question left Gabriele with such a profound sense of relief that she was tempted to laugh. Michael was still alive, perhaps even across the border by now, but it may still be necessary to play for time. At once every nerve in her body was fully awake and aware.

"Who?"

"Where is the Jew!"

"I don't know what you are talking about. I'm here with my husband."

The cold eyes suddenly blazed hatred.

"Liar!" He lashed out with the back of his hand and the blow knocked Gabriele across the bed.

"Where is he?"

"My husband took an early train back to Berlin." Her voice was weak. The men exchanged the briefest of glances.

If they had not apprehended Michael on the border, Gabriele realised, there could be only one other source of their knowledge. Her forger, Hans, had turned betrayer.

"Search the building and radio an alert to all border posts!" The order was issued tersely and it was received with a snap of the heels and a brief salute.

Within minutes, Gabriele heard, above the concerned voices of the hotel owners, the slamming of doors and shouts of the men. Her guard rested his gun within easy reach on the bedside table, and lit a cigarette. His movements were languid and he watched her with detached interest.

"Why a Jew, liebschen? Are German men not to your taste? It seems there are always some who would prefer to eat dirt even when they are offered bread!"

Gabriele's eyes narrowed but she remained silent. A sharp rap on the door caused the officer to grind his cigarette out in an ashtray and pick up his pistol.

"Come in!"

"He's not in the building, Herr Kriminalinspektor!"

"Then I think this little lady has a few questions to answer," Gabriele's guard suggested pleasantly.

"We know Michael Segal is not your husband, and we also know he is not on the morning train to Berlin," he said. "So perhaps it is time for you to drop the pretence and co-operate for your own good."

Gabriele thought swiftly. There was no doubt that Hans had informed the Gestapo; there was nothing to be gained in lying. Had she and Michael worked to Hans' plan and contacted the guide before attempting the crossing, everything would have been lost but there was an excellent possibility that Michael was already in Switzerland.

"We travelled here together and had dinner," she said.

"Michael left shortly afterwards without saying where he was going."

This time it was the junior officer that hit her. Gabriele fell back under the blow and her hand flew to her cheek. Her bottom lip was split and there was the metallic taste of blood in her mouth.

"Lying bitch! This bed has been slept in by two people, on that law alone we can convict you. You have cohabited with a member of the Jewish race and you have aided his escape from the authorities. You are a traitor to the German Volk. You won't get away with this."

She raised her head wearily. "Michael and I did not sleep together, but neither was it because he was Jewish and I, German."

The officer's laugh was unpleasant. "What! You have standards?" he mocked.

"What time did the Jew leave?" the Kriminalinspektor interrupted.

Gabriele shook her head vaguely. "I don't remember. Perhaps around ten."

"This was important to you! Your lover was leaving, perhaps forever. You would have been vitally aware of the time."

"I didn't check my watch."

"Perhaps we can jog your memory?" The Kriminalinspektor lit a cigarette beneath a cupped hand, habit causing him to protect the flame. Gabriele watched as he drew deeply blowing smoke from the corner of his mouth. The cigarette glowed red between his fingers as he stepped towards her.

"I can give you a more accurate time."

He laughed cynically. "So easy, liebling? For all your pretended scruples, you would sell your Jew without a fight?"

She lifted her chin and for a moment anger blazed in her eyes. "Michael left at midnight. We waited until we were certain everyone was asleep."

"How did he get out?"

"The key was on the inside of the door."

The Kriminalinspektor glanced at his watch, it was already 8.30am. If he had managed to evade the border guards, the likelihood that Michael Segal was still on German soil was negligible. He was a small fish, hardly worth losing sleep over. The guards would have the dogs out and if he was still around they would haul him in. He stifled a yawn.

"Take her in for interrogation," he ordered. "Make sure they throw the book at her. We don't need filth like this in Germany."

Chapter 2
Twice-Born

"Destroy this temple and in three days I will raise it up."
If the disciples of Jesus of Nazareth had at first failed to understand the implication of his words, certain learned men of the priesthood had not. During the night trial, witnesses were brought who had been prompted to focus on those words alone in order convict him. But their witness proved contradictory and Caiaphas had been forced to back away from this line of prosecution. Though the common people had understood Jesus of Nazareth to be referring to the literal temple, Caiaphas had discerned otherwise.

During Friday, the second day of the Passover and the day following the crucifixion, Caiaphas knew suddenly and with certainty that a guard must be placed at the tomb of the dead man and he waited out the remainder of the day with great impatience gathering a few of the chief priests together at sunset. It was the High Sabbath,[15] the eve of the Saturday Sabbath, a time when Jewish law restricted both work and travel but the high priest argued that the violation was necessary to prevent a national disaster. The delegation went to see Pontius Pilot at once.

"Sir," they said, "we remember that while he was alive, that deceiver told his followers he would die and be resurrected on the third day. Give us a guard lest his disciples steal the body and tell the people that he is arisen from the dead. Then the last error will be worse than the first."

Pilot nodded shortly, "You have a watch. Go your way and make it as secure as you can."

Caiaphas accompanied the priests and the Roman guard to check that the tomb was in order but he was not content to leave it at that. The corpse was rendered shapeless by the aloes and spices that Nicodemus had packed around the body and their smell permeated the

---

[15] John 19:31

tomb cloaking the smell of death.

"Uncover the face!" Caiaphas ordered.

Somewhat reluctantly his servant approached the body and pushed the shroud to one side. Beneath it, the head was firmly bandaged in the manner of the Jews and encrusted with congealed blood, which had flowed copiously from the nose.

"Remove the head covering!"

His servant fumbled with the knot. The linen strip had been wound around several times making it necessary to lift the head and disentangle the encrusted bandage from the hair.

Caiaphas moved forward delicately, eyeing the broken face with distaste. He nodded briefly and stepped away.

"It is he. Cover him." He turned and left the tomb.

The servant glanced down uncertainly at the bloody cloth in his hands, then, of habit, he folded it neatly and set it down on the earthen floor near the wall. Turning back to the body he drew the shroud over the broken face and followed Caiaphas.

An official seal was placed on the stone and the guard was set. Although he had made himself ritually unclean by his visit to the grave, the high priest slept peacefully that night.

Mary Magdalene, Mary, mother of James, Salome and Joanna set off to the sepulchre just before dawn on the first day of the week, taking with them spices they had prepared after the crucifixion for the anointing of the body. The early hour had been decided on both for fear of the authorities and out of necessity. The body had lain in the grave for three days and three nights already and decomposition would have begun to set in. It was better that they do what must be done before the heat of another day.

They had no way of knowing that Nicodemus had already hastily anointed the body of Jesus before the Passover evening began. Nor did they know of the measures that Caiaphas had set in place on the Friday evening. The women would have been startled to arrive at the tomb and find a Roman contingent on guard. Their one concern as they set off on the journey was how they would manage to move the stone in order to do their work.

They arrived before the sun had risen and stood in amazement.

"It's open!"

"Is it the right place?"

"I came with them when they brought the body. It is Joseph's tomb!"

They crossed the garden, clinging to one another in superstitious dread. The yawning opening of the tomb was black as pitch and, in the semi-darkness they could see, just off to the left, the heavy rock that had sealed the grave.

Mary Magdalene plucked up courage and stepped forward bending down to enter the darkened cave and feeling tentatively for the shrouded body, which had been laid out on a flat rock with the head towards the mouth of the tomb. It was empty. Mary blinked in disbelief and went back to the women.

"He's not there!" she whispered urgently. "His body has gone!"

Mary, mother of James laid her bundle of spices on the ground.

"Joanna, you and Salome wait here. Mary Magdalene and I will call Peter and John."

By the time the two disciples reached the garden, the sun had fully risen. John outran Peter and arrived at the tomb first. Stooping down he looked inside and saw immediately that it was empty. The linen shroud lay to one side where it had fallen and the napkin that had bound Jesus' head had been folded and left against the wall.

"He's gone!" John said bitterly as Peter arrived breathless from his run.

"Where have they taken him?"

"I do not know, but the others must be told."

Unable to keep up with the men, Mary had followed more slowly and arrived at the tomb after they had already left taking Salome and Joanna with them. All the pent-up emotion of the past week culminated in that moment and Mary Magdalene wept bitterly as she returned to the sepulchre and bent down to enter it.

"Why do you seek the living among the dead?"

Two angelic beings sat on the stone where the body had been laid. Their radiant presence filled the tomb with light so pure and unearthly that she was unable to speak.

"Fear not. The one that you seek has risen. Go and tell the

disciples and Peter that he will go before them into Galilee."

Mary backed away slowly; her heart was pounding and, still blinded by her tears she could not comprehend what she was seeing and hearing. As she turned from the grave, a man stood before her on the path.

"Woman," he said. "Why are you weeping? Who are you looking for?"

She shook her head, almost unable to speak. "If you have taken him, sir, please tell me where you have laid him."

"Mary."

She looked up filled with amazement.

"Master!" She fell at his feet and reached out to hold him.

"Don't touch me, Mary," he said gently, "I have not yet ascended to my Father. But go and tell the brethren that I ascend to my Father and your Father; to my God and your God."

As Mary ran joyfully back to Jerusalem, she thought of Jesus' words: my God and your God: my Father and your Father, and her thoughts turned to the words of Ruth many centuries before.

"Wither thou goest, I will go and where thou lodgest, I will lodge; thy people shall be my people, and thy God, my God."[16]

Naomi had taken Ruth from a foreign land and brought her home to Israel. Ruth had adopted Naomi's family, her people and her God. Mary of Magdala knew with an inner certainty that Jesus was saying she was now adopted into his family. The way had been opened for his Father to be her Father, and the Father of all who believed in the Son.

The Roman guard was in trouble. By fleeing their post when the earth shook and the stone rolled away, they had effectively signed their death warrant. No mercy would be shown under Roman law to soldiers who deserted.

It was just before dawn as they re-entered the sleeping city and they faced one another uncertainly.

"If we return to the Antonia now, it's all over for us."

"There's one possibility," one soldier said. "The guard was set

---

[16] Ruth 1:16

by Pilot to help the high priest secure a Jewish sepulchre. There's just a chance that if we go to the priests they may be able to help."

They looked from one to another with a flicker of hope and set off across the city in the direction of the Caiaphas' residence.

The initial response of the high priest as he met with the men in his cobbled courtyard was fury.

"You are lying!" he charged them. "Pilot will hear of this! No doubt you slept and allowed the man's disciples to rob the grave."

"No sir!" the centurion answered definitely. "A Roman soldier does not sleep while on duty. I think you know sir, that it is death to us if we do."

"And you are deserving of death, all of you! You have failed miserably in your duties. Was it such a difficult task, to guard a tomb throughout the night?"

The men stood at attention, eyes downcast as they listened to the Caiaphas' words. He was a man of formidable bearing with a luxuriant grey-streaked beard that rested on his chest. Heavy eyebrows jutted out, forming a hirsute canopy over dark, intense eyes. His lips, within the bristles of his facial hair, were broad and moist and his tongue played over them incessantly.

The sun was just up and the high priest had already performed the prescribed ritual for the first day of the new week during the feast of Pesach. Before dawn he had gone down into the Kidron Valley and, as the first rays of the sun lightened the sky, had picked the leaf from a new plant, raising it up before the God of Israel, Isaac and Jacob. It was the sign of resurrection life following the ritual slaughter of the lambs. Passover reminded every Jew that a lamb had died in their place when the angel of death had passed over, killing the firstborn of the Egyptians. A Lamb had died at the time of the slaughter of the lambs and a resurrection had taken place at dawn three days later; Caiaphas could not afford to make the connection.

"The stone was rolled away and the seal was broken!" he shouted again, wiping the sweat from his brow with the back of his hand. The sun was already hot, although it was not yet the eighth hour. "You are telling me that you were awake and this was a supernatural act?"

With as much confidence as he was able to muster, the Centurion to whom the guard had been relegated nodded.

"It was, sir! There was a rumbling, the earth trembled and the stone rolled away from the entrance. We saw light in the sepulchre; very white light, spilling out from the mouth of the tomb. A figure stood within the light – it was too bright, we couldn't see him clearly. We were filled with terror and we fled!"

Caiaphas felt his tongue cleave to the roof of his mouth and for a long time he was unable to speak. The words that had leapt into his mind were so clear and so pertinent that they caused his heart to palpitate and his limbs to freeze in horror.

And he made his grave with the wicked, and with the rich in his death; because he had done no violence neither was any deceit in his mouth;'

It was not possible! Could this man, Yeshua the Nazarene, who had met his death with the wicked and been entombed in a rich man's grave have been Messiah? Was this the man of whom the prophet Isaiah had spoken?

'Yet it pleased the Lord to bruise him: ... thou shalt make his soul an offering for sin, he shall see his seed, he shall prolong his days... [17]

He shall prolong his days… Caiaphas held onto the pillar of the porch for support. Yeshua had said that the temple would be destroyed and raised again in three days! Isaiah had declared that Messiah would, like the temple lamb, be cut off for the sin of many but would prolong his days!

His face had lost its blood and his head swam. The people must not hear of it! If there was a suggestion that he, Caiaphas, high priest of Judaea, had been instrumental in betraying and putting to death Messiah, his position would be lost. It was possible that public sentiment would be so enraged that they might not hesitate to kill him! He tried to think. It was imperative that he present a good face before the Roman guard. His legs felt as though they lacked bone and his hands shook but Caiaphas was fighting for his existence. He raised his head and stepped forward.

---

[17] Isaiah 53:9,10

"I realise that if the governor hears what has taken place today, you good men will lose your lives," he said. Clapping his hands, he ordered his servants to bring food and drink for the centurion and his three men. "We will need to put a different aspect on the story for the sake of the common people. If they hear what you have told me, there may be a Jewish uprising and, inevitably, many will die. I would like you to spread a version of the story that will calm the city. I will pay you well of course for your silence. You must understand that peace in Judaea is very important to me."

The men glanced at one another and nodded. This encounter was turning out to be far more to their advantage than they had dared to expect.

Caiaphas rubbed his hands together, palm against palm. Despite the heat they were cold and clammy.

"We will say that the disciples of Yeshua bar Joseph came while you were sleeping and stole the body."

The centurion protested, "Sir, if that comes to the ears of Pontius Pilot we will be immediately put to death."

Caiaphas shook his head. "Do not fear," he assured them. "If he hears anything of the sort, I will personally smooth it over with the governor."

The High priest sent the contingent of guards away with a handsome purse of money, and the story was spread abroad that the body of Jesus had been spirited away. But the rumours that something else had happened just before dawn on that day, persisted. And in the weeks to come the story grew wings.

Chapter 3
Twice-Born

Austria 1938
Wolfram von Seivers, head of the Ahnenerbe, the Nazi Occult Bureau, slowly ascended the steps of the Weltliche Schatzkammer. Already the Heldenplatz was decorated with the red white and black of the Nazi banners and ranks of black uniformed SS troops stood guard before the Hofburg.

Von Seivers had been sent into Vienna several days before the Anschluss with the dossiers his department had drawn up of all the Hofburg personnel. He had not anticipated trouble and he had not encountered any. Once it was made known that Vienna had fallen into Nazi hands, officials had simply handed over the Hofburg keys. Austrian President Miklas had made a token gesture of resistance by sending special reinforcements of police into the inner city to protect government buildings, but they fell back when it became obvious that the German forces were in control.

The halls of the Hofburg were silent as Seivers made his way from the back room where he had switched off the building's alarm system earlier, then up the narrow staircase to the room where the spear was kept. He shifted the roll of drawings under his arm and walked more quickly now, down the central aisle to the familiar glass cabinet. A voice startled him.

"Heil Hitler." Major Walter Buch, Nazi legal expert, stepped out of the alcove where he had been sitting.

Wolfram Seivers returned the salute, trying to bring under control the sudden swift pounding of the blood through his body.

He had been so certain that he was alone. He wondered if he would have seen Buch if he had not spoken.

"The preparations seem to be going well," Buch was saying. "When I arrived this morning they were already erecting the reviewing stand.

Seivers nodded. "I just came in myself to check on things

here," he said. "Herr Himmler is expected tomorrow morning and he'll want to be shown around."

"What have you got there?"

"The full layout of the Hofburg. I've been running a check of our plans against theirs." Von Seivers was beginning to sweat under a uniform that suddenly felt too tight.

"I wouldn't mind taking a look at those," Buch commented. "It's a fascinating building."

"Perhaps we could get together for a few moments this afternoon over schnapps," Seivers suggested.

"I might hold you to that, but I'm sure you have things to do. Excuse me, Herr Seivers." Clicking his heels, Walter Buch gave the Nazi salute. He swung away, and his boots beat a steady retreating tattoo on the marble floor of the aisle.

Wolfram von Seivers breathed a sigh of relief. He waited until he was certain Buch had gone before opening the glass cabinet that held the Spear of Longinus and lifted the blackened spear from its case. Carefully unrolling the drawings, he revealed the slender parcel hidden at their core. Von Seivers took the second spear from its wrapping and drew a sharp intake of breath as he laid them side by side. They were identical: Himmler's forgers had done their job to perfection.

Von Seivers placed Himmler's spear in the battered leather case and closed and locked the cabinet. Then he swiftly wrapped the Spear of Longinus in the soft cloth and rolled it into the Hofburg plans.

Himmler had had a new grey uniform designed and made in readiness for the Austrian Putsch, for although it was Adolf Hitler who would be at the centre of public attention, this was Himmler's greatest moment, and he wanted to be at his best for it.

The weather for the flight to Aspen Airport near Vienna was bad. The sky was a surly, resentful grey and the overloaded aircraft bucked and dropped through the turbulence.

Heinrich Himmler leaned with his back against the door in the tail plane, shouting instructions to Walter Schellenberg over the high-pitched drone of the engines and the clamour of the men in its belly.

"When we get in, we'll contact Karltenbrunner immediately,"

he yelled, "and assuming there is not too much resistance, we'll leave Vienna in his hands while we go through to Linz to prepare for the Führer's reception."

The aeroplane dropped through an air pocket and gave a sickening lurch as it hit the bottom, like an inexpert diver flopping belly-first onto the water. Himmler fell forward and gripped the back of a seat in an attempt to steady himself but was flung like a rag doll back against the door. Schellenberg, also caught off-guard, stumbled across the seats behind him and recovered with difficulty. Alarm crossed his features as he glanced at Himmler; without warning he lunged forward, flinging his arms around the Reichsführer's waist and throwing him to the floor. Several of Himmler's bodyguards leapt to their feet.

"What in the hell do you think you're doing?" Himmler shouted, disengaging himself from Schellenberg's grasp.

"Forgive me, Herr Reichsführer. The door!"

Himmler scrambled to his feet and looked uncomprehendingly at the aircraft door.

"The safety catch is off, Herr Reichsführer. I apologise for startling you. I hope you aren't hurt?"

Himmler straightened his jacket and dusted himself off. It was a moment before he trusted himself enough to speak but when he did, his voice was deliberately controlled.

"I must thank you Obergruppenführer Schellenberg. I believe you may have saved my life. Perhaps in the future I may have the opportunity to do the same for you."

Adolf Hitler was waiting for Himmler in Linz and he was both elated and nervous. He greeted Himmler eagerly.

"How has it gone, Reichsführer? Can I expect to be well received?"

"I believe your reception will be beyond anything you might have hoped for, mein Führer. All well-known anti-Nazis are being arrested, but they are certainly in a minority. We found Vienna to be in a state of anticipation!"

"What about security? I must have top security for my entrance into the city. This would be an ideal opportunity for an attempt on my life."

"Every precaution is being taken for your protection, mein Führer." Reflected light glanced off Himmler's pince-nez so that his eyes seemed to fade away behind them.

Adolf Hitler distractedly brushed the stray lock of hair off his forehead. "I want the guard doubled in the area of the Heldenplatz when I make my address. Bring extra plain clothed men in and let them mingle with the crowd. I can't afford to take any chances!"

Himmler shifted his neck under the tight collar of his uniform. "This will mean a delay, mein Führer..."

"Then let there be a delay!" Hitler waved a hand vaguely. "I'm not ready for Vienna anyway. I want to pay a visit to my mother's grave tomorrow." He sat back in his seat and his mood switched suddenly to elation. "Sit down, Reichsführer, and tell me what arrangements have been made to take the spear."

Himmler sat awkwardly in the seat opposite the Führer; he was more at ease when there was a desk between them.

"As you know, mein Führer, von Seivers was sent in a few days early to make sure that nothing was removed from the city. The Spear of Longinus and all the other Hofburg treasures are being carefully protected."

Hitler nodded his satisfaction. "With the spear back in German hands," he said, "We hold the key to world domination."

"Have you decided where you will keep it?"

"It will go back to Nuremburg," Hitler replied definitely. "The Reich's treasures were taken from Nuremburg to Vienna and it is right that they are returned to Nuremburg."

"I see, mein Führer."

Hitler glanced at him keenly and laughed. "Do I detect a note of disappointment? Am I right in thinking you had hoped the spear would go to Wewelsburg?"

"It did seem to be a fitting place for it," he replied awkwardly.

"I had a vision before we came away," Hitler said. "I saw the spear in the hall of St. Katherine's Church in Nuremburg. St. Katherine's will be made into a museum where the German people can view the treasures we bring back to the Reich."

Heinrich Himmler shifted into a more comfortable position in his seat and folded his legs neatly.

"I understand, mein Führer," he said. "Perhaps, as you say, it would be better for the people to view the spear that's part of their heritage, rather than to keep it for the select few."

The Ringstrasse was lined with crowds that had overflowed from the Heldenplatz and, as Hitler's cavalcade drove slowly past, he was greeted by a tumult that grew in power and depth. Arms stretched out towards him through the bank of black uniformed SS, the hysteria growing as he left his motor vehicle and took the steps to the reviewing stand in front of the Hofburg. Wave upon wave of adulation rolled towards him as he lifted his arm in a salute and then established itself in a clear chant that crashed and broke between the catchment of the buildings.

"SEIG HEIL! SEIG HEIL!"

It was minutes before he was able to speak and when at last he did, his voice was steady, even pious, but there was an expression on his face that was close to ecstasy.

"Grace has been given to me to unite my homeland to the Reich. I would give thanks to Him who let me return to my homeland in order that I might now lead it into the German Reich. Tomorrow, may every German recognise the hour and measure its import, and bow in humility before the Almighty, who in a few weeks has wrought such a miracle upon us."

Austria had spawned him and spurned him and now she capitulated like a woman to a more powerful lover. Adolf Hitler looked out over the people of the ravished city of Vienna and, as a man who has used the obliging body of a whore, despised her. It seemed only natural thereafter that she should be stripped of her finery and left in bondage.

It was after midnight when Adolf Hitler left the Imperial Hotel with Heinrich Himmler. He had cancelled the civic dinner and reception that were to have been held in his honour and refused a grand tour of the city. Hitler had known Vienna only too well. He was afraid that someone from the flophouses he had frequented might recognise him.

Wolfram von Seivers and Walter Buch were waiting for the two men outside the Hofburg and, with Hitler's personal aides, they stood by whilst the two men made their way into the building and up the steps to the Schatzkammer. Himmler felt the sweat break out on his brow as they approached the glass case in which the spear lay. He wiped his hands down the seams of his trousers and watched Hitler's expression anxiously as he looked down at the spear.

"I have waited for this moment for a long time." Hitler glanced briefly at Himmler as he spoke. "Perhaps, Reichsführer, you would not mind leaving me alone. I will be with you shortly."

Heinrich Himmler clicked his heels and walked quickly back towards the entrance. It was all he could do to prevent himself from breaking into a victory jig.

The Reichsführer SS, Heinrich Himmler, locked the door of his room in Wewelsburg Castle and leaned against it for support. He was breathless with fear and elation. Walking a trifle unsteadily, he stood looking at the faded leather case on his bed before leaning down to open it. The spear, blackened with age, lay in its place. Halfway down the blade, in a central aperture, the beaten nail head was secured by a cuff threaded with wire. In a familiar ritual, Himmler lifted the spear from its case and held it in his upturned palms. The gesture was one of supplication, an offering to the gods. But this night was different, the spear in his hands was the actual Spear of Longinus and the sense of its presence filled the room in a powerful way. The fear he had experienced dropped away, and his body became the receptacle for something infinitely deeper and darker. He was at that moment possessed by a spirit of such power and magnitude that he reeled as though intoxicated.

The vision, when it came, was swift and forceful. The heavens were ripped asunder before his eyes and Himmler knew with clarity that it was he, and not Hitler, who as claimant of the spear, would control the forces of history. He witnessed a Beast come forth from the body of a woman. It leered as it rose to a position of supreme power over the earth and, from its seat of glory; it tore with its teeth the flesh of a nation. Overshadowing the Beast, and empowering it, was the form of a dragon. Heinrich Himmler knew that he was not the Beast, but the one who was destined to bring it forth and the dark power that possessed him would be the driving force.

As he lay on his bed later that night, only the memory of the moment remained with him. The fear had returned, licking at his soul, and it seemed that Wewelsburg was filled with shadows as never before. His eyes burned like coals in his sockets, and his hands, clenched into fists as his sides, were damp and icy cold.

The voice of the dragon had spoken. What Heinrich Himmler envisaged, the total annihilation of the Jewish race, would not be completed in his lifetime. Yet it was imminent, little more than two generations away. Only then would the Aryan race be able to rise unhindered from the dust, with nothing to sully or restrain the magnitude of her cosmic destiny. But firstly, a rebirth of the Jewish State must take place; the Jews would be gathered back to their homeland, and the Beast would arise to carry out the Final Solution.

Chapter 4
Twice-Born

Herod dispatched his man-servant, Chuza, to the tomb of Joseph of Arimathea as soon as he heard the news, to establish for himself what had taken place there. Chuza returned before noon bearing the grave clothes.

"There is a rumour that the disciples stole the body," he told Herod frowning. "If that's the case, then they removed the clothes first and took the body away naked. I, personally, find it impossible to believe. Caiaphas was given a Roman guard by Pontius Pilot – I saw the remains of their seal on the sepulchre. Is it likely that unarmed fishermen would risk death by robbing a tomb of its body when Rome had set armed soldiers to protect it? And if the disciples had indeed passed a sleeping guard, would they have been able to roll back the stone without awakening them? And then of course, it leaves the question of the grave clothes."

He held up the blood-stained bundle to make his point. "They apparently undressed the corpse and folded the grave clothes before leaving!" He shook his head darkly. "Something else took place there last night, sir. Something that we're not being told about."

Herodias had slipped into the room silently on her cat-like feet and Herod started guiltily when he saw her.

"Herodias, what is it?"

"I heard that Chuza had visited the tomb of the Jewish deceiver and found it empty?"

Herod nodded. "Someone has spirited the body away."

Herodias' eyes were on the bloodied cloths that Chuza was holding. "Are those the grave clothes?" she asked sharply. The chief steward glanced at his master. Herod nodded.

"What are you doing with them? They are soiled and disgusting. Give them to me and I will ask my servant to get rid of them."

Chuza took a step backwards. "My Lady, do not disturb

yourself. I will dispose of them immediately."

Herodias' expression was brittle. "I will take them," she said. "Give them to me!"

The two men looked after her helplessly as she left the room.

Both Helen and Simon Magus laughed gleefully when Herodias returned with her prize, but it was only after the contradictory rumours of theft and resurrection began to abound in Jerusalem that the Magus disclosed the notion that was formulating in his mind.

"Where was the body of the Baptist laid?"

Herodias, who reclined languidly at the table, broke off a small piece of unleavened bread and used it to scoop a portion of spiced brown beans from one of the many dishes before her.

"I think his family was from the hill country in Judaea. His father was a priest. No doubt there was a family sepulchre. Why?"

"His bones must be brought to Machaerus."

"You are mad!" Herodias retorted. "We have the head of the Baptist; for what reason would we want his body?" But she and Helen were regarding him with interest.

The Magus laughed. "Ladies, I have a plan that is not revealed to me by flesh and blood. I will tell you what it is in due time, but first we must locate the tomb of John the Baptist."

* * *

The high priest awoke from a troubled sleep and threw back his covering. Despite the crispness of the night air, he was sweating profusely. The dream was more vivid than any he remembered. In it he had taken the sacrificial knife to the Passover lamb and at the moment that the knife slit the bared throat had found himself looking into the quiet eyes of Yeshua the Nazarene.

He remembered the meeting of the council only days earlier, after Lazarus had been raised from the dead by the Nazarene.

"If he's not stopped," certain Jews told the gathered assembly, "all will believe in him and the Romans will take decisive action against us. We will lose our nation entirely!"

"Don't you realise that it is expedient for us that one man

should die in order that the whole nation should not perish?"

Caiaphas remembered his words and trembled. Was it possible that he had spoken prophetically?

"Surely he has borne our griefs and carried our sorrows; yet we did esteem him stricken, smitten of God and afflicted... For the transgression of my people was he smitten."[18]

The Isaiah prophecy haunted him. Beside him his wife murmured softly in her sleep and tucked a hand under her cheek. The high priest sat up. The pieces were fitting together so neatly in his mind that he was appalled and terrified.

The Law of Moses required that on the tenth of Nisan each household take an unblemished lamb and examine it for imperfections before the slaughter on the fourteenth day. Caiaphas clenched his fists at the memory. It was no longer a sign of fury but of sudden recognition.

Yeshua had ridden into Jerusalem on the tenth of Nisan and on watch night, after his arrest, he was examined by the Sanhedrin. Traditionally this was a night during which all Jerusalem would stay awake until dawn and speak of the things of redemption. Death could not be mixed with the Passover. Therefore it was imperative that the prisoner be taken to the Roman prefect to receive the death sentence. Pontius Pilot had examined him: Herod had examined him!

He had to think! If there was just one point of the law that Yeshua had failed to uphold as the Paschal lamb then he, Caiaphas, could rest again without fear.

The High priest arose quietly and walked to the window looking out on the night. It was pitch dark, a thin layer of cloud that had drifted in at evening obliterated the stars. Nothing moved except the tumbling, frenzy of his mind.

The slashing of the temple curtain and the darkness, which had shrouded the land during the period of the crucifixion, had been supernatural; there was no doubt of that in his mind at all. That occurrence had left a strong residue of superstitious fear in the hearts of every temple priest. It had proved as impossible to cover-up as the purported resurrection and all Jerusalem was filled with talk of it.

---

[18] Isaiah 53:4,8

Every priest present that day had gathered in awe in the outer courts of the temple precinct and discussed what the incidents meant and whether they had bearing on the death of the man, Jesus. Several even swore he had been seen in the city after the event.

As Caiaphas understood it, he had done his duty in delivering the heretic to Pilot. But if this Yeshua was the Paschal Lamb sent by God, he had failed as high priest.

He, Caiaphas, had sometimes recognised that the process of sacrificial offering was flawed. He could bring no man closer to God through the offering of gifts and sacrifices for sin, but he supposed that YHWH had known what he was doing by implementing such a bloody ritual. As high priest he donned his robes and performed the slaughter but as for those for whom it was performed, they walked out of the temple and, unfailingly, fell back into sin. An innocent life was sacrificed to make them perfect for a moment.

It followed that there was a need for a perfect and final sacrifice by a perfect and eternal high priest. There were many who declared Caiaphas was not high priest at all as he had not been elected by the Sanhedrin but by Rome. As for perfection, he was mildly aware of his own susceptibility to sin but he deemed himself safe so long as he followed the ritual laws of cleansing before he entered the inner sanctuary of the temple.

The memory of the dream that had woken him was chilling. Had he sacrificed an innocent Lamb, one born to die for the sins of the nation, as the prophet Isaiah had foreseen? If he, Caiaphas were an imperfect high priest, so were all the sons of Aaron and, according to the Torah, so was Aaron himself. Who then was worthy to sacrifice Isaiah's Lamb? Only God himself fitted the role.

Caiaphas trembled. Yeshua the Nazarene had claimed to be the Son of God. Was it possible that YHWH had come into the world, as a perfect High Priest, in order to make sacrifice of himself for the sin of men? Caiaphas was aware that his breathing was laboured and his head had grown light. The room seemed to sway around him and he leaned on the window ledge for support.

If the Nazarene was the Lamb sent by God, Caiaphas reasoned, his actions showed that he had known who he was. He came into the city at the right moment; he appeared to have lingered in the Garden of Gethsemane waiting for his arrest – by all accounts he had made no move to evade capture and had rebuked his followers when they had attempted to fight. From this time onward, Caiaphas realised, only he and the elders of the priesthood had handled Yeshua, unwittingly following the Mosaic instructions regarding the preparation of the sin sacrifice.

All through the watch-night interrogation Yeshua had refused to respond to their questions, saying that his time had not yet come, '*He was oppressed, and he was afflicted, yet he opened not his mouth; he is brought as a lamb to the slaughter.*[19]' Then at dawn the council had put the question again.

"Are you the Son of God?" And he had answered directly.

"I am."

Caiaphas had immediately torn his robes in a ritual that symbolically cut Yeshua off from the nation of Israel condemning him for blasphemy on the words of his own testimony. From then on, to preserve their ritual cleanliness, the council had depended on Rome to sentence him to death. He and Annas had accompanied the prisoner themselves. As a lamb to the slaughter. Why had he not seen before that the man had waited until the dawning of the day of Redemption before declaring himself?

At the first Passover, God had poured out his wrath on Egypt's firstborn when Pharaoh refused to allow the Hebrew slaves to be set free. Israel was again under the yoke, this time of Rome, but Caiaphas knew there was a more subtle bondage, which enslaved mankind – the slavery of sin. Israel desperately needed a redeemer. Was it possible that Jesus *was* the Son of God as he declared himself to be? If so, God had poured out his wrath on his own Son in the place of Israel! Yeshua had known and submitted himself as a sacrifice of redemption! The High priest dashed the rivulets of perspiration from his forehead with the back of his hand. Why had he failed to see it?

'*...thou shalt make his soul an offering for sin. He shall see the travail of his soul and be satisfied... he hath poured out his soul unto death; and he was numbered with the transgressors; and he bare the sin*

---

[19] Isaiah 53:7

of many... [20]

Caiaphas gripped his beard with both hands as though he would tear it from his face as he realised he had taken the knife to the throat of the sacrifice for sin in the temple at the very moment the man, Yeshua, had died. He could still see the eyes of the lamb in his dream: quiet, gentle eyes, yet anything but passive. They reflected understanding, acceptance and something he had never fully experienced himself - love.

Caiaphas, high priest of Israel, held onto the window ledge until his knuckles showed white. How could he have been expected to recognise Messiah who came to the temple, not as a conquering king, but as an itinerant Rabbi – a small town preacher; a Nazarene from Galilee?

If it were true that he, Caiaphas, had been responsible for the death of Messiah, he was desperately vulnerable. Even with Israel under Rome the power of the high priest was recognised. He was consulted, sought out; men listened to his counsel. Pontius Pilot himself asked his advice in the governing of Israel. If there was so much as a hint that he was wrong he would be rejected and condemned.

He looked down at the shadowy form of his wife on the bed. There was innocence in sleep, he thought. His wife was no longer a young woman but she had served him well. She was a woman of godly bearing who had supported him in his position. He could not let her down. Whatever all this meant, it must be kept from her and indeed, from all of Israel. It was his duty as high priest to preserve the peace of the nation while under the Roman yoke. If these events were given any credence it would stir the masses and the final outcome would be worse than the first.

As he considered the matter further, his agitation ceased. It could be argued that he had acted in innocence but in absolute accordance with the plans of YHWH. If, indeed, Yeshua was the Lamb sent into the world, his sole purpose was to die as a sacrifice for sin. If he, Caiaphas, had prevented his death, he would have been guilty in thwarting God's will. There was no doubt he had acted rightly in putting the people of Israel before his personal convictions. God would

---

[20] Isaiah 53:10,12

honour him for that.

Satisfied in his own mind he had done what was right; he lifted the covers and slipped into bed. His wife stirred and reached out to touch him and for a moment he held her hand.

Chapter 5
Twice-Born

Gabriele was assigned to the custody of two Gestapo officers during the train journey back to Berlin. She sat near the window watching the endless flow of scenery until it became a meaningless blur in her mind. Beside her, the two men played cards across the centre table, effectively locking her into a corner of a compartment filled with a nauseating cloud of cigarette smoke, but Gabriele harboured no thought of escape.

Michael was free and she had helped to secure that freedom. It was the one thought that would carry like a pure refrain over a dirge, in the weeks following her arrest.

Her face was bruised and her lip broken, she was treated with open contempt by her guards and she had not eaten since her last meal with Michael at the hotel nearly twenty hours before. Neither man had made any move to offer her food or drink but there was tap water in the toilet and with a man standing guard outside, Gabriele had been able to both drink and briefly wash.

When the train arrived in Berlin station the following day, she was met by officers of the Nazi Party Office for Racial Purity, handcuffed and taken by car to their building in Ringstrasse.

"Gabriele Hoch?"

She nodded. Her interrogation officer was a man whose flesh seemed to have been sucked in against his bone structure. He wore a non-descript grey suit, shiny at the knees and patched with leather at the elbows. Reading through her personal details in a toneless voice, He glanced up now and then to receive verification of the facts. Gabriele watched him with distaste. His cheekbones were pronounced, his eyes set back in their sockets and his skin was like pale parchment folded into deep vertical lines around a thin mouth. From a receding hair-line, dry, light-brown hair thinly covered his skull and compacted under the grimy collar of his shirt. A bull-necked soldier stood guard at the door.

"What is your relationship with Michael Segal?"

"I worked with Michael until he was forced to leave his post at the university."

"But you formed a more intimate relationship."

"I have no idea what you mean by 'intimate'!"

"You were involved with the Jew sexually."

"I have already told the man who arrested me that I was not!"

At the door, the bull-neck leered but the expression of the interrogator exhibited no discernible change.

"The bed in your hotel room had been slept in by two people and you shared a sleeping compartment."

Gabriele shrugged. "In themselves, those two facts mean nothing," she retorted. "But if I had had an affair with anyone, I would not share those details with you!"

"You have broken German law," he snapped. "You are accused of having sexual relations with a Jew and of aiding his escape. If you know what's good for you, you will stick to answering my questions without any additional commentary."

"I was not involved sexually with Michael Segal," Gabriele said through gritted teeth. "But we were close friends."

"Close enough for your forged documents to reflect that you were married."

"I considered that travelling together as a married couple would attract less attention than if Michael had travelled alone."

"And to that end, you paid for documents to be fraudulently drawn up, although you were fully aware that you were in breach of the law."

"Of course. I would do the same for any friend that was in similar danger."

"In defiance of the State?"

"If necessary."

"The Jew, Segal, could have left Germany legally. There was nothing to prevent him. Why did you find it necessary to encourage him to cross into Switzerland using such complicated subterfuge?"

Gabriele's laugh was short and bitter. "How many Jews are managing to get out of the country?" she asked. "Thousands are clamouring for papers and few have made it out."

"Nobody wants them," he shrugged. "It's obvious."

"Michael is out. He is no longer in danger of harassment by thugs or arrest by officials. Germans seem to have abandoned all morality when they persecute human-beings simply for their racial affiliation!" she said.

The RPA official glanced at her sharply.

"You are altogether too free with your tongue," he said. "And you seem to be unaware of the trouble you're in. You could be looking at serving a long prison sentence; a pointless waste, if you ask me." He stood up, a slight, nondescript figure of a man, and tucked his notes into a file cover. Nodding at the guard, he said:

"I'm finished here. Lock her up."

"When is my case likely to be heard?"

"I have no idea," he said. "It might be days, or weeks. There is a big case load before the courts at the moment."

"I am due back at my lecturing post." It was a small plea, her first sign of weakness and the official smiled. When he replied there was a note of triumph in his tone.

"Your licence to teach has already been withdrawn," he said and he left the room.

Chapter 6
Twice-Born

Peter and Cleopas left Jerusalem in the afternoon and took the road to the tiny village of Emmaus, which lay seven miles to the north-west of the city. When Cleopas said he was going to relay the news of the past few days to his mother; Peter had immediately offered to accompany him.

"I can't stay here any longer," he said. "I need to walk to clear my thoughts."

It was the final day of the Passover and the road out of Jerusalem was quiet: tomorrow, it would be filled with travellers returning home after the feast.

"It has been a Passover most people will remember," Cleopas said glancing back to where the city lay behind them peaceful and resplendent in the warm glow of the afternoon sun. It reflected nothing of the turmoil and agony of the past few days. "It seems impossible to believe that just a week ago the crowds hailed the Master as he rode into Jerusalem."

"One day they were calling him Messiah, son of David," Peter said bitterly, "and a few short days later, shouting for his death!" He shook his head, "It still makes no sense, especially after this morning! What do you make of it Cleopas? His body has gone; Mary of Magdala says she has seen the Master alive, yet at first she failed to recognise him. Surely, she is mistaken?"

"The master raised Lazarus after four days in the grave," Cleopas reminded him. "Is it not possible that he, himself, could be raised?"

Again, Peter shook his head in confusion. He dared not hope; he had witnessed the crucifixion and seen with his own eyes the broken, lifeless body that was taken down from the cross. If he dared to believe in the face of what he had seen, his hopes might once again be dashed. He could not countenance that possibility. At the back of his mind nagged the shame of his denial of the Master. He remembered Jesus' words while he, John and James were found sleeping in the Garden of Gethsemane:

"Could you not watch one hour? Watch and pray lest you enter into temptation. The spirit is indeed willing but the flesh is weak."

They walked quickly, occasionally gesticulating as they spoke, trying to make sense of what had happened. Grief was a close companion, and one that could not yet be shaken off lightly. The road became rockier as the city fell behind but the view spread out before them, a panorama of green and gold broken only here and there by a gnarled tree, which had clung tenaciously to life despite the harsh Judaean climate, and grey rocky outcrops brushed by gold lichen.

They were completely unaware of the other person until he drew level with them. He raised a hand cheerfully in greeting as they half-turned, startled by the sound of his footsteps.

"You men were deeply engrossed in conversation," the stranger said. "Where are you headed?"

"To Emmaus," Peter replied.

"I am going that way as well. Mind if I accompany you?" He fell in step beside them without waiting for an answer. "So, what manner of discussion is this that keeps you blinded to all else? You appear to be sad."

"Are you the only one to come out of Jerusalem this morning who knows nothing of the events that have taken place there?" Cleopas asked.

"What things were these?"

"Concerning Jesus of Nazareth. He was a prophet, mighty in word and deed before God and all the people."

"The chief priests and rulers condemned him to death and delivered him to be crucified," Peter said. "Yet we expected that he was the one who would redeem Israel. And today, some women came from the tomb and astonished us when they said his body had gone. They swore they had seen a vision of angels who declared that the Master is alive."

"Is it so strange to you? Think about the scriptures for a moment. All these things had to happen to Messiah. Did Moses not prophesy that another would come in his likeness?"

They looked at one another and nodded.

"God poured out his wrath on the firstborn of the Egyptians and only then was Moses able to lead the children of Israel out of Egypt," the man pointed out.

"And the Master called himself the firstborn of the Father!"

"That was done because of the disobedience of Pharaoh," Peter protested. "We were witnesses to Jesus' obedience. He never did anything or said anything that he did not hear his Father saying."

"He was obedient unto death?" the stranger suggested.

"Exactly so. He went willingly."

"John even said that when Jesus appeared before Pontius Pilot, he told him that he had the power to lay his life down and the power to take it up again," Peter said, light suddenly dawning in his face.

"So, if he laid down his life in obedience to the Father, it follows that it was the Father's will that he perished."

Peter and Cleopas glanced at one another again. The stranger's summation carried certain logic.

"But if he was indeed the Son of David, Messiah, why did he not redeem Israel?"

"Perhaps redemption could only come with death?" The stranger was walking slowly, matching their pace. "There is no redemption without the shedding of blood. Think of the lamb sacrificed at Passover,"

"A sacrifice for sin."

"Then," said their fellow traveller; "does it not follow that the Father would give his only Son for the sin of the world. Who but God could offer the spotless lamb necessary for complete redemption of his people?"

"What fools we are!" Peter said, clapping the palm of his hand to his forehead. "We were looking for the Master to redeem us from the Roman bondage, not from the bondage of sin!"

"Justifiably, perhaps," Cleopas said with a grin; "did not the judges free Israel time and again from the yoke of the Philistines?"

"The yoke was only there because of their sin," the stranger reminded him. "But consider; what does the prophet Isaiah say?" And he continued expounding the prophets to them until all too soon, the village appeared ahead; moon-pale geometric houses tucked into a hollow of the earth, tempered by deep green palms. Clusters of brown-faced sheep stood quietly in the late-afternoon sun unperturbed by the arrival of strangers.

"Please," Cleopas urged when the man seemed set to continue on his journey. "Won't you stay the night with us? The hour is already late."

His mother, delighted to receive guests busied herself with the preparation of the food. News of Jesus' arrest and death had reached the village on the day following the crucifixion and she had waited, anxious for word that all was well with Cleopas, his wife, Mary, and the other disciples.

The three men were served around the table in the small central room of their mud-walled home. The elderly woman, her face softened by a sea of wrinkles, peered from the folds of her robe beaming as she wished them good appetite. It was simple fare; a stew of vegetables, unleavened bread and wine.

The stranger took one of the loaves, blessed and broke it.

Peter and Cleopas raised their heads, astounded.

"Master!"

In that instant of recognition, Jesus was gone from their presence. The meal was forgotten as they gazed at one another in joyful amazement.

"How did we not recognise him?" Cleopas said.

"Did our hearts not burn within us as he opened the scriptures to us, along the way?" Peter asked. "We must go back immediately and tell the others. He is indeed risen!"

Cleopas' mother tried to restrain them.

"Go tomorrow morning!" she begged, but seeing their resolute expressions she softened and laughed.

"I'll pack your meal for you. You will be hungry along the way."

Jesus appeared to the disciples many times before his final ascension to heaven. During this time, they were instructed and prepared for the tough and exhilarating journey that lay ahead. But for

Peter, the encounter on the road to Emmaus was the beginning of a release from guilt. Jesus had sought him out personally to comfort his heart and in the weeks and months ahead it was often Peter, impetuous as ever, who took the lead in preaching the gospel that Jesus had entrusted to them.

Chapter 7
Twice-Born

The Samaritan, Simon Magus, who was born in the town of Gitta, spent his early years in Alexandria, Egypt. Following the death of his father, he travelled extensively with his father's younger brother, Joseph, a tin merchant, and before his eighteenth year had tramped the mines of Southern England and learned the tin trade. In later years, Joseph would join the inner circle of Simon's band of disciples, becoming an ardent adherent of his nephew.

From Alexandria, the Magus gained an intimate understanding of the panoply of Egyptian gods; in particular, of the cult of Isis and Osiris, and while in England, he was brought in contact with the Druids. It did not take long for him to recognize the interrelationship of the Babylonian gods of Samaria with the gods of other nations. Alexandria was the ideal city for a study of this sort and Simon Magus began to pour over the scrolls in the great library, drawing connections between the various systems of worship in the known world. There was a large Greek and Jewish community in Alexandria and it was among these Jews that the Magus gained his first grounding in Judaism. The fascination for Magus was in the point of departure of the Jewish religion from all others.

The Jews were, of course, monotheistic and their God demanded total allegiance to himself and a rejection of all other gods. Jewish history was carefully recorded and, as the people of the book, the Jews considered their scriptures and their laws superior to all other writings.

There was a clearly demarcated system of punishment and reward which was dependent upon their obedience to God; where disobedience abounded, punishment in the form of attack, military defeat and dispersion resulted, a demonstration of the power of their God to perform in accordance with his word. When the king walked in obedience to the Law of God, the people followed his example and the land lay at peace.

As a Samaritan, the origin of his own people was recorded in these writings. During the reign of Jeroboam, in the years after Solomon's death, the ten tribes of Israel separated from the tribes of Judah and Benjamin. Realizing that the people would need some form of worship to replace the temple worship of the Jews, Jeroboam had set up golden calves at Dan and Bethel and Israel slipped back into a form of Osiris worship that they had never quite shed after the years spent in slavery in Egypt. Jeroboam's priests were 'sons of the lowest people', and not part of the Levitical priesthood instituted by God through the descendents of Aaron, the brother of Moses.

The Israelites were taken captive by Nebuchadnezzar of Babylon leaving only the poorest Jews on the land and Babylonian tribes repopulated Samaria bringing their own gods with them. When wild animals began to ravage the area, the Babylonians perceived it as a sign of displeasure from the God of the Jews, and called for a priest to teach them the ways of this national God.

A man from northern Israel was sent to Samaria to fulfil this role but the priesthood had, by this time, been separated from the temple worship of Judaea for many years and the religion the priest introduced to the inhabitants of Samaria was a hybrid mix of Judaism and paganism. This heterodox became incorporated into the existing forms of Assyrian and Babylonian worship.

The Samaritans called themselves God's people but continued to serve their graven images in the manner of the Babylonians. Because of their mixed background and the marked divergence in their worship of Jehovah, orthodox Jews had no dealings with them.

The Baptist's place of burial was not difficult to locate. In the hill country of Judaea, a sepulchre was the chosen method of burial for those who were able to afford it. Zachariah had been of the tribe of Abijah, and a member of the temple priesthood. Although he had never been a man of great means, neither was he of humble status. He and Elizabeth had a family tomb, which had been purchased by Zachariah's father. It was, therefore, natural that the disciples should have interred the body of Baptist in the family sepulchre.

Neither did the Magus and the two men who accompanied him

on his grisly mission experience any difficulty in removing John the Baptist's body. They operated in the dead of night at a grave site beyond the precincts of the sleepy Judaean village; wrapped the remains well and placed the load on the back of a donkey cart. The stone was rolled back and damage to the bruised grass and vegetation repaired as best they were able. As, in accordance with Jewish law, there was no veneration of the dead, neither of relics or images, his disciples gave no thought to the removal of John's remains. The theft was never considered and therefore never discovered.

Simon examined the corpse carefully. Even with the method, practised by the Jews, of wrapping the body with aloes and spices, and the comparatively low temperature of the tomb, John's headless corpse had suffered great deterioration.

"There will have to be another way," he said. "But we will keep the Baptist's body. It may serve some other purpose."

A few days later he put his thoughts to the inner circle as they gathered in the subterranean room known as the King's Chamber.

"Is there a way to smuggle the body of a crucified man out of Jerusalem?"

"The bodies are dumped in the valley of Hinnom," Marcus said. "It must be possible to remove one before it is burned."

"Then it must be accomplished soon. The work ahead will require great secrecy and cunning. I believe, brethren, we will need to invoke the intervention of the gods."

Chapter 8
Twice-Born

In July 1937, Marie Denarnaud received a visit at her home, the Villa Bethania in Rennes-le-Chateau. A storm had overshadowed the peaks during the night, clearing as the morning broke, allowing the sun to break through with crystal clarity. Shadows deepened the copses of trees and blackened the mountain crevasses.

The two men were in plain clothes, but Mme. Denarnaud knew without being told that they were Gestapo. They flashed their identity cards at her and introduced themselves.

"M Barbie and Karl Wolff. We have a few questions."

They ignored her sullen expression and stepped past her into a living room that was comfortably furnished.

Barbie shrugged out of his top coat, folded it neatly and placed it on the arm of the chair with his hat on top. He was dressed in a dark grey suit with a maroon and grey silk tie over a white shirt.

Although it was close to midday, Marie Denarnaud was still in a floral housecoat and a pair of misshapen slippers. Her hair, an unconvincing auburn, was grey at the roots and uncombed.

"We're conducting an investigation into the death of the curé Béranger Saunière," Barbie said. He sat back in the deep armchair and crossed his legs, looking relaxed and at ease. "You were his housekeeper?"

"That was a long time ago," she replied. "He died in 1917, why would you be investigating it now?

"Certain people are convinced the curé was murdered," Wolff replied, "and murder is a serious offence no matter how long ago it was committed."

"He was an old man," Mme Denarnaud protested, lifting her hands. "He died of a stroke. There was nothing unusual about it as far as the doctor was concerned."

"And yet five days earlier, when the villagers insist that the curé was in rude health, you purchased a coffin for him?"

"That's not true!"

Wolff held up a piece of paper. "We have a copy of the receipt."

Marie blanched and her heavy body sagged visibly. "I have nothing to say about that."

"I think you will find," Barbie said, "that there is nothing that you will be prepared to withhold before this interview is over." His voice was deceptively pleasant. "Perhaps you will tell us how you are managing to live so well, although I understand you have not worked since Saunière died in 1917."

Marie's hands worked together in her lap. "I have a private income."

"Left to you by Béranger Saunière?" Barbie prompted.

"Some of it."

"Yet his will showed him to be penniless."

"Look," she said suddenly, "I don't know what this is all about. Are you accusing me of something?"

"Just be so good as to answer the questions," Wolff interjected.

Barbie smiled unpleasantly. "Was the money Saunière's?"

The curé gave me money before he died," she said. "In appreciation for what I did for him."

"In return for favours?"

"I don't know what you mean."

"I think your relationship with the curé was more than that of a housekeeper. Isn't it true that you were his mistress?"

Marie Denarnaud's voice was bitter. "I was his housekeeper," she insisted.

Klaus Barbie raised his eyebrows in apparent disbelief.

"But there was a certain Emma Calvé who was his lover?" Wolff said.

Her chin tilted defiantly. "I was not aware of any irregularities in their relationship," she retorted. "Mme Calvé visited us regularly. They had certain things in common."

"She was known as high-priestess of Paris' esoteric sub-culture," Barbie said. "As a Catholic priest, I would have expected Beranger Saunière to have had very little in common with her."

"What did you think of her?" Wolff asked curiously.

"She was an operatic prima donna. Paris society loved her, but I found her to be a flighty bit of nonsense!" Marie retorted, taken off guard by his tone. "Full of city airs and graces. She acted as though she owned the place and she obviously had the curé under her thumb in the early days."

"By the 'early days', you mean after Saunière found the parchments in the church?" Barbie said. "That appears to have been the turning point in fortunes and finances for both of you. Suddenly we see the good curé's income jump from a paltry six pounds a year to a point where the man was spending millions towards the end of his life."

Marie Denarnaud shrugged. "The parchments were worth a lot," she said.

"On their own, the parchments were not worth a great deal," Barbie contradicted. "But the curé's find led him to something else that was worth a lot more."

Marie's lips curled. "What does anyone know?" she said. "The curé outsmarted them all. He found what they were all looking for and he used it to make money."

Barbie shot a glance at Wolff and then turned back to Denarnaud.

"We have it on good authority that the bulk of that money came from the Abbé Henri Boudet, curé of Rennes-le-Bains."

Marie Denarnaud shrugged carelessly. "I've told you," she reiterated, "I know that the curé made money, but I don't know where it came from."

"But the Abbé employed you to keep an eye on Saunière and to carry information between the two of them. Saunière appeared to be more a pawn of Boudet's than a friend," Wolff said.

The woman's eyes shifted uneasily. "I don't know what you mean."

Klaus Barbie stood up. He was not a tall man and his face was pleasant, even featured; a face that most women would have found attractive. He smiled down at Marie Denarnaud, so that she was unprepared for the sudden backlash of his hand. She gasped in pain and her hand flew to her face.

"You were an agent," Barbie grated, "and the money you received came mostly from Abbé Boudet!"

The woman moaned but remained silent.

Barbie gripped her by the hand, hauling her to her feet, twisting her arm savagely behind her back. "Answer me!"

She shut her eyes to blot out the image of his face and nodded. She was whimpering in pain. Barbie pushed her back into her chair and turned contemptuously away. He took a packet of cigarettes from his pocket and offered one to Wolff before lighting his own. Turning back to Denarnaud he drew deeply on the cigarette, gripped her by the hair and slowly and deliberately ground the burning end of the cigarette into her neck. Barbie waited until her screams had degenerated into ragged weeping before he addressed her again.

"Every time you refuse to answer a question," he told her conversationally, "I will find a new place to burn you, and believe me, you will find I am very inventive."

"Where did Boudet's money come from?" Wolff asked. His attitude had remained unthreatening throughout the interview and she looked up at him, pleading with her eyes.

"I don't know," she whispered. "But I think it was from the Organisation. He and Curé Saunière belonged to a group of Freemasons. The Abbé was very high up, but he still received orders from others. He instructed the curé in the way he should decorate the church and in the building of the Tour Magdala and this villa."

"Some interesting features have been brought into the church," Wolff commented. "'Terribilis est locus iste. This place is terrible!' An unusual inscription to set over the entrance to a church, don't you think?"

"And in the Stations of the Cross, a child dressed in Scottish plaid." Barbie added. "Presumably an indication of the curé's affiliation with Scottish Rite Freemasonry."

"I don't know," she implored. "Some of the things did seem strange to me, but I never questioned them. The curé was a good man, he treated his parishioners well and he used his money to improve the village."

Barbie cut in impatiently. "You said that Saunière found

something else," he said. "Did the Organisation know about it?"

The woman's face was red and swollen with weeping and she looked down unseeingly, at the hands that lay upturned in her lap.

"Not at first," she replied, "but they suspected. That's why Emma Calvé was sent in. She had no personal interest in the curé, I'm sure he was just one of her many conquests, but he loved her."

"You say the Organisation sent her in to spy on Saunière?" There was a spark of interest in Wolff that had not been there previously.

Marie Denarnaud's chin lifted in defiance once more. "She was certainly one of them. What would a woman like her have wanted with a village priest? He didn't tell her a thing at first. The curé became a very powerful man in the time that followed his discovery. He developed powers."

The men exchanged a swift glance.

"What sort of powers?"

"I don't know. There was a strength about him. He could lay his hands on people and they would get well." Her voice trailed off uncertainly.

"What did he find?" Barbie demanded. He leaned so close to her that she recoiled from the breath that fanned her cheek.

"He never told me a thing!"

Barbie straightened up and reached into his pocket for his cigarette case. Denarnaud saw the gesture and her hands fluttered uneasily. As the lighter flared into life, she moved back into the armchair in a futile gesture of escape. Klaus Barbie drew on the cigarette causing the tip to glow red. This time he leaned down, pinning her back against the seat and ground the burning end of the cigarette into her inner thigh. She shrieked wildly, her hands clawing at his arm, but the steady pressure of the cigarette hardly wavered.

"He discovered a tomb!" Her voice was pitched very high, on the edge of hysteria.

Barbie relaxed and his expression was that of a schoolteacher who had just received a correct answer from his student. He slowly ground his cigarette out in the ashtray and sat back to wait for Denarnaud to compose herself.

"Go on!"

Her eyes were wild and she was shaking violently, but she had brought the sobbing under control. "He bought a copy of a painting with him from Paris. It was Poussin's painting of a shepherdess and two shepherds examining a tomb. There was an inscription on it in Latin, 'Et in Arcadia ego'. The curé recognised the peak of Rennes-le-Chateau in the background and searched the area until he found the grave."

"What was so important about this tomb?" Wolff prompted. He was leaning forward in his seat and somehow Marie Denarnaud knew that her story meant more to him than to Klaus Barbie.

"There was a cup entombed with the bones."

"You mean a goblet?"

She nodded, "A golden goblet of great importance, the curé said. He believed it to be the Grail."

Klaus Barbie's expression was incredulous. "He believed it was what!"

"The Holy Grail," she whispered.

Again there was a swift exchange of glances between the two men.

"Was there anything else?"

Her glance shifted and she tugged nervously at her earlobe.

"Nothing more. Just a skeleton."

"She's lying!"

Barbie grasped her by the hair and twisted her head round so that she was forced to face him.

"What else?" he demanded. "That can't have been all."

"There was the skeleton. Please, you're hurting me!"

Barbie made no move to release his hold. "Speak to me!" he said. "When I'm certain you are telling the truth I will consider letting you go."

"The skeleton was headless, but there was an embalmed head. Béranger said it was the head and skeleton of Christ because of the genealogies buried there. Earlier than those he found in the church. He believed the papers were vitally important."

She was still afraid, but it was becoming easier to believe they would leave her alone as long as she gave them what they wanted.

Barbie's eyes flashed in triumph and Karl Wolff was hanging onto every word.

"What happened to these remains?"

She shook her head and her face reflected renewed fear. "The genealogies were sold into the hands of men from Paris and they took away the bones.

"The head and the cup," Wolff said. "Where are they?"

"The curé kept them but he may have intimated something to Emma Calvé about the head. They came looking for it before his death. In the end Béranger gave it to them."

"And the goblet?"

"I don't know what he did with it."

"Liar!" Barbie lashed out with the back of his hand the blow caused blood to trickle from the corner of her mouth. She was whimpering now, like a wounded animal.

"It may have been hidden in the church. Asmodeus is the demon protector of secrets."

"I am certain you know where it is," Wolff said conversationally. "Did you murder the curé out of a fit of jealousy, or did you decide to get rid of him knowing you would become a wealthy woman?"

He read the look of cunning beneath the fear of the hunted in her eyes.

"Let me guess," he said. "You started out as the Abbé Boudet's agent, but over the years, you fell in love with the curé. You were bitter against the Organisation that used Emma Calvé to seduce Saunière and your loyalty after that was only to Saunière himself. When the Abbé died and Saunière confided in you, you told no one the secrets, knowing that in time you could use them to secure your own position."

She shook her head adamantly. "I didn't kill him! I loved him!"

"But three days before his death you bought a coffin for him."

"I had no choice, they ordered me to. I'm sure the curé became careless! He realised the extent of the power he possessed through the relics and tried to use it against the Organisation. In 1916, some men arrived here and there was a quarrel. That was when the curé gave them the head. They instructed me knowing precisely when he would have the stroke that killed him."

"Why didn't you tell Saunière?"

She looked down at the hands that twisted together in her lap. "I was afraid. They were very powerful people."

"Then who killed him?" Barbie snapped.

"I don't know," Denarnaud replied wearily. "I don't know who did it, or how it was done. No one came near the house in those three days. I think they simply cursed him and he died."

"You're lying!" Barbie spat and he made a move towards her.

Wolff stopped him with a movement of his hand. "So, all these years, you've lived in the grand Villa Bethania, guarding your secrets. How is it, if this organisation is as powerful as you claim, they didn't get the cup from you?"

Barbie swung back towards her to gauge her reply.

"They never knew it existed," she answered. The curé told me about it after Abbé Boudet died and I never told anyone else. The curé loved Emma Calvé, but he never trusted her." She shook her head triumphantly. "I was the only one he really trusted!"

Barbie stood over her, irritated by her attitude. "The goblet, where is it now?"

Her jaw tightened and she looked away.

"There is a murder charge against you," Wolff reminded her. "It will be a simple matter to make it stick."

For a brief moment she defied them and then she averted her eyes. The vivid red blotch on her neck bore testimony to Barbie's tactics and she knew without saying that she had only been given a taste of what he was capable of.

"I'm an old woman," she said wearily. "This was a curse to me from the beginning. Perhaps if I get rid of it there will be peace for me in these last years. The goblet is still guarded by the statue of Asmodeus. If you come with me, I'll show you how to get it."

Wolff glanced across at Barbie. "Tell Otto Rahn to come in here. We'll leave the recovery to him."

Chapter 9
Twice-Born

The newly crucified corpse was retrieved from the valley of Hinnom even before rigor mortis set in and before it was scorched by the fires that burned there ceaselessly. The Magus had stressed certain criteria to his men, knowing the gods would do the rest. It was essential that flogging should have taken place; that the crucifixion had been carried out in the same manner as that of Jesus of Nazareth, and that no bones were broken. But there was an unanticipated problem.

"This man is not a Jew!" Marcus breathed urgently as they loaded the body onto the cart.

"Do we wait for another? It could be days!"

"The hands will have to cover the penis. It will be seen that the body was laid out that way as an act of decorum," Thaddeus said. "Hurry now, we must get out of here before we are seen!"

The corpse was covered with a load of flax and the cart trundled its way out of Jerusalem, a hazardous journey at night and one not lightly undertaken. Robbers abounded on the roads outside the city waiting for the unwary traveller. Thaddeus and Marcus walked cautiously at the head of the donkeys for the first watch of the night while seven of the Magus' men rode on the back of the cart, their sword-arm at the ready.

Their first stop was a solitary dwelling among the hills and at their approach a lamp was lit in a lower room. Before the cart was brought to a halt the door opened and a gaunt figure, wrapped warmly against the chill, beckoned them in.

"You have the body?"

Thaddeus nodded.

"Bring it this way."

They followed the man around the house and down some steps into a cellar; Marcus and Lucius bearing the corpse between them. He indicated a waist-high stone slab.

"Lay him down there."

The disciples took in their surroundings in some astonishment. They were in an underground pyramid and the surface on which the body rested was positioned below its apex.

The embalmer smiled. "The power of the pyramid preserves the corpse while I am working. Now, you said that you did not require full embalmment?"

Thaddeus nodded. "The head is to be removed," he said. "Lucius will take care of that. The body must be able to withstand desert elements for eight days."

"It can be done," the embalmer said slowly. "The weather is still cool, which is fortunate."

"Only one opening can be made in the cadaver," Thaddeus said, "and that is through the right side." And he described the piercing of the Roman lance.

The embalmer nodded, his eyes all the while on the rigid body laid out on the slab.

"Remove the head," he ordered. "Then the corpse must be washed."

As a butcher, Lucius was best able, with one blow of the sword, to dismember it cleanly. The embalmer retrieved the head by the hair and tossed it carelessly into a basket. Several stone jars stood in the corner of the room, some of which were used as receptacles for the fluids and internal organs. Still others held camomile oil and the embalming tar, a strong mixture of cedar and juniper resins, which would be used to paint the cavities of the body. Speed was of the essence and the embalmer used none of the delicacy that he had employed in the work on the head of the Baptist. The initial work was completed by dawn.

"You and your men will wait today and sleep," he instructed Thaddeus. "Making the journey at night will minimise the deterioration."

He continued his work during the day, allowing fluids to drain and filling the body cavities with rags. By evening, when they were again ready to travel, he was content that enough had been done.

"Whatever you intend to do, do it swiftly," he said. "I wish you good fortune."

Simon Magus had remained behind and passed the first day at Machaerus in the company of Helen and Herodias. On his return to the Dead Sea dwelling with the head of the Baptist he spent two more days seeking the will of the gods with Helen, his hierodule. The Magus was fully aware that the task he had undertaken could be done only once. There was no room for failure. However, he had woken on the morning of the third day in the full knowledge that a trial representation of the head must be made.

Already the screens were erected awaiting the return of his disciples and he set to work urgently. When the men returned with the body, of necessity the screens must be free.

"Give me your veil," he said to Helen, "and I will make it an icon!"

By the time the sun was fully risen, Simon was prepared and the head of the Baptist set in place. Within the dark room, Helen watched entranced by the sight of the inverted image cast upon the soft fabric of her veil.

"It is powerful magic," she told the Magus, "such as nothing the world has seen before."

Simon removed the fabric from the screen on the evening of the third day and he and Helen ran down to the beach to wash the silver from the cloth. In the failing light the result was disappointing and Helen's features fell. A series of stains were imprinted upon the cloth in the colour of old blood.

"You've ruined it!" she pouted angrily. "And you promised me the image of a god."

She left him and went to bed. For Simon Magus, sleep was impossible.

It was almost dawn on the following day when he heard the disciples arrive. Simon Magus went out to meet them, dark lines etched beneath his eyes. In the back of the cart lay the embalmed body of the crucified man. Everything was ready but he was now convinced it was all in vain.

He listened to their chatter as they unhitched the donkeys and unloaded the cadaver. They were exhausted by the journey but there was no thought of sleep. It was a race against time and the elements if they were to accomplish the task ahead.

"Simon!" Helen shouted and waved from the cottage. She was never an early riser and the Magus looked up, startled. Running towards them across the thin winter grass, Helen held the corners of her veil in both hands so that it ballooned in the wind. The men glanced enquiringly at Simon.

"You did it, Simon! You created an idol!" She held up the cloth in the sunlight and at once they saw it. The likeness was watery, ethereal, but, unmistakably, in the full light of day, it was an imprint of the mystical features of the Baptist.

Simon had prepared the heavy frame from which the body would be suspended, allowing for it to be supported at the groin and under the armpits. But first, a ritual of dedication was carried out in the King's Chamber; the Magus was seeking not simply to make an image of a man but that of a deity.

The body of the crucified man was more muscular about the shoulders than John had been and it was necessary to drive a stake down into the torso on which to rest the head of the Baptist. The stake served a dual purpose as the body was tied back to its support at this point, preventing it from slumping. The head was raised on a short plinth upon the shoulders of the cadaver and secured there, so that, as far as possible, the beard disguised the severance at the neck.

It was late morning by the time the preparations were carried out to Simon's entire satisfaction and they were ready to begin.

The white linen cloth, which Chuza had recovered from the sepulchre in Jerusalem, was attached upside down to a screen in the dark room, its fringes wound around nails on the wooden frame to prevent it from damage. By adjusting the position of the frame on which the corpse was hung, it was possible to make the height of the body correspond to the imprint on the shroud. Simon Magus did the work in the darkroom himself, meticulously matching bloodstains to body parts where the inverted image fell on the cloth. Before Marcus painted it with silver nitrate, a fine crease-mark was deliberately formed in the fabric slashing the inverted image across the line of the throat.

Three tense days followed while the men guarded the area to

ensure that no one approached. The Magus was certain that three days were enough. He himself had spent three days in the Khufu pyramid at Giza; Jesus had spent three days in the tomb before the resurrection. The image would need three days to make it a god. In fact, it would necessitate twice three days. It required delicate and meticulous work to turn the cadaver and to prepare the screen in the dark room to receive the image of the back view. Again the provocative crease was made at the neck where the thick band of hair fell between the shoulder blades concealing the severing of the head.

At last the fabric was detached from its frame, the silver was washed out on the sea shore and the fourteen foot shroud laid out to dry. Light was dark and dark was light: the result, however, was unmistakeable. Imposed on the length of white linen was the full life-size front and rear likeness of a man laid out in death; a scorched, sepia-coloured image rendered, it seemed, supernaturally. The watery nature of the figure suggested that the eyes were open in the hollows in the skull, rather than closed in death and at the neck was a pale line, a defect or crease, effectively separating the head from the torso.

"Sleep evaded me once again," the Magus confessed to Joseph, his uncle, the following morning.

"Why, Master?"

"This work has been done for future generations, Joseph. Do you think it is possible that they will fail to make the connection with the Nazarene?"

Joseph rubbed his chin thoughtfully. "If the story fades from living memory, which it will, no doubt, in time, the shroud will be of no further consequence," he said at length.

"But if the memory of the death remains," Simon Magus persisted, "will the connection be made? Is it enough?"

The older disciple shook his head. "It could be said, rightly, that this appeared to be the shroud of a crucified man," he replied hesitantly, "but there is nothing which connects it to the Nazarene."

"The association must be made or we have failed in our task!" Simon said. "Let us speak to the others."

It was agreed that certain objects should be used. Helen gathered plants and flowers common to the region, the Magus made a whip and found a reed such as the soldiers had given Jesus to carry as a sceptre. He was already in possession of the crown of thorns, the nails and the lance.

Using a length of linen as a backdrop, the objects were placed in such a manner as to surround the existing image that hung once again in the darkroom. As a final gesture, two shekel coins, the temple tithe, were placed to cover the eye sockets and, positioned beside the left leg, Simon Magus suspended a board. On it, carefully mirror-imaged, he had inscribed the words in Hebrew, Latin and Greek in similar fashion to that written by Pontius Pilot, 'Jesus Christ, King of the Jews'.

To their disappointment, when the job was done, the images of the objects surrounding the body were scarcely discernible to the naked eye.

"We must believe that it is enough," the Magus said. "We cannot do more."

The cloth was dried, folded and placed in a camphor chest similar to that which held the head of the Baptist.

"Master," Thaddeus said later; "we cannot stop here; this is an unknown art that we could use to make great gain."

"We will make no other," Simon said. "The method we have used is to be destroyed and forgotten. It must never be spoken of again. But the shroud will live on; the gods will preserve it. You remember the record in the Jewish scriptures of Nebuchadnezzar's dream?"

"The image with a head of gold?"

The Magus smiled. "The same! According to Daniel, the head represented Babylon."

The men looked at the magician uncomprehendingly.

"We have taken the head of the Baptist, Jesus' cousin, and placed it on the corpse of a gentile to create the icon of a false god. In so doing we have recreated the Jewish Messiah in the image of Babylon."

"The law of the Jews ensures that they will never accept a god whose likeness is worshipped," Joseph said.

"Especially one rendered on a death shroud!"

"And pre-eminence is afforded to a minor prophet, the cousin of Messiah."

There was laughter among the men. They had failed to see all that was in the Master's mind and they marvelled.

"This is the beginning of a new religion. By our actions, we have undermined the Son of God, and in time, what we have accomplished will be used to destroy faith in those who might have been tempted to believe!"

"How is that?" Lucius questioned, still not fully comprehending. "Generations will see this likeness and believe in the resurrection."

"In accordance with the Jewish God and his Son, the worship of icons is idolatrous, simply because the focus is upon the image and not on God himself," Simon Magus said. By creating an image of the resurrection we have apparently given image-worship the sanction of both Father and Son. We have dealt a death-blow to the work of the cross."

Chapter 10
Twice-Born

Michael Segal bought a postcard and a copy of Le Journal de Genève from a lakeside kiosk.

Years before the war, Switzerland's tourism had begun to die. There was little indication of real poverty but the country was showing signs of stress. The League of Nations had failed to bring peace; disarmament was a dream that no one had really believed in. The League was as good as dead; the dream was in ashes and once again Germany was on the march.

"Hitler is mad and Germany is mad!" the woman at the newsstand declared. "How extraordinary are these people! They inflict their madness on the world. What will they gain from this war? Once again they will carry home their corpses! Is this what the wives and mothers of Germany want?" she wrung her hands impotently and Michael smiled in sympathy. He knew too well what it meant to be exposed to Germany's madness. Many Swiss expected the Bosch to march through Basle this time and the tension was tangible.

From a lakeside café he sat down to write to Gabriele. He longed to say all that was on his heart but for the present, their pre-arranged signal would have to suffice. Michael's first exhilarating flush of freedom had been quickly tempered with concern. Had she made it home alright and would his disappearance result in repercussions for her? None of these questions could be asked. He wrote instead about his holiday on Lake Geneva, added that he hoped to hear from her soon and signed it Siegfried, a name rooted in the words, victory and peace. Then for a long time he gazed out at the lake in all its tranquillity and longed with all his being for Gabriele to be there beside him.

Like the rest of Europe, the Swiss were fully preoccupied with the invasion of France and their own vulnerable position. No state bordering Germany could consider itself secure; however, Switzerland's traditional position of neutrality rested more in her bankers than her borders.

Michael had a limited amount of money and there was a pressing need to find work or move out. In a country that had become a haven for refugees, a job would not be easy to come by. Unemployment, he was assured, was already high, particularly for those involved in tourism.

He considered his position and boiled down his choices. Obviously he would first exhaust the possibility of lecturing positions in the universities; secondly he would try schools. Failing which, writing was another option. But, as he thought about it, Michael realised that if it were at all possible, writing was exactly what he wanted to do. He would happily shelve the teaching and use his background in history to write and perhaps even expose the men and the machinations of this present war.

It was Le Journal de Genève that provided Segal with his first glimpse of direction. An article on the assembly of foreign ministers and their secretaries at the hotel Beau Rivage for a meeting of the League of Nations provided a list of personalities. Among them was a name he instantly recognised. Chaim Freiberg was accompanying the British Foreign Secretary, Anthony Eden, on his current peace mission. It might just be possible that he would spare a couple of hours for a friend.

They met for drinks on the terrace of the Beau Rivage and Freiberg shook his hand enthusiastically.

"You made it out! How did that happen? I was convinced that you were one of those who would stick things out to the bitter end!"

"I had someone who persuaded me just how bitter that end might be. I admit I was eased out on a shoe horn." He described his escape and Freiberg whistled softly. He gripped the knot of his tie and eased his neck under his tight collar. He was a florid man, overweight and balding and although Michael knew he was only in his thirties, he judged that his health was already beginning to fail.

"Is your family still there?"

Michael nodded. "I couldn't persuade my parents to leave. Yours?"

"Most of them got out when they felt things heat up. Inevitably there were those that stayed. We heard that an uncle and his family have been resettled in the East but we've lost touch with them." He shook his head soberly. "Who knows what is happening to Jews in Germany at the moment. There have been terrible reports. But you haven't come here to discuss that. What can I do for you Michael?"

Darkness had fallen and twinkling lights defined some of the far edges of the lake. On a bandstand in the corner of the terrace a pianist, accompanied by a violinist and cellist, played some of the more popular classical pieces. Candlelight flickered on tables decked in fine linen and waiters glided like ghosts filling glasses and attending to the needs of the rich and influential.

"Obviously, now that I am in Switzerland, employment is my next consideration. I'm thinking of turning to writing."

Freiberg nodded.

"What sort of thing?"

"I would like to examine the stuff that goes on behind the scenes at a time like this. An exposure of some of the elements that lead countries into war. Why the objective of the League has failed – that sort of thing."

Freiberg drew a handkerchief from his trouser pocket and mopped his face liberally.

"You're crazy of course. A crazy Jew!"

"Maybe," Michael smiled. "But I would need a source, someone high up with a finger on the pulse."

"Whooa!" Freiberg shook his head and shifted his chin in another attempt to ease his collar. "At a time like this no one's talking to anyone unless it's to tell them what they want them to hear!"

"I'm not tapping you for state secrets, Chaim. I'm an historian. I'm looking to bring things to the light in a way that no one else is doing. I want to encourage the common man to look deeper than the surface. You and I both know that international bankers are the only winners in war."

Chaim Freiberg laughed heartily. "If you're going to expose bankers, Switzerland might become a little unhealthy."

"I've thought of that," Michael grinned. "Any recommendations?"

"Publish outside the country under a nom de plume."

"Will you help?"

"Within strict limits," Freiberg said guardedly. "You will have to understand my position if I suddenly choose to raise the barriers."

"Of course."

"I'm in and out of the country at the moment. Living in Britain actually, old chap!" He affected the accent. "I'll let you have my address." He was thoughtful for a moment. "Any articles that you want me to look at could be collected here. Just leave them in an envelope at the desk. And if I might make a suggestion, stay with things that are safer to publish until after this war's over. How about looking at the Jewish problem? Very few are attempting to expose what's really going on there. People in this Nazi resettlement plan are disappearing – permanently. Check it out for yourself, Michael. Someone needs to!"

He mopped his face copiously and stuffed his handkerchief back in his pocket. "If you'll excuse me, I have things to prepare for when the delegates arrive tomorrow. Don't worry about the bill; they'll put it on my tab." He stood up and the two men shook hands.

"Be careful what you write, Michael," he warned quietly as he turned to leave, a corpulent figure in an outsized brown suit. "You're opening a can of worms if you interfere with the bankers."

Chapter 11
Twice-Born

13 March, 1939.

Snow lay in deep drifts as far as the eye could see forming a pristine garment to the sea of peaks, breathtaking in their beauty as they were touched by the softening rays of the late afternoon sun. To Otto Rahn, the Tyrolean Mountains seemed at that moment to echo the amor of the Cathars. Theirs was a love as cold as ice, incisive as a sword; a love which aspired to conquer the human condition and reach the Kingdom of the Mortals, the Ultima Thule. He stood for a long time allowing the peacefulness of the scene to seep into his soul.

At thirty-four years old Rahn had lived a dream, attained an icy and precarious pinnacle and descended into hell. Thinking back to his university years, it was his professor, Baron von Gall who had persuaded him to study the Albigensian Crusade, and Catharism held him captive from that moment on. By his twenty-fifth year he knew his life would be centred on achieving where others had failed. Otto Rahn was set on a determined quest to discover the Holy Grail.

He prepared to make his descent. Clouds were coming in from the North and squalls of wind whistled through the crags but there were still some hours of daylight left. It was not unusual for Rahn to climb alone; he loved and respected the mountains but seldom found the need for the company of others. He turned his face from the magnificence of the peaks, fixing his sights on the valley below.

Rahn had established a definite link between the Gnostic Cathar and Druidic beliefs. It became obvious to him as he probed the two systems that the Cathar parfaits were akin to the Druid priests. His spiritual perception probed into the words of the troubadours and beyond, and the clues in the Parsival led him to the Languedoc, certain in his mind that Munsalvaesch or Montsalvat, the mountain of salvation, corresponded to Montségur.

His first book, Crusade Against the Grail, had brought his work to the attention of the Reichsführer SS and Heinrich Himmler called him in to discuss it. Rahn remembered how he had felt in receiving such recognition, stumbling, so unexpectedly, upon a soul-mate in the Nazi hierarchy. When the Reichsführer offered Rahn a position of SS-sponsored research in the Ahnenerbe he accepted it with pride and within weeks Himmler had promoted him to SS-Untersharführer.

Rahn stumbled over a branch half-concealed under the snow and almost sprawled headlong. Dusk was falling and he retrieved the torch from his rucksack, his gloved hands fumbling clumsily with the latch. He was aware that he would need to use the flashlight sparingly if he was to preserve the battery.

The Lombrives cavern in the French Pyrenees was indescribably beautiful. White limestone stalagmites and brilliant rock crystal were offset against the rich brown walls of the cave. Accompanied by one of the locals, Rahn had followed the path into the bowels of the earth both entranced and afraid as though he was intruding on something so sacrosanct that it should not be disturbed. The cave had opened into a natural cathedral; a hall two hundred and sixty feet in height with crystal walls and marble crypts containing the bones of parfaits and knights who had perished centuries before. They had worshipped there hidden from the excesses of the Papists who had invaded the Languedoc and laid siege to the Cathar stronghold of Montségur.

The natives of the area related well to Otto Rahn. He spoke their Provencal language fluently and they willingly recounted the traditions of the area.

"The parfaits," they assured him, "escaped Montségur with the magical regalia of Dagobert II, and with the cup of the Grail."

He was so close that success seemed only a hairbreadth away but the holy relic remained elusive. Rahn turned to a study of the Cathar and Templar markings on the walls of the caves and to a revision of the sacred geometry of the area, but the clue arose, ironically, from a different direction.

Heinrich Himmler urged him on, sharing in Rahn's enthusiasm and commiserating with his disappointments and it was the Reichsführer who intimated that the research of the Ahnenerbe had taken them on another path.

"There was a Catholic priest, the curé of Rennes-le-Château, who had ties with esoteric groups in Paris," he informed Rahn. "He made far more money than a village priest should have done. His house-keeper is still alive and I intend sending Karl Wolff in to interview her."

"Do you think this priest found something in the area?"

"Almost certainly," Himmler said. "And if he discovered the Grail, you will be informed before anyone else. I know how much work you have put into this project."

Recovery of the gold chalice from Béranger Saunière's hiding place under the altar in the village church had been anti-climatic and knowing that the housekeeper had been tortured for the information left Rahn with a nauseating sense of revulsion. Karl Wolff had returned immediately to Wewelsburg Castle with the goblet.

Darkness had fallen. Otto Rahn sat down on a fallen tree trunk and shone his torch on his surroundings. The base camp was still a long way off. The wind was now full-grown and it soughed through the pines and moaned in the crevices. The cold was intense but it had not penetrated his clothing. Only Rahn's face was numbed and he pulled his scarf up over his nose. Switching off the torch, he allowed his eyes to adjust once again to the dark.

Himmler had ignored Rahn's pleas to make the find of the Grail cup public and instead had placed a gagging order on him. Rahn had sought meetings with the Reichsführer but suddenly doors were closed against him and when, finally, he had forced a confrontation with Himmler in the parking lot of the Reich Chancellery, he was placed under a disciplinary restraint and assigned several weeks of guard duty at Dachau concentration camp.

A sulky half-moon imparted an orange glow, hiding now and then behind the drifting cloud. Rahn played the light of the torch over the ground computing the conditions several steps ahead with a practised eye. He avoided watercourses where the undergrowth grew thickly and the way would be strewn with boulders. The undulating terrain offered few challenges so long as he followed the ridges. The snow had thinned during the day over the more exposed areas, but the weather had not been warm enough to cause a thaw and it still lay in heavy drifts, deathly pale in the light of the moon.

Theodor Eicke, commander of the first Death's Head detachment of the SS was also first commander of Dachau. After the purge of the SA, Hitler had handed control of the concentration camps over to Heinrich Himmler's Waffen SS. Dachau's interns were political prisoners as well as Jews and guard duty was the exclusive domain of the Death's Head units.

Rahn still woke at night, sweating with horror as his dreams replayed the screa-s of men who were systematically and coldly broken under the expert hands of the Himmler's men. Hangings and shootings were daily occurrences under Papa Eicke's stringent regulations and twenty-five lashes would be meted out to any man or woman for the most minor offences. Obersturmführer Rahn lived out the months of his punishment sickened to the depths of his soul. He resigned from the SS the following year.

There is so much sorrow in my country, he wrote. It is impossible for a tolerant, liberal man like me to live in the nation that my native country has become.

Metres away, Rahn caught sight of the black geometric shape of his tent in the torch light. Among the massive rocks was the place where he had kindled a fire earlier that day. A group of young pines huddled together some distance away, stark against a deep runnel of snow and a bitter wind still howled – like Dachau's prisoners, Rahn thought as he unbuttoned his jacket. He tossed it above his head and the wind caught the garment and swept it away. Rahn watched with detached interest as it snagged in the branches of one of the trees. Then he sat down and took off his boots and socks and lay back in the snow.

Chapter 12
Twice-Born

Among the Samaritans, Simon the Magician had become known as Nous, the 'Great Power of God'.

"You have been entrapped in a body of flesh by the wicked deeds of angels," Simon Magus taught his followers. "And I have come into this earth as a man to free you from their bondage. Mankind has forgotten its root: it sleeps, lost in ignorance. You are children of the Boundless Power. I have descended to the lower regions to awaken you and reunite you with myself."

He taught that all human desire should be extinguished except for one human quest, that of attaining its lost complement: an ecstatic reintegration of the male and female components of the soul.

His Gnostic doctrine was not understood by all but the force of his personality was. Women, aroused by his sensuality, flocked after him; men lusted after his power and sought to know the secret.

Although the Jews despised the Samaritans, Jesus had spent time among them and many believed in him. So it was, when the apostle Philip arrived in Samaria, people flocked to him wanting to know more of the death and resurrection spoken of across the length and breadth of Israel. Simon the Sorcerer watched the miracles and healings taking place and saw his influence rapidly diminish. Unless he acted quickly, he would lose all he had worked towards. The Magus was under no delusions; if he was unable to destroy the enemy from without the camp he must engage them from within. He was baptised with the rest and followed Philip closely, determined to grasp for himself a clear understanding of the apostle's doctrine.

Peter and John followed Philip into Samaria but where Philip had water-baptised the new converts in the name of the Lord Jesus, they baptised them in the Holy Spirit.[21]

---

[21] Acts 8: 9-25

Peter, Philip and John were seated in the shade of a tree sharing a meal of bread and red lentils when the Magus approached them. He squatted down on his haunches, allowing the hood of his cloak to fall away from his face. The dappling of the sun through the leaves caused light and shadow to play over his brow.

"Have you eaten, Simon?" Philip asked.

He shook his head. "Thank you, I am not hungry. Do you have water?"

They passed him the skin of water and he drank and handed it back to John. His eyes though, were on Peter, the big fisherman.

"I have seen your power among the people," he said. "Tell me what it is that causes lives to change when you touch them."

"The power is not ours," Peter corrected. "It is the same power that raised Jesus Christ from the dead,"

"The power of the Holy Spirit?"

Peter nodded.

"It's a remarkable phenomenon," Simon said. "Even the simple gain a new zeal. I have seen men and women speak in strange tongues and prophesy." His glance slid over the faces of the three men and back to the horizon. "Others are healed of sicknesses and released from the bondage of spirits. A remarkable phenomenon!"

Between the trees some distance away, a dust devil spun furiously whipping leaves and sand into the air before dying as swiftly as it had arisen. John sat up and wrapped his arms around his knees. He was watching the Magus keenly.

"Philip says that you have shown great interest in what is taking place," he said. "But what is it that really interests you, Simon?"

"I desire the gift that you and Peter have."

"To receive the Spirit of God?"

"Of apostleship," the Magus said. He took his moneybag from the pocket of his cloak and turned to face them directly. "I am willing to pay well to receive the power you have."

Peter's face darkened and John placed a restraining hand on his arm.

"May your money perish with you!" Peter said. "Do you imagine you can buy a gift of God?" He shook his head. "You have no part in this matter because your heart is not right in the sight of God. Repent and pray that your sin may be forgiven because I perceive that you are poisoned by bitterness and held in the bond of iniquity."

A prophecy was concealed in this statement. The bitterness that is in you, Peter was saying, will bring corruption and lawlessness to others.

Magus looked Peter in the eyes. His face was the picture of innocence.

"Pray to the Lord for me," he said. "That none of what you have said will come upon me."

Peter looked at the man before him and, perceiving the depths of his subtlety, knew he was facing a deadly enemy.

* * *

The Magus had chosen one of his most intimate disciples to take the shroud to Edessa and had prepared him well.

"Make certain that you do not tell him that you are one of the twelve of Yeshua of Nazareth," he warned. "It is possible that such a profession will be discovered. The men closest to the Nazarene are well-known to many."

"Then who do I say I am?"

"There were seventy followers who were sent out into all Israel. He sent them to minister the word of his so-called kingdom to towns and villages. You will tell him you were one of those."

"Then Master, I will go in my own name."

"You will proclaim Yeshua, crucified, dead and resurrected, even as the apostles do," the Magus said. "I will do the same. We will, in almost every manner emulate their ways. Most people have a common desire, they want righteousness but they cannot attain it. They are therefore content if their deeds are seen to be righteous. Your role will be to provide a virtuous cloak that will satisfy. With the relics we have in our possession, we will fulfil another quirk of the human heart. Superstition. Season the truth with a little variation; a little poison; a little magic; a little lust of the flesh, until it becomes a new reality. Do not content yourself with being mere apostles when you can become super-apostles!"

"I will not allow you to let Thaddeus take any of the icons!" Herodias informed Simon sharply.

"Indeed, my dear Lady, you will!" The Magus bowed low over her hand and kissed it but his eyes were raised to hers in mockery.

"The relics are mine!" She raised her voice imperiously. "I cannot permit them to be removed."

"Madam, you have no idea what you are saying," Simon Magus returned. "Nothing we have is yours! But listen, I want you to see into the distance with me. Our mission is far greater than what you can at present envisage. We are going to entrust certain things into the Will of the Universe. They will be set adrift upon a stream, an underground stream, over which you will have no control." He sought her eyes with his own, compelling her understanding. "You will soon grow old and die but we will have given birth to something eternal."

She shifted, seeking to break away from his grip.

"This time," she told him, "you will not have your way. The icons will stay in Judaea where they belong. You know nothing of this foreign king!"

"The shroud is going to Abgar," he said. She heard the iron will of the Magus in the words, but still she fought back.

"Not the shroud! If you must send something with Thaddeus, send the cup! Let us keep the shroud."

An enigmatic smile touched the lips of the Magus and he stood back, knowing that a small battle had been won.

"The shroud will go to Edessa, my Lady. I have heard the instruction from the head of the Baptist! The image is to go to the east; the cup to the west and the sword will remain concealed in Israel. The Baptist's head will stay with us. We, dearest Lady, are about to be moved from Judaea, which will soon become too dangerous a place for us to abide. For such a move, I will need you to apply your greatest subtlety to your husband."

* * *

Although successive generations would wipe away all evidence of the grandeur of Edessa, it was, during the time of King Abgar V, a beautiful city.

As Thaddeus entered the gates, he was struck by the lush greenery of the gardens in comparison with the barren desert landscape beyond. The citizens of Edessa were generally richly clad in brightly coloured silks and the women looked regal and distinguished in their tall headdresses. Shaded pools teemed with silvery carp that rippled the quiet waters with their bodies. It would take little to persuade him to stay in such a paradise, especially with the current signs of upheaval in Judaea and Samaria.

Abgar was delighted that after a long silence, "Jesus of Nazareth" had finally sent word that one of his disciples was on his way to the city and sought audience with him. The leprosy that was slowly eating at his body had almost immobilised him and his position was now desperate. His physicians were no longer able to assist and could, by their potions, only marginally ease his discomfort. Abgar V knew he was reaching the end of his life but the letter from the great prophet of Judaea brought a nudge of hope. He had promised to send with his disciple an image of himself.

'If indeed you desire to look bodily upon my face, I send you a cloth on which know that the image not only of my face, but of whole body had been divinely transformed.'[22]

Thaddeus sought out the contact, whose name had been given him by Simon Magus.

"Ask for Tobias, son of Tobias." he said. "His father was a Jew from this region. You will stay with him."

The home of Tobias pleased Thaddeus immensely. That he was a man of great means was immediately evident. The dwelling was built in the style of the Babylonians, around a courtyard shaded by tall palms. The interior was cool and spacious; the floors intricately decorated with mosaics.

That night, Tobias was shown the cloth. The viewing was made, at the insistence of Thaddeus, without his wife and children. The Jew gazed in awe at the sepia tones of the image on the shroud. In the

---

[22] A Vatican library codex 5696 fol.35; a 12th Century version said to be Christ's letter to King Abgar.

flickering light from the lamps the face appeared almost liquid and mobile. The negative image created hollows in the skull that were light in place of dark, so that the eyes appeared wide open. A deep sense of awe and worship filled the room and Tobias fell to his knees; Thaddeus of Paneas too, prostrated himself before the holy image.

It was later that night, when the shroud had been replaced in its casket that Tobias spoke what was on his mind.

"You cannot take a burial cloth before the king."

"You are speaking as a Jew," Thaddeus protested.

"The cloth is stained by blood. It is unclean in the eyes of any man. But I have a plan, Thaddeus. There is one, Aggai, maker of headdresses to the king. He is man of great influence. We will approach him on the morrow. So that the king will not reject this image, let us present him with a portrait acceptable to him. You can tell him that the image was created when this great prophet wiped the sweat from his face."

"I dare not cut it!"

"No, no! But it can be carefully folded!" Tobias said. Aggai is a skilful worker of cloth. We will instruct him to encase the image in a framework of gold."

Three days later Thaddeus of Paneas stood waiting outside the throne-room of Abgar V. Aggai, maker of silks and headdresses to the king, had done his work well, folding the shroud and placing it within a trelliswork of gold cloth in such a way that it was transformed into a mystical portrait. He too was spellbound by the image of the Baptist and, as he worked, Thaddeus had patiently expounded the gospel to him. What was taught was a delicate alchemy, incorporating the Gnostic teachings of Simon Magus into the life and death of Jesus Christ. Aggai became a faithful disciple and would ultimately give his life for that which he perceived to be truth.

Thaddeus waited until summoned into the presence of the Abgar V, and then walked slowly in the direction of the throne. The monarch's shrivelled frame gave him a diminutive almost child-like appearance. Several paces away from where he sat, Thaddeus raised the image of the Baptist so that it covered his face and waited, immobile, for the power of the icon to do its work.

Shock registered in the pale countenance of the king. In the shadow of the room he saw what was apparent to no other. Thaddeus masked by the image appeared as a visage shining like the sun. Abgar grasped the armrests of the throne and shifted himself forward, urging his frail body to respond to the life-force that was flooding through him. He raised himself with difficulty and staggered towards the image and with each step his strength increased. To the astonishment of his courtiers, when he reached Thaddeus, Abgar V dropped to his knees at the apostle's feet and worshipped.

The unearthly portrait of the Baptist became known in Edessa as the Mandylion, from the Arabic Mandil, which meant veil or handkerchief. The shroud had undergone a metamorphosis and became accepted as the cloth with which Jesus Christ had wiped the sweat from his face at the height of his spiritual conflict in the garden of Gethsemane. The blurred pigmented image leant itself to such a notion and because of the lack of detail there was nothing to suggest the eyes were closed in death. Indeed, all future artistic renditions of Jesus from the Orthodox Church, seeded by this episode, appeared to have been influenced by the shroud and were similarly depicted with eyes that stared from the hollows of the skull.

Accounts from the period reveal that Abdu, the man second in the kingdom, was also healed by the Mandylion and, as a result, Thaddeus was permitted to preach the first Christianised sermon. Many of the city's pagan altars were thrown down by those who heard the message and believed. Under Thaddeus and seconded by Aggai, maker of "the silks and headdresses of the king", a form of Christianity arose from Edessa.

After the death of Thaddeus, Aggai became responsible for the burgeoning church and became the first martyr to the new faith. While he was preaching, soldiers of King Abgar's son, the second to ascend the throne, forced their way in and broke both his legs, resulting in his death. From this point until the sixth century, the Mandylion disappeared from the pages of history.

Chapter 13
Twice-Born

SS-Standartenführer Reinhard Heydrich introduced Marianne von Ingolstadt to Karl Wolff suggesting that she might be well-suited to work in the Ahnenerbe. She was twenty years old when Wolff employed her and for two years her drive and determination was quietly noted by her superiors. Her work within the organisation consisted mainly of the restoration to the German culture of the old folklore and legends of the past. Within the Reichsführer-SS's blood and earth policy, the ties linking the peasantry to their land had gained a vital new importance. A revival of the simple folk customs of maze running, midsummer bonfires and Yule lights had been encouraged. The Ahnenerbe endeavoured to strengthen the roots of the German people, free, as Hitler declared, from the 'Jewish Christ-creed with its effeminate pity ethics'. 'If a people is to become free,' he said, 'it needs pride and will power, defiance, hate, hate and hate again.'[23]

A tough breed was needed to create a new Order, a people unafraid to do what was necessary to make things happen, and this was the path to which Marianne von Ingolstadt was committed.

The relationship Marianne shared with Obergruppenführer Karl Wolff was friendly. He would have chosen to take it onto a deeper level and had at times attempted to do so. She liked him, but as a married man and her superior, she made it clear that the physical attraction he felt for her would remain unreciprocated.

Marianne was attractive in a boyish, athletic way. Slim hipped, with legs that were long and sleek; small, well formed breasts, and facial features that were neatly moulded around a good bone structure. Her hair was straight and dark and hung almost to her shoulders. Wolff felt instinctively that if she would allow him to penetrate the barrier she had erected, he would have been able to release within her a depth of femininity and passion that until now she had suppressed.

[23] Mein Kampf

The suggestion that Marianne should be considered for the role the Reichsführer had in mind first came from Reinhard Heydrich who had been in frequent contact with her during his visits to the Ahnenerbe. He sought Wolff's opinion before an approach could be made to the Heinrich Himmler.

"I do have some reservations," Heydrich said.

"Obergruppenführer?"

"Her fixation for Hitler could prove to be a stumbling block."

"With your permission, Obergruppenführer, I could deal with that."

Heydrich smiled. "I'm sure you could."

"Was there anything else?"

"Not really." Reinhard Heydrich appeared thoughtful. "I've run a thorough check on her pedigree of course and that's entirely in order. What's your opinion of the girl, Obergruppenführer? Is she made of the sort of stuff necessary for the job?"

Wolff's expression was emphatic. "If you hadn't brought her name forward, I would certainly have done so myself. I believe the Reichsführer will be impressed with her."

"In that case, Obergruppenführer Wolff, I'll leave it to you to bring the girl to the Reichsführer's attention at the appropriate time. I will most certainly second the motion.

It was with certain reluctance that Karl Wolff submitted her name to the Reichsführer-SS for the special assignment, but in affairs that touched on the future of Germany, no personal feelings could be allowed to stand in the way.

"I believe, Reichsführer, that Fraulein Marianne von Ingolstadt meets all our requirements. You will find her a satisfactory candidate. Obergruppenführer Heydrich has completed the check on her background. I have a photograph taken from the file for your personal perusal. As a von Ingolstadt, her bloodline is impeccable; it can be traced right back to Charlemagne."

Wolff had joked privately to Oswald Pohl that if they could create an ancestral link to Heinrich der Vogler it would clinch the deal for Heinrich Himmler. He watched the Reichsführer's expression as he glanced down at the photograph but it was inscrutable.

"You know her well, are you satisfied that she can do this, Obergruppenführer?" Himmler asked. "Everything depends on her being the right woman for the work in hand."

Wolff nodded. "You will not be disappointed, Reichsführer!"

"In that case, Obergruppenführer Wolff I'll leave it to you to deal with the next phase. Work with delicacy, it is imperative that you don't frighten her off!"

As Karl Wolff left the office, Heinrich Himmler took his magnifying-glass from the drawer of the desk and leaned over the black and white image of Marianne von Ingolstadt.

Chapter 14
Twice-Born

It had been firmly decided that the sword would remain in the land of Israel. The weapon, which the Magus had fused together, was held in awe by his disciples especially since spells and magical symbols were inscribed on the blade, while on its hilt was the symbol of the integrated pyramids – the star of Shalem. To every man who held this 'desire of kings', ownership became an obsession. The scabbard made especially for the sword was a thing of beauty in itself, constructed from silver inlaid with precious stones and hung with intricate tapestries but the sword was a weapon that would make a warrior feel he was invincible.

"It is like the sword that King David saw in the hand of the Angel of Death over Jerusalem," Demetrius said. "A magical weapon that would instil fear into the heart of any man!"

Simon Magus regarded his disciple with interest.

"That account is written in the scroll of the Chronicles of the Kings," he mused. "Did it not say that King David no longer dared to go to the high place in Gibeon where the tabernacle and the altar of the burnt offering was for fear of the sword?[24]"

Demetrius nodded. "As a consequence, the threshing-floor of Ornan the Jebusite was made the new place of the sacrificial offering," he said. "Which during Solomon's reign became the site of the Holy of Holies of the temple."

"Gibeon," the Magus spoke the name thoughtfully. Demetrius watched him in silence knowing that something was forming in the Master's mind. "The Gibeonites fooled the children of Israel by their trickery," Simon said at length. "They made league with Joshua by pretending to be from a distant country and so preserved Gibeon from certain destruction. Was it not also the city over which the sun stood still? There is a parable here, Demetrius. We must take horses and ride to the seat of Benjamin."

---

[24] 1 Chronicles 21:28-30. 22:1

"All of us, Master?"

The Magus shook his head. "Not yet. You and I will ride alone."

They set out just after sunrise on the following morning, taking the north road from Jerusalem. By the third hour, the sun was already causing steam to rise from the sweating flanks of their mounts. Gibeon's walls were in sight and, encompassed within, lay a scattering of pale houses that appeared to have been eked from the rock on which they were built. Here and there on the hillside, a tree permanently bent and twisted by the force of the wind clung on tenaciously and a dusting of green grass embraced the thin soil between the limestone. The men reigned in their horses, feeling the sun on their backs and the hot wind in their faces. Then Simon Magus spurred his steed and Demetrius followed screwing his eyes up against the dust, which arose in small clouds from the thundering hoofs of the horse ahead of him.

A group of youths loitering within the city gates brightened when they saw the strangers.

"Who will show us Gibeon's pool?" Demetrius called out and at once received an enthusiastic response.

"We need a lad to tend the horses," the Magus said. "We will pay him for his trouble."

Leaving the horses to be rubbed down and watered they followed the boys up onto the wall and gazed down into the limestone pit which had formed the pool of Gibeon. It was totally dry. Around the periphery a spiral staircase, hewn into the rock disappeared into the depths.

"Will you take us down?"

"The women used to fetch the water from here," one of the youths told them. "But it has not been used for many centuries."

As they made their descent they could see that rubble had gathered at the foot of the pit, rocks and shards of broken pottery.

"Is the spring dry?" Demetrius asked.

They shook their heads. "There are times when the water still rises but the walls of the cistern leak now. We will show you the pool."

In total, ninety-six steps lead down to the subterranean cistern but it was pleasantly cool in the man-made cavern.

"Is there another entrance to this place?" Simon asked.

The boy nodded. "There is a door in the wall. Up there." He pointed to a place above the water-line beyond their point of vision.

The Magus dismissed the boys who ran noisily back up the steps, invigorated by this small intrusion into their day.

"There is a tunnel up there, which fills the upper pool when the water-level rises." Demetrius said looking up towards the narrow funnel that cast a circle of daylight onto the surface of the water.

"And it seems that the pool is fed from the horizontal tunnel yonder." The Magus pointed to the far end of the cistern.

"One of the youths said it leads to the spring, beyond the walls of the city."

Simon Magus exhaled audibly.

"Bethlehem's star pin-pointed the birthplace of Jesus," he said. "But the sun over Gibeon will point to the birth of so great a conspiracy with the nation of Israel that the Sun God himself will replace the God of the Patriarchs. Mark me, Demetrius, when I say that a new thing is born here this day in a cistern hewn from the earth by the hands of man. The sword will be concealed here in the cleft of the rock and a sign will be left to those that follow us, a mystery that must needs be resolved. A chosen king in the type of Solomon, whose name means Peaceable, will draw the magic sword from the rock, bringing wisdom, wealth and healing to the land. He will capture Israel, but not by force, and wipe the seed of the Almighty from the face of the land as a woman wipes the inside of a cup."

The Magus pushed his hand up into the deep cleft and smiled in satisfaction as he discovered a pocket within the stone that seemed to have been created by the Fates for this moment in the earth's history.

"You will write this prophecy Demetrius, so that it may be passed down through the ages. The sword has broken once and has been mended. It will be broken a second time and healed after many years and when the children of Israel return to their land. The nation will be born in a day in accordance with their scriptures[25] and the tribes will be brought together as one. Then will come a time of great disaster when chaos reigns over the world. In that day one named Peaceable

---

[25] Isaiah 66:8

will take up this sword and he will heal the blade. His coming will be announced by a great sign in the sky – a bright star that will be seen by all the ends of the earth. The children of the God of Abraham, Isaac and Jacob will perish from the face of the earth in that day and those of Samaria will reign in their place. The day of trickery is born this day in Gibeon, under the rock." Simon Magus smiled. "Let the sword perform its work!"

Chapter 15
Twice-Born

Herod had been told that the bones of John the Baptist, which were carried out of Israel in a sealed casket among the possessions of their household, were those of the father of the Magus.

The presence of Simon Magus was only tolerated among their copious entourage because Herod knew that the alternative was losing his wife. It was impossible to ignore the magician's powerful hold over Herodias and Herod's hatred of the man and his concubine, Helen, was enflamed by the secretive nature of their alignment. That the relationship was sexual was obvious. He could have accepted that Herodias had taken a lover, even as he saw no harm in his own extra-marital affairs, but what frightened him was her subservience to the sorcerer. It was also apparent that Herodias feared Helen, yet she insisted on keeping her. The fire in his wife's spirit, which had so captivated Herod, was doused in their presence and in its place was something so malignant, so dark and so intense that Herod no longer only feared her, he feared *for* her.

Following the death and resurrection of Jesus, Simon Magus had become a great man in Israel; an apostle among apostles. On the surface, he was the pillar of respectability and his church following grew rapidly. He trained men for ministry and he preached the gospel. He also sold relics to fill the coffers: splinters of the true cross, which seemed to abound, and crowns of thorns. The gospel was, in almost all respects, a carbon copy of that preached by the apostles of Jesus Christ, with just enough magic to cause a deviation towards the Gnostic and just enough sorcery to bind his flock captive to superstition rather than true faith. His preaching was a mocking parody of that of the apostle Paul, his arch-enemy and he used his own words against him; to the confusion of many of Paul's followers.

The Magus had birthed a parallel religion distinguishable from the true gospel only to the most discerning believer. Around him he gathered a tight inner circle of thirty disciples representing the lunar cycle as opposed to the twelve disciples of Jesus, which, according to the Magus, corresponded to the twelve solar months. Helen was numbered among his disciples but, as a woman, she betokened half a man leaving the number incomplete as in the course of the moon.

"Let the women weep for Tammuz and the men yearn for the Virgin of Heaven!" he taught his cabal. "But by no means intimate to your proselytes that the Heavenly Queen does not exist! Let them remain celibate and burn in their lusts. Twist the teachings of Paul of Tarsus to justify it. Everything must encompass a veneer of truth!"

Only when he was fully satisfied that the work in Israel could continue without him, did Simon Magus prepare to embark on the next stage of his operation. It was also with the prescient knowledge that came to him through the head of the Baptist that Jerusalem would soon be thrown into turmoil and would only rise again from obscurity after many years. Armed with this foreknowledge, the Magus used the events that took place shortly afterwards to persuade Herodias that Herod Antipas should urgently petition Caligula.

Herod Agrippa, Herodias' brother, had been imprisoned in Rome for treason under Tiberius Caesar, after a coachman had reported an ill-conceived remark he had made to his friend, Caligula. Meanwhile Philip, the husband of Salome, Herodias' daughter, had died three years before, leaving Bashan temporarily under the administration of the province of Syria. Once Tiberius was dead, Caligula released Herod Agrippa and appointed him the tetrarchy of Bashan, with its revenues and, in addition, the title of king.

At the insistence of Herodias, Herod Antipas had set aside his deep misgivings and journeyed to Rome seeking similar favours from Caligula. The tetrarch's intention in making this journey was leaked to Agrippa, and the Magus also ensured that an agent, who had been sent from Herodias to Salome carrying further damning information against Antipas, was intercepted by Herod Agrippa's men.

Simon Magus' plan worked without hitch and an urgent missive from Herod Agrippa exposing his brother-in-law arrived in time for Herod Antipas' interview with Caligula, so that Caesar was fully prepared.

Caligula, son of Rome's beloved Germanicus, had held such

great promise for the restoration of the empire after Tiberius' death that the character differences between father and son, which would have been obvious to a dispassionate observer, were at first overlooked. His first gestures were magnanimous. He offered reprieves to prisoners, political and criminal alike and he publicly burned Tiberius' carefully gathered evidence against the activities of his family – after taking care to first copy all the documents. However, after a period of illness Caligula underwent a transformation, and came forth a self-proclaimed god. It was doubtful whether Herod Antipas could have anticipated Little Boots' increasing megalomania. His behaviour was erratic, often violent and unpredictable.

Herod Antipas arrived at Puteoli and managed to see Caligula at Baiae. He stood nervously before the emperor, carefully outlining his case and his fitness to receive the crown of Palestine in the place of his brother-in-law Agrippa. All the while, Caligula thumbed through a lengthy letter and hardly raised his eyes to look at the man before him until Herod fell silent.

"Is it true," Caligula asked him at length, "that you have weapons and equipment enough for seventy thousand troops?"

Antipas blanched. "I don't know what you mean, Princeps."

"I have a letter from Herod Agrippa that accuses you of conspiring with Sejanus during the reign of my Uncle Tiberius. He also tells me that you have entered into a treasonable alliance with the Parthians against Rome. Of course, Tetrarch, I can have your armouries checked to see if your brother-in-law's accusations are correct."

"I do have weapons, Princeps, but it is purely with a collector's eye that they have been assembled!"

Caligula's glance was childishly triumphant. "Sufficient for seventy thousand troops! You expect me to believe that!" His voice rose. "You realise that I could wipe you out in an instant? Squash you like the bug that you are? Death would be too quick, though. I choose to exile you. Consider yourself stripped of your tetrarchy forthwith, but you can tell your pretty wife that she can stay in Rome." He sat in silence for several moments staring hard at Herod Antipas. "Only because she's Agrippa's sister of course. She can stay because of him."

Herod Antipas spluttered his thanks and withdrew from

Caesar's presence, fortunate indeed to escape with his life. He was banished with immediate effect to Lyons in the South of France.

Antipas was not the first of the Herodian exiles. An uncle had preceded him, becoming well-established in the Languedoc, and Herod himself had bought much property in the area over the years. He owned an estate that would make an admirable place of retirement. The countryside and the weather were gentler than that of Palestine and the prospect of growing old in peace was hardly unpleasant.

Exile could have been deemed as a welcome rest from his labours if it were not for Herodias. She was an ambitious, power-driven woman and, if anything, the prospect of Caligula's retribution was to be dreaded less than the inevitable confrontation with his wife. Herodias would not accompany him to Lyons, of that he was certain. She would choose to return to Palestine rather than suffer the disgrace of exile with him. Or perhaps she would indeed accept Caligula's invitation to remain with her friends in Rome. Herodias was still passionate and attractive. She would have little difficulty in finding company in keeping with her extravagant tastes and absence of moral values that so well suited the present Roman society.

As the chariot turned into the gate of their residence he felt the familiar tug of fear in his bowels. She had ruled him from the beginning; he was a fool in her presence and he knew it.

Simon Magus was with the Herodian family in Rome when Antipas returned to their lodging still stunned by the outcome of his audience with Caesar Caligula but already resigned to his fate. The ship that was to carry him to the South of France was docked in Ostia and Herod was to depart within days. For once Antipas was relieved that the magician was present to placate Herodias so that he would not experience the full fury of her wrath.

Herodias was even more hysterical when Simon Magus informed her that while he would go with them to the Languedoc, it was his intention to return to Rome.

"You said that you would go with me!" she screamed at him. "How could you lie to me concerning such a matter?" She pummelled his chest with her fists. "You made me a promise!"

Simon Magus grasped her wrists and held her at arms length.

"Be still and listen to me!"

"I have given up everything for you!"

His grip was unyielding and he viewed her tousled appearance dispassionately. Herodias' dark hair had broken loose from its bands and strands adhered to her damp cheeks. Her face was blotched and raw from weeping and kohl had formed ugly smudges under eyes. The noble lady was aging, he noted, and it became embarrassingly evident when her carefully applied makeup was removed.

"I have lost my position and my home because I believed you! You are a liar and there is no truth in you at all!"

The Magus gripped her violently by the shoulders and shook her.

"I said, be silent!"

The menace in his voice sobered her. She dropped her head into her hands and allowed the angry sobs to subside.

"Now listen!" he commanded. "I have told you before, this is bigger than you. You are simply a piece in an intricate design. My Lady, the fates have ordained a vital role for you, if you will but place yourself in my hands. I am the Standing One. Nothing will remove me from my place in history. Do you want to be part of me?"

"You know that I do."

"Then listen! Your launching point is from France; mine is from Italy. I will send Salomon with you. He is one of my most trusted disciples and one you well like."

Herodias looked up and pushed her hair away from her face. Anger was replaced by a sly interest. She had lusted after Salomon; the Magus knew her appetites well.

"In due season, I will come. By that time you and Salomon will have prepared the way."

"And I will have in my possession the head of the Baptist?"

He regarded her with irony. "You will, my Lady. For it is with the head that you will launch the new Order. The east has the shroud; England will gain the cup and Rome, Rome, my dear Herodias, will have me! Now, my Lady, wash your face, you are looking most ill."

When Herodias returned to the room, she had refreshed her makeup and her maid had rearranged her hair but to Simon's critical eye, even in the past few weeks, she had physically aged. The lines around her eyes and the sagging of her mouth and cheeks could no longer be disguised. Herodias was a woman who had relied on her face and her body to grasp for the things that were out of reach. The long journey from Palestine compounded with Herod's loss of position had taken their toll.

"What of the lance?" she asked in a voice that was now composed and steady.

"Ah, the lance! The lance, my dear Lady, will be with me in Rome. It is to become Rome's symbol of power! The lance opened the side of a god and spilled his blood onto the earth and it will become a sign to all who comprehend it! The blood of that dead god will be carried out from Rome to the ends of the earth but, while the lance exists, Yeshua of Nazareth will not be able to come down from the cross that held him! Whoever claims the lance will hold the destiny of the world in his hands – for good or for evil!"

"How do you propose to do all this?" Sensing his contempt, her tone was scathing. "You have no social standing in a city where such things are all important!"

"In Judaea," he prophesied, "I raised the head. In Rome, I shall raise the whole body."

Chapter 16
Twice-Born

Two weeks after his arrival in Switzerland, Michael Segal had still heard no word from Gabriele and he began to experience an overwhelming sense of impotence. At the risk of compromising his parent's position, he waited another week before writing to engage his father's help. It was a further two weeks before he received a reply.

"I telephoned the university from a call-box," his father wrote, "but when I asked to speak to Miss Hoch they said she had left and refused to give me any more information. I then telephoned the friend you mentioned in your letter. She said that Miss Hoch had been arrested several weeks ago. I'm sorry to tell you this, Michael, as I know she is a good friend of yours, but she is being held in the Berlin prison. Obviously, as a Jew, there is nothing more I can do for you. Your mother and I send you our love."

The letter fell from Michael's hand; he stood up and stumbled across the room blindly. Rage hit him like a thunderbolt. He picked up a chair and flung it forcefully against the wall then he dropped to the floor and wept like a child.

This letter was the last communication Michael Segal would receive from his parents. He never knew whether the telephone calls his father made on his behalf had precipitated their arrest, or whether they were simply caught up like fingerlings in the fine net of the Gestapo.

"You won't sell these articles," Chaim Freiberg said. "You'll never be allowed to expose the ties between international banking and Freemasonry at a time like this! In any case, it's written with too much *angst*! What the hell has happened to you, Segal, you look terrible!"

Michael shook his head and tossed back the whisky that Freiberg had ordered him. His money had almost run out by this time. For the past week he had lived on bread and coffee but he did not bother to relate any of those things to a man who had no conception of what it was to go without.

"Gabriele Hoch," he said, "the friend who helped me to escape from Germany. She was arrested and imprisoned."

Freiberg offered a murmur of sympathy. "I'm sorry to hear that, old chap, terrible news!"

Michael could see the sweat marks that were beginning to darken the fabric under the arm-pits of Chaim's over-sized suit.

"It's warm out here," he offered. "Shall we sit inside?"

They moved into the spacious sitting area of the Beau Rivage where fans were churning the air. Freiberg sank gratefully into an armchair and eased the knot of his tie.

"Chaim, I need your help," Michael's voice was low and urgent. "You're the one person I know who might be able to make contact with Gabriele for me."

Freiberg looked thoughtful. He clicked his fingers at a passing waiter and ordered another round of drinks and then, with unaccustomed sensitivity, glanced across at Segal again.

"Bring us some sandwiches as well," he said. "I've an idea my friend here could do with something to eat."

"What makes you think I'm in any position to influence events in Germany?" he asked. "I'm as much of a refugee as you are, if it comes to that."

Michael shrugged helplessly. "You're with the League," he said. "There are still points of contact with the Reich."

"In case you haven't noticed, Europe's at war with Hitler's Germany."

"But Switzerland isn't! You know men who can move mountains."

The waiter refilled their glasses and set before them a plate heaped with sandwiches.

"Eat!" Chaim Freiberg ordered as he helped himself. "So, if I do know someone who may be able to speak to people in the Reich, what are you expecting to achieve? Presumably, this young woman, what did you say her name was?"

"Gabriele."

"Gabriele, yes," he spoke around a mouth full of sandwich.

"Presumably if she was found guilty of helping you to escape she's been correctly sentenced. One could not circumvent the law."

"What do you suggest?"

Freiberg shrugged and wiped his mouth with surprising delicacy on the white linen napkin. "It would be amusing," he said, "to see if their legal system can be moved if certain nerves are touched." He took a diary from the inside pocket of his jacket. "Write down the lady's name and address here. And her status within the university. I will see what can be done. Now, let's talk about these articles." He pushed crockery and cutlery aside and laid the first set of handwritten pages on the table in front of him. "Too much *angst*. You've lost your humour, Michael."

"Put it down to a bad week."

"Okay. I may have someone interested in the article you did on the Jewish problem if you're prepared to rewrite." He opened his wallet and slapped some notes on the table, "Count this as an advance on his behalf. How soon can you have it done?"

"Give me a day or two."

"I'll get it translated into English," Freiberg said. "If you publish here, the Swiss will have you deported back to Germany."

He thumbed through both articles and slipped them into the envelope, handing them back to Michael. "This is good bread-and-butter stuff but I may have something else for you."

"Such as?"

"Show me what you can do with this and we'll talk," he said.

Chapter 17
Twice-Born

God sendeth the men in secret, but the maidens in light of day...
Parzival, Wolfram von Eschenbach.

AD 41

Simon Magus' initial inner circle of disciples dwindled as they were dispatched to preach his gospel. It was essential to counter Christianity wherever it was disseminated in order to shake the young roots of the budding church. Simon therefore initiated a second wave of Samaritan adherents before departing for Rome and each man was called to take a woman with him. The Magus was not content to simply counter the gospel; he was determined to imitate every work of Israel's God as he perceived it. By creating a new Chosen Race he intended to undermine those Jews who, in their arrogance, had looked upon the Samaritans as the least among nations. He would use counterfeit Jews to confound Jews, and counterfeit Christians to confound Christians.

Most of the men travelling with him had assumed Jewish identities, some even daringly expropriated from men within the Sanhedrin.

"In the conflagration that will soon come upon Judaea," Simon told them, "the deception will never be discovered. If the temple records survive, who is to say in generations to come, that Joseph of Arimathea did not leave Israel, or that the family of Jesus did not flee to the Languedoc?"

Women of childbearing age were essential to the plan but contrary to the word that was preached. Gnostic teaching promoted a lifestyle of celibacy as an escape from the evils of procreation but, for the Samaritan race, which would henceforth be divided into two forces, Christian and Jewish, procreation would be vital.

The Magus had also chosen a Samaritan woman for his own purposes. She was selected for her beauty, for strength of character, and for her complete devotedness to himself as master. It was given to her to assume a new identity and to learn a new language and when Simon Magus was certain that she was perfect for the task ahead, he renamed her. Henceforth Mary became his most ardent and committed follower. She would be granted the highest role of any of his disciples and was destined to play a part more visible and infinitely more enduring than that of Simon himself.

The ship, which followed Herod into exile, carried Herodias and three Marys into Province. It was driven off course by high winds and failed to reach the port of Marseilles. At nightfall after several days of storms, the hull was scraped by a submerged rock and, realising they had drifted perilously close to shore, the sailors sounded the depths and dropped anchor. They were shipping water despite running repairs made by the crew and throughout the night as they fought to bale the vessel, she was lashed by raging seas and howling winds. Huddled below deck, the passengers listened to the creaking of the timbers in the storm and wondered whether they would see the light of another day.

As dawn broke, the wind dropped at last and the rain ceased. The captain inspected the damage and made the decision to weigh anchor and head for a natural harbour formed by the tributary of a river, not far from where the vessel lay.

"It is unlikely that we will make it to Marseilles without effecting proper repairs," he informed Simon Magus. "But now that the sea has subsided we can row ashore to the village you can see from here."

The Magus leaned over the ship's rail and looked out at the land that lay sharp and clear to the eye after the storm. The Camargue was a wild stretch of marshy coast, the haunt of water birds, broken into myriad pools by the discharge of the Rhône into the Mediterranean.

Two women stood with him, one black and slender robed in white linen with her braided hair caught up in a matching turban; the other a Samaritan, dressed simply in deep blue. She glanced at the Magus and smiled.

"We begin here," she said.

"We begin here! I bequeath this land to you, Mary. France will always be deemed your country." Then he turned his gaze on Helen.

"Your role will not at first be obvious, my Ennoia. You will disembark as a servant, but you, also, will reign in France as a goddess. Webs are woven in the open places but spiders remain hidden."

The one known as Mary Magdalene caught up her long hair, expertly securing it with combs in the nape of her neck. They were moving steadily closer to land and the village was now clearly in sight. An excited group had gathered at the quay to greet the approaching vessel. This was not their expected starting point, but one ordained by the gods.

The party that disembarked caused no small stir among the villagers. The women, well-robed, some heavily made-up, bejewelled and obviously wealthy, were rowed ashore and carried by men-servants through the shallows. But there was something even more unusual about this company that drew the attention of the locals and seared the landing of this ship into the communal memory beyond any other such event. So much so, that the village became known, and is known to this day, as the Saintes-Maries-de-la-Mer. In time, the three Maries would become one in the minds of the inhabitants of the area with a triple spring known as the Oppidum Priscum Ra.

"It is a place where a three-fold water goddess has been worshipped for centuries," Simon Magus told his followers much later. "The Celts worshipped here and the Romans established a temple to Mithras on the same spot. The gods have indeed been kind. Our three Maries will supersede both Celts and Romans. Christianity will mark this spot and my Maries will be venerated here."

While the men were still ferrying their belongings from the boat to the shore, a woman stood up on the worn steps of a tavern and began to address the curious crowd of onlookers. She appeared to be in her middle thirties, and had about her a look of pride and untamed beauty that instantly riveted the attention. She was olive-skinned, even-featured with large expressive eyes and a well-shaped mouth and her hair was caught in a loose chignon. It was not her appearance alone that riveted attention. As she spoke, her words and her voice beguiled her listeners and her stories moved them. She introduced herself as Mary of Magdala and she communicated in the French tongue but not with the fluency of a native.

"We come here with a message of life," she told her listeners. "A message of real freedom! And I trust that we will bequeath upon you, precious sons and daughters of the Languedoc, perpetual hope for the present and for the future. God has recognised your struggles, he has seen the anguish and the hurt in your lives and he has sent us with answers for you."

"Who is this god and how can he give us answers?" The old crone sucked her lips in against her toothless gums and stood, arms akimbo, challenging the speaker.

"Oh, he knows you," Mary said with absolute assurance. "He tells me that you are Sophie; that your husband, Philip, is a drunkard and that you have been forced by the work of your hands and the sweat of your brow to care without his help for seven children."

There was a gasp of amazement from the villagers. Sophie's weathered hand fluttered to her mouth and her eyes widened.

Mary's smile was gentle. "And you, Nicole. The Father says he saw your tears when your baby died of a fever but He will wipe them dry. You will conceive and bear again. In a year from now, you will hold a son in your arms."

At these words, the young woman buried her face in her hands and wept. The crowd pressed closer, enraptured and attentive now; each heart secretly longing for some personal revelation from this God who knew them so well.

"Let me tell you about this God," the Magdalene said. You have many gods here in France, but there is a supreme God who loves you and wants to bring you into a closer relationship with himself. He has sent me to you because he knows that you have receptive hearts. This God sees your worth and wants you to become his treasured possession."

Again, the Magdalene's eyes strayed over the upturned faces and came to rest on that of a middle-aged man.

"You are Jacques?"

He nodded shortly. "I am." By his expression Mary recognised a studied resistance to her words.

"You will believe in me," she said, "and become an ardent

disciple. It is your destiny to be a great knight in the service of the Magdalene and the Christ. Forsake all and follow me. Your reward will be great and your faithfulness will be a sign to all who know you."

The man's face softened under the woman's penetrating gaze and he averted his eyes.

The Magdalene spoke of the birth of Jesus in the far-off land of Judaea and of the visit of shepherds and kings: of a king who had been born in a stable and placed in a manger. The small crowd listened attentively. Few could resist the story of a baby.

"The Master's promises extend beyond the boundaries of this life. He offers spiritual life to all who will receive it!"

When she had finished addressing the crowd, Jacques came forward and dropped to his knees at her feet.

"My Lady," he said. "Show me how to serve you and I will do it with my life!"

Jacques helped all who had left the ship to find lodging that night. Among those afforded rooms in his own home were Mary Salome and Mary Jacobi. The older women were presented as aunts of Jesus, witnesses to the crucifixion and of those who had visited the tomb on the day of the Resurrection.

The Magdalene was attended by a personal servant, a black woman with smouldering eyes, who had stood silently by as the Magdalene preached in the village. Mary introduced her as Sarah the Egyptian.

As a wealthy land-owner, Jacques was a useful adherent, and one who would indeed become numbered among Mary's closest disciples. Mary Magdalene moved out into the streets of Marseilles under his personal protection.

In an obvious identification with the goddess, she preached on the steps of the temple of Diana. In the fullness of time, new temples would be raised in Marseilles and beyond; cathedrals built to the glory of a new goddess; one known as the redeemed prostitute - Mary of Magdala.

Mary the shaman invited true seekers to herself. The hungry, the thirsty and the gullible were drawn to these gatherings, captives of her charismatic fire. These were often the hurt and broken, people who had a place in their heart for worship. Many more were drawn by Mary the prophetess who spoke the words they longed to hear. When she touched them they could feel the stirring of their spirit so that they chose to believe she was filled with the power of God. Some fell to the ground in a deep faint; others writhed and twitched as they fought the battle between the spirit in the Magdalene and the evil inherent in themselves.

She taught the gospel story, in almost every point similar to that propounded by the apostles of Jesus Christ. However, in the place of miracles, she brought magic, in the place of truth, she wove riddles and fables and, instead of scriptural prophecy, she brought clairvoyance. In this, she fed the masses smoke in place of bread.

In giving Southern France into the hands of Mary Magdalene, Simon Magus deliberately re-established goddess worship, an aspect of paganism that otherwise would have been lost to the masses under the spreading of Christianity. Simon's mission was to remove the manifest practices of paganism and rebirth them under a Christianised covering.

In this he adopted the idea of the two faces of the Roman god, Janus. One face represented the visible church, which would dispense a diluted and blurred gospel; basing worship on superstitious practices. The images of Saints would replace the plethora of gods that preceded the Christian faith. The garb of the priests; the mystical rituals, incense and candle burning, the relics; all these would carry over from the Simon Magus' Babylonian root and, like weeds, choke out the simplicity of the Christian gospel.

As there was a dark side to the moon, so the dark face of Janus instituted a principle that would persist through the ages. Helen the Egyptian came to France ostensibly as a servant and, as such, a statue would be erected to her in time to come in the church of Saintes-Maries-de-la-Mer. Behind the scenes, Helen was to play the Mary Magdalene of the inner circle. She was initiatrix to the Magus' initiator; elevating the prostitute to the position of Queen of Heaven. This was the Black Madonna who symbolised Semiramis and Isis. The Magus had chosen his consorts well.

Chapter 18
Twice-Born

Rome was ripe for Simon Magus. The madness, which had arisen incrementally under Augustus and Tiberius, reached a new climax under the Emperor Caligula.

Caligula had closed the granaries for ten days when he considered that his last wild beast show had not been met with enough enthusiasm, but on the day of the great Palatine festival had scattered largess to the crowd. The assembly encouraged by his apparent forgiveness had called upon him for more bread and less taxes. Angered again by their impudence, Caligula ordered a platoon of his German henchmen to restore discipline. They passed along the benches striking a hundred heads from their shoulders. The scheduled show continued. Hours later, a small group of conspirators waited for "Little Boots" to emerge from the theatre and murdered him.

Caligula's uncle, Claudius, was seized by soldiers after the assassination and, much against his will, was made emperor. Herod Agrippa, who was in the city on that fateful day, threw his powerful support behind him. Once in control, Caesar Claudius sought to right Caligula's wrongs and to restrain his excesses.

It was obvious to Simon Magus that he and his handful of disciples could not launch their new religion unaided. In order to carry it to the ends of the earth the Magus sought to marry it to this great and most dissolute of the world's empires. That which he was about to sow would take many generations to bear fruit, but seed is capable of long dormancy. He was convinced that what was planted in this generation would never be lost.

By the time the Magus came to Rome, she had supplanted Greece as the heart of paganism. The root was still indisputably Babylonian and the gods, adopted chiefly from the Greeks, were undoubtedly Assyrian, Babylonian and Egyptian in origin.

Simon Magus undertook to shift a mindset. Rome's many gods must be cemented in one. Her Vestal virgins and goddesses would unify. The equation was simple but the final sum of it would take time. Nimrod and Semiramis, Osiris and Isis, Jupiter and Juno would be assimilated into the persons of Jesus and Mary - God and Goddess of Heaven.

The beauty of the ancient city was breathtaking. The seven miniature hills with their rocky outcrops and steep sides distinguished Rome from other cities. Dominated by the raised temples of Jupiter Capitolinus and Juno Moneta, the Forum Romanum was cradled in the valley between the hills and incorporated the majestic arches, basilicas and temples of the city's emperors and gods. This was one of several areas designed to reflect the corporate life of the city; a gathering place for the citizens of Rome. The grandeur of these buildings with their marble and stone columns and arches decorated with intricately carved friezes and reliefs gave way to mansions, many bearing the triumphal war trophies of generals, and to gardens and fountains. Then there were wooden houses, several storeys in height and, beyond, the simple shack dwellings in the narrow winding streets of the poorest parts of the city.

Simon, self-styled apostle, soon moved his open-air meetings to the Roman forum. It was his aim to attract the largest audience and the highest attention to his preaching. His ultimate target was no lesser person than Tiberius Claudius.

Claudius had trained to become a priest of Mars at an early age and had written extensively on subjects regarding religion and history so, although he was considered socially inept and physically weak, he was, intellectually, not the fool his family believed him to be. Simon Magus was interested in the person of Claudius only insofar as he was able to ensnare and manipulate him. To enjoin himself to the emperor was to enjoin himself to Rome.

Miracles attracted the crowds as surely as they had in Israel when Jesus healed the sick, cast demons out of those possessed, fed five thousand on five loaves and two fishes, and raised the dead to life. Simon's miracles enthralled the superstitious and manifested his power, yet they were of a different nature to those of Jesus of Nazareth. Yeshua performed miracles based on his intimate relationship with the Father: Simon Magus performed similar miracles by the supernatural forces of will-power. Jesus healed the sick out of compassion: the

Magus acted out of self-aggrandisement. Nonetheless, the citizens of Rome gathered in droves to see the signs he performed and stayed to hear the gospel that he preached.

Claudius was being carried in a sedan on one of these occasions and ordered his men to stop and to place him in a position where he could observe the proceedings. A demon-possessed youth had been brought to the sorcerer. The boy, not more than fourteen years of age lay at Simon's feet foaming at the mouth and shrieking obscenities. The crowd pressed in about him, straining to see what would next take place.

Claudius could restrain himself no longer and stepped down from his carriage. There was a murmur from those at the back of the press as they observed him.

"Caesar!"

The multitude parted, allowing him to pass. There was silence as the slight man with his characteristic limp made his way to the front and stood facing Simon. The people of Rome had learned to respect Claudius, despite the mockery of his forebears. The changes he had instituted after the assassination of Caligula had followed his nephew's reign of terror with a new period of quiet stability. He had refused most personal honours and, like Augustus, worked intuitively and tirelessly for the good of the empire, building up the depleted coffers and refilling empty granaries.

Simon looked upon his guest with neither surprise nor deference. He bowed slightly and smiled.

"Hail Caesar. You have arrived at a good moment. I am about to release this young man from the spirit that tears him."

Claudius nodded and watched gravely.

The Magus leaned down to where the boy lay. He was grinding his teeth and spittle had dribbled from the corners of his mouth, flecking his tunic. His eyes were rolled back sightlessly but the threshing of his limbs quietened at Simon's touch.

The crowd whispered and shuffled.

"In the name of the Standing One and of Jesus of Nazareth," Simon commanded. "Come out!"

Again the youth arched and twisted wildly and blood mingled

with the foam around his mouth as he bit into his tongue.

"Come out of him!"

Simon pulled the boy forcibly to his feet and, grasping him by the shoulders, shook him. For several moments the youth's eyelids closed over the blank eyeballs, his face sagged and the terrible writhing ceased. He opened his eyes once more. The pupils were fixed and sightless. Simon the apostle laid him back on the ground and murmured words in his own tongue. Within minutes, the youth had scrambled to his feet unaided. He wiped his mouth on the back of his sleeve and looked at his surroundings as if for the first time. The crowd laughed at his confusion, especially as he realised that he was in the presence of the emperor of Rome.

Claudius bowed his head in deference to the Magus' power.

"To what do you ascribe such skill?"

The boy looked around and, realising that no one paid him further heed, slipped into the crowd unnoticed and disappeared.

"I am a priest, Caesar, much like yourself," Simon replied.

"Your Latin is good," Claudius said, "but you are not a Roman."

Simon shook his head. "I am a Jew, from Samaria."

"The Samaritans cannot claim to be Jews."

Simon smiled. "We are Jews, good Caesar, when it pays to be Jewish. When the Jews are in disfavour we Samaritans remember that we are of Babylonian stock!"

There was some laughter from the crowd: the emperor remained grave, but his eyes twinkled.

"Then," Claudius said, "it might not be wise to tell me that you have lived in Alexandria, as I have found both the Jewish and the Greek community there to be quite quarrelsome and intolerant."

"In which case, I plead my Babylonian heritage, sir."

"I see you are a man possessed of the wisdom and the wit of the gods." Claudius said with the merest hint of a smile and he turned to leave.

"Will you stay, Caesar, while I expound the Christian gospel to the people?"

The emperor glanced towards his sedan.

"If the telling of it is not too long," he said.

Over supper that night, Claudius spoke of all he had heard to his young wife Messalina. His first wife, Urgulanilla, who had been given to him in a clumsily arranged marriage, had been repugnant in every way: devoid of learning, talent or beauty. That the beautiful Messalina, who was many years his junior, accepted him even before he had had a hope of becoming emperor of Rome, was a joy to Claudius' heart.

"It appears that this cult eat the flesh and drink the blood of their god in some symbolic sense similar in manner to the early Babylonians," he said. "And they also practise a form of regenerative baptism."

His wife looked at him questioningly.

"They believe that such an immersion will bring them eternal life, not in the underworld, but rather, like that of the gods in heaven."

Messalina laughed. "Do they suppose that by some simple rite the gods will give access in their midst to the commoners of Rome?" she asked. "I find that a most distasteful suggestion. Imagine, Claudius, that Jove and your grandfather Augustus would allow such a degrading of their position."

Caesar smiled. "It is my grandmother Livia's response that would be most fascinating," he admitted lightly. "I have no doubt that she would find a way to banish or poison the lot of them!"

He had honoured the promise made to his grandmother and deified her after he came to power so that she could move from Hades and assume her rightful place at her husband's side. Although Livia held Claudius in contempt until her death, she had been convinced, even when power was still in the hands of Tiberius that both he and Caligula would become emperor. When her words came to pass, Claudius had offered the prophecy to the senate as one of the proofs of her divinity and persuaded them to include his grandmother among the goddesses of Rome.

Tiberius Claudius Caesar considered the words of Simon long after his conversation with Messalina. There was no doubt in his mind that Simon the Magus was a man of superior intelligence and that he was endued with extraordinary power. He decided to seek him out again, as one priest to another to learn more about him. It would be an interesting exercise and necessary if he was to accept the growing sect of Christianity in Rome. Claudius had already launched an investigation into the various cults imported into the city from other cultures. The Greek philosophers who worshipped the qualities of the gods, such as chastity, beauty and intelligence, and denied the immediacy of their interaction in human existence had, through their abstraction of the deities, shifted the focus of Roman worship. As Romans began to accept the Greek way, they had lost the fear of divine retribution and had even allowed their worship of minor deities to replace their focus on the gods of Rome. It was important for the emperor in his role of priest of Mars to make every effort to reverse this trend.

Chapter 19
Twice-Born

1939

On Monday September 4th, the day after Britain declared war on Germany, Marianne was working at her desk. Beyond the window there was still bird song. The day was unblemished. Nature at least remained unmoved - or uninformed. But as with that pregnant moment when the seasons change, life had shifted in a mysterious way into uncharted territory.

"So," said Karl Wolff as he entered her office, "the English have risen to the defence of Poland."

"They won't last."

"Of course not. They're not prepared for war. They won't be able to stand against us for long."

He sat down opposite her and placed his fingertips together in a precise gesture beneath his chin. As always in his presence, she was aware of his underlying strength; controlled brutality under a refined veneer. His features were pale, clean cut and strikingly handsome beneath a head of meticulously groomed blonde hair. He wore the uniform of the SS like the vestments of a priest or a magician, an open expression of his power. Each officer was well aware of the esoteric nature of his dress. The dagger was a revival of Pagan tradition, a weapon sacred to the old gods, engraved with the initials of the SS. In part it was derived from the Vehmgericht, the Secret Tribunal that had instituted a reign of terror during the dark ages. The SS ring symbolised the office of Gothi, priest of the Old Gods, and the runic symbolism of their badges was designed to instil a sense of invincibility.

Karl Wolff was more powerful than Marianne realised. Himmler looked for an extra quality in the men of the SS, and only those of outstanding potential ever rose to a position of trust. Wolff had demonstrated that he was a man of unusual ability and he moved swiftly through the initiations required for the SS, gaining Heinrich Himmler's coveted inner circle, that of Knight of the Black Order, the inner priesthood of the Schutzstaffel. Of the twelve, Wolff was the man closest to the Reichsführer; his right-hand man.

Marianne closed the file on her desk and with it set aside any further pretence at working.

"Do you really think it will be over quickly?"

Wolff shrugged. "There's no way of knowing. The war is necessary if Germany is to be rebuilt. That can only come from a complete cleansing of the land."

"We have the greatest leader the world has ever produced," she said proudly. "Ultimately, Europe will have to submit to the Führer's leadership."

He straightened imperceptibly. "Marianne, there's something in my office I want you to see."

She glanced at him in surprise. "Now?"

He stood up. "Now!"

The file that he took from the wall safe was heavy and its outer cover well worn.

"Shut the door!" he instructed.

She obeyed him silently.

"What I'm about to show you here is in the strictest confidence," Wolff said. "For the moment you won't understand what this is about but you have my word that there is a good reason. I believe Marianne, that I can trust you?"

She nodded, waiting for him to continue.

"The Ahnenerbe was instructed by Adolf Hitler, to investigate his racial background."

Marianne drew a deep breath. It was the avoidance of Hitler's title that gave her a swift premonition of what he was about to impart. Wolff was watching her.

"You know of course, that all racial backgrounds must be impeccable. We in the SS must produce an ancestral record that goes back unblemished for at least two hundred years."

She nodded again, not trusting herself to speak.

"We have proof that Hitler's background is racially mixed."

"What sort of proof?" Her voice sounded strangled.

"His father, Alois Hitler, was the illegitimate son of a woman known as Maria Anna Schicklgruber. Hitler's grandfather was said to have been a man named Johann Hiedler but there is no conclusive evidence of that. Hiedler married Maria when Alois was about five years of age and never legitimized the child. Thirty years after Maria Schicklgruber's death when Hiedler was in his eighties, he reappeared having changed his name to Hitler and testified that he was Schicklgruber's father. Alois adopted his surname when he was forty years old. A curious story, don't you think?"

Marianne shrugged. "No more than many other stories of illegitimacy," she retorted.

"There is another aspect that I haven't mentioned. At the time of her conception, Maria was employed as a servant in a Jewish household in Vienna, and when the pregnancy was discovered, she was sent home to Spital where Alois was born. We are certain that Hitler's father was in fact, the son of a Rothschild."

"A Jew!"

He nodded.

When Marianne spoke at last, her voice was so quiet that Wolff had to lean forward to catch the words. "Has the Führer been told?"

"He'd seen the evidence but has naturally enough, chosen to disbelieve it."

"So why did he take the name Hitler and not Hiedler?" she demanded defensively.

He shrugged. "Hitler is neater, don't you think? Perhaps it was simply a matter of personal preference. But it is interesting to note that a sum of money was paid to Alois Schicklgruber at the time of the name change. It was said to have been a legacy, but we believe it was a bribe." His grin was cold and sardonic. "Perhaps Baron Rothschild was granted a vision of the future and couldn't bear the thought of a leader, seed of his loins, being hailed as Schicklgruber." He snapped to attention and raised his arm in a Nazi salute. "Heil Schicklgruber! It lacks something, don't you agree?"

Marianne stood up, her eyes blazing. "You disgust me!" she said and she stalked out of Wolff's office, slamming the door behind her.

Wolff sat down and rested his feet on the file on his desk. He whistled softly and tunelessly through his teeth. He had anticipated her reaction and now it was necessary to wait. Time would tell whether he had gained or lost her.

Now that it was out in the open, it seemed so obvious that she wondered how she could have been so blind. His features were Semitic and his hair, darker even than her own. Yet he surrounded himself with blonde, blue-eyed heroes who epitomised Aryanism and there was not a German who seemed even to be aware of the paradox. Marianne von Ingolstadt stood at the entrance to the building and laughed. The sound was harsh and bitter and she knew she was close to tears.

Nature was wearing her most gentle face. The grass, lightly beaded by the previous night's shower, glistened almost white in the sunlight, and trees, rippling and swaying under a light breeze, still shed small drops of water from their leaves. In the park across the road, women sat in the sunshine and watched their children at play on the swings. They had abandoned their heavy topcoats and brought out brightly coloured sweaters, but it was still too cold to discard the headscarves. Inactivity caused them to huddle defensively into themselves on the benches.

Marianne wanted to shout at them, to blast them out of their stupid complacency. Didn't they know there was a war going on? Didn't they realise their beloved Führer was a dirty Jew? She began to run, with the brittle sound of her laughter trailing behind her, so that people turned to look. She stopped abruptly, just before the road on the far boundary and leaned her back against the trunk of a tree. The chill touched her for the first time and she drew her jacket around her to suppress the sudden uncontrollable shivering. Perversely, she experienced a nudge of pleasure in the roughness of the bark against her back and the wind in her face, as though nature had the power to reach out and heal.

A week passed during which time Marianne kept Karl Wolff at a distance. Gradually, the inner turmoil faded and there was a need to personally weigh up the evidence. On Monday morning, she knocked on the door of his office.

"You said you had good reason for revealing what you did," she said bluntly.

"Yes."

"Then, with your permission, I would like to look at the file for myself."

He opened the safe and placed the folder on the desk.

"Examine it here," he replied shortly. "Take as long as you like." And he turned and left the room, shutting the door behind him.

It was the final step in dealing with the bitterness of betrayal. Now that the Führer had been stripped of his image she was able to dispassionately scrutinize the man. She was left with a cardboard cut-out of a stranger.

"Sit down," Wolff gestured towards the other chair. "You haven't spoken to anyone?"

She looked at him directly for the first time. "What do you think?" she asked sarcastically.

He grinned. "I think it's the last thing that would cross your mind!"

The vestige of a smile touched the corners of her mouth, but she did not give him the satisfaction of a reply. Karl Wolff picked up a pencil from its position next to the green-edged blotter on his desk and drummed it against the arm of his chair.

"You will understand that I'm not at liberty to reveal everything to you at once, Marianne," he said slowly. "I am under orders. What I pass on to you will only be what I'm permitted to reveal. It's sufficient to tell you that you are to be offered a job of the highest priority and of the greatest secrecy. I know that your loyalty has always been to the Führer first. I am asking you to give your primary support to the National Socialist cause but to continue supporting Adolf Hitler as leader of the Reich."

He waited for a moment, hoping to gauge a response, but Marianne did not intend to play her hand immediately. She was punishing him for his part in Hitler's exposure and Wolff wondered whether her trust in him had also been compromised.

"If there is anything I have learned about you since we began working together," he continued, "it's that you have a vision broader than most people of your age. We have a plan for the future of Germany that we would like you to share in."

"Involving the Führer?" she asked dryly.

"Hitler may not be the right man to lead Germany into the new era, but he is the man to lead us now. He is a component of the whole picture and he has a destiny to play out. Our part is to ensure a future for Germany beyond Hitler."

She looked up knowing that the sense of mission, which had always been part of her, may have foundered in direction, but had lost nothing in purpose.

Her gaze was steady. "I'm ready to be part of it," she said.

Chapter 20
Twice-Born

"There must be writings," Simon Magus said. "I have told you the legends of Alexander the Great, which are penned in many languages. Tales of wondrous temples built of gold and precious jewels, where the king lies silent upon his couch and a dove speaks and prophesies in the voice of a man."

His disciples nodded. The stories of Alexander's travels and battles were among the favourites of those recounted from memory by Simon.

"A good story must have many objectives," he said. "It must excite the imagination and capture the senses. More than that though, it must arouse a holy desire and purpose in the breast of the hearer."

"A quest, or a call to battle!"

"And more! It must encompass a mystery so complete and unfathomable that a man will seek a lifetime to unravel it."

The Magus nodded his satisfaction. "I will begin to tell you such a story," he said. "Matthew will write it and each of you will teach it to all those who are initiated. In time the tale may grow and change but there are certain elements that must be retained. Alexander was led on his journey when his curiosity was aroused by a fish. We will focus on a fisherman." He looked up at his men who were reclining around the fire. It was night and in the woods beyond the walls of their lodging an owl issued a haunting repetitive call.

"This fisherman," said Simon Magus, "is a wounded king, a man of high-bearing and the keeper of a secret, a magical object that can only be discovered by one of his own lineage."

"Orpheus," Matthew laughed. "He is the fisherman, is he not?"

"Exactly! And Orpheus hearkens back both to Osiris and to Nimrod. It was he who introduced the orgies and the mystical ceremonies into Europe from Egypt. But using the fish as an image relates also to the feminine."

"The goddesses of love and fertility, such as Venus or

Aphrodite, take the symbol of a fish," Demetrius offered.

"Also Frig, the wife of Odin," the Magus agreed: "who gives her name to the sixth day of the week. It is in memory of the goddess that many Israelites eat fish on Fridays; they brought the custom back with them from the Babylonian dispersion. In my story however, I may use the image of Simon Peter, Jesus' fisherman, to direct the seeker to a certain vessel, a container of holy blood."

"The Blood Chalice!"

His disciples leaned forward, fascinated by the concept that the Magus was unfolding.

"And much more than the chalice! This lost component of the earthbound soul will remain nameless: an entity of light and beauty; an object of ecstatic passion and desire. The Pagan root of the tale must bear the guise of Christianity. But we will begin this story with the quest of a fool who has no notion that the Fisher King is his uncle."

"What is the secret?"

"You know, Demetrius, that the end of a story cannot be revealed at the beginning!"

Joseph's sharp retort was met by derisive laughter.

"Joseph is right," the Magus said. "But what I *can* tell you at the outset is the wound inflicted on the king means he can no longer sire an heir, and the sin which led to the infliction of the injury means that his land has fallen waste. Only the fool's successful completion of his quest can bring healing to both the king and his country."

"And manhood to the fool?" Demetrius asked.

Simon Magus nodded and showed his teeth in a smile. "I have given much thought to his name," he said: "and I have borrowed the meaning of the name of Solomon - peaceable. The wisest of Kings will show that a fool on our path is wiser than he. His name will be Parsival. Such a title will also suggest to a true seeker that a Zoroastrian Parsi of Persia is closer to our truth than what our words outwardly declare. Marcus, throw some more logs on that fire and I will begin my tale."

Simon Magus had conceived an enduring story, details of which would change marginally from country to country as it was recounted by his disciples. The much-desired secret would become known as the

Grail, a bright and otherworldly promise upheld by a virgin of ethereal beauty who fed the ailing king a wafer, or host, brought to the Grail by a dove.

The suffering King had, the Magus said, failed in his divinely designated task but another would arise to replace him. Increasingly, the magician would ensure that the fish became the designation of Jesus, thereby covering his tale with another layer of metaphor. The sacred function of substitution would fall to a Parsival. By sleight of hand, a descendant of the stock of Simon Magus was destined to become surrogate for Jesus Christ.

The Gnostic gospels were also conceptualised and begun by the Magus and would be completed by close followers of his teachings over the next two centuries working with the material contained in the four Gospels of the New Testament. In all, more than fifty of these gospels were penned. There was a trend common to them all: the elevation of Mary Magdalene; the snide belittling of Peter the fisherman, and the deliberate demotion of Jesus. When the popes later claimed to have succeeded Peter, they wore a symbolic fishers' ring. These Rich Fishers, wounded between the thighs, were to hold the seat in Rome for the restorer to come.

"I have made you apostle of apostles," Simon said after reading one of these writings to Helen, "You have been ranked above all the other apostles. Do you see how Peter hated you for your closeness to Jesus?"

Helen was illiterate when she met Simon, and although he was teaching her to read she had, until now, shown little desire for the written word, but this project of Simon's held her spellbound.

"You are subtle in your portrayal," she declared proudly and read his words slowly back to him, her finger tracing each syllable. "'Peter makes me hesitate: I am afraid of him because he hates the female race,' and what was the other quote?"

"'Women are not worthy of life'?"

She nodded. "Is he really the dangerous type? In the brothel the other girl who was black, as I am, was strangled by a man like that."

The Magus laughed. "I have met your Peter and in reality he's harmless! But I have put words in the mouth of that fisherman that will cause women to fear and hate him in time to come."

Simon had already directed the accusation of misogyny at the apostle Paul at every opportunity in his preaching. It was a weapon used with deliberation. He knew that women were instinctively drawn to the church by the message of love and peace, but let them think that those apostles were wolves in sheep's clothing and they would run the other way.

Sexual lust was as natural to Helen as drawing breath and the subtle implication of how the Magdalene's relationship with Jesus could be twisted to discredit him was lost on her until Simon explained it.

"Yeshua's mission was to rescue man from the jaws of hell, which the Christian Gospel claims is the consequence of sin. It was incumbent on him to become man to die for man while at the same time, to remain God."

"Why?"

He shrugged. "Blood must be shed to atone for sin – that's the essence of the Jewish sacrificial system. The Son was the final sacrifice! He died so that man did not have to pay the ultimate price – death and hell."

Helen shrugged contemptuously, "So, what does fornication have to do with that? If the Magdalene was really the consort of Jesus, how would that change his mission?"

"It's to do with Moses' Law," the Magus explained. "Such relationships outside of marriage violate the law. It is said that if a man breaks one part of the law, he breaks the whole law. If the sacrifice came from God it must necessarily be unblemished."

She laughed and the sound was harsh. "So, your implication of an intimate relationship with Mary Magdalene makes him a law-breaker?"

"Exactly that! I had to create the suggestion of a weak point in Jesus' character in order to denigrate him."

"Why didn't you simply find another part of the law that he *had* broken?"

"I could find no evidence against him. It's humanly impossible to keep the Mosaic Law, yet by all accounts he kept it!"

Helen looked at him thoughtfully. "Under your own argument, if you are saying that no fault was found in him, you yourself are implying that he is God."

The Magus smiled but she knew him well enough to recognise a moment of uncertainty. "So, he's God!" he agreed dismissively, "That's why it's up to us to forcibly defame him! Do you want to be told that your fornications will send you to hell? Humanity has no need of a God whose perfection would make us uncomfortable with ourselves. We will fight him with every weapon at our disposal!"

"There is still something that I do not understand," she said. "You have said that fornication is not permissible under Jewish law yet you have implied marriage between this Jesus and the Magdalene woman, how could that be that counted against him? Even I know that it is expected of Rabbis that they should wed."

"Marriage usually results in the establishment of a bloodline. Therefore, worship would shift from the God to his children."

Light dawned in her face. "So we have created the bloodline to turn the worship of this God to our own offspring!" She smiled and took him by the hand. "You have brought into being the perfect plan!"

Chapter 21
Twice-Born

Both in prehistoric times when Celtic tribes inhabited the Languedoc, as well as under Rome, the southern Pyrenees region was deemed sacred. When Simon and Helen arrived in Rennes-le-Chateau in approximately AD 40, the town was a thriving community. Contrary to the approach he and his disciples had adopted in Edessa, Rome and Britain, the Magus did not minister openly. He had come to create a mystery religion and his mission was to the chosen few.

Whereas Rome would constitute the outward face and expression of Simon's new religion; Britain and Byzantium the limbs; the Languedoc was to be the coven heart.

The nucleus of the inner circle planted at Rennes-le-Chateau consisted of Helen and the Magus' highest initiates; all of them married men and all Samaritans. This inner circle was made up of three groups of thirteen with Simon Magus at the head. This rule was to pertain to all generations and would constitute the Languedoc's future nobility; the breeding pool of the Samaritan race. The head of John the Baptist was committed into the perpetual care of these covens, and the teachings of Simon Magus were recorded by them to be passed down in secret until all things were accomplished. Within this intimate circle the Magus became known as the incarnation of Osiris, and Helen as the new Isis.

When they arrived, Helen was already in the fourth month of her pregnancy. The Gnostic teachings, which salted Simon Magus' Judaeo-Christian gospel, deemed that adding to the species was an evil perpetuating the separation of man from his final perfected state. Therefore, to justify Helen's condition to the initiates of the second level, the Magus formulated a way to turn this to his own advantage. It was time to strengthen the goddess aspect of his new religion.

The group of nine men were instructed to take the route to the castle of a local nobleman on foot. It was early evening and the sun created soft shafts of light through the massive trunks of the trees. The narrow forest path wound upward to where they were afforded glimpses of their destination; grey stone walls subdued in the fading light rose sheer above an outcrop of rock. Their focus was on the path so that they stumbled upon the clearing suddenly and without warning. As a man they stopped and stared in silence at a crimson cross planted in the ground almost fifty yards away. The atmosphere prickled with tension. As they watched, a pure white stag, spectral in its beauty and lightness of foot, bounded across the glade. Close on its tail was a pack of baying hounds and the one that led the pack drew alongside the deer and leaped for its throat while the others attacked its hindquarters. It fell and was savagely torn apart.

The onlookers were stunned into silence but the scene had not yet played itself out. A knight walked swiftly from the trees and, following more slowly behind him, was a woman, lithe and slender, her face hidden in the folds of her robe. In their hands they carried golden vessels into which they gathered the flesh of the stag. They then kissed the cross before disappearing into the forest on the other side.

"Is it a vision?" The question was spoken softly, verbalising all their thoughts.

"If it's not, there will be the blood of the animal on the ground as evidence," one young man said. He stepped forward boldly and approached the spot where the beast had fallen. Then, suddenly and as though mesmerised, he turned his face to the cross and fell on his knees before it, weeping with passion.

"Get away from there!" a voice shouted angrily and a priest in a hooded robe stepped into the fading light of the clearing. "You have no right to approach!"

The youth scrambled to his feet in confusion and retreated a few paces as the priest prostrated himself, kissing the base of the cross in rapt adoration. But even as he knelt there, another, similarly robed and hooded, ran towards him with a rod in his hand and attacked the suppliant, beating him across his back and shoulders so that he staggered away and disappeared into the trees. While the men looked on in astonishment, the second priest lashed out with his rod and, knocking the cross to the ground, he trampled upon it in a fury.

"Do you call yourself a priest?" The young man drew himself up in anger and would have lunged at the robed man to disarm him, but one of those who had stepped out behind him grasped him by the shoulder, drawing him back.

"Wait," he said urgently, "we are intended to learn something from this!"

"He has brought shame upon himself," the youth protested. "See what he has done!"

But even as he struggled to free himself, he realised that the priest had disappeared with the rest and they were alone once more. The cross lay on the ground, a discordant red, the one remaining sign of the strange scene that had been played out before them. Only after they reached the castle did they realise that they had forgotten to check the ground for blood.

"The stag in all its purity and beauty was brought down by the pack many centuries ago," the Magus said. "Nimrod was the one who opened the way for man's conscience to be freed from guilt. Osiris the Egyptian god was one with him. Each time, the hounds have taken down such initiators and ripped them to pieces."

"Who are these hounds?" the young man asked.

"Religious men in the image of Seth, men who know nothing of freedom, determined to place mankind in spiritual bondage," the Magus replied. "From his murder of Osiris, we know Seth as the god of Chaos. There is an Approaching-One, Parsival, who will restore the king and bring healing to the land. You will teach what you have seen today through all generations to future proselytes who take the oath of celibacy, but only the highest initiates will be permitted to know its meaning."

"The cross," another asked. "Is it to us a symbol of good or evil?"

"It has to be good," protested the youth who had fallen down before it. "I was consumed by its glory. I have never experienced such sweetness as I felt when I was faced by it today."

"You saw the two priests," Simon said. "They will reflect the two faces of this order. Outwardly it is sweet, as Gregory has said, and that is what will be conveyed to those who are not of this circle. The second priest displayed the truth. The cross of Christ deserves nothing but contempt and hatred, as does the so-called son of God who hung on it. It epitomises everything we stand against.

In the weeks ahead I will open your understanding to a great many things; mysteries that only the chosen will comprehend and you will, in time, become prosperous leaders of generations to follow."

The castle, which clung to the ridge high above the forest, was to be the home of the disciples for many months to come. When they left, they would be permanently transformed; men of immense power and the keepers of a secret so fantastic, so extraordinary, that hundreds of generations hence, men would still be selling their souls to become party to it.

None of the celibates of the second circle had yet laid eyes on Helen and the Magus had not spoken of her, but in her third trimester, and the sixth month of her pregnancy, a feast was planned.

It took place in the banqueting hall of the castle hung with silk banners, which shimmered like cascades of water in the smoky light from the torches. For the first time since the arrival of the initiates, there were invited guests at the meal; each of them trusted disciples of the Magus. Herodias was seated in a place of honour, and beside her Salomon who was attendant on all her needs. The face of Herod's wife was powdered a chalky white and her hair hennaed to expunge all signs of grey but she was unable to disguise the sagging skin in her throat or the plaintive quaver that had crept into her voice.

Simon Magus' consort, Mary of Magdala sat on his left side; her long hair caught up in a soft chignon and decorated with drop pearls. She was still a woman of strong bearing and alluring beauty; a woman destined to turn heads and hearts. The ornate seat on the Magus' right was empty.

The hall resounded with laughter and chatter. For Simon Magus' initiates, this was the first light relief from weeks of intensive training. None had failed the tests he had exposed them to; they had bound themselves to the oaths and participated in the rites imposed on them by the master without question.

The first dishes were brought in by servants who placed them on the table and withdrew. As lids were lifted, silence fell on the gathering and they looked questioningly at Simon who sat at the centre of the head table. Every dish was empty.

A knight entered bearing a new platter and placed it on the table before the Magus. A small smile played over his lips as he removed the silver lid. The assembly gasped at the powerful white light that emanated from it forcing them at first to avert their eyes. A strange head with matted hair and beard gazed out across the hall with every appearance of life. The eyes set in blackened hollows glowered with magnetic intensity. Simon rose to his feet and lifted the gruesome relic high. Besides the Magus, not a soul was able to remain in his seat. All fell to the floor in fear and worshipped.

"Arise, all of you!" The voice was mesmerizing and, unaccountably, afforded them the strength to obey. Every eye was upon the head so that the shriek of the knight who entered from the room behind them shattered the spellbound silence. Instinctively the men felt for their swords yet knowing they had surrendered their belts at the door. Brandishing a lance, gory from a kill, the knight circuited the hall and left by the main door through which he had come. And while the men still stared in shock at his departing figure, a woman entered in his place. She was small and slender but her belly bulged with child. Helen was dressed in a simple blue robe, and her dark-skinned face was framed by a hood of the same material. In her hands she bore a jasper drinking bowl within a golden chalice, which shone with dazzling, unearthly radiance.

In stark contrast to all that had just transpired, the ethereal figure of the woman radiated quiet tranquillity. Walking slowly to the head of the table, Helen took her stand at the right side of Simon. In one swift gesture, the Magus stretched out his arms and at once he was transfigured before them. His naked torso was drenched in blood and blood flowed from a crown of thorns that pierced his brow. A powerful wind emanated from the head table, swaying the onlookers on their feet.

"I am the Christ, the son of David, and you are witnesses that the Christ spirit dwells in me! This is my most intimate disciple, the Black Isis, Mary of Magdala," the Magus said. "Her body is the reliquary of the Holy Blood. You, my disciples, are to be the protectors of the secrets of this bloodline through the generations until we achieve the fulfilment of all things. Again, you will speak to your generations of the things you have witnessed today, but only the highest initiates may know their meaning. You have sworn oaths under the darkest of circumstances, which are intended to sear them into your souls. None of you will ever speak to any initiate below your level, of the true meaning and intent of the things that have occurred within this castle."

He took the cup and raised it above his head. The vision faded and they saw again that he was dressed in his white robes that bore no stain of gore. As the goblet was passed from hand to hand, each drank from it and fell down before the Christ in worship.

"Remember these words; bind them in your hearts and minds!" Simon Magus cried. "In the ritual played out before you today there are four vital elements, and there is a fifth and a sixth, which will complete the picture in generations to come. When all the pieces are assembled together beneath the Holy Mount, wherein lies the spring of all sacred knowledge, one man will draw the sword from the rock and use it to smite the old Order and usher in the new."

They drank in the words of the prophecy without comprehending the meaning.

"Take," the magician ordered, "and eat." He lifted the head of the Baptist in both hands as if in a sign of blessing over the assembly. "That's right," he shouted. "Whatever your heart desires to eat tonight will be yours! Visualise it there before you! Concentrate as you have been taught! As keepers of the secret, you will never hunger. While the Fisher King is worshipped, your land will be filled with plenty and your purses with wealth."

Before their eyes an astounding thing took place. The dishes on the table were filled to overflowing and the air was filled with their rich aroma.

The white Magdalene sat at the left of the Magus while the black Magdalene sat at his right side. As always, Helen ate sparingly, showing little appetite for food. The child kicked within her belly. It would be a boy, of course. History required that she give birth to a son.

Chapter 22
Twice-Born

The conquest of Britain by Claudius Caesar opened the way for the new religion to be brought into the West. The ritual magic of the lance in conjunction with the will of Simon Magus and his inner circle of disciples had succeeded in doing its work in bringing Claudius, the least bellicose of the Caesars to war. Two Roman invasions of Britain had been instituted by Julius Caesar more than a hundred years before; the first landing proved unsuccessful and the second yielded only marginal victories. But what Claudius Caesar lacked as a warrior, he made up for in tactical knowledge gained from his study of history and this time Britain fell and became a vassal of Rome.

Simon Magus' uncle, Joseph, was assigned to take the last of the relics westward. The jasper drinking bowl, which had come into the hands of Herodias, wife of Herod Antipas, was contained within a golden chalice reputed to have been given to Abraham by the ancient priest-king Melchizedek.

On the night of John the Baptist's death, Herodias had caught some of the blood from the severed head in the goblet and she and her daughter Salome drank of it. Henceforth, this cup had been set apart in a specially carved reliquary to be used in only the most important rites. It was the goblet taken to the crucifixion of Jesus the Nazarene, but the magician's efforts to fill it had been thwarted by the Roman guard. Nevertheless, as Simon Magus declared, the blood of John the Baptist was sufficient. They had his head, the shroud they had created from it, and the cup, which had held the Baptist's blood. Through their influence and the heritage of the relics, it appeared certain that the Baptist would become even more significant than Christ. The one who in life had been preparer of the way for Jesus had, in death, become the Opener of the Way for his usurper.

Christianity would be taken into Britain through the cup – the first of the blood relics. The shroud had gone to the east; the cup would go to the west, but the lance and the head of the Baptist were delivered into the head and the heart of Europe.

As a wealthy man and a member of the Sanhedrin, Joseph of Arimathea had been a well-known figure in Jerusalem and Herod had been delighted to tell Salomon all he knew of him, information that was passed on to the other disciples. Antipas had become rheumy-eyed and maudlin since his exile. Far from gaining the love and respect of his wife by bowing to her will in petitioning Caesar Caligula, he had lost her completely with the loss of his kingdom. He was fully aware that Salomon had taken the place of Simon Magus in his wife's bed and was almost past caring, instead he ate and drank excessively and agitated constantly about his failing health. Life was now centred entirely upon himself, and if there was an audience for his stories, he was delighted to entertain it.

Joseph of the inner circle left the Languedoc with one of the three covens; twelve more of the Magus' closest disciples. Their destination was an area in the south of England where there was a powerful energy centre formed by a convergence of the ley lines; a point of entry into the underworld. Glastonbury's rounded hill, or Tor, rising five hundred feet from the plains formed a triangle with the stone circles of Stonehenge and Avebury. It had been a centre of Druidic worship until the advent of Rome had placed Druidism under a stranglehold, but even before that, lost in time, the Tor had attracted the creators of the stone circles who wove their mysteries between earth and cosmos.

In the days when Joseph of Gitta and his men arrived in the vicinity of Glastonbury, the sea still lapped at the foot of the Tor and almost encircled the knot of hills to form what was known as the Island of Avalon or Avallach, the demigod ruler of the underworld. It was whispered that where land and sea kissed, the dead were gathered and drawn into the nether regions.

It was not Joseph of Gitta though, who set foot on Wearyall Hill just below Avalon's Tor, but Joseph of Arimathea. Joseph disembarked with his men, exhausted from the journey and legend has it that he thrust his staff into the ground and lay down beside it to rest. When he awoke, the staff had taken root and sprouted. The thorn bush that grew became known as the Glastonbury Thorn and it marked the newcomers instantly as powerful magicians or priests.

"Melchizedek, the great king of Jerusalem, drank from this cup and gave it into the hands of Abraham, Father of the Jewish nation," Joseph of Arimathea taught many months later. "At the last supper, Jesus the Christ drank from this goblet as he gave us the mystery of the sacrament of Holy Communion. On the following day, while the Saviour hung on the cross, I caught his blood in this same cup before laying him in my own tomb." His voice caught in sorrow and he buried his head in his hands. "Could there be a vessel more sacred to the Christian faith than this? Knights of the Church of Christ, every time you drink of this cup, you will draw a little closer to heaven."

He looked out over the gathering of men in the mud-brick building they had constructed, with some satisfaction. Many of them had already made vows of chastity and wore the brown hooded robes of the new Order.

Later that day the men congregated near the edge of a river and Joseph netted a large fish and tossed it flapping helplessly onto the grass where the men were sitting.

"There was a certain king," he said, "a rich fisherman, who ruled over the kingdom of Logres[26]. This king owned a golden chalice, a cup of blessing, which produced an abundance of food for those that desired it and wine aplenty. As protector of so great a gift, the king had to lead a life worthy of the cup but he sought after earthly love and slept with a beautiful virgin. On the same day, he engaged in combat with a knight and was sore wounded in his thigh by his own lance. The king rode back to his castle knowing he had betrayed the trust placed in him."

The men had gathered round and were listening intently.

"The Fisher King could no longer look upon the golden cup, so he covered it and placed it in a niche beneath the dome in the hall of feasting. As you know, a king is wedded to the spirit of the land, therefore his sin caused blessing over Logres to cease and the land suffered and was laid waste. His wound failed to heal and he endured

---

[26] Britain.

grievous pain, day and night for many a year. The King's subjects lamented the fall of their king and waited with deep longing for the pre-eminent one who would release him from this sad enchantment."

"Who could release him?" someone asked.

"Only one of his own family had the power to set him free and restore the land to its former glory," Joseph said. "The one pre-destined would twice heal the enchanted sword of the Rich Fisher. But he must first ask the right question of the king."

The fish had ceased its flapping and lay still, only its gills opened and shut fruitlessly.

"Then, one day, a young knight rode up to the castle gate," Joseph continued. "His name was Parsival. A Parsi is a great priest or magician, and he was such a one and most valiant in all his exploits."

"And he asked the question of the king?"

Joseph shook his head sadly. "Alas, he failed this time in his quest for not one of the king's servants was permitted to instruct him and he knew not that the question should be asked. On the following day therefore, when the sun arose, Parsival found himself in the ruin of a castle with no sign that the wondrous events of the previous night had ever taken place."

Joseph of Arimathea continued his story and brought it to its climax with the healing of the king by Parsival who assumed the throne in his place. That evening Joseph placed the baked fish on the table and his chalice beside it.

"Father," the men protested laughing, "your fish can never serve so many of us!"

"Then you reckon without faith in the vessel."

And Joseph gave thanks and broke the fish in his hands and to the amazement of the men, there was sufficient for everyone that night, and some left over. From that time Joseph, and later his son Alain li Gros, was known as the Fisher King, or the Rich Fisher.

Joseph's chalice was a potent vessel of life-within-death to everyone who drank from it. It opened the understanding of the initiate becoming a cauldron of rebirth, focussing his vision on heaven, on the Magdalene, and Mary the blessed Virgin.

The Druids had taught a religion of life-in-death similar to the

Osiris cult in Egypt. They worshipped among others, Mabon, a sun-god who was symbolised by a white bull. The immortality of the soul was demonstrated through the daily death and rebirth of the sun and through the annual cycle of the sacred oak tree. The religion Joseph and his disciples brought to Avalon harnessed many of the teachings of Druidism fusing them to a Christianised base.

Joseph perceived the astuteness of Simon the Magus and shook his head shrewdly. Certainly the Master was more than man. His wisdom was that of Lucifer himself. In his hands, the Christian faith had become a spiritual journey of superstition and mystery centred not on Christ but on relics. The form of Christianity Joseph of Arimathea planted at Glastonbury was as foreign as the oriental thorn bush was to English soil. It was a religion born of a bitter root and it was destined to snag and claw at the truth. Paul of Tarsus would have described it as a thorn in the flesh.

Chapter 23
Twice-Born

Freiberg was waiting for him at his usual table on the terrace. The day was overcast and he had pushed his hat back on his head and loosened his tie. Small white yachts skimmed the surface of the lake like bugs.

"Take a seat, Segal, I've ordered lunch."

Michael set his own hat down on the table and reached across to shake Chaim's hand.

"You're looking better fed than you did when I last saw you," Freiberg commented. "You've lost the desperate look."

Segal grinned wryly. "I'll be even better if the news you have is promising."

"Hard to tell if it's good or bad," Freiberg shrugged. "Contact has been made, your girl's still inside and there's some arm-wrestling going on. No positive news so far, I'm afraid."

"Did your contact say how she was?"

He shook his head apologetically. "Sorry old chap, it didn't occur to me to ask." His lapses into English were becoming more frequent and self-conscious as though he was trying to dispense with his German background and create a new persona.

"Alright," Segal said covering his disappointment. "You had some thoughts on direction for these new articles?"

"Ah yes." There was a pause while he mopped his brow and stuffed his handkerchief into his trouser pocket. Lunch arrived at that moment and Michael Segal noted with approval that the Beau Rivage Hotel was not constrained by any form of food rationing. The meal was served with a good red wine and for the first few minutes Chaim Freiberg attacked his steak with relish. He was not a man who lightly mixed his culinary enjoyment with business.

"I was thinking more in terms of a book," he said suddenly as though there had been no break in conversation.

"A book!"

"Yes, newspaper articles are published one day and are

forgotten the next. A book has a more enduring quality. Think you are up to it?"

"Sure, but I would need to find work to keep me going while I'm writing."

"More about that later." Freiberg dismissed the thought as though it was of scant importance. "Look, Segal, this might not be exactly up your street, so tell me if you're not prepared to do it."

"Sure." Michael picked up his wine glass and pushed his plate aside. Within seconds a waiter appeared from nowhere and spirited it away.

"I have an area of interest that I have been studying for years. Have you heard of the Turin shroud?"

"Can't say I have."

"It's a Catholic relic, purported to be the shroud of Christ."

"A Catholic relic!" Michael looked at him in stunned disbelief.

"Okay, okay! So what would a Jewish guy be doing studying a Gentile shroud?"

"Exactly! What's the point?"

Chaim Freiberg scratched the bristle on his chin and leaned back in his chair.

"This shroud has a figure superimposed on it," he said. "An image apparently not made by hands."

"What do you mean?"

"For one thing, it's in the negative. When it's photographed it reads more strongly. The face on the cloth is quite ghostly, almost watery in appearance." He nodded at the waiter who hovered at his elbow, wine bottle in hand and waited while he refilled their glasses. Chaim lifted his glass to the light, admiring the ruby liquid for a moment before taking a sip. "The shroud appears to have been imprinted supernaturally – and obviously, according to the Church, the image was made at the moment of the resurrection. It's not easy to argue against something as concrete as a shroud imprinted with the naked body of a man who appears to have been crucified."

"So, it's obviously a fake!"

"Quite likely, but a very good one. If the shroud is as old as they say, then it's a remarkable image, but there are those who postulate a medieval forgery."

"What is your point of interest?" Michael asked curiously.

"You may remember, my mother is Jewish but my father was Catholic. I was brought up in the Jewish faith, but my father couldn't quite escape his roots and the shroud was the sticking point. In his estimation, if there was such a clear proof of the deity of Jesus Christ and possibly the resurrection, then Christianity had to be correct. I suppose, as a result, I've always harboured an element of confusion."

Michael raised his eyebrows but made no comment. In his mind he was trying to find a polite way of declining the book offer.

"As I've studied the shroud," Freiberg continued, "I've recognised its influence on Byzantine religious art. The picture that most people have of Jesus Christ is one that comes down from those early works."

He looked at Michael's closed expression and sighed. "Okay, look, I realise that this was probably a bad idea but I thought I'd ask. I'd write it myself if I had the ability."

"Just how much information have you got on this shroud?"

"A lot. Several people have made a study of it."

"Any likelihood that the church would allow a viewing?"

Freiberg shook his head. "I attended the last exposition in '33. Rome doesn't readily allow access to the public."

"Tell me your impressions."

Chaim scratched the back of his head pensively. "Disappointing in one sense. I had to battle the crowds and the authorities were anxious to keep us moving. It was displayed horizontally behind glass, and although the image is unmistakeable at a distance, it becomes softer and more diffused as you approach it. It has a sepia tinge and there's an almost imperceptible tonal difference to the bloodstains but the image is clean. There's no sense that you're looking at a bloodied cloth."

"The church presumably owns the relic?"

He shook his head. "It's owned by King Umberto II of Savoy who was deposed as king of Italy around the time of the exhibition. I doubt whether even he's seen it since!"

"Give me the information to look over, and I'll let you know,"

Michael said. "But to be honest, Chaim, you were right; this is not my cup of tea."

Yet, surprisingly, as Michael Segal examined the reports, newspaper clippings and photographs that Freiberg had collected, his interest grew.

The first photographs had been taken by an amateur photographer, a man by the name of Secondo Pia, in 1898. The fourteen foot cloth had been hung above the altar in the Turin Cathedral of St. John the Baptist, and Pia brought in electric lighting and built a scaffold to raise the camera to the right level. His initial attempt, on opening night of the exhibition proved a failure as the screens of his flood lamps cracked in the intense heat. On the night of May 28th, after the last visitors had left, he tried once more, making two exposures of fourteen minutes and twenty minutes respectively, and hurried back to his darkroom to develop the plates. He was awestruck when an image appeared on the glass negative, for he was faced, not with the subtle, shadowy representation of the shroud but with a definite photographic likeness. The face was clear and lifelike, and bloodstains were brought into sharper focus, white against the dark background, and could be seen to flow from the wounds of the body.

Further pictures were taken in 1931, when the cloth was displayed over a period of twenty days to celebrate the wedding of Prince Umberto. Owing to the advances in technology, these were photographs of far superior quality and Michael examined the large prints that Chaim had obtained with fascination. There was no possibility that the images had been tampered with. They had been taken and developed under the scrutiny of many witnesses including a specially appointed commission of expert photographers who were present to check every procedure. In these it was possible to see that the flow of blood on the lower arms had trickled back from the wrists towards the elbows from the angle of the arms during the crucifixion. If the shroud was a forgery, it was accomplished with significant expertise.

"I'll write your book."

Chaim Freiberg beamed his approval. "What made you change

your mind?"

Michael Segal looked thoughtful. "I have very little interest in the shroud as a relic," he said at length. "But I want to know when the image was made and what made it. I find it hard to believe that it could have been done at the time of Christ but even a forger in the middle ages would have had to have been an expert to carry off a job like that!"

Chaim nodded. "An early forger could not have known what we know now," he said, "that the representation becomes lifelike when the light value is reversed. It is intriguing." He glanced at Michael with some embarrassment. "I would like to be involved as much as possible," he said. "Not exactly a ghost writer, you understand, but in collaboration."

"And your name included on the cover?" Segal said with no hint of mischief in his expression.

"Exactly! And in the meantime, I will pay your expenses here in Switzerland and engage a publisher."

"You realise that this could take a while?"

"Of course! Where do we start?"

Michael shrugged. "Let's look at the history. If the shroud has been around for a while, there must be some evidence."

Chapter 24
Twice-Born

Once the foundation of the Magdalene cult was firmly established in the South of France, Herod and Herodias sought to leave the Languedoc pleading Herod's ill health. Although they were not permitted to return to Judaea, Emperor Claudius allowed them to leave Lyons and awarded them, at their request, an estate in Spain at the seaside town of Cadiz, a situation closer in climate to that which they were accustomed.

They would leave following the birth of Helen's child and Salomon and several of his disciples were to accompany the Herodian court. His instruction from Simon Magus differed from that of the other disciples. Instead of introducing a relic around which the new faith would be built, he would establish the Order of the Temple steeped in his own speciality – esoteric Judaism in the form of Cabala.

Simon Magus referred to his inner circle of Samaritans as a sacred hierarchy which would become known as the White Brotherhood. This cabal of supreme initiates was intended to overarch all monarchies and governments and would, in the fullness of time, reign from behind the scenes in whatever nation in which they settled. It would gain the ear of kings, create agents in high places in government and, through the power of the Order, steer and control future events. Its aim was to absorb the ancient priesthood of the Jews which had never turned from the worship of Baal, while by all means seeking to convert and pervert the faithful. The ultimate goal was the rebuilding of the Jewish Temple in preparation for the return of Osiris.

"A girl!" Simon Magus' face was white with fury. "That's impossible! How can she have produced a female?"

Salomon placed a conciliatory hand on his master's shoulder, but the Magus shook it off.

"It cannot be my child!"

"Master, consider Helen, do not raise your voice," Salomon pleaded.

Simon Magus regarded him contemptuously. "I care nothing

for what that whore thinks or feels," he retorted. "She was to give me a son. The whole plan rests on it! What use is a female to us?"

Both men were faced with the depths of the failure. For once their invocations and their magic had let them down, and on a point so crucial. Simon had no desire to see the product of their union, which at that moment bellowed gustily forth from the adjoining room. Upon witnessing the Master's fury, the midwife, bearer of the bad new, had returned hastily to Helen's side, leaving the two men alone

There was no question of substitution. The bloodline was crucial and the skin colour of their off-spring made such a change impossible. Elimination was equally out of the question. They had prepared meticulously for this moment and should there be no child the final outcome would be worse than the first. The Grail feast could not be re-enacted.

But a girl! Nimrod and Semiramis had presented their adherents with a son. Isis and Osiris produced Horus. Mary had brought forth the one called Messiah. It was unthinkable that Simon Magus and Helen; the new Jesus and Mary Magdalene should initiate their most holy, magical bloodline through a female!

In the next room, Helen lay rigid on her bed, refusing to look at the little dark-skinned child that the woman was holding. It had not been necessary to hear every word of the conversation between Simon and Salomon; the unthinkable had occurred and she, Helen was blamed for the outcome. She heard the outer door slam shut.

"Here, mistress, hold her," the midwife urged, offering her the tiny scrap of humanity now tightly bound in white cloths.

"I want nothing to do with it," Helen retorted. "Take it away and leave me alone!" and she turned her face to the wall.

When his anger was past, Simon Magus named the child Sarah in acknowledgement of Sarah the Egyptian, the name under which Helen had travelled when they first set foot in France. He presented the child to the initiates on the eighth day after her birth, having determined that a daughter should not be allowed to ruin his plans. If the gods had ordained that Helen should bear a female, he would wrest what advantage he could from the situation.

So it was that Mary Magdalene, the Black Isis of the inner circle, clothed in a dress of Arabian silk, held the child tenderly to her breast on that day; the epitome of motherhood. Salomon spoke in place of Simon Magus introducing the little one as the Perfection of Paradise. He gave Helen also, a new name.

"This is how the Magdalene will be known through all generations," he told them. "She will be called Répandre de Choix, because her seed will be propagated and spread abroad, and her land will be known as Terre de Choix, the Chosen Land.

"No disciple of the Master may ever allow the question to be asked, 'What is your land?' or 'Where do you come from?' If you, or the generations to follow, allow such a question, you will be cut off and the blessings of long life and prosperity will be forfeited. You will conceal your heritage at all costs. You will call yourselves Jews or Christians as it has been allotted to you, but you will never let it be known that you are of the chosen land of Samaria!"

Simon Magus stood up and the room fell silent. His face was deathly pale and his eyes appeared to have sunk back into his skull.

"The Jewish/Christian God sent his Son," he ground out. "The Standing One has given an answer. From henceforth, I give you the Black Rose. Two symbols will stand together in perpetuity hiding the true nature of the cross, the rose and the cross – the female principle in combination with that of the male. The goddess will receive the worship intended for the Son; the Mother will be elevated above the progeny. Rex Mundi, god of this earth has made his reply!"

The Magus showed no further paternal interest in Sarah, but committed her into the hands of trusted disciples to bring up. Helen turned her back on her with equal disinterest and the wife of Salomon found a wet-nurse for the child from among the local community.

An Order had indeed been initiated, which would act as the protector of the Grail. The little half-caste waif, placed in the hands of the family who owned the Castle of Montsalvat was already promised in marriage to the infant son of Salomon. This would create a continuing pattern. In the Languedoc, an imported nobility would spring up from the loins of Simon Magus and his Samaritan order. They were destined to become men of great wealth and power. Sarah carried the chosen bloodline of Simon Magus and the black Magdalene into Europe. In the fullness of time it would become the lineage of kings. But she, as a woman, would never be privy to its secrets.

The final resting place of the bones of John the Baptist was designed to embellish the mystery. In the mind of Simon Magus, nothing was wasted; no detail lost. Each element was woven together in a web that would endure and widen through the generations until the ordained point of culmination. The plan was not his own. Its fountainhead lay in a mind infinitely more devious than that of the Magus. But the imparting of it to a single individual lay in his willing subjugation to the one who led him. He was fully prepared to plumb the depths of human depravity for a transient life-time of power. A human being reflects that to which it is enslaved.

The outer circle of his cult was designed to display light, so their white Magdalene assumed the outward adorning of love and virtue. She shone as the Virgin. But like the planet Venus, the harlot rotated in another direction. Venus was always a fly trap, attracting victims through an ostensible beauty but filled with a stench that only flies could be drawn to. The Lord of the Flies, Beelzebub himself, baited the trap.

The head of the Baptist and the heart of the Magdalene captured the Languedoc region: Biblical faith was never at issue. Mary Magdalene preached a gospel designed to attract the people and laced it with arsenic. This was Venus at her most appealing. Had Mary not lured the townsfolk with her prophecies and titillated the senses with the hint of something hidden and infinitely more profound, her words would have been lost forever. The Magdalene enticed the innocent seeker but the dark inner core revealed the true nature of the Order and none touched by the one escaped the tarnish of the other. The head and the heart; magic and mystery; these were the elements, and their path culminated in death.

The Magus was aware that in the years ahead many would seek the Languedoc's treasures; therefore it was imperative to bind cunning upon the hearts of those he was to leave behind and the secrets of the Order were burned into the hearts of every initiate. The inner circle consisted only of men of Samaria and Edom; knights of the finest calibre.

Simon Magus was approaching the end of his life and there was still work to accomplish in Rome. The foundation had been laid in the Languedoc; it was time to depart. The entombment of the bones was one of his final acts in France and the ceremony took place in the dead of night on the property of one of his knights. The crypt, which had been especially built for the remains of the Baptist, was situated about six miles from Rennes-le-Chateau and close to the village of Arques. It was to serve as a repository for the Baptist's bones but also, in times of necessity, as concealment for the head. A curse was placed on the sepulchre preventing any soul, other than the most highly initiated, from disturbing it.

Perhaps it was fitting that many centuries later Nicolas Poussin should have painted shepherds examining the tomb. After all, shepherds were the first group to visit the Christ-child after his birth, why should they not visit the resting place of the one who had been made his usurper?

The day following the interment, Simon Magus made the journey to Marseilles and took leave of Helen and the three Marys. Within the week he had boarded a ship bound for Rome. What he had left behind was destined to endure. For centuries to come, wherever the cult abounded, Mary Magdalene and the Baptist would be elevated while Christ Jesus would be moved inexplicably into the background.

Legends of the Baptist and the Magdalene would henceforth be associated with the Cathars and Templars, who were rooted in the Languedoc and Champagne regions. There would never fail to be whispers of a Black Madonna and a mysterious head around which Templar worship seemed to centre.

PART III

Chapter 1
Twice-Born

St. Denys is accredited with introducing Christianity to Paris in the third century. He was said to be an Athenian named Dionysius, a name which, in the Greek, defies all interpretation. But in the Chaldee, the name becomes D'ion-nuso-s and signifies "The Sin-Bearer"
St. Denis was beheaded and thrown into the Seine, but, so the legend goes, he climbed up onto the river bank with his head under his arm and marched away with it to his place of burial. The Catholic Church canonised St. Denys making him the patron saint of Paris. Until 1789, when for a time his office was abolished, a hymn was sung in the Cathedral of St. Denis in Paris commemorating this fable.
"The corpse immediately arose;
the trunk bore away the dissevered head,
guided on its way by a legion of angels."

From the beginning of time the severed head was an object of worship. In Norse mythology, Odin embalmed the head of Mimir and it became his prized talisman; an object that caused Odin to be regarded among the people as a god. Catholicism still venerates bones and body parts and has in its possession a vast number of skulls and embalmed human heads quite apart from the ghastly Capuchin Crypt in Rome, which is decorated with the skulls and bones of departed monks.
The story of St. Denys is the story of the death of Orpheus in Thrace whose head floated on the waters of the Hebrus. The name Orpheus is a synonym for the Babylonian God Bel, whose name means "to mix" or "to confound". Orv or Orph, signifies also, "to mix". The form of Christianity that Paris gained through St. Denys and his martyr's death was an unsavoury mix of Christianity and paganism and wherever such alchemy takes place, Christianity is lost.

The capture of Paris in the summer of 1940 was smooth and marked with very few unpleasant incidents. There were a handful of people, including the Mayor of Clichy, who over the days that followed the occupation chose the route of suicide rather than submission to the enemy. Otherwise the events took place in a calm and orderly manner. Swastikas were raised over key buildings; hotels were requisitioned and paid for.

German soldiers, after a victory parade down the Champs-Elysees, forgot the war for a moment and became tourists, flocking to the Eiffel Tower, the Arc de Triomphe and the Tomb of the Unknown Soldier. The Chabanais, one of Paris' better known brothels, sensed the atmosphere and posted notice that its doors would re-open for business at three o'clock that afternoon.

The evacuation that preceded the German army had been carried out at the height of the panic, almost draining the city. Officials and citizens alike had simply left, carrying with them what they could; in their haste, abandoning homes, pets, jobs and responsibilities. Little, apart from personal safety, appeared to matter. A frantic stream of humanity crammed the road south, cars and trucks travelling bumper to bumper; others on bicycles and on foot, some with no more than a hand-cart or a baby's pram.

As the remainder of the city's populace settled back into an uneasy calm after the occupation, many refugees slipped quietly back. A subdued Paris picked up life where she left off, but now it was the Germans who held the reins.

René de Bar had been among those who had quietly departed. His position as a journalist had allowed him to sense the inevitable once the German army had crossed the Meuse, so that the warning he received from the Organisation had not come as any surprise. He left while the battle against the Second Army was still being fought, avoiding the hordes that jammed the roads days later. His return to the estate would have appeared to his acquaintances to have been a fortuitous coincidence rather than a flight ahead of the enemy.

Sweat steamed from the flanks of his mount and the breath from her nostrils rasped against the chill morning air. The ride had been exhilarating. He handed his mare to the groom and strode up towards the house. The sun was beginning to dapple the valley, bathing some areas in light and throwing others into deep shadow. Vineyards on the terraced slopes created an orderly foreground to the hills

The smell of coffee welcomed him as he entered the hall, heels of his riding boots clicking as he crossed the marble floor. Windows had already been thrown open to the sunlight and servants were quietly at work. René de Bar sat down on the terrace where a table was set for breakfast, helping himself to fruit and croissants and, as the butler poured his coffee, he picked up the daily paper to peruse the headlines.

"There was a phone call while you were out, sir. I was asked to tell you to call Philip at 9.15 this morning."

De Bar nodded his thanks and opened the newspaper. Reports of the occupation were restrained and no doubt had been thoroughly censored. He glanced briefly through the pages and set it aside.

De Bar was tall and big boned and of an aristocratic bearing. His dark eyes beneath heavy lids were distant and strangely devoid of expression, but in conversation he was animated, quick witted and humorous and there were few that could match him intellectually.

At 9.12 am René de Bar took the stairs to his own suite and made a brief call from the telephone beside his bed.

"Hello Philip, Alain here."

"Ah yes, Alain," the voice responded. "I've been asked to tell you to return home immediately. Simone has been asking for you."

"Where?"

"Chez Jean Marc. July 10th at 10.00 am."

"I understand."

At the other end of the line there was a click as the receiver was replaced. De Bar massaged the end of his nose thoughtfully. So they had a job for him. It was time then to see how Germany had imposed herself on Paris.

For René de Bar there was very little bitterness or grief involved in the occupation. He was not a man given to sentiment and there were other far more important considerations to be taken into account. He was gratified that Paris had remained unscathed and cynically amused that France's army had fallen with such consummate ease. De Bar was not a natural pugilist. The science of war was far more fascinating than the fight itself. There was a crudeness to modern warfare that he found repulsive. He was a fencer, and the artfulness involved in the parry and thrust of a sabre was much more in his line. But there was an end to which the war was working, and the means by which it was achieved was unimportant.

Signposts had appeared directing military traffic, and clocks were advanced an hour to correspond with the Greater Reich time. An eleven o'clock curfew was imposed but it was rumoured that even that would soon be extended. All the speculation that the newspapers could not print was debated openly in the bars.

On the window outside Café Jean Marc where de Bar was to meet his contact, a notice had been placed: 'Hier spricht man Deutsch', and across the road a poster depicting a blonde Aryan looking down tenderly at a child held in his arms read: 'You have been abandoned. Put your trust in the German soldier.' The suggestion was to the average Parisian paradoxically both humiliating and comforting. For some, this was not a time for introspection, but rather for taking refuge in projected blame. It was a simple matter to believe that France had been abandoned by Britain and thrust into the arms of the Germans.

To René de Bar the poster and its sentiments were contemptuous and he despised the weakness and apathy in the faces of those around him. Everything was amazingly normal. Certainly there was tension in the air as if a shadow had been cast across the city, but some seemed hardly aware of it, while others were already blatantly profiting from the occupation.

Café Jean Marc bustled with activity as usual. The atmosphere was warm and heady with the smell of coffee and tobacco. The proprietor, Jean Marc, with a white apron tied around the girth of his large stomach, served at the tables himself.

De Bar was five minutes early for his appointment and he waited while a patron at a table near the door searched his wallet for change before leaving. He had left a rolled copy of La Gerbe on the table and de Bar glanced at it curiously as he sat down. La Gerbe was a collaborationist newssheet that had just hit the Paris streets and it carried an opening interview with Petain, explaining how collaboration would be a 'network of complementary activities'. De Bar knew the editor, Alphonse de Chateaubriant. He had come away from meeting with Hitler in Germany in 1936, with an attitude of mystical fervour that matched the most ardent Nazi. De Bar skimmed through the article and allowed himself a smile. The rhetoric was pure German National Socialism and was not, as such, designed to engage the intellect. He folded the news-sheet and laid it down.

"Bonjour."

If he had an expectation of the woman he was to meet, this first glance erased it instantly from his mind.

"Alain?" She had used his code name, a name deliberately chosen by René de Bar to reflect an ancestry that stemmed from Alain li Gros many centuries before.

He nodded, keeping his expression distant. "Won't you join me?"

She was stunning. Dark hair worn in a bob and fringed over hazel eyes. Her lashes were thick and heavy, adding a sleepy look to a face whose mouth was softly inviting and a nose slightly upturned. He allowed his glance to stray for just a moment to the long legs that she had crossed to one side of the table, before shaking himself mentally. Alain offered her a cigarette, which she accepted graciously, taking it from his silver case with slender, well-manicured fingers. He leaned over to light it for her.

"I am Simone."

She was quietly self-assured, obviously accustomed to attention. He ran a practised eye over her clothes. Her manner of dress was stylish and expensive. The collar of her ivory silk blouse was consciously turned up as a frame to her face and, befitting the fashion season, the shoulders of her grey jacket were padded to the correct shape and coupled with a narrow skirt in matching fabric.

"Coffee?"

She nodded.

They waited until Jean Marc had placed the cups on the table before speaking. She leaned towards him and took his hand, speaking intimately to him as though to a lover. Although the smile he gave her was sardonic, he entered into the role play without hesitation.

"Chérie." He kissed her fingertips. "Have I ever told you that you have the most sensational legs?"

She ignored him. "I've been asked to pass on instructions from Emil."

"Wonderful, chérie. I trust he's well?"

She was not to be baited. "You are to create a resistance movement in Paris," she said. "But Emile says that it is imperative that you remain in the background and are protected at all costs." This time she allowed a smile to play around the corners of her mouth. "Apparently you are considered too useful to be sacrificed!"

He shrugged. "They're just concerned that if I'm captured I might talk. I have a very low pain threshold."

She laughed and the sound was warm and attractive. "Emil wants you to train leaders. You will know the people that are right for the work."

He nodded.

"You are on no account to make contact with Emil directly. All contact should be through me.

"Ma'amselle," he assured her, "it will be my pleasure."

De Bar's curiosity in the occupation was purely objective. It was always fascinating to observe whether the puppet would dance in the way it was intended when the strings were pulled.

Two months after the invasion of Paris on August 13, 1940, a decree was passed, outlawing secret societies. A few days earlier, Arthur Groussier, president of the Grand Orient, anticipating the move, sent Petain a letter voluntarily announcing the dissolution of the Masonic Organisations. The Gestapo had come into possession of a list of names of Masons after searching Groussier's home, but de Bar, a practising Freemason, was unperturbed. At its lower levels, Freemasonry in France and elsewhere was no more than a charitable organisation and the Germans would find little evidence of the magical practises they were seeking. His own name would not appear on such a list.

At the beginning of October that year, René de Bar attended the opening of the German exhibition of Freemasonry that was held in the Petit Palais. It was well attended, with only a handful of the working class, distinguishable by their cloth caps, to be seen among the well-clad businessmen. There was nothing on exhibition that de Bar was unfamiliar with, the symbols and rituals of Freemasonry had been part of his life since childhood. The German pre-occupation with secret organisations and their apparent need to expose them was of more interest.

Freemasonry, posters declared, was responsible for stealing jobs from the average French citizen. These men, bound together by ritualistic practises, shared out the most lucrative jobs between them, regardless of personal skill or merit. He scanned the posters and was struck again by the vulgarity of this German movement. What passed as art to the Nazi mind, from the swastika to the plethora of posters such as these was, in fact, just crass propaganda.

"A Jew cannot help being what he is, but to be a Freemason is a choice," Petain pronounced. For de Bar, there had been little choice. Freemasonry was part of his inheritance. To refuse the path offered to him would have been to refuse his birthright.

He considered the father whose ancestry had conferred this distinction on him, with a mixture of respect and irritation. He had been a distant, authoritarian figure with an unyielding and single-minded way of manipulating those around him. He was a man who had never shown a predisposition towards affection, but it was from his father that René de Bar had acquired his insatiable thirst for power and Freemasonry was one of several levers toward gaining those things he considered most important.

He slowly descended the steps at the entrance to the Petit Palais. The dissolution of Freemasonry in France was a nuisance; the lists that had fallen into German hands would no doubt mean that some persecution would take place but they were simply dismantling the surface structure. As with most arcane organisations, there was the visible and the invisible. De Bar was part of the substrata, an adherent of its hidden face.

Chapter 2
Twice-Born

The woman stood against the grey stone building. She was well dressed in a tan skirt and white chiffon blouse. The tan hat, worn over shoulder length blonde hair, held a wisp of a veil that did not quite cover her eyes. It would have been difficult to tell her vocation at first glance, were it not for the over-tight cling of the calf-length skirt and the side-slit that exposed the top of her stocking. The slouch though was characteristic. The angle of her hips was insolently provocative as she leaned a shoulder against the wall, watching the passers-by. In one elegantly gloved hand she held a tortoise-shell cigarette holder, which she drew on languidly, allowing smoke to escape slowly between slightly pursed lips. Her mouth was painted bright crimson, an effect startling against her sallow skin.

The war had been good for business. Soldiers were exceptionally vulnerable beneath the brave façade of their uniform, and the uncertainty of the future made them behave in ways that might otherwise have been out of character. That she was Jewish would probably not have accounted for much if her clients had suspected it, although even in Berlin there were always those who were fastidious, even in respect to their association with prostitutes. For Ruth Leiman, life held little meaning beyond the physical needs and desires of her body. She worked with some skill and little pleasure to obtain the means to tend it for further use.

Until Kristallnacht at the end of 1938, when the organised mob ran rampant through Germany, destroying Jewish shops and businesses, few shops and restaurants bore the 'Jews not wanted here' notices.

During the war years in Germany, Jews either abandoned hope or resorted to ingenuity and even guile, in order to survive. There were beatings and casual murders in the streets, and Jewish shops were either boycotted or looted. Yet, still nurturing the hope that the common decency of the German people would prevail, the majority of the Jews remained in Germany.

Ruth was a survivor. In this early part of the war it was still, in Berlin at least, possible to keep one step ahead of the Gestapo. Deportations from the city had not yet become commonplace and, either under the protection of a sympathetic Gentile, or by remaining detached from the system; one could avoid harassment and arrest. But the Gestapo did not generally wear uniform, and their ability to blend with the general populace made them a more terrifying adversary.

Ruth Leiman acted independently working a street for only a few nights before moving on to find another base. Her rooms were in a run-down apartment block in Ludeckestrasse, one of the older sections of the city; a characterless building, owned by a man who asked no questions as long as the rent came in on time. As it was essential to remain as inconspicuous as possible, Ruth never took her clients home, taking care to compartmentalise her existence in the preservation of anonymity. Seldom using the shops and other facilities in her area, she shunned human contact beyond the brief liaisons of her profession. Relationships constituted danger, and she had learned to avoid contact with anyone who might jeopardise her freedom. Ultimately, it was the scrupulous care she had taken to cut herself off, that was to make her the perfect target. Her lifestyle was to become the signature to her death warrant.

She knew the man who approached her was a prospective client even before he came close enough to address her. A short man, and somewhat corpulent, his step was uneasy and he glanced about quickly, checking the street. She waited. His type was easily frightened off by any overt move before they were ready. He stood on the kerb with his back to her for a few moments and she saw the conscious straightening of his shoulders when he reached his decision. He turned to face her, smiling in a way that was intended to display confidence. Ruth returned his smile and beckoned him with a small nod of her head. It was the moment to take the initiative. She knew his type well; he would want the odd combination of sex and mothering, a breast to blubber on if necessary. She walked ahead of him and he followed obediently at a discreet distance. Ruth waited for him just inside the entrance to the building she was using and then led the way upstairs.

The room was not much. The carpet once patterned in greys

and greens had become threadbare and almost uniform in colour, and the bed, although large enough for her purposes was hardly inviting. He was not the sort of client who would have noticed it. His breathing was ragged from the exertion of the climb up the stairs and the excitement of the moment.

"How much?" He asked shortly.

She told him. He nodded and she noticed with distaste the movement of the heavy roll of fat that formed a second chin. Anyone that could afford to eat so well at a time like this could obviously afford to pay.

Chapter 3
Twice-Born

Claudius Caesar was delighted that Simon Magus had returned to Rome. He had fretted in his absence. The Magus was a good listener and a fount of wisdom. He had become a confidant and a father confessor, and if Claudius was honest with himself he might have recognised that he had come to trust the Samaritan with much that was unwise. He stopped short of divulging the more delicate details of state, but nonetheless allowed himself the unaccustomed luxury of speaking at length about himself and his family. Apart perhaps, from Messalina, no-one had ever shown any interest in what Claudius thought or felt and those that did always had ulterior motives. Simon Magus appeared to listen to him merely as a friend and a counsellor, offering no gratuitous advice and asking nothing in return for the Emperor's friendship.

Unlike his antecedents, Claudius had at first ruled Rome without selfish ambition, purely for the good of the country and its people. He worked ceaselessly to undo the terrible harm that the excesses of Caligula and Tiberius had wrought on the empire and had succeeded to a large extent. Although he was not universally loved or respected, the people had learned to trust him. His wife, Messalina, however, was hated.

Since the birth of their second child, at Messalina's request, she and Claudius had lived separately. Both her ambition and her promiscuity were insatiable and she had used her sexual charms to establish a power-base for herself, granting sexual favours, receiving bribes and making or breaking lives of senators and knights as the whim took her. While her deeds were apparent to all, Claudius, blinded by his love for his wife, saw no fault in her. He carried out executions at her caprice and began in fact, to assume a perverse enjoyment in dispatching his perceived enemies. In AD 48, however, Messalina overstepped the mark and exposed herself.

Messalina had plotted to depose Claudius, marry another and restore the republic to Rome. Broken by the treachery of his wife and forced to consent to her death and the inevitable purge that followed, Claudius had been brought to the point of madness. Simon Magus seized the day, using Claudius' misfortune to increase his hold on the Empire.

He began by exploiting the grievances of the Jews in Rome. They were angry with the Christ followers who had brought the belief known as The Way into the city.

"Until now, the Jews have afforded Rome very little trouble," Claudius said cautiously. "I have always been very tolerant of the religious beliefs of all of Rome's inhabitants. However, I cannot ignore these disturbances between these disciples of Chrestos and the Jews. I am forced to take some action."

Simon Magus nodded thoughtfully. "I understand, Caesar."

"As an accepted leader of these people, what do you suggest I should do?"

Simon Magus saw the opportunity to increase his advantage and took it without blinking. He folded his hands behind his back and thrust out his bottom lip pensively.

"Sadly, they have become swayed by the fanatical teachings of a Pharisee known as Paul of Tarsus who claims to have become a Christ-follower," the Magus said. "Conflict between these supporters of Paul and the orthodox Jews is inevitable. His disciples are rabble rousers of the worst kind. Wherever they go trouble results."

"What of the Jews who have instigated the riots? Should there be any retribution towards them?"

"The best action, Caesar, would be expulsion. Failing which, the disorder will only increase."

Under pressure, the emperor's nervous tic took hold of his whole head causing an uncontrollable jerking motion from one side to another.

"Such a move would be greatly opposed by the Senate," he said without concealing his unease. "Many of the Jews are wealthy businessmen and bring much revenue into the coffers."

"If I may say so, there are times when it is right to do battle in order to avert a fall from within. I know the Jews. When their religious beliefs are aroused nothing dissuades them from their path. They will doubtless fight the followers of Christ."

Claudius nodded. "I well remember the intractable attitude of the Jews in Caesarea under Pontius Pilot," he said. "It was the governor's first major problem on his new post. The Augustan Cohort was sent to Jerusalem bearing the emperor's likeness on their ensigns."

The Magus glanced at him and smiled. "I can imagine that the medallions infuriated the Jews!"

"It was perceived as a violation of their law. A delegation was immediately despatched to Caesarea to meet with Pilot who, quite naturally, refused to bow to pressure."

"But the Jews would not let the matter go?"

"Not at all! The protest grew until thousands gathered outside the Herodian Palace. It was a bleak and rainy November. Pilot allowed them five days of discomfort before calling a tribunal. He heard the Jewish petition and gave Rome's answer. No one moved. Finally he declared them guilty of treason and pronounced judgment of death against them if they would not disperse."

Simon Magus smiled. He knew the story well, but he allowed Caesar to continue.

"Again they refused. The governor ordered his cohorts to unsheathe their swords. The Jews moaned in fear but sat their ground and bared their necks to the soldiers declaring their intention to die rather than see the violation of God's Law. Pilot was compelled to back down and declare clemency. It was either that or mass slaughter."

"They are a stubborn nation."

"And you foresee that they will cause further disturbances in Rome?"

"Paul of Tarsus has converted many Jews from the old paths and these will continue to enflame the rest," the Magus said. "Should you fail to deal with the problem at the inception, your time will be taken up with tiresome judgments between aggrieved complainants or, worse, retrieving the bodies of the dead from the gutters."

Claudius' chin jerked spasmodically. "The senators can be very difficult about things of this sort!"

The Magus glanced at him gravely. "I believe, good Caesar, it is within your power to bring them to recognise that expulsion is a painful necessity."

So, for the remainder of Claudius' reign, while Jews, including those who had chosen the way of Jesus Christ, were prohibited by law from entering the city of Rome, the followers of Simon Magus grew like weeds. There was little to choose between their Christianised beliefs and the existing pagan worship of the Romans.

Claudius and the Magus met again some months later, in the Gardens of Lucullus, gardens that had been presented to Messalina during her lifetime, as a peace-offering by the Valerian family. It was a quiet spot away from the clamour of the city and the two men seated themselves on a bench in the shade of a spreading cedar. Claudius' German guards posted themselves a discreet distance away.

"Both Tiberius and Caligula were unable to resist the worship of man and paid the price of insanity," Claudius told Simon only half jokingly. "Augustus received a little deification before his death but his only real madness was my grandmother! I, I am the weaker of all of them, therefore my lunacy would be the greater."

"It is not to your credit that you refuse such honours," Simon assured him seriously. "Since the invasion, the Britons at Colchester have worshipped you in your grandfather's temple as a god. This is something that you must promote."

Claudius shook his head in frustration. "I know what I am," he said. "I am a man fraught with weaknesses. It would be nothing short of hypocrisy to allow the people to think anything else. What is happening in Colchester or any other of the provinces is not of my own making and is not to be encouraged!"

"The Jewish God declared in his word: 'Ye are gods.[27]'"

Claudius glanced at him with interest. "I understood that the Jews were monotheistic? Why would your God say such a thing to his people?"

The Magus' reply was rehearsed and slickly delivered. "It means that if we, as humans, are made in his image, we also bear the image within ourselves of his deity. We all have the potential of godhood, but only some, like yourself, Caesar, ever attain it."

---

[27] Psalm 82:6

Claudius shook his head. "No matter what your God might say, I know my human frailty. I have no imprint of the gods within me!"

Simon Magus bowed his head deferentially to hide the slyness of his smile.

"Forgive my words, good Caesar, if they offend you. You have believed that the citizens of Rome deserve kindness and charity. They perceive it as weakness and they have despised you. You treated your wife with gentleness and understanding and she returned such goodness with contempt. You have reached a crisis that must be turned to the good of Rome. It is time to seize your godhood but it requires a decision from you!"

Claudius was viewing him with amazement as he spoke. "Good Father, I don't understand! Are you saying that the people need leaders like Tiberius and Caligula who care nothing for their needs or their feelings?"

"Only under such leadership will the nation become powerful again," Simon Magus assured him. "War brings strength to a nation. Extended peace brings dissipation and apathy. Man is only honed under adversity. Confirmation of that truth is reflected in nature."

"The destruction of the weak and the survival of the strong..."

"Precisely that, Caesar! But if you continue to degrade your own image, you degrade the vigour of Rome. If you treat men with consideration and gentleness they will become weak. Rome will be destroyed through their indifference."

Claudius put his head in his hands and for a long moment he was silent. The Magus waited knowing that he had achieved his ends.

"Claudius the fool!" Claudius said at length and raised his head to look at Simon. "I confess I have never seen things in this light before. You are like a mirror, Father. You alone have the courage to show me the true image of myself! So, the fool will set aside his folly and take up his deity." He smiled sadly. "This is indeed an important moment in my life and I will need time to gather my thoughts. Kindly leave me now, Simon."

The Magus gathered the folds of his toga over his arm, stood to his feet and bowed. "I know that you will do the honourable thing, Emperor. For Rome."

Claudius remained in the Garden of Lucullus for some hours after Simon Magus had left. Calling for his guard to bring writing materials, he penned his thoughts in an orderly manner until he reached his decision. Until this moment, believing it to be in Rome's best interests, he had planned to reinstate the republic and to step down as Emperor within the year. But would Rome really be grateful? The Magus was right. He had been far too benevolent. It was time to change – Rome must again bow under a bloody tyrant; one that would be in Caligula's mould; wasteful, lustful, capricious and mad! He would again whet the blade of tyranny and give violent remedies for violent disorders. But it would not come from himself: let another reign and release the poisons that lurked in the cesspool. He massaged his temples thoughtfully. His own son, Britannicus must not be allowed to rule, there was too much of himself in the lad. He was too soft for Rome and inevitably he would destroy the empire and it would destroy him. But there was a woman with the right son for the job. If Rome did destroy Lucius Domitius, so be it. He, Claudius would have done his utmost for the empire. But, Lucius Domitius, Claudius was certain, would make Rome!

Claudius entered the gardens a man, and left them, a god.

Chapter 4
Twice-Born

Dr. Felix Kersten was a Finnish citizen, born in 1898 of Baltic German parents. Although he was living and studying in Schleswig-Holstein when the First World War broke out, he enlisted in the Finnish army and fought against the Russians in Estonia. Kersten would have liked to have become a surgeon but the cost of training was beyond his reach and instead of taking up a career in medicine, he became a masseuse. After receiving his degree in manual-therapy in 1921, he moved to Berlin where he studied further under a Buddhist monk from Tibet. By 1940, Kersten had established a lucrative practice with rooms in Berlin and The Hague, where he numbered members of the Dutch royal family among his patients.

In Berlin, a wealthy industrialist introduced him to Heinrich Himmler who was intrigued by Kersten's Tibetan connection. Himmler was fascinated with Tibet and had brought Buddhist monks into Germany to assist him in the Ahnenerbe, the Nazi Occult Bureau.

Whereas doctors failed to diagnose or treat the acute abdominal pain suffered by the Reichsführer, Kersten's massages brought immediate relief. As a result, Felix Kersten became the one person who, by gentle persuasion during his sessions, was able to sway Himmler for the good.

"Kersten," the Reichsführer was quoted as saying, "wrenches a thousand lives from me with every movement of his miraculous hands."

Chaim Freiberg had met Felix Kersten in The Hague shortly before the outbreak of war and sources had kept him informed of the Finnish masseuse's rise to a position of vital influence within the Reich. He therefore placed one more soul on Kersten's long rescue list.

"Have you heard of Gabriele Hoch, Herr Reichsführer?"

"No." Himmler's voice was muffled against the towel. Kersten had finished massaging his abdomen and was now working on his lower back.

"She's a professor of music," the masseuse said. "I gather she was teaching at the University of Berlin."

"Was?"

"A tragic affair," the Finn said sadly. "She fell in love with a young man and aided his escape to Switzerland."

"A Jew, no doubt."

"An affair of the heart." Kersten's fingers worked methodically. "Love is blind, Herr Reichsführer. There are times that it hits, despite race or class, and its victims act in an irrational way."

"So, this Gabriele was caught and is no doubt languishing in prison as you speak. Where do you find these cases, Herr Kersten?"

"It is a particularly tragic situation, Reichsführer. She's a young woman and very talented. It will be difficult for the university to find a replacement for her. She has already served many months of a long sentence and I have absolutely no doubt that she deeply regrets her impetuosity. Such a shame to leave her there!"

"And you want me to release her!" Himmler exclaimed into his towel. "The law is the law, Kersten. You expect the impossible."

"I would never ask you to circumvent the law, Herr Reichsführer, naturally. I realise that the process must be followed. But it could be said that she has already suffered enough for what she has done. She has lost the man she loved; lost her livelihood and the respect of the community and she has already spent nearly a year in prison."

Himmler sat up. The colour had returned to his face and he appeared relaxed and almost jocular now that the pain had gone.

"I tell you what, Kersten," he said. "I'll look into the case personally. I would be interested to meet this young woman to see whether she's the paragon of virtue you describe."

Kersten bowed and clicked his heels.

"That would be most kind, Herr Reichsführer."

Chapter 5
Twice-Born

It was raining, a fine cold drizzle. A trick of the light caused the Paris streets to shine like mother-of-pearl. Thin dark trees protruded from the pavements and sketched leafless branches against the grey sky, as motionless as charcoal on canvass.

Paris had become a silent city since the occupation. There were few cars on the streets and those which ran were mostly German. In order to beat the fuel rationing and because drivers automatically aroused suspicion of collaboration with the Germans, most chose alternative ways of getting around. Paris had become a city of bicycles. The first winter of the occupation had been exceptionally cold, a situation compounded by food and coal shortages. And now the country was moving uncertainly into her second winter.

Simone dismounted, wheeled her bicycle onto the pavement and chained it to the railings. Before taking the brown paper bags from the basket on the front of the bike, she set the angle of her beret and checked her make-up in the mirror of her compact. Making her way downstairs to the basement, she knocked at the door.

"Qui est ce?"

"Simone."

The door opened and the young woman smiled a greeting.

"Bonjour Jeanette, is Alain here?"

The girl nodded, shouting to make herself heard above the machinery.

"He's in the back office I think. He was working on some proofs."

De Bar looked up, sensing her presence. She was leaning against the door watching him and he was struck once again by the fluid, almost feline poise of her body.

"Look what I've found," she said, holding the parcels aloft. "Sausage, bread and wine. Care to join me for lunch?"

He took the packets from her and set them on his desk and took her into his arms.

"So, did you sell your soul, or just your body?"

She laughed. "I'll leave you to guess. Let's just say that the age of chivalry is not yet dead. Do you have any glasses?"

"There are some in the kitchen."

"We'll need a knife and some plates as well!" she called after him.

René de Bar had known from the first moment that he saw her that he would sleep with Simone, but he had not counted on their relationship developing as it had. They had both agreed to conceal their real identities from one another until the war was over. That way, should either of them be arrested, it would protect the other. De Bar knew that it would not be difficult for him to find out who she really was, and if he had chosen to do so, no moral obligation would have prevented him. But the constraints of the war added a dimension of intrigue to the relationship and he chose to leave things as they were.

She had taken off her coat and hung it behind the door.

"I love coming here," she said. "At least your machines give off some heat. My place is bitter."

He grinned. "I wondered why you were coming so often. I thought for a moment that it might be me."

"You are incredibly self-opinionated."

He stood behind her and nuzzled the back of her neck, his hands feeling her body through the heavy wool of her jersey. She turned to kiss him. He kicked the office door shut and drew her close, seeking her mouth again.

"Marry me once this war is over," he said.

She drew away from him a little so that she could examine his face.

"Do you mean that," she asked seriously, "or is it just war talk?"

"Of course I mean it. I want you."

"Do you love me?"

"Enough to bind me to you for life."

She pulled away from him and sat down. "Alain," she said quietly, "ever since we first met, I've wondered what I would say if you asked me to marry you."

He sat down opposite and looked into her eyes. "And what are you going to say?"

She shook her head. "The war could go on forever. We could be arrested at any time for what we are doing. Considering something as long term as marriage doesn't seem feasible at the moment."

"There's something else in your voice, something that you aren't saying."

She looked at him directly. "I don't think you have ever really loved anyone, Alain. I feel as though there is an element missing. I think you love what you want from me, rather than what I am."

She had expected him to react angrily but instead he laughed.

"I didn't know you were an amateur psychologist. Who have you been studying, Freud?"

She broke off a piece of bread and put it on his plate, hiding her chagrin behind the hair that spilled across her face. He reached over the desk and took her hand.

"You're far too serious" he told her. "But don't worry; I'm not going to pressure you for an answer.

She looked up at him and although the colour still heightened her cheeks there was no sign of emotion in her expression. He was once again impressed with her strength. Never permitting himself to be disadvantaged by Simone was a game to him, yet he was aware they were well-matched.

As a front to de Bar's printing activities he turned out regular newsletters for the Roman Catholic Church, but on a monthly basis he printed a magazine destined for the Resistance. So far most members of the Resistance had come from the ranks of the Communists in Paris and acts against the German occupation force had been on a hit and run basis. Gradually however, as agents were parachuted into France, groups were banding together, meeting on a daily basis at rendezvous throughout the city and although there was continuous friction among the various parties, some cohesion was beginning to take place. It was Simone's job to gather intelligence from agents and to deliver it to de Bar. He would sort and classify it and divide it into dispatches, which were coded and passed on for radio transmission. The risks were high, there was always the uncertainty that an agent might, in actuality, be working for the Gestapo, or that the friend who had been picked up the night before, might break under torture or turn traitor to save his own skin.

René de Bar's own game was a little more intricate than most, and his sifting of information, more complicated. Only certain intelligence would be passed on to MI6 in Britain, but there was nothing of importance that was not dispatched to his own organisation.

De Bar poured the last of the wine and handed Simone her glass.

"I have tickets to Jean Cocteau's latest play on Saturday night," he said, "Are you able to make it?"

Simone shrugged. "I'm free, and hopefully the theatre will be warmer than my apartment."

"But you don't enjoy Cocteau?"

"He's a little avant guard. I usually come away from his plays feeling as though I have missed the point."

He sipped his wine and set his glass down on the desk. "To appreciate Cocteau you have to understand his use of symbolism and myth."

She wrinkled her nose. "I never cared much for mythology."

"Then it's because you've taken it at face value. Mythology is a fore-telling, there's a prophetic aspect to it that's unveiled only if you seek it."

She laughed. "You sound as if you really mean that!"

"As you begin to explore, you'll find it's like Persephone, forced underground by the attentions of Zeus. Mythology is an underground stream, full of hidden whirlpools." He laughed at her incredulous expression. "Every myth contains clues that point to a momentous climax in our earth's progression," he said. "Cocteau understands that and he uses it."

"This climax. Is it something that has already taken place?"

"There have been cataclysms, but the climax is still to come."

She looked at him in exasperation. "I've never known you so full of mystery," she said. "But I'll come with you on Saturday and you can explain what Cocteau's trying to say afterwards."

He laughed and stood up. "I must get back to work. I'll meet you outside Café Bientot at seven."

She turned to wave briefly as she left, still ruffled by the discovery of yet another facet of the man that was beyond her reach.

Chapter 6
Twice-Born

April 1942

A black Opel drew up against the curb and the man who leaned out of the window to appraise her, grinned. He had a cigarette resting on his lower lip and his grey felt hat was pushed back on his head, affording his a jaunty air.

"Hello, liebling," he called.

Ruth Leiman moved slowly across the pavement towards him and, flicking back her blonde hair with a provocative movement, she leaned down to place a manicured hand on the open window of the car.

"Looking for someone?"

"You look just the type. Fancy a ride?"

"Sure, why not?"

He leaned over to open the passenger door for her and she slid into the seat next to him.

"I have a place to go if that's what you want," she said.

He shook his head, slipped the car into gear and moved off into the street. The traffic was sparse at this time of night, and there were few people around.

"I'd like to take you to a place of my own."

She sat sideways in the seat and watched him. He was good-looking which pleased her; it removed the tedium from the work and created something more akin to pleasure. His light brown hair curled appealingly over his forehead and his features were strong yet somehow boyish. She judged him to be in his early thirties and out for some fun. He glanced across at her and grinned.

"So, liebling," he said, picking up her hand and kissing the fingers lightly. "What can I expect for my money?"

"Just tell me what you like, sweetheart and I'll deliver."

Not three blocks from where he had picked her up, he pulled in to a parking place and took the key from the ignition.

"Here we are, liebschen," he told her. "Let's go."

Ruth Leiman felt the first prickling of uncertainty as they left the car together and approached the building. There was a subtle shift in his attitude. His hold on her arm was unyielding, altogether too possessive. She glanced up at the building. It was an old apartment block, built in dressed stone with slim, arched windows neatly outlined with a projecting stone surround. As they entered the foyer her unease turned to fear. Ruth had been in this game long enough to have an intuitive feel for atmosphere, a necessary tool of self-preservation for any prostitute, and she knew that this place was wrong. Looking round swiftly, she considered making a run for it, but her escort anticipated the move and blocked her. The grip on her arm now was forceful and officious, and there was an aloofness to his expression that had not been there before. A second man moved swiftly from the shadows in the stairwell, and at that instance she knew that whatever her companion wanted from her, it was not sex. She had walked straight into the hands of the Gestapo.

They had watched her for months before making the pickup, familiarising themselves with her movements. They noted every link, every contact she made. Ruth Leiman was perfect for their purpose, a true loner.

The apartment on the second floor, to which Ruth was taken, had been turned into one of those innumerable specialised Gestapo offices in the city. It was clean and well furnished with glossy oak desks and upholstered chairs in the waiting room. Heavy drapes in an embossed maroon fabric covered the windows, cutting out almost all the natural light and most of the noise from the street and adding a sombre note to the atmosphere.

"Identification!"

Ruth sullenly opened her handbag. The young officer snatched it from her, emptying the contents out onto the desk top. He pocketed the papers and pushed the rest of the things towards her. His expression conveyed nothing but contempt and Ruth wondered briefly whether the bantering joviality she had witnessed earlier, existed at all in his makeup, or whether he was simply a clever actor.

"Come with me!" he demanded, and took her by the arm again, his fingers bruising her flesh, so that she had to bite her lip to keep from crying out. Knocking sharply on an interleading door, he opened it and propelled Ruth into the office ahead of him. The officer behind the desk, wearing the formidable black uniform of the SS, stood up as they entered.

"So, Weigand, you have her!" he exclaimed with satisfaction.

"It was simple, Gruppenführer, she fell into my hands like a ripe plum."

The Major-General laughed. "I'm hardly surprised," he said. "You were chosen for the task by your rather dubious reputation."

He took Ruth Leiman's identity document from Weigand, perused it swiftly and slammed it onto the desk.

"This document is falsified. Where are your proper papers?"

Ruth shook her head. "I don't know what you mean. These are my papers."

"Liar!" Weigand struck her across the face with the back of his hand and Ruth gasped in pain. Her hand flew to her cheek and her fingers fluttered uncertainly around the broken skin of her lip.

"I'm not lying." Her voice was faint.

"We know who you are. Do you think you can hide anything from us? Where are your papers?"

Her expression was surly. "I destroyed them years ago when I left home."

"You are Esther Seligman." It was a statement of fact.

Briefly, she closed her eyes. "Yes."

"Our mission here is almost wrapped up," the Gruppenführer said to Weigand. "We should be able to close the office and move back to HQ. The Reichsführer will be well pleased." He offered the younger man a cigarette from the silver box on his desk and took one himself. "You will relay the order for the mop-up operation immediately. Every hotel that she has used must be hit. And any of her regular customers: the landlord who owns her block. You know the routine."

He walked around the desk and ran his eyes over Ruth. She glared back at him defiantly.

"A Jewess," he said thoughtfully. "Soliciting German men on the streets of Berlin." His hand shot out suddenly, gripping her by the hair and wrenching her head back. "Defiling Germans!" The colour suffused his face and for a moment it seemed as though he would gladly snap the neck that was contorted under the power of his hand. Then just as abruptly he released her.

"You dirty whore!" he said softly. "Filthy Jewish whore!"

He turned away, suddenly disinterested. "There are guards standing by outside for her transportation," he said to Weigand. "Get her out of here."

They drove through the night after her arrest, in a small unmarked van. Ruth sat huddled into one corner in the back, feeling the icy cold penetrate the metal walls of the vehicle and seep into her bones. Senses that had necessarily been heightened on the streets to effect her preservation, now grappled to interpret new information. There was no window in Ruth's prison; nothing to indicate their direction, but the air sweetened and the cold became more intense, and after some hours the labouring of the engine told her they were entering mountainous country. It was almost morning when at last they reached their destination and the guards opened the back of the van and ordered her out. Her body, stiff with cold, at first refused to respond and her knees buckled under her, so that she collapsed into the thin dusting of snow that covered the flagged floor. The boot in her ribs almost knocked the breath from her body.

"Get up! Schnell!"

There was a brief impression in the dawn half-light, of massive stone walls towering above a generous courtyard before she was dragged down a flight of stairs and along a passage that led to the cells. Ruth leaned her back against the door as it was slammed shut behind her and took the room in at a glance. There was a rough pallet with a blanket on a narrow cot, and a toilet bucket placed directly opposite the small viewing panel set into the door. A single light bulb screwed into a raw fitting against the ceiling cast an uncompromising light on the room.

Face to face with the fear that had always lurked a pace behind her, Ruth felt an overwhelming sense of desolation. The isolation of this moment seemed to justify all the nebulous feelings of alienation she had ever experienced. It was as though deep inside, she had known her limited resources must sooner or later fail. Ruth had never faced the certainty of death, but now, in her isolation, it was to become a spectre larger even than life. Everything to which she had attributed permanence and reliability stood in mockery against her. For the first time, she faced the inevitable. Even the body she had tended with such care was subject to an inexorable process of decay. She took the blanket off the cot and, wrapping it tightly around her, sat huddled against the wall and wept.

Perhaps it was a clumsy effort to use what she knew best in one last gamble for freedom, or simply the desire for some human comfort that caused her to try to proposition the guard some nights later. She sat on the edge of the bed, her skirt drawn up to reveal her long thighs and undid the button on her blouse, exposing the sensual curve of her breasts. The guard, who set the tray of food down on the table near the door, straightened up and turned to leave. Ruth tilted her chin provocatively and beckoned him with her eyes. He was middle-aged, a man with obvious appetites that had built a bestial quality into his flesh and facial features. She knew instinctively that she was facing a gamble. His glance flickered over her body and changed abruptly to contempt.

"You whore!" he spat. "Do you imagine I would touch you?" He swung at her with an open-handed blow that sent her sprawling across the mattress. She lay still, fighting tears of humiliation and pain, not daring to look up again until she knew that he had gone. She heard the key grate in the lock behind him, then realised with panic that he had taken her food and water with him.

Two men came for her the following morning and pushed her ahead of them towards the shower room. The guard she had attempted to seduce leered at her.

"Strip!"

Ruth licked her dry lips and as she read the implacability of their expressions, in what seemed like a horrible parody of her past, she took of her clothes.

"We're under orders not to mark her face," the guard told the other conversationally, and he sauntered over to where Ruth stood. His right jab delivered to her solar plexus caused the breath to whistle through her teeth and she sank to her knees, clawing with her hands at her stomach and fighting for breath. The second guard gripped her by the hair and yanked her to her feet. He was young, clean-shaven, with clear blue eyes and soft blonde curls. He looked incongruously angelic; there was no vestige of malice in his expression. His fist hooked into Ruth's ribcage and later she was to recall his smile as the bones cracked beneath his knuckles. Pain coursed savagely through her body; pain that did not ease hours later after they had raped her and thrown her back into her cell, and it continued to wrack her throughout the night and for days to come.

That evening, the guard that set down the soup, bread and water on the table was a woman. She left Ruth's cell without a word.

Chapter 7
Twice-Born

Shortly after Claudius met with Simon Magus in the gardens of Lucullus, the Emperor announced his intention to remarry. That the death of Messalina had changed him was obvious to all that knew him but his choice of a bride still came as a shock. Claudius' niece, Agrippina, the sister of Caligula, was even more debased than Messalina had been; she was promiscuous, vicious and unprincipled but she had two important points in her favour. She was an astute politician and she had a son, Lucius Domitius who was as corrupt and degenerate as his mother. As the marriage was considered incestuous it was necessary for the senate to first revise the law. Already fear of arousing Agrippina's ire had gripped the heart of the Empire and the motion was passed without a dissenting voice. Terror would increase as Claudius willingly abdicated all political responsibility in favour of his wife.

Messalina's daughter, Octavia, had been divorced from her husband when he was caught in incest with his sister. Agrippina sought Claudius' consent for Octavia's marriage to her son, Lucius Domitius. Claudius went a step further and adopted him into his family under the new name of Nero. The stage was fully set. The god Claudius had sown the seeds of his own destruction and the downfall of many. The lance in the hand of the Magus had met its mark.

"Messalina's astrologer Barbillos has confirmed the words of Thrasyllus that I will die in my sixty-third year," Claudius told Simon Magus. "I intend to enjoy the handful of years I have left to me. He is extraordinarily accurate, you know. The reason I agreed to divorce Messalina before her death is because Barbillos predicted that her husband was to die within the month. She persuaded me that if I was to save my life she should marry another."

The Magus raised his eyebrows. "Was she not put to death because of her marriage?"

"It was to have been a farce at which I was to have officiated. She assured me that she despised the senator she was to marry and that it was to be a marriage in name only!"

"And instead, she married while you were engaged in business outside the city."

Claudius looked rueful. The episode still hurt him far more deeply than he cared to admit. "A debauched affair! I was informed by a friend and returned to Rome with all haste. Certainly, it was more than a marriage in name but to Messalina it was just another in a multitude of liaisons. That fact I discovered when my freedman presented me with a long list of names of her lovers! The marriage had nothing to do with saving my life but everything to do with seizing ultimate control of Rome through the declaration of a republic." He smiled crookedly. "Barbillos was right though, her husband, the senator, died within the month and that at my command!"

"So your death will be in your sixty-third year according to the astrologers?"

Claudius nodded. "I have decided to honour you, Father, before the fates cut my strings. You have been a fount of wisdom to me, a Pethor."

The Magus bowed his head, "Your interpreter always, good Caesar."

"The Pethors were always the superior gods," Claudius said. "Neptune, Saturn, Mars and Janus were all Pethors and, of course, there was the supreme god, Zeus-Peter as the Greeks would say, or, in our tongue, Ju-peter[28]."

Indeed, the Magus was well aware that the Greeks called Artemis and Bacchus, Patora or Peter-gods, and that in Egypt the Ammonian priests were known as Pethors. Every pagan oracle temple had as its sacred symbol a phallic Peter stone. And although the word petra could signify any rock or stone, in the religious sense it was related to Osiris or the sun-god, Baal.

"You will be called Pethor," Claudius said. "I have decided that your Christian sect should be honoured. You have after all, given me the gift of eternal life with the gods, even while I still abide on earth. You will be granted the same honour insofar as I have the power to grant it. I have had a statue made in your likeness, which is to be

---

[28] Jupiter.

dedicated in the Temple of Janus. You, my Father, will be remembered to all generations. Every man in the empire will know that there has been a Pethor in Rome! Simon-Peter, interpreter of the Mysteries."

The Magus' smile was one of quiet satisfaction. This choice of name was pre-ordained by the gods! It would no doubt cause some annoyance to Simon-Peter the fisherman and apostle of Jesus.

A statue to a new Roman god, one Simon of Gitta, was erected on the River Tiber between the two bridges. It bore an inscription to 'Simoni Deo Sancto' – to Simon the Holy God. 'He persuaded those who adhered to him that they should never die, and even now there are some living who hold this opinion of his... All who take their opinions from these men, as we before said, call themselves Christians.'

Claudius Caesar died exactly in accordance with the prophecies of his astrologers in his sixty-third year, the fourteenth year of his reign, and was officially deified. It was said that his wife Agrippina served him a dish of his favourite mushrooms containing a slow poison and when it seemed that his body might purge itself she administered the lethal dose. Nero himself confirmed this through his frequent use of the Greek proverb about mushrooms being the food of the gods.

Before Claudius' death Nero had endeared himself to the nation with his affected modesty, charm and somewhat effeminate good-looks. Claudius as his adopted parent had placed all that he needed to rule squarely in his hands, including a liberal education – even recalling Seneca from exile as his tutor, although he despised the man.

For his own son, Britannicus, he had chosen a very different route; his instruction had been tough and old-fashioned, designed to make a man and a soldier of him. Claudius had hoped to move Britannicus out of danger before Nero became emperor of Rome, but the youth refused to leave and the Emperor died knowing full-well he had signed his son's death warrant.

In AD 54, at seventeen years of age, Nero assumed power in Claudius' stead and all attempts by Simon Magus to build a relationship with Rome's new emperor were thwarted. Agrippina, suspecting the influence Simon had exerted over Claudius, discouraged any contact with her son. She continued her destructive reign of Rome through

Nero even as Livia had ruled through Tiberius and when he attempted to break away from her iron grip she sought to retain her hold through entering into an incestuous liaison with him. Simon Magus therefore, chose to follow a more subtle route bringing his Jewish arm into play.

Nero married Poppaea twelve days after his divorce of Octavia, the daughter of Claudius.

"She bores me," he explained to his friends on one of the occasions on which he had attempted to strangle his wife. "She complains of being miserable. Surely, being married to the emperor should be enough to make her happy?"

Despite Nero's excuse that Octavia was barren, the divorce proved unpopular with Rome's citizens. His remarriage to Poppaea, who was already married to a knight, was the more so. In an attempt to exonerate himself, Nero accused Octavia of adultery and had her executed.

Except for the period under Emperor Claudius, Jews in Rome had enjoyed full religious liberty and minor government offices were open to them. The Magus' inner circle comprised both 'Jews' and 'Christians' and while the Christian element had gained much influence in Rome under Emperor Claudius and openly proselytised; his 'Jews' pursued a different line. They were the financiers of the Magus' enterprise and their main source of income was through the trade of slaves. Simon's men extended their trafficking to include the moving of perfumes, jewels, drugs and liquor and became heavily involved in the business of prostitution.

Ya'akov the 'Jew' was everything Nero was not. He was tall and muscular and carried himself with an air of confidence. His features were well-defined, his brow distinctive and he was altogether pleasing to the eye.

When Poppaea's infant child, Claudia Augusta, died Ya'akov was on hand to offer comfort. Nero was too self-consumed to notice Poppaea's vulnerability and Ya'akov's seduction was subtle. The relationship developed swiftly and passionately. Once again, Simon Magus' influence was being brought to bear on the Empire.

"Emperor, I must warn you," Seneca said; "the Jews are becoming altogether too powerful. Unless they are stopped, they are destined to destroy you and Rome."

Seneca, Nero's erstwhile tutor, a well-known writer and philosopher, had for many years been the Emperor's closest friend but his interference was not well received. The Jewish insiders supported the emperor against his perceived enemies while encouraging and financing his insatiable greed. When his first palace burned down they financed its rebuilding. The Golden House, as it was called, had a mile long pillared arcade and a statue of the emperor in its entrance hall which stood a hundred and twenty feet high. A massive pool was surrounded by buildings made to resemble cities and part of the house was overlaid with gold and studded with precious stones. Nero was fully inclined to keep such men close to the centre of power.

When the emperor refused to listen, Seneca took up his pen to expose the corrupt practices of the money-lenders. The writer was a popular figure in the empire and his works were widely read. By this time though, the 'Jewish' power-base was too firmly established and pressure was brought to bear on Nero to act against his friend. If Seneca did not stop his pernicious writing, he was told, the flow of money feeding Nero's ever-swelling lusts would cease.

"Damn you, Seneca, why can't you leave things alone? Don't you realise what sort of problems your misplaced principles are causing me?"

Seneca regarded him gravely. "Caesar, you are being blinded," he said. "These men will bring about your downfall."

"You know nothing! If you were really my friend you would not speak. Let these things alone, Seneca."

Seneca tried one more tack. "Caesar, the man Ya'akov: mark him! He has the ear of your wife, Poppaea and he is exerting too much influence over her."

"How dare you!" Nero screamed. "What are you insinuating? Don't you realise I could have you killed for saying such things? Leave me at once, Seneca, you presume too much on our friendship!"

That night, when Nero came home from the races, Poppaea lay on her bed. She was several months pregnant and her face was pale and tear-stained.

"Why do you keep leaving me alone, my husband? Does my

pregnancy displease you? Do you seek other company in my stead?"

Nero gazed at his wife dispassionately. He crossed the room, gripped her by the hair and dragged her coldly from the couch. As she screamed in terror he kicked her savagely to death.

However, so as not to further upset the sensibilities of Rome's citizens, the emperor decided against having Seneca killed and, instead, forced him to take his own life.

In public Simon Magus' round table of Christians and Jews were strangers; in secret, a brotherhood. Their bond would never be made clear neither would any indication of their nationhood be made known: these were men of one blood and one spirit and even over many generations their purpose and direction was destined to endure. They were Simon Magus' illuminated ones – the Illuminati.

For ten years after the death of Caesar Claudius, the Magus moved between Rome and the Languedoc creating new converts to his pseudo-Christian faith. These disciples comprised men and women who, as adherents to Simon Pethor's Gnostic Christian teachings, committed themselves to God in a vow of celibacy and good works. Some of the male converts were invited to enter the Order of the Temple. Of those initiates who rose to the upper levels, many were rewarded with governing positions. A power base was being established through a process of gradualism.

In Rome, where Simon Magus was treated as a god and attracted a huge following, it was inevitable that Nero, threatened by his presence, would seek an excuse to kill him.

Chapter 8
Twice-Born

April 1942
Ruth was alerted by sounds in the passage. People were approaching and their footsteps were purposeful. She was on her feet when the heavy metal door opened, hands clenched at her sides and her eyes reflecting naked fear. Heinrich Himmler stood in the doorway and examined her for a moment in silence. She knew who he was. There were few in Germany who were unfamiliar with the Reichsführer-SS. He turned to the officer who stood waiting in the background.

"The likeness is commendable, don't you agree Obergruppenführer?"

The conversation was not new. They had compared the photographs many times, but this was the first instance that Himmler had seen her in the flesh.

"Her height and build are almost identical, and there's a good similarity in the features. I don't think the job will prove to be too difficult."

"You know the work I've been doing with Dr. Rascher at Dachau." Himmler's eyes were back on the girl. "He's been carrying out extensive experiments on condemned prisoners, their reaction to a low pressure chamber that we've installed there. Fascinating results!"

Karl Wolff nodded.

"After only minutes in the chamber, sweating occurs and the head begins to roll. Then there are spasms that increase in intensity." His tongue flicked daintily to the corners of his mouth. "After a while the subject looses consciousness and respiration slows until it ceases entirely. The whole process usually lasts about thirty minutes." Momentarily his glance slid back over Wolff's face, as though to assess his response, but then he turned back to Ruth. "I instructed Rascher to extend his tests to include freezing. It is of course, essential that we have this information for the war effort. Airmen are often brought down in icy waters…"

Again Wolff's contribution to the conversation was little more than a murmur.

"All experiments are scientifically conducted. We have tanks of ice water in which to immerse the prisoners, or, if there is snow, we simply leave them out naked overnight. I am particularly interested in the most successful methods of re-warming." He was thoughtful for a moment, his eyes still watching Ruth, serpent-like in their intensity and yet curiously without expression. "We bring in prostitutes from Ravensbrook. Then we take a man who is unconscious from a long period of immersion and see how long it takes him to recover when laid alongside these women. I've been thinking of using two women, one on each side of the subject to accelerate the process. When I visited Dachau recently, I was interested to see that most men recover their sexual urges very quickly." He turned reluctantly from his scrutiny of the girl and faced Wolff. "The men who take part in the pressure chamber experiment and survive have their sentences transmuted from death to life imprisonment. I believe in a system of reward."

The door swung shut behind the two men and their footsteps receded down the passageway. Ruth collapsed heavily onto her cot. She recognised the type, it was not the first time she had encountered a voyeur, but never before had she experienced such intense fear in the presence of any man.

"The time it will take will depend entirely on the amount of work that will need to be done," the surgeon said. He turned to address the young woman. "Would you mind standing next to her for a moment?"

Marianne von Ingolstadt nodded briefly and walked to where Ruth was standing, taking care that their bodies should not touch. Ruth was watching the proceedings uneasily, her face pale and drawn in the artificial light created by the single pendant over her cell. The doctor's minute inspection of Ruth's features was clinical; she might simply have been a laboratory specimen. He turned back to Wolff.

"You can see," he said, "that most of the work will have to be done on the nose. We will have to build up the bridge and alter the appearance of the tip, here." Karl Wolff compared the two women carefully and nodded his agreement.

"It will also be necessary to heighten the cheekbones. Her bones are more pronounced - they will need to be built up, so." He demonstrated, tracing his fingertip over the area below the orbit of Marianne's eye."

"Can you do it without leaving any scars?"

The surgeon rubbed a finger down the length of his nose thoughtfully. "Inevitably there will be some scarring," he said, "but there are ways of minimising it so that it will be scarcely noticeable. With the nose, we would take it from here, just inside the tip, and insert two slivers of split rib, one of which would go upward, towards the forehead, the other, down towards the incisor teeth. This will build up the bridge of the nose." He looked across at Wolff to see whether he was following him. "Of course, taking the rib will inevitably leave a scar, but we could take it just below the breast, that way the scar would be less obvious."

"Couldn't we take the rib from some other source?"

The surgeon shrugged. "It's possible. It has been done, but it increases the possibility of rejection."

"You mentioned the cheek bones."

He nodded. "There we would make the incision just under the lower eyelid, which would leave no discernible scar, then we would tunnel down towards the cheek bones and build them up with bone either from the rib or the hip."

"Will it be difficult to create a good likeness?"

The surgeon examined the two women again. "They are very similar in looks. Where her hair is beginning to grow through it appears that the colour is right, and the eyes are very similar. A relative of course, or a friend, would undoubtedly not be deceived at close quarters, but I have no doubt that we are capable of doing a job that would deceive her acquaintances, always supposing the young woman can do her part."

"Herr Doctor," Obergruppenführer Wolff said quietly. "You have been chosen for this task because you are the foremost man in this field in Germany. What I am asking you to do here must be a work of genius. This identity change is essential to the war effort and must be as close to perfection as possible. Do you understand?"

The surgeon bowed stiffly.

"Perfectly, Obergruppenführer."

Wolff turned to leave. "What sort of team will you require?" he asked.

The doctor removed his spectacles and massaged his eyes thoughtfully. Replacing them, he looked back at Wolff.

"An anaesthetist, at least one competent assistant and a qualified person to deal with instruments. You will allow me to pick my own team?"

"We will give you the opportunity to put forward the names of those you would like to use."

Wolff nodded to the guard and Ruth heard the familiar sound of the locks sliding into place. They had made no effort to conceal what they were doing from her, behaving in fact, as though she lacked the normal faculties of hearing and comprehension. Ruth sank down heavily on her bed. A feeling of numbness had begun to overtake her. Of all the Jews in Berlin that they could have chosen, why her?

Lieutenant-General Wolff dismissed Marianne von Ingolstadt and took the arm of Doctor Kraus, steering him towards the library. Opening the liquor cabinet, he took out a bottle and two glasses.

"Schnapps?"

"Thank you."

"I don't need to tell you, Herr Doctor that what has passed between us, is a matter of the utmost secrecy."

"Naturally, Obergruppenführer."

"Then you will understand of course, if I tell you that a surgery has been set up here at Wewelsburg and that you will be detained until your work is complete."

Doctor Kraus stopped with his glass at his lips and replaced it slowly on the table next to him.

"That is impossible, Obergruppenführer!" he protested. "I have my practise in Munich, and my family! They have no idea where I am and it would be most inconvenient if I was to simply disappear for the duration of the job without some explanation."

Karl Wolff leaned back against the cabinet and took a sip from the small glass of schnapps. His eyes were steely as he looked down at the doctor, but his tone remained polite.

"Herr Doctor," he said, "I'm certain you will enjoy your stay at Wewelsburg. You will find it is a most fascinating castle. Please don't concern yourself with your family or your practise. An explanation will be given to all that will be entirely satisfactory. I'm sure your partner, Doctor Heckleman, will hold things together for you until you return." Wolff emptied his glass and placed it on the table. "If you'll excuse me, Herr Doctor, I have things to attend to. I trust you will find everything is to your comfort. Perhaps you could let me have that list, so that I can make final preparations for your assistants to be brought in? In the meantime I will arrange for a full set of photographs of the girl to be brought to your suite." He nodded affably. "Thank you for your time, Herr Doctor." Wolff clicked his heels together and raised his arm in the Nazi salute, then swinging round he left the room.

Chapter 9
Twice-Born

In the autumn of the year 67, Simon Magus heard from Alexander the coppersmith that Paul, having been arrested for a second time, was in Rome. Paul had aged on this his final journey. His hair and beard had turned almost white and hollows had formed in his cheeks, but the sternness and anger, which had marked his early years, had softened under physical hardship and in the upheavals he had experienced in the churches, into a quiet authority. In his close fellowship with God he was a man at peace with himself.

The coppersmith was a big man with hair and beard not dissimilar in colour to the metal he worked with. He was born and raised in Ephesus, which was where he first met and followed Paul. Later, after the reign of Claudius, Alexander moved to Rome where he married Antonia. Two sons and a daughter were born of this marriage and all were still under the age of eight.

During his first incarceration, to avoid being turned over for trial to the Jews in Jerusalem who would have put him to death, Paul of Tarsus, a Roman citizen by birth, had appealed to Caesar but the process had delayed any possibility of an early release. When at last he was brought to Italy as a prisoner of Rome and incarcerated in a house on the outskirts of the city, Alexander was among those believers who regularly met with him.

Many who had suffered under the successive Caesars gladly received Paul's doctrine of righteousness and the hope of an eternal destination unsullied by man. The single Roman guard who had been assigned to his keeping treated Paul as a father and offered no prohibitions to those who visited the rented house.

"It is," Paul had admitted on one of these occasions, "a strange situation I find myself in. Since being imprisoned, I have had the opportunity to share the gospel of Christ with governors Felix and Festus, with King Herod Agrippa before his death, and Bernice his queen, as well as to the full council of the Jews, both Pharisee and

Sadducee. None of these things would have been possible without my arrest. During the great storm off the coast of Crete, I was able to witness to all aboard ship. In a dream, an angel told me that there would be great material loss, but that no lives would be forfeited, and indeed, those who sailed the ship believed me in the end and even cut loose the lifeboat they intended to escape to shore in!"

"Tell us again what happened on the island of Melita[29]," Alexander urged. He sat on the floor at the apostle's feet; his muscular arms locked around his knees as if to contain his enthusiasm; red curls in disarray around his burly face.

Paul smiled at him and obediently recounted the events of the storm that resulted in the loss of the ship and the cargo.

"The soldiers were all for killing us prisoners and making their own way to shore and would have done so if my centurion had not intervened. He believed the word I had received from the Lord, that all souls would be saved and deemed it bad fortune if they had lifted their swords against us!"

Most of Paul's listeners had heard the story before and knew the best was yet to come.

"So, we cast ourselves on the mercy of God and leapt into the raging water. Some managed to swim, others clung to pieces of flotsam, but every man made it safely to shore! We were met by the people of the island, barbarous, unlearned folk who nevertheless treated us kindly and kindled a fire to warm ourselves by."

"And you gathered sticks and set them on the fire yourself," Alexander prompted.

"Only to have a viper appear from the bundle and, in escaping the flame, attach itself to my hand!" Paul said joining in the general laughter. "I shook if off into the fire where it perished. But the people, both those from the vessel and those from the island alike, decided that having escaped the shipwreck, I was obviously guilty and would die from the snake bite. They watched me with great caution for some time, waiting no doubt for my body to swell. When nothing happened, the inhabitants of Melita decided instead, that I must be a god! It was some time before I could dissuade them of that!"

---

[29] Malta

"How long was it before you were rescued?" another man had asked.

"We were on the island for three months. During that time God was at work among the people and many received healing. They showed us great kindness and when we left made certain that we were laden with all we needed for the journey. A ship from Alexandria that had wintered there brought us as far as Puteoli where we found some of the brethren. The rest you all know."

During the two years of his house-arrest Paul taught openly in Rome but ultimately his appeal to Emperor Nero was heard and he was released. He left Italy soon after his acquittal in the spring of the year 62, visiting the churches at Ephesus and Colossae. It was at this time that he heard with sorrow that James, the brother of Jesus and leader of the church in Jerusalem, had been stoned to death.

For the next four years, Paul had journeyed on to Macedonia, to Asia Minor, Spain, Crete and finally back to Macedonia and Greece where he was once again arrested during a disturbance.

To his Christian followers in Rome who were already suffering persecution under the hand of Nero his second incarceration came as a shock and as a presage of their own doom.

It was Alexander the coppersmith who brought Paul news of the other apostle in Rome. He arrived at the house one morning in a great state of excitement.

"The apostle Simon is in the city!"

"Simon?" Paul was puzzled.

"Have you not told us yourself of Simon the fisherman? He is here in Rome!"

"If Simon Peter was in Rome, I am certain I would be the first to know about it."

"I have seen him myself. He has just returned from the south of France where he has visited Herod Antipas."

"Then you can be sure that we are not speaking of Simon Peter," Paul said wryly. "He is not likely to be found willingly in such company! You no doubt mean Simon the Magus, who is no apostle of the Lord Jesus."

Alexander looked crestfallen. "But he is! I heard him preach last night. He is as much a preacher of Jesus as you are!"

Paul glanced at him sharply. "Alexander, hear me. This man is a most dangerous enemy of the cross of Christ. Stay well away from him."

His companion's face flushed with anger.

"From what I heard he spoke the truth!" he retorted.

"Peter and John met Simon the magician in Samaria," Paul said, "where he attempted to buy from them the power of the Holy Spirit. What he really wanted was apostleship! They saw through him and called him to repentance. Simon Magus has been a thorn in the side of the church since! What he teaches is the Babylonian mysteries under a Christian guise."

The coppersmith changed the subject and they spoke of other things. However, later that day, Paul discussed the news with Mark. Simon Magus was subtle. His teachings had stirred huge controversy in Samaria, Judaea and throughout almost all the areas where the word of God was preached. Rome had received him with open arms and, before his death, Caesar Claudius had set up a statue to him. It had become evident that the church was to face increasing trouble from false teachers in the time ahead.

"Simon Peter is visiting the Jews in Babylon," Mark said. "He sent a letter to the churches in Turkey warning them against the Magus' teachings."

"Has the magician visited Turkey?" Paul was surprised.

"Timothy shook his head. "He sent Thaddeus, one of his closest disciples, who persuades the people with what he claims, is an image of Jesus Christ; a portrait made without hands. Peter is greatly concerned. Many are being deceived and are turning away from the true faith to a form of idolatry."

Paul sighed. "We well know that the presence of Simon Magus in Rome bodes ill for the church here," he said wearily. "I should have warned Alexander more fervently. When he next comes I will advise him of the trouble which comes of Simon Magus."

It was a month before Alexander visited Paul again. He was annoyed that Paul had attempted to prevent him from attending the meetings of Simon but had ignored the apostle's counsel, ascribing it to jealousy. Antonia had gone with him to see Simon Magus once out of curiosity and since then enthusiastically attended every meeting. It was good to have his wife at his side. She disliked Paul, proclaiming his teachings too narrow and even boring. In her opinion, his manner, unlike that of Simon, lacked flamboyance or excitement. Then there was the fact that Paul, as a prisoner of Rome, was bound to remain in his house, relying on visitors to come to him for teaching. There was something positively unsavoury, Antonia said, in the idea of an old man trusting in some supposedly all-powerful god, yet still unable to attain his freedom.

Simon captivated the superstitious. The lower social classes of Rome were given no access to the mystery religions of Cybele, Isis and Apollo but they found ready acceptance into the religion preached by the Apostle. They were attracted by Simon Pethor's magnetic speech and the sense of excitement generated at every gathering and the disciples who accompanied him were almost as powerful as Simon in the signs they performed.

Alexander was both animated and defensive; a man on a mission.

"I know you said I shouldn't go back," he said, "but I needed to see for myself what it was that you had against Simon."

They were walking together in the central courtyard of the house and Paul waited without comment for him to continue.

"You have to see him!" Alexander was unable to contain his enthusiasm and, as always when he was excited, gesticulated widely. They were an unlikely pair; the large, almost ungainly coppersmith with his untamed hair, and Paul the Pharisee. For although he now followed the Way, which was the name given to the budding Christian faith, Paul still bore himself with the quiet dignity of the priestly class.

"The only reason you condemn him is because you haven't seen him! Simon was a close personal disciple of John the Baptist before his death and he speaks much about him."

"Alexander, the man is a deceiver," Paul's tone was quiet but firm, "have you heard nothing of what I have told you about Simon and his doctrines?"

"I've heard and understood." The coppersmith's voice was patronising. "You are a prisoner in Rome and Simon is a free man. For reasons of his own, he has not come to see you. I am sure that this must have wounded you deeply."

"No, Alexander!" Paul said, cutting him short. "None of these things are hurtful to me. What does wound me is that you have chosen to ignore good counsel and follow a man who is no more than a scoundrel and a sorcerer! You have left the hope that was given you in Christ and have followed a lie. This will not count to your eternal good."

Alexander turned on the old man angrily. "You always stood as judge and jury! What gives you the right to assume that you are the only one with the truth, or have discovered the only path to heaven?"

Paul sighed. "There is only one truth," he replied. "Jesus Christ the Righteous. He is truth."

"That which irks you most is the women who follow him!" Alexander said. His attitude was triumphant as if he had produced his trump card. "Your hatred of women is obvious! The reason your own power is so limited is because you refuse to recognise the woman's role!"

"Do you fully understand what you are saying?" Paul's voice was steady, but it was obvious that he was fighting for control. "I have nothing against women or, indeed, against marriage, although some have said that I do. Simon Magus degrades women through his teachings, making them no better than the temple prostitutes. Do I need to tell you that if you seek evil perversions, you will find the Father of all evil?"

"Jesus kept a whore at his side!" the coppersmith retorted. "You can't deny that!"

Paul stood up, his face dark with anger. "I know nothing of Mary Magdalene's past sins, but whatever they were, she repented and never revisited them! Leave now, Alexander and never let me see you here again!"

Alexander laughed bitterly. "I won't be back!" he promised.

When Paul wrote to Timothy, during the last months of his

incarceration, it was evident that although he encouraged his young 'son' in the Lord, he was deeply saddened.

"I am now ready to be offered and the time of my departure is at hand," he wrote. "I have fought the good fight, I have finished my course. I have kept the faith. Henceforth is laid up for me a crown of righteousness, which the Lord, the righteous judge shall give me at that day. And not to me only, but to all them also that love his appearing.

"Alexander the coppersmith did me much evil. The Lord reward him according to his works. Of whom, thou beware also for he has greatly withstood our words. At my first answer no man stood with me, but all forsook me. I pray God that it may not be laid to their charge."

It was obvious from his epistle that Peter, the apostle of the Lord, was not in Rome. Paul would not have failed to mention his presence and Peter would certainly not have abandoned him in his hour of deepest need.

Chapter 10
Twice-Born

Once Heinrich Himmler had obtained the release papers, he visited the woman's prison in Berlin. He persuaded himself that the act was altruistic, certain that Felix Kersten would be impressed with his personal intervention. But the truth was that the Reichsführer SS was curious. What made a woman fall in love with a Jew? And what possessed her to defy the law in aiding his escape? He wanted to see her for himself and he wanted Gabriele Hoch to know that he, Heinrich Himmler, was her benefactor.

Within the cold breast of the Reichsführer lurked a romantic streak. In the realms of his imagination, he was a chivalric knight; a celibate of the Teutonic Order, living a life of selfless courage and unrequited passion. He desired a woman who would instantly recognise these qualities and would adore him from afar.

Gabriele Hoch was summoned from her cell and taken by a prison guard to the warder's office.

She had lost weight during her incarceration; food rationing in the prisons was stringently applied. She was thin, angular and pale but her auburn hair still grew with a life of its own. She had combed it and captured it with her few precious hair pins after her weekly shower that morning. As she approached, Himmler surveyed her with interest. She was a good-looking woman, the sort he would have gladly married off to one of his prime SS men had she not defiled herself.

Gabriele entered the office and stopped short in amazement. The puffy features of the Reichsführer were instantly recognisable from his newspaper photographs. He was impeccably dressed in his black SS uniform with its silver deaths-head insignia, ritual dagger and highly polished black boots. Light reflected off his eye-glasses from the single bulb lighting the room so that behind them his eyes were rendered invisible.

It was impossible to discern what this visit might mean but Gabriele knew the reputation of the leader of the SS. It did not bode well.

"Take a seat Miss Hoch!" His voice was cool but civil.

He sat down opposite her and watched her for several moments without speaking. She waited, determined not to allow herself to be intimidated.

"You were arrested for aiding a Jew to escape across the Swiss border."

"That's correct."

"You were further found guilty of cohabitation."

She shook her head wearily. "It hardly matters any more, but no, we were not 'cohabiting' as the court euphemistically called it."

"You were friends?"

"We were work colleagues until Michael lost his job under the Nuremburg Laws."

"And you are a music teacher?"

"I was in the music department at the Berlin University."

Himmler nodded; he had never managed to overcome his shyness with women and suddenly found himself at a loss for words. This moment had occupied his fantasies, but faced with the reality, the dream had shattered. There was no awestruck maiden yearning for him with her eyes; rather, a woman in a shapeless grey prison dress who regarded him with cautious hostility and he was unnerved.

"I have signed your release papers," Heinrich Himmler said frostily. "I think you will find the university will be quite open to you reapplying for your old post."

Gabriele stared at him in disbelief.

"Why?"

He shrugged uncomfortably. "The Reich is not opposed to leniency," he said, "in certain circumstances." He bowed his head formally, clicked his heels and left. Gabriele looked disbelievingly at the papers he had handed her. At the bottom of the second page appeared the signature of Heinrich Himmler, far bolder than one might have expected from the appearance of the man, and the official stamp of the Reichsführer SS.

The warder was hurrying down the corridor towards the woman who stood on guard outside the office door.

"Fetch Miss Hoch's personal possessions!" he ordered. "She is to be released immediately."

Within the hour, Gabriele Hoch stood on the pavement outside the prison walls gripping her cloth bag. She felt dazed and disorientated and for the first time that day she allowed herself the luxury of tears.

One of her first acts of freedom was to write a postcard to the address Michael had given her.

Chapter 11
Twice-Born

In July of the year 64, fire broke out at the northern end of the Circus Maximus in Rome causing pandemonium. Many of the older buildings were built of wood and the dry timbers burst readily into flame throwing sparks and thick smoke heavenward creating a brown pall over the city that blocked out the sun. The fire spread rapidly and citizens gathered their children together and fled in panic before the conflagration with what possessions they could carry. For six days, Rome burned while Nero watched from the Tower of Maecenas, playing his lyre, enraptured by the beauty of the flames. Much of the ancient city's tenements, mansions and monuments were reduced to ashes.

It was obvious that it had been deliberately set. Consuls caught Nero's attendants on their properties, armed with oakum and blazing torches, but were unable to interfere. He had been bored, he said, with the drabness of the buildings and the narrowness of the city's streets.

In the wake of the fire, no one was permitted to search the ruins of their homes. Nero declared that the corpses and rubble from the devastated buildings would be removed without charge but what was promoted as an act of charity was a wonderful opportunity for personal gain. It was also an auspicious moment to deal with some of his perceived enemies, many of whom, having lost their homes, had taken refuge in the tombs and the catacombs.

Shortly thereafter, a plot to assassinate Emperor Nero was uncovered and those involved were condemned to death, exiled or afforded the opportunity to commit suicide. This attempt on his life tipped the scales and unleashed the full force of Nero's madness. Christians were subjected to the fury of his wrath as Rome bowed beneath a reign of terror. Some of his victims were painted with tar, tied to stakes and set alight to form human torches in his pleasure gardens; others were dressed in animal skins and thrown to the wild beasts in the Circus Maximus for the Emperor's entertainment.

Simon Magus was well-protected and it took time to run him to ground; ultimately though, two years after the great fire, his hide-out in the catacombs was discovered and he was dragged forth by Nero's guard and brought before the Emperor.

Nero was consistently jealous of the talented and the powerful, and he was especially afraid of the Magus. The Standing One, renamed Simon Pethor by Claudius, who declared that he was Father to the Samaritans, Son to the Jews, and appeared among other peoples as the Holy Ghost, had gathered an avid following. Nero perceived it as a threat. If there was a living god among them it was possible that Rome might rise up and proclaim him king. Nero was despised and feared, and his position was becoming increasingly vulnerable. His mother haunted his dreams. Rome's lowest citizens knew it and, penning his guilt in verse they posted it on the walls.

'Acmaeon, Orestes, and Nero are brothers,
Why? Because all of them murdered their mothers.'

To take his mind off the turmoil in his country, Nero prepared to leave for Greece. The Greeks, he declared, were a far more cultured nation than his own and greatly appreciative of his musicianship. But he was determined that he would see Simon dead first.

Nero had committed many murders. He had killed his wife, Poppaea, his mother and the aunt who raised him as a child. Britannica, Claudius' son was poisoned at his hand and he was personally responsible for the deaths of many knights and senators. Yet, superstitious fear caused him a sleepless night before Simon Pethor's brief trial and, facing the man, he trembled. It was reputed that the magician had conjured the spirit from a young boy and kept it chained in his room, and Nero feared for his own safety. It would stand the magician in great stead to hold the Emperor's spirit captive and he had no doubt as he looked upon his prisoner that he was capable of such a feat.

Simon Magus appeared not in the least cowed by his predicament. Despite his days of internment in Mamertine Prison where he had been chained in a cell several feet underground he stood physically erect and spiritually unbowed. The Magus' gaolers had not permitted him the liberty of a wash; his face was smudged, his hair and beard wild, and his robes soiled.

His haughty air, Caesar thought, would not save him today neither would the fury of his supporters account for anything after this. Tossing his blonde ringlets away from his face with one bejewelled hand, Nero surveyed the prisoner with nervous satisfaction. By evening, he would be dead and Rome would no longer be troubled by the man. Nero voiced his accusations of sedition and arson.

"You deliberately fomented unrest among your Christian followers and many were later seen setting the fires," he said. "Witnesses have come forward who will swear to the fact."

Simon bowed his head ironically, "And I could produce many trustworthy witnesses who would declare that your own men were responsible, Caesar. History will judge between us."

Nero's eyes hooded but he refrained from answering. He knew, the fewer words spoken with this man, the better.

Witnesses were produced. They were well coached and spoke with conviction, and within the hour the Emperor had passed sentence. Nero arranged the folds of his toga over his arm and stood up to leave.

The powerful voice of Simon restrained him. This was Simon Pethor, the Interpreter; Simon the god.

"Your own death, Caesar will follow. Within the year you will be forsaken by all and die by your own hand."

Nero's pale hand rose as though controlled by a puppet-master and flicked nervously across his cheek. Slender, effeminate fingers found a curl and twisted it. Almost, it seemed, his thumb, like that of a young child would have strayed to his mouth but he resisted it.

Simon Pethor's fanatical eyes mocked him. "For your sins, Caesar, you will burn in eternal hell. Know this! You may crucify me, but in three days, I will rise again."

The Emperor stepped backwards, stumbling clumsily over his own feet. As he left, he spoke briefly to the centurion who was standing by. The man barked a sharp order to his soldiers who fell in beside the Magus, spears at the ready, and he was led away to be crucified on the Ostia Road.

Many of Simon Magus' disciples followed and gathered at a

short distance from the cross. Simon shook off the hands of the two soldiers who restrained him and, removing his outer garment, he hailed one of the disciples by name.

"Menander. Here, take my cloak. From this time on, you will wear it and Rome will follow you. Have no fear; I will rise again after three days. Tell Helen not to mourn for me."

"Father, I will hold your cloak for you against that day…"

Menander was pushed roughly aside and the soldiers again laid hold of Simon Pethor's shoulders manhandling him roughly to the ground.

"Wait." Simon's tone compelled them. "I will not be crucified in the same way as *he* was," his expression conveyed his contempt. "If this is how I must die, then crucify me upside down."

The soldiers looked questioningly at the centurion who shrugged. "Let him please himself," he said and as they drove in the nails with the mallet, he turned away. Simon Pethor's death, though hideously painful, was hastened by the way he was hung. Menander and two others waited until it was over and, under cover of darkness, they took down the body and carried it away.

Paul also, had been transferred to the notorious Mamertine Prison and was incarcerated for several days in a cell not far from the Magus. The only access to the subterranean chamber was from a grating above. Paul spent his final days chained to the damp stone wall in almost total darkness but he sang praises to the Father of his Saviour, Jesus Christ, in a voice that was a little rough and off-key until his mouth was too dry to continue. He rejoiced that his end was coming. Soon, very soon, his heart told him, he would see his Lord face to face. He had run the race and he would receive the crown of eternal life.

Paul was dragged from the cell and, blinded by the intensity of the sun and weakened by the lack of food and water, he stumbled out of the prison gates under heavy guard. As a Roman citizen he was afforded a brief trial before being marched out of the city. Many others were taken in the same company and Paul was able to exchange a warm glance or a quiet word of comfort with some. He was beheaded on the Ostia Road; a more merciful death than that afforded to Simon Magus.

Simon's disciples waited out the three days besides the body of their Lord but at the end of their vigil on the third day they looked to Menander who, unlike the rest, showed no sign of unease or confusion.

"I have prayed," he said, "and I have reached a conclusion."

The men and women gazed at him wordlessly. Flaming torches cast restless light over the blackened walls of their underground room and teased the pallid face of Simon Peter with a suggestion of life but the body, its terrible wounds cleaned by the women, lay pallid and immobile.

"You will remember Simon Magus' words on that last day, both before Nero and at the cross. He first said that Nero's death would follow his own. He knew of a certainty that he was going to die. He gave also a message for Helen, saying that she should not mourn him. Why also, would he have given me his cloak and with it commissioned me with leadership? It was the gesture of a departing master."

"But without doubt, he said he would rise on the third day..."

"The scriptures say that to God a day is as a thousand years, and a thousand years as a day."

They looked at him without comprehension and Menander smiled. "Our master will indeed rise; he alone is the Standing One but first there must be the fulfilment of all things." He stood to his feet wrapping the Magus' cloak around him as he did so. The little group of disciples were hushed as they gazed upon his face, which darkened as the power came upon him.

"Hear, little children," Menander prophesied, "many centuries will pass before the culmination of all things takes place. When all the parts of the puzzle, from the east and the west, the north and south fit together under one great nation, the Standing One will again set his feet as Parsival upon the earth. He will unite all men and bring all things together in himself. In time to come, many nations will strive for this prize but there can be only one who receives the victory wreath."

As he resumed his seat, Apollonius spoke. "Let it be in accordance with the words of Menander. The waiting is over, tonight we will bury the master. Let the women prepare the body. It is time to let Simon Peter go; there is much work to be done."

The remains of Simon Magus were buried in the dead of night

in the pagan cemetery on Vaticanus Hill. Menander, still wearing the master's cloak, spoke the words at the tomb.

"Simon Pethor, be it as you have said. In three days, O god, rise again from the dead. Your disciples await your return."

PART IV

Chapter 1
Twice-Born

The Emperor Justinian of Constantinople had sent his own engineers to Edessa, which had become part of the Byzantine Empire, to aid in the reconstruction of the city after the flood, and it was while repairs were made to the city's walls that the Mandylion was rediscovered. It had been bricked into a niche under a tile made in the image of the shroud's visage. A lamp had been set with these objects, after the manner of the Jews for the burial of their dead. The year of the discovery was 544AD; a portentous year in world history, said to mark a time when, once every seven hundred years, the earth's treasures surface.

The letter purporting to have come from Jesus himself had been carefully preserved in the city's archives, held by Edessa as a talisman of protection. Now, the citizens shifted their trust once again to the image made without hands. A domed cathedral was built to house the Mandylion, a Hagia Sophia built of stone and surrounded by water, beautiful to the eye and intricately decorated within with mosaics.

"Exalted are the mysteries of this shrine," a hymn exclaimed, "…it contains the very essence of God."

In Constantinople, Justin II who, despite the conflict between the Monophysites and Orthodox believers with regard to the formation of religious images, called for the creation of a dominant figure of Christ enthroned to be set above the imperial throne. The face was executed in the likeness of the Mandylion. Papal legate to the court of Constantinople during the reign of Tiberius II, Justin's successor, was the man who would later become Pope Gregory the Great. He was intrigued and excited by what he saw and, during his stay in the city, commissioned the painting of a similar icon to take back with him to Rome.

In the early part of the 940's, Byzantine Emperor Romanus Lecapenus ordered an incursion into what had again become Muslim territory. His aim was to seize the Mandylion, the image of images, and bring it to Constantinople.

Thus, on a spring day in 943, the Byzantine army under the command of General John Curcuas encamped outside the walls of Edessa and emissaries were sent on horseback to make their terms known to the emir.

"Edessa will be spared," they proclaimed, "and two hundred high-ranking Muslim prisoners released. Furthermore, we will pay twelve thousand silver crowns and the city of Edessa will be given perpetual immunity from attack by the emperor."

The emir listened in silence. He was fully aware that Curcuas' campaigns had already caused the fall of other Muslim cities and Edessa was vulnerable to attack.

"What are you seeking in return?" he asked.

"Just one thing. The Christian community are in possession of a religious icon known as the Mandylion. The emperor requests that it should be moved to Constantinople."

The emir shook his head despairingly. "Allow me time to negotiate," he said. "Meeting your request will not be easy. There will be strong opposition from the Christians who revere this image and gain much trade from pilgrimages to Edessa."

"We will wait," the emissary said and they mounted their horses and rode out of the city gates.

Riders were dispatched to Baghdad and the problem was debated at length by the Caliphate. John Curcuas kept his men occupied with minor incursions into neighbouring territories until eventually word was received from Baghdad.

"Give them what they want and let the prisoners be released."

Curcuas had brought in Abraham, the bishop of the neighbouring town of Samosata, to identify and receive the Mandylion; one of the few men who had seen the genuine image. It soon became apparent that his expertise was essential as two separate attempts were made to pass off copies, but despite a running battle between the forces of the emir and the city's Christians, the true Mandylion was taken. General John Curcuas signalled his men to break camp and turned his steed towards Constantinople.

Chapter 2
Twice-Born

"That bastard Himmler killed him, I know he did!" Lina Heydrich screamed. Her fists beat at the chest of the SS-Sturmbannführer who had brought her the news. He tried with some embarrassment to restrain her.

"I'm afraid you don't understand, Frau Heydrich," he assured her. "Your husband was murdered by Czech agents. The Reichsführer had nothing to do with it."

Lina threw back her head and laughed hysterically. "You obviously don't know our Reichsführer!" Her eyes were wild, shifting as though in the grip of a fever. "He has powers behind him, he's capable of anything!" She began to weep again, a ragged horrible sound.

"He was very badly injured by the grenade," the Major replied awkwardly. "Everything possible was done to save him."

"You just don't understand, do you?" She gripped desperately at his arm. "Heinrich Himmler is afraid of Reinhard, because he knows his position as Reichsführer-SS is built on my husband's brains and abilities. Without Reinhard, Himmler is nothing! Himmler has always lived in his shadow!" Her mood changed abruptly and she smiled a small wistful smile. "He never missed an opportunity to excel," she said. "Did you know he was head of the Central Security Department, Chief of Security Police and the Gestapo as well as President of the International Criminal Police Organisation, with thirty-three countries under his control?"

"Obergruppenführer Heydrich was a remarkable man," the major agreed obediently, relieved to find himself on more comfortable ground."

Unexpectedly she laughed and, loosening her grip on the Major's arm she walked towards the window.

"It was most amusing when Reinhard detailed himself for action in the Luftwaffe. You should have seen Himmler's face when he realised he'd been sent on a mission over England. You could just see him trying to imagine whether he'd hold out under torture!"

The major smiled. "I believe he was officially grounded after that."

She nodded. "And he would have been court-martialled for insubordination later, if he hadn't been awarded those decorations for bravery when his plane was shot down behind Russian lines! He had continued flying under an assumed name, but that finally blew his cover! At least it meant they got him out fast when they realised what had happened!"

She swung round to face him and her expression was bright, almost brittle.

"The Führer would never have known a thing about it if it hadn't been for those damned decorations. He has an eye for those sorts of details! You know of course that Reinhard was given the silver bar for combat missions and the Iron Cross, First Class? Heinrich Himmler was downright jealous of his achievements, especially the sporting achievements. We all know it took Himmler months of practice before he could even attempt the Reich Sport Badge. Even then the officials had to pretend he'd passed to shield him from further embarrassment." She was pacing the room restlessly. "Himmler did it," she muttered. "I just know he did it!"

The Sturmbannführer's shoulders straightened. "Frau Heydrich, I assure you, the Reichsführer couldn't have had anything to do with your husband's death. He was in Germany…"

Lina's chin tilted defiantly. "My husband was transferred to Czechoslovakia at a time when he constituted the greatest threat to Heinrich Himmler!" she ground out. "Nevertheless, Reinhard was doing an excellent job here and Herr Hitler was well pleased. That wouldn't have suited our Reichsführer-SS at all, would it?" Her expression darkened again. "When they hit the car last week," she said, "he leapt out, shooting like some Wild West hero. He didn't even appear to be hurt. Klein, his driver, didn't realise he'd been hit."

"I'm sure that was how your husband would have chosen to die," the major offered. "He was a tough man, a man of polished steel, and he died the way he lived, a hero."

Lina's expression softened, but only for a moment.

"No!" she contradicted sharply, "you're wrong. He lived a hero's life, but he died a fool's death, weakening slowly on a hospital bed. That's not what he would have chosen. He wasn't even killed by the grenade, which would have been a noble death; he was killed slowly by the car's upholstery springs, and by some dark curse Heinrich Himmler placed on his life."

She threw herself at the major, weeping bitterly, her fingers biting into his arms. He took her by the wrists gently and stepped back.

"The doctor will be here in just a moment," he said awkwardly. "I'll call one of the women to stay with you." He eased his collar with one finger as he retreated hastily from the room. Behind him, Lina collapsed onto the sofa, like a marionette whose strings have been suddenly slashed.

The transfer of Reinhard Heydrich to Czechoslovakia had indeed come at the most opportune moment for Heinrich Himmler. For years Heydrich had used every tactic within his means to wrest control of the concentration camps from him; instruments of terror that were a vital key to ultimate power in the Reich. What had begun to take place between the two men was a life and death struggle, always played out beneath a façade of pleasantries. Sooner or later the strongest must win.

On 27th May, 1942, immediately after Reinhard Heydrich was fatally wounded by two Czech patriots who had been parachuted into German-occupied Czechoslovakia from Britain, SS General Odilo Globocnik began preparations for 'Operation Reinhard' with the deportation of Jews to the death camps. In a reprisal action in Czechoslovakia, 199 men and boys were murdered in the mining village of Lidice and the village was razed to the ground. On the day of this massacre, thirty Jews were driven from Theresienstadt to the ruins of Lidice and were compelled at gun point to work for thirty-six hours without a break to bury the dead.

"Such a tragic affair!" Himmler confessed to Felix Kersten. He was lying on his back on the high, white-sheeted bed while the capable fingers of his masseuse gently manipulated his stomach.

"Tragic, Herr Reichsführer," he agreed.

"At the funeral, the Führer referred to him as the 'man with the iron heart'. I thought that was an apt description of Heydrich." His eyelids were closed and Kersten thought he had not seen the Reichsführer look so relaxed in a long time.

"There's no doubt he was tough," he agreed cautiously.

"On the surface, yes. A very tough character. But underneath, like all men of divided race, there was a deep-seated unhappiness that nothing could eradicate."

"You are saying that Obergruppenführer Heydrich was of mixed blood?" Kersten asked, astounded.

"Certainly!" Himmler gave a small definite nod.

"There were rumours of course, which were very persistent as he gained power. But he sued for racial slander?"

Himmler's eyes flickered and closed again. "As head of SD, he had no trouble in dismissing any accusations of that sort, but they were not without foundation. Both the Führer and I were well aware of the situation, right from the early days. Checks had been done of course, and we were in possession of documented evidence. I, myself, felt it would have been correct to have expelled him, but the Führer was of the opinion that the Party could make good use of his exceptional talents. He was aware that Heydrich was highly gifted, but also a dangerous man. Because of the deep bitterness he felt for the trick fate had played on him, he was the ideal man to use against the Jews. In that sense, he was truly 'a man with a heart of iron'. Almost without conscience! He never showed mercy or pity in any of his dealings. So, it turned out, of course, that the Führer's instincts about him were right."

Felix Kersten drew his strong hands in smooth strokes from just below Himmler's ribcage, down towards his lower abdomen.

Kersten's face was rounded, almost indistinct from the neck that bulged uncomfortably above a tight collar. His mouth was small and earnest, and his eyes, beneath the long forehead, were bewildered and self-effacing. But Kersten was raised to a position above mortal men by his remarkable powers of healing.

"So, his death will be a blow to the Reich?" Kersten spoke lightly, but his words probed and dug even as his hands did.

Himmler's mouth hardened perceptibly. "He was always a

great help to me in my work, but I managed without him once the Führer had him transferred." He was silent for a moment and then he opened his eyes and looked directly as his masseuse. "It was as if some dark fate snatched him away at the zenith of his power," he said. "Very tragic!" He shook his head and closed his eyes once more. "You know Kersten, it made me feel quite strange walking behind the coffin at the funeral, holding the hands of those young mongrels of his."

"I can imagine."

"In my eulogy, I felt it my duty to leave the impression that his bloodline was clear for the sake of the family. I think my words were: As he has continued the line of his ancestors and done them nothing but honour, so he will live on with all his qualities, noble, decent and clean in his sons, who are inheritors of his blood and his name." He looked to Kersten for approval and was rewarded with a congratulatory smile.

"I understand the funeral was an impressive affair?"

"A fitting tribute to a man of his calibre," Himmler said as he sat up. "I feel his wife must have been entirely satisfied with the way it was conducted."

Kersten glanced at the Reichsführer as he began to dress himself and thought of the rumours that circulated about *his* background. By all accounts, Heydrich was not alone in the impurity of his ancestral line.

Chapter 3
Twice-Born

Chaim Freiberg brought the news of Gabriele's release even before her postcard was delivered into Michael's hands.

"Your girl's out, Segal!" he told him triumphantly.

"What do you mean?"

"Do I need to spell it out for you? I mean Gabriele Hoch has been released."

Michael sat down suddenly and gazed wordlessly out over the lake.

"Are you alright, old chap?" Freiberg asked, sounding concerned. "You're not going to have a collapse or anything like that are you? Look, I've got champagne on ice here. This is deserving of a celebration."

"How the hell did you do it?"

"Put a bit of pressure on the Reichsführer-SS!"

Michael laughed. "No, seriously, Chaim."

"I am serious. Let's open the bubbly." He nodded in the direction of a waiter who opened the bottle and filled their glasses.

"It was surprisingly simple," Freiberg said and once the waiter had withdrawn he recounted his meeting with Felix Kersten.

Michael Segal shook his head in amazement

"You're a wonder! Gabriele and I are forever in your debt."

"In that case I'll expect an invitation to the wedding," Freiberg said, failing miserably in an attempt to appear humbled. "Look, I'd better order something to eat with the champagne if you want to walk out of here later."

Lunch at the Beau Rivage was becoming something of an institution. Chaim had been in town for almost two weeks and they had discussed the book on several different occasions over the hotel's superb meals. This time, when they finally got down to business, it was with more hilarity than usual. Michael was feeling more liberated than at any time since his crossing from Germany and he realised how deeply he had felt Gabriele's incarceration. He set his thoughts of her aside reluctantly and attempted to give Chaim Freiberg his full attention.

Paul Vignon's book, written in 1902, was the obvious starting place as he undoubtedly had laid the groundwork of any serious study of the shroud. Michael had focussed his attention on both the book and a subsequent lecture by Sorbonne's professor of comparative anatomy who had worked with Vignon.

"As an agnostic, his talk was particularly convincing," Segal admitted. "He was certain the wounds represented on the shroud were anatomically flawless and that there was no trace of known pigment on the fabric."

"And he also demonstrated the senselessness and difficulty of anyone working in the negative," Chaim reminded him.

"He sounded as though he had suddenly got religion," Segal said. "Not surprising that the lecture caused a furore in the scientific community!"

They discussed Vignon's study of the distinctive markings on the facial features of Pia's photograph and the comparison of these features in eastern and western art.

"There's no doubt in my mind that most of the representations of Christ have arisen from a common source," Freiberg said.

"I understand the gospels don't give any sort of portrayal of the man," Michael said.

"Much like the Jewish scriptures," Freiberg agreed, "generally there's no engagement with the physical or the emotional. But we do know Jesus was beaten about the face and the body."

"And that he was lashed before the crucifixion. It's agreed by the medical experts that the injuries seen in the photographs are in complete accord with the gospel records."

"And we also have evidence, documented by Vignon, of the representations made by artists of Edessa's Mandylion. These portrayed a face on a light background, ranging from monochromatic sepia to rust brown, very similar to the shroud's image. We're left with the same question as Vignon et al."

"Are the Mandylion and the shroud one?"

"Exactly."

"The Mandylion was a portrait."

"Set in some sort of gold trellis-work. It's possible that it folded out into a full-length shroud."

"Why would it have been folded in the first instance?"

Freiberg shrugged. "To hide the fact that it was a shroud? We know that no Jew would knowingly have touched it! Perhaps it was presented as a portrait to make it more acceptable to the king of Edessa."

"The evidence is circumstantial but I don't know if there would be enough to stand up in a court of law."

"I'm expecting you to make a good case."

Michael laughed. "And if I disprove it, am I fired?"

Chaim Freiberg was remarkably sober. "I needed a sceptic to write this for me," he said. "And preferably a Jewish sceptic! I trust you will try to your utmost to discredit it, but that you will be honest in your findings."

"I hope the results won't disappoint you."

"I have no idea what I want you to find, Segal. But when you find it I don't think it will disappoint me. I've got a meeting at three. Let me know how things go."

He heaved himself to his feet, a heavy figure in a Homburg and an outsized suit. Leaning across the table, he shook Michael's hand. Segal wondered if he should mention that his tie needed straightening, but thought better of it.

Chapter 4
Twice-Born

582 AD

The boy pressed closer to the camp fire. They were talking about him, he knew they were. From his vantage point among the camels, he could see some of the faces of the men touched by the orange glow of the flame. They had arrived in the oasis when the sun was at its zenith and while servants unburdened the camels, watered and fed them, Muhammed went with his uncle to greet the monks who had arrived the day before. The desert made brothers of strangers and oases were havens, which forged unusual bonds between those who sought refuge from the furnace of the sands.

Muhammed leaned his body against the hump of the nearest couched beast. Briefly, it swung its head in the boy's direction, grumbling volubly and baring its teeth. He ignored it. His uncle often spoke about him, even to strangers; the boy knew the stories well but never tired of hearing them; it pleased him to be the centre of attention. His uncle's words came clearly to his ears and at first he was disappointed.

"Abd Al-Muttalib, my father, received a vision from God," Abu Talib was telling the monks. "He was shown the situation of a well in Mecca in which the treasures of the Kaaba were hidden. Many men had sought it, but it was the vision given to my father that brought these riches to the surface."

"A deed for which he was doubtless highly esteemed by the people of your city?"

Abu Talib nodded smiling broadly beneath his bristling moustache.

"My father was of the tribe of Quraish, a descendent of Abraham and his son Ishmael," he acknowledged proudly. "He was a famous man among our people - and rich; very rich!" He glanced around at his audience. His own men followed the familiar tale with rapt attention. "I am one of ten brothers," Abu Talib continued, "which was also an answer by Allah to a prayer of my father. Abd Al Muttalib had promised to sacrifice one of his sons at the Kaaba if this prayer was answered."

"A supplication made too lightly perhaps?" The monk's teeth were darkened stumps between fleshy lips and his countenance, as he grinned at his own joke, was unpleasant.

Abu Talib nodded wryly. "In a divination ceremony, the lot fell to Abd Allah, the youngest son – his favourite."

"Father of the boy who travels with our caravan," one of the men elucidated.

"Muhammed?"

"Just so!"

In his hiding place, the child squirmed with excitement. This was his part of the story.

"Abd Allah was obviously not sacrificed; the son bears testimony to that fact."

"Abd Al-Muttalib visited a seer to plead for his son's life and was told that the god Hubal would accept the sacrifice of a hundred camels in the place of the child. The substitute was accepted and his life was spared."

The monks were following the story with interest.

"Where is his father?"

"Dead before the birth of the child. His mother's death followed, before the boy reached his sixth year. My father took the child until his own death a little more than three years ago. Muhammed now travels with me and, in accordance with our custom, receives training in the ways of the desert. My father always believed the boy had a special destiny among our people. He called him Al-Amin, the trustworthy."

Two of the monks glanced at one another.

"Bring the boy, we would see him."

Abu Talib hesitated. "He is no doubt asleep."

"It is important that we should see him."

There was a scuffle among the couched camels and Muhammed stepped forward, self-consciously, into the circle of men.

"I am awake."

There was a burst of laughter from the Arabs but the monks were silent.

"Come here boy!" Father Michael seized Muhammed's thin wrist in an iron grip and drew him closer. The boy stood obediently before the monk and gazed fearfully at the thickset face and broken teeth in the face partially concealed beneath the cowl of his robe. For a long time, the holy man was silent. At length he turned to Abu Talib.

"Be on guard against the Jews," he said harshly. "They will construe evil against him!"

"Go to your tent, Muhammed."

The child turned away trembling and left the circle of the fire.

Father Michael walked away from the gathering and gazed out towards the horizon. The moon was in its first quarter; a finely etched crescent hung against the starry sky. It was like an omen.

"Your father, Abd Al-Muttalib, did he believe in the One God?"

Abu Talib's face became guarded. "He believed the Kaaba was built by Abraham, father of the Jews. It is the knowledge he passed on to his sons. It was my father's desire that the Kaaba be cleansed and rebuilt."

"Cleansed of its idols?"

Abu Talib nodded. The subject was unpopular, even among members of his own tribe and it was dangerous to speak of such desires too openly.

"In not many years it will be rebuilt," the monk prophesied. "I see it as the destiny of your nephew."

Abu Talib glanced at him uncertainly and then back at the dying embers of the fire. "He's still a child," he said. "He may not survive the rigors of the desert."

"He will survive."

Muhammed lay on his mat but sleep was a long time in coming. Something strange had happened, as though the old monk's eyes had opened a place of buried knowledge in his soul. The words of the monk echoed in his mind: the Jews would construe evil against him. Yet, his grandfather had taught him that Abraham, father of Ishmael, patriarch of their people, had also fathered the Jews, and it was said among the Arab people that Abraham had even built the sacred Kaaba in Mecca.

The Jews were therefore brothers. Would his brethren construe evil of him? He tossed restlessly, falling at last into a light sleep. Somewhere, as he wrestled in his dreams, he discovered what he perceived as the truth. The Jews were indeed his mortal enemies. Towards dawn, two men in white robes appeared to him and laid him down upon the ground. In his dream he saw them remove the heart from his chest and take from it a black clot, which they cast away.

Chapter 5
Twice-Born

In June, 1937, Himmler's knights of the Black Order opened the Wigpurti Crypt. The deed was not done in the light of day but in a magical ceremony at the hour of midnight.

Heinrich Himmler was a middle-class nonentity at the head of the SS elite. He could lay no claim to a meaningful lineage and had no legitimate tie to the aristocracy, however Himmler had become more and more convinced that he was reincarnated from his namesake Heinrich I. By communicating with der Vogler's spirit, he fashioned for himself a bond that in his estimation transcended any blood lineage. Whereas his men moved from one room to another at Wewelsburg in order to familiarise themselves with the historical personalities represented by each; Himmler's room, which was decorated to reflect Heinrich I, was his alone.

For the second year running on 2 July, the cobbled streets of Quedlinburg were decorated with Nazi banners and resounded to the roll of drums and the slow goose-step of the SS. Heinrich der Vogler's remains were interred in the crypt below the Cathedral. The man, who, in his lifetime, had rejected the anointing of the pope, would not have been disappointed with his final resting place.

Himmler made a pact that he would keep until the end of the war. At midnight, on the anniversary of Heinrich der Vogler's death he would worship the king in the crypt of St Servatius. It was during one of these sojourns that the intricate plan to counter the Jewish-inspired World Revolutionary Movement was transmitted to Himmler from beyond the grave by Heinrich I: a plan that involved summoning up the Beast.

Six years later, on the night of 2 July 1943, Himmler planned his ultimate desecration of the Quedlinburg crypt.

There is a legend associated with the Armenian, St. Servatius suggesting that he was distantly related both to John the Baptist and to

Jesus himself. There exists a statuette of Memelia, his mother, standing like the Madonna with the infant, complete with bishop's mitre, in her arms. Servatius zealously opposed Arianism and, in his wanderings, as far afield as Trier and Edessa, denounced Arian bishops and testified against them.

It was said that Servatius was priest and guardian of the Holy Sepulchre in Jerusalem before being sent by the Spirit to Tongeren where he succeeded Valentine as bishop. Later he became bishop of Maastricht and built a church over the Roman temple of Fortuna and Jupiter. The threat of attack on Tongeren by the Huns encouraged Servatius to make pilgrimage to Rome where he kept vigil at St. Peter's tomb. There, in a vision, Peter forecast the destruction of the city and handed Servatius the key of heaven. The priest returned to Tongeren, transferred the precious relics to Maastricht as Peter had instructed him and died a few days later in May 384. Among the relics associated with the saint are the key to heaven, and a chalice.

Heinrich Himmler's annual pilgrimage to der Vogler's tomb at the midnight hour in 1943 differed dramatically from any previous visit. Twelve Obergruppenführer accompanied him and two women; Marianne von Ingolstadt and the Jewess, Ruth.

Over the four years since Marianne's recruitment, she had been subtly and systematically initiated into the arcane beliefs of Himmler and his twelve Obergruppenführer. The transition was not difficult; her training in the Ahnenerbe had already stripped away any remnant of Christian credence replacing it with a form of paganism; Karl Wolff hastened her shift into the occult by the use of the drug, peyote. From that point on, it was a simple matter to make her believe that what she was about to do was vital to the war effort and ultimately for the greater benefit of humanity.

The gnawing pain in Himmler's abdomen had dramatically increased as the day wore on and, as he and his entourage moved quietly through Quedlinburg's dark, deserted streets, he found difficulty in remaining upright. Sweat rolled off his face and his entire body felt clammy and disorientated, as though the life-force was being drawn from him.

Karl Wolff parked the army vehicle and they walked the last stretch of road up to the church building, their footsteps echoing between the stone walls. Even if they were heard, no soul would consider challenging the authority of an SS contingent on the streets at such a late hour.

Himmler had chosen this location for the burial of the king of the First Reich with Machiavellian deliberation. The church had emerged in the 900's from the residential chapel of his hero, Heinrich der Vogler. It was named for a saint who had, like Godfroi de Bouillon, been called guardian of the Holy Sepulchre. And Quedlinburg was the birthplace of Karl Ritter, the German whose plan the Nazi's had adopted in their war against the Jews.

Ruth Leiman was brought bound and gagged into the silent church and pushed ahead down the steps into the vault. Two men of Himmler's inner circle lit flaming torches and fixed them into holders on the walls. Ruth took in her surroundings fearfully. Flames played over the walls, illuminating stone ceilings, which arched upward from the pillars. The cellar was decorated with the pagan symbolism of the SS. Ruth recognised the swastikas and thunderbolts but the other runic signs meant nothing.

Her eyes fell on a stone slab that had been placed in the centre of the crypt and she knew, without being told, that her life would end on that altar.

As she lay against the wall, her presence forgotten in the initial rituals, Ruth tested the ropes that bound her wrists, but there was no possibility of loosening them and eventually she lay still. Numbing terror coupled with the disjointed sensation of having stepped back into a past era left her staring uncomprehendingly at the scenes that were being enacted before her. They were deliberately invoking the spirit of the Beast and the intense power of some dark presence permeated every crevice of the crypt.

Shortly before midnight, they laid Ruth naked upon the icy stone of the altar and removed her gag so that they could hear her screams. It was Himmler himself who, with the ritual dagger, carved the sign of the swastika into her chest before he killed her.

On the stroke of midnight, on the grave of Heinrich der Vogler, in accordance with accepted SS doctrine, a perverted sexual act brought about conception of a child who would receive the spirit of his esteemed ancestor. Memelia, the Madonna-figure would, in due course, bring forth another who would don the mitre of religious authority.

The story of St. Servatius was a prophecy. Himmler was also building on the foundation of Ju-Pethor and the goddess of fortune. Tonight the chalice was filled and a Key to the future was turned. A Beast, claiming to be the Christ would arise as a consequence of this night to become guardian of the Holy Sepulchre in Jerusalem: a keeper of the Keys.

For three days, many years hence, vigil would be kept for him at St. Peter's tomb and within a year, Germany would meet the same fate as Tongeren; the Huns were already at the gates. Like the saint, Himmler would rescue the holy relics and spirit them to safety.

St. Servatius was also associated with three wooden shoes. The first to leave a lasting imprint on German soil was Heinrich der Vogler. The second shoe was leader behind the scenes of the Second Reich, Heinrich Himmler. The third, the leader of the hidden Reich, would also leave his footprint in the earth. He would come as a white knight; a saviour of the earth. But without doubt, he would be the most terrifying beast of them all.

Chapter 6
Twice-Born

595 AD

"He has as yet shown no interest in marriage," Father Michael said. "Abu Talib describes his nephew as a serious young man with a fine mind and delicate tastes. Most of the Quraish tribe are steeped in idolatry but the boy's grandfather, Abd Al-Muttalib of the Hashimites, passed on certain knowledge to his sons. They claim to be descendents of Ishmael and followers of the Jewish Baptiser; God of the holy image."

The Pope smiled. "Muhammed displays a sense of destiny?"

"I believe so."

"Then, if you are certain this family is part of our brotherhood, it is time to thrust his fate upon him. Tell me about this widow, what did you say her name was?"

"Khadija. She's a wealthy member of their tribe and a convert to the Mother faith. Recently she donated all her money to the Church and retired to a convent."

"She's old. What makes you think he will be interested?"

"At forty she is still beautiful. If she appeals to his spiritual calling she will capture him."

"And you have spoken to her?"

Father Michael revealed his broken teeth in a smile. "I have, Your Holiness. She is most willing to be used by God for His purposes. I have personally trained her cousin Waraqa. He is a faithful disciple who will guide Muhammed in the spiritual disciplines and enlighten his soul. The sign of the Master is upon him. I believe we have discovered our Arabian Messiah."

At the request of his uncle, Muhammed conducted the camel train of the widow Khadija to Syria and his obvious competence earned her approval. There was an attraction between them which, at first, had little to do with the flesh. Khadija was a mature woman, intelligent and fascinating. Her deep spirituality was indeed a magnet to the young man. What he discovered was a meeting of minds – a woman with whom he could converse as an equal and one who encouraged him with all her heart to step out and embrace the fate for which God had prepared him. Muhammed was twenty-five years old when he took Khadija in marriage and she was fifteen years his senior. It was a union of blessing and tears. Of the six children born to them, only their three daughters survived. The best known, Fatima, would later be married to Ali, Muhammed's successor.

"Iqraa!"

Muhammed cowered with his face to the ground. The cave was filled with an unseen presence and darkness closed in about him.

"I cannot."

"Iqraa! Read!"

There was no doubt that this was not something invented in his own mind – unless, indeed, he was on the brink of insanity.

"I have never learned to read."

The power that embraced him turned his limbs to water. He could not move. Words forsook him and even coherent thought became impossible. It was as though he was squeezed by some force so mighty, so supernatural that Muhammed was certain he was being held in the fist of God himself.

"Recite in the name of your Lord who created!" the voice reverberated as though through his very being. "He created man from that which clings. Recite! And thy Lord is most Bountiful."

There was no release from the intense crushing of his body. He was fighting now for every breath, certain he was on the edge of death.

"He who has taught by the pen, taught man what he knew not. Iqraa – recite!"

This was one of forty-year old Muhammed's many retreats to Mt Hira, but the first of his revelations. He fled the cave in terror, determined never to return.

"Cover me!"

"What has happened?" Khadijah took him by the shoulders and looked into his ashen face. "What is wrong?"

"Cover me!" Muhammed's eyes cast about wildly as though

seeking escape.

"Tell me what has happened!"

She wrapped a blanket around his shoulders and eventually the trembling of his body ceased. At length, hesitantly, he described his experience.

"I will speak to my cousin," she assured him. "You know you need not fear. You are a good man. Allah will not let you down."

Waraqa listened with bowed head to Muhammed's story. "You have been greatly blessed," he said at length. "I believe it is the Archangel Gabriel who appeared to you, even as he did to Moses."

Muhammed shook his head in confusion. "Gabriel? No. You don't understand. This being was dark - a creature of boundless terror! I was in fear of my life."

"He is a mighty being. Any man would be afraid. Understand Muhammed, you have been chosen from among men for a great work. You cannot run away from the destiny that is before you."

"I cannot go back!"

"You will go," Waraqa said. "You need only surrender to him and he will become to you as an angel of light. Succumb!"

"I don't know..." There was still doubt in Muhammed's eyes, but a new sense of conviction was beginning to overtake fear. Had he not always known that he was destined for greatness? The monks themselves had spoken it when he was a child. And then there was the dream. People called him al-Ameen, the Trustworthy. They too recognised his difference from other men.

There were many visitations after that. Over a period of twenty-three years, verses were penned on whatever materials were available, memorised and taught to his followers. Gabriel authenticated the accuracy of the revelations and gave the order in which they were to appear in the Qur'an. They were the commandments of Allah to his people. Muhammed's mission was to restore the worship of the One True God and to demonstrate the moral laws to his creation.

Muhammed's attention was drawn by raised voices from the courtyard and he knew without being told that, once more, the problem was the sacred stone. The time had come in the rebuilding of the Kaaba to position the stone in the wall, but factions of the Quraish were once again fighting for the privilege.

"Muhammed!" Several men hailed him. "Decide this for us. Which family should set the stone in the wall?"

Muhammed wiped his sweaty palms down the length of his robe and gazed silently at the agitated group. It was a delicate moment.

"Give me my mantle!" he ordered.

Someone retrieved the outer garment from where Muhammed had hung it earlier and passed it forward through the crowd. He laid it on the ground beside the stone.

Al-Lat and al-Uzza, moon goddesses, and Manat, the goddess of destiny, were all worshipped in the form of a sacred stone. When Muhammed entered Mecca victorious and smashed the three-hundred and sixty idols of astral worship, the black stone of the Kaaba, dedicated to the moon goddess al-Uzza was the one token of the ancient religion he had permitted to remain. According to the legend, the patriarch Abraham, and his son Ishmael, had discovered the stone when they were gathering rock for the building of the Kaaba. If this was true, how could such a stone be considered an idol?

It was, in fact, more the colour of burnt umber than black. Muhammed picked it up and cradled it in his hands. It was warm from the sun and there was something compelling in its touch.

"I know well that you are a stone that can neither do good or evil," he said, "but I invest in you the power to draw all men unto yourself." Unexpectedly, he bowed his head and kissed it.

Placing the sacred object on his mantle, he called one elder from each of the four bickering factions to come forward.

"Each of you take a corner of the garment," he ordered, "and lift it. So!"

Under his direction, the stone was set in its place in the marble plinth and the men stood back, awed and somewhat chastened by Muhammed's wisdom.

"The job is done," he said. "Let us return to work."

His own work was only just begun. Converts came slowly and Muhammed was scorned, maligned and often in fear of his life, even from those of his own tribe. Battles would yet be fought, and blood shed, before men bowed beneath this new religion. Idolatry was a way of life and one not easily surrendered in favour of worship of the One God proclaimed by the prophet. In the year 615, it became necessary for Muhammed and his Muslim followers, as they were known, to flee to Abyssinia for safety. Negus, the Roman Catholic king, granted his support, recognising the close similarity of his own beliefs to the doctrine of Muhammed. During this period, the Quraish outlawed Muhammed's family, the Hashimites, only removing the ban in 619, the year of Khadija's death.

"They will never surrender the Hajj," Abu Talib said emphatically. "It is expecting too much!"

"It is symbolic of their idolatry," Muhammed retorted. "It must go, or I have failed."

"You have allowed the stone of the moon goddess to remain, and the Kaaba, which is her sanctuary. So, what harm can there be in keeping the Hajj? It is a festival central to the unity of our people. Already, Muhammed, there has been so much resistance; so much bloodshed in the name of this new religion. It is time for compromise."

Muhammed shook his head wearily. "Uncle, you know that the Hajj is the autumn rite of persecution of the dying sun. The people stone the three pillars of Mina and invade the abode of the God of Thunder. Women offer themselves promiscuously to the pilgrims. Adultery is something I have endeavoured to stop."

"It cannot be halted completely, Muhammed. Men need such an outlet. According to the law of the Hajj, there is no further contact between the man and the woman and the offspring of such unions are considered blessed. They are well-treated."

"It is not what I want!"

"Consider, nephew. You have won a few converts but they are ill-received. If you want to conquer Arabia you must give heed to the needs of the people. Father Michael himself has shown us how such concessions have benefited the Roman faith."

Waraqa nodded. He had instructed the Arabian in the spiritual disciplines of the Church of Rome and now acted as interpreter of his visions.

"It is a simple matter of adaptation," he agreed. "In time, the root of such practices is lost. The common people have short memories. If you retain the Hajj you will satisfy this generation. Later it may even form the heart of the new religion." He looked at the Kaaba, which was still devoid of its outer covering. It stood on a marble plinth; the single room a majestic fifty feet in height. Within, were three tall pillars supporting structure of the roof. In time, it would be swathed in black, becoming a reminder of the sacred stone set in the south-east corner of the foundation.

"It is said that at the time of Adam, when the stone fell from the sky, it was pure white," Abu Talib offered. "It cleansed worshippers and absorbed their sin. That is why, today, it is black."

The sun danced off the white sand dazzling their eyes. Muhammed felt the trickle of sweat beneath his robes. It was not unpleasant.

"It is well to remember that Jesus Christ is seen as the cornerstone of the Christian faith," Waraqa said. "There is a clear reference in the Psalms. 'The stone which the builders refused is become the head of the corner.' By allowing this stone to become the focus of worship by your followers it can be said that all the references in the Bible relate to the sacred stone of the Kaaba."

Muhammed gazed at his cousin with renewed interest.

"So!" he said at length. "We will allow the moon stone of the Kaaba to replace the man-god of the Christian scriptures."

In the minds and the hearts of those who followed the Prophet a barrier was erected, a black stone that would forever form a stumbling-block to their vision of the true God.

Chapter 7
Twice-Born

2 July, 1943

Ernst Karltenbrunner used the butt held between his nicotine stained fingers to light another cigarette before grinding out the first in the loaded ashtray.

"How long have I been head of the RuSHA," he demanded of Martin Bormann, "and yet I'm still constantly bypassed."

Bormann shook his head sympathetically. "Himmler was clever," he admitted. "He had to make sure you wouldn't take over where Heydrich left off, so he removed the responsibility for personnel and economic questions from the Security Department. The Reichsführer couldn't afford to have a repetition of Heydrich's struggle for power."

"He died at a very opportune moment for the Reichsführer," Karltenbrunner conceded. "Given another year and Himmler might have found himself an inmate of Dachau. Heydrich was an unscrupulous man." He drew deeply on his cigarette and thrust his bottom lip forward funnelling the smoke towards the ceiling. "I've realised there's more to it than just a question of politics. If you're not one of Himmler's chosen few, you don't stand a chance. That's the power base of the SS, and I'm an outsider."

Bormann smiled to himself. He had initially been somewhat surprised at Himmler's choice of a successor to Heydrich. Ernst Karltenbrunner, an attorney from Linz was by comparison with the men whom Himmler normally surrounded himself, almost unkempt. He was tall and loose limbed with a scarred face and fingernails that were invariably cracked and dirty. Karltenbrunner was more the sort of man Adolf Hitler had surrounded himself with in the early days of National Socialism.

"Himmler's a very little man," Bormann commented. "He buries himself in his mysteries in order to create an appearance of power. But Heydrich was a sly bastard, he knew just how to crawl when the Reichsführer was around, yet he manipulated him. No doubt, he pretended to be party to his Knights of the Round Table crap, and Himmler was convinced he was a true disciple, meantime Judas was laughing up his sleeve."

Karltenbrunner massaged the scar on his cheek thoughtfully. "How much does the Führer know about what goes on in the upper ranks of the SS?"

Martin Bormann leaned forward in his seat, his sharp features intense. "No-one in the Reich really knows what goes on. That's why a loyal supporter in the upper hierarchy would be of great benefit to the Party. The Führer, of course, is convinced of Himmler's total allegiance. His ingratiating little Ignatius Loyola always gives the appearance of absolute faithfulness. Hitler indulges the Reichsführer's secrecy as harmless game-playing, without realising that he could be building a power-base right under his nose that might ultimately topple him. Himmler's more ambitious than he looks, I'm convinced of it."

Karltenbrunner examined the burning tip of his cigarette reflectively. "I needn't tell you that you can count on me at all times to keep you informed," he said. "The Führer has my absolute loyalty and support."

4 July 1943

"Are you ready for this?" Karl Wolff asked.

She turned her head away. The finality of it was terrifying. Her face had lost its colour and over the past weeks her features had become pinched as the strain threatened to engulf her. Wolff longed to cry out to her to stop - to hold her in his arms and tell her it no longer mattered. Again and again he marvelled at the strength manifested in a frame that hardly seemed built for it. And now, at the penultimate hour, he was not sure that she would be able to pull it off.

Wolff put his arm around her shoulders.

"Marianne?"

He wondered for a moment of brief panic, what he would do if she wavered, but she gave him no opportunity to find out. Looking up at him, her eyes were like flint.

"I'm ready."

"I'll be leaving in five minutes," he spoke tersely. "I'll wait for you at the appointed spot. Leave in approximately twenty minutes but make certain there are witnesses. At least two people should see you go."

"And the body?"

"It's already in the boot. Everything is in order. Be calm and drive slowly and carefully. We can't afford to have any mishaps."

She managed a small smile. "Karl?"

"Yes?"

"Hold me."

Wolff took her in his arms and drew her to him. She felt small and vulnerable, her body unexpectedly compliant. Impulsively, Karl Wolff leaned down and kissed her. Her mouth was soft and responsive beneath his and for a long moment she clung to him.

At length he drew away and cupped her face in his hands. "I must leave. Berger will be waiting for me. Will you be alright?"

"I'll be fine, don't worry."

Marianne heard the car start up in the courtyard below and stood a little back from the window to watch the two men leave. She could still feel the pressure of Karl's mouth on her own. Abruptly she turned away and poured herself a schnapps, drinking it neat, allowing the searing heat of the raw liquid to burn strength into her. The unreality of the moment was accentuated by the effect of the drink, so that when she descended the stairs to the courtyard fifteen minutes later, she felt a pace removed from all that was about to take place.

As Marianne approached the gate, she deliberately clashed the gears of the Mercedes so that the small knot of soldiers grinned and exchanged snide comments when they saw a woman at the wheel. Nodding at the guard on duty, she drew out onto the road.

It was not uncommon for Marianne von Ingolstadt to be seen at Wewelsburg, although the presence of any woman at the Reich SS leader's school was the exception rather than the rule. Her work with the Ahnenerbe brought her into contact with many members of the SS hierarchy and she was a well known figure to many of them. Over the years since her inception into the Ahnenerbe, she had matured into a woman whose quiet poise was offset by a steely determination. She was fascinating rather than beautiful. Men were vitally attracted to her and puzzled by her enigmatic character.

She took the road from the training barracks, driving slowly and steadily as Karl Wolff had directed. All the time she was aware of the unnerving presence of the corpse in the trunk behind her, and her knuckles were white on the steering wheel as she sought to direct her attention to the road. The engine of the car began to toil and Marianne shifted into third gear. She glanced at her watch. In just under five minutes she would reach the spot and it would all be over. Looking up, her eyes widened in horror. She had veered over into the middle of the road and a lorry, approaching rapidly from the opposite direction was bearing down on her.

Marianne caught a glimpse of the shocked expression of the other driver as he fought to contain his vehicle. She swung her steering-wheel forcing the Mercedes back onto the right hand side of the road, and felt the jolt of impact as the car grazed the bank and slewed to a halt several meters on. The truck's horn blared and receded as the vehicle passed, leaving an uneasy silence in its wake. Marianne's legs were unsteady as she got out to inspect the damage. The fender was dented and there was a long scrape down the side of the car, but the tyres were unscathed. She climbed back in and started the engine, leaning her head on the steering wheel for just a moment before shifting into first gear and pulling out onto the road.

The vehicle that Karl Wolff and Gottlob Berger were driving was parked just off a hairpin bend, protected from the drop by a low, dry-stone wall. Wolff's eyes widened as he saw the car.

"What the hell happened?"

Marianne shook her head. "I'll tell you later. Let's just get this over with."

He nodded, but his mouth was tight with anger. "We must hurry," he said. "There's not much traffic on the road, but we can't afford to waste any more time."

Gottlob Berger slipped behind the wheel of the Mercedes.

"Gottlob, please be careful!"

He grinned at her. "Sure," he promised. "Don't worry about me. Just keep well out of the way."

They watched as he drove about a hundred meters down the road and turned the car around. He revved the engine hard as he approached the bend and at the last instant hit the brakes so that the tyres screamed in protest. He impacted the low wall at just the right angle, with sufficient power to scatter the rocks without carrying the car and himself the extra couple of meters over the edge. Wolff whooped his approval as Gottlob climbed out of the car grinning broadly.

"Do you think there's a place for me in the movies?" he asked.

Marianne wiped her damp palms down the seams of her skirt.

"Let's get moving," she urged, "before someone comes!"

Wolff examined the front of the vehicle and nodded his satisfaction.

"There's a couple of rocks to be shifted before she goes over."

Berger opened the boot of the Mercedes and Marianne turned away leaning her weight against the back door of the car. She had no wish to see the woman again or dwell on the events that had taken place in the crypt two nights before. She heard the crunch of the men's shoes on the gravel and felt the Mercedes sag as they set the body behind the wheel.

"The petrol, Marianne!"

She acted on the order immediately, fetching the can from the floor of the other vehicle. The Gerry-can was heavier than she had expected and by the time she hauled it over to them, they had already pushed the car to the edge of the precipice.

"Hurry Marianne!" Berger called urgently.

Wolff took the can from her and doused the body and the front seat liberally. They were working fast, aware that at any moment they might hear the engine of an approaching vehicle. The woman's lifeless features stared at Marianne from behind the wheel, waxy pale. Blood that had trickled from her nose and her mouth had dried and blackened, giving her a ghoulish appearance. Marianne suppressed a shudder as she accepted the empty can from Wolff and turned away.

The two men put their backs to the boot of the Mercedes and pushed. It gained speed suddenly and they turned to watch it go. The right front wheel went first and for a moment it seemed to hang clumsily over the edge as though undecided, then it tilted and rolled.

Mesmerised they watched its descent, praying that the body would not be thrown free. The noise reverberated throughout the valley as it smashed from ledge to ledge in a slow motion fall. There was the flash of an explosion and it became a fireball tumbling with the loose rock and ripped metal, seeking a final resting place. It caught, rocked and stopped. Nothing moved.

A bird sounded a few tentative notes into the lingering silence and then burst into full-throated song. Black smoke drifted quietly upwards, creating a steady undisturbed funnel. The men looked at one another and grinned.

"Congratulations Marianne, you are officially dead!" Gottlob Berger said and slapped her on the shoulder.

Wolff took in her expression at a glance. She was almost as pale as the corpse that had gone over the cliff in her place, and her mouth was vulnerable as he had not seen it before. He realised she was close to tears.

"Let's get out of here!" he said urgently.

They examined the area swiftly to ensure nothing was left behind. Marianne slipped into the back of the car and Wolff glanced back at her. "Get some rest," he instructed. "You deserve it."

Chapter 8
Twice-Born

A clatter of hoofs on the cobblestones of the courtyard brought servants hurrying to the door to meet the newcomers. It was night and the flare of the torches illuminated the steaming flanks and frosty breath of the horses. The loose cowls of their coarse brown robes threw the faces of the monks into deep shadow so that their appearance in the uncertain light of the flame was frightening. The horses shuddered and wheezed in the cold air as their riders dismounted and, at a word, they were led away to the stables by young grooms who were trying with their knuckles to force the sleep from their eyes.

The year was 1070 and the domain was that of Godfroi de Bouillon on the edge of the Ardennes Forest.

Food was called for; servants were summoned to provide for the needs of the company. De Bouillon left his wife's bed, washed his face and made his way downstairs to meet his guests. He was a powerful figure, both in stature and in influence. Long dark hair, tousled by sleep, met with an untrimmed beard but Godfroi's features were those of a cultured man.

The leader of the monks threw back the cowl of his robe as the master of the house entered the room. He was well-known to him and, indeed, had acted as his tutor when de Bouillon was a youth.

"Peter," Godfroi, greeted him. "Where do you hale from and why this night visit? Do you come in peace?"

Peter the Hermit laughed briefly. "We hale from Calabria, in Southern Italy and we come in peace," he assured him. "We have journeyed many days to get here."

De Bouillon called for a glass of wine but refused the food his man-servant offered him.

"Then you are on a mission," he said. "Are you passing through, or does this involve me?"

"It involves you directly," Peter the Hermit answered. "But I beg to speak with you privately."

Three of Peter's monks accompanied the two men into an ante-chamber where a fire had been newly set and burned strongly. Peter stood before it with his hands linked behind him allowing the warmth to permeate his bones; his crown was tonsured and thin brown hair covered his ears and the nape of his neck. His eyes were black and penetrating over a beak of a nose and there was a merciless twist to his thin mouth.

"All my men can be trusted to the utmost," the Hermit told de Bouillon, "These three I trust with my life. Nothing you or I say will go beyond these walls."

Godfroi de Bouillon pushed his fingers through his beard and scratched his chin.

"So tell me," he said. "What is your business here?"

"Ursus has made a call. The time is right to seize Jerusalem. In a little while there will be a call to arms."

De Bouillon raised his eyebrows and leaned forward in his seat.

"The Holy Land," he breathed. "It is as I had hoped. Since the Mandylion was captured by the Turks we have eagerly awaited an order to move."

"Ursus asks you to prepare the way in France. We would have you donate a tract of land for my monks."

He nodded. "Where?"

Peter the Hermit drew his lips back in a humourless smile.

"Orval."

"The site of Dagobert's death?"

"It is holy ground."

"I will seek the patronage of my aunt the Duchess of Lorraine. The land will come to your Order in her name."

Peter nodded his satisfaction. "There is another matter."

"Speak."

"It will be necessary to ensure the election of a pope sympathetic to our cause, a charismatic man who will rally the people. The call for a holy crusade must come from him."

"Ursus has a man in mind?"

"You know him. Odo, Abbot of Cluny." Peter the Hermit surveyed Godfroi de Bouillon through slitted eyes. "He is a nobleman of some intellect and a man of tact.   We need one who can bring about a new understanding with the Byzantium Church. But that is enough for the night," he said. "My men have ridden hard and will need to rest. We will meet again on the morrow."

It was after midday when the meeting was reconvened. Servants had laid a meal on a trestle table under a spreading oak on the lawn and the men ate with good appetite.

"When Jerusalem is taken," Peter the monk said, "the rightful king must assume the throne."

Godfroi's eyes were carefully hooded and expressionless. He had spent the remainder of the night in deep contemplation and he had anticipated their thinking. By inheritance, he was of the Merovingian line of kings, one of several pretenders to the throne but the fates had ordained that he was the most eminently apposite. While there were others who could lay some claim to Jerusalem's throne, none, apart from King Tafur himself, possessed Godfroi de Bouillon's pedigree.

King Tafur, also known as Ursus, headed the inner circle of the Black Order and, should the Holy Land be taken, only he had the power to crown Jerusalem's King. The fingers of destiny were closing; several of the holy relics were already in de Bouillon's possession. The Mandylion remained elusive: the Mandylion, the sword, and the city of Jerusalem.

"I am here to instruct and prepare you to establish a secret order at Orval," Peter said. "This is to be a holy knighthood; fighting men carefully chosen and fully prepared for battle. My men and I will remain here to aid you until all things are readied then we will ride ahead of you into the Holy Land. With the aid of the new pope, Europe will be called to arms against the infidel and Jerusalem will fall into our hands."

"King Tafur has chosen the man to head the army?"

"Ursus has spoken," Peter the Hermit confirmed. "You will lead and your brother Baudouin will ride at your side. If you make it alive into the Holy City, you will be given the throne. Once it is captured, it is committed to my monks to carry the Head of Wisdom into the Holy Land."

Godfroi looked up in awe. "Our most sacred relic?"

Peter's narrow lips compressed into a smile.

"The Head belongs in Jerusalem. May God go with you. You do not venture alone."

Chapter 9
Twice-Born

1943

Jean Cocteau's thin, sharp-featured face was drawn in a petulant pout. Aware always of the impression on an audience, even when none was present, he had arranged his body carefully on the couch and the hand which held his cigarette drooped languidly. His head was drawn slightly back and his eyes hooded against the smoke.

Opposite him, Jean Marais, an actor from South Africa, and Cocteau's current lover, was sprawled out in an armchair reading a book. Marais' acting career had begun in earnest in 1937 after Cocteau saw him audition and offered him a role in his play Oedipe-Roi, and their association had begun from that point. Marais both admired Cocteau and recognised a need to profit from the Cocteau's reputation. As an eccentric, and a prolific and somewhat controversial writer, Cocteau attracted reflected glory for Marais whenever they were seen together. By sharing Cocteau's bed he had also gained leads in his latest plays. 'La Machine a Ecrire', which Cocteau had written when Marais was demobilised, was playing at present, offending the critics with its homosexual undertones, but drawing audiences nevertheless.

Jean Cocteau stubbed out his cigarette and stood up.

"Where are you going?"

"Out. I'll be back later."

"Do you want me to come with you?"

Cocteau shrugged into his fur coat and combed back his thick hair, checking his reflection in the hall mirror.

"Not tonight Jeannot." When he turned to face the younger man his expression softened the words. "I need time alone."

Marais said nothing but smiled to cover the twinge of resentment. He stood up and adjusted Cocteau's tie; the gesture was intentionally intimate, like a wife seeing her husband off to work."

"I hate being left alone when you go out," he chided.

Cocteau touched his cheek. "I know, I don't expect to be too long but I need to walk a bit, I have some ideas for a new play."

An icy breeze found its way between the buildings, chasing leaves and scraps of paper. Cocteau drew his coat more firmly around him and set off purposefully down the street. It was dusk and from the scudding clouds he suspected that before the evening was out there would be more rain. Cafés and bars were doing brisk business with those who had just left work and a steady stream of people was heading for the Metro. In contrast with the streets, the underground was warm and a hot, dusty wind preceded the train. The station was packed with evening commuters forcing Cocteau to elbow his way through to reach the open doors. An elderly man tipped his hat as he passed and from further down the train a woman stared at him curiously. Wherever Cocteau went in Paris there were those who recognised him, a fact which in most moods he found gratifying, but tonight was simply an irritation. He tilted the rim of his hat a little lower, throwing his face into shadow, and turned up the collar of his coat.

Even before the war, Cocteau's acclaim had spread beyond the borders of France and his personality was such that he was constantly surrounded by admirers and hangers-on. The occupation of Paris had scarcely affected his lifestyle; it was still possible to live well with the right means and the connections, and Cocteau had both. His only expressed concern was whether he would continue to find a supply of opium, but even that had not, so far, proved to be a problem.

Paris had a need to be entertained and Cocteau obliged with a steady stream of plays. The Germans encouraged the performance of the arts as a witness to the world that Paris, although occupied, was not oppressed. It added credence to the collaboration. Even Germany's acclaimed Arno Breker, a friend of Cocteau's, was brought in to exhibit his sculptures, which seemed at this sensitive period of time to depict the perfect Aryan male.

Jean Cocteau appeared to have no interest in politics as long as his own lifestyle remained unruffled. Apart from a few scathing comments directed at Vichy and the Nazis, remarks expected of him as an artist, there was nothing to link him with the Resistance. He had in fact, warm ties with Germany and consorted with a number of German intellectuals during the occupation, yet it is possible that Jean Cocteau was one of the most influential figures in Europe during the war period.

The newsreel was already in progress when René de Bar took a seat, three rows from the back of the theatre. It was one of Goebbels documentaries on the Jewish Question and it was almost played out when Cocteau slipped into the seat beside him. De Bar made no acknowledgement of his presence and it was not until the main feature started that he handed Cocteau the manila envelope. The two men exchanged words quietly without taking their eyes off the flickering screen and then de Bar stood up and left. Cocteau waited until the closing scene of the film before he too made his way to the exit and shrugged into his coat as he felt the bite of the night air. On the street corner a German soldier leaned over to take a light for his cigarette from the cupped palms of his friend and his face was illuminated for a moment in the flare of the match. Cocteau waited until they were gone before stepping out onto the pavement.

He made his way back across the city to the Theatre Hebertot where his latest play was being staged. He needed time to study the intelligence that de Bar had passed him and with Marais in the apartment, it was too risky. The theatre was empty and silent; there would be no performance until the next night. The janitor nodded at him as he passed and went back to sweeping the foyer. Cocteau switched on a light in the small office and locked the door behind him. The smell of smoke had become a permanent part of the room and, as if it triggered a response in Cocteau, he took his silver case from the inside pocket of his coat and lit a cigarette before opening the envelope. The room was cold and he could feel the chill working up through his feet. Sitting down, he thumbed through the typewritten pages. De Bar had done a thorough job. With the information coming in from Paris and the network that was beginning to operate, somewhat hesitantly, across the rest of France, a clearer picture was developing. His organisation would ultimately control most of the intelligence fed to both the Allies and the Germans.

He took a sheet of paper from the drawer and sat down at the desk. The outline of the play was already formulated in his mind, but it was now necessary to weave the information de Bar had given him, into the structure employing codes and ciphers whose true meaning would be understood by only a handful of chosen men. Jean Cocteau's selection for the task by the organisation was by no means co-incidental.

It was late when he finally left and the cafes were beginning to close, people were hurrying once again in the direction of the Metro to catch the last trains. A light still burned in Cocteau's apartment. Jean Marais was still reading, and it was clear from his expression that he was peeved. Cocteau's elation was not to be dampened. He stripped off his clothes and walked across the room to the bed, feeling the deep pile of the carpet beneath his feet. Light from the lamp played over his body. As he removed the book from Marais' hands and laid it on the bedside table he recognised behind the mask of boredom in the younger man's face, a flicker of interest in his eyes.

Chapter 10
Twice-Born

12 July, 1943

Frau Anna von Ingolstadt received the news of her daughter's death with such calmness that Matthias was frightened.

Now in her mid-forties, Anna was still an attractive woman, although tension and weariness often gave her the appearance of severity. She sat quietly in her armchair staring into the empty fireplace, her hands, usually so busy, lay upturned in her lap. The fine lines around her eyes had deepened and become laced like the web of a spider, and her mouth was compressed to a thin line with the effort it took to keep control. Underneath her right eye a small tic was the only betrayal of her inner turmoil.

For as long as her children could remember, Anna von Ingolstadt had pinned her long, straight hair back into a bun at the nape of her neck; to see her with her hair down seemed almost as shameful to them as it would be to see her naked. Discipline was central to her nature and the home pivoted on Anna's created order. Now with the swiftness and cruelty of one blow, that order was destroyed and the family looked on helplessly as Anna fought a hidden battle with this crisis.

A week had passed before Matthias at last took the courage to try to reach her. He had been feeling desperately alone as though the loss of his daughter's death had dealt him a double blow and his wife had been taken also.

That night as they prepared for bed, he placed his hands on her shoulders.

"Anna, we must talk."

She turned her head away, avoiding his eyes. She had loosened her hair and brushed it out and it fell, long and sleek over her shoulders. This time of intimacy, when the bedroom door was closed on the day's troubles, was one that Matthias still cherished. Anna's body was no longer as perfect or as supple as when they had first married, her breasts had lost their tautness and her stomach swelled gently after the births of their children. Still, after all these years, his love for her had not diminished.

"I remember that first night at Dieter's party," he said. "You stood out among those flighty young things, and to me you were the most beautiful."

She looked up at him and he was alarmed to see death written in her eyes.

"We've lost her," he said, "and we have to accept it or we'll lose ourselves with her."

"How can I? Marianne's dead! Do you really expect me to move on as though nothing has happened?" She pulled away from him angrily and sat down on the edge of the bed. Matthias sat next to her, feeling the iciness of the brass bedstead against his back. He could see the ashen reflection of her face in the mirror above the washstand.

"I'm not asking you to pretend that nothing's happened. I'm asking you not to cut yourself off from Horst and me. I want to share in your grief, and I need you to share mine."

For the first time he saw with relief that she was close to tears.

"How can you know what I am feeling?" she flung at him suddenly. "How can you possibly know what I've felt all these years?"

"What do you mean?"

She flung herself at him, beating his chest with her fists. "You don't know me at all!" she screamed. "You have never stopped to think what I was going through."

Matthias caught her by the wrists and held her. He was confused and uneasy.

"What are you talking about?"

Anna's face registered her contempt. "Have you forgotten who I am? I am a Jew. I am a Jew, Matthias. In a house where my children express hatred of Jews. Living with you and my son in your SS uniforms, going out day after day to help in the slaughter of my people! They have taken my son and filled his head with pagan beliefs and given him the uniform of the Death's Head. And now, they have sent him, a Jew, to work in Saschenhausen!"

Matthias von Ingolstadt released her hands and shook his head slowly.

"Why didn't you tell me what you were feeling? All these years, we've been happy. I thought everything was fine. Why didn't you say something?"

She laughed bitterly. "What was there to say? Did you imagine that by changing my name I had somehow changed my being? Did you think that Judaism was so totally expunged from my nature that I felt nothing for the suffering of the Jews?" She dropped her head into her hands. "In this separation from my people I have finally understood what it is to be a Jew. And now the God of Abraham, Isaac and Jacob is allowing me to share in their suffering. Did I think that I could hide myself from him when I assumed a new name?"

She began to weep and the sound of it tore at his heart. He could think of nothing to say to her.

At length, Anna lay back on her pillow. Her face in the dark frame of her hair was very pale and her eyes were swollen.

"At least Marianne went to her death never knowing that her mother was Jewish. I could not have born it if she had died hating me."

Adolf von Ingolstadt turned his face away. They had drawn their curtains but it was suddenly as though the darkness had pushed through into the sanctity of their bedroom. The sounds of the night closed in on them and a chill reached into Matthias enclosing his heart like a fist.

Richard Heydrich had made him pay bitterly for his silence. Anna would never know that he had also been made to suffer for their deception. But the secret that had died with Heydrich still hung over them like a curse.

It seemed like hours before the regular pattern of Greta's breathing told Matthias that she was asleep. He slipped from the bed and went downstairs to the darkened living-room.

"What have I done?" Not since the last war had Matthias von Ingolstadt wept but he was crying now.

It was too late for such stark clarity. He longed desperately to change the decisions made so long ago but vision is often slow in coming and when the axe falls there is no going back.

"What have I done?"

For the first time, the self-deception was stripped away and Matthias knew the depths to which he had fallen. He had systematically capitulated to the SS until it stripped him of everything.

The Anna he had married was irretrievably lost to him the moment he entered the Schutzstaffel yet he deliberately chose the Order over his relationship. Greta, he now knew, had helplessly watched the systematic indoctrination of her children, as they were swept away from her with the tide, yet he had not lifted one finger to prevent it.

"When an opponent declares, "I will not come over to your side," Adolf Hitler said in a speech in 1933, "I calmly say, 'Your child belongs to us already.'"

Marianne and Horst were children of the State; obedient, robotic Nazis who, at a tender age, had sworn to live and die for the ungodly tyrant who ruled not just Germany, but the hearts and minds of Germans.

Sanity mocked him and slipped further from his grasp. Matthias von Ingolstadt hammered his forehead with his open palm. He was sweating with anxiety; tumbling out of control through pitch-blackness.

He had willingly surrendered his faith in God for the dubious reward of promotion in the SS. When the Concordat was signed between Hitler and Cardinal Pacelli of the Roman Catholic Church, Matthias persuaded himself that God had sanctified Nazi beliefs. Had he really believed it? Surely he had recognised in making his vow to Adolf Hitler that he was selling his soul?

It was crystal clear to him now that the Nazi Party first removed the church then occupied the vacuum. The Reichsführer-SS had stringently regulated every aspect of their existence and then demanded their souls! Christian marriages were outlawed; Christian baptisms were forbidden and a priest could not be brought in to bring absolution to the dying. The anti-Christian nature of the Order could not have been more apparent.

Matthias von Ingolstadt remembered how Hitler had impressed everyone with his great works in the beginning. He created employment, raised health standards, improved working conditions, built roads and expanded industry. He had given priority to the education and training of the youth and introduced social security and benefits for the aged. The people were more than ready to trade individual freedoms for peace and security. But even that, he realised, was a mirage.

"The world can only be ruled by fear," Hitler had declared. "Terror is the most effective political instrument!" And Matthias recalled another of the Führer's speeches: "In all confidence we can go to the limits of inhumanity, if we bring happiness back to the German people."

Adolf Hitler's idea of happiness began with a process of elimination of the enemies of his regime and went on to remove the retarded, the mentally weak and the aged. Reintroduction of the old racial stereotypes of Jew and Mongolian were generally popular as they served to glorify Germans. How easily Matthias had obliterated Anna's past from his mind. In the process, he had seldom stopped to consider how she viewed the hounding, beating, incarceration and murder of her people.

The Wehrmacht, the SA, the SS and the Gestapo had become vehicles of terror, which were formed to consume, devour and destroy. By a process of methodical indoctrination, the Nazi party had sucked the soul from the German people replaced it with hatred, hatred and more hatred. Nazism in all its forms, Matthias realised, was the creation of Adolf Hitler and therefore the only true reflection of his character. He sat forward in his arm-chair, suddenly riveted and chilled as this realisation struck him.

The Waffen-SS, was a machine; well-oiled, immaculately turned out and with all the cold, pristine beauty of a weapon of war. It was totally devoid of warmth or compassion; it was obedient to the death and its very nature was destruction. Whether intentionally or otherwise, the SS was the outward persona of the Reichsführer whose monster it was and it utterly demonstrated Himmler's satanic core.

Matthias had made the Nazi will his will and therefore their guilt was his guilt. He had chosen the regime over God and that, he knew, was enough to damn him.

Chapter 11
Twice-Born

A hot breeze blew in off Lake Geneva causing both men to sweat uncomfortably in their suits. Although it was only mid afternoon, Freiberg's heavy jowls were already dark with stubble and he was beginning to relish the thought of a shower and shave.

They had chosen to walk along the edge of the lake. The weather was slightly overcast but it had, as yet, brought little change to the heat-wave. Flowers grew in neatly tended beds; a profusion of mauve and orange; their colour accentuated by the grey backdrop of the water.

"Doris would have loved those," Chaim said. "She was a great flower lover."

"You've never told me what happened to your marriage."

"We were divorced a couple of years ago," Chaim said. "I think she got tired of waiting for me to come home. I always put my career first and assumed she would understand."

Michael glanced at his friend. "It's a common mistake."

"I was sure everything I was doing was for her," Freiberg said. "By the time she pointed out that she married the man and not the politician it was too late."

"Would you have done things differently had you known?"

Freiberg sighed. "That's the silly part," he confessed. "I think I would have done it exactly the same. It was actually for me, not for her and it was only after she left that I realised how much I had lost." He paused in his stride and looked directly at Michael. "Don't make the same error, Segal. Secure the relationship you have with Gabriele as soon as you can and make sure you hold onto her."

Michael smiled. "I'll do that," he said.

A pavement café with bright yellow umbrellas shading the tables caught Chaim's attention.

"Care for a coffee, old chap?"

They seated themselves at a table and Chaim leaned on his

elbows and toyed with his the brim of his hat as they waited for their order to arrive. Conversation turned, as usual, to the subject of the book.

"Paul Vignon had the idea that the shroud was a contact print made by the body of the crucified man. There's a lot of urea in sweat, which he thought may have reacted with certain of the spices used in the burial process," Michael said.

"Such as?"

"Myrrh and aloe spread on the shroud causing discolouration."

"What do you think?"

Michael shook his head. "Unlikely," he replied. "Vignon did some experimentation and came up with a couple of roughly human-shaped stains on his fabric. Nothing with any detail."

"There's an abiding problem with the body contact theory," Freiberg added.

Michael smiled. Chaim had covered most bases in his own study on the subject.

"Distortion of the cloth?"

"Exactly."

"The cloth naturally drapes itself over an inert form and any image would definitely distort," he agreed. There's no suggestion of any warping of the shroud image."

"So, what are we left with?"

"There may be other natural phenomena, which we are unaware of, that could project an image," Michael said, "but no matter how it was created, if the cloth was draped over a body, there would be distortion. Vignon experimented with a direct contact print of a head. The reproduction was far wider than the head itself. The shroud image was definitely not made by direct contact with the body."

"What about supernatural intervention?" Chaim put the abiding question with a degree of embarrassment.

"Look at it this way," Michael said. "Even if this was a divinely inspired resurrection of a dead body, certain natural laws still pertain."

"Cloth draped over the body would still distort."

Michael nodded. "That's my feeling. This thing is a mystery, and at the moment I don't have the answer."

The coffee was ersatz and not particularly pleasant. Chaim emptied his cup without appearing to notice. Michael wished he had ordered a beer.

"Have another look at the possibility of forgery," Freiberg said. "I know men like Vignon have found no trace of pigments on the linen and there is nothing to suggest brush strokes. What about scorching?"

"It's a possibility," Michael said. "In which case, it has been carefully and even delicately executed. But then we're back to the old question, why in the negative?"

"It makes no sense," Chaim agreed. "Whenever the shroud image was made no forger could have imagined that a later generation would photograph it and view the representation as it was intended." He scratched himself thoughtfully behind the ears; examined the inside rim of his black Homburg and, holding the dented crown delicately between fingers and thumb, set it back on his head.

"So, really, the only answer that fits the bill is the one that is most impossible."

Michael Segal raised his eyebrows. "What's that?"

"It has to be an early photograph."

Chapter 12
Twice-Born

1088

Odo, who had been an abbot at the Benedictine monastery at Cluny, was elected Pope in 1088 taking the name Urban II. Under this papacy, penitential pilgrimage was to become a vital expression of spirituality, and Bernard was the man raised up by the unseen powers to join him in inciting a crusade to capture Jerusalem.

Bernard of Fontaine-les-Dijon, a young Burgundian nobleman, was slight, small-boned, with blonde hair, a ruddy complexion and a beard that tended towards red. There was fire in his expression, fervency in his actions and in his eyes an unearthly light. He had arrived at the Abbey of Citeaux only three years before, with a group of thirty-five friends and relatives whom he had persuaded to enter the monastery, bringing new zeal and a revived asceticism to the weakened Cistercian order.

Bernard's influence would also later serve to draw men into the ranks of the Templars. This was an era, more than any other, in which personal desires were abnegated in favour of zealous, and even militant, Christianity. His spiritual power and charisma were far-reaching and almost irresistible. From one end of Europe to another, men rallied to the call of the cross and the service of Christ.

"The Holy City of our Lord has been trampled by the infidel!" Pope Urban II shouted to the crowd. "The most holy things of God have been desecrated and trodden underfoot. Is it fitting for us to ignore the pleas of our Byzantine brothers who are crying out for help? Can we who are free fail to heed the cries of oppressed?"

In 1085 a small contingent of knights had been dispatched from Robert, Count of Flanders, to Alexius Comnenus of Constantinople. Ten years later a group of Byzantine delegates approached the Pope for help in stemming the tide of the Seljuk Turks which, by taking Nicaea, less than a hundred miles from Constantinople, had succeeded in reducing the Byzantine Empire to a small Greek stronghold. Pope

Urban II graciously lifted the ban of excommunication on the Byzantine Emperor Alexius, but the impassioned call to arms was less about the relief of Constantinople than the reclaiming of Jerusalem for the Mother Church. The seizure of the Holy City would not be without apparent reward for the common knight.

"I am calling on you to become knights of Christ! Any man among you could die tonight and rot in Purgatory for your sins without any hope of release. I am offering you not only indulgences for yourselves but for your dead, who cannot participate in this spiritual journey. Is there a man among you who does not desire to release the souls of those who are bound in chains and languishing in the horrors of eternal darkness? Until now, the Church has kept herself from bloodshed in accordance with the will of our Lord, but power is granted to me by God Himself to make a decree binding on earth with certainty that it will be bound in heaven!

"I declare today, by the will of the Almighty, that pilgrims will be armed to prevent the Saracens from grinding the faithful of God beneath their feet."

Pope Urban, fearful in his golden robes, towering mitre, golden chains and rings, stretched his hands out towards the gathered throng.

"If you want to ensure your own salvation, take up your sword and fight! All those who bind themselves to this cause with penitence and show no base motives of greed or vengeance will earn full remission of his sins and no further earthly penances will be imposed upon him by the Church!"

"God wills it!" the people shouted.

The papal throne had been set on a platform in a field outside the eastern gate of Clermont where a great crowd had gathered. Cardinals and bishops distributed cloth crosses to be sewn onto the outer garments of the deluge of penitents as an assurance that their wives and families would be given the protection of the Church of Rome.

One other man, besides the Pope and Bernard, most credited with the call to arms for the first Crusade was Peter, known as the Hermit, who claimed he was in possession of a letter from heaven granting him a sure mandate for such a mission. The monks from

Calabria in Southern Italy, under the patronage of Godfroi de Bouillon's aunt, had been housed in a monastery built for them at Orval. Godfroi and his brother Baudouin were receiving intense preparation and training for the task that lay ahead of them at the hand of Peter the Hermit and his men. The shadowy Order seeded in the soil prepared by Simon the Magician was about to make a concerted effort to gain the world.

Chapter 13
Twice-Born

October 1943
Officially, Marianne von Ingolstadt was dead. The process of change was tediously slow, but gradually her new identity was beginning to take shape and a new face was emerging from the old. She had been unprepared for the psychological impact her 'death' was to have on her, coupled with the long-term imprisonment within the walls of Wewelsburg and her isolation from other human beings. She was like a small craft adrift on a vast and dangerous expanse of water and there was little to anchor herself to. On one of the rare occasions that Karl Wolff came out to Wewelsburg, she clung desperately to him.

"I don't know if I can cope with this Karl, I'm still the same person inside. I don't know how to be anyone else and I don't want to be Ruth Leiman!"

"You can do it." Karl drew away from her, gripping her upper arms firmly. "You were chosen because you were the one woman we were sure would make it."

She shook her head and tears of despair flowed down her cheeks. You don't understand!" she flung at him. "You don't know how lonely this is. I don't even have the comfort of looking in the mirror and know that it's me I'm looking at. My past has gone, my family has gone and I don't even have the familiarity of my own face. I'm afraid, Karl. I'm terribly afraid of what I've done."

"Marianne, look at me!" He tilted her chin and waited until she was able to meet his eyes. "Not only can you do it," he said, "but you no longer have a choice. There is no going back. What you've done can't be reversed. In order to cope with it you have got to reach that point of acceptance and make the future work for you. Before Quedlinburg you were committed to doing a job because you believed it was your destiny. Has that commitment changed?"

She stood quietly looking up at him. "No," she said.

"Then take courage and go forward. Sometimes, in order to

gain the world, we must first lose ourselves. Nietzsche says that when you venture into the seas of unexplored emotions, clench your teeth, keep your eyes open and keep a firm hand on the helm. Sail straight over morality and past it. You will flatten and crush what is left of your own morality by daring to undertake such a voyage."

She smiled and drew away from him. "I think that any remaining vestige of morality was surrendered with my innocence, and I left that behind at Quedlinburg."

Wolff laughed and kissed her lightly. "A big speech from one who is still a child," he teased, and then added more seriously. "Wherever this path leads, Marianne, I won't be far behind."

In the forth month she felt the first fluttering movements of the child within her womb. With it came the knowledge that the period of intense mourning was passing and she was experiencing a related stirring of life within herself.

Dr. Kraus' work was over and at the request of the Reichsführer he and his surgical team met in one of Wewelsburg's more intimate dining rooms for a celebratory dinner before they were due to leave for Munich. Light from the corner standard lamp added a glow to the room already warmed by the fire.

Heinrich Himmler bowed slightly as he greeted the surgeon. "I must congratulate you Herr Doctor you have done a fine job."

"Thank you Reichsführer," he said stiffly.

"I trust you have found your time at Wewelsburg comfortable?"

"We have been very well cared for, Reichsführer, but my team and I feel that the work could have been accomplished far more easily in Munich."

"What do you mean?" There was a chill in Himmler's tone.

"I mean that these months spent here in Wewelsburg, separated from our families have been fruitful but could have been done just as well in conjunction with our normal lives."

"You were aware that there were unusual circumstances involved. This task required the utmost secrecy."

"With all due respect, Reichsführer, I believe we could have worked with the same level of secrecy in Munich, and with far less frustration to myself and my team."

Himmler nodded and in a conciliatory gesture indicated the chair beside him. "Please be so good as to sit down, Herr Doctor. I apologise for what you have been through, but I assure you it is essential to the war effort. You are flying back in the morning, I believe?"

Dr Kraus nodded. "I understand there is a light aircraft standing by to take us back."

"I want you to know that the work you have done and the time you have spent here will be more valuable and far-reaching than you realise," Himmler assured him as the waiter set bowls of steaming soup on the table in front of them. He picked up his spoon. "I trust your flight back will be most pleasant."

The morning air was crisp and clear and the sky above the mountain peaks a startling blue. The pilot already had the engine running and was performing a methodical check of the instruments as they came aboard. He raised a hand in greeting.

"Welcome, welcome aboard. We have excellent flying weather this morning."

The two men and the nursing sister were in good spirits, anxious to return and pick up the fragments of their lives after the long disruption and now that they were away from the atmosphere of Wewelsburg, there was some laughter and light hearted banter.

"So, how long will it take us to get home?" Dr. Kraus leaned over the seat to attract the attention of the pilot.

"As long as we don't meet any British en route, roughly an hour and a half," he replied, grinning at his little joke.

The engines changed their pitch and slowly the aircraft began to roll out, bouncing a little over the uneven runway. The car that had delivered the surgical team to the airstrip, turned away and headed back in the direction of Wewelsburg. Moments later the peaks of the mountain range lay beneath them, forming a broken sea of green and grey.

"There's Wewelsburg," the pilot called, pointing down at the castle, small and insignificant against the magnitude of its surroundings. The plane found its altitude and evened out as the pilot pointed its nose south.

"There's coffee in the flask down there, if one of you would care to pour it," he called out.

Kraus passed him a tin mug of steaming coffee and poured some for the others. He was about to pour a cup for himself when the pilot stopped him.

"Hold this for a moment, will you?" He passed his mug back to the doctor and glanced down at the instrument panel.

"Something wrong?"

"I don't know. One of the engines seems to be overheating. I'm heading back for the landing strip."

The aircraft banked and then as it made the turn, it coughed uncertainly, a thin line of smoke issued from beneath the wing and trailed behind them.

"Can we make it back on one engine?" The nurse asked anxiously.

There was no reply from the pilot and it was doubtful that he even heard the question. The gauges showed unmistakably that the second engine was overheating. They were still ten minutes from the landing strip and losing altitude fast.

From the grounds of Wewelsburg Castle, Heinrich Himmler, flanked by Obergruppenführer Wolff and Pohl, watched the approach of the light aircraft, his hands clenched tightly at his sides. The sound of the engine came to them across the distance, ragged and uncertain.

"Will they make it?" he asked anxiously.

Wolff shook his head, "It's almost impossible, there's still too much distance to cover."

The drone of the engine cut, caught and cut again. The plane glided for several more minutes before plunging silently into a suicidal dive and disappearing from sight behind the crest of a mountain. It was too far away to hear the impact, but a pall of black smoke rose to mark its position.

Himmler turned to face Wolff and smiled his relief. "It's done." He said.

**Chapter 14
Twice-Born**

Gabriele's postcard arrived later in the week and Michael read and reread it several times. The contents, as he had expected, were simple and innocuous, written in reply to her uncle Siegfried. She had apologised for the delay in writing and hoped he was having a wonderful holiday on the lake. She was, she said, missing him and longing to see him again. For Michael, at the present, it was enough.

Work on the book was progressing rapidly. Chaim Freiberg had been away for several weeks and Michael spent long hours in the library researching and making copious notes. He had traced the history of the Mandylion; its arrival in Edessa; its subsequent disappearance at a time of Christian persecution and its reappearance nearly five hundred years later from the niche in which it had been hidden, over the Kappe Gate of the city.

Concealment of the Mandylion would have taken place in about AD 57, possibly even before the first gospels were said to have been written, and the hermetically sealed niche had served to protect the relic from four major floods. Although the exact date of the cloth's rediscovery was not recorded, the Syrian born historian Evagrius recorded that it was employed as a talisman to protect the city against an attack of the Persians in AD 544. Michael read the account of how the citizens had tunnelled under their own walls to set fire to a mound of timber gathered by the Persians by which they intended to scale Edessa's fortifications. There was insufficient oxygen to set the timber alight but in their quandary, the Mandylion, "...the divinely made image not made by the hands of men, which Christ our God sent to King Abgar when he desired to see him.[30]" was brought out. Water was sprinkled over the image and then over the wood, the account read, and immediately the timber burst into flame.

---

[30] Evagrius, Ecclesiastical History, original text in Migne, Patrololgia graeca, vol. 86.

Michael Segal read it with considerable scepticism convinced that, in keeping with the times in which it was written, the account was laced with superstition; nevertheless, the Mandylion was undoubtedly an historical reality. When the image was taken from Edessa to Constantinople in AD 945, the sons of the king had remarked in obvious disappointment upon its watery, indistinct nature. That description alone excited him. Could they have been looking at anything other than the shroud? Segal was convinced that it was becoming more and more unlikely that they were dealing with two separate images.

By the time Chaim returned to Switzerland, five chapters were ready for proof-reading and another five mapped out.

"I'm impressed," Freiberg said. "This is deserving of a little celebration."

As all Chaim Freiberg's celebrations involved both food and drink Michael was not unduly surprised to once again receive an invitation to supper at the Beau Rivage.

He set his knife and fork down and picked up his wine glass.

"I've found something quite interesting," he said. "There was a time when the Mandylion was housed in the Pharos Chapel in Constantinople that reference was made, almost by the way, of Christ's sindon."

"The shroud?"

Michael nodded. "There were references in various places to shrouds, even as there were of crowns of thorns and lances, but the shroud of Constantinople was definitely imprinted with a full length image of Jesus Christ. I've found references to the Mandylion being carried in a procession in 1036. In 1058 it was seen in the Haggia Sophia. Sometime between then and 1130 the shroud with its full length image came to light."

"How do you know that?" Chaim Freiberg was perspiring in his black dinner suit and red satin bow tie. He used his napkin to wipe his face liberally and took a mouthful of white wine. Michael could never dispel the notion that he was better suited to cloth cap and workmen's overalls in some German beer hall.

"Pope Stephen III spoke of the full-length cloth in a sermon.

Better than that, he tied the shroud back to the image sent to Edessa. He said that Christ had stretched his whole body on a cloth, so that his image was divinely transferred. There was also a monk named Ordericus Vitalis who wrote a History of the Church around the same time. He also claimed that a full-length likeness of the body of Christ was sent to Abgar V."

Freiberg whistled softly. "That makes a nonsense of the notion of a fraud perpetrated during the Renaissance."

"In addition to that, about this time, Jesus' death began to be depicted differently. The mummified form, bound in strips of cloth gave way to pictures of Christ laid at the foot of the cross on a double-length piece of linen, which would cover the head in the same way as Turin's shroud. There are several early examples, including an eleventh century ivory at the Victoria and Albert museum, showing the body laid out with the hands crossed awkwardly over the loins, right over left, exactly like the shroud."

"As I understand it, the sindon wasn't seen as a shroud?"

Michael shook his head. "The body was presumed to have been washed, which is inconsistent with the blood marks on the cloth. So this was thought to have been a cloth the body was laid upon when it was taken down from the cross, prior to the entombment"

"Would it have been washed?"

"In other words, was this the shroud?"

"You're also a Jew, is the body washed before burial?"

"Of course."

"And if the death is violent?"

Chaim shrugged. "I'm not certain. I have an idea the blood would not be washed away."

"The life is in the blood," Michael quoted.

Both men were silent for several moments, lost in their own thoughts.

"So what do you think, Segal? Is this the burial shroud of a man resurrected from the dead?"

Michael shook his head. "I don't know, Chaim. Ask me again when I've finished the book."

Chapter 15
Twice-Born

October 1943

René de Bar stepped out into the street and shaded his eyes against the late afternoon sunlight. Reaching into the breast pocket of his suit for his dark glasses, he set his hat at a more sober angle and ventured out into the flow of humanity that constituted the exit of some of Paris' white-collar workers from their places of employment.

The two Gestapo officers that fell in on either side of him seemed to have come from nowhere and he was given no time to react. Their grip on his elbows was brisk and businesslike as they steered him towards the black Mercedes parked just round the corner with the engine idling.

There was an individual in the front passenger-seat dressed in a tan trench coat and a hat of a slightly deeper shade. He turned as de Bar was pushed into the back and tilted the hat back off his eyes.

"M de Bar, we meet at last." He took a cigarette from his silver case and cupped his hands around the flame as his driver leaned across with a light.

"What do you want with me?" de Bar demanded. He was gratified to find that his voice was controlled. He was well aware of the identity of the man and his presence signified that they did not consider him an insignificant catch. The car moved off into the street, held back for a moment by a velo taxi. Its two passengers, German soldiers, saluted as the Mercedes passed them, but their woman driver peddled on without so much as a sideways glance.

Klaus Barbie drew on his cigarette and exhaled thoughtfully without bothering to respond to de Bar's question. He had positioned himself with his back to the door from where he could observe de Bar more easily.

"De Bar," he mused. "Could that be a Jewish name perhaps?"

"It's French."

"But Bar, it's Hebrew for 'son of' such as son of Jonah. Can you prove you're not Jewish?"

"I can offer you a physical demonstration if that's what you want," de Bar replied testily.

Barbie dismissed the notion with a wave of the hand. "Physical proof says something about whether your parents were practising Jews or not, it says nothing about your ancestry."

De Bar made no reply. He was flanked on either side by the two men who had affected the arrest. Through the windows of the car he could see the crowds of cyclists making their way home in the early dusk. His thoughts turned briefly to Simone. He was to have met her this evening. How long would it be before she realised that they had him?

"You know who I am." It was more of a statement than a question and de Bar had no intention of gratifying Barbie with an affirmative answer.

"I have no idea."

The movement of the cigarette to Barbie's lips slowed almost imperceptibly and de Bar noticed with satisfaction the flash of irritation that crossed his features.

"I am Klaus Barbie," the German said coldly, "and I have a feeling that it's a name you will remember from now on."

The Mercedes took the turn into Avenue Foch and stopped outside the Gestapo headquarters. The driver walked swiftly round the car and opened the passenger door, clicking his heels as Barbie got out. The sun had dropped behind the building, taking with it the last vestige of the autumn warmth. Dusk blurred the images without softening the coming darkness. Barbie stood a little way off scrutinising de Bar for signs of fear. He considered himself an expert in the interpretation of emotion. He had witnessed the expression of the full range of human feeling and knew just how to make use of weakness.

René de Bar knew his opponent well by reputation; not for nothing was he known as the Butcher of Lyons. Behind the suave, handsome features was a man who enjoyed the process of humiliating and breaking people under torture. For the first time, it occurred to de

Bar that he might not live to see the end of the war.

They led him directly to an interrogation room on the first floor of the building and Barbie hung his coat on a peg behind the door.

"Sit!" he ordered, indicating a wooden chair in the middle of the room. As de Bar obeyed Barbie drew a second chair across, turned it around and sat with his legs astride and his gloved hands resting on the back.

"We had Jean Moulin here a few weeks back," he said conversationally. "A brave man. It took a lot to break him." He stood up and walked across the room, dismissing the guards with a gesture.

"There were several things we wanted from Moulin," he continued, "but the identity of Alain was of special importance to us. I am an expert in interrogation methods M de Bar, but in the end we had to settle for only one fact from Moulin's lips before he succumbed. A very brave man..."

He smiled at de Bar who was again struck by the pleasantness of the Barbie's face that contrasted so sharply with his vicious reputation. Something slipped into place in de Bar's memory. Information on Moulin's death had inevitably leaked back to the Resistance, and a man who had bathed Moulin's face before he lapsed into a coma had heard him whisper one word: "Allein".

De Bar cursed himself for his stupidity. The single word had been taken to mean Moulin was, in his delirium, speaking of his solitary confinement, although no one had ventured an explanation as to why he should have used the German. Too late, he realised that the one man who knew the identity of Alain, had been trying to issue a warning to the Resistance.

As Klaus Barbie continued his monologue, de Bar realised that he was relishing the opportunity to vaunt himself.

"I was under orders from Reichsführer, Heinrich Himmler to send Moulin to Germany for interrogation, but I knew I was better than any of his men at extracting information. I had no intention of handing him over until I had what I wanted." Barbie smoothed his hair back off his face with the palm of his hand. "Primarily of course, I am a detective in the employ of the criminal police here in France and I excel in my work." He smiled benignly. "I believe I got out of Moulin what no other man could have and as a result I received a personal commendation from the Reichsführer-SS. Once Moulin cracked, I put him on a train to Germany but he never reached his destination. With the information we received from him, it was simply a matter of time before we brought you in."

Barbie began to peel off his gloves, at the same moment barking an order to the men posted outside. The pleasantries were over. The first of the two Gestapo was a massive brute with none of Barbie's outward refinement. He stood by with semblance of a grin on his face, waiting for orders.

'Strip!"

De Bar did not respond immediately but realising he would gain nothing by stalling; he stripped naked except for his underpants.

"Get those off!"

As de Bar bent down to slip them over his ankles, Barbie delivered a blow to the side of his head that knocked him off his feet.

"You lying bastard!" he ground out. "You are a damned Jew! Get up!"

"My family has circumcised all males for generations," he returned quietly as he stood to his feet, "but we are practising Catholics."

Barbie sneered. "You expect me to believe that? No Catholic in his right mind uses circumcision." He nodded to the guard. "Search him."

The man forced de Bar's mouth open and examined his teeth.

"Bend!" he ordered, "Spread your legs."

His Gestapo side-kick acted with sadistic pleasure, dragging him back into upright position by the hair and with a deft twist of de Bar's arm, forcing him to his knees at Barbie's feet.

"Who are your associates?" Barbie snapped. "Who are you working with? I want names, places of operation…"

The questioning was restrained, almost routine, as though they were holding back on de Bar for a reason. Later, he was force-marched naked along a corridor and down two flights of stairs into the basement. He was thrown into a cell with such force that he was propelled violently into the opposite wall and his clothes were tossed in after him.

René de Bar sank down and lay with his face against the concrete. Then slowly and clumsily he dressed himself, lay down on the straw pallet in the corner of the room and slept.

Chapter 16
Twice-Born

Like the eye of a hurricane, Switzerland waged peace while all others waged war: a calm atoll in the European heartland, she was the slave of many masters.

Although there was still no end of the conflict in sight, rumours of plans by the Allies to launch a major cross-Channel attack abounded. America's part in the war was growing and two major decisions made by Eisenhower effectively wrested strategic command from Britain.

The first was his own appointment as Commander in Chief of operation Torch, the second was General Marshall's posting as Supreme Allied Commander. Marshall assumed that Britain was deliberately dragging out operations and extending the conflict rather than focussing all effort in a final push across the channel, perceiving it as Churchill's desire to control Arabia after the war. British strategy had always been to force the Axis to disperse her troops by launching smaller strategic missions. Allied talks were bitter. Italy had begun to collapse and was in contact with Eisenhower's headquarters to discuss terms of surrender and the possibility of joining the Allies against Hitler. German forces massed in Northern Italy and occupied Italian positions in the Balkans. The Axis was showing signs of disintegration and Britain felt certain that her tactics were justified. In September of 1943, the Allied forces agreed upon an invasion of Italy but they failed to achieve the element of surprise and were met with a vicious German counterattack; six divisions almost succeeded in driving the Americans into the sea. They hung on until reinforcements turned the tide and the German front collapsed. Salerno cost the Allies fifteen thousand of their best men confirming Churchill's doubts about the D-Day invasion. Germany's intelligence was excellent and the Wehrmacht was still an efficient and formidable fighting force. The war was by no means won.

Michael's primary concern was whether Gabriele and his parents, left behind in Germany, would survive the conflict. Gabriele wrote regularly, if guardedly, to her uncle Siegfried fully aware that letters were opened and read by the censors and Michael's replies were penned with equal caution. It was therefore a shock to him when he received a letter telling him that his parents had disappeared.

"I went past the house where your parents used to live with certain nostalgia," she wrote. "It's always sad to pass a home where one has spent many happy hours and find it empty. No one lives there now, although things are much the same as it was when you were a child. I spoke to a local baker and he assured me that he remembered your family and the time they moved away."

Michael sat with the letter in his lap for a long time. Reports of Jewish suffering were coming out of Germany with increasing persistence. Everyone had heard the horror accounts of Jews transported to the east in cattle trucks; of detention camps and work camps. There were continual rumours, each more frightening than the last, but ultimately the whole truth would not be known until it was all over. He was forced like so many others, to wait out the remaining period in uncertainty.

Once the notion that the shroud image was formed photographically had been laid out on the table, it seemed to Michael Segal to be the only logical option. No imprint made by body contact could have been so free from distortion and it was unlikely that a fake could have been fabricated with such delicacy and without any obvious pigmentation of the fabric. It was also extremely doubtful that an early forger would have consciously decided to create a work of art in the negative. But if an early photographic likeness was formed, the forger would have had no means of using it to create a positive representation. At first, Michael could find nothing in his research to suggest that any such knowledge might have been available during the first century.

"You might be looking in the wrong place," Chaim Freiberg said, when he reported his lack of success.

"What do you mean?"

"Most early advances were made by alchemists. I think you

might find your breakthrough there."

Weeks later, when Chaim was back in Geneva they met at Michael's apartment, which had gained some furniture and a semblance of order in recent months.

"I've found some clues," he announced, opening a bulging research file. "There's not a lot of written information, but photographic knowledge was around early, a lot earlier than we give it credit."

Chaim was perched uncomfortably on Michael's typing chair but he listened intently to the information that his friend had sourced.

"As early as 1536, during the Renaissance, there was a book by someone called Fabricius, which describes how certain metals can capture an object's true likeness when light has been allowed to fall on them. Before that, during the eleventh century a man called Ibn al-Haytam wrote a clear description of the camera obscura in his book Kitab al-manazir."

"Camera obscura?"

"A crude early version of the camera. A darkened room, or box, with a pinhole. His book dealt with optical science, so it's likely that he had some knowledge of lenses."

"Nothing earlier than that?"

"Al-Manazir makes it clear that this knowledge was not discovered by him but that it came from an earlier source."

"Did they have the ability to capture images?"

"Arab alchemists had developed substances with photochemical properties - silver nitrate and silver chloride were described as early as the ninth century. They may well have been known a lot earlier and passed down among initiates by word of mouth."

"We're still nine hundred years out of our timeframe."

Michael nodded. "But a lot closer than we were the last time we met."

Chaim grinned. "You're right. Anything definite on the creation of lenses?"

"Nothing at this stage. Glass had been around for a long time of course. But quartz lenses[31] are needed for photography." He shrugged,

---

[31] Lenses used in Old Kingdom – Egypt. See appendix 1.

"We're still a long way off, but I sense we're on the right track!"

Chaim stood up. "Then I think we have some cause for celebration," he said.

"A beer?"

"A couple. And perhaps a bite to eat somewhere."

Michael grinned to himself as he followed Chaim out of the apartment and locked the door behind him.

Chapter 17
Twice-Born

As the first wave of crusaders under Peter the Hermit made their way south across Europe, Jewish communities were slaughtered without mercy. The intention was clear. Jerusalem was about to be seized, not for the Jew, but for those who had assumed the name of Christ. This was the People's Army, also known as the Tafurs. A sacred college at the heart of this army was presided over by the King of Tafur, a shadowy figure from Calabria, perhaps Peter the Hermit himself, who wielded the power to make kings.

Alexius Comnenus had immediately recognised the threat this great army posed to his city when the People's Crusade, under command of Peter the Hermit, which was the first to descend upon Constantinople, became restless and began to ravage the city's suburbs. The Byzantine Emperor promptly dispatched the crusaders across the Bosporus billeting them in a military camp close to territory under control of the Seljuk Turks. During raids into enemy territory French and German forces were trapped and when the main army went in to attempt a rescue, the People's Army was virtually annihilated.

The Frankish knights who led the second wave of crusaders were a warrior class, many of them descendants of those who had fought alongside the Merovingian and Carolingian kings, soldiers highly skilled with the sword and the lance and, although this was the elite force the Emperor had envisaged, Alexius was justifiably suspicious of their intentions.

If the Crusade leaders had intended to capture the shroud and the other holy relics in the safe-keeping of the Emperor of Byzantium, they did not at this stage play their hand. Instead a pact was entered into with Alexius in which they promised to return to him any of the cities captured en route to Jerusalem. When Nicaea fell to the invading army, the Turkish garrison surrendered to the Byzantine fleet and the Crusaders kept their promise and moved on.

The going was hard. Temperatures were high; there was a

desperate shortage of water and little food. A savage battle was fought at Dorylaeum against the army of Kirij Arslan and only the rearguard action under Godfroi de Bouillon saved Bohemond's army from certain defeat. This time the crusaders' spirits were buoyed by the plundering of the Turkish army's camp.

After resting as guests of the Armenians, the army marched on Antioch and laid siege to the city. What followed was eight months of hell for the crusaders in which pestilence diminished their ranks and famine forced them to eat many of their remaining horses. But just as news of an approaching Turkish army brought the men to their lowest ebb, Bohemond of Taranto won them a reprieve.

Feigning a retreat from the city's walls, they returned under cover of darkness to three towers kept by Fairuz, a Turk who had succumbed to a bribe offered by Bohemond. The walls were scaled and the city was taken but the tables were turned almost immediately and the besiegers became the besieged. Beyond the Antioch's walls the great army of Seljuk Turks prepared to make an assault on the crusaders within.

In a chapel a group of monks prostrated themselves before the Blessed Sacrament and prayed late into the night for deliverance from their enemies.

In the early hours of the following morning one of their brethren, a priest from France, Peter Bartholomew, aroused them from their beds.

"I have received a vision!" he told them breathlessly. "The sacred lance is buried here in Antioch in the church of St. Peter. I need men to help me retrieve it."

They stared at him.

"How can you be certain?"

"I know it! It is an answer from the Blessed Virgin. There is no doubt in my mind. So, will you come?"

It was first necessary to receive the permission of Adhemar de Le Puy, appointed by Pope Urban II as the spiritual leader of the crusade. It was he who had led the army to Antioch. His hooded eyes showed the merest flicker of interest when he heard of the mission of the group of monks before him. Peter Bartholomew was a monk unknown to him and of no noble standing therefore it would not do for Le Puy to betray the stirring of excitement that these words aroused.

"A vision?"

"Of the Blessed Virgin. She appeared to me herself, bathed in great glory!"

"What were her words to you?"

"She told me, Your Worship, that the sacred lance, which pierced the side of her dear Son, is buried here in Antioch."

"Go on."

"She said that I should select twelve good men and search beneath the paving before the altar in the church of St. Peter."

For a long time, there was silence from the legate and he studied Peter Bartholomew coolly before speaking once more.

"How can I be certain that this vision is true?" he asked.

"I beg your indulgence, sire," Bartholomew twisted his hands together to cover his impatience. "If it is true, I will prove it by producing the lance. It will ensure our victory before the Turks."

Once more his words met with no immediate response but this time Le Puy was moved by the young priest's sincerity. Eventually he nodded.

"You have my permission. But you will ensure that any damage done to the Church is repaired."

"Thank you, sire."

For a day and a night, Peter Bartholomew and his twelve friends dug to no avail but the young priest's conviction never wavered. His faith in the Virgin's word was absolute. It was on the morning of the second day that he stepped down into the pit they had created and reached into the rubble.

"I think I have it!" he shouted.

An oiled cloth had been wrapped around a crafted wooden box and within it lay the Roman lance. The head was of simple design, crafted of iron blackened with age and fitted with a wooden shaft.

"The spear of Longinus!" Bartholomew breathed.

The monks covered their bare heads with the hoods of their cowls and knelt before the relic in worship.

The news of the find swept through Antioch empowering the

crusaders spiritually even as food and drink found in the city had strengthened them physically.

Inspired by the lance as a portent of the favour of God, two hundred horsemen rode out against the mighty army of the Seljuk Turks with their talisman held high. They were followed on foot by the knights who had lost their steeds and, unaccountably, the Turks fled at the sight of them.

"An army rode with us," the crusaders exulted. "Chariots and horses of fire defeated our foe. It was not flesh and blood that won this battle for us but the lance that pierced the side of Christ!"

Months before, only days after the death of his wife, who, like many other women, had accompanied her husband on crusade, Baudouin de Bouillon, brother of Godfroi, had ridden off with a small contingent of knights on a mission of his own.

Edessa was a desirable prize; a wealthy city on the trade route between Constantinople and the east. It was also an attractive spiritual prize. Although it was known that the Mandylion had been captured by Constantinople and lay closely guarded within the Byzantine city, it was just possible that Alexius held a skilful copy of the true shroud. Baudouin intended to ascertain the truth for himself. There was a third reason known to only a handful of men. Peter the Hermit was very specific in his instruction of the de Bouillon brothers.

"In the early days, disciples were sent to Edessa and a letter is still preserved there, written in the Master's own hand. If we are to bring the Magus' plan to fulfilment there are brothers among the sons of Ishmael who must be united to our cause. It is up to you to find them."

Edessa was not ruled by the Turks but by the Armenians and its capture would require the sort of subtlety of which Baudouin de Bouillon was fully capable.

The citizens pleaded with the Edessa's ruler, Thoros, to allow Baudouin and his knights to protect their city and Thoros welcomed them in. He was a man frail with age and it was recognition of his own vulnerability that persuaded him to trust the Crusaders.

"They are strong," he confided to his closest advisor. "If I reject them, even although they are small in number they could return with a greater army and take Edessa by force."

His advisor nodded. "And they have gained the hearts of the people who have seen their successes against the Turks. They know that it will be of great advantage to have them with us."

"Besides, Baudouin is a man of noble blood and a good Christian," Thoros said. "Such a man is to be trusted."

There was a moment's hesitation on the part of the other that could have been interpreted as doubt.

"He is a strong deterrent to the Turks," he said at length, "it would indeed be foolish to reject his offer of support."

Baudouin made a deep impression on the old Armenian, and it was not long before Thoros, who was childless, adopted the Frank as his son. It was an ill-considered move. Thoros was an unpopular leader and Baudouin a heroic figure. Within a month Thoros was struck down as he attempted to flee, leaving Baudouin de Bouillon the sole ruler of Edessa.

Meanwhile, in defiance of the pledge to Emperor Alexius, Bohemond was crowned King of Antioch and there followed a period in which the impetus of the crusaders was lost. Plague broke out in Antioch and one of those who fell victim was the papal legate, Adhemar de Le Puy. Many left the city to escape the sickness and conducted raids on Muslim held coastal towns.

It was during this time that Peter the Hermit's men, known as the Tafurs, consumed the bodies of the men they had slaughtered striking abject terror into the hearts of the local inhabitants.

Radulph of Caen wrote: "Our troops boiled pagan adults in cooking pots: they impaled children on spits and devoured them grilled."

The sacred lance was doing its work for evil in the degenerate hearts of those who held it.

Chapter 18
Twice-Born

October 1943

He sensed the approach of dawn before the change came. One moment they were driving through inky blackness with nothing revealed beyond that which the headlights picked out on the road ahead, and the next it was as though he had moved from blindness into partial sight. Shapes wreathed in mist were silhouetted against a sky, shyly exposed, like a virgin before a lover, touched with pearly blush as each passing moment she surrendered herself more fully to the caress of the morning light. Night's heavy blanket fell away from the mountains and they emerged resplendent; snow-whitened peaks challenging the dark smudge of the pine forests on the lower slopes.

Two SS officers flanked René de Bar in the back of the Mercedes, while Klaus Barbie sat at the front with the driver. They had travelled throughout the night, crossing the border into Germany at Strasbourg, and appeared to be heading north on a route that avoided the main centres. There had been little communication in the back of the vehicle during the drive, but it was obvious that Barbie was a man expecting imminent promotion. He chatted to the driver, scarcely bothering to suppress elation and, when there were lulls in the conversation, he whistled tunelessly between his teeth.

Wewelsburg Castle was both an integral part of the mountain scene and aloof from it. De Bar could see the unusual configuration of the building, three circular turrets forming the apexes of a triangle. Its Germanic exterior was stolid and oppressive, and although from a distance it achieved the appearance of age, de Bar realised as they approached that much of it was in fact, newly constructed.

One of his travelling companions lit two cigarettes and passed one to him without speaking. De Bar drew on it gratefully while their papers were cleared at the gates. The guard stepped back from the car, saluted smartly and allowed them to pass.

"Heil Hitler!"

Barbie acknowledged the salute with a cursory wave of his hand. The Mercedes entered the courtyard, nosed in against the stone wall of the main building and stopped.

"Get out, schnell!"

De Bar shifted across the seat and stood up gingerly, feeling his joints protest from being in one position for so long. After the stuffiness of the vehicle the morning air was icy. The large flag-stoned courtyard was silent and, apart from the guards at the gate, there was no other sign of life. At close range, the building was even more intimidating. Vast walls bore down on them from three sides, and those doors which punctuated the base of the stone at ground level appeared blank and uninviting. Steps rose to the more imposing main entrance but de Bar was led to a side door on the left, not far from where they had parked. Two guards wearing the black uniform of the SS were sitting on a bench just inside the door, playing a hand of cards. The older of the two, an officer, deftly flicked a cigarette to the floor and ground it out with his heel, and both men snapped to attention.

"Herr Barbie, this way please.'

The officer led the way down the corridor, unlocking a heavy iron door beyond which was a row of grey metal doors with viewing grids inset at eye level. The cell, which was unlocked for René de Bar was cold and empty apart from a slop bucket and a straw pallet with a thin blanket. Klaus Barbie leaned against the door jamb watching him.

"Welcome to Wewelsburg."

De Bar's expression was inscrutable. "I can't say the name means anything to me."

"Wewelsburg is a leaders' school of the SS. I'm certain that your time spent here will be very pleasant; I'm leaving you in good hands. But you will need time to unpack." Barbie grinned at his own joke and clicked his heels. "Enjoy your stay." He turned away and the cell door was closed firmly behind him, the sound of it echoed through the block.

At eleven that morning the two SS guards came for him. The younger man hauled him to his feet and shoved him unceremoniously out of his cell but before de Bar could properly regain his footing, the second man booted him from behind and sent him crashing into the wall opposite.

"Get up. Fast!"

They propelled him down the passage with the butt of a rifle pressed to his spine.

"In here!"

At the far end of a large room were a couple of latrines and a shower, partitioned, but without doors, and against the same wall, a stained urinal. In the opposite corner was a deep sink with a draining board, but otherwise the room was empty. The floor was untreated concrete with a slight fall towards a shallow drain. De Bar took in his surroundings in an instant without any expectation that he might have been brought in for a hot shower.

The older guard, a man in his early fifties, had the lean chiselled features of an aristocrat, a face sensitively drawn, with long narrow nose and well-shaped lips. He moved smoothly, with shoulders erect and hips forward-thrust. De Bar noticed that his fingers were long and tapered and the nails well-manicured. The second man could not have been much more than twenty years old, his skin was as soft and smooth as a woman's and his eyes were a deep, magnificent blue. One blonde forelock curled softly over his forehead and his smile as he balled his fist was beatific.

They beat him up on a daily basis in the week that followed his internment, with perverted punctiliousness. If he lost consciousness, they put his head under the tap in the sink to bring him round before dragging him back to the isolation of his cell, his body battered and bleeding. Yet de Bar was fully aware they were going easy on him and that he had at no time been subjected to any interrogation. They were playing games, softening him up, and he knew it was imperative on him to stay alert for the next phase.

Six days after his arrival at Wewelsburg, the routine was abruptly broken. Their steps took them beyond the washroom and through the bowels of the castle into upper passages that suggested daylight, fresh air and luxury. The walls were decorated with oil paintings and tapestries, and the passageways were richly carpeted, deadening the heavy tread of the boots of his guards. He was alarmed to discover how exhausted he was. His breath rasped through the back of his throat from the climb up the stairs, so that the cough that had begun to plague his sleep at night, racked his body and he grimaced with pain.

"In here."

Heinrich Himmler was alone; an insignificant figure at a desk which dwarfed him. He dismissed the guards with an impatient motion of the hand, leaned back in his seat and surveyed de Bar with unfeigned interest from behind his rimless glasses.

"So, M Alain," he said, using the name given to de Bar by the Paris resistance. "I have anticipated this moment for some time."

Cocteau, de Bar thought fleetingly, would have found the incongruity of this moment amusing. The Reichsführer-SS, son of a school teacher, even more chinless than his photographs suggested, was fastidiously groomed and dressed, while de Bar, the aristocrat, his prison clothes dirty and blood encrusted, swayed on his feet before him. Himmler's pale eyes travelled down the length of de Bar's body and flicked back to his face, the prim set of his mouth reflecting his distaste.

"I see they have been mistreating you," he commented, tapping the leather switch delicately against his fingernails. "My men are inclined to be a little unrestrained. I encourage brutality of course. It's absolutely essential that fighting men show no sign of sentimentality in their treatment of the enemy. Only in that way can we create a nation of men truly refined in the nature and principals of war." He looked up into de Bar's expressionless face and with hardly a change in tone, spoke words which were at once startlingly familiar.

"'I am forbidden to ask either your name or your race, for if I ask that question of you I know I shall not have your help any longer.'"

The words were from Wolfram's Parsival, and although not faultlessly quoted, could hardly have been coincidental. De Bar was intimately acquainted with the poem, and it was obvious that Heinrich Himmler knew precisely who he was dealing with.

"You had better take a seat, M Alain," Himmler suggested. "There are areas of your life that I wish to discuss and the interview could take some time. May I offer you a cigarette?"

René de Bar savoured the first inhalation of smoke without allowing the enjoyment to cloud his thinking. The Reichsführer had left his seat and walked behind his prisoner setting himself at a new advantage before speaking again.

"Your resistance work was a front for something much bigger," he said.

De Bar drew on his cigarette. Himmler moved back round the desk to face him, stalking in cat-like silence. Even in this position of power, there was an element of uncertainty about the man and de Bar felt it.

"I know a lot about you, M Alain. For example I know that you are a Scottish-rite Freemason of the highest degree, and that information alone would afford you time in a concentration camp whether you were in Germany or in occupied France.

De Bar looked steadily back into Heinrich Himmler's eyes. The man was good; there was no doubt about it. He had not gleaned that information from any of the usual sources.

"I'm also aware," Himmler said as he resumed pacing, "that it was your organisation that first issued the Protocols of Zion. An invaluable tool in our hands at the present time, wouldn't you agree? It's amusing to witness the gullibility of the masses. If they would only take the time to study the document carefully, they would see the glaring anomalies for themselves. But I find that people have a tendency to see what they want to see and to ignore anything that contradicts their opinion."

De Bar spoke for the first time. "The protocols are undoubtedly a forgery," he said.

"You and I know they are not. There's an unusual quality to that document. A spiritual steeliness that places it on another plane. You will realise by now, M Alain, that I did not bring you here to interrogate you. I have men skilled in the art of that sort of thing, and that route may yet prove to be unnecessary in your case. My intention is to offer you certain information." He had commenced pacing again and spoke as though he was conducting a lecture. "The organisation responsible for the protocols, left Jerusalem having unearthed one of the treasures of the Temple, one hinted at in the songs of the medieval minnesingers."

"A fascinating historical observation, Reichsführer, but what has any of this to do with me?"

"'Seeing that your sword is shattered, all your skill in war cannot save you from death unless I am pleased to spare you. It is more fitting for us to be friends than bitter enemies.'"

Not for the first time during this interview, de Bar was taken aback. The man's mind was either unbalanced, or as intricate as a maze run. It was impossible to tell where he was leading. Once more, the quotation had come from the Parsival and this time, he remembered, it was at the meeting of Parsival with his infidel brother and fellow knight. Perversely, de Bar was beginning to enjoy the matching of minds, while still determined to conceal the fact from the Reichsführer. But without warning Himmler changed his tack.

"Let me compliment you on your excellent German," he said. "May I ask you where you studied?"

"My father was a linguist. He insisted on the same direction for his children."

Himmler's features rearranged themselves into an expression that could almost be interpreted as affable.

"Excellent. Excellent!"

Abruptly the Reichsführer turned away and barked an order and the two guards who had been in position outside the door, entered and without a word marched de Bar back down to his cell.

Chapter 19
Twice-Born

Abbot Bernard received his visitor with a bow of his tonsured head and showed him into a quiet room off the dining hall. Victuals were set before him, several slices of meat and bread, and a glass of red wine.

"It is humble fare," Bernard said without apology.

"And I give thanks to God for it," said the Pope and bowed his head for a moment of muttered prayer.

Bernard watched him eat and contemplated what such a visit could mean. Odo finished his meal at length and wiped the grease from his hands and mouth with a napkin.

"I have an assignment for you and the monks of Citeaux," he said crumpling the cloth and tossing it onto the table. "I am told you have the ability to put words together well. The hidden doctrine of the Catholic faith must be re-written for our time."

"Speak on, Holiness."

"We have reached a turning point in history, perhaps even the moment of which we have all dreamed and towards which we have all striven. Jerusalem may soon fall into Christian hands and although Godfroi de Bouillon is ill, it is yet possible that by the grace of God he may be crowned."

"If he dies, his brother Baudouin will doubtless take the throne in his stead."

The Pope shook his head. "He is a brave knight," he said. "But he is a man who has no heart for the things of God. Baudouin de Bouillon is proud and arrogant and he seeks the love of women. It was a sad day when his good wife succumbed to the hardships of the crusade. It freed Baudouin once more to pursue his own lusts."

"Power, wealth and women." Bernard spoke with a grimace of disdain. "These are not the marks of a true knight, your Holiness. If Godfroi perishes, this quest will perish with him. God will not set his favour on such a man."

"Pray, Abbot Bernard," Pope Urban II said. "Beseech the

Blessed Virgin for the health of Godfroi. It may be that he will find healing."

They were pensive for a long moment. Sun poured in through the high window of the sparsely furnished room and a fly buzzed around the mouth of the Pope before settling on his empty plate.

"You desire me to write the hidden doctrine because you believe it is possible we have not yet reached the end of the journey," Bernard said at length.

Odo sat back in his chair and linked his hands. "I fear we have not. We must prepare ourselves for whatsoever comes to pass."

"The writing of it then would assume the nature of our time while the elements passed down remain unchanged?"

"Very soon our knights in the Holy Land will seek the sword," the Pope said. "It will doubtless be found from the clues given in the ancient tale but it seems that once again it must be broken. For now, the platter remains empty although we are apprised of the whereabouts of the Head of Wisdom. The Virgin is yet keeper of the cup and with it she upholds the light of the heavenly vision. But there are two further things. In your writings, Abbot, you are to emphasise the centrality of the Eucharist. You and I know that the Divine Substance, communicated in the Eucharist is the Grail, the secret doctrine of the Church of Rome and of the mystery religions. When it is consumed mystically, the sensitive seeker, the one whose election and calling are guaranteed, experiences the awe-inspiring enchantments of real knowledge. This is to be intimated and even emphasised."

The Abbot's eyes shone with excitement and he reached across the table, grasping the hands of the Pope in his own.

"The Eucharist, so taken," he said, "is the way back from whence we came. It is the final reintegration of the stone into the crown of Lucifer. Our names, Your Holiness are engraved upon that stone."

"Then you will write it?"

"With joy, Holiness! To the true seeker, the mystery of the Divine Substance constitutes the language of the zenith. It is the wind under the wings of the eagle. The romance of the Parsival conveys the essential and vital role of the Eucharist in the high theology of the Mother Church."

Odo smiled and disengaged himself from the grasp of the Abbot.

"I would ask you and your monks who undertake this task, to emphasise the Fisher King's reliance on the Grail alone for sustenance – on the blood from the lance and the wafer laid upon the stone by the dove. I would also have you combine the tales which come of the Celts, for it is they who received the doctrine from the mouth of Joseph of Arimathea."

Bernard ran his fingers through his luxuriant red beard and smiled, "It is well that we knit together the words of the Master with those of Joseph. In such a way can we bring all the richness of the tale to light and every facet of the doctrine can be laid out for future generations."

"Yet obscured to all but the true seeker of the faith," the Pope agreed. "Every pope stands in the stead of the Fisher King, wounded between the thighs for the kingdom to come. Simon Pethor bore only a daughter and therefore the offspring of Joseph of Arimathea carries the royal blood." His fingers caressed his cheek and he looked beyond Bernard into some hidden place of his mind. "As eunuchs for the faith we bear no offspring, yet we abide in the deeply satisfying love of the Virgin, giving suck to her perfect breasts. It is appointed to some of us to be knights for the kingdom and some to be monks. Together, we represent the final kingdom and the victorious king."

"Parsival in the borrowed garments of the Red Knight?"

The Pope laughed. "'Who is this that cometh from Edom with dyed garments from Bozrah?'" he quoted. "'I that speak in righteousness, mighty to save. Wherefore art thou red in thine apparel, and thy garments like him that treadeth in the winevat?'"

"'I have trodden the winepress alone; and of the people there was none with me: for I will tread them in mine anger, and trample them in my fury and their blood will stain all my raiment.[32]'" Bernard's expression was markedly cynical as he completed the quote from the book of Isaiah.

"Let the one who comes in the borrowed clothing assume his rightful place as King of Jerusalem," the Pope said. "Then no-one will

[32] Isaiah 63:1-3

dare to stand with the Ancient of Days! The defeat of Jesus of Nazareth will be complete. Our brave knights will stain their clothing with the blood of Jews and Muslims when the Holy City falls to the Christians, and I and my Cardinals will continue to wear the red apparel of Edom until the kingdoms of this world fall into our hands!"

"In that day the true Parsival, Nimrod Twice-Born, will assume the place of the Pope," Abbot Bernard said. "And perhaps if Godfroi survives, that hour is already upon us."

Chapter 20
Twice-Born

November 1943

Another two days passed without change for René de Bar, then in the early hours of the morning he was torn from his sleep by a sound what he was at first unable to identify. He lay still, listening to the uneven beating of his heart. In the extraordinary stillness it seemed that the heartbeat of the universe was pounding in unison with his own. The scream, when it came again, ripped through the silence jarring every nerve in his body.

It seemed like hours before the last tormented shrieks weakened and subsided. De Bar lay in the darkness; sleep had deserted him. He was oppressed by an almost physical presence of fear that lay across his chest and impaired his breathing. If the torture of a man at such close proximity was intended to have an effect on him, he was aware that they had achieved their purpose.

Day broke rudely with the clatter of the guards' boots in the passage outside. The light in his cell was switched on and de Bar lay for a moment looking up at the naked bulb, which was attached slightly off-centre to the raw concrete ceiling. He relieved himself in the bucket and sat down on the edge of the mattress to wait.

Since his interview with Himmler he had taken to amusing himself by quoting out loud, passages that he could recall from the Parsival.

"He who seeks to gain instruction from this tale, must not wonder at the contrary elements brought to light therein. Here he must learn to flee away, there to chase, how to avoid, when to blame and where to praise. In him alone who is expert in all these possibilities will wisdom be confirmed.'

'The contrary elements brought to light'; it was less the contrary elements of the Parsival that now destroyed his meditation, but the contrary elements of the position he now found himself in that greatly disturbed de Bar. It was obvious that Himmler had used the words of the Parsival intentionally. The direction of his conversation had only served to entrench his words more deeply.

The sudden rattle of the door startled him and it was opened before he had fully regained his composure.

"Come!" The guard gestured with his rifle. De Bar stood up slowly and moved towards the door. Someone was waiting in the passage outside. He wore the high-ranking uniform of an SS-Obergruppenführer and between his fingers a cigarette burned, the smell of it tantalising de Bar's senses.

"Will you come this way?"

It was a request rather than a command although the presence of the guards made it difficult to decline. Once again their route took them up into the more spacious corridors of the castle, but this time the Obergruppenführer opened the door to a private suite.

"You will find a bathroom through that door," he told de Bar, "and there are clothes in the cupboard. Take your time. Someone will be back for you later."

He heard the key turn in the lock as the man left the room. Left alone, he looked around, assailed by a sense of unreality.

Food set on a corner table attracted his immediate attention; fresh white rolls and real coffee with an assortment of German sausage and cheese. It was the first palatable meal since his arrival ten days ago and he ate swiftly with a deep sense of enjoyment, waiting until the hunger pangs were assuaged before turning again to examine his strange surroundings. The heavy oak door had been intricately carved by a master craftsman. It took as the centrepiece of its design, a chalice engraved with patterns and symbols inset in silver and jade.

The room, he had noticed almost at once, was dedicated to Frederick II Hohenstauffen, and this theme was carried throughout the sumptuous decor. On the walls were pictures relating to the period of Frederick's reign and, in a glass case, beautifully scripted, was his history. Before going through to the bathroom, René de Bar walked across the room and drew back the heavy brocade curtains from the high windows and gazed down across the thickly forested slopes of the mountainside. It was one of those late autumn days, which the sun had painted with her clearest palette. Perhaps his incarceration had caused him to see with greater clarity. The sky appeared bluer than usual and the trees were a blaze of colour from the sombre greens of the pine, to the deep red and oranges of those touched by the coming fall.

De Bar glanced at himself wryly in the bathroom mirror and met the eyes of a stranger. In the few days since his capture, his face had become drawn and pallid and his eyes surrounded by bruised hollows. He bathed, shaved, and changed into his own clothes, which had been freshly laundered.

Once his creature comforts were met, he focused his full attention on his unusual predicament. It was obvious that they knew him. He had from the beginning, not been treated as a normal resistance prisoner. Himmler was playing an intricate game which, it seemed likely, would result in some sort of an offer from the Germans. How many players were involved and how high the stakes were, there was no way of knowing. His own loyalties were uncomplicated, he bore few allegiances. There was only one aspect of his life that he was prepared to die for, and to that end he had sworn an oath.

He stopped at the glass case to read the familiar history of Frederick II but, as he glanced through the illuminated script, he froze. How could he have allowed something so obvious to slip by him? Frederick II Hohenstauffen had lived from 1812 to 1850 and had launched himself into the scenario of European politics, shaking it to its foundations. He was a charismatic personality, a man of legendary arcane powers, one who believed in astrology and practised the art of alchemy. A patron of the arts, Frederick spoke six languages fluently, and was a lyric poet in his own right. Both a king and a chivalrous knight, he had inspired his minstrels to chant their tales of the Holy Grail. De Bar glanced at the cup engraved into the oak door and walked again to the window. This time the view did not absorb him. Frederick II had centred his life on one prized possession, the spear of Longinus, using its power during the Crusades and the running battles with the Italian states and the papal armies. There were those, Germany's Wagner among them, who rightly equated not only the cup with the Grail legend, but also the heilige lance, the spear of Longinus.

De Bar rubbed his chin pensively. Generally, in order to dominate a situation, it was necessary to stay a step ahead of the enemy.

This time, he had the uneasy sense that his enemy was a pace ahead of him.

The last rays of sun played on the mountain peaks plunging the valleys swiftly into darkness. Wewelsburg castle drew the shadows to herself becoming just another mountain crag in the falling dusk.

De Bar slept for some hours, waking to the deep silence of his surroundings. He watched the night from his window as he waited for the heaviness of sleep to leave him. An orange moon was beginning to rise behind a distant peak and bats wove swift patterns across the grey backdrop of the sky. Some foreshadowing of what was to take place conveyed itself to him through the scene outside his window, causing the adrenaline to course unexpectedly through his body. Even before the first sounds reached him, he knew they were coming for him and he stood up to wait.

The setting of the great hall was deliberately medieval. Spanning the walls from ceiling to floor were brightly coloured banners bearing the heraldry and armorial insignia of each of Himmler's chosen Obergruppenführer, his order of Black Knights. A fire crackled and sparked in a massive fireplace and the room was fragrant with the scent of wood smoke. The two men who had come for de Bar took their places on the seats surrounding a large trestle table set as if for a banquet.

Each of the men was dressed entirely in black, except for Himmler, seated at the head of the table. De Bar drew an involuntary breath and his last doubts were removed with such force that it left him reeling. The Reichsführer was wearing a cloak made of black and grey skins over his clothing.

"Come and sit here with me," Heinrich Himmler instructed. "'If I let you sit further away, I would be treating you like a stranger.'"

This time there could be no doubt. Himmler was quoting directly from the ancient poem and by the words he used and the cloak he wore over his shoulders, he was styling himself on Wolfram von Eschenbach's Fisher King. The effect was incongruous, Himmler with his prim austere features, draped self-consciously in sable, yet de Bar was not tempted to laugh. He knew the charade held some deeper purpose and that his own fate was somehow intrinsically bound up in this moment.

He sat down slowly. If Himmler was playing the Fisher King, then his words and actions intimated that he was addressing Parsival. At their first meeting, Himmler's words clearly showed that he knew de Bar was of the Grail family and must not be questioned about his name or background. De Bar ran a hand through his hair and looked around him. There was tension in the atmosphere that touched all of the men in the room.

At a signal from Himmler the men filled their plates and returned to the table. They relaxed a little as they ate, but pitched their conversation low and the sound of laughter was rare. De Bar was ignored. He toyed with his food, waiting to see what would unfold. One by one, plates were emptied and set aside. Apart from his first words to de Bar, Himmler had not chosen to address him again. Watching him, de Bar realised how consciously he controlled himself. Each movement of his body was executed with care and precision so that he revealed nothing beyond his deep discomfort with himself.

The black knight burst through the door at the far end of the hall, his face a hideous mask, lips drawn back off his teeth and eyes bulging. In his hand he brandished a lance, and blood from the long tapered point of its head spilled back down the shaft and flowed over the hand that flourished it. The knight ran around the periphery of the room, playing out the ancient rite of the poem. As he left, the vacuum of his parting was emphasised by the small sounds of the logs burning in the fireplace. No one looked in de Bar's direction but he knew without any doubt that they were waiting for him. Whatever Himmler's game was, he was prepared to play along, partly out of curiosity to see where this was going, and partly because he was well aware that the Reichsführer-SS held the power of life or death over him. If he left the questions unspoken, de Bar had little doubt that his own fate would not have been like Parzival's in its lenient ending.

"What was the meaning of the lance?" The words sounded hollow and ridiculous to his ears.

"The one who owns the lance holds the power of the world in his hands," the Fisher King answered. "The power is in the lance and the blood."

The spear of Longinus, Wagner's heilige lance. But unlike Wagner, Himmler had recognised that there was another element to the fulfilment of the Grail legend.

A woman entered the room now, no more than a girl, with long dark hair that swept almost to her waist as smoothly as a fall of water. She walked with her chin held high and a touch of defiance in her stance and in her hands she bore a golden chalice.

By the colour and styling of her long dress de Bar was immediately reminded of the tapestry in the Musée Cluny in Paris, La Dame a Licorne. He had studied the picture's symbolism in detail as a child. But this flesh and blood woman was no virgin. Beneath the flow of her dress her body bulged with child. The girl walked across the room to where René sat and set the goblet on the table before him. He picked up the chalice and gazed incredulously into the red jasper cup cradled within. There was no doubt that this was the Grail treasure; the elation in his spirit told him it could be none other.

And then, without warning De Bar experienced a shift in time. He was seeing the king reclining before the hearth, wrapped in sable skins. A large ruby glowed as it was touched by the light of the fire, jarringly red against the grey fur of his hat. The men spoke in the soft lilting accents that were both foreign and yet familiar to him, so that he understood the words without knowing anything of the language. He knew without seeing that beyond the castle, cold mists enveloped the hill of Tara, and the knights surrounding their king were touched by an unearthly sorrow.

The king was dying. Death had already placed her mocking touch on his features and yet with the young man's coming, he was making a final grasp at life. A cup of red jasper within a golden chalice was offered and all those in the room watched him as he drank of it. A pageant was played out before the youth, but afraid at first of revealing his gaucherie before the knights and ladies, he suppressed the questions that begged an answer.

'The son of a woman, whose mate will not be known,

He will seize the rule of many thousands'.

With the words of the ancient prophecy the vision had faded as swiftly as it had come and de Bar was back at the side of Heinrich Himmler. This time he spoke with more confidence.

"What is the meaning of the chalice and the woman who carries it?"

"This cup has borne holy blood. Now the cup-bearer is the chalice of the blood of one who will rule the world."

He was speaking in riddles and yet de Bar knew exactly what his words implied.

The girl was waiting for de Bar to drink. The goblet felt smooth and cold to his touch, yet as he swallowed the liquor it burned like fire through his veins.

"He who drinks well will see God

He who quaffs as a single draught will see God and the Magdalene."

The words slipped into René de Bar's mind and lingered there. He watched the young woman leave. Her movements were fluid, athletic and fascinatingly feminine.

Again he experienced the turning back of time and witnessed the woman they had brought before him.

"I give you Mathilde, my daughter," the king was saying. "She is a woman of high standing and one who will serve as an alliance between our nations. If God wills it, she will bear you heirs that will continue the line of your blood through the ages."

By his pronouncement the king of Tara had revealed the youth's own royal lineage.

"There is one more gift that I give you," the Fisher King said. He shifted himself uncomfortably on the couch on which he was lying drawing the animal skins more closely around his body. A servant ran forward and quickly built up the fire, so that the flames roared, sweeping up the chimney of the great central fireplace that warmed the room. The king beckoned one of his knights and spoke a few quiet words. Struggling into an upright position, the Fisher King called upon the youth to draw nearer. As he knelt at his feet, he was touched on either shoulder with the blade of the old man's sword.

"Arise, go forth," he commanded. The young man raised his head and the knight bowed his knee before him. In his hand he bore a cushion of white velvet and upon it lay the jasper goblet. "Take this cup with you," the Fisher King said, "its powers will regain you your kingdom. Guard it well. Strive with all your might as a Knight of Christ to bring the pieces of the sword together!"

For some reason, de Bar knew that the year was 666, and the youth the lost King Dagobert II.

Chapter 21
Twice-Born

Jerusalem eventually fell to the crusaders in 1099. It was smaller than Antioch but the walls were well fortified. The Fatimid caliphs of Egypt were the occupying power and, until the crusade, they had raised no objection to Christian pilgrims visiting the city from Europe.

Before the arrival of the armies there had been ample opportunity to build up stocks of food and water in preparation for a long siege. Christians had been expelled, but the Jewish population remained within the walls.

A swift overthrow was imperative if the crusaders were to avoid a repetition of the happenings of Antioch, but wells outside the walls had been blocked or poisoned, there was little food, and those who laid siege were themselves vulnerable to attack. The crusaders had no siege towers with which to scale Jerusalem's walls and there were no trees in the area. But a reconnaissance group discovered a cache of prepared timber, which they saw as an act of God. Towers were built and, about a month after their arrival, the walls were breached and the crusaders swarmed into the city.

Jerusalem's inhabitants were indiscriminately put to the sword and the streets flowed with blood. The Jews fled to their synagogue for safety only to be burned alive as the crusaders put it to the torch. The Al Aqsa Mosque also proved no place of refuge to Muslims and they were slaughtered without mercy. In all the streets and squares, heads, hands and feet lay in mounds and those who walked there were up to their ankles in gore.[33] But the first of the relics had been carried to the city and as with all holy events; it was only fitting that a great blood sacrifice be offered.

Shortly after Jerusalem's overthrow, a secret conclave was held by a select group of men. Chief among them was Peter the Hermit but

---

[33] Testimony of Raymond of Aguilers, chaplain of Raymond of Toulouse.

other notables were Hugues de Payen, Hugues the Comte de Champagne, and André de Montbard, uncle of Bernard, the Cistercian abbot of Citeaux. Present also were the leaders of the armies that had overthrown the Saracens, Godfroi de Bouillon and his younger brother Baudouin; Bohemond who had seized Acre, as well as Raymond, Count of Toulouse. The purpose of the secret meeting was to elect a king.

The Comte de Toulouse was a strong contender for the throne but the outcome was a forgone conclusion.

"There is only one that is of a royal tradition equal to any of the regal houses of Europe, and indeed, greater than any of them," Peter the Hermit declared. "That is the one descended from the loins of Joseph of Arimathea."

Those of the conclave nodded their heads and all eyes were turned upon Godfroi de Bouillon. That he was ill was already obvious and it was that reason alone that had caused them to give consideration to Raymond's claim. The Crusade with its severe reversals had taken its toll and it was unlikely that de Bouillon would recover.

Godfroi rose to his feet with difficulty.

"I cannot accept the kingship," he said. "That will, no doubt, in a short while fall upon the shoulders of Baudouin, my brother. If the Order of Sion is in agreement, I will assume the title of Defender of the Holy Sepulchre, and may God help and strengthen me to fulfil the charge that has been given me.

Odo, Pope Urban II died two weeks after the fall of Jerusalem before the news of the victory reached him. Godfroi de Bouillon succumbed within the year and Baudouin was recalled from Edessa. On Christmas Day 1100, he was crowned king of Jerusalem.

The ascension of a French King from Lorraine, with the blood of Samaria in his veins, to the throne of the Holy City, brought Simon Magus' religious Order of the Temple full circle and it might have seemed that this was the crowning point of history. But, as yet, not all of the precious relics had been assembled. Jerusalem was captured but the hold over it was tenuous. The sacred lance was in Baudouin's hands and the cup, which his family had possessed for centuries, had been borne by Godfroi de Bouillon to the city during the crusade. Once Jerusalem was captured, the head of Wisdom was brought to the city by the monks of Orval. The Mandylion, however, was still in the keeping of the Byzantine emperor and could only be taken if Constantinople was overthrown. As it was only a matter of time before the Turks seized the rich prize of Constantinople for themselves, it was imperative that the city be captured by the Latin forces to prevent the shroud from falling into the hands of the infidel. In accordance with the prophecy of the Magus, it was only when all these were assembled in one that the eternal king would rule from Jerusalem.

There were yet two other pieces of the puzzle to be discovered: the sword, known as the Desire of Kings, and a sacred room hidden beneath the Temple Mount. The inner sanctuary built by Hiram, hierophant and master-craftsman of Tyre, Simon Magus said, was to become the repository of the sacred objects for all time. With Jerusalem in the hands of the crusaders, it was now possible for the work to commence without interruption.

In 1112, nine men from the Champagne region of France were chosen and committed to the task of finding the secret temple. They were all related, either by birth or by marriage and each formed part of the inner cabal of the Samaritans. De Payen, vassal of Hugues of Champagne, was sworn in as Grand Master over the eight knights of La milice du Christ.

"You will be billeted in a wing of the palace on the Temple Mount," King Baudouin said. "I need not inform you that the undertaking must proceed in the utmost secrecy. Not even my official chronicler will attest to your commission. If questions are asked, it will be said that you are charged with the protection of pilgrims in the Holy Land."

Hugues de Payen bowed his head, "Thank you, sire. It is understood."

The Al Aqsa Mosque was built on the Temple Mount, a situation sacred to Islam and significant to the Jew. To the Jew it was where Abraham had prepared to sacrifice his son; it was the threshing floor of Ornan and the site of Solomon's Temple. To Islam, it was the place from which Muhammed, in a dream, had ascended to heaven on the back of his steed. To some Jews, it bore a different connotation. The Mosque was built over a rock known as the Eben Shetiyyah, the stone of foundation, which stemmed the fountains of the abyss. On it was inscribed the Holy Name of God. Were this rock lifted, the legend said, it would institute a second flood.

For the next nine years, the temple mount would become the focus of a Templar search. The knights tunnelled at first vertically under the Mosque to a depth of twenty-five meters and then struck out horizontally towards the Dome of the Rock. At length a second tunnel was created at a lower level, running parallel to the first.

"It has proved fruitless, sire." Hugues de Payen confessed to King Baudouin at last. "Several years of labour have realised little beyond a few buried artefacts."

"You should have struck the chamber by now," Baudouin said. "There has to be a mistake in calculation."

De Payen's expression was weary. "We have reviewed the instructions time and time again, sire. There is nothing to suggest that we have fallen into error."

"Summon your men to the palace tonight!" King Baudouin said. "We will bring the knights from the priory and together we will seek verification. We cannot delay any further!"

Immediately after the crusade, an Augustinian abbey had been built on Mount Zion over the ruins of the Byzantine, Mother of All Churches. In 1108 the monks from Calabria left the monastery at Orval without word. Many months later they joined Peter the Hermit in the Holy City and occupied the new monastery, taking the name Chevaliers de l'Ordre de Notre Dame de Sion. Sion housed the inner cabal; the Temple was destined to become the visible order.

Jerusalem was in darkness when the thirty men proceeded to the Mosque after first meeting with the king. He had stressed the urgency of the matter. A second crusade was needed to hold Islam at bay, yet Europe appeared to have lapsed back into torpor. Few fighting men remained in the Holy Land and it was uncertain whether the city could be held for much longer.

"Everything, brethren, is invested in this quest! Much blood has been spilled to gain us this vital foothold. Our future, and the future of our Brotherhood, is in your hands!"

Fiery torches illuminated the procession that wound up the steps to the temple mount. The monks, faceless beneath the cowls of their robes in the uncertain light, bore on staves a camphor casket. It was carried by four men with great care and worship, while the others walked in rows of three, before and behind them.

Ahead, the Dome of the Rock loomed black and forbidding against the moonless sky and, as the monks mounted the steps and entered the precinct, they began to chant, their voices rising and falling in unison drowning the shuffle of their footsteps on the stone floor. The dominance of the Islamic edifices on the mount did nothing to ruffle them. Until some future reconstruction of Jerusalem's Temple, the Dome covered the true temple beneath the earth and the focus of worship was the rock, Eben Shetiyyah.

Templars clustered silently beneath the great dome waiting for their brethren to assemble. The casket was placed on a folded samite cloth on the rock, the chanting ceased, a monk prayed aloud in the Latin tongue and the box was opened.

Peter the Hermit took the head of the Baptist in both hands raising it high and monks and Templars fell on their knees before it. There was silence. In the semi-darkness the grotesquely pallid face of the relic was barely visible in the mass of tangled hair.

A pure white light flickered and grew out of nowhere until it bathed the rock, illuminating the head. As the men gazed, awestruck, the facial features changed and it seemed to the assembly that they were gazing at the countenance of an angel. Inexplicably, the sound of sweet music sprang from somewhere high in the dome and the air was filled with a heady fragrance. Within the breasts of these hardened men stirred a great yearning as that of a lover for his beloved. For a long time, there was no need for words. No earthly love could so stir their souls or saturate and fulfil their beings. None moved. The glow enveloping the head burned brighter and then faded once more.

"Eben Shetiyyah is the stone on which the Holy Name is engraved; there is a sure womb beneath." The words emanated from the ancient relic although there was no discernable movement of the mouth which spoke them. "Only the true seeker will discover it. Three members of the cross lie above the clay; it is for the valiant knight to unbury that which lies hidden beneath the earth. You soldiers of the cross will prosper in your quest and unite symbolically the sword and the lance with the cup and the platter. Masculine and feminine elements will become one and will bring the promised Christ to birth from the secret womb. Go back to the Spring! The quest is complete in the person of Galahad; the question will be spoken and answered. The time is almost come."

"It is impossible that we have missed it!"

It was not the first time Hugues de Payen had spoken those words that night and Peter the Hermit nodded distractedly, his eyes shifting back to the black outline of the dome that overshadowed and pinpointed the spot.

"You are certain the tunnels end there?"

"And go beyond."

"Then you are undoubtedly on the wrong level." The words contained judgment and de Payen was annoyed.

"We have followed the instructions," he retorted sharply. "There can be no mistake."

"Yet the chamber is not found."

"Brethren," Archambaud de Saint Armand reminded them quietly. "Our time would be best spent in examining the word. "If there is something that we have missed, the clue is best sought in unity. Let us see the cross planted into the ground as a sword is plunged into the heart through Eben Shetiyyah, the rock of foundation."

Hugues de Payen bowed his head briefly in acquiescence. "First," he said, "it would be fitting to take the Chevaliers to the mouth of the tunnel."

He walked swiftly, still smarting with anger but knowing that help was necessary. He had failed the king and any further setback might cost him his position in the Order. It was becoming obvious that King Baudouin's health was failing, a fact which added to the monarch's impatience – that, and his own inability to produce an heir.

The first tunnel sloped gently beneath the foundations of the Al Aqsa Mosque and a few chosen men followed it in single file and viewed the black mouth of the vertical drop. A rope lay coiled to one side of the well, anchored to a metal bolt hammered into the rock face. But at night there was nothing to be gleaned from the excavation itself except to salvage something of de Payen's pride.

"A sword wound into the heart of the rock," Archambaud mused as he gazed down into the man-made pit. "Another such wound was made by King Hezekiah at Gihon's spring."

Peter the Hermit glanced at him sharply. "We're all aware of Hezekiah's tunnel, but it goes away from the temple, in the direction of the Pool of Siloam outside the walls of David's city."

"But it begins at the spring," Archambaud said. "A place of great significance to us all. Solomon himself was anointed there as king after David."

The Grand Master was no longer staring moodily into the entrance to the tunnel but was listening to the exchange with keen interest.

"Hezekiah was subtly changed towards the end of his reign," he said, "so that he made allies of foreign powers and no longer heeded the council of Isaiah the prophet. Was it not he who disclosed all the treasures and secrets of Judaea to the Babylonian king, holding nothing back?"

Archambaud nodded. "Is it not possible that the good king's tunnel intercepted another at its source, one which led in the direction of the temple?"

"May I remind you that Gihon is said to be one of the four rivers of Paradise?" Peter the Hermit's eyes glinted in the light of the torches as the three men glanced at one another.

"Is it possible we have overlooked the obvious?" de Payen said. He massaged his eyes between finger and thumb. "What do you suggest?"

Discussion continued into the night and two hours before dawn the Chevaliers de l'Ordre de Notre Dame de Sion slipped away into the darkness.

On the following morning exploration began in the tunnels at Gihon's spring.

Chapter 22
Twice-Born

"Many people have become aware that this coming year will be one of awakening; the fulfilment of the promise of the Grail," Himmler was saying. "Until now, no one has held all the pieces of the puzzle. I have brought the lance and the cup together and now the hour of completion is almost at hand."

The embers were fading and Oswald Pohl threw more logs onto the fire. The smoke moved this way and that around the wood before the first flame crawled tentatively from beneath the pile.

De Bar was silent, waiting for the Reichsführer to continue.

"Adolf Hitler believes himself to be the reincarnation of Landulf, Europe's most evil magician, who was said to have been the Klingsor of Wolfram's Parsival." This statement was made baldly as though he expected de Bar's full understanding.

De Bar leaned forward in his seat. "And you are the wounded Fisher King!" His tone was sardonic. "The only obvious wound that Hitler has inflicted on you is to block you from leadership of the Reich, if that's what you wanted."

This statement was rewarded by a small triumphant smile. "But it was I who clipped him smooth between the legs!" he declared, once more reverting to the imagery of the poem.

Again de Bar watched him, choosing to wait his cue.

"I own the real Heilige Lance," Himmler boasted. "Hitler displays a forgery in St. Katherine's Cathedral, believing it will lead him to world domination. Adolf Hitler has never been more than a puppet." His voice was contemptuous. "Dietrich Eckart declared on his deathbed that it was he who controlled Hitler, and now I control him. All these years, Hitler has been dependent on the voices in his head for guidance. My men and I provide the direction. He follows."

"And you are telling me that the true leadership of Germany stems from Wewelsburg?"

"Just so! The Führer makes no move without the voice of

prophecy to guide him. It was that which brought him to power and it's that which will destroy him." It was not possible to keep the pride from his voice. "Your organisation has directed the affairs of Europe from behind the scenes for centuries, but we now dominate Germany, and for the moment we control Europe."

Once again, de Bar chose not to comment and for a while the room was again silent but for the sparking of the fire.

"The Parsival conceals the clues to an ancient bloodline." Himmler leaned back in his seat and watched de Bar, seeking some sort of affirmation in his expression.

"What bloodline?"

"I believe you know the answer to that. You know the history of the Merovingians. They were no ordinary kings and although their origin was lost in legend, there were clues as to where the bloodline emanated from. Mérovée, the first king of the Merovingian line was said to have had two fathers."

De Bar allowed himself a slight smile. "Legend has it that his mother was bathing in the sea when she was raped by a sea creature."

"But when one examines the myth, it was probably just another way of saying that he was fathered by one from across the sea."

De Bar's shrug was non-committal.

"It's strange that the same legend weaves its way into the Welsh story of Bran," Himmler said. "He too was said to have been fathered by a sea creature."

"Another ancestor from foreign parts?" de Bar suggested politely.

"Or an interconnecting of the same legend. Bran was the Welsh version of Parsival and the story of the sea creature creates the link with the Merovingian dynasty."

De Bar ground out the cigarette he had been smoking and lit another. "So you are saying that Parsival was a Merovingian?"

Himmler's face was triumphant. "According to history, Dagobert II was the last of the line of the Merovingians. Legends have a way of concealing great truths, but truth, like concealed treasure, has to be discovered."

"So?"

It was plain that Himmler was enjoying his moment. The men were gathered round, each one listening intently to the conversation, yet remaining apart from it. Someone had replenished the beer steins, but Himmler was drinking small cups of black coffee from a pot that had been set near him on the table.

"After Dagobert's murder by Pepin the Fat and the disappearance of his only male heir, Sigisbert, there was a flagrant attempt to remove all mention of him from the pages of history. Yet, nearly two centuries later, his remains were exhumed and reburied and Dagobert was canonised by the Catholic Church. He was even awarded his own feast day, December 23rd, the anniversary of his death. I believe that when Wolfram von Eschenbach wrote the Parsival, he concealed clues that spoke of this bloodline surfacing again. Clues that would lead mankind into a glorious new future."

"And where do I come into this, Reichsführer?"

"I trust I am not boring you, M de Bar." It was the first time since his arrival at Wewelsberg that de Bar had been addressed by his correct title.

"Nothing about this evening could possibly have been described as boring," he replied truthfully.

"Then, if you will bear with me, I will give you the rest of the history as briefly as possible." The schoolmaster's son was most at home in this sort of lecture. "The main line of Merovingian descent did not end with Dagobert's death. Sigisbert IV was said to have been rescued by his sister and in 681 he was taken to the Languedoc, the domain of his Visigoth mother, Dagobert's second wife. He inherited the title of his uncle, Duke of Razes and Count of Rhedae, or Rennes-le-Chateau and gained a new name, Plant-ard, from the French, *rejeton ardent*, the ardently flowering shoot of the Merovingian vine. Many years later, as we can glean from the legend of Lohengrin, the line of Plantard was knit with de Bouillon, and Godfroi de Bouillon, the swan knight, set forth to conquer Jerusalem."

Himmler stood with his back to the fireplace, his hands linked behind his back. Even in so natural a pose, he still appeared tense and awkward. He had folded up his cloak and set it aside and with it his Fisher King masquerade. His immaculate uniform with its deaths heads insignias and ritual dagger seemed so much a part of the man that de Bar wondered if he ever wore civilian clothes.

You are the direct descendant of the Grail family, and pretender to the throne of France through the Merovingian line."

"I know my heritage," de Bar said. "If you have brought me here to reveal that to me, you have wasted your time."

"I have brought you here," Himmler said coldly, "to offer you the means to take back what rightfully belongs to you."

Despite himself, de Bar felt the uneven pounding of the blood through his veins.

"I don't know what you mean."

"Allow me to demonstrate."

He nodded at Wolff who brought a box and laid it on the table. The Reichsführer opened it and carefully removed a scroll and several yellowed documents from their wrapping.

"Do you know what I have here?"

De Bar shook his head, but as he looked down at the documents he felt a stirring of excitement.

"Genealogies," Himmler qualified, "but these are far more ancient than those presently in the possession of the Prieuré de Sion. These were among the possessions of the Knights Templar and, I believe, coupled with later documents establish a direct lineage from Mary Magdalene who bore the child of Christ. The later genealogies trace the line of the Merovingians from the year 544 to 1244." He glanced up at René de Bar knowingly. "Dates, you would agree, that are significant, especially as next year the Grail is expected to surface once more?"

De Bar's polite smile in no way reflected the sense of incredulity he was feeling.

"How did you lay your hands on these and the cup?"

Himmler smiled enigmatically. "It was not difficult. The Ahnenerbe is an extremely efficient organisation. Perhaps sometime we will fill you in on the details."

Getting up from his seat he crossed the room and nudged a log into place with the toe of one highly polished boot. "I'm sure you have realised that I have an offer to put before you."

De Bar lit a cigarette and was not surprised to find his hands were shaking. He had not forgotten that he was still a prisoner on enemy territory.

"There is a sword that must be mended."

"You gambled that I would know the Parsival," de Bar said,

"It was not a gamble, I knew your background. It would have constituted an essential part of your training. What about the sword?"

"It will withstand the first blow," de Bar said, "at the second it will shatter. If you take it back to the Spring it will become whole again from the flow of water."

Himmler nodded. He was as eager as a schoolboy now, scarcely able to contain his excitement. A small flush of colour had appeared over his cheekbones. "Von Eschenbach was speaking of bringing together certain relics to heal the land under a promised king," he said. "But it will take one man to reunite the pieces of the sword."

"Parsival?"

"I am prepared to give you the genealogies that will establish proof of your heritage and the spear of destiny which will afford you total control. You will be able to rise to the highest position of power in Europe. A position from which you are destined to begin to bring Europe to unity."

"Why?"

"Germany is heading for destruction. I knew at the beginning that this was a war we could not win. But war was the only possible vehicle for the implementation of my plan. It was the only way to obtain the spear from Austria and to gain access to the treasures of France. Without war, the prophecies of the Parsival could not come to pass."

De Bar waited for him to continue.

"Once the spear is taken from Germany, her defeat is inevitable. It will not take long. A few months perhaps." The moment had arrived where his proposition must be placed before de Bar and Himmler felt suddenly afraid. He had gambled everything on this response. If de Bar refused, there was nothing beyond. "I have one condition," he said.

"Go on."

"You saw the girl was expecting a child."

De Bar nodded briefly.

"I am offering you an alliance," he said. "A marriage. The girl is a Jewess." He acknowledged de Bar's look of surprise. "Oh yes," he said, "there's nothing I haven't thought of. I know that the Jews will never accept a Messiah who is not of Jewish stock, so I have provided a Jewish mother."

"Messiah?" de Bar echoed.

"I have read the Protocols," Himmler commented dryly, "I am aware that the future world leader will be of the seed of David, and for such a man to be accepted by the Jews as Messiah, his mother must be Jewish. Ruth is in fact a distant cousin of yours, although one who separated from her family in her early teens. I will let you have her papers, so that you will be certain in your own mind that she is of good stock. But I want this child to be brought up as your own."

"And you, I trust, are the father?"

Himmler did not reply directly, but he could not disguise his look of personal triumph.

"Why are you doing this? What's in it for you?"

"There are two reasons," he said. "The first is that in fulfilling all the provisions of the Grail I will have affected the destiny of the world for all time. I believe it is my calling. This unborn child will complete what I have begun. He will wipe every Jew and every Christ-follower from the face of this planet and therefore prevent the Second Coming! In little more than one generation, the planet will be given back into the hands of Lucifer. You will need time to consider your answer. It's late and I suggest we retire. Gentlemen!"

He stood up and clicked his heels together, wheeled around and left the room, a small stiff figure in his black SS uniform.

Two of Himmler's Obergruppenführer fell in beside René de Bar and escorted him back to his suite. They were still taking no chances. It was well past midnight but De Bar was stimulated beyond any possibility of sleep. Heinrich Himmler, Reichsführer-SS was undoubtedly a megalomaniac and history would either denounce him as insane or worship him. De Bar lay back on his pillow in the darkened room, his eyes fixed sightlessly on the dim glow of his cigarette.

Himmler had spoken without compunction about the

extermination of the Jews to a man he believed was a Jew, knowing that he was a high Luciferic initiate. Their methods differed but their motivation was identical.

Chapter 23
Twice-Born

November 1943

He noticed without surprise that the door was locked behind him. The cell was still just a choice away. It reminded him of Nietzsche's unfree will; if he chose the moral it would mean almost certain death, whereas the reprobate course constituted an unmitigated rise to power. On the surface there was no contest. If he took the logical direction, would there be a point at which he could regain his freedom of choice? He lay awake well into the night, avoiding the temptation offered by the supply of liquor in the corner cabinet of the room. He needed his mind to be absolutely clear in order to calculate every risk.

"If I am to go along with you," René de Bar said, "I need to know what your other conditions are."

Heinrich Himmler shifted in his seat and adjusted his glasses. His expression betrayed nothing. "May I offer you a brandy, M de Bar?"

"Thank you, I would prefer coffee."

Himmler spoke a few words into the telephone on his desk and turned his attention back to his prisoner. "There are a few minor considerations," he said. "Personally, I would like to secure a political position in the new Germany once the war is over."

De Bar's expression was dubious. "I will obviously do whatever I can but I doubt it would be possible. If the Allies win this war, they're not going to deal too kindly with the Nazi hierarchy."

Himmler waved a hand in airy dismissal of such a notion. There was a sharp knock at the door and a uniformed officer entered bearing a tray of coffee. Himmler passed de Bar a cup and waited until the officer left before continuing with the conversation.

"With the level of power that I am placing at your disposal," he said, "I doubt whether it will present a problem, but should it prove for some reason to be impossible, I will expect you to arrange safe passage out of Germany for myself and any of the men who might wish to accompany me. Also, I will require thereafter, protection and safe passage for any senior member of the SS who seeks it."

De Bar nodded his agreement. "It's possible to use the network within the Catholic Church to move men and their families out of Germany. Further?"

"Concerns access to the child. I would require a certain amount of participation in his training."

De Bar regarded him thoughtfully. "The training of any child within the Prieuré de Sion is carried out at the discretion of the organisation," he said. "It would not be easy to bring in an outsider."

"Nevertheless, I consider this an imperative. It will remain up to you to find a way to implement it. Naturally, I will create my own form of insurance. The spear will be given to you when you leave Wewelsburg, but the genealogies will be put in trust. Copies will be placed at your disposal. However, the originals will not revert to you until the child has come of age. Should anything untoward happen to me prematurely, the genealogies will be destroyed. Do you understand, M de Bar?

"Perfectly." He had to admire the gall of the man.

"The Grail cup will be hidden for safe-keeping in Germany and I will ensure that it is released to you when the child celebrates his Barmitzvah," the Reichsführer continued.

"And if I refuse to work with you?" The question had to be asked.

"I think you may have already calculated that answer."

René de Bar smiled wryly. "Then I accept your offer, Herr Himmler. Where do we go from here?"

This time the Reichsführer was unable to disguise the triumph in his face.

"I insist," he said; "that you take a little brandy with me. Such agreements should be ratified with a toast."

De Bar nodded.

Himmler set two deep-bowled glasses down on the desk and carefully poured two fingers of the amber liquid into each.

"I'm certain that whatever this child learns from me will be in harmony with the teachings of your organisation. We're both aware that mankind is on the edge of a new era, an age of spiritual evolution that will have a profound effect on the whole planet." His eyes gleamed behind his spectacles and he raised his brandy glass in a salute to de Bar. "A new root race is being established," he said, "a race characterised by gifts utilised by only a chosen few, such as mind-control and the manipulation of the vril, the earth's forces." He was on his feet now, his drink untouched, pacing restlessly as his thoughts sought an outward expression in words. "The Aztecs understood the need for blood sacrifice to delay the end. Their timing was wrong, but ours is not. This war was necessary for many reasons, but one of the most vital was the aspect of human sacrifice." He swung round to face de Bar. "I believe you understand what I am saying?"

De Bar nodded.

"These beliefs are the foundation of the Reich. Adolf Hitler himself believes humanity is reaching a new stage in its metamorphosis, but his understanding is more simplistic. The human species is in a decline, just managing to hold on, but every seven hundred years, it achieves a step up."

"And you recognised that the seven-hundredth year was imminent."

Heinrich Himmler's smile was self-congratulatory. "Had we not made the blood sacrifice, 1944 might have been the end of the age. By my intervention, I believe it will continue as the Mayan calendar predicts, until 2012, at which time our man will have assumed control."

De Bar allowed himself a smile. "Your research has been very thorough."

"The Spear of Longinus has given me a role in the history of this planet that mankind will probably never recognise," Himmler said. "I have been the saviour of this era. There has been an enormous blood-letting, but every drop that was shed on the earth was necessary. Treasure will indeed come to the surface next year, in the form of a child. He will be the new Parsival and his destiny will be to usher in the sixth root race."

Despite himself, René de Bar felt his flesh tingle.

"You may have heard of Lebensborn, my breeding scheme," Himmler continued. "I've gone about it scientifically just as one would go about creating a new strain of plant. Using the SS as my starting point I have taken men of pure, Aryan blood and allowed them to breed with only racially pure women. I myself have given preference to men who appear to have the right sort of affinity for spiritual things. With a little human intervention, Germany will play a leading role in the creation of Homo Noeticus. I see myself as architect and perhaps even Father of the coming New Age."

"And yet, you have chosen a Jewess to be mother of your new world leader?" There was more than a suggestion of irony in de Bar's tone.

"In order to infiltrate the child into your organisation. It would not have been from personal choice," Himmler returned coldly. "Every requirement had to be perfectly met. This Jew is different though, like you, she has taken a Luciferic initiation. In exceptional circumstances such as this, it sets her apart from her race."

Perhaps his real genius, de Bar mused, lay in his ability to appear benign. Already many writers and historians had discounted his importance to the Reich. The power of the SS was a true reflection of the man behind it, and the deeds of the SS were an outworking of the camouflaged reptile at its heart.

"There is one more thing," M de Bar," Himmler was saying. "Is there anyone in France who would know that this association with Ruth could not have taken place?"

It was many moments before René de Bar could bring himself to answer the Reichsführer's question.

"Just one," he said at length. "Her name in the resistance is Simone. I can tell you where to find her."

Chapter 24
Twice-Born

Hezekiah's tunnel at Gihon's spring led to another meticulous search, which bore little fruit. It was the Calabrian monks who, in their study of the history of the area, once again turned the search around.

"Solomon's limestone quarries lie to the north of the city," they told Hugues de Payens. "A natural cave in the side of the hill marks the entrance. It is said that the excavations extend deep under the city itself, perhaps even to the very door of the inner sanctum."

"The place is known as the cave of Zedekiah," Peter the Hermit added. "The king is said to have hidden there before attempting to make his escape."

"Was he not the last of the kings?"

The Hermit nodded. "His children were slaughtered before the Babylonians put out his eyes. He died in Babylon."

"Ride with me Peter!" de Payens said urgently. "Perhaps this is the very place we are seeking."

They tethered the horses below an outcrop of rock and forced their way through the undergrowth to examine the cliff frontage. Flies buzzed around their faces and sought to settle in the sweat and dust in the corner of their mouths and eyes.

"Here it is!" Peter the Hermit's cry was triumphant.

Lighting the oil lamps, which they had brought with them, they stepped through the narrow opening. In the flickering light, beneath a sweep of solid rock, a vast chamber opened up before their eyes. Both men stood still allowing their vision to adjust to the gloom. It was deliciously cool after the merciless heat of the afternoon sun.

"Is this the place? I see no sign of quarrying."

Peter the Hermit did not reply but instead strode purposefully into the depths of the cave. De Payens followed the uncertain light from his companion's lamp, which cast eerie shadows as he walked.

"There are other chambers. Man-made. Hewn from the limestone," the Hermit called back. "Certainly, this is the quarry!"

"Then we must bring our men on the morrow. Let us see if the last king of Judaea will lead us into the earth's womb. Perhaps, Peter, our digging is over at last. A way has been prepared already."

It was another month before the entrance to the tunnel was discovered. Exploration of the chambers was arduous. Multiple galleries were hewn deep into the limestone and in some, massive blocks, still locked into the rock had been abandoned.

A rough engraving of what appeared to be a cherub chiselled onto the rock face in an antechamber was the first clue that something might lie beyond. When tapped by a hammer, the sound was hollow. What remained was to discover the mechanism by which it would open.

"Describe it to me!" King Baudouin clutched at Hugues de Payens sleeve.

"Sire, it is breathtaking; words can scarcely convey the beauty of the place. A vast circular room overlaid with gold and precious stones. The dome, sire, is encrusted with sapphires set with carbuncle to mark the position of the stars of heaven. It is filled with the richest treasures befitting our coming King and Pope." De Payen fell on his knees before the king. "Within the room we discovered the greatest treasure of all!"

"The sword?" he asked eagerly. "Do you have the sword?"

"My men are still searching, sire. As yet, we have failed to find it."

The king's countenance fell. "What then?"

"The Ark of the Covenant, sire."

Baudouin inhaled sharply.

"Mon Dieu!"

"We have in our possession those things of which kings and popes have only dared to dream! Just one step more and we will seize the kingdom and the elect will be reunited with Lucifer in his perfected state as he existed before the fall."

"Hear me," the king's voice was hoarse. "The Head of Wisdom must be placed within the Ark."

The Grand Master bowed his head. "It is most fitting, sire. He is our living word. It is fitting that he is the Law within the ark."

"It must be done in a ceremony before I die," Baudouin said eagerly. "That will be his resting place."

King Baudouin's health was failing rapidly and it was obvious now, even to him, that his deepest desire to see the chamber for himself would never be realised. He would never survive the rigours of the tunnels. As he lived the wonders of the inner temple vicariously through Hugues de Payen, his eyes blazed with the old passion. Certainly he had dared to dream of immortality but it had eluded him. How frail and how transient was the flesh. Like the dry grasses of the Holy Land which blossom for a moment and are consumed. In his heart, he had always known he was no Galahad who bore within him the guarantee of election. He knew that the latent desires in Parsival had been burned away in the hermitage but he, Baudouin, had made little attempt to control his own fleshly lusts. The king fell back in his chair and his breathing became laboured.

"We are so close," he mourned. "But not all the relics are within our grasp. You must rally another crusade, Hugues. The sword must be found; so much is possible if you possess it. And funding! They will give you all the money you need now that you have located the chamber. We must repel the Saracen and secure the Holy Land until the relics can be gathered together."

"It will be done, sire. God wills it!"

In 1117, shortly before his death, King Baudouin I negotiated an official constitution for the Order of the Templars at St. Leonard at Acre. It was his cousin, therefore, Baudouin of Bourg, who, once crowned, dispatched Hugues de Payen on his vital diplomatic mission to Europe.

The newly formed body of knights was to persuade Fulk of Anjou to marry Baudouin II's daughter Melisende making him heir to Jerusalem's throne. The new king had fathered three daughters but no sons and it was imperative to create a standing dynasty not only to stabilise the country, but for the continuance of the line. At the same time, de Payen sought papal sanction for the Order of the Templars which, in essence, was simply a continuum and the visible expression of Simon Magus' own order.

The third part of Hugues de Payen's mission was to raise a crusader force to launch an attack against Damascus. Baudouin II was negotiating from a position of strength. Much of Outremer was now in Christian hands and if Damascus could be toppled the Moslem threat would be greatly diminished.

News of the discovery of the hidden 'spring' beneath Jerusalem's temple mount was delivered only to those worthy souls that constituted the progeny of Simon Magus' cabal. It sent a shiver of anticipation through Europe's underground stream and Hugues de Payen was received by Henri I in England 'with great worship'.

The mission met with every success. Funding poured in for the Templars and the second crusade. Fulk of Anjou moved to Jerusalem to marry Melisende shortly after his son, Geoffrey, was married to Matilda, the daughter and heiress of Henry I of England further strengthening the alliance between the three powers.

De Payen's greatest challenge however, was his appeal to the church council at Troyes, which was held at the Court of the Count of Champagne, to secure the endorsement of his order of military knights. The teachings of Christ had never sanctioned violence; it was still forbidden for knights killed in jousts to be buried in consecrated ground. The morality of war was under scrutiny.

In 1115, Count Hugues of Champagne donated the Valley of Wormwood to the charismatic Cistercian Abbot Bernard for the creation of a new monastery, which was renamed Clairvaux. The abbot's young uncle, Andrew de Montbard, was a founding member of the Order of the Templars. Because of these and other intimate connections between the Cistercians of Clairvaux and the budding Order in Jerusalem, it was natural that Hugues de Payen should write to seek Bernard's help in obtaining apostolic confirmation for the Templars and drawing up a Rule of Life for the Order. The Abbot of Clairvaux therefore was among the attendant churchmen under the presiding Papal Legate, which included ten bishops and seven abbots. When five of the Temple's knights appeared with the Grand Master before the Council, Bernard proved to be a strong partisan and all opposition was swept aside. In 1128, the church council at Troyes officially recognised the new religious and military order of the Knights

Templar.

When, two years later, Hugues de Payen returned to Jerusalem with three hundred knights, the Order of the Templars was already greatly enriched by donations of land and money.

It had become clear that the sword was not concealed within the inner temple and it was given to the monks of the Order of Sion to discover its whereabouts. For several months, they searched examining the words passed down from Simon Magus in the light of clues in the scriptures. In this manner, one unlocked the secrets of the other.

One morning, shortly after Hugues de Payen's arrival, Michael of Molesme signalled to a companion.

"I may have something," he said. "In the Celtic tale of Peredur, son of Evrawc, it is said that he slew a lion cutting the chain which bound him, and dropped his body into an immense pit. There is a similar account in the first book of the Chronicles of the kings. It is written that Benaiah, who was numbered among King David's mighty men, slew a lion in a pit on a snowy day."

"What has that to do with the sword?"

Michael shrugged. "Perhaps nothing. But I know there is a deep pit carved into the rock in Gibeon where there is said to be an underground spring. I have heard," he added, "that the area was used for wine-making and jars were stored in cellars beneath the pit. Could it be that the three drops of blood in the snow, which so engaged Parzival's attention in the tale, pointed to the Biblical account of the snowy day?"

They looked at one another thoughtfully.

"The sun stood still over Gibeon, did it not, perhaps implying a union with the Sun God and the Temple of the Sun?"

The first monk nodded. "Gibeon was a Levite city allotted to the tribe of Benjamin," he said. "There is a great stone, which was thought to be the place of the altar of burnt offering where the tabernacle was kept before the building of Jerusalem's Temple."

"And it was at that pool that David's men wrestled with those of Saul's remaining son. Ishbosheth's men concealed their swords and in the fight, each produced his weapon and killed his opponent."

"A place of motionless suns, hidden swords, and dead lions," Michael of Molesme said with a thin smile. "Is it possible that the lion slain represented that of Judah?"

"Perhaps it is time to put this information in the hands of Hugues de Payen," his companion suggested. "It may be that his knights will make something of it."

A party of knights were despatched on the following day, de Payen at their head, and the village inhabitants watched from an uneasy distance as the horses clattered through Gibeon's gates. The knights were girded with swords over their white surcoats and their steeds, draped in clean white linen, snorted and tossed their heads so that their highly polished brasses gleamed in the sun. At a word, the local blacksmith came forward to assist with the animals and pointed the way to Gibeon's pool.

More than a thousand years had passed since Simon Magus and Demetrius followed the same worn steps, which spiralled from top to base of the sheer cylindrical rock.

Hugues de Payen, hearing the rattle of boots on stone magnified and captured within the confines of the space, experienced a sudden surge of exhilaration: a ghostly premonition as though the soul of the long-dead magician whispered an urgent refrain. The chill of the subterranean cavern enveloped him and he stopped, allowing his eyes to adjust to the gloom before descending into the depths where an unexpected circle of light from above made him aware of the water. Looking up, he saw the same channel of daylight that had captured the attention of Demetrius so long ago and he breathed the old familiar words:

"If you take it back to the Spring, it will become whole again from the flow of water. If the pieces are not lost and you fit them together properly, as soon as the water wets them, the sword will become whole again, the joinings and edges stronger than ever before."

His three knights had gathered beside him on the rocky ledge above the waterline.

"This is it!" de Payen said. "We have found the place, I am certain of it! We can but trust that the sword is not already discovered."

The men fanned out, examining the area methodically for

possible places of concealment for the ancient relic. Hugues de Payen did not move. Let the earth reveal its treasure, the whispered voice of the Magus urged him. Looking up towards the source of light, his eyes followed the crack that began there, widening as it meandered down through the rock face to a point above his head. The Grand Master stretched a hand up into the gap, allowing his fingers to probe the rock. Then, not six inches from where he stood, deep within the cavity, he felt a subtle change in the texture of the surface.

"James!" he called. "Come! Feel this!"

"What is it, Master?"

"There's something up here."

James worked one hand along the natural lip of the stone, fingers pressing the smooth metallic face of the object that seemed firmly entrenched there. Then, further down the fissure, resistance gave way and the panel shifted beneath his pressure causing the furthest end to swing outwards. Hugues de Payen grasped the exposed object and between them they rocked it gently back and forth until it could be released from its niche.

The Grand Master moved into the natural light which spilled down from the top of the pit. He was holding a sealed oblong box and a gleam of gold could be distinguished in the gouges made by the force of extrication. As James rubbed away some of the grime from the metal, they could see that the surface of the box was engraved with ancient designs and writings.

"We have it!" Hugues de Payens said in a voice husky with emotion. "Let us return to Jerusalem. The King must hear of this!"

Chapter 25
Twice-Born

April 1944

She was like a trapped creature fighting for survival in a situation from which there could be no escape. Her eyes shifted restlessly, dark and wide against the startling pallor of her skin. Perspiration beaded her face and matted her hair into damp strands. Another contraction wracked her body and, at the height of the pain, a scream tore from her lips; a sound pitched high, animal-like in its fury. She threshed violently on the hard delivery table, refusing to submit to the demands her body was making.

"The baby is lying breech," the physician told Himmler. "We could be facing complications with this birth. It's highly likely that we will have to perform a Caesarean section and I suggest that we hospitalise the young lady immediately. If you will allow me to call an ambulance, I believe it will be safer for her and the child."

Himmler regarded the doctor coldly. "The child will be born at Wewelsburg, Herr Doctor. There is no question of moving her. But I am holding you personally responsible for the safety of mother and child. Wewelsburg is well-equipped for any eventuality, and you are among the most experienced doctors in your field. You have been selected to do the job and we expect you to complete it.

"Of course, Reichsführer," Doctor Graf clicked his heels and returned to the delivery room. It was just after one in the morning and she had already been in labour for twelve hours. The nurse straightened up as he entered.

"There is no dilation, Herr Doctor, but the child's heartbeat is still sound."

He glanced down at the figure on the bed and not for the first time experienced an unprofessional flicker of fear. She was out of control and strangely, the drug he had administered seemed to have had little effect on the level of pain she was experiencing. The whole business was ugly. Even if this was the Reichsführer's bastard, the level of security to which he and his nurse had been submitted was strangely disproportionate.

Nearly another three hours passed before Himmler would allow the operation to take place. The doctor had heard of the Reichsführer's obsession with numbers but this delay was criminal. The situation called for urgent intervention, but not until Himmler was certain of the timing, would he allow the surgeon to make his incision. It was exactly 4am of the 4th April, 1944 that the child entered squalling into the world. For a few moments, Doctor Graf allowed the small, bloodied body to be placed in the hands of the Reichsführer and he held it up to examine it. A smile played across Heinrich Himmler's thin lips. On the baby's chest, over the heart, was a birthmark; a strawberry red blemish that bore a strong resemblance to a Templars cross. The patience of the world, ripe for its Messiah, was soon to be rewarded, for its time was almost come.

On the following day, a pagan ritual took place at Wewelsburg as Himmler's eleven Black Knights of the inner circle brought a handful of soil from every district in the land and placed it under the crib; a mystic ritual of blood and soil intended to bind the new-born infant to Germany. As the men gathered around the crib, they saw that his eyes, the colour of slate, were open. As he looked up at them, strangely alert, it was as though he had brought with him into this life, some past secret knowledge.

Later, René de Bar sat down beside Ruth on the bed. The child slept with his head against her breast.

"Here, you take him."

He took the baby from her and rested it awkwardly on the crook of his arm. It seemed incredible that within this little scrap of humanity lay the potential for so much. The child slept on, but occasionally the partially opened mouth worked and the small pink tongue curled at some dreamlike memory of his mother's milk.

"There's something you must see," Ruth said and she leaned across de Bar unwrapping the blanket. The child stirred and stretched, but his eyes remained shut. De Bar gazed down at the splayed strawberry birthmark across the baby's exposed chest, feeling detached from the scene as though his spirit had torn loose from its bonds and he was looking down on the child from a long distance. It was some moments before he trusted himself to speak.

"He is the chosen vessel," he said. "The son of Lucifer."

It was a fortnight before Doctor Graf and his midwife assistant were permitted to leave Wewelsburg castle. Ruth had made a swift recovery from the Caesarean operation but because of the importance that the Reichsführer placed on the patient and her infant, the doctor had been forced to remain far longer than he would have chosen. Herr Himmler had made it abundantly clear that any complication would be laid at his feet, and the specialist left Wewelsburg with a deep sense of relief that the job was finally accomplished. It was good to be going home. He settled himself comfortably in his seat for the long drive back to Hamburg.

"A very strange business!" the midwife said, without turning her gaze from the window. "I don't see how the birth of that child could possibly have had anything to do with the war effort. The Reichsführer is such an old woman that he couldn't allow his fancy lady to be seen outside Wewelsburg!"

Graf shot an uneasy glance at the chauffeur, but the glass panel that separated the cab from the back of the vehicle seemed to create a soundproof barrier. The chauffeur, obviously relaxed now that he was beyond the bounds of authority, was leaning to one side as he drove, his elbow resting on the open sill of the window. His SS cap sat neatly above his ears, and his hair had been well trimmed above the base of his skull. Even beneath his uniform, Dr. Graf could detect the massive breadth of his shoulders.

Frau Zeigner shifted her bulk on the seat beside him. She was a large woman with hips that ensured her a dominant position on the seat but the midwife's work capabilities had never been diminished by her size. Dr. Graf had worked with her with confidence that came of a long partnership.

He smiled. "It's possible the child was not the Reichsführer's anyway," he suggested. "I have it on good authority that he already has a well-established mistress."

"There you are then!" Frau Zeigner retorted triumphantly. "Of course he couldn't allow Miss Ruth off the premises. Two mistresses and a wife! You wouldn't think a little man like that would have it in him, would you? He looks far too proper. Like a head-master, I would say. Just shows though, you can't go by looks, can you?"

Graf shrugged. "The Reichsführer has always encouraged the birth of more babies into the Reich."

"Aryans! He encourages the birth of Aryans through his Lebensborn project. He even gives a special grant to babies born on his birthday. But let me tell you something, Herr Doctor, his fancy woman was no Aryan." With difficulty, she twisted her body round to face him. "I've known some Jews in my time and that woman was a Jew."

Dr. Graf looked at her for a moment without comment before turning back to his scrutiny of the countryside. She was right of course. He had not been able to shake off the grey depression that had beset him since the start of this assignment, which had left him feeling flat and somewhat irritable. Initially it had been easy to feel flattered that he had been chosen to undertake a special mission to aid the war effort, but spending two weeks away from his family and his practice to deliver Himmler's Jewish mistress of a child was less than palatable.

Time spent in the Reichsführer's presence had confirmed his former impression of the man. He was insipid and ridiculously authoritarian. His pedantry became obvious after only a few minutes in his company, so that one became swiftly overwhelmed by a frustrating sense of boredom. In appearance, Himmler was almost effeminate; short, especially so when surrounded by SS studs. But set into the chinless caricature of a face, were eyes terrible in their coldness. Never before had Dr. Graf found difficulty in meeting a man's gaze, but each time Himmler looked at him with pale, reptilian eyes and the light glinting off his spectacles, Graf had been compelled to avert his glance. It was difficult to put his feelings into words. It was not as if the Reichsführer wielded extraordinary charisma, rather, he sensed, there was a vital quality missing from the man.

The source of Dr. Graf's depression was National Socialism itself. When the Nazis had assumed power in 1933, the glory of the nationalistic cause had swept him along with the flood. Germany had once again become a nation, which made one feel proud to be German.

Everything had seemed clean and incorruptible then. Perhaps it had been reflected in the youthfulness of the men at the top. Himmler was only twenty-nine when he was made Reichsführer-SS; Heydrich was twenty-seven when he took over the SD and he was head of the Secret State Police and the National Criminal Police by the time he was thirty-one. Inevitably, it had tarnished. The very element that had added vitality to the political scene at the inception of National Socialism had ultimately been responsible for the rot. A young man given power before he had had a chance to gain wisdom was almost certainly open to corruption.

The drone of the engine was unchanged. They were more than an hour-and-a-half from Wewelsburg Castle and travelling through open countryside. In another half-an-hour they would reach the suburbs of Hamburg.

When the time-bomb, neatly taped to the body-work of the vehicle behind the back seat, exploded, Dr. Graf's thoughts had just turned to lunch.

Chapter 26
Twice-Born

April 1944

Michel Hervet had slipped so neatly into René de Bar's place after his arrest that hardly a ripple had been felt in his parting. It was only then that Simone realised just how effective Alain's cover had been. Somewhere, she was certain, there must be relatives who were missing him, but she knew nothing of his real background or identity. It made her loneliness and sense of isolation even more complete.

Outwardly nothing in Simone's existence was allowed to change. Her own life and the lives of others depended on her ability to successfully compartmentalise her life and to keep a clear head. Paris was becoming an increasingly dangerous place to operate from. Agents disappeared overnight and their radios were seized by the Gestapo so that with each transmission there was a heightened risk that locations would be exposed.

Perhaps she simply imagined that the spring of 1944 was colder than any she remembered. The chill penetrated Simone's apartment, making each morning bleaker and more difficult to face. She sat in front of her bedroom mirror to do her make-up, wearing her street overcoat over her nightdress, and with her neck enveloped in a thick woollen scarf. The cold seeped into her fingers, making her movements clumsy. Putting the finishing touches to her mascara, Simone ran a brush through her hair, slipped on the dress that had already been laid out on her bed and sat down to draw on her nylons and fasten the suspenders. She was pleased with the shoes she had found on sale in the side street: navy-blue patent-leather with neat red bows on the front and practical heels perfect for the female cyclist. Picking up her handbag, she glanced around to see that everything was in order. Then she left the apartment, locking the door behind her. Simone took her bicycle from its place behind the stairs and wheeled it down to the street.

It was only after René's arrest that she had realised the love she had felt for him was genuine and not just infatuation heightened by the special circumstances of war. Even then, she knew that she had fallen for a man who, like an old jigsaw puzzle had several vital pieces missing from the picture.

The buildings lining the Seine appeared to be huddled together for warmth against the greyness of the city. Hundreds of tiny chimney pots, haphazardly lining every roof were like stunted fingers raised in mute appeal. A barge moved slowly under the St. Michel's bridge and the river roiled darkly in its wake; little waves sucking at the edge of the canal caused clusters of debris to bob and agitate.

There were two mail drops to be checked; the first at an apartment in Rue St. Dominique where an agent would leave notification of any radio transmissions received from London. The second was a tobacconist not far from the interrogation cellars. The information was taken from there to a café on the Boulevard St Germain, where Simone was to meet with Michel Hervet.

Hervet was a short, softly spoken man with a perpetual self-effacing smile, who worked under the code name of Paul. Simone often wondered if he was as he seemed, simply a vassal, or if beneath the gentle facade there lurked a man of sterner stuff.

"Ca va?" he greeted, patting the padded bench beside him to indicate that she should sit. "Have you had a good day?"

He had already ordered coffee and she poured herself a cup, cradling it in both hands to feel the luxury of heat against her fingers.

"It's been fine." She placed the folded newspaper on the table between them and after a few minutes he set it down between them on the bench, knowing that it contained the letters he was waiting for.

I see you're not reading the collaborationist news sheets yet?" he teased.

Simone tossed her head with a snort of contempt.

"There've been more arrests in Lille," he told her quietly. "There could be leaks that will affect the Paris operation. The Bosch are still jumpy after the burning of the locomotive shed down there."

She nodded.

"I haven't heard whether any more transmitters have fallen into their hands."

"Who was arrested?"

"I know of Yvette and Francois, but there have been others."

Simone looked down at the table so that her face was in shadow. They all knew the high cost to the SOE of every agent that was arrested and every transmitter that was captured. Even when she had not met other agents personally, their code names were familiar to her, and their arrests or deaths touched her and brought home afresh her own vulnerability.

"Pass the word around," Paul was saying. "I'm particularly concerned about our radio operators at present. Celeste has been carrying her transmitter from house to house with her to keep one step ahead of the Gestapo."

"I'll be in touch with her tomorrow, I'll find out how it's going." She stood up to leave.

"Bon chance, Simone," Michel Hervet said quietly. "Take care."

Simone parked her bicycle and ascended the stairs slowly. The depression she had felt when she awoke had not lifted and it enveloped her now like the cold, reaching deep into her bones.

As she slid her key into the lock, Simone froze and a feeling of panic engulfed her. Her thoughts were racing. The door was unlocked and she knew with a certainty that she had locked it when she left. Everything now rested on a cool-headed response. She stepped quietly away from the door and turned back towards the stairwell. The sound of a boot scraping on a rung of the fire-escape was so slight that under normal circumstances she might not have heard it. Her eyes widened with terror; riveted on the dark opening. At the same moment she heard the door of her apartment open behind her and she swung around. There was no escape. The man on the fire escape stepped out quietly with his eyes on her face and his Mauser aimed at her chest. He was smiling as he addressed her and although the words he spoke were French, the uniform was that of the Gestapo.

That night, in the notorious cellars beneath the Sicherheitsdienst, they slowly broke Simone's body, then strung her up by the arms and shot her at point blank range.

Chapter 27
Twice-Born

Hugues de Payens died in 1131 and was succeeded by Robert de Bourgogne[34] as Grand Master of the Templars.

The election of Pope Innocent had been contested, and a rival, who was given the backing of the Norman King of Sicily, was elected, taking the name of Anacletus II. Innocent II fled to France, where he was championed by the Abbot Bernard of Clairvaux. Such was Bernard's influence that the kings of France and England rallied behind him followed by King Lothair III and the German bishops.

Immediately after the death of Anacletus, Innocent II returned to Rome and the schism was healed. Doubtless, as a reward for Bernard's support, Pope Innocent published a bull, Omne datum optimum[35] granting the Templars wide-ranging privileges.

Under the rule, the Order was exempt from all other ecclesiastical jurisdiction, independent of the diocesan bishops and answerable only to the pope himself. They were permitted to receive tithes but need not pay them, a privilege, prior to which, had only been granted to Bernard's mushrooming Cistercian Order.

On Christmas Eve, 1144, Edessa fell to the army of the governor of Mosul and the news reached the newly elected Pope Eugenius III several months later.

Eugenius had been drawn to the order of Clairvaux as a monk under Bernard. It was with something of his old Abbot's passion, that he addressed a bull to Louis VII of France, urging him to take up the cross. King Louis was just twenty-five years old when he accepted the challenge but initially the idea of a second crusade was ill-received. Louis' brother, Henry of France, had also just joined the Cistercian

---

[34] This is according to information given in Holy Blood and Holy Grail, by Michael Baigent, Richard Leigh and Henry Lincoln. Other documents name Robert de Craon as Grand Master, and set de Payens death at 1136.
[35] Personal prelature of the Pope.

community at Clairvaux and, predictably, the young king approached Bernard for his support. Abbot Bernard consulted with the Pope, and in March, 1146, Eugenius reissued his papal bull and assigned Bernard the task of promulgating it in France.

Starting at Vézelay with the King at his side, Bernard again gave the rallying cry to a crusade. The Germans too came under the persuasion of Bernard's tongue and, much against his will, King Conrad was urged to lead the crusaders.

On the last day of Easter, April 1147, Pope Eugenius III and Louis, King of France met with the French Templars in their enclave north of Paris. It was an occasion of great pomp and solemnity and one which placed the final stamp of authority on the Order. The new Grand Master, Everard de Barres had summoned his pre-eminent men from Portugal and Spain and the bearded knights in their white habits impressed the gathering.

But it was in private council with the Pope and Abbot Bernard of Clairvaux later that night that Everard de Barres placed before them a request on behalf of the Templars.

"The Order of the Temple humbly desire the permission of Rome to wear on our mantles a red splayed cross." He laid the design before the two men.

Bernard glanced at the Pope who was gazing at the tunic thoughtfully.

"Perhaps you would explain why you have chosen this emblem?" he asked at length.

"You will recall the ancient romance of Parsival," Everard said; "when he was entranced by the three drops of blood in the snow. And in the similar tale of Galahad likewise when he saw three drops fall from the sacred lance onto the tablecloth of the Fisher King?"

Pope Eugenius nodded.

"I was drawn to contemplation of these three scarlet drops on their background of white," Everard continued. "It appears that the trance state which they incurred in the two men bore considerable import on the tale."

"Earthly things, even the threat of death or great reward, could not draw away their eyes from the blood," Bernard said.

Everard looked at him keenly. "Precisely so! A heavenly vision was revealed to these great knights, born out of earthly symbolism. Parsival's thoughts were set on the beauty of his wife, while Galahad thought to kiss the drops of blood on the cloth. But I believe their hearts were enraptured with a higher, more intimate vision of the goddess of heaven, symbolised by scarlet on white." He stood up and walked to where a fire crackled in the great hearth. Standing with his back to the flames he went on:

"It is a custom of the Jews and others that the wedding sheet is the token of virginity is it not? Such a token with its drops of blood is held by the father against any subsequent attempt of the husband to seek divorce by accusing his wife of infidelity before the marriage."

Bernard was smiling broadly, knowing full well where this conversation was leading. The Pope made no comment.

"Go on."

"It would seem fitting that the Temple should, in like manner make their pledge of chastity here on earth against that day of ultimate consummation with the Holy Virgin in heaven."

"Your croix pattée may be deemed to express symbolically four drops of blood."

"Three drops for the arms of the cross exposed on earth," Bernard of Clairvaux interjected, "the fourth implicit in the promise of heaven."

"Three drops inevitably form the sacred triangle," Everard agreed. "The fourth creates the square. In the meeting of those two triangles arises true knowledge."

"Gnosis."

"It is so. If the triangles meet apex to apex heavenly knowledge can be poured into an earthly vessel as with the Grail cup. But it is in death the triangles meet face to face and the cup broadens to a platter of knowledge. We will know all things as we are known."

The Pope stood up and smiled. "You have your request," he said. "Let the garments of the Temple henceforth bear the mark of the blood cross as a sign to the powers on earth and to the powers of heaven."

Fighting at the side of Louis VII in the second crusade were the Templars in their distinctive white outer-garment with its powerfully symbolic splayed rose-cross.

Shortly thereafter, ninety-five monks of the Order of Sion left the Holy Land with Louis VII carrying with them two of the greatest treasures of their Order. The golden chalice and the lance were being returned to France but the head of the Baptist still remained in the hands of the Temple in Outremer.

The majority of the monks took up residence at a priory at Orleans, donated to them by the king, while seven were incorporated into the fighting ranks of the Templars. The remainder, in two groups of thirteen entered a small priory at St. Jean le Blanc close to Orleans. This constituted the inner order of the Priory de Sion in France. Their leaving of Jerusalem with the relics undoubtedly presaged the fall of the Holy Land.

Chapter 28
Twice-Born

The German people were beginning to taste the bitter inevitability of defeat. The first flaming glory of the Reich had burned from embers to ashes.

Hitler called up boys from fifteen to eighteen, and men between the ages of fifty and sixty, and pressed them into a final defence. Despite the dire consequences for desertion, it was not unusual to see youths with grotesquely blackened faces and swollen tongues strung up on Berlin's ornamental lamp-stands, their bodies decorated with the declaration of their treachery.

The Reichsführer clung to his illusion of power, still controlling those around him with his violent rages, but it was obvious now that the Nazi god was a broken, prematurely aged, human being.

Gabriele Hoch willed the war to end. Her job was restored on her release from prison but she was ignored and rejected by the university staff. The reason for her imprisonment was no secret; she had consorted with a Jew and she was not going to be allowed to forget it. In the end though, the rumours reached the ears of her students and a coordinated protest forced her resignation. She left feeling humiliated while at the same time relieved that it was all over.

Weeks later, Gabriele found a job as a seamstress and milliner in a small factory with a very different class of girls. They regarded her with suspicion at first but in no time Gabriele had won them over.

Air raids were taken in their stride and a quick sprint to the shelter was an excuse to light up a cigarette and spend time in laughter and idle chatter. There was no debate on the rights and wrongs of the war, just girlish nonsense about the colour of a lipstick or the attributes of a beau.

Gabriele realised that the bravado masked the deeper unspoken issues: fear of death, of homelessness, of hunger and of losing the war; a possibility that loomed ever more likely as the weeks passed. They were afraid of the Allies, but more particularly, they were afraid of the approaching Russian army.

A letter arrived from Michael in October 1944. There was a brief preamble ending with the words: 'I have heard from a friend of mine that you should visit Brunswick and I would encourage you to make the trip as soon as you are able.' He assured her of his love and, as usual, signed it Siegfried. There was no doubt that it was an instruction; a warning.

Getting out of Berlin would not be simple. Gabriele was informed by a Reich official that it would take days, possibly weeks, for a pass to be issued, unless it could be shown that there was a family emergency or that she was on military business.

She left the offices and, tying her scarf more tightly under her chin, leaned into the bighting wind. The city was battle-scarred, reeling under continual air-attack. Roads were blocked by bomb-craters; buildings had collapsed leaving a shattered façade or a hollow shell, spilling rubble and glass across the pavements and into the streets. Gabriele now scarcely noticed the floating ash, or the smell of burning, which permeated the air. Refugees were still leaving the city on foot but without a pass it was likely many would be turned back. There had to be another way.

The shop was one she naturally frequented, being just across the street from her apartment and Gabriele's question was addressed quite innocently to the baker's wife.

"How do you manage to get flour at a time like this?"

"We're rationed, of course," the woman said as she handed Gabriele her half loaf of black bread and accepted her coupon. "The van goes to Magdeburg every Tuesday, which is where we collect our supplies. But like everything else, it's becoming increasingly difficult."

The answer was providential. If she could stow away in the back of the van, Gabriele reasoned, it might be possible to make her way north from there to Brunswick.

Late on Sunday night, she slipped down into the deserted street and checked the vehicle. The rear door was unlocked and opened easily. Switching on her flashlight, she was relieved to see that a mesh screen divided the cab from the load area and behind the seats lay a disorderly pile of about fifteen or twenty flour sacks.

"Perfect," Gabriele breathed. "That is exactly what I need!"

She closed the door of the vehicle quietly and went back upstairs to her room. It was not going to be a comfortable journey, but with any luck it would be her ticket out of Berlin.

Chapter 29
Twice-Born

Heinrich Himmler was certain that once he released René de Bar and sent the spear of Longinus back with him to France, the Reich's dominance over Europe would be shattered. He therefore held de Bar until the end of 1944, trying in his ordered way to arrange every detail to his satisfaction before he let him go.

The Reichsführer, Adolf Hitler, had anticipated a year of massive significance during which time he would see the gods act in his favour. He watched it slip by with growing panic. In 544AD, Benedict, holder of the Grail secret, had died, while in the same year, the Mandylion resurfaced in Edessa. Seven hundred years later, in 1244, with the Cathars under siege, the Grail was spirited out of the mountain fortress of Montségur. It was anticipated that 1944 should have brought it to the surface once more. In desperation, Hitler sent a contingent of men to the Montségur area of France to institute his own search. To possess the Grail would be to save Germany from defeat. As the year came to an end, Hitler's spirit was broken and his health began to deteriorate. From this point onward his grip on reality slipped away and the nightmares, which had terrorised him for so many years, broke the bounds between waking and sleeping to dominate every area of his life. His gods had become a plague of evil spirits that sought to consume his soul. He spent the night hours with his light on and guards stationed outside the door; but still the demons stalked him.

The Grail *had* surfaced in 1944, but it was lost to Hitler. The baby with the slate grey eyes and the mark of the Templars over his heart slipped quietly into Switzerland shortly after his birth to an apartment that Klaus Barbie had arranged for mother and child on his way back to France. Ruth Leiman's papers showed that the infant had been born in Switzerland and that she, a German speaking Swiss from Zurich, was unmarried. It was from Zurich that she posted the letter addressed to René de Bar telling him what he already knew - that he had become a father.

The butler took the mail through to M Charles de Bar in the

afternoon and laid it on the table. De Bar nodded his thanks and finished the sentence he was writing before setting his pen aside and sorting through the pile of letters. He was an imposing man, tall and more heavily built than his son. His dark hair, well cut and oiled to hold its sweep back from the forehead had begun to silver over the brow and temples. De Bar had not mellowed with age, his face was characterised by a dogmatic mouth, an intractable jaw-line and a strong beak of a nose. His eyes were small and heavily-lidded and the dark pupils were flat and unapproachable.

The letter in his hand was addressed to René and he weighed it indecisively for a moment before opening it. It had obviously been written by a woman. The hand was neat and youthful, the letters tightly formed and self-conscious. Charles de Bar would have preferred to have set it aside in the hope that his son would return to deal with it himself, but there was no guarantee that he was ever coming back. It was already almost seven months since he had been taken by the Gestapo and despite his best attempts at tracing him, there was still no clue as to his son's whereabouts. All enquiries had been met with silence.

De Bar shook his head and slid the letter from its envelope. Adjusting his spectacles he scanned the contents. His attention was riveted by the second paragraph; he re-read it and laid the letter aside thoughtfully. After a few moments, he went in search of his wife.

Martine de Bar was a woman in her late fifties, with all the carefully constrained neuroses of the upper class. She was brittle, and artificial, immaculately groomed and charming in company. She had dyed the grey from her hair, rouged the bloom back into her cheeks and in similar manner had painted the intrigue back into a life that may otherwise have become tiresome, through a series of illicit liaisons.

Charles found her on the terrace and she replaced the lid of her nail polish delicately as he approached, taking care not to damage the crimson varnish on her nails. She greeted de Bar with no discernible change in expression, fluttering her fingers before her face to dry the polish.

"Shall I ask Pierre to bring you some coffee?" she asked as he sat down.

He shook his head and, taking an embossed gold case from his breast pocket, offered her a cigarette.

"Light one for me, will you chéri?"

He passed her the cigarette and she set it gingerly into her ivory holder. "Is something wrong?"

"There's a letter in the mail for René that I think you should read."

"Oh, who is it from?"

"A girl by the name of Ruth Leiman. Has he ever mentioned her?"

"I don't remember anyone by that name. What is it about?"

He handed the letter to her across the table. "It claims that René is the father of her son."

Martine looked at him, stunned. "Do you think it's true?"

"I have absolutely no idea," he snapped. "Why don't you read it and decide for yourself?"

Martine read the three page letter and set it down on the table. "It certainly sounds genuine," she said at length. "But she obviously doesn't realise that René is in custody. What shall we do about it?"

"I am going to reply," Charles de Bar said irritably. "She'll need to know what has happened. If this really is René's child, then he's our direct heir and I will want him looked after. Especially if René doesn't come back."

"Charles, I wish you wouldn't say things like that. Of course René's coming back. Now that the occupation's over the war could end in a few months and he'll be back with us."

"My dear, I'm asking you to be realistic..." He glanced at her brightly set smile and shrugged. Nothing he said would make any difference, so any pursuit of the conversation was pointless.

"They appear to have met before the war," he commented, "and renewed the relationship when she came to Paris a year ago."

"But he never mentioned her," she protested. "He never said a word about a young woman in Switzerland."

He nodded. "Don't worry. I'll check it out. This is certainly not something that can be taken at face value. But it's possible that there were many things René did not bother to tell us about."

Martine raised her eyebrows and turned away petulantly. "Do you realise," she said at length, "that would make me a grandmother?" She lightly touched the line of her hair, flirting with him. "Do I look like a grandmother, Charles?"

De Bar drew on his cigarette and deliberately turned his head away to avoid answering her question. She was an infuriating woman, full of petty vanities, but she knew he still found her attractive and she played on this.

"If this girl is genuine, I'll want her and the child to stay here."

"Of course you will, chéri. And I shall want to see the little mite myself. Do you think he will want to marry the girl, Charles? Perhaps he will be appalled at the idea of fatherhood?"

Charles de Bar stood up. "I don't have the faintest idea," he said stiffly. "I only know that the existence of a male heir in the circumstances is of vital importance to our family. And this is something I cannot afford to overlook."

He called an extraordinary meeting of the Prieuré de Sion the day after he had seen Ruth Leiman. The thirteen men of the Arche of the thirteen Rose-Croix gathered in the Paris home of one of the three Croisé; a M Francois Benoist.

Benoist poured drinks from an oak cabinet and joined the others around the table. The room in which they met was dominated by a long table, which dispensed a mellow gleam in the light from the standard lamps. There were one or two eighteenth century antiques and two family portraits dating back to the same period. Sounds in the room were subdued by the deep pile of the carpet and the floor-length drapes that covered the windows.

Certain formal rituals had to be undertaken before the start of any meeting. Charles de Bar was one of the nine Commandeurs of the third grade of the Prieuré de Sion, and its head Nautonnier, or Grand Master, was the playwright and eccentric, M Jean Cocteau.

For the sake of security, wartime meetings had been kept to a minimum but, since the liberation of Paris in August, there was a new freedom of movement that had found itself expressed even in the ranks of the Prieuré.

Once the initial formalities were dispensed with, Jean Cocteau at the head of the table turned his chair to one side and stretched his legs. Cocteau was the youngest of the men present, chosen for his hereditary right to his position rather than his suitability. Yet his remarkable skills as a writer had kept the organisation informed of vital events throughout the occupation. It was assumed by his audiences, that Cocteau alone understood the imagery and language of his plays, which had continued to play to full houses, but there were men to whom his words spoke volumes.

"So, Commandeur de Bar, you have convened this meeting. I gather you have something of importance to tell us?"

Charles nodded, inhaled deeply on his cigarette and flicked the glowing tip against the edge of the ashtray.

"As you know," he said, "there is still no news of my son, but two weeks ago, I received a letter from a young woman in Switzerland, claiming that René was the father of her child. The boy was born on the 4th of April this year."

There was a stir amongst the men, an exchange of glances.

"Gentlemen, two days ago, I visited this young woman in Paris. I had invited her to come to France as I wanted to know whether this infant was genuinely my grandchild." Charles de Bar drew on his cigarette once more and glanced around the assembled group. "The girl's name is Ruth Leiman, a Jewess. She and René met before the war and spent a brief time together a little more than a year ago. I was satisfied that the story she told me was correct." De Bar leaned forward over the table and there was a light in his face that none of the men had seen before. "During the time that I was with this young woman in her hotel room, she had occasion to change the child and he was lying naked on the carpet while she folded the napkin. He has a strawberry birthmark over his chest. In the distinct shape of the Templar cross."

There was a hissed expulsion of breath from the company of men. Francois Benoist struck the edge of the table with his fist.

"The Merovingian mark!"

Charles de Bar nodded. "Almost as definite as if it had been stamped on."

They looked at one another in silence for a moment.

"This can't be coincidence," Benoist said at last. "We are well aware that Commandeur de Bar is a direct descendent of the Merovingian line. And the date of the child's birth…"

"The fourth of the fourth 1944," Cocteau mused. "We anticipated this year would be one of importance. Events are falling into place. It is essential, Commandeur de Bar, that we find the whereabouts of René. We need him to confirm that the child is his."

"I have little doubt," Charles de Bar said. "But you are right. We must have the confirmation only René can give. If we can't take a vote at this stage to admit the child to the Prieuré de Sion, I would like to suggest that we expend all our efforts in finding my son."

The men murmured their assent.

"What has she named the child?" Cocteau asked curiously.

Charles de Bar smiled. "Perhaps it's just a coincidence since the girl is a German speaking Swiss," he said. "No doubt with his French paternity in mind she has named him Jean. His second name is an even stranger choice. She has called him Jean Lucis."

The young playwright smiled. "Lucis. The composite of Lucifer and Isis. Perfect."

Concerted efforts had already been made to trace the whereabouts of René de Bar. As a prominent member of the Prieuré de Sion, he was not short of friends in influential positions, either in France or Germany. Moves however, had to be made with subtlety and diplomacy for fear of further endangering his life.

For sometime it seemed as though René de Bar had ceased to exist. There was no doubt he had been arrested and was in the hands of the Gestapo but beyond that there was silence. With the liberation of Paris in August 1944, it could finally be established that de Bar was no longer on French soil and the feelers, which had been put out through Sweden and Switzerland, were intensified.

In early October, Dr. Jean-Marie Musy, President of the Swiss Altbund declared himself ready to discuss the fate of the Jews with Heinrich Himmler.

"What do you think?" Himmler asked René de Bar. "Do I meet with him?"

De Bar nodded. "It's the contact you've been waiting for.

We're ready for the final move."

"Perhaps," Heinrich Himmler replied cautiously. "But so much will depend on how quickly things happen once you leave Germany."

René de Bar shook his head. He had come to anticipate Himmler's objections and his pre-occupation with detail.

"No matter how fast the changes take place," he assured him, "We're prepared for every eventuality. Are you ready to give the order to abandon the 'Final Solution'?"

Himmler nodded but de Bar was aware that he was agitated.

"It's the first time that I'll be openly setting myself against Hitler. The extermination of the Jews has always taken precedence over the war effort and I have no idea how he will react when the order goes out."

"It's my guess," René de Bar suggested, "that he's so preoccupied with his military failures that he won't react at all."

"Do I have your assurance that my men will be protected?"

It had become a recurring and increasingly urgent theme of their conversations. The Reichsführer's concern for the SS was deepening as the prospect of Allied reprisals became a reality.

"Herr Himmler," de Bar's use of his name rather than his SS rank jolted him into hearing: "we have discussed this at length. Everything will be done to ensure that the SS are given safe-haven. After this is over, my agents will spread the word that Rome will give them aid. Anyone taking refuge in a Catholic Church will be given assistance in getting to the Vatican. For those who don't make it, we will give legal help wherever possible. I can't vouch for everyone."

Heinrich Himmler nodded dumbly. He had handed over the reigns of power and felt as though the horse he was riding had bolted.

The Reichsführer Heinrich Himmler met Dr. Jean-Marie Musy in the conference room of a quiet hotel near Vienna. Himmler was accompanied by a small entourage of men, including Walter Schellenberg who had been instrumental in setting up the meeting. Musy was accompanied by one other man who acted as his secretary.

"You will no doubt be aware, Reichsführer," Dr. Musy was saying, "that the eyes of the world are on you. Many people are certain that you will succeed Adolf Hitler as Führer in the near future and it's therefore imperative that you establish a strong, positive image abroad. Any move at this stage, in favour of the Jews would be propitious. My organisation would strongly urge you to discontinue all action against them and allow them safe passage to Switzerland."

"My personal conviction," Himmler replied, "has always been against the killing that has taken place. At the outset, we encouraged the Jews to emigrate. Unfortunately, for the most part, they were reluctant to leave Germany and, of course, their immigration was certainly hampered by world opinion. Nobody wanted them!" He raised his hands in a small deprecatory gesture.

"So you would consider my proposal, Reichsführer?"

Himmler inclined his head. "Certainly! It's time a stand was taken against this whole unhappy business."

Musy smiled his satisfaction. "Should you manage to pursue this course, I think you will find you have the support of a number of very influential organisations. Perhaps we could discuss this further over a drink? Would you care to join me in the lounge, I have something of a more private nature to ask of you?"

Dr. Musy waited until he was certain they were alone before proceeding.

"We are trying to find someone, Reichsführer, whom we believe may be in Germany. We were wondering if you could use your considerable influence to trace him for us."

"If I can be of assistance, certainly."

Musy fingered his neatly trimmed beard. "He is a Frenchman by the name of René de Bar. A man of considerable influence in France. He may be known to the Gestapo by his name in the Resistance, Alain de France. He was arrested by the Gestapo in August last year and hasn't been heard of since. There is an organisation in France who will be willing to negotiate an excellent settlement for his safe return."

The Reichsführer nodded. "I see. If your M de Bar is in Germany and is still alive, I will do my best to find him for you." He stood up, clicked his heels formally and held out his hand to the doctor. "Now, if you will excuse me, Dr. Musy, I will retire. May I thank you for a mutually beneficial evening?"

Two weeks later René de Bar was released from Wewelsburg Castle and given safe passage back to Zurich where his father, Charles de Bar, was waiting to meet him. In the attaché case, which René de Bar carried with him, was a worn leather case containing the head of the spear of Longinus.

Chapter 30
Twice-Born

In the early hours of Tuesday morning, October 15th 1944, Gabriele Hoch climbed into the back of the panelled bread-van parked in the street below her room. She was carrying a cloth bag with food for the journey, a few clothes and her personal papers. Over her dress she wore a full length coat both to keep out the cold and the flour. As the sun rose, Gabriele concealed herself under the flour sacks, created a breathing space against the back of the passenger seat, and settled down to wait. The elderly baker was a punctual man. She knew he left at 7.30 sharp once the first loaves were in the oven and the second batch was rising.

She heard his footfall on the pavement outside the vehicle and held her breath as he checked briefly to see whether the rear door was secure. He cranked the engine and the vehicle spluttered into life. The driver's door slammed shut. It was imperative that she remained as still and as silent as possible, knowing any movement might serve to betray her presence. Gabriele could hear the baker muttering irritably to himself as he negotiated the new obstacles in the street and once he was forced to reverse when his usual route was blocked. Tyres slipped and churned as they sought to find a grip over a pile of rubble and the van slowly bumped its way forward until it reached level ground.

There had been several air raids over the past nights and it was becoming increasingly difficult for the city's support units to cope. Few men were left to clear the streets or to drive ambulances and Adolf Hitler's policy that women should not be used to fill men's positions in factories and essential services had led to increasing chaos.

They reached their first roadblock shortly after 8.00am and the van rattled to a halt.

"Papers!"

Sandwiched between the sacks, Gabriele's breathing quickened. She was grateful that the baker kept the engine running, certain that silence would have betrayed her presence.

"Name?"

"Heinz Breuning."

"Where are you going?" The voice was immature, pitched too high for the right degree of authority.

"To Magdeburg."

"Anything in the back?"

"Nein. Nothing."

Gabriele could hear the crunch of the soldier's boots on the gravel. The back door opened and remained open for what seemed like a long time. Then it slammed shut.

"Proceed!"

She heard Herr Breuning's slight chuckle and the disparaging remark he made under his breath as he pulled back onto the road. They were on the road with Berlin behind them and Gabriele wondered if she would ever see the city again.

It was less than an hour before the next roadblock and this time the check was more thorough than the last. The soldier ordered Breuning to open the back doors but again the baker left the engine running.

"As I said, nothing but flour sacks."

The soldier grunted and thrust at the pile with his rifle-butt missing Gabrielle by inches. He straightened up.

"Go on your way, old man!"

The baker walked round to the cab and shut the door behind him. The tyres spun momentarily on the loose gravel as the vehicle pulled off the verge.

"Wait!"

"Ja?"

Again the back door opened and Gabriele froze. Had something alerted the guard to her presence? She did not move a muscle but her heart pounded uncontrollably.

"Your door. It was not properly shut."

It slammed again and she heard the shifting of the handle.

"That's it. Proceed!"

The bread van drew away slowly and within moments they had left the post behind. Gabriele put her hands to her face and allowed silent tears of relief to flow unhindered.

There was one other checkpoint before they reached Magdeburg but this time the baker's papers were perused briefly and he was waved on.

Ten minutes later, the vehicle drew to a stop, the engine was switched off and the driver's door opened and slammed shut. Gabriele pushed her way out of the sacks and sat up. There was no sound from outside. Through the dividing grille she could see that they were parked in front of a warehouse and Heinz Breuning was walking purposefully towards the office at the entrance.

Gabriele wriggled her way swiftly to the rear of the van, dragging her carpet bag behind her.

"Please," she muttered grimly to herself, "don't let there be anyone outside."

She unlatched the door carefully, pushing it open a crack and blinking for a moment against the sunlight. It was a suburban area and although a few people were labouring some distance away, no one noticed the dishevelled figure that emerged somewhat clumsily into the daylight. Gabriele walked swiftly towards the road without a backward glance at the baker's van. The beige overcoat she had chosen with her hiding place in mind was a shade lighter but looked surprisingly good. Gabriele checked her face and hair in the mirror of her powder compact and grinned wryly. Stepping back into the cover of a copse of trees she attempted to repair the damage. A vigorous brushing removed much of the flour from her hair and her handkerchief sufficed to put some colour back into the pallid cheeks. She shook a cloud of dust from her coat, recovered her hat from her overnight bag, pinned it in place and slipped on her gloves. Then, with a little more confidence, Gabriele Hoch stepped back onto the pavement. Magdeburg lay in sight ahead of her and with any luck she would find a hotel for the night.

Much of the city already lay in ruins and the inn was one of the few buildings in the town's centre that was still unscathed.

"If Germany loses this war she will lose bravely!" the innkeeper's wife told her with a fatalistic toss of her head. "Her greatest sons have fallen as heroes and many more will fall in the days ahead."

"Have you lost children?"

"My oldest son was killed in Italy," the woman said matter-of-factly. "The younger boy is at the front. Now they have called my husband up in defence of Berlin."

She took Gabriele's plate. "Can I get you something to drink?"

"Water will be fine, thank you."

"The Americans and the English," the innkeeper's wife pronounced the names of the enemy bitterly, "are not like us. We are a great people and we will arise again victorious from Germany's ruins. You will see! Our blood has not soaked this land for nothing!"

"I need to get to Braunschweig," Gabriele said as much in an attempt to change the subject as to find the information. "Are there any routes open?"

"I think the main roads are being used by the army," the woman said doubtfully. "Most other people are on foot. As you know, there is little fuel."

Gabriele nodded. She knew she had been lucky to get out of Berlin; there were few private vehicles left on the roads.

"Then I'd better get a night's rest," she said with a short laugh. "I might have a bit of a hike ahead of me."

The land was green and lush. Cattle grazed peacefully on open pastures and once three young horses watched Gabriele's approach from the far end of a field before lifting their tails and cantering across to view her more closely. The weather was cold but clear, perfect for walking and she made good time on that first day, deliberately keeping off the main routes to avoid checkpoints and determined to make the best of the journey. She had managed to buy a loaf of black bread and a small block of cheese from the innkeeper's wife who had also directed her to a farm just east of Helmstedt.

"Just mention my name," she said, "and they will give you a bed for the night."

Gabriele nervously approached the farmstead late that afternoon. She had covered more than twenty miles and the unaccustomed walk had left her exhausted. A dog barked as she neared the house and a buxom woman watched her suspiciously from the back door.

"What do you want?"

"I have come from Magdeburg," Gabriele said. "Frau Schmidt from of the Drei Mohren Gasthof told me I could find you here. She asked me to send her greetings." The woman's face broke into a smile that instantly changed her features.

"Frau Schmidt! Wonderful! It's been weeks since I last saw her. Come in, come in. You are very welcome."

Two young girls watched Gabriele until the younger overcame her shyness and introduced a kitten to the guest and soon they were both chattering away companionably.

The farmer had been called up only days before.

"He was wounded in France," Frau Giesler said. "He had only just begun to fully recover." She shrugged philosophically. "There is nothing to be done, the enemy is pushing into Germany and must be held back by any means. Sacrifices must be made."

Supper was an extravagant meal. Gabriele's eyes widened at the sight of fresh milk and butter in the larder and sides of bacon hung from the ceiling. Glass jars of preserved fruit and vegetables were neatly stacked on the shelves.

Frau Giesler insisted that she stay and rest another day.

"It is our privilege to have a visitor," she declared as she lit the way to the guest bedroom in the attic that night. "I am sure Braunschweig can wait!"

As Gabriele settled down to sleep under the plump eiderdown, she decided that another day on the farm would suit her well.

Chapter 31
Twice-Born

"According to the Arabs, these men are all-powerful. They are Shiites, of the Fatimids, a sect known as the Nizari Ismailis. The Sunni call them Assassins."

The bearded man seated opposite looked at him questioningly.

"A name derived from the word hasheesh in the Arabic," the knight illuminated. "It is said they consume the flowers from a plant and enter battle in a trance, which renders them fearless."

The Grand Master rested an arm across his stomach, cupping his chin in the other hand. He surveyed the young informant with interest.

"You say their origins are in Persia?"

He nodded. "From the Elburz Mountains on the Caspian Sea. Their leader is one known as Hasan ibn-Sabah. He despatches his devotees to carry out a campaign of terror, to slay the Sunni sultans and capture their fortresses."

"Then we have a common enemy."

"And, I believe, common interests. These Ismailis are learned men, philosophers, with highly-developed religious doctrines. Their power, which is the cause of deep consternation to their foes, arises from certain mystical beliefs."

"It seems they have set their sights on seizing the strongholds of the Franks," the Grand Master said thoughtfully. "It is perhaps time to defeat them at their own game. Set up an ambush and capture one of their leaders, I would personally see the calibre of these men."

The prisoner who was led before Robert de Bourgogne, Grand Master of the Temple, was not the wild-eyed rebel he had expected. Several men had been held in the ambush beyond the castle of Qadmus, which had fallen to their possession, and this man was easily identified as the leader of the group. He stood before de Bourgogne, his head high and his expression haughty.

The Grand Master addressed him in faultless Arabic.

"Your men call you Khwaja. Is that your name?"

"It is a title of respect meaning master. My name is Malik Abu Hanifa."

Robert de Bourgogne was seated on a chair of carved ebony placed on a dais so that he was deliberately elevated above the captive. Two other Templars sat with him; the red crosses on their white tunics dominating the room.

"Why are you in Outremer?"

"We are sent to make converts and to destroy the power of the Sunni in the region."

"You have also crossed swords with the Franks."

Abu Hanifa's shrug was non-committal. "If they are in our way they will be treated as the enemy."

"Who sent you?"

"Our leader is an old man. He lives in Alamut."

"Hasan ibn-Sabah?"

The man nodded showing no surprise at the level of the Templar's information.

"The Ismailis are a sect of the Shia religion," de Bourgogne said. "Where do your differences lie?"

Abu Hanifa raised his chin and for a moment it seemed he would not answer but he chose at length to give only such information as was already common knowledge to his Muslim enemies.

"The Ismailis are Seveners. We accept seven Imams after Ali, the cousin of Muhammed, whereas the other Shiites recognise twelve. All history is divided into seven periods, each commencing with a prophet followed by six infallible Imams. The last Imam was Al Mahdi, Ismail, who will return to conquer the world."

"Who were your prophets?"

"They were Adam, Noah, Abraham, Moses and Jesus followed by the greatest of them all, Muhammed."

The Grand Master nodded. "Go on."

"Each prophet has an interpreter who taught the secret meaning of the Imam's teachings to a small circle of initiates."

"Who were the interpreters?"

"The six were Seth, Shem, Isaac, Aaron, Simon Peter and Ali."

The Templars glanced swiftly at one another.

"Simon Peter?"

"He was interpreter to the one known as Jesus."

Robert de Bourgogne stood to his feet abruptly and signalled to a guard at the door.

"Humphrey," he said, turning to the man on his left, "Return this man to his cell. See that Abu Hanifa and his men are treated well. They are to be our protected guests."

Once the prisoner had left the room, de Bourgogne left his dais and paced the room.

"A meeting must be convened," he said at length. "We must parley with their leader. How many prisoners were taken?"

"We have ten in the hold besides the man, Abu Hanifa."

De Bourgogne swung round and smiled slowly. "Eleven in total? Excellent! As did Joseph when he desired to reveal himself to his brothers, we will send the ten and retain the leader, Hanifa. Perchance we will gain a response from the father."

Fulk d'Aguilers smiled and nodded.

"See that they are first fed and treated favourably. We want them to send a good report." He fingered his beard thoughtfully. "Simon Pethor, the Magus!" he said at length. "These are men who have, it seems, arisen from the same root as we. Can you believe it, Fulk? We have the same interpreter as these desert savages. I believe we have discovered our half-brothers!"

A cautious approach was made to the Temple by the Assassin leader, Ali ibn Wafa. After ongoing negotiations and with studied reluctance, the Templars released their hostage. Early formalities were followed by deeper encounters and, at each, they probed to find the common ground the Grand Master already knew with a certainty existed between them.

They found it in Jethro.

"The Druze worship Shu'ayb, the one buried in Tiberius."

"Are the Druze brothers to the Ismailis?"

Ibn-Wafa shrugged. "The faiths have diverged. But their leaders are high initiates. Seveners like us."

The Grand Master shook his head, "Shu'ayb?"

"Jethro, the father-in-law of Moses." Abu Hanifa declared. "And high priest of Medina."

The Templars looked at him with undisguised interest.

"When the Israelites came out of Egypt they did not go north," Hanifa continued. "They crossed the Red Sea and Moses led them into the great wilderness."

"They left signs. Their seven branched candlestick is carved into the rocks in many places," Ali ibn-Wafa added. "Moses took them to the home of his wife. They stayed there many moons."

"While the cloud rested, they stayed."

"It was a powerful sign of the God of Moses. Moses was a great prophet. He was feared and respected by all people."

"Jethro, priest of Medina instructed some of the leaders of the Jews; men who understood the nature of these things. He revealed to them the black stone," Ibn Wafa added.

Robert de Bourgogne met the glance of d'Aguilers over the head of their guests.

Abu Hanifa laughed shortly. "When Moses later constructed a tabernacle for the God of the Israelites, there was jealousy among the Midianites. They demanded a house for the moon stone."

"And the priest of Midian built it a covering," Fulk d'Aguilers nodded.

The Ismaili showed his teeth in a smile. "A black cube. The Kaaba in Mecca today follows Jethro's pattern."

Robert de Bourgogne spoke thoughtfully, "The common factor is the Master, Simon Magus."

"If an alliance is to be formed to our advantage, it is necessary to demonstrate Templar pre-eminence."

"They must be shown the head."

"That is impossible," Fulk d'Aguilers said. "These men are heathen and this is our most sacred relic. It must not be done!"

"They are indeed heathen," de Bourgogne acknowledged; "but there is a common foundation, which cannot be ignored. Simon the Magus led their patriarchs as he led our own. Spiritually, we are one."

"Then let them convert."

"No! As Muslims, they are serving an eternal purpose. Should they assume the mantle of Christ they would be of no further use in the East."

"Then what point is there in revealing the head?" Fulk argued stubbornly. By permitting them sight, we risk their indiscretion and will have lost far more than we have gained."

"The Master was their teacher; they will be apprised of the relics," de Bourgogne said. "Their own belief doubtless emanates from the image on the shroud. And do not underestimate the power of the head of the Baptist! Have you forgotten the terror in its revelation? None who see it would dare speak of its mysteries."

Fulk stood to his feet and paced the room. "You speak truth," he admitted at length. "But if there is a double-cross, we will destroy them!"

He turned to the remaining ten men of the inner circle. "Are you in agreement?"

There was a unanimous raising of hands and the vote was taken. The Ismailis would be taken captive spiritually and bound to the Order of the Temple.

The Ismailis dubbed the relic Baphomet the father, or fount, of Wisdom. The Old Man of the Mountain, Sinan ibn-Salman grasped at this new source of authority.

"We will convert to your faith!" he pronounced some months later.

Robert de Bourgogne shook his head. "The Assassins must not convert!" he said. "Islam must play its own role. We will however covenant to form an enduring brotherhood. The Templars and the Assassins will be mutually supportive."

In 1149, at the Battle of Inab, Ali ibn-Wafa fell as he fought alongside Raymond of Poitiers, and three years later Raymond II of Tripoli was murdered by the Assassins. The Ismailis supported the Templars in war, removed their enemies in times of peace and paid the Order an annual tribute of 2000 Besants. In return, the Templars made no move against Assassin bases. The alliance was yet weak, but it stood.

Baudouin III's mother, the feisty daughter of Baudouin II, had ruled in the place of her son, only releasing her tutelage when arms were raised against her. However, the young king died without heir at the age of thirty-three and the reins of the kingdom were placed in the hands of his younger brother, Amalric.

Relationships between King and Temple soured during Amalric's turbulent reign. Abortive sorties into Egypt left Outremer at risk and Nur ed-Din attacked Antioch laying siege to the fortress of Haranc. Bohemond III, the son of Constance and Raymond of Poitiers, led a force against him and Nur ed-Din retired. Against the advice of his more experienced men, Bohemond pursued and his troops were ambushed by the Muslim forces. Sixty Templars were among those killed.

Six years later, in 1166, Nur ed-Din attacked and besieged the cave-fortress in Trans-Jordan, garrisoned by the Templars. Amalric assembled an army and set out to relieve the stronghold only to discover that the twelve Templars had surrendered without a fight. The king ordered them hanged. As a result, two years later, the Temple refused to accompany the invasion of Egypt.

"Amalric has entered into negotiations with the Old Man of the Mountain."

It was the year 1173 when the current Grand Master addressed the Temple chapter with the news. Francois Othon de St Amand placed his hands squarely on the table before him and leaned forward. His expression was dangerous.

"I have had word that Sinan ibn-Salman is speaking once again of conversion to Christianity. He has sent an envoy to Jerusalem to negotiate a settlement with the king."

"It is a blatant act of treachery against the Templars," Robert said. "He must be stopped at all costs."

"More than that, it must not be known what part the Temple has played with the Assassins. Such knowledge would bring the Order into disrepute and may even cause its downfall."

The men of the inner circle nodded. Amalric was seeking any excuse to defame them.

"Walter of Mesnil," the Grand Master said, "take a party of knights and intercept the envoy when he leaves Jerusalem. Amalric will give him safe passage so there will be no expectation of attack. Make very certain that he understands that the Temple will not tolerate any attempt by ibn-Salman to convert and what his end will be if he does."

Walter of Mesnil stood up and bowed his head. He had lost one eye in battle but his good eye gleamed and his hand was already at the hilt of his sword in anticipation of the attack. Mesnil's smile exposed broken teeth.

"We will issue a strong warning," he said. "The envoy will be sorry that he entered Outremer."

"Spare his life but change his heart."

The attack on Abdullah and his men had the desired effect. Sinan ibn-Salman ibn-Muhammed spoke no more of receiving Christ, but King Amalric was furious. He refused to countenance the rights of the Temple to act unilaterally under the papal bull Omne datum optimum, which exempted the Order from secular jurisdiction. Walter of Mesnil was dragged from a meeting of the Templar chapter in Sidon and imprisoned, but the king's intention to petition the pope and the monarchs of Europe to dissolve the Order was frustrated by his untimely death a year later.

Chapter 32
Twice-Born

It was obvious that the war was coming to an end. Hitler had made one final and brilliant attempt to turn the odds, amassing a formidable spearhead of ten Panzer divisions. He planned to launch the 5th Panzer division through the Ardennes Forest and across the Meuse River cutting the American forces in half and bottling up the British and Canadians in Holland and Belgium. In forcing a retreat into France he calculated that the Allies would have to abandon fuel and ammunition dumps, supplies desperately needed by Germany. He was prepared to throw a quarter of a million men and two thousand tanks into this offensive, and to back it with massive air support, gambling almost all the fighting power Germany had left. German agents in Holland, Belgium and France kept General Rundstedt well informed and Adolf Hitler was apprised of the position of almost every enemy division.

As they awaited supplies, the Americans had slackened off their offensive and had no expectation of a German counter-attack. Morale had undergone a subtle change. Soldiers were anticipating the end of the war; home beckoned; there was the sweet promise of a future and their sense of self-preservation increased accordingly. No-one wanted to die this close to the finish line.

Germany, on the other hand, had everything to gain and nothing to lose. On December 14th and 15th 1944, as the weather cleared, Rundstedt launched his offensive; a shockwave that sent the Allies reeling in complete disarray. Divisional and Corps headquarters were forced into retreat, communications broke down, and German flying bombs added to the sense of panic and unreality. A brigade of English-speaking Germans in American army uniforms had been sent in ahead of the Wehrmacht driving trucks and tanks bearing American markings and they deliberately built on the confusion by misdirecting traffic and countermanding orders. Chaos was increased by snipers parachuted in behind American lines and 'friendly' divisions, which attacked when approached.

The Americans rallied and fought as never before, holding the strategic town of Bastogne against massive odds until General Montgomery's British troops were able to turn the tide. It was the last major battle of the war and resulted in heavy losses on both sides. However, although the Allied invasion of Germany had been set back six weeks by the offensive, it weakened the resistance and expedited the end for the German Wehrmacht.

Adolf Hitler's eyes were glazed and rheumy and his face deeply lined; weeks spent underground had drawn the colour and life from his flesh leaving it as pale as a death mask. The air in the bunker was foul despite the air-conditioning and the scream and thud of the shells caused a continual reverberation through the walls and floor. The Russians were concentrating their bombardment on the area around the Reich Chancellery, intent on reducing Hitler's once magnificent show-piece to rubble and dust.

After the first expression of rage aroused by Hermann Goering's attempt to assume leadership of the Reich, Hitler had sunk deeper into despair and the atmosphere in the bunker had moved to the knife edge of madness.

It was late evening when Heinz Lorenz scrambled over the ruins of the square. Around him Berlin burned and smoked like some Wagnerian funeral pyre. Hitler, who was in conference with Ritter von Greim when the Reuter dispatch was handed to him, made no attempt to steady his trembling hand. Germany's despotic ruler, who had dominated by the power of his will, was a broken man. He had come to accept that the tremors of his body were as much beyond his control as the thud of shells over the bunker. He apologised to von Greim for the interruption and opened the dispatch. The Führer's eyes bulged horribly as he read the note and his face turned purple with rage. He gripped the edge of his desk and a scream that seemed to form in his depths tore from his lips.

"TRAITOR!"

Ritter von Greim leapt to his feet. "Mein Führer?"

"Traitor. They are all traitors!"

He flung the dispatch across the desk and von Greim picked it up and glanced swiftly at its contents.

"Heinrich Himmler! Surely not, mein Führer!"

Hitler's face was distorted, apoplectic. "The one person I believed in. The one person I thought I could trust! Even he has betrayed me. Goering at least had the decency to inform me of his intentions but Himmler simply went to the enemy behind my back."

The word spread swiftly through the bunker. Der treue Heinrich, a traitor! There were righteous expressions of indignation. Here in Berlin, their lives were being laid down in support of the Führer, while Heinrich Himmler carried on a flirtation with the Allies through Count Bernadotte, attempting to consolidate his own power over the head of Adolf Hitler. Eva Braun, Hitler's longstanding mistress wailed in distress when she heard.

"My poor Adolf! After all he has been through. He doesn't deserve this!"

The Führer, armed with the news of Himmler's betrayal and the knowledge that the Russians were now only a block away from the bunker, reached a final decision. In a brief ceremony in the early hours of the morning of the 29th April 1945, he made Eva Braun his wife as a reward for her years of faithfulness, and immediately thereafter dictated two new wills, one of which expelled Heinrich Himmler from the Party and pronounced Admiral Doenitz his successor.

All that was left to him now was the promise from Odin that he should be received into Valhalla, the Great Hall of immortality. On Walpurgis Night, the witches Sabbath, Adolf Hitler and his wife of a few hours, Eva Braun, took their lives in the bunker below the Reich Chancellery. Twelve years of hell for the Jews in Germany and Europe were drawing to a close.

Heinrich Himmler had not entered into negotiations with Count Bernadotte lightly. He was a man whose code of loyalty was intended to be absolute. As a knight served a king unreservedly until death, so Himmler desired to be seen to serve the Führer. Pressure from Walter Schellenberg to enter into talks with Bernadotte however, had been subtle and increasingly persistent, and he still considered himself indebted to Schellenberg for saving his life on the flight to Austria after the Anschluss. Heinrich Himmler, never a man of iron strength and resolve, had slowly buckled. He nevertheless waited for some sign before empowering Bernadotte to communicate with the Allies on his behalf, and that had finally come with the report of Hitler's conference on April 22nd. Adolf Hitler had declared his intention to remain in Berlin and die in its ruins. Berlin was about to fall and Hitler was as good as dead. Himmler told himself that he could now, with good conscience, open negotiations for a peace settlement.

On May 5th, at Flensberg, he participated in his last staff conference, one to which he was not invited. Heinrich Himmler had become a major embarrassment to the Führer's successor, but the Reichsführer was cheerfully optimistic, even arrogant in his assumption that, despite the contents of Hitler's last will, Doenitz would include him in the new government. Himmler stated that he intended to establish a reformed Nazi administration which would conduct peace negotiations with the Western powers as an independent government in its own territory. He left the meeting obviously well satisfied with his contribution, leaving even the SS leaders uncomfortable with his illusions. On the following day Doenitz fired him.

His four Obergruppenführer were forced to lean across the table to catch Himmler's words. He was speaking softly, urgently.

"I have received another dispatch from Sweden. De Bar has assured me that there is no possibility that I might remain safely in Germany. There's no political future for us here, but he's offering us safe passage to France and a change of identity."

The men glanced quickly at one another. They had realised long ago that the time for vacillating was over, but their persuasions had fallen on deaf ears. Himmler had waited in the hope of some miracle, even after the treaty of unconditional surrender had been signed. Udo von Woyrsch spoke up.

"It's imperative, Reichsführer, that you leave the country immediately. Many senior members of the party are already in the hands of the Allies, and it's now only a matter of time before they reach Flensberg."

Himmler sighed. "I had hoped to hear something from Schellenberg before I left. You don't think I should wait for Field-Marshall Montgomery's reply to my letter?"

"We must move now, Reichsführer, before it is too late."

Von Woyrsch shot another glance in Karl Gebhardt's direction. All his men were fully aware that Walter Schellenberg had no intention of contacting Himmler. It was said that he blamed Himmler's uncertain approach to the talks with Bernadotte for their ultimate downfall.

"Did de Bar set out details of the escape plan, Reichsführer?"

Himmler nodded resignedly. "He has planned the death of the Reichsführer-SS and my resurrection under a new name. It will appear that I have committed suicide." A flicker of emotion crossed his features. "My death is to be afforded maximum publicity. I am certain that my men will be devastated when they hear that I have taken the easy way out. It will seem to them a betrayal of everything I stood for."

"It's essential to our plan that you should go, Reichsführer." Gebhardt's voice was urgent.

Himmler left the table and turned away from his Generals so that they would not see the fear in his face.

"I would have liked to have seen a political solution," he said failing to hide the wistfulness in his tone. "I would have been content with even a minor position within Germany's new government."

The four men struggled to mask their frustration and Gebhardt spoke with patience, as though to a child.

"Reichsführer, you still have a hundred and fifty men here with you at Flensberg. Every day you remain, increases their danger. If you leave now it will give them time to disperse and look after their own interests. They're confused and anxious but their loyalty demands that they remain with you."

Himmler nodded and when he turned back to face his Obergruppenführer, they were relieved to see a return of some of the old determination in his expression.

"De Bar wants me to go to Bavaria where I'll be picked up by a British command in two days. I'll put the word around that I'm heading for Sweden. Naturally, there's the possibility that I may fall into the wrong hands. The mission is not without its hazards." He rubbed his chin thoughtfully. "I'll require at least two men to go with me. They mustn't know anything of course, but they will be important witnesses to the course of events." He placed both hands squarely on the table and leaned towards them. "But what about you?"

The men glanced at one another for a moment.

"I'm staying," von Herff said definitely. "My family's here in Germany and who knows," he shrugged with a grin, "perhaps we'll get off lightly.

Von Woyrsch nodded. "I'll stay on as well."

"I'd like to make the journey south to the check point with you," Ohlendorff said. "I'll hand myself over and take my chances with the British.

Gerhardt grinned. "You can count me in with Ohlendorff. That way we can be sure you make it through."

The moment for Heinrich Himmler was not without dramatic irony. De Bar had specified that he dress in the despised uniform of the common soldier, shave off his moustache and wear an eye patch as a form of identity. Only those of his inner circle were aware of the greatest incongruity of all; that of the identity of Himmler's rescuers. The secrecy of the mission would have been impossible had all those who played their part not been Freemasons and were therefore under oath to a higher authority than that of the military.

The Reichsführer had already carried out his own reconnaissance of the post on a previous occasion, disappearing without a word to his staff two weeks previously after receiving an outline of the plan from de Bar.

This time, several other men elected to go with him, among them Dr. Rudolf Brandt, Himmler's secretary, and Werner Grothmann, his military adjutant. Carrying a pass in the name of Heinrich Hitzinger, a man similar to him in appearance who had been condemned to death by a People's Court, Himmler set off on 20th May, 1945, on foot in a southerly direction from Flensberg.

One way or another, the Reichsführer-SS, Heinrich Himmler, faced his end and the thought was sobering. Despite his belief in reincarnation, he was still afraid of death. He had never entirely managed to expunge his Catholic background and he was haunted by thoughts of hell and eternal damnation. As they left Schleswig behind and crossed into the gau of Holstein, each step became one step deeper into fear.

Himmler deliberately turned his thoughts to the past. It was unfortunate that he had had to leave Hedwig without a proper opportunity to say goodbye. He remembered her as she had been when she first came to his office as his secretary. Haschen, as she was known by her friends, was twenty-eight years old with blonde hair cropped stylishly into the nape of her long neck and curling softly above the high bones of her cheeks. Her skin bore a translucent sheen lightly bruised beneath gentle eyes, touched by fright like some woodland creature. Her mouth was crushed and tender, so that she was more child than woman. As Marga had been to him like one of the Valkyrie, Haschen was a wood-nymph.

In 1942 she had born him a son, Helge, and their second child, a daughter whom they had named Nanette Dorothea, was now little more than a year old. He wondered how the news of his death would affect Haschen. Her financial position was secure, and he had also made sure that Marga and his daughter Gudrun would be well taken care of.

Perhaps his most difficult decision had been the dynamiting of Wewelsburg Castle, but Himmler was determined that his centre should never fall intact into the hands of the enemy. He had left them nothing. The SS had stripped the Reich of most of its treasures and now they lay in vaults beneath Zurich, a policy of insurance for the Fourth Reich of the future.

At least, Himmler thought, nothing had been in vain. His Lebensborn project may have been considered a failure by some, but it was like seed, a starting point that seemed small and insignificant, but which was destined to grow massively and flourish. How many children he speculated, had been born in the Lebensborn maternity homes, children of pure Aryan blood. How many had been conceived in the graveyards of their ancestors and were growing, even now, mighty in their inherited spirit. These would be the men and women, visionaries of the future, who would bring the New Age to pass. Many Germans of good blood had fallen in this war, but it had been a necessary beginning.

As an agriculturalist Himmler knew that before the ground was planted it must first be ploughed and cleared of weeds. His role had been the weeding out of the inferior nations, the preparation of the ground and the planting of the right seed.

His most perfect work, the seed that still required his nourishment, was the child already safely in France. He had birthed Homo Noeticus in Germany and created a perfect leader for this new species.

There was just one step that must still take place before the implementation of the new era. Mankind must experience a massive spiritual awakening.

Himmler and his party of men crossed the Elbe west of the city of Hamburg on the afternoon of the 20th May and made their way towards Bremen. The British post had been alerted to their presence in the area, it would now only be a matter of hours before they were picked up.

Chapter 33
Twice-Born

"The young King is dead!"

The words were whispered through the courts. This death signalled the end of a dynasty and more than one monk who dared not speak the words aloud pondered in his own heart whether the house of Baudouin de Bouillon had been cursed by God from the beginning. In March of 1185, the leper king Baudouin IV had succumbed to his illness and was succeeded by his nephew, the son of Sibylla, sister to the leper. Raymond of Tripoli, who had acted as chief minister to Baudouin IV, became regent to Baudouin V and, in this office, negotiated a four year truce with Muslim leader, Saladin. Now, a year after assuming the throne of Jerusalem, the eight-year old king was dead and there was no obvious heir.

A stipulation of the will of Baudouin IV was that succession should be decided by Pope, Emperor and the Kings of England and France.

"Such an action will not be necessary," Sibylla informed the hushed court. "I am sister to King Baudouin IV and mother to King Baudouin V, therefore the subject of succession is not under question."

"Had your husband, William of Montferrat lived," the Grand Master of the Hospitallers said deferentially, "you would indeed have been considered for succession. But sadly, Ma'am, he is dead of malaria and your new husband has nothing that recommends him to the throne."

"My brother, King Baudouin himself gave his consent to my marriage to Guy of Lusignan," Sibylla retorted. "He, obviously, did not share your sentiments!"

Sibylla's supporters murmured their agreement.

"If I may remind you, Ma'am, it was pressure placed upon your brother by both your good self and your mother that caused the king, who was in ill health, to succumb to your desire to marry Guy of Lusignan."

"The king was fully aware at that time that the issue of my succession was probable," Sibylla insisted, "Yet, he did give consent! The Patriarch, Heraclius has agreed to the coronation. You, sir, must see that you are over-ruled."

"No so, Madam! I hold the key to the royal regalia and I refuse to relinquish it. This coronation will not take place."

"And I hold the second key!" Grand Master of the Templars, Gerard de Ridefort, reminded him as he stepped forward.

A hush of disbelief fell over the entire gathering. That the Orders of Temple and Hospital should squabble in public at so significant and delicate a moment in the history of Outremer was unheard of.

"I say, Sibylla is Queen and she must immediately be crowned."

"No, sir!"

Gerard de Ridefort stood before the Grand Master of the Hospitallers and looked into his eyes.

"It is done," he said quietly. "I too hold a key."

Heraclius stepped forward and opened the casket. As the crown was placed on Sibylla's head, she stood imperiously to her feet.

"Guy of Lusignan." She received the second crown from the hands of the Patriarch and, with her husband kneeling at her feet, crowned him king.

Once the Templars had discovered the entrance to the tunnel, which penetrated the underground temple, they reopened and explored the original passages. One of the secret entrances was indeed through Gihon's spring. An ancient water source from deep within the Temple Mount had eroded the rock naturally, and Hiram of Tyre's artisans had simply widened the channel and hewn steps into the rock.

In Hezekiah's time, his diggers of the water conduit had accidentally penetrated this shaft and doubtless pursued their exploration until they uncovered the inner temple itself; a find which must have caused great excitement and consternation to the king. Certainly it was the desire for spoil that brought the Babylonians against Judaea during the reign of Manasseh, Hezekiah's dissolute son. Perhaps Hezekiah, in his foolish disclosure of Judaea's treasures had also chosen to reveal the hidden mysteries in the depths of the earth

The Templars rebuilt and fortified the tunnel walls and blocked and concealed their earlier excavations with rubble. Knowledge of the discovery was a closely guarded secret and worship in the subterranean temple was limited to the very elect.

It was unprecedented for Gerard de Ridefort to venture into the inner sanctum alone but, had his movements been observed, it is doubtful whether any member of his Order would have questioned him. As Grand Master of the Templars in Jerusalem, he was trusted and highly esteemed.

He lit his lamp and drew the door shut behind him. The indescribable opulence of the temple caused him to stand in awe as yet undiminished by familiarity. De Ridefort was aware of the unnatural pounding of his heart. This was no ordinary mission and the inner sanctuary itself seemed to be filled with eyes of ancient watchers within the looming shadows. He moved swiftly to the Ark and lifted the golden lid. Within, on a crimson cloth, in place of the tablets of stone, lay the sword. Gerard de Ridefort lifted it out and withdrew it from its scabbard, weighing the weapon in his hands. Its beauty lay in its simplicity of design and the engraving along the length of its powerful blade. The desire to fight with this sword; to own it, had consumed him for months. De Ridefort slid his own sword into the scabbard with its tapestry hangings and put it back in the Ark of the Covenant. Glancing once more at the magic sword, he thrust it into the scabbard that hung against his thigh. Turning swiftly, he retrieved the lamp and left by the way he had come.

A rift was occurring in the Latin forces exacerbated by Raymond of Tripoli who had approached Saladin to oust King Guy. He had acted as regent to Sibylla's young son, Baudouin V, before the child's death and refused to accept the new monarchy. As an act of his patronage to Saladin, he had agreed to allow a non-belligerent Islamic reconnaissance force to cross his country. Word of it reached the king who, with a party of knights including the Grand Masters of the Templars and Hospitallers, was en route to Count Raymond seeking reconciliation.

Without hesitation, Gerard de Ridefort rode to castles in the area and summoned another ninety knights as well as forty secular knights from Nazareth and the small force set off in pursuit of the Muslims. It was as they crested a hill that they first caught sight of the formidable body of men below. Most had dismounted and were watering their horses at the springs of Cresson.

"They are too many for us," Roger des Moulin, Master of the Hospitallers, said as they gazed out at the Egyptian reconnaissance party spread across the valley. "It would be foolish to attack with such a small number of men."

James de Mailly nodded. "I agree. We are vastly outnumbered."

"And you love your blonde head too well to want to lose it!" Gerard de Ridefort ridiculed. "So you would let these infidels live because you are too cowardly to fight!"

The Templar Marshall turned in his saddle. "I shall die in battle like a brave man," he said. "It is you who will flee like a traitor!" He raised a hand to the knights behind them.

"Prepare for battle!" and he spurred his horse and led the attack down into the valley below.

Gerard de Ridefort dropped his visor and, couching his lance, followed de Mailly into the fray. The blood pounded in his temples as he engaged the enemy. Many of the Muslims had managed to leap into their saddles as the knights charged and blood-curdling cries split the air as the two forces came together. Weapon clashed against weapon and resounded as they glanced off the armour of the knights. Horses whinnied in terror and screamed in pain. Ahead of him de Ridefort saw James de Mailly strike to the right and to the left with his sword then he too was caught up in the heat of the battle, unhorsing several riders before his lance shattered.

De Ridefort drew the sword from its scabbard knowing with a certainty that with it he was invincible. Man after man went down before him as he lashed out unerringly at those on foot. He turned just in time to see de Mailly's horse fall beneath him at a deft sword stroke from a foot-soldier. The Templar Marshall landed heavily and, before he had time to recover, his assailant raised his sword with both hands and struck a mighty blow beheading him instantly.

De Ridefort struck the man at full gallop and the power of the blow from his sword-arm clave the skull of the Muslim. At the same instant, the sword broke in two. Mindless of the danger, de Ridefort spun his horse around and leapt from the saddle to retrieve the broken blade. The battle was almost over. The Grand Master lifted his damaged weapon aloft and galloped towards the hill. Only three blood-bespattered Templars and a handful of other knights followed him from the field. The Grand Master of the Hospitallers was among the dead.

Gerard de Ridefort's conduct provoked a howl of fury from the Orders of Sion and Temple in Jerusalem.

"His actions in leading his men to their death on the battlefield were impetuous and foolhardy, but that he should have taken the sword... That is worthy of death!"

But de Ridefort had come prepared with an answer.

"It was an act of God," he said calmly. "I wish you to all hear me on this. I know I was led to take the sword and use it in battle. If I had asked, you would have denied me."

His words were met with an uproar of angry protest. He held up a hand for silence.

"I have asked you to listen. We can all read the signs. None of us can deny that when the other relics left Outremer our time was already over. But it was prophesied that the sword had to be broken a second time. That was the token that would spell for us the end of the quest."

"We were not called to create a self-fulfilling prophecy," a monk protested.

"And I did not do so. Every action I undertook on that day was beyond my control. Forces were at work and I was a mere tool in their hand. Did we imagine that the sword would shatter itself to prove to us that our time in Jerusalem is drawing to a close? Surely it is evident that the powers would use one of us to accomplish the word that was spoken?"

There was silence from the gathering. De Ridefort knew he was fighting for his life, but he had created enough doubt to tip the scale in his direction.

"Jerusalem was finished when Baudouin II died a penitent in the robes of a monk," he said. "Can we argue that it is not so?"

No one spoke.

"A queen on the throne means that Jerusalem is already lost. I say the inner temple should now be closed and sealed. The sword must be left to rest in the Ark of the Covenant against the day when the true Parsival takes his place as King and Pope and brings healing to this desolate land."

"And I say you are a traitor, Gerard de Ridefort!"

"You are not worthy of your position in the Order!"

"He has spoken truth," a Templar shouted back. "Our time in Outremer is at an end."

"The sword was not his to take. He is worthy of death!"

The words between the Temple and Sion were flung back and forth and the tension in the hall was tangible. The Templars stood with de Ridefort and the Grand Master narrowly escaped with his life and his position intact, but a rift had been created between the monks of the Order of Sion and the Temple that would not heal in the time ahead.

"The Templars will continue to be the repository of the secrets," de Ridefort said to his men later that night. "From this time forth all our churches will be built to reflect the true temple, the circular womb beneath the rock of foundation, in memory of Jerusalem."

A carefully hewn rock was slipped into the entrance of the sanctuary and the tunnels were sealed. All traces of the Templar excavations were erased. Simon Magus' magical sword was left within the womb of the earth symbolising the act of penetration. Although centuries were destined to pass before the feminine principal united with the dominant masculine, Gnostic alchemy was at work and would ultimately bear fruit.

King Guy summoned all forces to gather at Acre leaving fortresses and cities deserted of their men. On the first day of July, Saladin crossed the Jordan and divided his massive army in two.

Reginald of Châtillon and Gerard de Ridefort called for an immediate assault to relieve the city of Tiberius, which had fallen to the enemy, while Raymond urged restraint.

"What does this coward know?" de Ridefort taunted. "He claims to have broken his pact with Saladin and now he's playing into his hands. You have blood on your hands Raymond of Tripoli. It is your fraternisation with the enemy that has brought this to pass."

"My wife is in Tiberius," Raymond said quietly. "Do not suppose that I have no care that she is rescued. I call for caution only because we are in danger of losing the kingdom!"

"You are a fool and a coward," Reginald of Châtillon laughed bitterly. "Has Raymond of Tripoli not already proven himself?" he asked, turning to King Guy who, as always remained indecisive in the face of stronger men. "He made a pact with Saladin to overthrow you. He deserves to be put to the sword. I concur with the Grand Master. It is time to act. I say we march on to Tiberius."

The order was given to advance. In the late afternoon it encamped at Sephoria.

They were met by a messenger who informed Raymond that his wife was trapped in the citadel of the town. His sons begged him to go to her rescue but again Raymond urged caution. At stake were the Christian kingdoms.

"Is it right," he said; "to lose our advantage and risk the army for the sake of Tiberius and my wife?"

Later that night, Gerard de Ridefort came to the king's tent.

"Sire, would you heed the advice of Raymond of Tripoli, a man who has betrayed you?"

"He has fully repented of that betrayal."

Gerard's pitying look did not escape the king.

"Sire, I urge you. Press the advantage while you have it. If you hold back now, you surrender all."

The king looked uncertain. "The heat at this time is intense," he countered. "If we go forward there is no certainty of water for man or beast."

"And if we hold back we have gained nothing! My Templars would rather put aside their white mantles and sell and pawn all they have than lose this chance to avenge their brothers who died at the springs of Cresson."

Reluctantly, King Guy ordered the men to march at dawn. They took the northern route over the hills and by midday they were desperate with thirst. Muslim archers harassed them constantly and when they reached the village of Lubiya, the Templars at the rear called for them to stop for the night. The well at Lubiya was dry and men sent out to scout for water were ambushed and killed.

Raymond of Tripoli threw up his hands in horror. "My Lord God, the war is over. We are dead men. The kingdom is finished!"

They encamped at the desolate Horns of Hattin. Saladin's army waited below and that night the Muslims set fire to the brush that grew on the hills so that the smoke intensified the thirst of the soldiers.

Saladin's men attacked at first light. The Latin forces were crazed by thirst, while their armour and helmets only served to exacerbate the heat. The clash of metal and the screams of the wounded filled the air. Below them, a lake gleamed in the early morning light. Desperately, the infantry tried to break through the enemy ranks to reach the water but they were cut down or captured.

Count Raymond broke through the Muslim phalanx with a group of knights and, unable to return to the main army, fled to Tripoli. The Bishop of Acre, holding high a piece of the 'true cross' was cut down and the relic captured. King Guy and Gerard de Ridefort were taken prisoner along with other eminent men, including Reginald of Châtillon who was personally beheaded by Saladin when he taunted the Muslim leader with his need for Christ.

More than two hundred knights were given the option to turn to Islam or die. All were put to the sword on the following day. The King and the Grand Master were spared.

Only two knights were in Jerusalem to defend the city and, to extend their numbers, knighthood was bestowed on thirty bachelors of the bourgeoisie. The city was filled to overflowing with terrified refugees, most of them women and children. It was clear that no fight could be made.

"We can encourage Saladin to parley," Balian of Ibelin told Queen Sibylla with a confidence he did not feel.

"How?"

"We hold the Muslim holy place, the Dome of the Rock. We will threaten to burn it if an attack is made on the city. We will sue for peace and safe passage for every citizen, Saladin is a shrewd man and just; I have no doubt he will listen."

The Muslim leader demanded a ransom for every person and when it was finally raised he entered the city in triumph. In essence, the Holy Land had fallen back into the hands of the infidel.

Chapter 34
Twice-Born

As a Jew, Michael Segal knew that a relic such as the shroud was unlikely to have been fabricated for the early Christian church, which had budded from a Jewish root. No Jew would accept either the shroud or its image as a symbol of their newfound faith, knowing how offensive both were in terms of Moses' Law. In which case, if the forgery had been made at that time, it was by Gentiles and for Gentiles.

It was possible, of course, that the grave-cloth, which was numbered among Constantinople's religious relics, was not the Mandylion but if not, why was there no record as to when and where such a hugely important find was made? The shroud undoubtedly bore the full-length image of a crucified figure presumed to be Jesus Christ. That, at least, was well documented. On the other hand, if the shroud and the Mandylion were one, the records indicated that it had been taken to Edessa shortly after the crucifixion of Christ well before the Roman overthrow of Jerusalem. In fact, the Mandylion was hidden in its niche above the Kappe Gate several years before the destruction of the temple took place in AD 70.

He was forced by the evidence to concur with Freiberg that the shroud was either created supernaturally, or it was an incredibly early photographic image.

Michael had been reluctant to examine the Biblical evidence for the shroud. He had no desire to know more about the Christian God and even a clinical investigation of the evidence was distasteful. Reminding himself that forensic scientists and garbage collectors had to get their hands dirty if they wanted results, and that his book could hardly be considered complete without the New Testament background, he set himself grimly to the task.

By the end of his first reading of the Gospels, Michael Segal was surprised to find that, increasingly, he liked this Jew who had dared to approach the Jewish Law with such freedom. It was not a response he had anticipated. However, the claims Jesus made about himself were obvious, especially to a Jew. The man was either a lunatic, which did not square with his words and deeds, or he was who he said he was, the Son of God, Messiah.

Segal examined the prophecies in the Jewish scriptures and discovered that more than sixty found their fulfilment in the gospels.

"Some of them could have been manipulated," he reasoned aloud. "But a man doesn't go to the cross to ensure that his hands and feet are pierced to equate with Psalm 22. Or, for that matter, give his back to the strikers and his face to those who would pluck out his beard to make sure he conformed to Isaiah 50." He massaged the back of his head with both hands and then dropped them back into his lap. "The only other option is that he was who he claimed to be – the Son of God. In which case, I'm left with two conclusions," he gave a wry grin. "I can either accept him as Messiah, or reject him."

Segal had begun this journey to work through a crisis in Chaim's faith and ended by deepening the unspoken rift in his own.

"So, where does this lead me in terms of the shroud?" He gazed into space, attempting to formulate his thinking. "It's irrelevant!" he concluded at length. "It's not the shroud that brought me to this point, it's the written Word. We Jews have that much right! You can't establish your beliefs on an image."

This, he decided, was the simple answer he would give Chaim when he asked. However, the two remaining questions stayed with him. Much later that night Michael Segal received an answer. It did not come by the intervention of a priest, neither through any relic. No mystical experience beamed heavenly light into his soul. There was no trumpet sound or drum-roll but rather a knowledge in the quiet place of his soul that the Word was truth. From this moment on, Michael knew he would be prepared to live or die for the author of that Word.

Chapter 35
Twice-Born

23 May 1945
Captain Thomas Williams, the commandant of Interrogation Camp 031 near Luneburg looked over the group of new arrivals.
"Who are they?"
"I don't know sir. They were making their way south and we picked them up between Hamburg and Bremerhaven. Lieutenant Shelton seemed to think there might be a couple of high-ranking Nazis among them."
Williams nodded and looked them over with practised eye. He was a big man with a deeply weathered face that looked as though it had been fashioned from leather. Blue eyes narrowed down to slits, fanning in the corners into deep laughter lines. There was no trace of humour in his expression now. Three men had caught his attention and in particular, there was something familiar about the short one with the eye patch. He was shabbily dressed and his pale cheeks were unshaven.
Williams tapped them on the chest. "You three. Step forward!" As they hesitated he repeated his command in German. "Let me see your papers!"
The short man reached into his inner pocket and brought out a pair of steel-rimmed spectacles with his false identity document. While his men stared grimly ahead, he removed his eye patch and put them on.
"Heinrich Himmler," he said quietly.
"Call military intelligence and tell them to get over here, fast!" Captain Williams barked. "And I want that bastard searched thoroughly. Make sure he doesn't have any poison on him."
The sergeant saluted smartly, swung around and left the room.
"Do you really think it is Himmler, sir?" Lieutenant Fitzpatrick asked curiously.
"I have no damned idea, Lieutenant. I've only got the newsreels and his word to go on. If it's not, he does a pretty good impersonation of the man. Judging by the expression of his mates out there when he

revealed his identity though, I'd say there isn't much doubt." He lit a cigarette. "I'm not sure who the other two are, but we'll leave them in solitary for the moment and concentrate on the little one. If we really have got Himmler, I'd like to bet they're a couple of his Lieutenant-Generals."

The sergeant rapped at the door and saluted as he approached the desk. "Radio ops have been in touch with Intelligence, sir. Colonel Michael Stokes is on his way over. We can expect him to arrive later this evening."

It was 23.00 hours when the truck finally drove in over the rutted road to the camp. The night watch warned Williams of their arrival and he took the steps down to the road entrance two at a time. Saluting smartly, he introduced himself to the two men.

"Captain Williams sir, thank you for coming."

The colonel returned the salute briefly. "This is Dr. Samuels who will be assisting me. I presume the prisoner has been searched?"

"Of course. Thoroughly, sir. We stripped him immediately. He was not carrying a weapon but we did find a phial of cyanide hidden in his clothing."

"Did you check his mouth?

"As best we could, sir. I'm reasonably certain there was nothing there."

The colonel nodded. "Right. Can I have a private word with you before I see the prisoner?"

"Certainly sir. Would you care to join me for a drink in my office?"

Williams poured two brandies and sat down opposite the colonel.

"We're positive the man you are holding is Heinrich Himmler," Colonel Stokes said. "He disappeared from the public eye two days ago with a number of his top men and we were expecting him to show up in this area if he hadn't already managed to cross the border."

Williams nodded.

"What I am about to say to you, Captain, is extremely sensitive. I believe you are a man of discretion?"

"I hope so sir."

"We have need of Himmler for top level investigation. He will be interrogated and once he has reached the end of his usefulness, he will be disposed of. For obvious reasons it will be essential that the public, both the Allies and the Germans, believe him to be dead."

Williams rubbed his nose uncomfortably. "I think I see what you mean, sir."

"Himmler, more than any other Nazi, is responsible for the wholesale slaughter of Jews," the colonel said bluntly. "Worldwide public sensibilities are going to be aroused when the full extent of the atrocities gets out. With Hitler dead, the Reichsführer will bear the brunt of public outrage but publicity will damage the effectiveness of our investigation, which is extremely delicate."

He swallowed the last of his brandy and stood up. He was almost as tall as the captain but with a presence that was imposing. His even features were offset by a clipped military moustache, and the hand that set the tumbler down on the desk was carefully manicured.

"Please understand that your cooperation in getting the prisoner out of here is essential, and so is your vow of silence. You have my personal assurance, Captain Williams, that Heinrich Himmler will pay for his war crimes once my investigation is complete."

"Yes sir, I understand."

"Dr. Samuels will sign the necessary death certificate. It will be said that Himmler had a second phial of poison concealed in a hollow cavity in a molar and that on investigation he bit into it and died shortly afterwards. I will brief you on the finer details once this is over to ensure that our stories agree."

"In order to do the job convincingly there would need to be a body, sir."

The colonel's thin mouth lengthened into what might have been determined as a smile but his eyes remained cool and guarded.

"There is a body in the back of the truck, Captain, similar in size and appearance to the Reichsführer. It has been mutilated to conceal the true identity and I've had Dr. Samuels remove the teeth for the same reason. In a couple of hours I want one of your men to take it out and bury it in a suitably remote spot. Choose a man who can be trusted to keep his mouth shut. There must be no possibility for anyone to discover the body and carry out an investigation that would prove to be an embarrassment for the British Army. Is that understood, Captain?"

Williams snapped to attention. "Perfectly, sir."

He was asleep in the corner of a room that was otherwise empty; a diminutive figure dressed in a uniform that was too big for him. The sound of their arrival awoke him and he got quietly to his feet and stood defensively with his back against the wall. Colonel Stokes greeted him shortly and turned to Captain Williams.

"Thank you, Captain. You can leave us now. I'll need you to give the doctor a hand with the parcel in the back of the truck in a while. I'll report back to you in person before we leave."

He turned to Himmler as Williams left and addressed him in fluent German.

"I am Colonel Stokes," he said. "I'll require your full cooperation, Reichsführer, in order to get you out of here before daybreak. You understand that as you are a prisoner of importance, your death will be of great public interest, so what we are about to do must be carried out thoroughly. The general public must be absolutely certain that you have died tonight."

Himmler nodded.

"We will take photographs as proof of your death," Stokes went on; "the first will reflect the effects of cyanide contorting your features and the others with your face in repose. I trust you will be prepared to co-operate with us?"

Twenty minutes later, Captain Thomas Williams woke a man from his sleep and spoke to him urgently outside his barracks.

"Officer Leigh, I have an assignment for you," he said. "There's a body in the back of my jeep that I want you to dispose of. If Gerry gets wind of where you've put it, we could have some sort of cult worship on our hands. Wrap the damned thing in barbed wire and bury it well, do you understand? Then forget where the hell you've put it."

Leigh saluted. "Yes sir." He hesitated momentarily and then asked. "May I ask whose body I'm getting rid of, Captain?"

Williams shrugged. "The knowledge might help you to bury it deeper," he said reflectively. "It's Heinrich Himmler, Nazi Reichsführer. He committed suicide here tonight. Now get on with the bleeding job, will you!"

Leigh grinned. "I was a dustman before the war, Captain. Disposal of rubbish is my game, and this load will be my pleasure."

Chapter 36
Twice-Born

1204

"They must be forced out of the city at all costs," Emperor Alexius IV said tersely. "Constantinople is a state of grievous tension, at any moment we can expect war with the Franks."

"If you don't pay them sire, they will not leave."

Alexius raised his hands despairingly and dropped them. The Franks, louts that they were, had regained him his throne, therefore indebting him to the leaders of this fourth crusade, but his predecessor had left him without the resources to pay so great an army.

At first, the army had poured into the city peaceably, awed by Constantinople's splendour. But these were fighting men who had not left their native land to gawk at beauty. They were on a mission to spill foreign blood. The glory of the first crusade had become legendary, firing the souls of new recruits and these men had nothing but contempt for the perfumed, bejewelled Greeks of Constantinople.

"They are billeted beyond the city walls," Alexius said. "Tonight the gates must be barred against them. We cannot allow them back in."

His advisor nodded slowly.

"Constantinople will be protected by the power of the holy cloth, sire, which you have placed in the church of the Blessed Virgin. We must not lose faith."

Alexius fingered his beard. "It is together with the robe of the Virgin," he said. "The Son is restored to his Mother. It is as it should be."

"Sire, your decision to display of the cloth has, I believe, brought hope to the common citizens. The Church of My Lady of Blachernae has become a rallying point - a place of great encouragement."

"We can do no more," King Alexius said. "Tonight, order the gates locked and barred and call the army to a defence of

Constantinople. The crusaders will not take kindly to this action against them."

In 1147 Count Henri II of Champagne had been royally entertained by the Byzantine Emperor Manuel I Comnenus in Constantinople who showed him many of the city's most venerated objects. And again in 1171 Amaury I the Frankish king of Jerusalem, had visited the Byzantine emperor who foolishly exposed the inner treasures and secrets of the palace and sanctuaries; nothing had remained hidden and nothing was revered too highly to be revealed to this king. The Emperor revealed to Amaury, all of Constantinople's precious relics said to be evidence of the Lord's passion. The cross, the nails, the sponge, the reed, the crown of thorns, the sandals, the holy lance and the *sindon*, the cloth in which his body was wrapped; all these were laid bare before the covetous gaze of Jerusalem's King.

The walls were breached not far from the Church of Blachernae and knights and foot-soldiers poured into the city with a determination born of righteous anger. From the moment of their arrival in Constantinople to restore Alexius IV to his throne, they had felt judged. But to have been locked out without their due payment was a slight that could not be lightly overlooked. They would teach these effeminate Greeks a lesson and see if their perfume and jewellery would help them in a fight!

Soon the battle was being fought from street to street and the sound of the clash of the swords against the armour of the enemy rang through the city, mingled with the terrible cries of the wounded and the fearful screams of the women and children.

A special detachment of knights had been entrusted with a mission. The first contingent was dispatched to the Church of Blachernae; the second to the Pharos Chapel. Their instructions were to bring out the sacred relics; to protect them with their lives and deliver them into the hands of the Count of Champagne.

Although the Byzantines resisted the enemy as best they could, the fighting did not endure long. Their leaders were no match for the experienced knights. The crusaders broke open wine cellars and swiftly became inebriated. Inevitably, pillage and looting followed as the soldiers rampaged through the streets. They desecrated the holy places; destroyed precious works of art and raped any woman they could find.

Once again, the shroud with the image of the Baptist was lost, apparently destroyed during the mayhem and revelry of the night.

Chapter 37
Twice-Born

Switzerland 1944

"Ruth?"

The coincidence was too great, but the Jewish features were unmistakable. She had grown the bleach out and restored the natural colour of her hair; otherwise she was the same woman who had sheltered him in her room during Kristallnacht. She looked at him without any spark of recognition and her glance was wary.

Of course she would not remember him, Michael Segal thought wryly. A prostitute who trades her body with any number of men could hardly be expected to remember one man, even if the circumstances had been unusual.

"Are you Ruth?"

She leaned over and tapped the driver on the shoulder. The action was urgent.

"Drop me here!" This was not the gentle voice he remembered. She was fumbling for her parcels.

"Here. Hold my baby for a moment, will you?"

She handed him the bundle and he took it awkwardly; he had never been at ease with babies. He looked down at the small exposed face in its swaddle of blankets. Ruth slid out of the car and assembled her parcels on the pavement at her feet.

The child's eyes were slate blue, but there was something in its look that penetrated Michael's spirit and momentarily his head reeled with shock. An icy hand gripped his heart and seemed to be squeezing the life out of him. Ruth was leaning into the taxi.

"Can you pass him to me?"

Michael appeared not to hear her and she gripped him by the shoulder and shook him.

"What's the matter with you? Are you deaf? Give me my baby, Jüden!"

Did he really hear the contemptuous, "Jüden," or had he

imagined it?

She snatched the child from him and slammed the door of the taxi. The driver turned around and stared at him.

"You all right?" he asked. "You look as though you've seen the ghost of your father."

Michael nodded slowly. "I'm fine, thanks. Drive on."

As the taxi pulled away from the kerb Michael looked back at Ruth. Her eyes did not meet his and her face was closed off and expressionless.

What *was* that? The question formed itself in his mind but the answer came from somewhere much deeper in his spirit.

The Man of Perdition. One who would carry the seed of all this hatred through to the next generation. Another Hitler: another much more than Hitler. Hitler had been the forerunner. This was the Man.

Michael Segal trembled. The cold refused to let him go. The war was not over; still, he sensed, a new time of preparation was just beginning. There would be a new genocide; a final attempt to eliminate all those who believed in the God of Israel. Where had this sudden knowledge sprung from: through a glimpse of something in the eyes of an innocent child? Segal shook his head to clear it from the startlingly unfamiliar thoughts that were gripping his mind. He should have choked the life out of the infant while it was within his grasp. Even with the murderous notion he was certain it had not been within his power to do so. The dark presence that surrounded it was the child's protection. There was nothing to be done. The book was written. The end was already accomplished.

Chapter 38
Twice-Born

1952

The sun was low, lying just above the undulating hills, streaking livid rays out across the valley. The day had been dry and hot, the earth exuding heat, which shimmered in waves above the ploughed earth.

René de Bar's father, Charles, stepped out onto the terrace and stopped in his tracks. Ruth was there dressed in a sleeveless cornflower-blue cotton dress. The child in her lap lay still, yet strangely alert, his naked body gleaming in the sun's late rays. Ruth's expression was distant and unearthly and Charles felt the breath catch in his throat. The sun was dying at her back and its light was captured in her hair, causing a nimbus around her head. He was looking at a cameo of Madonna and child; of Isis and Horus; of Semiramis and her son Ninus, the first of the Mighty Ones. At that moment he felt that he was in the presence of a goddess, one whose divinity, as with those ancients, was drawn from the deity of her son.

Jean de Bar's early childhood on his father's estate in Bordeaux was spent almost exclusively in adult company, removed from the influence of other children. His grandfather lived until Jean was eight years old during which time Charles was the undisputed patriarch. Even in those final years when his body was ailing, Jean was aware of the undaunted strength of his spirit. He was uncertain whether he liked the old man or not, but respect had been cast into the relationship by the attitudes of the people about him.

Jean had only once deliberately disobeyed his grandfather. He left the estate to meet with a boy of his own age, the son of one of the household servants. For a few golden hours they explored a stream bed and, where the trickling water formed a deep pool, fished for tadpoles with the mud sucking at their bare toes and the icy water slapping against the twisted tree roots that edged the pond. Jean would always remember how the sun bit into his shoulders through the thin fabric of his shirt, and the briars scratched his legs. But he would also remember the controlled anger in his grandfather's eyes as he had issued the order.

"Whip him."

The lashes administered by his tutor had ripped into his naked buttocks and upper thighs, raising ugly welts on the skin. He was locked in his room without supper and remained there until the following morning. The servant and his son were dismissed. The sin had been twofold, in mixing with people beneath his station and, even worse, disobedience to his grandfather. Jean had never crossed Charles again.

"Can I talk to you?"

René de Bar looked up from his work and nodded. Ruth was standing at the door to his study, her long hair loose around her shoulders. She was wearing a floor length gown of cream satin and the outline of her body was as sleek as when he had first seen her at Himmler's banquet. Although their marriage had in every sense been an alliance, de Bar had never failed to find his wife captivating. She was sensual and bewitching, the sort of woman who turned heads whenever she entered a room.

"Come and sit down. Can I get you a drink?"

She shook her head. "I wanted to talk to you about Jean."

René poured himself a whisky and sat down beside her on the couch.

"Has my father's death upset him?" he asked.

She shook her head. "It's not that. At the time Charles died, Jean seems to have had some sort of experience, a vision perhaps."

"What sort of vision?"

"He said someone walked with him in the woods, a creature. Half man, half beast with pipes in his hand. Jean said he stepped towards him and became part of him so that he was suddenly seeing the woods through his eyes."

He glanced at her sharply but said nothing.

"Could I have a cigarette?"

René lit two and passed her one.

"Was that it?"

She shook her head. "He said the glade was full of creatures. A faun ran across the clearing, a small spotted faun. Satyrs appeared from among the trees, caught it and tore it apart."

De Bar stood up abruptly and refilled his glass.

"I shouldn't have bothered you," she said. "I should have dismissed it as childish fancy."

He swung back to face her. "You don't know what you're saying," he snapped. "Forget it happened. I'll talk to him."

Jean was excited and disturbed by what he had witnessed.

"The creature had goat legs and although its head was human he had small horns," he said, "And he smelt like a goat! But he didn't kill the faun, the satyrs killed it."

"Show me where it happened."

Jean led the way along the path from the house; a diminutive figure against the hugeness of the forest. The trees closed in around them as they entered the wood; tall and dominant, whispering in the breeze that ruffled the higher branches.

The child bent down suddenly and retrieved something from the path.

"Oh, I forgot to tell you. The goat-man made this and put it on my head like a crown."

René took the ivy wreath from his son's hands and said nothing.

"After the faun was dead, he walked back with me to the edge of the forest and played a sad tune on his pipes."

"A tune of seven notes," René de Bar said almost to himself.

René knew the glade. He had played there himself as a child, but now it seemed smaller than he remembered it. Jean unexpectedly slipped a hand into his father's.

"There it is," he whispered.

René de Bar walked slowly forward and felt his skin creep. In the grass at his feet lay the mutilated body of a spotted faun. Its flesh had been savagely ripped and torn, and its severed head lay a short distance away. Sightless eyes, even in death, were wide with terror.

The death of Nimrod; the death of Osiris; the death of Tammuz, all were presaged in the tearing of the faun. This re-enactment and Jean's coronation carried the authority of those who lived outside the natural realm. Jean was the one twice-born who like Nimrod bore within himself the spirit of the gods.

This confirmation of the child's identity could not have come at a more portentous moment. Today Charles de Bar would be buried in the grounds of the estate and preparations were underway to receive guests later in the morning. He, René, would receive the baton of leadership of the organisation in place of his father. He experienced a stab of unreasoning and unreasonable envy that the spiritual coronation was not his own. He knew Jean carried the spirit of the Magus, yet the child was not his. There were no familial ties.

The funeral was well attended. Charles de Bar had been a person of some eminence and people gathered from all over Europe to pay their last respects. There were others who even in this moment of parting could not afford to appear with the family for fear of recognition. Heinz Halder was one of those who chose to stay away from the service and the gathering at the graveside. But he was well aware that the death of de Bar would increase his own influence in the life of Charles de Bar's grandson, Jean, and he was pleased.

Chapter 39
Twice-Born

In the year 1188 an incident occurred just outside Gisors in France.

There was a gathering of forces. Men and their steeds were gloriously arrayed for battle. Knights clad in blue and gold mingled with Templars wearing white tunics with its dominant red cross. Chain-mail and weaponry glittered in the sunlight. The heat was already intense, burning into the heads and shoulders of the soldiers within the constraints of their armour.

Puffs of dust were raised by the galloping hoofs of two horses and there was the clash of lances as opposing knights engaged in a friendly joust to ease some of the tension that was building.

Monks robed in the cinnamon and brown of their order stood in sharp contrast to the grandeur of the knights. They remained aloof, some of them mounted, others gathered in knots on the edge of the throng. In battle in the Holy Land certain among them had served as strategists and advisors to the armed forces and they were well respected and even feared.

It was the third day of parley and tempers were frayed. Henry II of England and his men had arrived early and taken up the shade under a mighty elm while Philippe II of France was left seated under a canopy erected for him in the heat of the sun.

A hot-blooded, lusty young man, Richard the Lionheart, son of Henry II, rode onto the field with his knights. He was a fearless warrior, well-respected as by both his own men and Saladin whom he had crossed as an enemy in the Holy Land.

It was difficult to say whether the heat of the day caused the fracas that followed; whether it was instigated by kings, knights or monks, or if there was another unseen force in the air desiring to create a prophetic word for generations yet unborn.

Philippe had given notice to Henry on the previous day that the elm was to be cut and, to prevent it, Richard the Lionheart had instructed his men to band the trunk with iron. The presence of Henry and his Templars under the elm strengthened the prohibition.

This was not about the tree. As a result of final act of foolhardiness by the Grand Master of the Temple, Outremer had fallen to the Saracen. After their capture by the Muslim forces, Saladin had freed both King Guy and Gerard de Ridefort on the understanding that they would commit no further act of war against him. In consultation with the Papal Legate, however, it was decided that a vow made to an infidel had no binding obligation and they had gathered a force of knights and marched on Acre, laying siege to the city. The besiegers came under attack by Saladin's forces and the Grand Master, de Ridefort, fell in battle. King Guy once again escaped and, with Conrad of Montforret, made another attempt to free Jerusalem.

Henry II and Philippe II of France knew that the opportunity was lost. Philippe had joined with the Order of Sion in accusing Gerard de Ridefort of recklessness and treason. Not only had he approved the marriage of Guy to Sibylla, placing on the throne of Jerusalem a parvenu of no standing or religious right, but he had stolen the sword of the Baptist and precipitated the battle that ultimately cost Christendom the Holy City of Jerusalem.

Both kings were aware of the symbolic finality of this act. Whereas Henry was prepared to stand with the Templars, Philippe was not. By cutting down a mighty tree reputed to be eight hundred years old, he was declaring Jerusalem irretrievably lost and the Templars cut off for their perfidy.

"We will try again," Henry said. "My son Richard is still prepared to fight for Jerusalem."

"It is finished!" Philippe replied bitterly. "You are fully aware that the Order of Sion left in '53. They knew that the end was coming and brought with them to Orleans all the sacred relics but the sword and the piece of the true cross. The Temple Grand Master broke the sword and lost the piece of the cross to Saladin by his impetuous advance on Hattin."

"But that is restored."

Philippe nodded grimly. "By no more than an act of God!"

"If we fight again we can still take Jerusalem."

"No! This fight is not one of flesh and blood; you and I know that full well. God will thwart any further attempt. Already, by cursing the line of Godfroi de Bouillon, his anger towards us for the sins committed in Outremer is abundantly demonstrated."

Henry's gaze shifted uncomfortably. He himself had sent vast sums of money for the crusades, much of which had been used to ransom the citizens and refugees when they were besieged by Saladin, but his love of creature comforts had prevented Henry from taking up the cross. It was not the first time he had wondered if he, as king of England and count of Anjou, was not partly instrumental in bringing God's anger upon Jerusalem.

"We will not take down the tree," he protested. "It is too final! I will raise another crusade and lead it myself. I don't believe it is too late!"

Philippe gazed at him scornfully. "Can you not hear?" he said. "Have you no ears? It is finished!" He raised a signal to his men and at once Henry's Templars stood to arms beside him.

"Stand back!" Philippe demanded. "The tree is to be cut down!"

Behind Philippe a phalanx of five squadrons, each under command of a lord, had formed to protect the men with axes and hammers that were to perform the task. A momentary hush fell over the field followed almost immediately by shouted threats and curses. Weapons were drawn and the Templars stood at the ready waiting only for a command from the King.

"Move aside," Philippe said tersely. "What is to occur is the will of God."

There was a wavering in the face of King Henry and for a moment it seemed that he would concur but one of his Welsh guards released an arrow in error, and a Frenchman dropped from his saddle. There was a cry of rage from the French and Philippe ordered the advance of his woodcutters. Richard the Lionheart plunged into the French vanguard with his Templars to cut off their advance and a short but fierce battle ensued, which eventually forced Henry's men to flight. They took refuge within the walls of the Templar stronghold of Gisors, and Philippe II ordered that the elm be felled.

Henry II called for a cardinal. It was after midnight and the summons was cause for immediate alarm. The king was pacing his chamber.

"Ah, Cardinal," he said. "There is an account in the Holy Bible of the cutting of a tree. I want you to read it to me."

Mixed emotions of confusion and relief were expressed in the face of the man of cloth.

"Permit me to fetch a Bible, Sire."

He returned with the heavy book and set it carefully on the table.

"I think the account you desire is that of Nebuchadnezzar, king of Babylon."

"Were there bands of metal placed around the base of that tree?"

The Cardinal looked at him in surprise. "There were, Sire."

Henry pushed the hair off his face. His cheeks were unshaven and his eyes were red-rimmed as though he lacked many nights of sleep. "Recount the story to me!"

"King Nebuchadnezzar dreamed of a mighty tree in the middle of the earth and while he still slept there came the voice of a watcher, a holy one from heaven. 'Hew down the tree and cut off the branches. Let the beasts get out from under it and the birds from its branches. But let the stump remain in the earth, even with a band of iron and brass.'"

The Cardinal looked up. King Henry was listening intently.

"Go on," he said.

"'Let it be wet with the dew of heaven, and let his portion be with the beasts of the grass of the earth: Let his heart be changed from a man's and let a beast's heart be given unto him: and let seven times pass over him.' This was the command by the watchers," the Cardinal continued, "that the living would know that the Most High rules in the earth. He gives the kingdom to whomever he wills and he sets the basest of men over it."

"What was the outcome of the story?"

"Daniel the prophet interpreted the king's dream warning him that he would fall because of worldly pride. It came to pass exactly as he had prophesied. For seven years Nebuchadnezzar lived as a beast of the field until his kingdom was restored to him."

"It was restored?"

"Yes, sire."

"You may go, Cardinal. Leave the Bible with me!"

For several hours, King Henry poured over the words in the great book and pondered their meaning. Was the Almighty speaking again through the humiliating events at Gisors? Or had Philippe's Priory of Sion arranged the cutting of the elm cognizant of its full symbolism? Certainly there were signs that all the men had deemed prescient. The year was auspicious in its numerology. 1188, twice nine: these were numbers that were held in high esteem by Sion and Temple. Philippe when speaking of the need for separation had pointed to the significance of the elm in the sacred field. The tree was said to have been eight hundred years old and its trunk so thick that nine men, arms fully extended, were required to encircle it. Had not the Order of the Templars begun with nine men, a Grand Master plus eight? And the duty of the Order was still to encircle and preserve the holy bloodline and the precious relics of the Grail.

What was begun with Charlemagne's coronation as Emperor in the year 800AD would again be brought full circle. Church and state would yet unite to birth a King of Kings. Philippe spoke truly. Although Christian strongholds remained in Outremer, when Godfroi's royal line died out, Jerusalem was inevitably lost. Perhaps the rift between Sion and Temple was God-ordained judgment following the fall of the Holy Land.

Henry himself had resisted what was inescapable by placing the metal around the trunk of the tree to prevent the felling. For the prophet Daniel, the bands placed about the trunk had signified that the root would remain in the ground.

By the will of God another king would arise and, in due time, Jerusalem's throne would be restored. Nothing was wasted. Men would live and men would perish; history would repair and repeat itself until the appointed time and even kings and secret orders could do nothing to hasten it. If it was the will of the Almighty, no amount of human machination would force his hand – what was done might have resulted from the error of man, but the timing of events rested in the hands of God. Henry closed the great book and took himself back to his bed.

Chapter 40
Twice-Born

Michael had instructed her to go to Brunswick and Gabriele knew he would somehow find her there.

She had arrived on a bicycle loaned to her by the farmer's children, which she left dutifully at the Catholic Church. There was little accommodation to be had in the city but for three months Gabriele worked on a farm and found a room in an old gasthaus in a village close by. News of the Allied approach was on everyone's lips. The Russians were not far from Berlin and the British and American forces pressed in from the West.

At the time of her arrival in December the beautiful old city of Brunswick was damaged but still intact but, by the middle of April when the city was taken, much of it lay in ruins or gutted by fire from the continual pounding of Allied bombing. For citizens and refugees alike, life was a continual battle for food and shelter - a fight to stay alive. Faced with the presence of the occupying forces some Germans were obsequious, expecting to be ill-treated. Few wept. Even the women for whom the human catastrophe was too great were generally beyond tears. They averted their faces from the occupiers in their Jeeps and foreign uniforms and scuttled away into the ruins.

British troops moved into the gasthaus and residents and guests moved out. Gabriele accepted with the rest the inevitable order of things and made her way back to the city. For her though, the arrival of the troops brought the first ray of hope. The bombing had stopped, most of Germany had surrendered. The war was over and Nazism was as good as dead. Most important of all, somewhere out there was Michael.

Gabriele discovered an underground shelter, a place where hundreds gathered each night crammed together on benches or on the concrete floor and for the next two weeks this became a temporary home. After the chill of the night air, the shelter was a place of foetid suffocating heat and often the cram of humanity was so great that there was no place to lie down and sleep. The enforced proximity both appalled and, paradoxically, comforted her. This was a last refuge to those who had lost homes and relatives, possessions and livelihood. There was little food and no medicine, no dignity, no privacy and, for the majority, no hope.

Just ahead of the Allies, posters of Adolf Hitler and symbols of Nazism had been removed from the walls of homes and businesses leaving faded squares on the wallpaper. For many years ahead, there would be nothing to replace emptiness that remained in the German soul. Ruin and desolation was Adolf Hitler's legacy to the German people.

Along with thousands of others who sought outside contact, Gabriele Hoch put her name on the Red Cross list and waited.

Adolf Hitler was dead. In the underground the news had passed uncertainly from mouth to mouth. There were no details but command had been passed, it was said, to Commander Doenitz. Gabriele saw little sign of sorrow; little change in the numbness that embodied their underground existence. Nothing beyond the terror of daily survival could touch them.

On the second day of May, Gabriele emerged from the concrete bunker below the ground into the daylight and breathed the fresh air. Overhead the skies were almost clear. In the area of the bunker the ruins lay as though poured out by some mighty hand. There were few geometric shapes to be seen. Bomb craters had pitted the roads; electricity and telephone cables hung from broken walls; severed water mains spewed precious water onto the streets. Gabriele stopped suddenly and, as she bent down, tears sprang to her eyes. A daffodil had pushed through a patch of earth and its single yellow blossom bobbed in the slight breeze. It was spring.

Perhaps it was the daffodil that caused her to return to the Red Cross that morning. Her heart skipped a beat as she found her name on the list and saw the colour-coded mark against it.

The Red Cross office had been set up in a block that was relatively unscathed and an official ran a finger down a list of names.

"Hoch Gabriele? There was someone asking after you the day before yesterday. A Chaim Freiberg."

"Chaim Freiberg?" She looked at him blankly. "There must be some mistake. I don't know anyone of that name."

The officer shrugged. "He could be looking for someone with the same name," he said, not without sympathy. "But I'd check it out, if I were you." He wrote quickly on a piece of paper and passed it to her. "This is the address."

She took it and moved out of the queue. The hotel, located several blocks away, was known to her but the route across town was difficult to traverse. Gabriele picked her way through the rubble and broken glass, disorientated by the lack of landmarks, and found herself in an area where several blocks had been missed by the bombers. British military vehicles were parked against the curbs and gangs of men, probably Germans, were involved in clearing the roads. All of a sudden she felt out of place and for a moment, as she looked up at the hotel building, considered going back.

"I'm looking for Chaim Freiberg."

The man behind the desk gazed at her in obvious disapproval and Gabriele was suddenly made aware of how she must look in his eyes. She was no longer just one of the hundreds in the bunker whose appearance reflected their own.

"Who shall I say is calling?"

Gabriele lifted her chin a little higher and spoke firmly to cover her discomfort.

"Gabriele Hoch," she said. "Please tell him Gabriele Hoch would like to see him."

The desk clerk picked up the telephone and spoke a few words quietly, his eyes never leaving her face. Willing me to leave, she thought, before any of his well-to-do visitors see me in his posh foyer.

"Hold on, please," he said. "Mr. Freiberg will be right down."

Gabriele stood looking at the plush red carpet, the gilt mirrors, and the chandeliers that had somehow remained unscathed during the bombing and felt a sense of unreality not untinged with anger.

"Miss Hoch?"

He had entered the lobby from the lift behind her. Gabriele swung round and her heart sank at the sight of the stranger.

"Miss Gabriele Hoch?"

She nodded, not trusting herself to speak.

He stepped up to her gravely and shook her hand.

"Let me introduce myself. I am Chaim Freiberg, a friend of Michael's."

"You know Michael?"

"Very well."

The receptionist was watching them curiously.

"There is a room booked for Miss Hoch," Chaim said. "See that she is given all that she needs."

The clerk smirked, "Do you have any luggage, Fraulein?"

Chaim Freiberg stepped up to face him, placing both hands squarely on the desktop. "We will be collecting Fraulein Hoch's luggage later," he said in a tone that was quietly threatening. "In the meantime, you make sure she is shown to her room!" He turned back to Gabriele. "Michael has sent the things he thought you would require," he said quietly. "If there is anything else, you can ring me in room 101. Will you do me the honour of having dinner with me this evening at seven?"

"Thank you. It would be a pleasure."

Gabriele's head was reeling as she was shown to her room on the third floor. The young page left and she looked round in wonder. This was luxury beyond anything she had dreamed of in years. She caught her reflection in the full-length mirror in the dressing room and grimaced. No wonder the clerk at reception had treated her with such contempt!

Chaim Freiberg was waiting for her later as she entered the dining room and he gave a silent whistle of amazement as he stood to his feet. Gabriele was transformed. She was wearing a simple dress of dark green satin and her auburn hair hung loose to her shoulders. Chaim saw her to her chair.

"Michael Segal is a lucky man." he said.

She laughed. "I believe I'm a lucky woman! How on earth did he know just what to buy me? I am so glad that he sent an emissary," she added. "I would not have wanted him to see me as I was when I arrived!"

Chaim ordered a bottle of French wine and when the waiter had left them alone with the menus Gabriele asked the question that was foremost in her mind.

"Is Michael still in Switzerland? And is he well?"

Chaim Freiberg looked up and smiled. "He's very well," he said and his glance strayed over her shoulder to the entrance of the dining room. "And I would say he is about to be even better."

Gabriele looked at him uncomprehendingly and then turned around just in time to see Michael Segal's stunned expression.

"Gabriele!"

Chaim Freiberg was grinning foolishly as Gabriele stood to her feet and Michael wrapped his arms around her.

"Chaim! How the hell did you do this? Where did you find her?"

"Actually, old chap," Chaim said, "Gabriele found me."

Chapter 41
Twice-Born

On the 4th April 1957, Jean de Bar turned thirteen. He had grown from a quiet child to an introspective youth, already broadening out into manhood. While his father was alive, René de Bar had never interfered in the administration of the estate, or in the meting out of justice to his family. Once his own position was secured, he became as autocratic and dogmatic as Charles had been. It was not that there was a lack of communication with Jean; rather that the relationship was more in line of despotic ruler and subject than father and son. Communication generally took place in the form of a summons to his office. The chair, opposite the broad expanse of mahogany that formed René's desk, seemed massive to the boy. It creaked as he moved and smelt faintly of leather.

"Do you have any problems you wish to discuss with me before we start?" It seemed that every interview was begun this way yet Jean could never recall an instance when he had chosen to use it to air a grievance. He would shake his head.

"No sir, everything is in order."

His father would consider where to begin. "What," he would ask, "is liberalism?"

And Jean would gather his thoughts and make his reply. Already his speech was clear and articulate, a fact which pleased his tutors and caused good reports to be issued to his father,

"Liberalism," he would reply, "is a weapon of our organisation. It is a fantasy of freedom that has been introduced to the masses to create a state of anarchy. All liberalists are anarchists, whether in fact, or simply in thought. Governments which have submitted to liberalism have voluntarily laid down their power and our organisation has been on hand to take up the reins."

"But we have another equally effective weapon which has set us well on our way towards the establishment of a New World Order," René de Bar would prompt.

The child would nod and without hesitation reply: "Collectivism, sir."

"Why?"

"Because it goes against nature. It submerges individuality. The law in nature lies in force. The weaker must submit to the stronger. In nature there is no equality and no freedom."

"But we have permitted the masses to seek freedom."

"Liberty, equality, fraternity. These are simply notions planted in the minds of the mob. In fact they are meaningless."

His speech would be rewarded by a smile from de Bar.

"What are some of the methods we have of manipulating the individual?"

"Success. Man loves to achieve what he sees as success and if you remove it from him, he will go to any lengths to restore it. The strength of our organisation has been that we have ignored short term success and kept our eyes on the ultimate Plan."

"What else?"

"Man's self-importance. The focus on self and selfish desires has helped to break down family units and the structure of society. Other things such as materialism, pornography, sport, television, entertainment and cheap literature cloud the thinking, paralyse initiative and focus the attention of the individual away from the real issues."

At last René de Bar would stand up, signalling an end to the interview and Jean would experience the momentary warmth of a hand on his shoulder. Together they would walk out onto the patio and his father would order lunch. Now talk would turn to lighter things.

Jean de Bar's education was infinitely broader than most young men of his age. It encompassed the usual subjects but involved also the careful dissection of history and the daily analysis of unfolding world events. Tutors were carefully selected from the organisation to impart their various skills. They were men in the business of moulding leaders, and although Jean's training was more intensive than most, all the children initiated into the Prieuré de Sion by their parents received similar tuition.

Heinz Halder had lived on the estate for as long as Jean de Bar could remember, but already, at fifty-seven years of age, he seemed to

Jean to be a very old man. A dusting of grey hair, as thin as the grass that grows on the balding mountain ridges, was cropped high over small neat ears. Halder's eyes behind his tortoiseshell glasses appeared so colourless and rheumy that they added a touch of death to his faded features. His face was hollow beneath the cheekbones, accentuating a weak chin and his rather puny frame was bent at the shoulders after years of suffering with arthritis and a stomach disorder.

Halder, though generally anti-social, had taken a personal interest in Jean's achievements, teaching him many things on a more informal basis than most of his tutors. He was delighted when Jean began to learn fencing. "No one truly reaches manhood without a fencing scar to show for it," Halder told the boy, and showed him the thin scar across his own cheekbone. "That I received at university. It's a badge a man can wear with pride."

Jean had surveyed him with renewed interest. It was seldom that he heard anything of Halder's past, although the old man would spend hours, like the most pedantic of school-masters, recounting his theories and philosophies. It was curious that his father permitted his ramblings. As a rule he disliked Jean to discuss anything that might contradict the teachings of the organisation.

Halder was not present at Jean's birthday celebration, which had taken place earlier in the day choosing, as was his habit, to avoid strangers. René de Bar had invited several families to a buffet lunch, which was served on the lawn in front of the house.

It was late afternoon by the time his guests had left and Heinz Halder was finally able to present Jean de Bar with his own gift, a pair of silver epees.

"I've had the inside of the hilt engraved," he pointed out. Jean read the bold inscription aloud. "Jean de Bar from HH. 4th April, 1957." He weighed one of the epees in his hand and smiled his pleasure. "They're beautiful, thank you sir."

From the front of the house they heard the dogs bark and moments later the butler came through to the drawing room to where Jean and Halder were seated.

"There is a man here with a special delivery from a lawyer in Switzerland," he said apologetically. "I'm afraid, master Jean that he insists upon handing it to you himself."

Halder was touched by a cold chill of presentiment. He shot a swift glance at the boy. Jean was already on his feet.

"Show the man in."

"Jean, perhaps your father should be here," Halder suggested uncertainly.

"It's probably a birthday present Herr Halder. It's addressed to me personally."

Halder nodded. That had to be it, a birthday present. He sat back in his seat aware that the sense of unease had not left him.

"Allow me to present myself." The lawyer was a man in his late sixties with hair almost white, thickening into a wave over the collar of his grey jacket.

"I am Herr Groener from von Laue, Groener and Herbst in Zurich. I have been instructed by a client to deliver a dispatch to M Jean de Bar on the occasion of his thirteenth birthday."

Jean directed him to a chair.

"Please sit down, Herr Groener. May I offer you some refreshment?"

The lawyer smiled and declined. "I have to be back in Paris this evening. I'm afraid I will need to leave immediately. I hope you will excuse me?" He opened his briefcase, removed a manila envelope and snapped the case shut. As he stood to his feet, he handed the letter to Jean. "If you don't mind gentlemen, I will leave. I'll see myself out." He bowed briefly and left the room.

Jean picked up one of Halder's rapiers.

"Let's see how sharp these are, shall we sir?" he said as he slit the end of the envelope. He removed the documents and looked at them curiously. "Well, it's not a birthday present," he said. "It seems to be a birth certificate – a woman's."

"Let me see that!" Halder's voice was tense with anxiety.

Jean handed the certificate over obediently and opened the accompanying letter. He began to read its contents aloud.

"Dear young de Bar," he read. "I'm afraid I have no idea what your name might be, so I am unable to address this to you in a more personal manner. No doubt however, my lawyers will find out the necessary details for me when the time comes.

"The birth certificate that I am enclosing, belongs to your maternal grandmother, Anna Lejkin, mother of Marianne von Ingolstadt, or, as you will know her, Ruth Leiman.

"You have a complicated background, but I shall endeavour to lay it out for you as clearly as possible. You will see that your grandmother was born in Poland in 1895. When she married your grandfather, a German from Berlin in 1920, she chose to change her identity to conceal the fact that she was Jewish. Her daughter, your mother, Marianne von Ingolstadt, believed herself to be a full-blooded Aryan. At the time of the writing of the letter, she is about to follow in her mother's footsteps and will change her own identity.

"As part of a plot to groom you for world leadership it was imperative that you were of the royal line of the Merovingians and to fit the prophetic image, you had to appear to be Jewish. The identity given to Marianne von Ingolstadt, your mother, is that of a Berlin whore, Ruth Leiman, a childhood runaway from the de Bar clan, a branch of your own family.

"I felt that this birth certificate would make a novel gift to you for your Barmitzvah. I would dearly love to present it to you personally, and indeed, if I manage to survive the present circumstances and live to see your thirteenth year, perhaps I shall. But I feel certain that there will soon be an attempt on my life and I am therefore placing this document in the hands of a lawyer now.

"Should Herr Heinrich Himmler be with you, which I am sure he will have made it his business to do, would you kindly extend him my compliments.'

It's signed, Reinhard Heydrich."

"Heydrich!" the name fell from Heinz Halder's lips like a curse. The youth raised his eyes from the document and appraised Halder. The old man's face had contorted and he was backing away slowly as though pursued by some unseen vision. On the floor before him lay the crumpled birth certificate. Jean walked over and picked it up. His face as he looked up was expressionless. Halder's back was against the fireplace wall as though he had crucified himself, his outstretched hands clawed at the unpolished stone.

Jean's face expressed little more than distant curiosity.

"Heinrich Himmler," he said thoughtfully. "Heinrich Himmler."

"You are Aryan," Halder protested. "Pure blooded Aryan. I made certain of it myself..."

Jean's lips curled. "I'm no Aryan," he said. "No more than you are!"

Himmler's face was white. "Aryan!" he protested. "You have to be Aryan..."

"Look at me!" Jean ground out. "LOOK AT ME! I'm a damned Jew!"

"You're my own son. Son of Himmler. Son of Lucifer. You are my legacy to the world. The new prince of this age. Through you the Jewish nation will be annihilated. DAMN YOU, HEYDRICH!" he screamed. Again his face contorted with pain and he tried to speak. A sudden violent spasm caused his right arm to drop limply to his side and he gripped savagely at his chest with the other arm.

The memory of the night of the child's conception was crystal clear in his mind and the words of the prophecy came back to him.

'Because of the dishonour to his body, he will bear no goodwill to man or woman.'

Once more the Parsival, and this time pure mockery.

"You bastard, Heydrich!" he breathed. "You've taken it all from me!"

His body sagged and he slipped slowly down the wall. His lips mouthed silently. Jean de Bar watched him with eyes like ice. Then he threw back his head and began to laugh.

Epilogue
Twice-Born

Michael Segal weighed up the facts as he knew them and jotted an outline down on his notepad.

Fact: the League of Nations had been infested with Freemasons.

The League of Nations gave way to the United Nations, which was fully committed to adopting Stalin's five goals towards global conquest.

Confuse, disorganise and destroy the forces of capitalism. Bring all the nations together into a single world economic system. Force the advanced countries to pour financial aid into the under-developed nations. Divide the world into regional groups as a transitional stage to world government; and ultimately bring the regions into a single world dictatorship.

From the outset, the USSR had seen the United Nations as an instrument in the liberation of colonial and semi-colonial nations and in spreading Communist dogma. It also gave Communists full diplomatic immunity to further their revolutionary aims in the USA.

Non-Communist member nations were encouraged to embrace Socialism as a transitional stage towards Communism. The final step would be the submission of their military forces to the UN making further resistance impossible.

Fact: The UN was the plaything of Communism.

Part of the shift to World Government was the Council on Foreign Relations founded by Elihu Root who led a small delegation at Versailles to operate beside the Inquiry team (Mandell House's secret insider elite) as advisors to President Wilson in 1918. They had been at the heart of the action in the USA ever since, producing most presidents from their ranks.

Fact: The CFR incorporated Inquiry becoming the most influential secret society in America.

There was a huge level of obfuscation. Jimmy Carter's election as President of the United States in 1976 was a prime example. Carter, while still a Democratic Candidate had written a book called, 'I'll Never Lie to You,' which constituted a lie, Michael thought ruefully, before the opening page.

"The insiders have had their chance," he wrote, "and they have not delivered. And their time has run out. The time has come for …Americans…to have a president who will turn the government of this country inside out."

Before the election took place, Hamilton Jordan, Carter's advisor said:

"If, after the inauguration, you find Cyrus Vance as secretary of state and Zbigniew Brzezinski as head of national security, then I would say we have failed and I would quit."

Both men, CFR insiders, were appointed to the specific positions spoken of by Hamilton, who, incidentally, did not step down.

Brzezinski and Vance were, after all, Trilateralists, as was Jimmy Carter, so they were all of the same millpond anyway.

Fact: The Trilateral Commission was founded by David Rockefeller in 1972, while still chairman of CFR. It followed, therefore, that the Trilateral Commission was just another arm of the CFR. The Trilateralists aim was to bring together US, Europe and Japan to create the foundation of a world economic power.

Although Michael was certain it helped him to process his thoughts, Gabriele always complained when he drank too much coffee. He took advantage of her absence to make himself a second cup, and settled down at his desk once more.

There remained another important facet to all this. Was there a powerful elite ruling behind the scenes, whose sole intention was to create a World Order?

He had studied the names of those who headed the international banking sector and of those in the Trilateral Commission and the CFR. Many, although by no means all, were ancestors of the German Ashkenazi Jews who had left Europe before the First World War. And in numerous cases the same names appeared in one or more of the secret organisations whose avowed intent was one world government.

Fact: There existed a wealthy elite who associated themselves with global control.

Implicit in world domination was a single leader.

There were two world leaders to come. The Bible clearly prophesied both. He, Michael, was certain he had seen the one, and he had come to an intrinsic faith in the other. So, whereas the conspiracy appeared on the surface to be political, there was a strong religious aspect to it.

There was a Babylonian system; a hollow image of the real thing exhibiting an outward piety in its robes, incense and genuflections. At the head was one who dared, in the face of the knowledge of the Word of God, to call himself Holy Father.

This harlot religion encouraged its adherents in the worship of images; its sanctuaries were replete with icons of the Queen of Heaven and imaginary saints. Worship of Jesus was reduced to a mystical performance in which he was raised up before the people as a piece of bread at the heart of the monstrance.

Fact: Church would be again married to State as in Roman times and the world leader would claim to be the Christ.

One last question arose from all these considerations. The elite comprised Communists, Fascists, Jews, Catholics, and possibly even Muslims. How did these disparate groups come together? The only likely answer was that these outward divisions were of no consequence to their plan and possibly even contributed to its implementation.

Fact: An overarching body, perhaps Freemasonry, or the Illuminati as the inner heart of Masonry, united these various groupings but it served their purpose to appear unrelated.

Michael was certain the baby he had seen in Switzerland was the final Messiah and that he would arise from within the Roman Catholic Church. Somewhere, even now, this man was readying himself to enter the world stage. Millions would receive him as Lord, yet he would be the epitome of all evil. World government would come about one way or another but he, Michael Segal would not be around to see it.

Two thieves were crucified with Jesus. One mocked and rejected Him; the other, recognising that his own death was justified, accepted Him. To him, Jesus said, "Today, you will be with me in Paradise."

"All of humanity was divided in two at that point in history," Michael said. "Sheep and goats!" He spoke aloud to himself much more now that he was old and it worried him less. "Those open arms invited all to come to Him, but most would not. Mankind is separated by the cross as east is separated from the west. If we reject the sacrifice He made on our behalf we choose our own fate. In short, hell."

The thief on his right hand had gone out that fateful day with the sure knowledge that he would die, yet he lived to become the first fruit of Christ's death. Michael Segal jotted his thoughts down on the pad in front of him.

'One died that day *for* sin, one died *in* sin and one died *to* sin. What strange irony!'

He glanced down at his shaky handwriting with a wry smile. "Lord, your servant is old!" he said.

The question that had haunted his youth had been answered. The God of Abraham, Isaac and Jacob had indeed accepted him 'in the beloved'. But without taking hold of that singular sacrifice and believing that His death atoned for his own sin, he would have shared the fate of the second thief.

Michael walked through to his bedroom. Gabriele found her husband there when she returned home several hours later. He was on his knees; his upper torso was slumped forward across the bed, his eyes were closed and his face reflected a calm repose.

Postscript
Twice-Born

Scholars generally agree that the source of the name of Jerusalem, city of David, is based on the word Yeru meaning foundation, and Shalem or Salem. Shalem was the designation of the Canaanite god of the evening star, twin of Shaher, Lucifer, or star of the morning. The blazing evening and morning stars are different aspects of Venus, known as the Goddess of Heaven.
The God of Abraham, Isaac and Jacob, the Great I Am, set his name upon Jerusalem, and allowed His Temple to be built upon Lucifer's foundation making it Yeru Salem, foundation of peace.

The Almighty God, creator of heaven and earth, spoke the universe into existence, setting sun, moon and stars in the heavens to divide the day from the night, and for signs of the times and the seasons.[36]
Lucifer appropriates to himself these secondary lights and through them seeks to display his nature and character. Shaher, the myths tell us, was cast to earth in the guise of the immortal serpent, Sata or Satan, father of lightning. The Bible confirms this and sheds more light upon who cast him from heaven and why.
How art thou fallen from heaven, O Lucifer, son of the morning! How art thou cut down to the ground, which did weaken the nations! For thou hast said in thine heart, I will ascend into heaven, I will exalt my throne above the stars of God...I will ascend above the clouds: I will be like the most High.[37]
The eternal, immortal, invisible, only wise God dwells in light unto which no man can approach[38]. The Word, which went forth from Him is light and can still be found in all aspects of His creation, right down to the waves in the quark of an atom, which can only be described in

---

[36] Genesis 1:14-16
[37] Isaiah 14:12-14
[38] 1 Tim 1:17

terms of light.

Satan, in his multiple guises, seeks to undermine every work of God. In return, the God of Abraham, Isaac, Jacob, and God of the Gentiles, has elected to build upon multitudes of shaky foundations the devil has laid. God works in the light, revealing all hidden secrets, Lucifer, angel of light, works in darkness, mystery and secrecy.

Jesus Christ chooses an elect, but not an elite. He chooses His people from the shipwrecks, the cast-offs, the depraved, the deprived, the bitter and the lost, and forms in those trembling, unstable lives a new foundation in His Son, Jesus Christ.

It will become even more vital to remember in the years ahead that the Creator God is in full control, despite the coming turmoil. He set the stars in the heavens and holds them in place. He made the mighty planets: by his Word they spin on their axes and circumnavigate the sun. When we, like climbers on a mountain face, appear to cling to life by our fingertips, afraid to look down, yet equally fearful of looking up, one heartfelt cry for help to the God of Gods through his Son, Jesus, brings Him near. We discover we are being held to the rock face not by our own efforts, but by the Father who loves us.

History focuses upon the Temple. Through the final sacrifice of Jesus, the Lamb, in Jerusalem's Temple, the Father dispensed with the sacrificial system of the Jews and chose to build his temple on the broken lives of men and women. More than that, he formed a Holy Place within the renewed heart of regenerate man and placed His Spirit there. As we confess our sin, he is faithful and just to cleanse us. He calls us to follow Him.

Amazing love, how can it be
That thou dear Lord, hast found out me?

And if it seem evil unto you to serve the Lord, **choose you this day whom ye will serve;** whether the gods which your fathers served that were on the other side of the flood, or the gods of the Amorites, in whose land ye dwell; **but as for me and my house, we will serve the Lord.**

Joshua 24:15

And after these things I saw another angel come down from heaven, having great power; and the earth lightened with his glory.
And he cried mightily with a strong voice, saying, Babylon the great is fallen, is fallen, and is become the habitation of devils, and the hold of every foul spirit, and a cage of every unclean and hateful bird.
For all the nations have drunk of the wine of the wrath of her fornication, and the kings of the earth have committed fornication with her, and the merchants of the earth are waxed rich through the abundance of her delicacies.
And I heard another voice from heaven, saying, **Come out of her, my people, that ye be not partakers of her sins, and that ye receive not of her plagues.**
For her sins have reached unto heaven, and God hath remembered her iniquities.

Revelation 18:1-5
(emphasis added.)

The Holy Blood and The Holy Grail Michael Esses et al.

I am indebted to the authors of The Holy Blood and The Holy Grail for their research, and have used their book extensively in the writing of both Nimrod Twice-Born and Opus Dei.

Appendix 1
Old Kingdom Lenses.

The illusion of the following eye of certain statues from the Old Kingdom in Egypt has been the subject of much research.

Professor Jay Enoch of the School of Optometry at U.C. Berkley delivered a lecture on the unique development of lenses among the ancient Egyptians.

Certain statues in the Louvre and the Egyptian museum in Cairo share the common feature of "the following eye".

An example of these early lenses, formed during 2600-2575 BC at Meidum, can be seen in the famous statues of Rahotep and his wife Nofret, and also appear in small statuary during the Fourth and Fifth Dynasties. It seems that the peak of development was reached circa 2475 BC.

The lenses are composed of polished rock crystal, either alpha silica or fused silica, formerly known as crystalline quartz and fused quartz, with a convex front surface and a near hemispherical concave ground pupil in a flat iris plane, which is generally covered in resin, at the rear of the lens.

This type of eye structure is known as a form of 'schematic eye' and indicates an advanced understanding of the anatomy of the eye for that time. This schematic eye may be best observed in the Louvre with the 'reserve eye' from Saqqara (E-3009), since it is not blocked with any resins. The accuracy with which these lenses were made suggests that they may have been turned on a lathe.

Information taken from the American Research Centre in Egypt – Northern California.

649

www.ingramcontent.com/pod-product-compliance
Lightning Source LLC
Chambersburg PA
CBHW061504020726
47502CB00006B/1925